The *Nanny* AND THE
HEARTTHROB

BOOK FOUR

USA TODAY BESTSELLING AUTHOR
KRISTA SANDOR

CANDY CASTLE BOOKS

Chapter 1
HARPER

Today was the day Harper Presley had to turn her disaster of a life around or she'd lose everything.

Failure was not an option.

And the best part, which might sound more like the worst part…

She had to do it in a cocoa-colored tutu while wearing a brown feathery mask.

If this wasn't hitting rock-bottom, she didn't know what was.

But first, she had to livestream an online music lesson.

From inside her car.

That didn't have working air-conditioning.

In the sweltering heat.

Yep, this had to be the rockiest of rock-bottoms. But if things went her way, in a few hours, she'd be living it up and walking on sunshine.

She balanced her laptop on her rusted Volvo's nicked dashboard and gazed into the camera. "Do re mi, sing along with Bonbon Barbie," she crooned, but before she could utter another word, some asshat pounded on the passenger side window.

Thunk, thunk, thunk, thunk!

She paused the livestream and released a frustrated growl. Shifting in her seat, she leaned over and rolled down her car's smudged window. The old gears whined a high-pitched squeal as the glass begrudgingly disappeared into the door, and a rush of hot desert air entered the vehicle.

"I'm working here," she quipped, sizing up a burly older gentleman clad in an ornate bellhop uniform. The ridiculous coat was adorned with sequins around the collar and *Luxe Grandiose Hotel Las Vegas* stitched across the front. He slipped a pack of cigarettes out of his pocket, then shoved them back inside the glittery coat.

"Lady, you can't sit here in your car," he barked in a thick New York accent. "This is the entrance to Las Vegas's Luxe Grandiose Hotel, not a parking lot."

Um…yeah. She knew exactly where she was. Did he think she was an idiot?

She scowled at the man, giving the shimmery dude a dose of the *go-screw-yourself* expression she'd been perfecting since kindergarten. This expression had served her well…until now.

Unfortunately, her attire seemed to tamp down the intended effect of telling the bellhop to take a long walk off a short pier. He fiddled with the pack of smokes again. He appeared to be jonesing for a nicotine hit, but his jittery movements ceased when he got a good look at her.

The man took a step back and cocked his head to the side. "What are you supposed to be? A half-naked piece of crap? This is Vegas. There are some outrageous shows here, but I've never seen anybody dressed like a piece of crap. And what's with the brown feathery mask? Are you the potty patrol princess headed for the toilet ball or would that be the toilet *bowl?*" he mused with a snort.

What a comedian.

She checked her outfit. As much as she wanted to tell the snickering bellhop to go to hell, she couldn't deny that her appearance was, for lack of a better term, absolutely batshit crazy.

Still, the unique ensemble was why she'd made the twelve-hour trek from Denver to Sin City.

She lifted her chin and gestured to the designs on her chest. "These are chocolate bonbons—the delicious candy. They aren't poop."

Point of clarification.

Poop emojis had been printed on the shirt, but she sure as hell wasn't about to admit that. She'd doctored the image to make the comical bowel movement into bonbons—the chocolate domes of perfection she adored. She usually wore a denim jacket over the brown top that skimmed her midsection, but it was too hot to wear a coat in the sweltering desert heat.

Of course, she realized how odd she looked, but there was a reason—a very good reason—she was dressed like a cocoa dessert.

Under the music teacher alias Bonbon Barbie, she was about to go bonbon big-time and become the internet's place to go for neurodivergent thinkers to learn how to read and write music.

At least, that's what she'd hoped would happen.

No, she desperately needed it to happen.

The idea of streaming music classes online under the guise of Bonbon Barbie had come to her a few months ago.

And nobody from her real life had any idea that she'd ditched teaching in-person piano lessons and created an alternate online persona.

She hadn't even mentioned her career shift to her best friends—something she felt awful about. She'd wanted to tell Penny Fennimore, Charlotte Ames, and Libby Lamb. Since

Miss Miliken seated them at the same table back in kinder-garten, the three women had been her people. She loved them like sisters, but her friends were living their best lives. They'd found love and abundant success in their fields.

And what was she doing?

The exact opposite.

Music was her calling, but she hadn't been killing it as a piano teacher, which wasn't that surprising.

Her general disdain for nose pickers, aka children, and most human beings, for that matter, wasn't quite a fit for working one-on-one in rich folks' places, cringing as overindulged pint-sized people banged away on pricey pianos.

Okay, she was fond of a few kids, but shlepping from house to house with a stack of music workbooks wasn't what she'd pictured herself doing when she'd decided to study music in college.

Once upon a time, she'd had dreams. Big, wild, beautifully elaborate dreams. Dreams that came with cheering crowds and glittering fireworks displays. She'd fantasized about having all eyes focused on her as breathless throngs of fans watched her every move and hung on her every word.

Some girls got a fairy godmother who bibbidi-bobbidi-booed their dreams into a reality. And more power to them if that was their jam.

But it wasn't her.

Harper Presley was the captain of her own ship. She, and she alone, was in control of her destiny, and whatever choices she made, she made them on her own terms.

But not every dream was destined to come true.

She'd put her dreams on the back burner six years ago at the tender age of twenty.

Still, today wasn't about chasing after the life she'd once yearned for.

Today was about survival.

And this type of survival demanded cash.

A boatload of it.

She didn't need the money for herself.

She needed it for her grandmother, her granny Babs.

Thanks to a douche nozzle at the bank who'd talked the woman into a creative financing loan to pay for updates to the heating and plumbing systems in their historic Denver home, Babs was up to her ears in debt.

Her grandmother was on a fixed income. There was no wiggle room when it came to her budget.

And what was the collateral? What would they lose if they couldn't pay back the loan?

Their home. Her grandmother's home.

But there was more.

Babs was getting older, and while she was still in good health for a woman closing in on seventy-five, she'd slipped and sprained her ankle a few months ago. Her grandmother had played it off as nothing, but the woman lived alone. Her grandfather had doted on her grandmother when he was still with them. She was the love of his life, and he was hers. He would have wanted to make sure someone looked after his beloved wife.

She owed it to her grandfather to be that someone, so she'd left the freedom of having her own place and moved in with her grandmother.

The day she saw the first bill from the bank, she nearly passed out. The woman had never been great with money. Her grandfather had handled the finances. She didn't want to worry Babs, so she'd kept the statement with the forty-eight-thousand-dollar price tag hidden and had called the bank and directed them to send any inquiries her way.

After that uncomfortable call, she'd gone for a walk to brainstorm how to make a pile of cash. After coming up with nothing and nearly settling on selling a kidney on the black market, she'd walked past a thrift store where she'd laid eyes on a truly bizarre window display.

A mannequin dressed in a brown tutu, a brown shirt that hit midriff with a poop emoji on each breast, and brown thigh-high boots stopped her in her tracks. The tan, brown, and black feathery mask covering the plastic lady's face had been the cherry on the top of the clearly crap-inspired outfit.

But when she saw it, she didn't immediately think of poo.

With her favorite bakery a few doors down and the scent of chocolate in the air, she'd seen past the potty emojis, and a plan solidified.

A crazy plan, but a plan, nevertheless.

She'd purchased the entire ensemble, frilly tutu and all. And with a few well-placed scraps of brown fabric, she'd transformed the crap emojis into bonbons.

As crazy as the outfit looked, it brought her comfort. Bonbons and music would be her ticket to turning things around.

She didn't know what else to do to help save the house.

But it was more than a house. The place had become her home when Babs and her grandfather had taken her in when she was five years old.

Babs had been a celebrated harpist, performing with the Denver orchestra, and her grandpa Reeves had been a gifted conductor. They'd made a decent living, but they didn't have much to spare. Despite their tight budget, they'd insisted on one sweet splurge.

Once a week, they strolled down to the Baxter Park Bakery, making up silly songs along the way, before purchasing three decadent bonbons. While she and her grandmother would choose a different flavored treat each time they visited the shop, butterscotch bonbons had been her grandfather's favorite. The man had passed away from a sudden heart attack when she was a teen, and she and her grandmother had continued the bonbon tradition in his memory.

Sitting outside the shop, it was like he was still with them, humming a melody as they noshed on the chocolatey confection. That hit of sweetness elicited a decadent rush of endorphins, and for a brief sliver of time, nothing weighed heavy on her heart.

She swallowed past the emotion in her throat as the muscles in her chest tightened.

If today was a bust, Babs would lose everything.

She couldn't fail.

Her grandfather would have wanted her to do everything in her power to keep the house.

And that's precisely what brought her to Las Vegas.

"Miss, you've got to move your car," the bellhop repeated, recovering from his bout of amusement.

She needed to get this guy to buzz off.

She checked her watch. "I'm expected inside the hotel shortly."

He reared back and took in her sad heap of a car. "You're staying at the Luxe Grandiose?"

She toyed with one of the mask's feathers. "Possibly."

"Possibly?" he echoed.

She plastered on a confident grin. "It depends on how things go inside. However, I'll have you know that I plan on working my magic and that should lead to a pile of cash. Then I'll take care of my car."

That's it. Exude confidence.

Harper Barbara Presley would be kicking ass today.

The man leaned in. "Are you a working girl, honey? Did some guy with a weird poop fetish hire you?"

Gross!

"No!" she chided. "I was invited to audition for a job.

That's why I'm wearing this outfit, but I'm a little early, and I have to teach a class online before I go in."

"You're teaching a class in that get-up?"

"Yes, it's a music class for neurodivergent children, teens, and young adults."

Confusion marred his features. "Neuro, what?"

She restrained herself from rolling her eyes. She didn't have time to explain the science of brain development, and she needed this guy on her side. "Listen, Mr. Bellhop, sir, I can't afford to pay fifty bucks to park my car, and I have to teach this lesson." She peered in her rearview mirror and spied several vehicles parked in the center of the hotel's elaborate round-about entry. "There are plenty of cars parked here. Why should I have to move?"

He snickered. "Yeah, lady, we've got Maseratis, Lamborghinis, and McLarens, not brown Volvo station wagons from the dawn of time."

Harper gasped.

How dare he insult Carol!

Yeah, she'd named her car.

"This Volvo wagon is not from the dawn of time. It's only twenty-six years old."

She was the same age as the Volvo her grandmother had passed down to her, and they'd been together forever. Carol was more of a peer than a machine.

Now, was Carol the Volvo the sexiest car?

God, no!

The minute she could afford to trade Carol in, she'd drop the turd-on-wheels in a hot second.

Sorry, Carol.

But she couldn't think about a new car at a moment like this.

She had to focus on bringing her A game.

The organizers of a contest called The Next Hot Online

Performer had reached out to her a few weeks ago and invited Bonbon Barbie to the Luxe Grandiose to, in their words, show them what made her hot and demonstrate how she got her viewers panting for more. The whole panting-for-more part was a little weird, but the offer was a godsend. It came with a considerable cash prize and the promise to be featured on multiple platforms with a robust advertising push.

And robust advertising meant more eyeballs on her and more views and subscribers.

That was the key to making it big as an online personality and how she'd pay off her grandmother's debt.

But first, she had to convince the bellhop to give her a break.

"Can you help a gal out? I'm begging. I need the hotel's Wi-Fi to finish my class, then I'll go inside the hotel and audition for this job. I'm sure that after they meet me, they'll hire me on the spot and be more than happy to pay for parking and put me up for the night," she blathered, praying that the word salad she'd spewed would become a reality.

In her heart of hearts, she had no idea what would happen once she stepped inside that hotel. Still, she had a feeling that her life was about to change—a tingling sensation telling her she was approaching a crossroads.

Whatever happened in the next few hours, there was no going back to the old Harper.

For real.

She'd most likely be down a kidney if this didn't pan out.

The bellhop removed the pack of smokes from his pocket and slipped a cigarette between his lips. "I'm going on break. I'll tell the doormen and the other bellhops to let you park here. But if the hotel manager catches sight of you, you're on your own. He'll have your car towed. That man doesn't play around. They run a tight ship here at the Luxe."

Sweet success! Score a point for Bonbon Barbie.

"Thank you," she gushed as the bellman disappeared around the corner with a trail of smoke in his wake.

He might be on break, but she had to get to work.

Her appointment with the Next Hot Performer people was in less than fifteen minutes.

She caught her reflection in the rearview mirror and stared at herself. Peering out of the dark feathery expanse, her eyes were a barometer into her psyche. Blue, brown, and gray with flecks of green and gold, it was as if her eye color changed with her mood. And her mood was currently a mix of adrenaline-infused exhilaration combined with a helping of hope. She exhaled a slow breath. She had to pull it together and finish the lesson.

Going back into instructor mode, she checked the number of viewers at the bottom of the screen.

Seven.

It was better than zero.

And it was time to wrap up this unconventional lesson. She'd never gone live in the front seat, but desperate times called for desperate measures.

And speaking of measures, she required a musical measure. She tapped the button to continue the livestream and picked up a small magnetic whiteboard with a treble clef written in brown marker and five horizontal black lines, making up one measure of music. She glanced at the grimy cupholders, searching for another teaching implement.

And yikes!

She wasn't the tidiest of twenty-six-year-olds, but the state of her car suggested a candy-crazed, chocolate-obsessed toddler had taken over. Gorging on bonbons, lollipops, and diet soda had left her car messier than usual.

No bother.

She'd give Carol a good cleaning once she returned to Denver.

She checked the timer.

She only had a few minutes to go.

From a mishmash of multicolored magnets and lollipops, she fished a red circular magnet and a red lollipop from the sticky console compartment. She placed the magnet on a makeshift musical staff, then ripped the plastic packaging from the red lollipop.

"Do is C. It's the first note on the C major scale. Do is where you go, and we always use red for this note," she continued, pointing at the magnet with the lollipop. "We use orange, yellow, green, teal, dark blue, and purple as we move up from line to space," she finished, adding the rest of the colorful magnets to the scale.

She skimmed the comments section.

It's so easy to follow the notes when they're different colors.

Her heart swelled.

"Keep using the different colors," she continued. "They'll help your brain track more easily. Download the practice sheets from the link below. Never forget, you can train your brain to read and write music." She grinned into the camera. "See you next time. I'm Bonbon Barbie, making music sweeter and easier to understand. Thanks for watching my live lesson. No matter your learning style, you can become a musician." She leaned forward and lowered her voice. "And if some giant jerk or big bully tells you that you can't because you have trouble processing information or remembering things, tell them Bonbon Barbie says…screw you."

Best to not beat around the bush.

"And don't forget to subscribe and check out the prerecorded classes, right here on LookyLoo, the internet's premier video sharing and social media platform," she blathered, finishing the session. She tapped the button to end the class, melted into the seat, then checked the total number of subscribers.

Thirty-three.

Thirty-freaking-three.

She'd read that hitting fifty thousand subscribers was the key to making real money.

Only forty-nine thousand nine hundred and sixty-seven to go until she started raking it in.

Usually, this unfortunate detail made her want to scarf down a tray of bonbons.

But not today.

If she played her cards right, those forty-nine thousand nine hundred and sixty-seven, and maybe even more, would be lining up to view her music tutorials and live sessions.

She slid the lollipop into her mouth and fanned herself.

No wonder they called this place Sin City. It was hot as hell.

She was about to close her eyes and go over what she wanted to say to the Next Hot Online Performer panel when her phone chimed. She stared at the screen. She only had ten minutes before her appointment.

That tête-à-tête with the shimmery bellhop with the thick New York accent had eaten into her prep time.

She grabbed the candy and the magnets from the cupholders and tossed them inside her tote, along with the whiteboard and her laptop. Forget the prep. She could demo the lesson she'd just taught. She'd wow them with her fresh approach to teaching kids. That had to be why they'd invited her. It was time to tuck away the growly, sharp-tongued Harper and channel the sweetness of Bonbon Barbie.

She stared at herself again in the rearview mirror. "Be Barbie. Don't let Harper screw this up. Do you hear that, H?"

"Are you talking to yourself, music teacher?"

Ugh! The bellhop.

"I'm heading inside. Can you keep an eye on my car?" she asked, sliding out of Carol. With her tote in one hand and her phone in the other, she kicked the door closed with the spike of her heel.

"I told you, lady. If the—"

"Yeah, yeah, yeah, the manager is a stickler for following rules at the fancy-pants Luxe Grandiose," she supplied. She clickity-clacked her way down the sidewalk, then came to a screeching halt.

What about her overnight bag? It was in the back of Carol.

Forget it. If someone wanted to steal a fresh pair of clothes and her toothbrush, they could have at it.

Teetering in the high-heeled boots, she strutted her stuff toward the entrance, when her phone rang and her dear friend Libby Lamb's picture appeared on the screen.

Seeing the woman's face comforted her until she glanced up and found everyone from the hotel staff to arriving guests staring at her.

She couldn't really blame them.

She was dressed like an over-sized mocha-colored ballerina in a bird mask.

"It's called a costume, people," she chided, then accepted the call and pressed the phone to her ear, like the badass she was.

A doorman did a double take as she sailed into the hotel like she owned the place.

"Hey, Libbs, what's up?" she said, ignoring the man and scanning the opulent lobby.

"We're checking on our favorite piano teacher," her friend chimed.

"We?" Harper repeated as she spied a kiosk. The Next Hot Online Performer event was being held in one of the ball-rooms, which, thanks to the map, she now saw was a hotel combined with an event center with multiple concert venues.

That had to be a good sign. This fancy-pants hotel

appeared to be the real deal, and if the Next Hot Online Performer was being held here, the contest had to be legit.

She studied the map next to the event listings, then continued her clickity-clack down a hallway as she set off toward the ballrooms and goose bumps peppered her skin. Going from the desert heat of her car to the chill of the icy air-conditioning sent a shiver down her spine.

"Penny and Charlotte are with me," Libby supplied.

"Hey, H," the women called.

"How's the piano teacher conference?" Charlotte asked.

That's right. She'd lied.

But it was a teeny-tiny white lie.

She was in Vegas because of music.

That was true.

It was easier to tell them she was attending a humdrum gathering of music instructors. Once she landed this gig, she'd spill the beans and introduce them to her bonbon alter ego.

"The conference is…whoa," she cried. Her eyes nearly popped out of the feathery mask as a trio of women clad in pasties, that left absolutely nothing to the imagination, and G-strings walked by.

This was Vegas.

"Whoa?" Penny echoed.

Focus!

"It's like whoa, hella amazing," she said, praying they wouldn't push for more details.

"That's good to hear," Libby answered, but there was concern in her tone.

That was never good.

"We called because I'm getting a weird vibe."

Oh no!

Libby was their resident yogi and spiritual maven. The chick had been tuned into reading vibes and sensations since they were in pigtails. Aside from a recent stint when her inner balance was out of whack, the woman could sense a shift in energy like nobody's business. And her yoga Spidey senses had been spot-on lately.

A tremor of trepidation worked its way down her spine. If anyone could pick up her frayed nerves, it was Libby.

"What kind of weird?" she tossed back, working to keep her voice steady as she passed two women dressed as sexy nurses.

"We wondered if you knew who else was in Las Vegas? We read about it online," Penny said gently.

What were they talking about?

Through the silence, she could picture the trio of women, her best friends, the people she loved like family, anxiously waiting for her reply.

They were full-stop, do-not-pass-go, one hundred percent worried about her.

But why?

She scanned her surroundings, and her jaw dropped.

She didn't have to ask her friends who they were talking about.

Anger roiled in her chest as the reason for their concern looked her dead in the eyes.

Chapter 2
HARPER

Harper glared at a life-sized cardboard cutout of the man who'd wrecked her six years ago.

She'd spent night after night with this douchebag, composing music, writing lyrics, and dreaming about bright lights and packed stadiums.

And…love.

She'd fallen head over heels. The sweet nothings the real version of this cardboard cutout had whispered into her ear had turned out to be a boatload of broken promises and twisted lies.

She studied his image. It was hard to believe she'd once cared for the creep. In the cardboard rendering, he didn't look like the sloppy musician who'd skipped out on her in the dead of night. With his highlights and trendy rocker apparel, the cutout of Vance Vibe, formerly Vance Viberenski, smirked at her like she was nothing, like she was another one of his fans swooning in his presence.

The total douche nozzle!

"Vance," she hissed into her cell phone, the syllable dripping with contempt.

But her anger couldn't compete with the blistering humiliation that burned her cheeks at the sight of him. An emotional hurricane threatened to destroy her resolve as a homicidal urge to kick this cutout in his cardboard balls prickled through her.

"We saw that he was performing at some hotel and event center called the Luxe Grandiose. Where is your conference being held?" Libby pressed.

"Not that one," she lied. She didn't need her friends worrying about her. And her brain was too busy thinking of ways to deface Vance's stupid cardboard smirk to muster up the name of another hotel.

She did have a rainbow assortment of markers and highlighters in her tote.

A pair of devil horns and some nose hair would improve his appearance.

She looked away, reining in her fury, when another cardboard face caught her eye. She peered down the glittering hallway. Vance's body wasn't the only life-sized cutout adorning the space. A cascade of corrugated cardboard celebrities lined the shiny marble floor, and another familiar face appeared.

"Holy shit, it's him," she whispered.

"H, are you okay, honey?" Charlotte asked.

That was a great question.

And the answer?

Hell to the no!

She flicked her gaze from the second cardboard cutout to throw her for a loop.

She had a contest to win.

She glanced at her watch.

She wasn't late…yet.

She had to get off the phone.

"Hey, girls, thanks for checking in," she said, her voice rising an octave. "I'm good. You don't have to worry about me.

Another session is starting. Treble clef versus bass clef. It's a real controversy in the piano teacher world. I have to go."

"H, one last thing," Penny said.

"Yeah?"

"Landon is in Las Vegas, too."

Landon Paige.

Damn her stupid heart for skipping a beat at the mere mention of the man. She concentrated on the cardboard cutout of the man and steadied herself. "Welp, Vegas is a big city. I doubt our paths will cross. Look!" she cried, doing a crap job of improvising.

"What is it?" Char asked.

"A brawl is breaking out between the clef clans. Love you! Talk soon! Bye," she chirped before ending the call.

She dropped her phone into her bag and stared at the cardboard cutout with perfectly tousled dark-brown hair, soulful brown eyes, and a body that would put a Greek god to shame.

There he was, in corrugated wonder, pop music's sinfully sexy heartthrob, Landon Paige.

Stop!

She could not allow herself to use the words *sinfully* or *sexy* when describing the man.

He was just a guy—no, a male platonic acquaintance. A male platonic acquaintance with a voice like velvet. A voice she used to secretly swoon over.

Who was she kidding! She still listened to his music—not that he'd put out anything new in years.

Landon Paige had exploded onto the music scene with his band Heartthrob Warfare when he was eighteen and she was barely out of elementary school. He was her first pop star crush back when she didn't know that most musicians were self-absorbed, self-serving douche nozzles. Now, the guy was in Denver and part of her extended social circle.

Insane, right?

And like the other stupid cardboard rocker, she had baggage with Landon. Well, not quite baggage, but a connection that felt more like an expectation.

An expectation she was hell-bent on defying.

An expectation tied to the nanny matchmaking maven, Madelyn Malone.

The woman worked exclusively with rich and famous single male caregivers. Over the last six months, the mysterious Ms. Malone, with her trademark scarlet scarf, rich Eastern European accent, and Fendi-fairy godmother vibe, had recruited Penny, Charlotte, and Libby as nannies. Her friends had each been given a position with a single male caregiver who was no longer single because her best friends were engaged to their nanny match bosses.

Yep, Penny and the hot nerd, Rowen Gale, found love through nanny matchmaking bliss. Charlotte and the hotheaded chef, Mitch Elliott, were next, and the British boxing sensation, Erasmus Cress, had recently liked it enough to put a ring on it with Libby. They were blissfully happy, breaking off into their trios that included a cute kid. And yes, she liked these kids. Phoebe, Oscar, and Sebastian were adorable. The nanny match lovefest was enough to make her gag most days, but she couldn't deny that they made delightful families.

But here's the thing.

There was one man left in the men's nanny match group.

Landon-freaking-Paige.

She didn't know the specifics about Landon's caregiver status.

Was he a dad, an uncle, a big brother? Could a stork have accidentally dropped a little nose picker on his doorstep?

She had no clue.

Whatever it was, the men kept that information hush-hush.

But she did know what her friends were thinking.

With a group of four women and a group of four men in need of a nanny, it only made sense that she and Landon had to be the last match.

But that wasn't how she rolled.

And there was no way in hell Landon could ever be her match—nanny-wise or romantic.

He was a musician.

And she sure as hell wasn't making the mistake of getting close to one of those again. That meant putting the kibosh on becoming the dude's nanny. Granted, the nanny gig paid well, but it wasn't enough. The debt she needed to clear came with far more zeroes than even the generous nanny salary promised.

And then there was one final salient fact.

Madelyn hadn't approached her regarding a nanny position, which was a damn good thing. The woman had hit the mark when she'd matched her friends, but her situation was different. Plus, she simply didn't have the disposition to act as a parental figure, especially after what her mother and father had done to her.

Dammit, why did her mind have to go there?

The empty place inside her, the place she hid behind a sharp tongue, a heap of sass, and a practiced scowl threatened to swallow her whole.

She removed her mask and dropped it into her tote. "You're about to become the next hot online performer. Focus on the future. Do it for Babs. Think of Grandad," she whispered, when a voice from her past cut through the air like a ripe fart.

"Harper? Harper Presley, is that you?"

Of all the hotels and event centers in this town, what was the chance she'd bump into Vance the prick?

Clearly, one hundred percent.

The universe seemed hell-bent on throwing every obstacle her way.

She steadied herself, ready to go off on the jerk, then remembered what she was wearing.

Universe, you really deserve a kick in the metaphysical balls.

She forced herself to meet Vance's gaze, then caught salvation out of the corner of her eye. She spied a sign with The Next Hot Online Performer Try-outs at the entrance to a ballroom only a few feet away.

She was so close to solving her problems.

Inches away from making it big.

She couldn't let this encounter with her ex throw her off. She shifted her bag to her other shoulder.

Don't let him get into your head.

"How nice to see you, Harper," Vance crooned. "Are you here to take in my concert?"

Gag.

"That would be a no," she shot back.

"You're certainly admiring my cutout. It's hard not to," Vance purred—no, oozed. The man oozed like pus pouring from a giant, gangrenous wound.

He sauntered toward her with a gaggle of busty women and a smattering of douchey bros in tow.

Despite raking in the cash, there was nothing remarkable about him. With mousy brown hair streaked with golden highlights, he'd become a cookie-cutter pop star. And he'd done it by stealing her work, her words, and her melodies.

"I'm here in a professional capacity. You'll have to excuse me. I'm expected in the ballroom," she touted while holding herself back from punching the smirk right off Vance's stupid face.

He looked over his shoulder. "That's what you're doing instead of making music?"

What did he have against online performers?

The guy's music was on every social platform. Like it or not, he was an online performer, too.

He looked her up and down. "I guess it's not too far from your wheelhouse. You weren't half bad in the sack."

She tasted bile. This man was nauseating.

Every cell in her body wanted to stomp on his foot and drive the spike of her heel straight through his gaudy, expensive shoes.

Stay cool, girl.

Don't let him take this away from you.

"I'm going into that ballroom, *jackass*. A girl's got to make a living. And what do you care what I do? I haven't heard from you since you slinked out of town. Or is it something else? Do you feel like stealing this opportunity from me, too?"

She couldn't help herself.

In the end, the snark always won.

And in this case, it was for a good reason.

He'd full-on passed off her music as his own. That's how he'd gotten his foot in the door. Yes, one could argue they'd somewhat collaborated on the songs, if you called being in the same apartment and breathing the same air collaboration. Vance had mostly played with his phone and taken selfies of himself while she worked, but by the time she figured out what he'd done, he'd already signed with a label.

And what was she supposed to do?

She was a broke college student when she'd heard the first bars of her song play on the radio with his heavily modulated voice belting out her lyrics. She'd been furious, and rightly so. But she didn't know the first thing about going after someone, nor did she have the resources to do it—or, more importantly, the proof.

The guy might be a first-class jerk, but he was smart enough to take every slip of paper, every notebook, and delete every audio and video clip from her phone that connected her to the music.

Even if she'd had the resources, it would be a he said, she said case.

It was a gamble she couldn't afford to take.

Vance tried to play off her comment, yucking it up with his entourage, but agitation rolled off the man in crashing waves. "Feisty as ever," he bit out, brushing her off, but she'd struck a nerve, and she wasn't done.

"This isn't feisty, Vance Viberenski," she replied, enunciating the syllables of his less than cool last name. "This is complete and utter disgust. How do you live with yourself?"

For a split second, trepidation flashed in his eyes. But before she could blink, a slimy smirk spread across his lips. "Isn't she hilarious?" he spouted to his crew of goons, then leaned in. "Still trying to pretend you're some badass and not the little girl nobody wanted. How very, very sad, *Harper Barbara.*"

The man might rely on Auto-tune and a bevy of sound techs to make him sound half-decent, but he sure had a talent for wielding cruelty.

The breath caught in her throat.

Only Babs called her Harper Barbara.

As much as she despised the guy, she couldn't heap the blame solely on him. She'd let herself be used. She was the one who'd shared her heart, her music, and the details about her parents with him.

Her lips parted, but nothing came out.

Vance's blue eyes glittered with brutal delight. He leaned in and lowered his voice. "My label has a team of lawyers. They're sharks. You throw an accusation at me like that again, and all I have to do is make one call. They'll slap a defamation of character suit on you faster than you can say the name of *my* hit song, 'Every Time You Break My Heart.'"

His song?

The hissing breath against the shell of her ear made her want to crawl out of her skin.

She took a step back, hating the man, but he wasn't wrong. He held all the cards.

What had she seen in this prick?

Her poor judgment in men wasn't the only thing gnawing at her soul.

Other slippery voices whispered in the darkest parts of her mind.

He took off because you're not a star. You don't have what it takes to make it in music. You're no good.

You're the girl who gets left behind.

She pushed the maddening thoughts aside. Her gaze grew glassy, and she looked away. She wasn't about to let him see that his verbal daggers had hit the mark.

"You'll have to excuse me," she said, willing her voice to remain steady. "I have an interview. I'm about to become the internet's next hot performer."

His eyes nearly popped out of their sockets. He peered at the ballroom doors. "You're really going in there? I thought you were kidding."

"I was invited, thanks to my...stellar online talents."

Take that!

Her ex shook his head. "Jesus, Harper, I never figured you'd amount to much, but porn? That's your plan?"

She stared at him. If she wasn't still standing, she would have sworn her bones had liquefied.

What the hell did he say?

Vance studied her expression, then burst out laughing.

Was he messing with her?

She had to set the record straight.

"I'm here because I teach neurodivergent learners how to read and write music through my online LookyLoo classes. That's what I'll be doing on a larger scale when

I'm chosen as the next hot online performer," she announced, then caught a fair amount of skin out of the corner of her eye. The gals in nothing but pasties and G-strings leaned against the wall, staring at their phones, as more scantily clad women sauntered around outside the ballroom doors.

"Yeah, sure, good luck with your neurodivergent porn gig," Vance remarked with a smug twist to his lips, when the ballroom doors opened, and a bearded man emerged with a clipboard.

"Bonbon Barbie?" he called, holding the door open with his foot as he glanced back and forth down the hallway.

This was it!

She ignored the swarm of near-naked women and waved to the guy. "I'm here."

"That's your porn name? Bonbon Barbie?" Vance could barely get the words out. His body convulsed as he busted out laughing.

What was wrong with him?

Had his celebrity existence and the perpetual party lifestyle left him a few notes short of a measure?

She blew the guy off and hurried toward the ballroom.

The bearded dude eyed her costume, then checked his list. "Bonbon Barbie, you forgot to send in a video."

What?

She could not be disqualified because of an error.

"You're mistaken," she said, her stupid voice rising a nervous octave. "When I accepted the invitation to audition, I attached a lesson I taught on coding sharps and flats with different colored highlighters."

Confusion marred the man's expression. "Sharps and flats? Isn't that musical stuff?"

Was everyone in this city a few notes short of a full measure?

"Yes, it's musical. I'm a music teacher."

The guy's brows knit together. He frowned, then angled his body toward the ballroom. "I need a little help out here."

A tall man with pasty skin and slicked-back hair joined them. "What's the problem?"

The bearded guy nodded toward her. "Bonbon Barbie says she's a music teacher."

The tall guy sucked in a tight breath and cringed. "Did you say Bonbon Barbie?"

"Yeah, it's here on the list. But there's an asterisk next to her name," the clipboard dude supplied.

An asterisk? Why would they put an asterisk by her name?

"I'm Bonbon Barbie. Your organization emailed me and invited me here," she chimed, doing her best to not melt into a pool of mortification. Heat rose to her cheeks. She could feel her douche nozzle ex-boyfriend's eyes boring into her.

"Shit!" the tall guy muttered, shaking his head. "I forgot to email you about the mix-up."

No, no, no!

She shifted her stance and fluffed her brown tutu. "Mix-up?" she replied, her voice rising another shaky octave like a jittery opera singer after pounding a case of energy drinks.

The pasty man tapped the clipboard. "We meant to invite *Bang Bang* Barbie and accidentally reached out to you. I got the bang bangs and bonbons confused."

He had to be kidding. But the man wasn't laughing.

Three, two, one.

Blastoff for planet humiliation.

This was really happening.

She'd accidentally been invited to audition to become a porn star.

It might have been funny if she hadn't pegged every hope she had on this contest.

A cacophony of laughter rang out.

She'd almost forgotten she had an audience.

Vance and his minions slapped each other on the back in blissful jubilation, taking pleasure in her catastrophic condition.

For the millionth time, what had she seen in this guy?

The tall man ignored the hubbub, took a step back, and undressed her with his eyes. He licked his lips.

Ew!

"You are hot," he said with eyes glued to her bonbons. "Your whole sexy poop emoji thing might really work for some of our kinkier viewers. It's working for me."

This could not be her life.

She crossed her arms, shielding her bonbons from this sleazeball. "I'll have to decline the offer."

"Then step aside, poop kink."

"Poop kink?" she repeated, to the delight of stupid Vance.

"We've got real performers to interview," he huffed, giving her the brushoff. He peered down the hall at the trio of brunettes clad in…G-strings and pasties.

"Step aside?" she seethed. "Shouldn't you apologize? I drove twelve hours to get here. I spent everything I have on gas."

The tall guy shrugged. "Like I said, it was a mistake."

A mistake that had led her on a wild-goose chase to Sin City.

White-hot anger and blistering humiliation flooded her system when Vance's voice cut through the corridor.

"Always great to see you, Harper. Keep fighting the good fight and vibe on," he called over his shoulder, convulsing with laughter as he dropped his douchiest of douchebag catchphrases and paraded down the hallway with his entourage.

It appeared rock-bottom wasn't as low as she could go.

This slice of humiliation pie had landed her in the special sub-level of rock-bottom: the poop kink level of hell.

The bearded dude with the clipboard drew a slash across

her name, then scanned the space. "We're ready for *Bang Bang Barbie*," the man called, then tossed her a wink.

Was she supposed to be proud of him for getting it right?

Her whole life was on the cusp of total ruin. She pinched the bridge of her nose when a clackity-clack and a woman's high-pitched squeal cut through the hum of conversation.

"I'm Bang Bang Barbie," called a blonde, Barbie-looking chick covered in glitter, and barely anything else, as she teetered toward them in shiny pink heels. "Sorry, I'm late. The roundabout was blocked because they're towing away some broken-down heap parked near the main entrance."

A broken-down heap?

Her jaw dropped. "Oh shit!"

"Yeah, the car looked like shit. It was brown," Bang Bang Barbie offered like she'd majored in color identification at Dingbat University.

This was too much for one woman to take.

She'd explode if she didn't release the anger roiling in her chest.

She marched up to Vance's cardboard cutout, released a primal scream, then punched his stupid flat face.

And…

"Holy shit, that hurt!" she exclaimed, cradling her throbbing hand as the people in the hallway stared at her, wide-eyed the way one would watch a train wreck.

Say something not crazy.

She straightened the paper version of Vance. "These cutouts are way more solid than they look."

Stop talking!

She had bigger problems.

She had to get to her car.

She turned on her heel, then booked it down the hallway. Tearing through the lobby like the coffee-colored version of The Flash, she burst through the doors. A blast of desert air took the breath right out of her as she watched a tow truck turn the corner and disappear with her Volvo.

"Carol!" she screamed, but it was no use. Carol, in her brown Volvo glory, was gone, swallowed by dark skies as the tow truck merged into a sea of traffic illuminated by flashing lights.

She ran her hands down her face. "How is this my life?" she moaned, then hit pause on her pity party when someone tapped her shoulder.

"Sorry, music teacher," the burly New York bellhop offered. "I hear the couple who own this hotel run a tight ship—real ball busters."

But she didn't have the strength to worry about some billionaire couple who owned this shiny event center.

"My car," she whimpered as her phone rang. Moving like a zombie bonbon on autopilot, she slipped the cell from her tote. "Hello?"

"Ms. Presley?" a man said, his tone all business.

"Yeah?" she eked out.

"It's been exceedingly difficult to get in touch with you."

"Who is this?" she stammered, working to regain her bearings.

"It's Richard P. Snodgrass, from the bank."

The bank.

"It's imperative we speak, Ms. Presley. You're running out of time before—"

As if she were caught in a slow-motion tornado, she hit the end call button and turned off her phone.

She could not deal with the bank. There was only so much mortification a gal could stomach.

"Here you go, music teacher," the bellhop said, pulling her from her stupor. Concern welled in his eyes as he pulled a slip of paper from his pocket. "It's good for one free shrimp cocktail at the bar," he explained, handing her a coupon.

Who knew rock-bottom's poop kink level came with a coupon for free shrimp?

"Thanks, sir, that sounds...shrimp."

Okay, she wasn't firing on all cylinders. That was to be expected. It wasn't every day a gal drove twelve hours only to learn she'd been mistaken for a porn actress while her song-stealing ex looked on.

She took a breath. "You're a sweet man."

"And one more thing," the bellhop said and fished another item from his shimmery coat. "It's the number for the impound lot."

She nodded and dropped it into her bag.

The man shifted his stance. "You don't look like you landed that gig."

"I didn't. They wanted a porn star, and I'm a singer and a songwriter."

What did she say?

Why had she chosen those words to describe herself?

She hadn't thought of herself in those terms in years.

"What will you do now?" the burly man asked. "You got any friends or family who can help you out?"

She did.

Her friends were successful gazillionaires. With one call, they'd be there in a hot second. But the thought of coming clean stung. Her pride, her drive to be Miss Snarky Independent Harper Barbara Presley, wouldn't permit her to wave the white flag.

Out of her group of friends, she was the tough one. The scrapper. The mouthy bitch. When she was in kindergarten, she could terrify the toughest of fourth-grade boys with one blazing glare.

She caught her reflection in the building's shiny exterior.

She didn't look so tough now.

The bite of failure had punctured her heart—and it showed.

She lifted her chin. What she required was a reprieve—a brief respite.

Her career was in the toilet, and there was a real possibility that she and Babs would lose the house, but she couldn't let her mind go there—not yet.

She held up the coupon triumphantly. "Tonight," she announced, "I'll enjoy a complimentary shrimp cocktail thanks to a very kind man."

If she was trying not to look crazy, she was doing a terrible job.

A wry grin stretched across the bellhop's face. She hadn't really looked at him until now. He had rosy cheeks and kind green eyes, and he had to be in his early sixties. And was he wearing make up?

"Off you go," the man said, then held the door for her.

Armed with the coupon, she entered the buzzing hotel, then stopped. Standing in the center of the lobby, she closed her eyes and remembered a piece of advice that had been with her since she was a girl.

If something's not working, try another melody, but never stop making music.

"Find another melody," she whispered and listened to the overlapping rhythms of rollicking conversations. Layer upon layer, she parsed out a tune. A warmth spread through her, recalling the silly songs she and her grandparents used to make up on their walks to the bakery for their weekly bonbon date.

"*Sweet, so sweet, hello to my favorite treat*," she sang, recalling the bonbon jingle she'd crafted on one of their strolls years ago. She sighed, prepared to stuff her face with shrimp, when someone tapped her shoulder. She opened her eyes, expecting to see her kind bellhop. Instead, she met the gaze of a slim, older woman holding a tray littered with brightly colored glasses topped with little umbrellas.

"Are you with the bachelorette group, honey?" the woman asked in a New York accent.

A decent number of New Yorkers worked here.

"What?" she asked, taking in the woman clad in black. With a cascade of silver hair, high cheekbones, and a prominent chin, the woman's face fascinated her.

The lady gestured over her shoulder toward the entrance to a dance club on the far side of the lobby. It was teeming with young women in tutus, laughing, dancing, and licking giant lollipops.

Tutus and lollipops? Kind of strange, but she couldn't knock the combo.

"The bachelorette group," the silver-haired woman repeated. "The party is in the Luxe Grandiose dance club." She pointed to a section of the lobby flashing neon. "And the wedding will take place across the lobby at the chapel."

"That's convenient," Harper mumbled. "I'm sure no terrible choices have been made with a disco across from a place to get hitched."

The woman chuckled. "I'm one of the hosts at the Luxe Grandiose. My job is to direct you to your intended destination."

Intended destination?

"Take this," she said, handing her one of the fancy drinks.

"Why?" Harper asked skeptically.

"Because of your attire, honey."

This lady thought she was with the bridal party.

Score one for the thrift store tutu.

"Okay," she answered and accepted the frilly beverage.

"You'll be drinking for free tonight, of course," the woman added.

Jackpot!

"Free? Like, I don't have to pay for anything, free?"

All right, universe, this was an improvement.

The hostess narrowed her gaze. "Yes, as long as you're with the wedding party. You're dressed like you're a part of the group."

Just go with it.

She plastered a grin to her lips. "I am definitely with the wedding party. I couldn't be happier for..."

Shit!

"Katrina and Jude," the hostess supplied, biting back a grin.

"Yep, good old Katrina and Jude," she replied and downed the fruity concoction before the hostess could yank it away. She might have to sell a kidney, but she was free and clear to put a dent in her liver this evening.

"I can take your bag and check it at the concierge. What's your name?"

"Harper Presley." She slid her tote off her shoulder and peered at the feathery mask. "I plan on drinking away my problems and making terrible choices tonight. I've had a crap-tastic day," she confessed, handing her bag to the hostess.

That was an understatement, but a night posing as part of a bride's entourage was precisely what she needed.

For one night, she'd go wild and let loose.

She scanned the lobby and noticed two women. One wore a T-shirt with Landon Paige's picture silkscreened across the front, and another sported Vance's stupid smirking face.

What a visual.

Her nightmare of a past and definitely-not-her-future represented in concert apparel.

She eyed the tray of drinks. If anyone needed copious amounts of alcohol, it was her.

She set the empty glass on the tray and picked up two more drinks.

"Double-fisting already," the hostess teased.

Hell to the yes.

She bit the top of the umbrella like a rabid beast and tossed it to the ground before downing drink number two. "Oh, yes. How much worse can this night get?" she mused, ready to drain the third glass, when the woman dropped the host vibe and waved her in.

"Honey," she said with a conspiratorial grin, "word to the wise. Never ask that question in Sin City."

Chapter 3

LANDON

"Landon Paige, Landon Paige!"

The energy in the concert hall thrummed as the crowd chanted his name. The syllables echoed in a thunderous roar. Whistles and whoops punctuated the air as the spotlight held him in a golden glow. He stilled and gave the crowd space to release the tidal wave of emotion. Breathless, his heart hammered and sweat soaked his T-shirt as he absorbed the adulation.

He used to live for this.

Yeah, *used to*, before the anger and clawing regret had taken over.

He used to peer into the crowd and rejoice in the phenomenon, savoring the moment when a group of perfect strangers ceased being individuals. Once he strummed his guitar and the lights hit the stage, the crowd became a single organism. It swayed to the beat, singing along and devouring his every move. The power that came with being a pop star used to leave him blissfully punch-drunk. The rush had him riding an endorphin high that could sustain him for hours, even days. Akin to being plugged into an IV of pure adrenaline spiked with unwavering creative energy, new melodies took hold. Lyrics buzzed around his mind in a flurry of activity.

He'd play a full set, then spend hours with the two people he loved the most in this world making music.

But not anymore.

It had been almost eight years since the stream of sweet euphoria had flowed through his veins.

Eight damned years.

Eight years ago, nothing seemed out of reach. Now, he knew what the future held. And it had nothing to do with spirit-affirming invincibility or harnessing inspiration.

He also knew when and where this reminder of his past life would rear its ugly head.

He sensed the crowd readying itself for the dreaded transition.

The boom of his name died out as two words took their place.

"Heartthrob Warfare, Heartthrob Warfare!"

He stared into the lights and softened his gaze, allowing his vision to grow blurry. He did everything in his power to zone out, disappear, and keep the sound from tearing him apart.

But it always got him.

Every damned time.

It didn't matter where he was performing. From New York to London to Dubai, and now to Las Vegas, the crowd always did this.

They thought they were paying tribute to two lost souls. They thought it brought him comfort.

It didn't. It did the opposite.

It was the ultimate reminder of what he'd lost.

But he couldn't show it.

He had to play the game, be the star, sing the songs, and accept the crowd's collective condolences.

He ignored the ache in his chest. With the encore complete, the torture was almost over.

Stand there and let them drink in the star. Let them shoot a video. Let them snap pictures.

But don't let them see the real you.

He swallowed past the lump in his throat.

Every person in the audience had paid their hard-earned money to see a pop star and feast on the pop god. He could be that for them, not because it was his passion, but because it was his job. And blessedly, it was time to bring tonight's performance to a close.

He glanced to his left and nodded to a musician playing bass. He spoke the man's name. He allowed the crowd to cheer, then looked to the right and gestured to the musician on the keyboard and followed the same routine.

It wasn't that he disliked these musicians. They were terrific people, but they were stand-ins, fillers, placeholders. Years ago, before the accident, when he'd complete the same movements, it was to acknowledge his best friend, Trey Grant, and his little sister, Leighton Paige.

Listening to the crowd, then acknowledging the stand-in musicians, was a bitter pill. It made him feel closer to Trey and Leighton while reminding him that he'd never share the stage with the pair again. It triggered the memories of the last words passed between them.

Harsh words he could never take back.

Caught in a cyclone of nostalgia spiked with crushing despair, he listened as the crowd chanted the name of the band he'd started with Trey and Leighton back when they were teenagers.

It was so easy then, snacking on junk food, jamming in a garage, and shooting videos of their backyard performances. They'd uploaded the clips onto social media for kicks. Sure, they'd dreamed of playing in major venues across the world one day. They were small-town teenagers with stars in their eyes. But they'd never expected to become household names in the blink of an eye.

"Heartthrob Warfare, Heartthrob Warfare!"

He remembered the day Leighton had blurted out the two words. At the time, they would have died laughing if someone had told them those words would grace the lips of millions of fans and be chanted in near-deafening waves of palpable sound.

It had been a rainy summer day in the Colorado foothills. After hours of fruitlessly trying to perfect a song, Trey had abandoned his bass and Leighton had left the keyboard. The two decided to take a break and play Scrabble on an old milk crate in the center of the garage. They often shifted gears when they struggled to come up with lyrics or something wasn't jiving with a melody. Some days, a word on the board would spark creativity. Leighton would call it out, and they'd play around with it, riffing and improvising, using the word to jumpstart their creativity.

But he never joined them around the game board.

Scrabble wasn't his thing. Reading and writing—any academics, for that matter—had never come easily.

They still didn't.

Leighton had gotten the brains when it came to school. Still, he had his own process when it came to music—a process that incorporated sound, movement, and another quality he still couldn't quite describe. With the murmur of Trey and Leighton's voices and the tap of the Scrabble tiles hitting the game board in the background, he sat on a stack of milk crates and strummed his guitar, experimenting with words and melodies. He couldn't see the notes. He felt them. He understood them, which was quite extraordinary since he'd never taken a music lesson.

His childhood had been too volatile.

He and Leighton had lost their parents when he was eleven and she was just shy of her tenth birthday. Their paternal grandmother had taken them in, but she soon fell ill. She was their only living relative, and by the time he was twelve, he and his sister found themselves in the foster care system.

Not many folks wanted to take on the combo of a moody preteen boy and a sharp-tongued spitfire of a girl.

Luckily, they only needed one couple to want them.

And one couple had.

The summer before his freshman year of high school, he and Leighton moved in with two eccentric sculptors, Tomás Medina and Bess Fletcher. With their wild manes of hair and hippie lifestyle, their new foster parents weren't like anyone they'd met. There weren't any rules in the Medina-Fletcher household like they'd experienced in other foster placements. They had free rein of the multi-acre property nestled near Evergreen, Colorado, in the foothills of the Rocky Mountains. It was the kind of wonderland that could spark even the surliest of teen's creativity.

The house was like a museum of oddities. Tomàs and Bess were collectors of the strange and the beautifully unusual. While their place was jam-packed with the tools of their trade, clay, plaster, chunks of wood, and hunks of metal, it also contained treasures and trinkets from their travels.

With their foster parents' easygoing vibe, he and his sister settled in and spent hours ignoring the dust bunnies and exploring every nook and cranny. They'd started in the attic, rifling through trunks, and they'd hit the jackpot. They uncovered a trove of *Rolling Stone* magazines from the sixties, seventies, and eighties and stumbled upon an old record player and a stack of dust-covered records.

They pored over the images. Between soaking in pictures of the Beatles, Jefferson Airplane, Led Zeppelin, the Eagles,

U2, REM, and the Police, they played the old albums and screwed around, singing into paintbrushes.

But the exploration didn't stop in the attic.

Their foster family encouraged them to tinker with whatever items they found in the house and on the property. That's when he and Leighton made a life-changing discovery in the dusty detached garage. Horns, a clunky tuba, a guitar, a trio of keyboards, and an upright piano sat linked together between spider webs.

The minute they'd entered the space and spied the guitar, a topsy-turvy tingle had passed through him.

It was as if he'd found his calling hidden beneath a layer of dust.

And he wasn't wrong. Discovering the cache of instruments had changed his life.

With tiny particles dancing in the rays of light pouring in through a pair of windows on the west side of the structure, nothing less than a miracle had taken place within the cluttered space. For a kid who hated school and wasn't keen on sports, it was as if he'd struck gold.

Like a pair of musical savants, he and Leighton learned they could play just about any song by ear on just about any instrument.

It was uncanny.

After a few weeks of living with Tomàs and Bess, they'd become decent musicians. Leighton had gravitated toward the piano while he couldn't get enough of the guitar.

And this gift, and the racket they were making until late into the night, had caught the attention of their neighbor, a gangly kid his age with a mop of sandy brown hair and sky-blue eyes named Trey Grant, who happened to play the bass.

And the rest was history.

The three of them spent every free moment in the garage eating, sleeping, and breathing music.

A couple of years in, Trey suggested they start recording their sessions, and Leighton had proposed they share their music online.

But one crucial component was missing.

They needed a name, and thanks to a handful of Scrabble tiles, one stormy Colorado day, they got one.

With the rain pounding the garage's tin roof, his sister had shrieked as she placed her tiles on the board. She added *throb* to the end of the word *heart* that had built off the *A* in Trey's word, *warfare*.

"LB, that's our name. Heartthrob Warfare," his sister had called, pointing out the words to him, letter by letter.

He could still hear the excitement in her voice.

"Heartthrob Warfare is going to war and fighting for what makes your heart sing."

That's how Leighton had explained it. She'd beamed, saying the words over and over like a spell.

Heartthrob Warfare, Heartthrob Warfare!

Was he sold on it?

Not exactly.

But that was the thing about Leighton.

Once she'd fallen in love with something, there was no talking her out of it.

The truth was, after a bit more consideration, he couldn't help but admit the name was catchy as hell. It possessed a lovely, melodious cadence to it.

And what did Trey think?

It was no secret that Trey had been in love with his sister since he'd set eyes on her back when they were kids. So of course, the guy had agreed, and thanks to a handful of letter tiles, Heartthrob Warfare was born.

But there was more.

Like magic, minutes after Leighton had spoken the name, a refrain came to him.

Heartthrob warfare, I'm fighting for your love.
Heartthrob warfare, it's a battle for your touch.
Heartthrob warfare, I need you, oh, so much.

The lyrics and the melody revealed themselves to him like they always did.

And Trey and Leighton pulled the song together like he could never do.

Like he still couldn't do.

Fifteen years ago, the song "Heartthrob Warfare" had been the catalyst. He and Trey were eighteen and Leighton was seventeen when the song went viral. Thanks to millions of views on the social media platform LookyLoo, before he could blink, they'd been plucked from obscurity. A manager had offered her services, and days later, they'd signed a contract with a music label.

That was either the point where everything went right or where his life began to unravel.

The music label had tweaked, no, completely changed, their acoustic-rock vibe.

The producers brightened their sound with techno beats and snappy pop refrains. The PR department turned the trio into the bubblegum version of their band, but they had allowed them to keep their name. And thanks to Mitzi Jones, their no-nonsense, tenacious manager who'd seemed to materialize out of thin air, they not only held the copyright to their music, but they also retained the rights to their sound recordings, which was a big deal and gave them control. Many an artist had gotten screwed over, not understanding the importance of both.

But the music label had screwed them in one regard.

They'd played up their youth and pegged him as the dreamy heartthrob lead singer and the face of Heartthrob Warfare, effectively pigeonholing the group as sugary-sweet pop artists.

They didn't mind the changes to their music at the time, and he'd be lying if he said he didn't enjoy the attention.

For the first time, he'd felt accomplished, even talented.

And nobody could see the parts he hated about himself.

He'd welcomed the tsunami of adulation.

They were three naïve teens from Colorado living the superstar dream. They'd agreed they'd get back to the music they wanted to play, one day. They'd harness the acoustic, edgier sound and focus on meaningful lyrics and melodies that stayed with people and lived in the listener's soul—the kind of music showcased at Colorado's Red Rocks Unplugged Concert.

There, artists didn't rely on synthetic sound and pulsing bass.

Raw talent was what got a musician on the stage.

But *one day* kept getting pushed back, and with each delay, frustration built and anger festered inside him, until the dream of returning to Heartthrob Warfare's original sound imploded.

Gone, in the space of a breath.

It almost didn't seem real—like a dream, no, like a nightmare.

Forget the fame and fortune. He'd give everything he had to go back in time to the three of them laughing and making music in that garage.

Back before the hard choices.

Back before the ultimatums and cruel words.

But there was no going back.

There was only the future—a future that, even from his perch on center stage with throngs of fans calling out his name, looked damned bleak.

He glanced offstage and caught his manager from the corner of his eye. Mitzi had known him long enough to tell that he'd zoned out. She gave him a healthy dose of stink eye, ran her hands through her spiky salt-and-pepper-colored hair, then signaled for him to wrap it up.

The woman was gruff but fair. She'd gone to bat for them back when they didn't know a thing about the music industry. He didn't trust many people, but he trusted her.

He nodded, then gripped the mic. "Thank you, Las Vegas. It's been an amazing run, and you've been an amazing crowd."

"Landon Paige, Landon Paige!" they chanted, the noise near deafening as one thought rattled around in his mind.

Was this the end?

This was his final concert at the Luxe Grandiose. For the last six months, he'd commuted between his home in Denver and a deluxe suite at the Luxe.

He'd gone through the motions, praying these shows would jumpstart his creativity.

They hadn't.

And worse than that, he feared he was on the cusp of a complete career collapse.

And he only had himself and his shortcomings to blame.

He pushed the vexing thoughts aside.

Play the part. Be who the fans need you to be.

Nobody wanted to see the man behind the pop star mask. They came to see a show, to experience Heartthrob Warfare's very own heartthrob, Landon Paige.

And that's what they'd get.

He sure as hell wasn't about to give them a glimpse of the real man. The man with glaring faults, humiliating deficiencies, and a secret.

Only a handful of people knew his secret, and that's how it had to stay.

He squinted, blocking the bright lights with his hand, and focused on the fans holding up a sea of signs. He scanned the jumble of letters, once, twice, and then for a third time before landing on one he recognized.

Landon Paige, marry me.

He could decipher this one. It had been a staple since the beginning.

Playing the part of the pop star, he pointed toward the ladies holding the sign. "Marry, you? I wouldn't dare. You're too good for me," he crooned as the women lost their minds, screaming and jumping up and down as the people around them held up their phones, recording the exchange.

The "dare" bit was his go-to dreamboat bullshit act. It always made the audience go wild. It used to make Trey and Leighton laugh their asses off once they were offstage.

But it wasn't total bullshit. Marriage would never be in the cards for him.

But make no mistake. He was no monk.

He'd screwed his fair share of women. He was the world's heartthrob. Supermodels threw themselves at him. But it never lasted, because he couldn't let them in. He couldn't reveal the heartbreaking secret behind the heartthrob.

Just as the thought crossed his mind, he pictured a pair of hazel eyes—eyes that glinted with mischief and seemed to change color with her mood. Not quite brown, not quite blue, and not quite gray with flecks of green and gold, these chameleon eyes belonged to the woman who'd become the absolute bane of his existence.

Harper Presley.

Chapter 4
LANDON

Harper Presley.

There she was, popping into his head again.

The roar of the crowd faded, and her voice was the only sound he could hear.

And why was that?

Six months ago, he'd heard her sing.

That might be a bit of a stretch. It was more of a taunt-laced, sing-songy one-liner. She chanted her friend's name and what sounded a hell of a lot like the word *weirdo*, which would have fit the scenario.

Penny, Penny, Penny, Penny, Penny and the weirdos.

Christ, it had stopped him dead in his tracks. He'd messed with his hat to shield his eyes to keep her from seeing that he was watching her and waiting, no, yearning for her to part her lips and tease her friend again with the snarky tune.

Still, it wasn't just her voice that left him dumbstruck.

She was simply stunning.

Her chocolate-brown hair fell in loose waves around her shoulders.

And that body! The thought of Harper Presley in a miniskirt got his pulse racing.

She wasn't spindly like the skin and bone models he'd dated. She was more of a petite powerhouse. This woman had curves that could render a man speechless—and that's precisely what she'd done.

The first time he'd seen her was when the tech billionaire, Rowen Gale, one of the men in his nanny match men's group, got set up with his nanny.

Yes, he was a part of a nanny match men's group. It sounded like utter bullshit, but it was the real deal.

The foursome included Rowen, the hothead chef, Mitch Elliot, and the boxing champion, Erasmus Cress, and himself, the world's pop heartthrob.

Mitzi had contacted the mysterious nanny match maven, Madelyn Malone, to help with the nanny selection. That's when he'd become part of a group of single male caregivers waiting for the matchmaker to place them with a nanny.

The other three guys had been matched over the last six months.

And now it was his turn.

He was the last to go.

In a little over a week, he'd employ a nanny, and his title of absent uncle would change to permanent caregiver when he took custody of his niece, Aria.

Aria.

It was a beautiful, flowing name. But don't be fooled by the delicate, melodious moniker.

His niece was a seven-year-old spitfire with enough boldness in her little finger to take out half the globe with one searing glance.

He loved the kid to pieces. She was the perfect combination of Leighton and Trey with her blue eyes and dark locks. A fact that made his heart swell and then crack into a million pieces.

She'd lived with Tomàs and Bess these past two years.

He'd always known this was a temporary arrangement.

But six months ago, an end date to his responsibility respite had been set.

His foster parents had been invited to lead a sculpting seminar abroad at a university in northern Italy.

They'd offered to turn it down and continue to care for Aria, but he couldn't let them do that.

It had been their dream to return to Italy to teach. Their fiftieth wedding anniversary fell during this time, and he'd insisted they celebrate the joyous occasion at his home in the region. He loved them. He wanted this for them. Still, when they'd shared the news a few months ago, this seismic shift felt lightyears away.

Now, only a little over a week remained before they departed.

It was time for him to step up and accept his role as Aria's legal guardian. He knew this, but it scared him to death.

If it was safe to assume he wasn't the marrying type, he sure as hell wasn't the parenting type either.

He needed help.

But this was where it got complicated when it came to the nanny situation.

Harper's three best friends, Penny, Charlotte, and Libby, had been matched with the three men in his nanny match men's group.

And how'd that go?

They were engaged.

All of them.

Every nanny match had turned into a nanny *love* match.

So much for maintaining a platonic boss-nanny relationship. It was hearts and roses with these three couples. And with Harper's three friends matched with his three friends, he didn't have to be a genius to deduce that he and Harper were the next match.

That couldn't happen. Love was not on the horizon for him. It couldn't be.

He didn't despise love. He was happy his friends had found it. He genuinely liked them, and he'd even connected with their kids. But none of that required him to give away much about himself.

So far, he'd existed on the periphery—a supportive onlooker in his friends' nanny match endeavors.

And that was close to love as he could get.

They knew him as Landon Paige, the pop star fussing over his number of fans or flipping his collar and sporting a cap to go unnoticed in a crowd. It was easy to play that version of himself. He'd been doing it for years.

As much as he cared about these people, he couldn't let them see the flawed man behind the glitz and glam.

And that was the trouble with Harper Presley.

The minute he'd seen her, he'd known that if anyone could see through his facade, it was her. He'd figured he could ignore her. But that was damned near impossible. There were a shit ton of reasons for them to see each other. Their friends' lives required a crapload of relationship interventions, which meant spending time with Harper at writing competitions, school carnivals, food truck stops, birthday parties, and even volunteer drives with the astronauts on the International Space Station as special guests.

Yes, the shit with these people was freaking bananas.

But it was the good kind of bananas—for the other guys. The men had found love and true companionship.

Still, that couldn't be his path. He would provide for Aria. He could do that. He had homes across the globe and more money than he knew what to do with. And Aria was wealthy in her own right. Once she was twenty-one, her parents' wealth and royalties would become hers. But even with his niece, his blood relative, he had to maintain his distance.

In the long run, it would be better for the child.

Five people had known the real Landon Paige. A little over two years ago, that number dropped to three. And that was the way it had to stay.

There was too much on the line—and he had a clock of his own ticking away.

He'd made a deal with his label.

These past six months were supposed to be a last-ditch effort to reinvent himself and pull together the music that he, Trey, and Leighton had promised each other they'd write. If he could do it, in a little over sixty days, there was a chance they could get him a spot at the Red Rocks Unplugged—the game changer of a musical event that could alter the trajectory of his career and show the music world he was more than a pop prince. It was the perfect venue to springboard in a new artistic direction.

But there was one not so tiny problem. He hadn't written one new song.

Not one.

And time wasn't on his side.

Not to mention, his lack of progress hadn't gone unnoticed.

He'd catch snippets of Mitzi's calls with the record execs whenever he was in Vegas.

They'd grown impatient with him.

He hadn't put out anything new in eight years.

Eight years.

A knot formed in his belly. He couldn't come up empty-handed. The last thing he wanted was for Heartthrob Warfare to be written off in the annals of music history.

That couldn't be his legacy.

He couldn't fail Trey and Leighton and be the one who let it go down the drain.

He had to figure out a way to create on his own.

This was his last chance.

With Tomàs and Bess leaving for Italy, he'd require a nanny to care for his niece while he tried to pull together the music—but this nanny couldn't be Harper.

She'd be the ultimate distraction—a distraction he couldn't afford.

It was bad enough that before he drifted to sleep, it was her voice that carried him into slumber.

"Landon Paige, I love you!" a fan cried, pulling him from his Harper-induced stupor.

Get it together and end this show.

He nodded to the crowd, thanked the musicians one last time, then walked off the stage as the roar of applause petered out.

Mitzi handed him a towel. "Jesus Christ, Landon, what were you doing out there? Meditating? These aren't laced with magic mushrooms, are they?" she asked and handed him a small bakery box with three butterscotch-filled bonbons.

He huffed a little laugh, popped one of the sweet treats into his mouth, then handed off his guitar to a stagehand. "You don't mince words. I'll give you that, Mitz. And no to both. I wasn't meditating or strung-out."

He ate the second bonbon and savored the creamy texture.

These bonbons were delicious, but they weren't like the ones he remembered from his childhood.

Still, they served their purpose.

"Well?" Mitzi pressed.

He stared at the last bonbon—the reminder of his child-hood that pulled at his heartstrings. He pushed the thoughts away and donned his pop star facade. "I was basking in the glow of my fans' elation," he replied, then ate the last bonbon as a young production assistant with her blonde ponytail swishing from side to side scampered toward them. She stared at him through her lashes, took the empty box, then handed him a fresh black T-shirt. He shed his soaked top, and the assistant's jaw dropped as all eyes fell on him.

And rightly so.

A pop god had to look the part, and he didn't slack off when it came to maintaining his physique.

And what about the bonbons?

They weren't exactly healthy, but they were a tradition, and he made an exception for them.

He'd always make an exception for them.

Mitzi rolled her eyes at the gawking PA. "This is why I'm glad I'm a lesbian," she grumped, then cleared her throat. "Focus, blondie. We need to walk. Landon's not done yet. Where are his signed photos?"

The woman blinked as Mitzi broke the pop god spell. "Um…the photos are right here," she chirped, pulling a stack of autographed headshots from her bag. "The superfans are excited about the VIP meet and greet."

He nodded. They always were.

"I should say that they're very, very, *very* excited," she elaborated, then cringed.

Dammit!

That was code for the fans waiting to meet him were a few slices short of a loaf.

But that was the job.

"Which ballroom?" he asked, wholly indifferent to these meet and greets.

"The ballrooms are being utilized. There's a porn thing going on in the one you usually use."

What the hell?

Had he heard her correctly?

He stared at the woman. "A porn star convention?"

"I'm not sure exactly. It's something like that. The Luxe

staff have you set up in the hallway," she stammered, her cheeks growing pink—and for a good reason.

He was Landon Paige. He didn't get sidelined.

Or did he now?

"The hallway?" he shot back, irritation coating the words.

"Leave it alone, Landon," Mitzi cautioned, but the woman wasn't paying him any attention. She frowned as she glanced at her phone as they weaved their way past stagehands tearing down his set. They emerged from the arena complex as two men removed a sign with his name splashed across it in bold lettering. Without a second glance, the workers tossed it into the trash bin.

Jesus!

"Oof, that's got to hurt."

Of all the people to run into at this very moment.

He looked up as Vance Vibe, with his streaky highlights, giant Rolex, and a gold chain that made him look like a wannabe rapper, sauntered down the hallway.

The asshat looked like the parody of a pop star. The dude might be raking it in, but the guy's smarmy demeanor always put him on edge. There was something not right about the man. But he couldn't seem to get away from him. They shared the same music label, and the execs had been pushing for him to collaborate with the guy.

Hard pass on that.

"Vance, what a nice surprise," he said with absolutely no niceness or surprise in his tone.

He and Vance had artist residency contracts to perform concerts at the hotel. He was usually able to steer clear of the man, but the universe had decided to throw him a curveball on his last night in Sin City.

"I was sorry to hear the news," Vance replied, his voice syrupy sweet.

Whatever the hell he was talking about, the guy sure wasn't sorry.

"What news?"

Vance toyed with his chain. "I heard they didn't extend your contract at the Luxe Grandiose?"

Mitzi cleared her throat.

He glanced at his manager. The woman shook her head. The movement was barely perceptible, but he'd caught it.

"I was ready to move on," he answered, then tossed Mitzi a look that said WTF.

"To work on new music?" Vance pressed.

The man was fishing for information.

He schooled his features. "Something like that."

"With a new label?" Vance continued, needling away.

Who was this guy? The pop version of Nancy Drew?

"Excuse me?" he growled.

"I heard rumblings that you may be out. I figured it was a mutual parting," Vance replied, feigning concern. "And hey, Mitzi Jones, I'm glad I ran into you."

Mitzi raised an eyebrow. "Are you?"

The woman could spot a poser a mile away.

"You've got a great reputation," Vance gushed. "You're always welcome on my management team if your situation changes."

What the actual hell?

"That's kind of you, Vance, but I have a job," she answered smoothly.

"Yeah, sure," the pop fool replied, eyeing the contents of the trash can.

This asshole.

He resisted the urge to remove the sign and hit Vance over the head with it.

"How's the writing going?" Mr. Twenty Questions continued, not missing a beat. "Have you been in the studio to lay down any new tracks?"

What was he digging for?

"Don't take this the wrong way," he began in a tone that projected the opposite sentiment, "but what I do musically is none of your business."

"But it has been a while, hasn't it? When was the last time you put out something new?" Vance mused. "It's been years, right?"

Landon held the man's gaze, but he couldn't correct him.

"The offer's always there to collab," Vance stammered, shifting his stance. "I'd be happy to throw you a bone."

This sucker just asked for it.

"A bone?" he seethed, getting in Vance's face. He was ready to punch this Auto-tuned asshole into next week. Landon Paige might be a heartthrob crooner on the stage, but years spent bouncing around foster care placements had taught him how to fight.

"Landon," Mitzi warned, resting her hand on his back. "We have the meet and greet."

Forget the meet and greet.

He didn't budge. He wouldn't be the one to back down.

Vance took a step back. "I didn't mean to hit a nerve, man. You're a pop god. Everyone knows it. 'Heartthrob Warfare' is a classic. I loved that song when I was a kid."

A classic?

He loved it when he was a kid?

Vance Vibe was only a few years younger than him.

Was this tool making a dig at his age now? Christ, he was thirty-three, not ninety-three.

"If you want to work on something together, or if you need some help, I'm offering," Vance eked out.

Help?

"I work alone, Vance."

"Didn't you collaborate with the other members of Heart-throb Warfare, or are you hiding something?" Vance asked, masking the question with a cluck of a laugh.

How dare this man bring up Trey and Leighton.

If he was going down in a blaze of pop-downfall glory, taking a swing at this prick wouldn't impede his trajectory.

He hardened his expression. "The only thing I'm hiding," he said, lowering his voice, "is a right hook that could really mess up that pretty Botox-laden face of yours."

Vance Vibe couldn't know his secret. There was no way. He was fishing again. He had to be.

"You're kidding, right?" Vance stammered, dropping his douchey swagger. "You wouldn't hit me, would you? We're both from Denver. That's a connection, and I heard you've been spending quite a bit of time there."

"Look at that. You're both from the Mile High City," Mitzi intervened, trying to keep the peace.

"I might be back there soon," Vance yammered. "We could meet up there and have a jam session."

Who the hell said jam session?

He narrowed his gaze, giving nothing away, when a piercing trill ricocheted through the hallway.

"Landon, Landon Paige, I made this for you," a woman shrieked.

He broke the staring contest and peered over Vance's shoulder. A middle-aged woman, clad in a shirt with his face on it, barreled toward him with a large sack in her hands. She stopped and gasped for breath. Huffing and puffing, the woman reached into her bag, then thrust something soft into his hands.

"It's a pillow," she gushed.

He stared at a cushion embroidered with the cross-stitch version of his face.

It was creepy as hell, but it couldn't have been easy to do.

He stared at the frighteningly accurate representation. "This is quite a gift."

"I made two. One for me, and one for you," the woman replied, drinking him in.

"Did you."

"Yeah, I sit on your face every night at dinner. Last night, I ate a burrito while sitting on your face."

"Uh-huh," he uttered because what the hell did you say to a person who admitted that they enjoyed eating burritos while sitting on your face?

"Here, honey," Mitzi said, swooping in. She took one of the photos from the PA. "Here's an autographed picture of Landon Paige. You can hang it on the fridge—or sit on it. Whatever floats your boat," she added and bit back a grin.

God help him.

The fan squealed with delight, then started digging in her sack of a purse. She held up a marker. "Landon Paige, can you write, to Norma Rae, my biggest fan and the best cross-stitcher in all the West?"

Shit.

He stared at the pen. His stomach churned, and Jesus, was the air-conditioning on? It felt like a heatwave had overtaken the space.

"Enjoy your fans and your cushion. Keep fighting the good fight and vibe on," Vance sneered with a syrupy smirk as he dropped his cringe-worthy tagline. The prick had recovered from their little tête-à-tête, and the trepidation that had rolled off him in waves had vanished. Vance looked from Norma Rae to the sign in the garbage to the line of Norma Rae lookalikes waiting for him. The creep flashed a cocksure grin before going on his merry freaking way.

Good riddance.

But the encounter with Vance had screwed with his head.

A muscle ticked in his jaw.

He knew what the guy was thinking.

No new music equated to no new fans. Landon Paige was a washed-up pop star—a relic who hadn't put out anything original in close to a decade.

Was it the truth?

He ignored the twist in his belly and zeroed in on the pen. It threw him into a tailspin.

Don't let anyone see the real you.

He exhaled a slow breath and pulled himself together. He mustered a grin for Norma Rae. "Thank you for the gift, but I don't have time to sign the photo. There's a pressing matter I need to discuss with my manager."

Norma Rae tittered with exhilaration. "Is it about a new song?"

He couldn't get a damn break.

"How exciting!" the woman yipped, not waiting for him to answer before hurrying down the hall toward a group of giggling women dressed in head-to-toe Landon Paige gear.

He could not handle a meet and greet—not tonight.

He turned to Mitzi. "I need to talk to you." He glared at the PA. "Alone."

The young woman gasped, then skittered away.

He didn't like pulling the overindulged artist card, but he was on the edge of losing it.

He led Mitzi down the hall. "What the hell is going on? That flash in the pan, Vance Vibe, doesn't know what he's talking about, does he?"

Mitzi exhaled an audible breath. "Honey, I was going to talk to you about your situation."

"Then talk."

"Vance wasn't that far off the mark."

"The label wants to drop me?"

"Possibly."

"Possibly?" he repeated.

She released a weary sigh. "Nothing has been decided. There are rumblings in the industry that the label might get sold to another entity. This is good for you. It buys us some time to broaden your appeal and reach new markets. Plus, they're still on board with your switch from pop to rock, which reminds me," she said, reaching into her tote. She handed him a piece of paper and a pen. "Initial here by the red arrow."

He eyed the document, and his blood pressure spiked. "What is this?"

"It's a waiver for an opportunity I'm looking into for you. Nothing's written in stone, but it's worth keeping an eye on," she added, and for the first time in a long time, his badass manager didn't look quite so badass.

Was she worried? Was his situation worse than he thought?

He stared at the jumble of lines and curves dancing on the page.

He hated the legal mumbo jumbo.

He spied the arrow, then scrawled his initials.

LBP

He returned the forms to her and swallowed past the lump in his throat. "I understand the label is getting antsy, and I'm grateful they're giving me a shot to branch out into acoustic rock. But my pop shows still sell out. I make them money."

Mitzi slipped the waiver into her bag, then pursed her lips.

He knew this face. It was her expression when she was trying to find the best way to give him shit news.

"Your shows sell out, but you're not generating new fans. Vance Vibe is an assclown, but he puts out new music constantly. I'm not sure how he does it."

Searing jealousy engulfed him. It killed him that posers like Vance Vibe had it so easy when it came to making music.

"The guy's got a handful of good songs. I'll give him that. But he can't sing. They manipulate his voice on his tracks, and he lip-syncs at his shows."

Mitzi's expression softened, which wasn't a good sign. He didn't worry when she was tossing out barbs and spitting venom. But her concerned countenance had him on edge.

"It doesn't matter if Vance Vibe lip-syncs or if he's the worst singer on the planet, which I agree, he is. He's racking up fans hungry for his latest hit. Your sales have tanked, LB. Your fans bought your music years ago."

She wasn't wrong, and she'd called him LB.

Now that Leighton was gone, no one called him that anymore.

And it wasn't good. Mitzi only dropped his initials when shit had gotten real.

He tried to steady himself.

But he couldn't.

It was as if he'd lost his footing when it came to keeping up the pop star facade.

It was too much. The pressure was too much.

How was he supposed to care for Aria and figure out how to write a hit?

He cleared his throat. "Is there any word on securing a spot for me for Red Rocks Unplugged?"

Mitzi frowned.

There was his answer.

"Let me guess. No new music equals no spot."

She reached into her bag and handed him his ball cap, cell phone, and glasses. "Skip the meet and greet. The event PAs and I will hand out photos. Go blow off some steam. You know what they say. What happens in Vegas stays in Vegas. But keep in mind, Landon, real life is about to hit, and there will be real consequences."

He stared at the embroidered pillow. "I'd say learning that I was about to be dropped by my label is the definition of real life."

Mitzi rested her hand on his chest. "I meant Aria. She needs you. You're her closest connection to—"

"Yeah, I know, Mitz," he said, cutting her off in a tumble of words, his voice thick with emotion.

"And," she added.

He scoffed. "There's more?"

"I wanted to wait to tell you this, but I spoke with Madelyn Malone earlier today."

His ears perked up, and thoughts of Harper Presley's sassy smirk and perfect ass invaded his mind.

Block. Her. Out.

"Go on," he sputtered.

"Madelyn said your nanny case was special. Unlike the other men in your group, she's taking an unconventional approach to your match."

An unconventional approach?

After observing Rowen, Mitch, and Raz's matches, he'd concluded that everything about Madelyn Malone's approach was unconventional.

How much more unconventional could she get?

He glanced away. "Did Madelyn happen to mention the potential nanny's name?"

Mitzi cocked her head to the side. "Why, do you have someone in mind for the position?"

All he could see were hazel eyes.

He shrugged. "No."

Liar.

He pulled his cap down and slipped on his glasses.

Damn it all!

It was time to do something reckless and lose control.

This evening might be his last chance to distract himself from an uncertain future.

"I plan on getting drunk tonight," he announced like a sullen teenager.

He needed a release. He had to do something to relieve the pressure building inside him and divert his thoughts from Harper Presley's enchanting chameleon eyes.

"Okay," his manager answered with an aloof wave of her hand.

He tucked the pillow under his arm. "I'll probably break some shit."

Mitzi shrugged. "You can get away with that. You're famous."

He released a mirthless laugh, then held the woman's gaze. "I'm lucky to have you, Mitz. I don't know why you reached out to us years ago, but I'm glad you did."

Great, now his emotions had him acting like a sentimental sap.

Mitzi's expression sharpened. "What the hell was that, LB? Are you getting soft on me?"

"No," he answered through a chuckle, seeing through her tough manager facade.

"Get out of here," she chided, swatting him on the arm. "Play Clark Kent in your hat and glasses and have some fun. Do something for you."

Do something for you?

He didn't even know what that meant.

"I can't have you getting mushy. Save it for your music. You know I don't put up with that shit," she added and bristled.

But he knew better.

He smiled at the woman who'd guided his career. "Yeah, I know," he answered as a flood of emotions rushed through him.

Christ, he needed a drink—or ten.

He set off for the main lobby and took in the scene. The Luxe Grandiose lived up to its name. This sprawling area was its own self-contained clubbing district, glittering in a sea of lights and buzzing with activity.

A man could get into a hell of a lot of trouble here.

And that's what he wanted.

He exhaled a slow breath, but that didn't quell the storm within.

It was like standing beneath a waterfall as a deluge of obligations and unknowns threatened to take him under. He rolled his head from side to side, working out the tension in his neck, when a pulsing techno beat drew him in.

It called to him like a siren's song.

Or maybe it wasn't the thrum of the bass calling to him but an actual siren.

He passed the wedding chapel and tattoo parlor and made a beeline toward the dance club, hardly able to believe what was right in front of him. His heart hammered in his chest as he trained his gaze on an enchantress.

A petite enchantress with dark wavy hair and curves that wouldn't quit.

No damned way.

The flashing lights in the club bathed the dancing beauty in shades of blue, green, red, and purple.

As if he were in a trance, he sauntered past a cluster of people, then stopped on the edge of the dance floor.

His heart was ready to beat itself out of his chest.

It couldn't be her, could it?

Chapter 5
LANDON

Dumbstruck, Landon stared at the dance floor, when his phone vibrated. Mindlessly, he pulled it from his pocket.

Three faces illuminated the screen, signaling a text from his nanny match group chat.

Yeah, they had one of those.

He focused on the screen as a boxing glove emoji accompanied a string of letters.

Erasmus Cress: Hey, heartthrob wanker, I have a favor to ask.

He stepped away from the pounding music but stayed close enough to observe his dancing beauty. He pressed the audio button. "What do you need, Raz?"

The words populated in the message box, and he hit send.

Erasmus Cress: Libby's getting a vibe. She's worried about Harper. She told me H is in Las Vegas at a piano teacher conference. Libby said she sounded off when they spoke earlier. I know Vegas is a big place, but if you see Harper, can you make sure she's okay, mate?

Hopefully, Libby wouldn't sense the accuracy of what he was about to say.

He swallowed hard, then pressed the microphone icon. "I doubt I'll run into Harper, but I'll keep her safe if I do."

Keep her safe?

Where the hell did that come from?

Then again, maybe he was seeing things. The lights could be playing tricks on him.

But the exhilaration thrumming through his veins confirmed it.

Not only was Harper Presley in Las Vegas, she happened to be dancing her ass off no more than twenty feet from him.

And God help him. She was a siren.

With her hands above her head, wrists crossed, and her hips swaying from side to side, she moved like the beat owned her body, like it lived in her soul, like she couldn't help but give in and submit to the swell of the refrain.

One with the music, she was pure sensuality. She gave off a raw sexual energy that flipped a switch inside him. A carnal urge flared. Like a predator, his vision narrowed, and he focused on his prey as every superfluous thought drained from his consciousness.

He observed her. No, he consumed her, drinking her in and memorizing her every move.

Jesus, he was screwed.

His phone buzzed with another incoming text, and he startled, blinking as his laser-sharp focus went blurry.

He checked the screen. The nerd face emoji popped up.

Rowen Gale: Have you talked to Madelyn? The countdown is on, right? Your niece is coming to live with you soon. Any word on the nanny situation?

His phone buzzed again, and he observed a salad icon.

Mitch Elliott: The nanny candidate must be Harper. It would only make sense.

Erasmus Cress: I agree. It's got to be her. Good bloody luck with that battle-ax of a woman, mate. I used to beat up people for a living and I wouldn't get in the ring with that wildcat.

He had to shut this down.

He pressed the microphone icon. "Gotta go. I've got pop god shit to do."

He hit send, then turned off his cell and slipped it into his pocket.

He returned his attention to Harper, and a dizzying current raced through his body. He'd had a strong reaction to her presence in the past, but it was nothing like this.

Why was that?

The answer hit him like a Mack truck.

He'd never had her all to himself. They'd been physically together plenty of times, but they'd always been in a group buffered by their friends.

This encounter was different.

Tonight, she was alone in Las Vegas. It was only the two of them in a city built for sin.

He zeroed in on the beguiling brunette, then frowned.

What the hell was she wearing?

Was that a brown tutu?

And what shapes were printed on her tiny top?

He squinted.

Were those bonbons?

And why was she wearing a sash like she'd nabbed the grand prize in a beauty contest?

He scanned the club and spied a group of women dressed like sexy ballerinas.

Was this a piano teacher thing? Did they moonlight as sexy, club-hopping, techno-loving dancers?

She turned, and he noticed something in her hands.

A lollipop?

Was she a sexy, club-hopping, bonbon-wearing, candy-eating ballerina on the down-low?

She lowered her arms, licked the treat, then slid the candy into her mouth.

And holy shit! Whatever she was, it triggered his entire blood supply to head south in one hell of a hurry. Harper Presley dressed like sexy chocolate and indulging in a lollipop while dancing like a sensual goddess had him hard in seconds.

But he wasn't the only one who noticed her.

A man on the dance floor moved in. This sweaty, Don Juan wannabe with one too many buttons undone on his shirt came up from behind and gripped her hips, grinding into her tutu-covered ass.

Who the hell did this guy think he was?

Despite the darkness, all he saw was red.

Harper swatted the dude's hands away. She didn't seem too bothered by the guy, but he didn't take the hint. He tried again and rested his hand on the small of her back. This got her attention, and she turned on a dime. Her serene musical goddess expression made way for a look he knew well. She glared up at the guy, then tried to push him away. But he didn't budge. Instead, he gripped her wrist and pulled her to his chest.

This prick just made the biggest mistake of his life.

The thumping bass faded along with the rise and fall of the house music. He couldn't hear anything besides the blood pounding in his ears. It was as if his sense of sight had funneled power away from his other senses. He left the cushion on a barstool and closed the distance between himself and the jerk manhandling Harper.

He rested his hand on the guy's shoulder and dug his fingertips into the man's skin. "Get your hands off of her," he snarled.

The guy shifted his stance, taking Harper with him in a

clumsy turn. "Who the hell are you?" the guy slurred. He was a run-of-the-mill drunken Vegas tourist reeking of cologne, cigars, and alcohol.

But he didn't give a damn if this guy was living it up on vacation.

He tightened his grip on the man's shoulder. "I'm about to become your worst nightmare if you don't fuck off in the next three seconds."

He hadn't met Harper's gaze, but he could feel her eyes on him.

And Christ, he liked it. But he needed some answers from her, like what the hell she doing here.

First, he had to get rid of this handsy tourist.

The wobbly man squinted and gave him a once-over.

The guy was big, but he was bigger. He had a few inches on him at six four and at least thirty pounds of muscle.

"Is she your girl?" the man slurred, confusion marring his expression.

Yep, he was another Vegas drunk.

But that didn't give him the right to drape himself all over women on the dance floor.

"Dude, is she your girlfriend?" the guy hollered over the beat, but he hadn't released Harper's wrist from his grasp.

That was going to be a problem.

He glanced at the man's beefy hand, then got in his face. "She's my fiancée, asshole."

Fiancée?

Where the hell did that come from?

It didn't matter. He was improvising.

"And if you don't back the hell off," he continued, "you'll return to whatever bullshit town you came from in a body cast."

Not bad—menacing with a dash of a veiled threat.

The drunk blinked a few times. "Do I know you, dude? Are you somebody?"

He could handle this. The guy was hammered. "Yeah, you know me. I'm the guy who's about to kick your ass if you don't let go of…" he trailed off and met Harper's gaze. Even in the darkened club, those eyes drew him in.

"She's your fiancée, yeah, I get it. I get it. Sorry, man, I was having some fun," the drunk replied. He let go of Harper's waist, then stepped back and raised his hands like he was being robbed. "Don't hit me, man."

"I'm not going to hit you," he answered, when Harper lunged in front of him.

"But I am. You need to learn to take a hint. Women aren't here for your enjoyment," she shot back and raised her tiny fist.

Dammit!

He grabbed her hand mid-swing.

"Why are you stopping me?" she cried.

So much for a thank you or even a hello.

"You can't be punching people," he replied, feeling the force of this woman. There was some real power behind her fists.

"You were about to hit him," she countered.

"I was just scaring him." He shook his head at the infuriatingly hot tutu-clad woman, then turned toward Mr. Drunk and Handsy. "We're good, dude. Give the ladies some space on the dance floor."

The drunk gave him a sloppy salute, then pointed at Harper. "You're a lucky guy. I'd marry her for her tits alone."

Just when he was trying to let the douche get off with a warning, the guy had to go and run his mouth.

He glanced at the glaring beauty by his side. Maybe he should let Harper punch the guy's lights out. It might knock some sense into him.

No, this guy wasn't worth the effort.

"If you know what's good for you," he warned and threw a cagey look at the petite powerhouse, "you'll get the hell out of here."

Luckily, the tourist got the hint and complied.

And look at that! He was already keeping Harper safe. Just as he was about to revel in his chivalry, she grabbed his chin in her ridiculously strong hand and forced him to meet her gaze.

"Are you drunk?" she snapped without an ounce of appreciation in her tone.

That's what she had to say to him?

"Are you?" he shot back.

"I wish. The drinks here are so watered down I'd need a couple gallons to get even remotely shit-faced." She scoffed. "And what the hell is wrong with you?"

Irritation coursed through his veins. "Nothing is wrong with me. In fact, I'm a hero. I saved your ass."

"Who says I needed to have my ass saved?"

Was she mad at him for coming to her rescue?

His whole white knight vibe drained away. "Jesus, Harper, just say thank you."

She lifted her chin. "I will not say thank you."

This ball-buster of a woman.

She pegged him with her gaze and morphed into interrogation mode. "What are you doing here?" she asked and licked her sucker.

That lollipop would be the end of him.

She started going off, and she looked pissed, but he couldn't focus on what she was saying. He stared at her mouth. She had beautiful, full lips. The kind of lips that would look damned hot wrapped around—

"Hey, heartthrob. What. Are. You. Doing. Here?" she hollered, punctuating each word with a jab of her lollipop.

He snapped out of it. "I work here. I just finished a concert. What are you doing here?"

"Me?" she snapped.

"Yes, Erasmus texted me and said Libby was getting a weird vibe off you. He mentioned you were at a piano teacher conference in Vegas. Raz wanted me to be on the lookout for you."

The beautiful brown ballerina battle-ax dialed back her outrage as panic marred her expression. "Did you tell him you saw me?" She'd tried to inject a fair share of badass into her question, but he detected an uneasy undercurrent.

What secret was she keeping from everyone?

"I told them Vegas was a big place and that I probably wouldn't run into you." He glanced around the packed club. "This doesn't look like a piano teacher conference. Did you lie to your friends?"

Her jaw dropped. That knocked her off her chocolatey-delicious high horse.

Exhilaration raced through his body.

Was he getting off on fighting with her?

She recovered and swished her hair over her shoulders. "What would you know about piano teacher conferences?"

Honestly, he knew nothing about piano teacher conferences.

He stared at her sash, trying to decipher the writing.

"It says *bridesmaid,* or are you trying to look at my tits, too?"

Yeah, he might have allowed his gaze to linger.

"And why did you call me your fiancée?" she bellowed at the top of her lungs.

"I did it to protect you. So yeah, for all intents and purposes, you're my goddamned fiancée," he belted.

A high-pitched squeal rose over the bump and grind of the booming house music. "Harper, why didn't you tell us you were engaged?"

He looked over his shoulder as a woman in a white tutu, a veil, and spindly heels tottered over with a glass of champagne and a giant rock on her ring finger. If that wasn't weird enough, a guy dressed as a gladiator was hot on her tail.

This was Vegas, but still.

"Harper, honey, are you okay?" the ballerina bride asked. Black smudges of mascara darkened the skin beneath her eyes, and her hair looked like she'd spent the last hour inside a tornado. Champagne sloshed in her glass. Droplets fell to the ground before she downed the remaining alcohol in one gulp.

"We saw that guy creeping up on you," the leather-clad gladiator added.

"But your *fiancé* got rid of him. How romantic," the drunk bride cooed, then raised her hand and gave him a sloppy high five.

He turned to Harper. "Are these your piano teacher friends?"

She looked from him to the oddly dressed couple, said nothing, then stuck the lollipop into her mouth.

"We're not piano teachers, silly," the woman cried, wobbling before gripping the gladiator's arm. "We're Katrina and Jude, the newlyweds."

This just got interesting.

"How do you know Harper?" He was almost scared to ask.

The bride did a happy dance. "Harper is Jude's second cousin's sister-in-law's niece's stepsister. Did I get that right?"

Harper gifted the woman with a plastic smile. "Yep."

"And Harper's engaged to you," the bride continued like she'd cracked a secret code.

He stared at his hazel-eyed fiancée interloper.

Why the hell had she crashed a Vegas wedding?

He turned to the cosplay couple. "Can I have a minute with—"

"Your fiancée," the ballerina bride and the gladiator supplied.

These two were a piece of work.

72

"Yes, with my fiancée," he echoed, then escorted Harper away from the dance floor. "What is going on here?" He glanced down and caught the designs on her little half shirt. Yep, he'd called it correctly. "And why do you have bonbons on your shirt?"

She touched the fabric. "You know what they are?"

"Yeah, of course, I do. Bonbons are damned delicious."

"They are," she agreed.

Bonbons were a part of his past, and now, here was this woman with two of them embroidered on her chest.

What did that even mean?

Nothing, it didn't mean anything. He brushed off the association.

"Are you dressed up like a chocolate ballerina bridesmaid for the wedding?"

There's a statement he'd never expected to utter.

She tapped the lollipop to her lips. "Not exactly."

"Those are your clothes? You put that outfit together on purpose?"

She scoffed. "Yes, I did. I'm damn proud of it."

This wasn't adding up. Who dressed like that on purpose?

He decided to change tack. "Why did you lie to crash some Vegas wedding? What are you really doing?"

Here's what he knew for sure: Harper Presley was dressed as a sexy bonbon, and the woman had conned her way into a gladiator-meets-ballerina Vegas wedding. And she'd lied to her friends about a piano teacher conference, but why?

She ran the slick lollipop across her bottom lip. The wheels in her head were turning. She glanced at Katrina and Jude, then pushed onto her tiptoes and rested her hand on his chest. "I'm going to level with you."

"I'm listening." He was listening, but that didn't stop him from wrapping his arms around her waist and bringing her closer.

It happened reflexively.

He inhaled, and sweet Christ, she smelled good enough to eat.

She tempted him like a piece of naughty, delectable candy.

Harper Presley proved to be the ultimate distraction in her bonbon ballerina disguise. And he knew that if he got a taste, he wouldn't be satisfied with only one bite.

This was the kind of temptation that could cost a man his very soul.

"Harper," he whispered, able to taste the syllables.

She chewed her lip, then waved for him to lean in closer. "I might have told a teeny-tiny white lie that got me added to Katrina and Jude's wedding party. Go with it."

"Just go with it?" he repeated.

She pulled back and looked him square in the eyes. "This has been the worst day of my life. I have one night to lose control and forget about tomorrow. I need this. I need Katrina and Jude."

"For what?"

"For the free watered-down drinks and unlimited shrimp cocktail." She rested her forehead on his chest. "I'm about to lose everything because I'm not a poop kink porn star."

Sweet Christ! He was not expecting that.

He tipped up her chin. "Did you say *poop kink porn star?*"

She gestured to the chocolates printed on her boobs. "I'm a bonbon, not bang-bang."

He cocked his head to the side. "Are you on drugs-drugs?"

This conversation was getting crazier by the second. He tried to assess her pupils, but it was too dark.

"I'm not on drugs," she lamented. "I'm a woman with zero prospects. They even took Carol."

And the bizarro factor amplified tenfold.

He cocked his head to the side. "Who's Carol?"

She leaned into him again. "My car. The hotel had my car towed."

"Your car's name is Carol?"

This was getting confusing.

"Yes, she's a brown nineteen ninety-four Volvo wagon. Of course her name is Carol." Harper pushed onto her tiptoes, glanced past his shoulder, then stiffened. "Katrina and Jude are watching us, and they look a little wary. They may be on to me. Please, play along."

"What do you want me to do?"

"You're the one who called me your fiancée," she barked, sneaking another peek. "Do something fiancé-ish."

He stared into her eyes as the music changed and the thump of a new track pulsed through the club.

A cheesy, overdone Vance Vibe track.

Of all the times for this bullshit music to come on, this had to be the worst.

He stilled, preparing for the deluge of maddening emotions.

Soul-crushing envy reared its ugly head and threatened to tear him apart.

Harper bristled in his arms. It was as if the song made her skin crawl as well. She gripped his shirt and twisted it in her hand like she wasn't sure what she hated more, Vance Vibe's music or a poly-cotton blend.

Were they both on the edge of a complete breakdown thanks to a Vance Vibe song?

"Hey, Mr. Fiancé? The ball's in your court. Do something before my shrimp cocktail privileges get revoked and those two figure out I crashed their wedding."

He knew exactly what he wanted to do, and he didn't care what the drunk newlyweds thought.

He focused every ounce of energy on her, and something remarkable happened. His spiraling thoughts ground to a halt, and time stood still. The layers of anxiety and uneasiness building in his chest melted away, and all he saw was her. His gaze dropped, and he drank in the apples of her cheeks and those plump, sexy as sin lips. Hungry to memorize every detail, he traced his index finger down her jawline.

The breath caught in his throat, and he repeated the motion. This time, he cupped her face in his hand.

He'd never touched her like this before.

Scratch that.

He'd never touched her at all, which made it even stranger that stroking Harper's cheek was like coming home.

How could that be?

Their bodies began to move. They swayed to the beat, but he didn't hear Vance's modulated voice. The sound condensed into a pulsating reverberation—a thrum that drew them together. She rested her hands on his shoulders, and her breasts grazed his chest. Her touch ignited a spark, and his blood popped and fizzed as a titillating buzz raced through his body. Cloaked in flashing lights, a blanket of breath and beat wrapped them in a melodic cocoon.

With one hand on the small of her back, he tangled the other in her mess of wavy hair. She stared up at him. It was too dark to observe the color of her chameleon eyes. Were they more brown or gray or blue? It didn't matter the color. Harper Presley had worked her magic and cast a spell.

Was Vance's song still playing? He had no idea. Whatever rhythm they were dancing to, they each heard it. Or perhaps, somewhere between watching her on the dance floor and claiming her as his fake fiancée, they'd created their own frequency—a melody only detected by the two of them.

Tucked against the end of the bar, he caressed her back, rubbing circles on her exposed skin before sliding his hand lower. His fingertips brushed against the coarse tutu fabric, and a scintillating thrill overtook him as he bypassed whatever the hell tutus were made of and squeezed her ass.

It wasn't like anyone could see what he was doing. It was too dark, and there weren't any couples dancing near the line of empty barstools.

Heated anticipation tore through him. It was as if they'd entered one of his dirtiest fantasies.

With an ass that didn't quit and those hazel eyes, of course, Harper had made it into his daydreams.

Unable to stop, he slipped his hand inside her panties and caressed the smooth skin.

Jesus, he was losing his mind in this sweetest of escapes, but he wanted more.

He rolled his hips, and she rocked with him. Like two halves coming together to create one entity, their bodies melded. His hard, muscular angles met her soft curves in a scintillatingly sensuous motion.

But this wasn't a demur sway.

This was what happened when longing and lust intersected, and his cock took notice.

He inhaled a tight breath. She had to be able to feel his hard length against her stomach.

The question was, what would she do about it?

As if the universe had read his thoughts, he got the answer.

She moved in closer and parted her legs as a dirty little grin pulled at the corners of her mouth. That sexy move ignited a firestorm of desire. Hot and unrelenting, it invaded every cell in his body as raw need took over.

She brought the lollipop to her mouth, held his gaze, parted her lips, then...yep, she sucked it.

Hard.

God help him.

He leaned forward, allowing his breath to warm her earlobe. "Do I get a taste?"

"Is that all you want?" she tossed back. She put up a tough front, but she trembled in his arms as she spoke the words. That tiny glimpse of vulnerability touched a part of him he hadn't felt in years.

What did he want?

It didn't feel like they were talking about candy anymore.

His heart was ready to beat itself out of his chest. Questions came at him faster than he could process them, but each boiled down to one central query.

Who was Harper Presley beneath the sassy exterior?

She pulled the sucker from her mouth and licked her lips. Her mask was back in place, and the raw vulnerability he'd observed had disappeared behind a beguiling twist of a smile.

"You can have a taste," she said, teasing him with the lollipop.

"What flavor is it?" he asked, tightening his grip on her supple backside.

She moistened her lips and hummed a sexy little sound. "Cherry."

That was all he could take.

He plucked the lollipop from her hand, then dropped it.

In the blink of an eye, she looked ready to punch his lights out. "What did you do that for? I was—" she protested, but he didn't give her a chance to finish.

He didn't want to lick her lollipop. He wanted to lick *her*.

Like a man driven to do nothing else, he silenced her with a kiss. Their lips met in a crush of cherry bliss. It was like coming apart and being put back together in one spiraling sensation. He ran his tongue along the seam of her lips, indulging in the sweet salvation. Soft and warm, her mouth welcomed his kisses. Exhilaration built between them, and each kiss led to another and another.

He was right to trash the candy. He'd take locking lips with Harper Presley over sucking on a lollipop any day of the week.

Wait!

He was kissing Harper Presley—and he liked it.

He shouldn't like it. He shouldn't like holding her in his arms and twisting her silky locks around his fingers. He shouldn't crave the electricity crackling between them.

But he did.

He loved it.

She moaned against his mouth, and he couldn't stop himself from having another lick. Their tongues met in a symphony of kisses and caresses. She tasted like an escape, a beautiful diversion.

The ultimate distraction.

She was the distraction he couldn't afford. But he sure as hell wasn't about to stop kissing her.

She threaded her fingers into the hair at the nape of his neck. "This is reckless," she whispered.

He inhaled her cherry breath. "Do you like being reckless?"

She broke their kiss, held his gaze, and rocked her hips. "I do tonight."

Game on.

He dipped his head and tasted the skin beneath her earlobe. "Nothing is off-limits."

"And every terrible choice is the right choice," she purred.

He stared down at her, ready to get back to kissing the dirty smirk off her face and start reckless make-out round two, when a high-pitched squeal popped their terrible-choices-or-bust bubble.

"O.M.G, Jude," the drunk bride shrieked like she'd won the drunken bride lottery. "I figured out who Harper's fiancé is!"

Chapter 6
LANDON

He and Harper broke apart like a bomb had exploded.

Thanks to her cherry kisses, he'd forgotten about the gladiator groom and the ballerina bride.

"You're the singer," the bride gushed. "You're Lan—"

"Bartholomew," Harper corrected, interrupting the woman's drunken declaration. "His name is Bartholomew," she sang like the town crier.

He stared at this enigma of a woman. But it wasn't her voice that grabbed his attention this time.

It was his middle name.

She couldn't have pulled that name out of thin air. Bartholomew wasn't a name that rolled off the tongue. She had to have known it was his middle name. Sure, if someone was dogged enough, they could find the information, but it wasn't common knowledge.

"People tell *Bartholomew* he looks like Landon Paige all the time. Isn't that right, *Bartholomew*?" she said with that plastic grin that said *play along or we're screwed*.

She wasn't wrong.

"It's a family name," he answered, telling the truth.

Harper wrapped her arm around his waist, playing the part of the fiancée. "I like to tease him about his strong resemblance to the pop god and call him my heartthrob."

"Pop god?" he repeated, raising an eyebrow.

"Did I say god? I meant pop goober," she tossed back.

"I bet you call him heartthrob because of Heartthrob Warfare," the gladiator thundered like he was on the drunk Vegas version of a trivia game show.

And from the gladiator's mouth to the DJ booth, the track changed, and a techno remix of "Heartthrob Warfare" pulsed through the club.

"I love this song," Katrina shouted and pulled Jude into the center of the dance floor for a little drunk newlywed bump and grind.

Away from the prying eyes of the hammered bride and smashed groom, he took Harper's hand as they watched the newlyweds dance their hearts out.

He wanted to revisit the whole pop god moniker, but there was a good chance if he brought it up, she'd bust out that right hook she'd nearly landed smack-dab in the center of Mr. Drunk and Handsy's shiny face.

He gestured toward Katrina and Jude. "What's the deal with their outfits?"

"It's honestly kind of sweet. Katrina always wanted to bang a gladiator, and Jude wanted to nail a ballerina," Harper answered, straight-faced, as Katrina twirled, then fell on her ass. The ever-helpful leather-clad warrior, Jude, helped his new bride to her feet while pumping his fist to the beat.

To each his own.

"If that isn't true love, I don't know what is."

Or did he?

Harper's posture stiffened. "You don't have to hold my hand, Landon. We don't have to pretend."

He peered at their joined hands. "Who says I'm pretending? You are my fiancée." It was his attempt at humor, but she wasn't laughing.

She removed her hand from his grip and bristled. "There's no way I could ever be your real fiancée."

That was blunt.

Was he not good enough—not smart enough?

"Why do you say that? Do you think there's something wrong with me?" He didn't mean for the words to take on a grating edge, but he couldn't stop his old, hidden wound from festering.

Calm the hell down, man.

"Yeah, there's something wrong with you," she countered. "And it's my number one dating rule. You're a musician, and I don't date musicians…anymore."

Anymore.

"What's the second rule?" he pressed.

She rolled her eyes. "Do not date a musician," she repeated. "It's every rule. I'd date a psychopath before dating a guy in a band."

Jesus! Message received.

But tonight wasn't about dredging up the past. Tonight, he'd help her forget, and he'd rely on her to help him do the same.

His career was hanging in the balance, and Aria was days away from moving in with him.

Shit was about to get real—but not yet.

"You could never be my real fiancée either," he fired back, giving her a dose of her own feisty medicine while keeping it light.

She narrowed her gaze. "Why?"

He tipped up her chin, then ran his thumb across her pouty lips. "I don't date bonbons."

"But you like kissing them," she countered. "And eating

them. I tasted chocolate and butterscotch when you…" She touched her lips. "When we…when that kiss…"

He couldn't blame her for not being able to form a cohesive thought on the topic.

He didn't have words to describe the kiss either.

He'd never kissed anyone like that before, but he had to play it cool.

He shrugged. "If I'm in the mood, I've indulged in a bonbon. What about you?" he continued. "You don't date musicians, but do you kiss them?"

She gazed up at him through her eyelashes. "If I'm in the mood, Bartholomew."

Bartholomew.

"How did you know my middle name?"

A lock of her chocolate-brown hair fell forward, and she allowed it to shield her gaze. "Is it Bartholomew? That's funny. I was just bullshitting. What a coincidence."

That was a lie.

"It's not a coincidence. How did you know it?"

And then he figured it out.

She had to be a fan.

"I must have read it somewhere. I don't know," she snapped, brushing the errant lock behind her ear.

Dammit!

He didn't mean to embarrass her. Oddly, he liked that she knew it. He liked imagining her singing along with him.

He softened his expression. "It was quick thinking, Harper. I appreciate you covering for me. I don't want to be recognized tonight."

"Why not?" she asked as the fight in her tone drained away.

"It appears we're in the same boat. I could use a night to forget a few things, too. Everything in my life is about to go to shit," he confessed as every muscle in his body tensed.

He shouldn't have said that. He couldn't let his guard down with her.

He braced himself, preparing for her to pepper him with questions.

But she didn't.

Her smirk of a smile reappeared, and she tapped the brim of his cap. "Does this incognito getup really work? Because you don't fool me."

That's what scared him.

It was what also made her the perfect companion for one night of debauchery.

He could work her out of his system. The reality couldn't live up to the fantasy, could it?

A slice of silence stretched between them, and he concentrated on the woman who seemed to be able to see into his very soul.

Stop!

"Then it's decided," he announced, swallowing his emotions. "We'll never get engaged."

"Deal. No engagement. And as a caveat," she added with a defiant twist to her lips, "I'll never be your nanny either."

Perfect. They were on the same page.

"Deal," he replied as they shook hands.

"This night is about terrible choices, heartthrob," she proclaimed. "For one night, we'll forget about tomorrow and make every stupid decision."

Amen to that.

"Nothing counts?" he asked, taking her hand and leading her toward a darkened corner of the club. "Everything's on the table?"

This time, she didn't pull away.

"Anything goes. What do you have in mind, heartthrob?"

Heartthrob.

Damn, he liked the sound of her calling him that.

He bit back a grin. She could have called him Mr. Giant Colossal Asshat. He was riding the buzz of holding her hand like a nervous preteen trying to make a move at a middle school dance.

Like she'd said, he was a pop god. Holding some woman's hand shouldn't be a big deal.

But like it or not, Harper Presley wasn't just *some* woman.

She was the woman who'd agreed nothing was off the table for the night.

And he knew how to start the evening with a bang.

He led her to a darkened stairwell. He knew this club well. He'd spent many a night here getting shit-faced, and he knew of a spot that would afford them privacy.

He pressed her back against the wall and caged her in. "If we're going big, it's time to up the ante."

The light from the stairwell allowed him to take in her hazel eyes glittering with mischief.

She narrowed her gaze. "I'm game."

He leaned in. "How far are you willing to go?"

She traced a line down his abdomen. "Further than you, heartthrob."

He'd been hoping she'd say that.

He took a step back and scanned the empty corner. Thanks to the flashing lights and the booming music, they wouldn't catch anyone's attention.

He dropped his gaze to the puffy tutu. "Take off your panties and give them to me."

If this was his last night to lose control, he wasn't about to pussyfoot his way around.

He'd happily give in to his dirtiest desires.

She twisted a lock of hair like a temptress. "You think I'm going to hand over my panties?"

"I dare you," he tossed back, turning his little stage-bit phrase into a challenge. "You said you want to be reckless."

"I did."

"And you want to go a little bit crazy?" he added, brushing the pad of his thumb across her bottom lip.

"Uh-huh."

"I'll only say this one more time, Harper. I dare you to take off your panties and give them to me."

He'd used the dare verbiage so often in his shows the word had lost its luster...until now.

"I *dare* you, Harper Presley," he repeated, and his lips tingled as he spoke the words.

"A dare?" she repeated as a sexy smirk bloomed.

He nodded. He was about to find out how far his siren of a bonbon would go.

As the bass pumped and a roaring techno beat pulsed through the room, he held her gaze. Moving to the rhythm, she swayed from side to side. Playing the part of the seductress, she ran her hands down her torso, paying particular attention to her breasts before slowly removing her panties.

He devoured her with his gaze, and his cock twitched in his pants.

Christ, he wanted her.

She lifted the scrap of black off the floor with the heel of her boot. "I'll take them off, but you've got to come and get them."

Always a ball-buster.

He gleefully dropped to his knees. Grazing his fingertips down her thighs, he moved past her boots, then procured the black G-string. He wrapped his hand around the fabric, relishing the bite of the lace and slide of the silky satin.

"These are mine," he growled, then pressed a kiss to her inner thigh.

"I've got a dare for you, heartthrob," she purred, beckoning him with her index finger.

He stood. "Let's hear it."

She closed her eyes and released a slow breath. "I dare you to make me forget."

She stared up at him, and his heart leaped into his throat. He'd expected a sassy comment. But that was her magic. That flash of vulnerability. One second, she was piss and vinegar, and the next, she was as delicate as a glass slipper.

It made him want to protect her.

That's what he'd told Raz he'd do.

I'll keep her safe.

The urge to gather her into his arms and whisk her away to hide behind the walls he'd constructed around his heart was nearly too strong to resist.

But he couldn't do it. It wasn't even a choice.

There was only room for one in the confines of his battered soul.

Still, there was one thing he could give her—one night. Nothing more and nothing less.

He pocketed her panties, then cupped her face in his hands. "I accept the challenge. But I need you to answer one question."

"Okay," she whispered as an invisible string drew them closer together. It anchored him to her in a heady haze of flashing lights and pulsing sound.

He trailed his fingertips down her jawline. "Harper Presley."

"Yes," she breathed.

He was drowning, lost in a sea of desire, and only she could save him. "Tell me what you want to forget."

Chapter 7
HARPER

What was she doing?

The breath caught in her throat. There was no going back, no hitting stop.

Landon's question hung in the air.

What do you want to forget?

At this point, what *didn't* she want to forget?

The bills. The house. Vance the douche nozzle. The porno contest mix-up. Her dwindling prospects.

Her entire life was a shit show. She longed to cast aside her worries and escape from her responsibilities.

And to do that, she needed a good dose of wild, reckless abandon.

And she clearly wasn't the only one.

When Landon swooped in like a white knight and sent the handsy drunk packing, palpable anger and clawing irritation had rolled off him in turbulent waves. She knew one thing for sure: he wasn't happy about the meaty drunk manhandling her, but the fury he'd rolled in with wasn't completely due to the handsy creep.

Landon Paige had charged in, guns *already* blazing.

Not that she needed to be rescued.

Not that she needed any man, especially a musician, to come to her aid.

Still, when she'd looked up and seen him, the tiny kernel of hope she'd locked away in her heart had sparked to life. The dreams of a ridiculous girl who'd once penned notebooks filled with effusive lyrics celebrating love took notice of the man's gallant response to her precarious situation. Did her stupid heart skip a beat?

Perhaps.

Fine, yes, she'd been rendered breathless, and butterflies had erupted in her belly.

But of course, she couldn't show it—especially not to the likes of Landon Paige.

And she'd done a good job of holding that sappy girl at bay. She'd fallen back on her take no bullshit persona…until he kissed her.

That kiss.

She could still taste the chocolate and cherry flavors coming together in a burst of deliciously raw desire.

And that kiss was no platonic peck. He'd kissed her like a man drowning in tumultuous waters—like a man searching for a miracle.

He'd revealed the depth of his soul with that kiss and surprised the hell out of her.

When they were with their friends, he played the part of the shallow, cookie-cutter pop star, but that kiss had shattered his plastic heartthrob facade.

This man was hurting.

Could he tell she was hurting, too?

Or was she kidding herself?

Was this simply her foolish schoolgirl side rearing its naïve head? Could it be her inner hopeless romantic trying to escape from the fortress of snark and sass? She'd hid her darkest parts here and locked away the question she'd kept hidden for as long as she could remember.

Who would choose Harper Presley? Who would want the abandoned little girl?

Maybe it didn't matter what the man thought.

They were two people who needed time to stand still for one night.

No matter how good a kisser he was, Landon Paige was not the man for her.

Nope. No way. No how.

She'd have to block out the echoes of the silly girl who'd once dreamed of the kind of true love found in the lyrics of her favorite pop songs.

Heartthrob Warfare, I'm fighting for your love.

Heartthrob Warfare, it's a battle for your touch.

Heartthrob Warfare, I need you oh so much.

Damn the lyrics that had been with her since she was an awkward teen.

Damn the dreams of that trusting girl who'd grown up and allowed a sleazebag of a musician to steal from her and break her heart.

Tonight was about one thing and one thing only—and it had nothing to do with love.

Tonight, she'd push every limit and lose control.

She schooled her features and held Landon's gaze, praying he couldn't see the naked fear behind the tough girl act.

Don't let him see the real Harper Presley.

"What do you want to forget, Harper?" Landon repeated, his voice a smooth ribbon of sound.

She ran her hands down his chest, then continued the descent, tracing the defined ridges of his abdominal muscles. "I want you to make me forget everything. And I dare you to do it with this," she added and palmed his hard length through his jeans.

And hello, Mr. Pop Star Giant Disco Stick.

Focus! Harness the snarky bitch within.

"I'm talking about no strings attached sex. You've got my panties in your pocket. Don't you think it's time you finished the job? It appears you're up to the task."

Yeah, and then some.

"That's the dare?" he asked, his voice a thick rasp.

"That's the dare," she replied, working him in slow, smooth strokes.

A muscle ticked in his jaw. "Are you sure you know what you're asking for?"

This was beyond reckless. But she couldn't stop.

"I know exactly what I want. Nothing counts tonight. Nothing is real. We'll go back to Denver, and it'll be like this night never happened. Safety check. I've been tested. I'm clean."

"Me too."

"And I'm on the pill. Tonight, we're two consenting adults with nothing stopping us."

He watched her closely, but she couldn't read him.

Was he about to reject her?

"I need this," she whispered, unable to hide the raw ache in her voice.

He gripped her wrist and stopped her from teasing his hard length.

Had she blown it with that sentimental slip?

"Do you need help, Harper? Are you in trouble? If you need anything, I—"

Shit!

She pressed her fingertips to his lips and doubled her resolve. "We're not talking about real life. There's only one question you have to ask yourself."

"What's the question?"

"Do you want me?"

She exhaled a shaky breath, but she'd gotten it out.

He tightened his grip on her wrist that sent a charge through her arm. The man exuded raw desire—that was his job. He was a pop star. But to have all that energy focused on her sent a wave of euphoria through her veins. A muscle ticked in his cheek again as he sharpened his laser focus. It was as if he were holding himself back from bending her over a barstool and taking her in the club.

Good, that was the vibe they needed.

He released her wrist and took her hand in his. "Come on. I know a place."

Relief washed over her—or was that disappointment? Was she disappointed he was okay with one night of debauchery? Did she want him to want more?

No, no, no! It didn't matter if he sang her a love song and begged on his knees.

He was a musician.

And there was no way in hell she'd ever date a musician.

Get it together, Bonbon Barbie.

Holding her hand, he led her up a spiral staircase. Unlike in the rest of the packed club, they didn't see a soul in this dimly lit space. Their feet clanked against the metal steps as a few naked lightbulbs hanging from the ceiling cast the stairwell in a golden glow. She glanced at Landon. It was the first time she'd seen him without the flash of colorful strobe lights. He caught her looking and smiled that dreamy pop star half-grin.

And there it was again. Her silly heart skipped a beat.

Do not fall for the pop star.

Pop star equals musician.

Musician equals heartbreak.

"Are you really up for anything?" he asked with a dirty smirk that got her pulse racing and knocked the equal signs out of her head.

"Are you?" she tossed back.

Landon drank her in. His eyes glittered with lust. "I was born ready, bonbon."

Bonbon?

She was about to give him hell for dropping such a cheesy line and calling her *bonbon* when a door appeared at the top of the stairs.

"Where are we?"

"Trust me. You'll love it up here."

He opened a door and gestured for her to enter the snug alcove hidden by a black curtain—the Vegas version of an opera box. She parted the thick drapes and gazed out into a sea of flashing lights. They were at least two stories above the packed dance floor. It was quite a view, and then the beat dropped, and she gasped as the floor vibrated with the thumping music.

She held on to the railing attached to the half wall. "What is that?"

"We're above some major subwoofers," Landon answered as he planted himself behind her. "They don't use this spot very often. I did a PR event up here a few months back. They had me throw T-shirts into the crowd."

She leaned over the railing, observing throngs of people dancing to the beat, lost in their own world. Hidden in this secluded nook, the track changed. A techno remix of "No Fear," another Heartthrob Warfare song, resonated through the club. It wasn't one of their more popular tracks, but it was her favorite.

What were the chances of hearing this song in this secluded location with a pop god she was pretty damn sure wanted to screw her brains out?

She closed her eyes, taking it in, then parted her lips and sang along.

"Nothing to fear with you sitting here.
Nothing to hide with you by my side.

We fly above the pain. Soaring like birds.
Open hearts.
Open minds.
Baby, baby, when it's all the line,
No fear can keep me from claiming what's truly mine."

With the bass rippling through her, the layers of worry and doubt peeled away. She swayed to the beat, soaking in the sound.

"Sing it again, Harper."

Her eyes fluttered open, and she looked over her shoulder.

Landon Paige looked ready to pounce.

"You want me to sing the refrain of your song...to you?"

He brushed her hair over one shoulder and kissed her neck. "That's exactly what I want you to do," he answered before taking her earlobe between his teeth.

Delicious anticipation hung in the air, and she stared down at the writhing bodies. There was nowhere for her to go. His muscled frame held her captive as his hard cock pressed against her, signaling his intention.

"Sing," he whispered against the shell of her ear.

"Nothing to fear with you sitting here," she began. *"Nothing to hide with you by my side. We fly above the pain. Soaring like birds. Open hearts. Open minds. Baby, baby, when it's all the line, no fear can keep me from claiming what's truly mine."*

She'd performed this song in the mirror while singing into a hairbrush more times than she could count. It was surreal to have the artist, the lead singer of Heartthrob Warfare, listening as she sang his words. She waited for him to respond, but he didn't make a sound.

"Landon?"

He gripped her hips, then slid the tutu down her legs. And in the blink of an eye, she was half-naked.

"Hold on to the railing and spread your legs," he instructed—no, demanded.

Her voice had done something to the man because he wasn't messing around.

And his bossy, take-charge tone was crazy hot. She hadn't expected it. Usually, she was the mouthy one calling the shots. But not in this alternate universe. And heaven help her, it got her hot, like do-me-in-a-balcony-alcove kind of hot. She complied with his order and felt him shift his stance as he undid his pants and shrugged them down.

This was really happening.

Sweet anticipation tingled between her thighs.

"It should be illegal to be that sexy, bonbon," he said, sliding his cock across her ass.

She inhaled a tight breath, but before she could exhale, a sliver of apprehension penetrated her sex-brain haze, and she glanced at the door. "You're not concerned about someone walking in on us?"

He teased her with his hard length. "It makes it more fun. Or are you chicken?"

"I'm no chicken."

"That's right. You're a bonbon."

"You bet your ass I am," she tossed back and swiveled her hips.

He held her close. "This night is about terrible choices, right?"

"It is," she purred, enjoying the thrill of living dangerously.

He slipped his hand between her thighs and rocked his palm against her sensitive bundle of nerves. "You dared me to make you forget."

"I did," she panted as he teased her.

"We're going to do whatever we want tonight. There's no thinking about tomorrow. This is Sin City. I have you all to myself, and I am not wasting a single, solitary second."

She rolled her hips. "What do you want to do first?"

He leaned in, and his warm breath on her neck sent a delicious shiver down her spine. "You."

He sang the word like a dirty lullaby, and she was there for it.

If she were a real bonbon, she would have melted into a pool of chocolatey goo. Luckily, years of playing the piano had left her with an iron grip. She tightened her hold on the railing as he teased her entrance with the tip of his middle finger and hummed his delight against her neck.

"You are so wet for me, bonbon."

She was.

She couldn't hide behind a sharply worded barb with this man working her into a heated frenzy. She arched into him as he massaged her sweet bud in deliberate circles.

"Sing the refrain to 'No Fear' again," he growled against the shell of her ear.

"Why?" she panted.

"Because your voice gets me so hard, I feel like I'm about to explode."

Her voice did that to him?

When had he heard her sing before tonight?

And how was she supposed to sing with him strumming her sensitive bud like he was a clitoral virtuoso? This man and his magic hand had her gasping for breath and teetering on the edge.

"I'm close. I'm so close."

"Sing the refrain," he commanded, dialing up the pace.

This was the sweetest torture she'd ever endured.

She'd be a liar if she said she hadn't fantasized about what it would be like to sleep with Landon Paige. The guy had been her first celebrity crush.

But nothing had prepared her for this.

She hadn't expected him to be so demanding. And she hadn't expected to like it.

She called the shots when it came to every aspect of her life. But in this hidden alcove, where they could be discovered at any minute, the rush of getting caught had her moaning.

He positioned his cock at her entrance. "Sing it, Harper. Sing the last line."

She gripped the railing as the lyrics came to her in a waterfall of sensations. "*No fear can keep me from claiming what's truly mine.*"

"Do you know how long I've waited for this?"

What was he talking about?

But before she could ask, he thrust his cock into her sweet, wet heat. She cried out, but she didn't have to worry about anyone hearing her. Her voice joined the pulsing cadence of the beat as her body welcomed his hard length. The ground pulsed beneath them. Erotic energy encircled them. She'd expected him to go to town, pumping and grinding like there was no tomorrow, but that's not what happened. Buried deep inside her, he stilled, then reached around and caressed her cheek. Savoring their connection, the gentleness of his action caught her off guard. Slowly, like he had all the time in the world, he kissed her neck and held her in place.

"Are you okay? I'm not hurting you, am I?"

The tenderness in his voice brought tears to her eyes.

Do not cry.

"I'm okay...unless that's all you've got. Then we might have a problem."

He chuckled. "Harper, we've only just begun."

He pulled out, then rocked his hips and thrust inside her. The decadent slide of his cock had her gasping within seconds. The man set a pace that would put an Olympic athlete to shame. The slap of their bodies followed the thrum of the beat. She held on to the railing and savored the ferocity of their connection. Her mind emptied. She didn't have to pretend to be strong. She didn't have to maintain her armor.

She surrendered to the rhythm of their bodies. There were no bills and no awful ex-boyfriends.

No expectations, no obligations.

No two-bit pasty-skinned dude telling her to get lost and make way for Bang Bang Barbie.

The only bang-bang on her mind was banging with her sexy heartthrob.

Her entire world became this man and the thump of the bass reverberating through the floor. They moved with the beat, one with the music, as he took her hard and fast from behind.

"Look how damned beautiful you are," he whispered against the shell of her ear.

She stared across the expanse at a mirrored wall.

There she was.

Thanks to the crush of people in the club, she hadn't noticed the walls. But from their perch above the packed dance floor, the flashing lights caught them in a whirlwind of rich color.

She drank in their carnal dance and caught Landon doing the same.

Watching him watch her had her weak in the knees. She reached back and gripped his arm. It changed the angle of penetration and allowed him to thrust deeper.

"Christ, you feel good," he groaned, dialing up his pace.

With his cock between her thighs and his hand caressing her most sensitive place, pleasure rippled through her body. She tensed, tightening around him as the flash of blinding lights and the swell of the music carried them on a wave of palpable desire.

Music and motion coupled with lust and longing.

A symphony of sensations carried them higher and higher.

The tempo shifted into overdrive. Reckless and on the

verge of flying over the edge, she bucked against him and released a primal, profoundly cathartic sound.

"Yes, yes, that's it. Take it. Take everything," he rasped.

"Harder, faster," she panted, and thank the stars, this man could follow directions. The force of his body was balanced by the deftness of his touch. He made love to her like he was born to do it. Intuitively, as if he could read her mind, he understood what she needed before she knew she wanted it.

And then, everything condensed. She pictured a measure of music with a four-count rest.

Four, three, two, one.

With an explosion of light and sound, they met their release in a cascade of melodic moans and a crescendo of lusty cries. His voice, that sweet, sexy rasp, carried her higher. Like a song, they rode the rhythm and submitted themselves to the pulsing beat.

She disappeared into the sound, lost in the rapture of bliss.

Their song ended, and she chased her breath, winding down from a dreamy ecstasy.

She looked up and caught his eye. "A girl could get used to a life of recklessness."

"Is that so?" he asked as a sated smile bloomed on his lips. But the expression disappeared when he flicked his gaze to the dance floor. "Oh shit!"

"What?"

"Down there," he said, pointing to a trio of security guards at the far end of the club. The men were pointing at them.

He pulled out, then hiked up his pants. "We've got to go."

Panic tore through her as she whipped the curtains closed.

"Landon, we cannot get arrested. Libby and Raz almost got arrested and that led to them hanging with donkeys all summer. I am not running around the mountains with donkeys."

"I hear you, bonbon. That's not us. Libby and Raz are the best, and their donkeys are great and all, but they smell like…"

"Like freaking donkeys," she shot back, ready to hightail it off the balcony.

They bolted out the door, taking the steps two at a time, when Landon glanced at her, then skidded to a halt.

"Why are you stopping?"

"Your tutu."

She looked down, shrieked, and covered her lady parts. "I'm half-naked. We have to go back and get my tutu. I can't go out there like this. Maybe if I had body glitter like Bang Bang Barbie, I could pull it off."

What kind of crazy was she spouting?

Had he bang-banged the sense clean out of her?

"I don't know what you're talking about, but we don't have any glitter. We can't go back." He whipped off his shirt and handed it to her.

Her jaw dropped as her naughty girl brain concentrated on his ripped torso. "I'm good with this wardrobe modification, but I don't think more nakedness will help us."

"It's for you," he said, shaking his head. "It's long enough. It'll cover everything."

She glanced up the stairs. "I love that tutu," she lamented, but the man was right.

She slipped his shirt over her head and followed him down the metal stairs, clanking as they picked up speed.

"What about you?" she asked as they neared the bottom. "Now you're half-naked."

"There are like twenty shirtless gladiators in the club for Jude and Katrina's wedding. They won't notice me."

Breathing hard, they made it to the first floor and peeked out the stairwell.

"Do you see them?" she asked, holding on to his arm.

"Yeah, they're closing in on this side of the club. Go

with what I'm about to do," he answered. Doing a duck and run, he led her around the corner, toward the bar, then lifted her onto a barstool. She plopped onto something soft as the guards plowed through the dance floor. Their heads swiveled back and forth as they scanned the area.

She blinked as one of them met her gaze. "Landon, I think we're screw—"

Before she could finish, he shut her up with a kiss. Instinctively, she wrapped her legs around him, pulling him between her thighs.

Breaking every rule seemed to be great for their libidos.

They made out like a pair of sex maniacs.

"Do you see them?" Landon murmured against her lips.

"Yeah, one is watching us," she replied as she licked his face, then knocked his hat clean off his head as she ravaged his perfect pop star hair. "Oh no," she moaned.

"Oh no?" he echoed as he stuck his tongue in her ear.

"A security guard is coming this way," she whispered, squeezing her eyes shut like a toddler. If she couldn't see him, he couldn't see her.

Landon froze with his tongue still lodged in her ear.

"Hey, buddy," the security guard barked. "I need to speak with you."

"Please, no donkeys," she whispered to the universe.

Her pop star retracted his tongue. "What can I help you with, sir?" he asked, adjusting his glasses.

She opened her eyes, pissed, but not surprised that the toddler trick hadn't worked. She glanced at the security guard and prayed Nevada didn't have donkey racing.

The stalky guard held up a ball cap. "You dropped this. I wouldn't want somebody to step on it."

Her heartbeat slowed.

Was that it? Were they in the clear?

Landon accepted the cap and placed it on his head. "Thanks, man."

The guard cocked his head to the side and gave Landon the once-over. "Anyone ever tell you that you look like Landon Paige?"

Crap!

She parted her lips, ready to regurgitate the Bartholomew ruse, when another guard waved to their curious bouncer.

"Spencer, come on," he called. "We'll cut them off before they get down from the balcony."

Their hat retrieval helper nodded, then set off toward the stairwell.

They were safe. He hadn't recognized them.

They sat, stock-still, until the three men disappeared into the stairwell.

Landon leaned in and rested his forehead against hers. "That was close."

She giggled. "Way, way too close."

"I guess there will be no donkey shenanigans for the heart-throb and the bonbon," he said as they broke into a rolling bout of laughter.

The heartthrob and the bonbon.

She wasn't about to get sappy, but that did have a nauseatingly cute ring to it.

The adrenaline receded, and she wrapped her arms around his neck. He kissed the tip of her nose and traced tiny circles on her back.

"No donkey duty for us," he said as an easy grin bloomed on his beautiful lips.

"Thank God," she offered, gazing into his eyes.

Sharing this collective relief felt as intimate as having him inside her—maybe even more so.

"Look," Landon whispered, cutting into her thoughts. He gestured with his chin toward the security guards exiting the stairwell—empty-handed. Two men fanned out and walked the club's perimeter while the third held up a tutu—her tutu—and inspected it.

Landon planted a kiss on her cheek. "Give me a second, bonbon," he said, then jogged over to the man.

What was he doing? They were in the clear.

She watched in horror as he greeted the man, then gestured to the smattering of tutu-wearing women on the dance floor. Barely able to breathe, she observed the exchange. They spoke some more before the big guard handed Landon the tutu.

Score!

He strutted toward her and raised the tutu triumphantly.

"Are you crazy? What if they recognized you?" she asked, accepting the garment.

"I told them I was with the wedding party and would be sure to return this to the bridesmaid who'd *misplaced* it."

She pressed the brown material to her chest. "You didn't have to do that. It was a thrift store tutu."

He touched her cheek. "Yeah, I did. You said you loved that tutu."

"I do-do," she sang like a total weirdo, but it made Landon smile.

Her heart swelled. She couldn't let this gesture go to her head.

All the man had done was retrieve the tutu he'd ripped off her to screw her into oblivion.

No, it was more than that. He cared enough to risk getting caught.

And there it was again—the kernel of hope warming her chest.

"Thank you, heartthrob," she said, and she meant it.

She'd promised herself she'd never swoon over a man again, but God help her, Landon Paige was wearing her down.

She leaned forward, prepared to kiss him until her lips went numb, when she shifted on the stool. "What the heck am I sitting on?"

His body vibrated with laughter. "That would be my face."

She gave him a healthy dose of stink eye. "I think I would know if I was sitting on your face."

A dirty grin stretched across his lips. "You would know. I guarantee it. Stand up. I'll show you. There's a design on the pillow."

She hopped off the stool. "Do you make it a habit to carry a pillow around Vegas with you?"

"It was a gift from a fan."

She narrowed her gaze, trying to decipher a design stitched on the pillow. "What is that? I need a little more light to see."

"Let's head to the lobby. I think we've worn out our welcome here." He wrapped his arm around her shoulders, and they left the club.

The Luxe Grandiose lobby still buzzed with activity. She turned the cushion around in her hands, then busted out laughing.

"Wow, this is kind of creepy yet really well made." She glanced at him, then ran her hand across the meticulous design. "It says a lot about you that your fans connect with your music. It's the greatest gift a performer can get."

He could do that. She already knew this because he'd done it with her.

A blush graced his cheeks. "The fan told me she made two pillows. One for me and one for her to sit on when she eats burritos."

She tried to keep a straight face. "A woman out there eats burritos while sitting on your pillow face?"

His pink cheeks bloomed scarlet. "Apparently," he answered as they dissolved into another round of giggles.

"This has really been quite a night for you, heartthrob.

You've engaged in cross-stitch kink, public indecency, and evaded hotel security."

"What about you, bonbon? You conned your way into a wedding, got yourself free cocktails and a shit-ton of shrimp, and did the dirty in public. I'd say we're truly a pair of badasses," he answered and drank her in with his warm brown eyes.

She bit her lip as the deliciously possessive behavior sent a tingle from the top of her head to the tips of her toes.

"What's next, heartthrob?" she asked, her voice barely a whisper.

Mischief glinted in his gaze, then vanished a second later as shock marred his expression. "Harper, get down!" he bellowed like they'd time traveled and were trapped in the middle of a World War II battlefield.

She fell back on her kindergarten duck-and-cover tornado drill training, wrapped her arms around her head, and pitched forward. Landon swooped in front of her and snapped a flying object out of the air.

"Why are people throwing things at us? It's not more embroidered cushions, is it?" she yelped, gaze trained on the shiny marble floor, bracing for whatever the hell would come rocketing toward them next.

"No, it's flowers," he answered, confusion coating his words.

She lowered her arms and stared at a bouquet of white roses.

"Harper and Bartholomew, it's a sign. You caught the bouquet," Katrina slurred joyfully, peering over the railing from the second floor.

Had they walked into the toss-the-bouquet part of the wedding?

She scanned the lobby and found a slew of tutu-clad women clumped together, clapping and whooping.

"Yeah," Jude the Gladiator Groom agreed. "You're in love,

you're engaged, and this is Vegas. Harper, you're family. Folks, we've got another wedding coming up. Let's hear it for Harper and Bartholomew!"

A mass of hammered gladiators roared something akin to a drunken battle cry.

Oh shit!

She met Landon's gaze. The man's mouth opened and closed, but he didn't make a peep.

"Cousin Harper?" Jude called.

Double shit!

She focused on the drunk gladiator. "Yeah?"

"You're my second cousin's sister-in-law's…" He scratched his head.

"Niece's stepsister," she supplied, barely able to keep a straight face.

"You're family, and Katrina and I want you to be happy. Granny Bootsy would want that for you, too," the man added, brushing a tear from his cheek.

"Who the hell is Granny Bootsy?" Landon asked without moving his mouth.

"I don't know," she tossed back through a frozen grin.

"Granny Bootsy would want you to get married," Katrina bawled, joining her gladiator husband in the blubber-fest.

Married.

"We dare you to do it!" the sobbing gladiator exclaimed.

Another dare.

That's what this night was about.

They'd struck a deal to lose control and throw caution to the wind.

Landon's gaze bounced from her to the bouquet. "We did agree that nothing was off-limits."

"And that we would make every terrible decision," she added as a topsy-turvy feeling took over.

Do not marry Landon Bartholomew Paige.

Do not marry Landon Bartholomew Paige.
Do not marry Landon Bartholomew Paige.

Still, she couldn't come up with a choice more inappropriate than getting hitched.

"Let's hear it, folks," Jude called through his tears. "Harper and Bartholomew! Harper and Barto-lala-mule! Harper and Barlo-kama-blue," the man slurred.

Despite the complete and utter insanity, a bubbly euphoria couldn't keep her from smiling at her heartthrob partner in debauchery.

"You're probably used to people chanting your name," she teased.

He grimaced. "It sounds better with my first name. Bartholomew doesn't really roll off the tongue, does it?"

"Harper and Bala-meow-la-mew," Jude continued, making her heartthrob's point.

She tried to get a read on the pop star.

Did he really want to marry her?

Was she considering marrying him?

He wrapped his arm around her, and it felt so right, so natural, like everything in her life had led her to this wild moment.

"You've got nothing to fear. You're among friends and family," Jude blasted as Katrina did a drunken happy dance.

Nothing to fear.

She'd have plenty to fear and consequences to face. But right now, with Landon Bartholomew Paige looking at her like she made up the entirety of his universe, none of that could touch her.

"We double-dog dare you," Jude and Katrina blasted through the cavernous space.

A double-dog dare?

She hadn't been double-dog dared since Penny double-dog

dared her to enter the school talent contest back in second grade.

She released a shaky breath and peered over Landon's shoulder toward the Luxe Grandiose wedding chapel, where she spied her bellhop and the hostess, standing side by side with their heads cocked to the side.

She waved to them, then gazed into the chapel.

What was she doing?

This was too much. Yes, she was for pushing the limit, but marriage was going too far.

"Landon, I don't think we—"

"Take these," he interrupted, trading the bouquet for the cushion and her tutu.

"Are we doing this—really doing this?" she eked out.

"Let me see your left hand," he pressed, tucking the items under his arm, then held out his palm.

She rested her left hand on his as he touched the tip of her ring finger.

"What are you thinking?" she asked. She felt ready to explode, like the grand finale of a fireworks display was going off in every cell in her body.

He flashed her that boyish half-grin.

It took her breath away.

"A dare's a dare, bonbon. And we've been double-dog dared. There's no turning back."

Chapter 8
HARPER

So much for the honeymoon.

Harper sat at her grandmother's kitchen table and stared at a box of bonbons and the latest statement from the bank.

$48,202.08

That's what was owed on the loan.

By October fifteenth.

She counted the days on the little calendar Babs kept on the table.

Fifty-two.

She had fifty-two days to come up with almost fifty big ones.

She closed her eyes and released a pained breath.

What she wouldn't give to go back to the carefree hours she'd spent in Las Vegas.

Scratch that.

She wanted to throttle the guy.

It had been a week since her night with Landon—a week since they'd let loose and gone wild.

And a week since she'd seen the man.

Now she understood exactly how Cinderella felt when her

coach reverted to a pumpkin and her dress was reduced to rags.

The sting of reality had hit.

And she'd really screwed up this time.

Just when she thought it couldn't get any worse, she touched her neck and toyed with the platinum circles hanging from a chain.

What had she done?

She tucked the necklace into her shirt, scowled at the balance due, then focused on the chocolate.

"All right, bonbons, we're in a real mess. How the hell will we get ourselves out of this one?" She picked up one of the delectable treats and waited for the chocolate to answer.

It didn't.

"You're no help, you tasty asshole," she grumped before popping the confection into her mouth.

The stairs creaked, and she listened as her grandmother padded down the hallway.

"Harper Barbara?" the woman called.

"Yep, I'm in the kitchen," she grumbled. She stuffed the bank statement into her pocket, then jammed another chocolate into her mouth.

"Are you berating bonbons again?"

Crap!

She needed to pull herself together. She could not allow her grandmother to learn what she'd done.

"I'm just talking to myself," she answered and glared at the box. "Chocolatey traitors," she whispered, scolding the sweets like a lunatic.

Babs removed her purse from the hook on the wall, checked the contents, then set it on the counter before tossing her a knowing look. "Harper," the woman repeated with an edge to the syllables.

She'd known this tone since she was a little girl.

"Fine, yes, I'm yelling at candy," she confessed.

She'd been yelling at chocolates all week since she'd returned from Las Vegas.

Over the last seven days, she'd blown almost every dollar she had on the treats. Like clockwork, she'd slip out of the house while Babs was napping or when the woman was playing her harp. Clad in fuzzy slippers, ratty sweats, and Landon's T-shirt—yes, she still had that T-shirt—she'd haul ass to the Baxter Park Bakery, which had recently changed its name to Cupid Bakery. She didn't care what the name was, as long as they kept a steady supply of the sweets.

She'd probably consumed her body weight in sugar and cocoa by now.

Was she eating her feelings? You bet your ass she was.

She'd only bathed once since she'd returned from Vegas, and that was five days ago. She'd caught her reflection in the mirror a couple of times. Rocking a Frankenstein's bride meets walk-of-shame sorority sister vibe, she was lucky the bakery's owner, Mr. Sweet, a man she'd known since she was a girl, hadn't called the cops the last time she'd stepped foot inside the store.

He had, however, cautioned her to ease back on her cocoa consumption.

And she'd wanted to—she honestly had.

But in a moment of weakness a few hours after the man had warned her to take a bonbon break, she'd paid a couple of teenagers to go in and buy her two boxes of sea salt butter-scotch bonbons. With the decadent filling and a savory dash of salt, she'd hoovered one of the boxes in under a minute to the absolute shock of her teenage accomplices.

That little stunt had gotten her banned.

So, yeah, she'd been a hot mess since she'd been double-dog dared.

She sighed and cradled her head in her hands.

"Enough is enough, little miss," her grandmother chided, bopping her on the head.

"Ow, Babs, what was that for?"

"I'm leaving for the musicians' retreat in an hour, and you're starting to worry me. Will you be all right on your own?"

The annual trip to New Mexico.

How could she have forgotten?

Actually, quite easily.

Between stuffing her face with bonbons and bribing teens to buy her more chocolate contraband, she'd been a cocoa-infused zombie.

"How long will you be gone?" she asked as Babs dropped a granola bar into her bag.

"Same as last year. We've got the house for six weeks. Just me and a couple of old symphony widows, playing music and reconnecting. No TV and no internet. Only the fresh air and good friends," the woman answered with a grin. "If you need me, I've left the caretaker's phone number on the fridge. She can get a message to me."

"Are you sure you should be going with your ankle? I wouldn't want you to fall and break it this time."

Babs steadied herself on the counter by the coffee pot, then kicked and wiggled her ankle like the appendage was possessed. "My ankle is fine. And may I remind you, I've been taking this trip for the last eight years. I can take care of myself, missy."

"I know." She slumped in her chair.

"Did you get everything worked out with the bank?" the woman asked over her shoulder.

She plastered on a grin. "Yeah, there are a few details to work out, but I'm on top of it."

"I appreciate it. Your grandad was always better with numbers than I was." Babs narrowed her gaze. "Now, what's going on with you, little miss? You've been skulking around the house and inhaling bonbons for the last week, like when you were a teenager, and you worked yourself into a frenzy going back and forth over whether or not you were going to mail that fan letter to—"

"Babs," she interrupted, not wanting to hear *his* name, "I'm recovering from my piano teacher convention."

"Really?" her grandmother replied, clearly not convinced, as she removed a mug from the cupboard. "I've been a musician my whole life. I know we can party. How do you think I met your grandfather? And why do you think he married me after three dates? I was a damned good time fifty years ago," she added, then flicked a lock of her long dark hair over her shoulder.

"Babs, I cannot stomach thinking of you and Grandad Reeves," she lamented as a picture materialized in her head. "Ew!" she moaned.

"Stop, love is love—even if it does happen thanks to a tequila bender," Babs answered, humming a cheery little tune as she poured herself a cup of decaf.

She couldn't even blame alcohol for her choices. She blamed music and a man who'd insisted she sing for him. Sensing his desire and having those soulful brown eyes trained on her had weakened her defenses. And when he'd handed her the bouquet, she was lucky she hadn't melted into a pool of swoon.

She'd promised herself she'd never lose her mind over a musician again.

Stupid sexy pop god musician.

"What's going on, Harper?" Babs called over her shoulder.

Too damned much.

She concentrated on the familiar sound of her grandmother making coffee and inhaled the heady scent. The predictability of the routine brought a sense of peace. The clink of the spoon in the sugar bowl and the splash of cream brought her back to a time when her legs had dangled from this very chair.

Mug in hand, Babs looked her over, then studied the bakery box. "You're a mess. I'm surprised Mr. Sweet hasn't cut you off."

Oh no!

"Wouldn't that be something—banned from bonbons," she answered, trying to play it cool.

"I wonder how his wife is doing?" Babs mused.

"Why do you say that?"

"It's been a while since I've seen her," her grandmother replied, then sat down across from her and grimaced.

"What is it, Gran? Does something hurt? Is it your ankle?"

"I told you, my ankle is fine. It's my nose that's bothering me, missy."

"Your nose?"

The woman nodded. "Between the scent of the bonbons and your body odor, you could stop traffic with that smell. If the Olympics had a body odor event, you'd take first, second, and third prize. Unfortunately, the hazmat team wouldn't allow anyone inside the complex to present you with your medals, thanks to the overpowering stench. You have heard of soap, haven't you? It's that little white object in the shower."

What a comedian.

She'd inherited her sass and mouthy vibe from good ole Grandma Barbara, but it could be a real bitch when the woman dished it right back.

"Somebody woke up like a ray of sunshine," she deadpanned, then discreetly sniffed her pits and...holy shit! She smelled like death by chocolate—and not the delicious dessert. No, she smelled like what happens when a chocolate bar falls into a port-a-potty in the sweltering heat. She nearly gagged at the thought.

"Tell me what's got you riled up and binging bonbons," Babs pressed. "You haven't even touched the piano since you returned. You know that's your tell."

Harper drummed her fingers on the kitchen table.

Even if she wanted to spill the beans, where would she start?

Still, it wasn't like her blistering irritation was unfounded.

She had a decent number of reasons to be well and truly pissed off.

Four, to be exact.

Reason number one: She was no longer a miss or missy, as Babs liked to call her. She was a Mrs.

Mrs. Landon Bartholomew Paige.

She'd married a half-naked L. Bartholomew Paige, surrounded by drunken ballerinas and boozed-up leather-clad gladiators while going commando and rocking brown boots and her fake fiancé's T-shirt.

Not exactly the kind of wedding most girls dream of—not that she'd ever been one of those girls.

Still, she figured she'd at least be wearing underwear when she said "I do."

Reason number two: thanks to their after-wedding escapades, she was pretty damned sure the marriage was legit.

In the movies, if the couple hadn't sealed the deal by bumping naughty parts, there was a chance the marriage could be annulled.

That's not how it went for Landon and her.

They'd bumped, pumped, and banged the hell out of each other.

They'd spent their wedding night locked in Landon's decked-out suite, doing the dirty deed.

No, more like doing the dirty *deeds*, plural.

They'd christened the bed, the bedroom floor, the shower, the bathtub, and the bathroom floor. They'd done it against the door to the suite, against the door to the bedroom, and against the refrigerator in the little kitchenette. Then, because it was another flat surface, he'd pressed her back against the wall of floor-to-ceiling windows that looked onto the strip and rocked her world with another trio of mind-blowing orgasms.

They'd knocked out an all-you-can-eat sex buffet bender for the ages.

Honestly, the entire night was a testament to the strength of female anatomy. Her lady parts had been licked, fucked, and sucked until her eyes rolled into the back of her head and her body erupted into orgasmic bliss, which sounded terrific until she woke up bleary-eyed and alone in bed.

Yes, alone.

And not the good kind of alone where a gal wakes up, glances around in shock before her attentive lover returns with a tray of pastries and fresh coffee—not that anyone had ever done that for her, but again, movies and pop songs painted this picture every day.

And this illuminated the third reason she'd self-medicated with copious amounts of chocolate.

Reason *numero tres*: when she'd woken up from the honeymoon boink-fest—*alone*—she soon learned that Landon was nowhere to be found.

She'd married an MIA pop star.

When she ventured down to the concierge to claim her tote bag, the woman working the desk informed her that Mr. Paige had been called away.

Called away?

Yes, that's right, her freaking sex god pop star heartthrob husband had skipped out on her in the early morning hours.

And he hadn't even left a note.

Still, he wasn't a complete dirtbag. He'd done her one favor that couldn't be categorized as sexual.

He'd retrieved Carol.

He'd paid her fine and had her Volvo returned to the hotel.

There was another piece of information that gave her a sliver of insight into her runaway husband. The chick at the concierge desk mentioned Landon had looked distraught when he checked out.

But this only tamped down her wrath for a few seconds before the anger volcano churning inside her erupted.

Her deadbeat husband didn't get to be distraught.

Um…hello, actual distraught is waking up in a Vegas mega-suite, rocking no underwear and a diamond the size of Texas, only to learn your husband has bolted.

That's the official definition of distraught—or it should be.

The second she'd wrapped her head around being married and abandoned, she'd wanted to reach out to Penny, Charlotte, and Libby.

But what was she supposed to say to them?

Hey, ladies, remember how I said I was going to a piano teacher conference? Welp, I lied. I thought I was trying out to be the internet's next big thing, except it turned out to be a porno audition. And I saw Vance Vibe, punched a cardboard cutout of the man, conned my way into a ballerina-gladiator themed wedding, then married Landon Paige. Oops, I almost forgot. Babs is about to lose her house, and I can't do anything to save it. So, what have you gals been up to?

No, that wouldn't work.

And it got worse.

She was married to a man, and she didn't even have his phone number or know where he'd been for the last week.

He'd completely cut and run.

He'd even taken her panties.

And that was the perfect segue into spitting-mad reason number four.

For a reckless, blissful, completely outrageous slip of time, she'd felt fearless with Landon by her side—like nothing could touch them. Like she and her pop prince were bulletproof and bound by more than a dare.

A euphoric elation had seeped into her soul.

And that was her biggest mistake.

She'd allowed herself to believe there was a chance that what they had was real. Her hopeless romantic heart had hijacked her brain. She'd done everything to keep her vulnerability hidden. She'd walled off her heart, boarded it up, and slapped a big old Keep Out sign on it, but that didn't stop her from tearing down the defenses for the night.

This was why she'd sworn off dating musicians.

She hadn't technically broken the rule.

They'd skipped dating, faked a thirty-minute engagement, then jumped right into matrimony.

But one glaring fact stood out. A fact she'd be wise to remember.

Aside from her girls and Babs, the people who she thought cared about her always left her.

A lump formed in her throat.

"Harper, have you spoken to your friends since you got back?" Babs asked, her tone softening like she'd read her mind.

Penn, Char, and Libbs had been texting and calling nearly nonstop. Luckily, thanks to their impressive careers and being caught up with cute kids and doting fiancés, they seemed to have just enough time to text but not enough time to pop over to the house, which had been a godsend.

She'd been able to keep them at bay with ridiculous replies like "So much to do, so little time." And "damn, I forgot to charge my phone. Sorry I missed your call."

"I've texted with them a few times, but I've had a lot on my mind."

Her grandmother watched her for a beat. "Whatever's on your mind, you don't have to carry the weight of the world on your shoulders. You'll figure out whatever you're wrestling with. You're a good girl, Harper Barbara."

She was more like a dirty, dirty married girl, but she was not ready to divulge that whopper. She swallowed past the emotion in her throat. "You're getting soft, old lady," she teased, but there was no bite to her barb.

"Perhaps, I am," her grandmother agreed. She chuckled, then schooled her features. "Now, what did your grandfather always say when an obstacle presented itself?"

Jesus, here they go.

Harper sighed, but she couldn't stop a smile from pulling at the corner of her lips. "He said a lot of sappy things, Babs."

"Yes, he did. Your grandfather was a true romantic, and that's why I fell in love with him. He balanced out my bitchiness."

"Babs," she groaned and released a much-needed chuckle.

"Now, come on, little missy. I know you remember what he used to tell you."

She did.

She flicked her gaze from the bonbons and studied a framed picture on the windowsill. "He said living a good life was like composing a song. If something's not working, try another melody, but…"

"But never stop making music," Babs finished. "The right melody always comes along—sometimes when you least expect it." She sighed a sweet, girlish sound. "That man was dreadfully upbeat, wasn't he? But he was right. And you get to choose another melody if you're stuck—or in your case, little miss, a *smell-ody*. Do you see what I did there?" her grandmother teased.

Smell-ody.

"Babs," she grumbled and pressed her hand against the two rings hidden beneath her shirt.

What kind of melody could change her situation?

"Are you sure there's nothing you want to tell me, little miss?"

Harper glanced away. She couldn't burden the woman with the bills, and she sure as hell couldn't cop to being married.

She took a bite of another bonbon. "No," she answered through a mouthful of chocolate like a toddler.

"If you eat every bonbon," Babs began, raising an eyebrow, "you won't have any left to give to Libby and her fiancé. You're expected there today for the housewarming party, aren't you? That's why I came down. I still have a few more things to pack before the ladies pick me up to go, but I wanted to make sure we got to say goodbye."

Dammit! Stupid chocolate zombie brain.

She swiveled in her chair, grabbed her phone off the counter, and checked the calendar app.

Babs was right. If she didn't leave now, she'd be late.

She surveyed the dwindling number of chocolates in the box—the box that was supposed to be a housewarming gift.

Gah!

There were six bonbons left. Not the dozen she'd planned to give to Libby and Raz, but a half dozen was still a respectable number of treats.

"I nearly forgot about the housewarming," she whined. She scrambled to her feet and scanned the room, searching for her tote.

"Your purse is on the hook," Babs said smoothly, biting back a grin.

Brain, start working!

"Which reminds me," Babs continued. "I forgot to tell you that I met Madelyn Malone."

Harper stared at her purse and froze.

Madelyn?

Her heart pounded. "You met Madelyn Malone, the nanny matchmaker?"

"Yes, she stopped over while you were at your convention."

Madelyn showed up at the house.

No, no, no, no, no.

"Exactly what day did she stop by?" she asked, going for nonchalance. "The day I left or the day I got back?"

This was hella important.

Babs took a sip of her decaf. "The morning of the day you returned. I can't believe I forgot to mention it to you. We've both been a bit scatterbrained."

Scatterbrained or not, she'd already been married to Landon by then.

But Madelyn couldn't have known about the wedding. And even if she did, and she'd mentioned it to Babs, her grandmother would have dropped the gauntlet and made her spill the details the minute she pulled up in Carol.

"And what did you and Madelyn talk about?" she asked as a bead of perspiration trailed between her breasts.

"We mostly spoke about music. She'd heard me play years ago when I was still with the Denver Symphony Orchestra. We had a lovely visit. I shared with her about my musicians' retreat. It just so happens, we both love visiting New Mexico."

"Uh-huh," she grunted, but that couldn't be all Madelyn wanted.

The matchmaker always had something up her sleeve.

"Isn't it marvelous how she's matched Libby, Charlotte, and Penny with their fiancés?"

"Uh-huh."

"Madelyn simply adores the four of you," Babs added.

Harper removed her tote from the hook but kept her back to Babs. "And she stopped over, out of the blue, and introduced herself?"

"Yes, she said she was in the neighborhood."

Unlikely.

"Did she mention anything about matching me for a nanny

position?" Her heart was ready to jackhammer itself out of her chest.

"No, she didn't."

Crisis averted.

She released a relieved breath. Maybe there was nothing to it. Penny, Char, or Libby could have mentioned Babs was home alone while she was in Las Vegas.

"But I asked Madelyn if there was a placement for you," Babs added.

Dial up the jackhammer.

"Why?" she asked in a high-pitched opera voice that exploded from her throat when she got crazy flustered.

"Because you need a job. I'm not sure I know what you're doing when I hear you singing and calling yourself Bonbon Barbie in your room, but I know you're not teaching in-person piano lessons, and it's not just that. You're a young woman. You need to be out in the world, working on your music and finding your way, not living here with your grandmother."

She turned and faced the woman who'd raised her. "I want to make sure you're okay, Babs."

Her grandmother got up and placed her empty mug in the sink. "I get around just fine, missy. And truth be told, you're cramping my style."

"I'm cramping your style?" she fired back. "Did my moving back in interrupt your three a.m. raves in the attic? It's what Grandpa would have wanted me to do." Along with making sure the house didn't get repossessed, but she left out that part.

"Harper, even if my ankle hadn't healed, I would be fine. You know better than anyone else that you can't allow an impairment to hold you back."

She did.

That's what had inspired her foray into online music instruction.

She peered into the living room, and a soothing warmth welled in her chest as she took in the piano.

Her piano.

She pictured herself as a girl, feet dangling as she sat in the center of the piano bench with Grandma Babs on one side and Grandad Reeves on the other. Armed with a box of colored pencils, there was no stopping her.

"I know," she whispered.

"Madelyn did mention one curious thing."

Here it comes. Sweet baby Jesus, don't let it be about Landon! She couldn't handle more lying.

"And what was that?" she replied, keeping her tone even.

"She's having trouble matching a client."

"Oh yeah?" she answered and cleared her throat.

"Her client is in the music industry. She wanted to get my opinion on the kind of nanny who'd work well with a musician."

The music industry?

It had to be Landon.

"Is that so," she answered, unable to keep her voice from rising an irritated octave as she worked to maintain her cool.

She bristled.

Why was she bristling? She didn't want to be the guy's nanny, right?

Still, the thought of Landon employing another nanny had her gnashing her teeth.

She was, at least on paper, his wife.

Pull yourself together, woman.

Thanks to the ample amount of sugar in her bloodstream, she was as jittery as a caffeinated Chihuahua. She caught sight of her sandals out of the corner of her eye and lunged for them. Why she thought she needed to reach for her shoes like she was engaged in an interpretive dance number was anyone's guess. She slipped and dropped her tote in a spastic convulsion.

The contents clattered onto the floor, along with a flurry of lollipops and lip balms.

Stop acting like a lunatic.

She sank to her knees and furiously collected the items, tossing them in willy-nilly.

"Are you okay, little miss?" Babs asked, squinting as she peered at the ground. "You seem a little...excited. Have you eaten a real meal since you got back, or have you been existing on lollipops and bonbons?"

"I'm super great. I'm doing a candy detox diet. First, you eat a ton of candy, then you detox," she shot back, not making a lick of sense as her voice climbed another octave.

She'd be singing opera if she didn't calm down.

"Is that a bird mask?" her grandmother continued, taking a few steps toward her. "What are you doing with a bird mask?"

She stuffed the feathery face-covering into her bag. "That old thing? I found it in the attic," she lied again. The lies were stacking up. "I wanted to show it to Libby. She's got a thing for birds. Yes, that's why I have a feathery bird mask in my purse. And speaking of Libby, I need to leave right now to make it to the housewarming party. Not a minute to lose."

"Give me a hug," Babs said, opening her arms. "I'll be on my way to New Mexico by the time you get back. Promise me you'll remember your grandad's advice. Music is part of your soul, little miss. Never forget that," she added as they embraced.

"I'll try," she whispered, tightening her hold.

"I know you will. And you should venture down to the basement."

"To your and grandpa's soundproof practice room?"

"It's an excellent place to revive your creativity and find your voice," the woman answered with a flirty little smile.

That was a little weird, but okay.

Babs sniffed the air. "And promise me you'll take a shower. Good heavens, missy."

"I promise. I'll acquaint myself with soap in the very near future. Have fun at the retreat. I love you," she said with a pasted-on grin. Her emotions were all over the place. Irritation coursed through her veins at the thought of Landon and some random nanny. Anger roiled in her chest at the thought of losing the house. And she might be twenty-six years old, but she still hated to be separated from her grandmother.

She sniffled. *Do not cry.*

She grabbed the box of bonbons, then hoofed it out the back door as she went over her conversation with Babs and one salient point stood out.

Madelyn was up to something.

Was she fishing for information? Was Landon about to get some random nanny?

And if he was paired with a woman, would he look at this nanny the way he looked at her?

This would be a terrific time to have her husband's phone number to get some answers.

She had more than a few questions for the runaway pop star.

She got into Carol, slammed the old Volvo's door, then crammed two bonbons into her mouth before reversing down the driveway like a brown bat out of hell.

She cursed herself for marrying the man.

The bolter.

The guy who hadn't reached out to her since he'd said I do.

She gobbled down three more bonbons.

Forget her one-night stand spouse. It was time to focus on what mattered.

She had to figure out a way to make some fast cash. She couldn't have the woman return home to find an eviction notice on the door.

"Come on, Grandad, send me a melody from the great beyond," she said, then popped another bonbon into her mouth at a stoplight as a Vance Vibe song—no, a Harper Presley song pilfered by Vance Viberenski—blared on the radio.

The guy probably made enough from her music to pay Babs' bills ten times over.

"Ugh," she bit out, then reached for another bonbon, and…nothing.

She glanced at the box and found a few flecks of brown.

What the hell was she supposed to give Raz and Libby?

She couldn't show up at the housewarming empty-handed.

She checked the clock. She had a little time.

She was only a couple of minutes away from the couple's ritzy Crystal Acres neighborhood. She spied a gas station and pulled into the parking lot. Okay, a gas station wasn't the ideal location to shop for a housewarming present. Still, her choices and her budget were limited. She cut the ignition, rifled through her wallet and found it empty, just like the bonbon box.

Dammit!

She opened the glove box. "Come on, Carol, there's got to be some cash stashed in here."

She rummaged through multiple pairs of broken sunglasses and more gloves than one girl could ever need, then gripped a slip of paper. No, not paper—a bill. A five-dollar bill.

"Bingo, bitches!" she hollered as an elderly woman walked past her car and clucked her tongue.

Was everyone on her case today?

She forgot the old bird, grabbed the fiver, and sprinted into the convenience store. She scanned the place like a rabid beast searching for prey, then zeroed in on the perfect housewarming gift.

Perfect might not be the best way to describe a wilting

houseplant in a ceramic pot. But the pot was indigo—Libby's favorite color.

"Score one for Bonbon Barbie," she announced and closed in on the plant. Bubbly jubilation surged through her when she spied the price tag.

"Three eighty-nine, people," she called out like a game show host.

She could buy this half-dead houseplant and have some extra cash. She trotted to the cashier as "Walking on Sunshine" by Katrina and the Waves played. The peppy music spoke to her, and she added a little spring to her step.

Her life might be a giant shit show, but finding this cheap plant was a win, albeit a small win, but a victory, no less.

She set the plant on the counter. Feeling like a million bucks—or a solid five—then spied a clear plastic jar bursting with cute little pencil erasers. Happiness took over as she spied a tiny hot dog, a mini donkey, and a cute camera eraser.

What a find.

Phoebe, Sebastian, and Oscar would go crazy for these. It was like the universe wanted her to be at this convenience store at this very moment.

She checked the price.

Twenty-five cents a pop.

Woohoo!

Not only would she show up with a housewarming gift, but she would also come armed with treasures for the kids—and school supplies, no less. With the school year starting in a couple of weeks, not only were these gifts *hella* thoughtful, they were *hella* practical.

Talk about being a considerate friend.

She collected the tiny items, then noticed a miniature piano beneath a hamburger-shaped eraser. "What's one more?" she mused before adding the small black and white rubbery instrument to the mix. She could use it in one of her Bonbon Barbie lessons.

She smiled at the cashier—a young man wearing a beanie with *High AF Good Vibes Only* printed next to a marijuana leaf. She wasn't into that scene, but she'd accept every drop of positive energy this day would give her. "I'll take these erasers and the…" She stared at the counter.

Where the hell was the housewarming gift?

She looked over her shoulder and found the old tongue clucker holding the plant—her plant—the perfect present for Libby and Raz.

"That's mine, lady. Hand it over," she demanded as "Walking on Sunshine" continued to play. She could direct a little sunshine toward the crusty gal. She grinned at the woman. "*Please*, hand over my plant," she said like the ray of sunshine she was. "I set the plant down to pick out erasers for my friends' kids. I'm buying the plant and the erasers because I'm a good person."

Boom!

The woman crinkled her face into a deep scowl. "You set it down. If you set it down, that means you don't want it."

All right, grandma, the gloves were coming off.

Harper scrunched up her face and lowered her voice. "I'm telling you, I will be purchasing that plant."

"I want it," the old gal tossed back. "I like the pot."

Dammit, Katrina and the Waves.

Screw walking on sunshine. It was time to channel some darkness.

She narrowed her gaze. "Listen, lady, I have five dollars to my name. And come hell or high water, I am buying this plant and these four erasers. You will have to fight me for this half-dead fern, or whatever the hell kind of plant it is. I'm not a botanist. But I can promise you this. I am prepared to die on this hill—this plant and eraser-laden hill. They'll have to erect my tombstone next to the cash register. That's how far I'm willing to go. Whatcha gonna do, granny? Are you ready to throw down for this plant?"

The woman gasped and set the plant on the counter with a pronounced thud. "Well, I've never seen such atrocious behavior," she hissed before making a beeline toward the soda dispensers.

"Atrocious Behavior is my middle name, sister," she called, then set the five items on the counter feeling like a gangster—a convenience store OG.

The clerk gave her the once-over, then sniffed the air.

Could she catch a break, please?

"I get it. I smell like chocolate death warmed-over," she snipped, riding her OG plant high. "Just ring me up, Mr. High *AF*. I'm in a hurry."

"Chill, dude, it's all good," the man offered with a wide grin, then rang up the items. "That's five dollars and eight cents."

Stupid tax.

She smoothed the crinkled bill on the counter. "Yeah, as you can see, I'm good for the five, but about those eight cents. I don't do public math, and I didn't really compute the tax." Her gaze flicked to the take a penny, leave a penny tray. "Would you mind if I borrowed a few of those?"

The cashier stared at her. "Eight isn't a few. Three is a few."

So much for good vibes.

"Eight could be a few," she countered. "I believe the range for a few is any number between three and nine, and eight is solidly between three and nine."

Let's hear it for kindergarten math. Miss Miliken would be crazy proud of her.

"No," the guy replied, stretching out the syllable. "I'm like one hundred and six percent positive eight doesn't qualify as a few. You've got to put something back, lady."

Oh, hell no!

She leaned in. "Listen, dude, if you know what's good for —" she growled, then froze mid-rant as a familiar energy radiated behind her. It was a presence she recognized.

"I can cover what she can't."

A delicious tingle danced down her spine.

Traitorous tingly spine.

But getting irritated with her vertebrae didn't change the fact that she recognized that voice.

His voice.

Her missing in action husband's voice.

Chapter 9
HARPER

Harper spun around and found herself eye to eye with the heartthrob.

Looking as gorgeous and as dreamy as ever, L. Bartholomew Paige whipped off his aviators. "Hey."

Hey? That's it? Those are his first words to her in a week?

"Hey?" she echoed, hitting a high note that would impress an Italian opera singer.

Landon pulled a one-hundred-dollar bill from his wallet and handed it to the cashier. "This is for my…"

"Wife?" she supplied, hitting a high note like she was Maria Callas in a performance of *Madame Butterfly*.

Her ear-piercing shriek had stunned everyone in the store.

And when the hell had Landon slipped in?

She glanced between the gawking old lady and the suddenly-quite-alert cashier. "Sorry, I don't usually bust out arias in convenience stores."

"What did you say?" Landon uttered, his stupidly perfect lips parting as his jaw dropped.

"Arias, like in operas."

"I know what an aria is," he threw back with a distinct edge.

He had no right to get all touchy with her.

Okay, so…this had gotten weird.

Well, more bizarre than it was ten seconds ago when she was yelling at an old lady and about to steal eight pennies.

"I don't usually sing arias in public…or ever," she added, flashing the cashier what she hoped wasn't a sociopathic expression. Still, the fear in the dude's eyes told her, quite explicitly, that she could never frequent this establishment again.

"Get your stuff, Harper," Landon barked. "We should get going." He turned to the old tongue-clucking plant-pilferer. "Ma'am, I'm happy to pay for your beverage."

The cashier held up the bill. "You want some change, man? Your girl only owes eight cents, and a drink is a buck ten."

"I'm not his girl," she snapped.

"Keep it for…" Landon huffed, then glanced at her. "For your trouble."

Trouble!

Who did this man think he was?

"I'll leave when I'm good and ready to leave," she shot back, pocketing the erasers and clutching the plant. She strolled past a display of key chains and studied one with the words *Hang in there* written in loopy lettering.

You hang in there, you dumb key chain.

She took a step back, studied a rack of beef jerky, then glanced at the cashier.

There was no reason to remain in the store, especially with the guy starting to twitch.

Landon looked her up and down. "Are you *good and ready* to leave?"

Dammit! She was.

"Yes, I'm ready to leave but not because you said it was time to go," she countered as he opened the door. She strutted her stuff, exiting the store, then caught her reflection in the glass.

Sweet Jesus!

Why was it that when she was dressed to the nines and having a great hair day, she didn't see a soul? But on those days when she looked like she'd been wrestling feral cats, she ran into her...her pop star husband.

And she was wearing his shirt.

Maybe he wouldn't notice.

And her appearance should not matter.

If anyone asked about her wardrobe, she'd say she was rocking a retro look. What retro look? Hell if she knew, but it sounded better than the truth. And on the topic of truth, she pegged Landon with her gaze. "What are you doing here? You didn't buy anything."

"I saw your car on the way to Raz and Libby's house-warming party, and—"

"And what?" she asked, cutting him off while wanting to pull her hair out. How had she not put two and two together? Of course Landon would be invited to the get-together.

"And I wanted to see you, Harper. I wanted to see how you're doing."

She threw her shoulders back and parted her lips, preparing to discharge a battery of zingers, but the man looked awful. Okay, not awful. Landon Paige had flawless bone structure and a sexy five o'clock shadow that would not quit. Even rocking a ball cap, she knew every hair on his head was in place. He looked as awful as a musical Adonis could look, which was still smokin' hot. But it was the wretched weariness in his eyes that gave him away.

Don't feel sorry for this man.

"How did you even know this was Carol?" she asked, pointing to her Volvo heap.

"I saw Carol in Vegas after getting her out of the impound lot for you."

Crap, he did do that.

"I didn't need you to do it, but I appreciate it. I'm a big enough person to give credit where credit's due," she replied in the least appreciative tone possible.

He took a step toward her. "I can tell you're mad."

"You can?" she fired back, feigning shock. "You should talk to Libby. She's clairvoyant, too."

He released a pained sigh. "Something came up, and I had to leave. I didn't want to wake you. You looked so peaceful."

That tiny kernel of hope in her chest warmed at the thought of Landon watching her sleep.

She stared at the half-dead plant. "Where'd you have to go in such a hurry?"

"I had to return to Denver."

"And how did you get home?"

"My plane."

"Your plane? How nice," she answered, reviving her mega-bitch tone. "I drove twelve hours in the heat in a 1994 Volvo with questionable air-conditioning."

Cool it, girl.

She wanted to take it down a notch. She truly did. But it hurt to see him after that night—that crazy night where she'd felt invincible. When he'd held her hand, it was as if a force field protected them, shielding them from the outside world and the nagging voices in the back of her head whispering she wasn't enough.

"I wasn't thinking clearly when I left, and I'm sorry." He removed his cap and ran his hand through his hair, then pulled it low to shield his eyes.

She stared at his left hand.

He wasn't wearing his ring.

Why did that hurt?

"You're not wearing yours either," he said, reading her mind.

"It's right here," she answered, touching the outline of the two rings through the— Oh no, that's right. She was rocking his shirt. He eyed the garment and bit back a grin.

He must have thought she'd been pining away for him like a lovesick Landon Paige superfan.

She was about to tell him she absolutely had not been pining for him, nor had she cross-stitched his face on a pillow, when he pulled a chain from beneath the collar of his shirt, and a platinum band caught the light.

"I've got mine, too." He stared into her eyes, and his gaze softened. "It's good to see you. You look—"

"I look like I'm vying for first place in a hobo contest or trying out for the part of street urchin in *Les Mis*."

He chuckled. "You do have a way with words. You can paint a picture. I'll give you that, bonbon."

Bonbon.

He looked away. "We should talk about—"

"—getting to Libby and Raz's new place in Crystal Acres," she blurted. Their situation was out of control, but she couldn't have the state-of-their-screwed-up-union conversation in front of a convenience store while cradling a dead plant.

He gestured to his Porsche. "Do you want to ride together?"

She waved him off. "I don't want our friends to get the wrong idea. I haven't told anyone about…"

"I haven't either." He shifted his stance and released an audible breath.

The man was in pain.

She wanted to reach out and touch him. The impulse was almost too much to bear.

But she didn't.

She hardened her features. "You go ahead. My lateness will be nothing new to my friends," she said coolly, gesturing with her chin toward his sports car.

"We should talk after."

"Okay," she whispered, the word coming out like a crack in thin ice, and suddenly, the rings around her neck weighed a ton.

"I'll see you there," he said, taking a step back but not looking away.

"Yeah, we'll act like nothing happened. I'll be my usual witty self, and you can be the self-absorbed pop star," she added, trying to make a joke, but it fell flat.

For a beat, their eyes locked, but she couldn't get a read on him.

Was it regret over what they'd done?

Disappointment over the fact that it had to end?

Or was it something unrelated to her, and she was the self-absorbed half of this marriage?

They'd gone into that night in Vegas saying it was a one and done—an evening to go wild, a time to forget their troubles and throw caution to the wind. But when he'd caught the bouquet and smiled that boyish half-smile at her, their connection had felt real.

A dare is a dare, and we've been double-dog dared.

"Go, you don't want to be late," she said, pushing aside her sappy musings.

He flicked his gaze to the ground and nodded. Without another word, he moved like a man who hadn't slept in a week and folded himself into the Porsche. The car's engine roared to life, and she watched the vehicle disappear into the traffic. She tightened her grip on the plant as her heart broke a little at the sight.

Cradling the plant in the crook of her arm, she leaned

against Carol. "He is your one-night-only husband, and no matter how wrecked he looked, he still left you and never called."

Images of Vance and her parents flashed in her mind, and she allowed the familiar angry impulses to blot out her sorrow.

What could be so important that he couldn't reach out?

Then again, he didn't have her number either and probably didn't want to ask the guys for it.

Could she blame him when she'd done the same thing?

She stared down at her shirt—his shirt—and huffed an irritated breath.

Yes, she could absolutely blame him.

He was the one who'd handed her the bouquet with that sexy, infuriatingly naughty, deliciously devious look in his dreamy brown eyes. If this marriage was anyone's fault, the onus belonged on him.

She buckled the plant into the passenger seat, then got in her car and rested her head on the steering wheel.

Her heart was ready to beat itself out of her chest. Seeing Landon after their wild night had sent her into a tailspin.

It was a crazy twist of fate that the man was in her life to begin with.

He'd been her first crush when she was a teen. She'd done a good job keeping it to herself—not that Penny, Charlotte, or Libby would have given her grief for it. But at the time, she needed something to call her own—something separate from her real life.

And now what?

It was time to get on with it.

She started Carol up and headed for the housewarming party.

But she couldn't stop herself from speculating on what would come next.

Landon would want a divorce.

Perhaps that's what had ignited the torment in his eyes.

She turned onto the parkway that led into the sprawling Crystal Acres neighborhood. The gate was open, and she sailed into the ritzy oasis in the heart of Denver. Mansions with ample acreage lined the tree-covered streets. Thanks to Charlotte living in this neighborhood, and Penny a few miles away in the equally fancy Crystal Hills neighborhood, she was well acquainted with this part of town.

She pulled up to Raz and Libby's sprawling mansion and parked on the circle drive, making sure to keep her distance from Landon's shiny Porsche.

She cut the ignition, turned to the wilting plant, and focused on the deep indigo vase. "I'll go in there and be my old sarcastically endearing self. This is no big deal, right?"

Like the bonbons, the pot didn't offer any words of encouragement.

She should probably stop requesting advice from inanimate objects.

She unbuckled the plant and got out of her car. "Your life is a dumpster fire," she muttered. "You married a musician on a double-dog dare, but you are still a badass to be reckoned with. Be the take-no-crap bitch," she finished, rocking a pep talk, then glanced down at her bright orange socks and sandals—colorful orange socks with a hole exposing her big toe. Not precisely the wardrobe of a badass bitch, but a gal had to work with what she had. "Charge inside and give them some classic Harper Presley sass."

Focus on Libby and Raz. It's their party and a day to celebrate their yoga-doing, donkey-racing, vibrator-testing bliss.

She could escape and play Auntie Harper with the kids. She could suggest a game of hide-and-seek and remain hidden for the duration of the party.

She had options.

Swallowing past the lump in her throat, she stared at the front door, gripped the knob, turned that sucker...

And...action.

She listened for voices and jogged through the enormous house, moving toward the overlapping conversations. She made her way through the kitchen and caught sight of everyone on the covered porch.

No one had noticed her yet.

She spied Landon.

Her breaths came hard and fast.

Do not act like a crazy person.

For reasons she couldn't quite wrap her mind around, she sprinted through the shiny kitchen, the size of a mid-sized organic grocery store, then burst onto the scene.

"Sorry, I'm late," she got out between puffs of air. "I wanted to get you a housewarming gift, and then I got into a fight with a lady over who was the rightful recipient of this plant, but as you can see, I was the victor," she announced and held the droopy plant above her head like a trophy.

Totally not-crazy people entered a party like that, right?

Wrong.

She surveyed the group as all eyes fell on her.

Mitch, Rowen, Raz, Penny, Libby, and Charlotte stared at her with crinkled brows. And, oh shit, Madelyn was there, too. The only person not focused on her was her husband. The man drained a bottle of beer like a star frat recruit, then peered into the bottle as if it held the answer to his prayers.

She could use a few prayers, too.

From the befuddled looks on her friends' faces, it was clear something was up.

And this something did not appear to be good.

She didn't need Libby's mind-reading powers to sense the tension in the air.

Do not jump to conclusions.

Perhaps it was her attire—or her scent. At least this gathering was outdoors.

But the stunned look on Landon's face led her to believe it was more than chocolate-infused body odor or her raggedy orange socks and sweats that had the group in a state of shock.

He glanced at Madelyn, then turned away from the nanny matchmaker and met her gaze.

No one spoke for what seemed like the better part of a decade.

"What happened in Vegas didn't stay in Vegas," Landon said as the color drained from his face.

She sucked in a death gasp—at least, that's what it sounded like, or maybe it was the sound of her brain cells working to piece together what everyone knew. Unfortunately, an all-consuming panic drowned out any connections her mind was able to make.

"I need a little more info, heartthrob," she said, trying to keep it light as her stomach dropped, and she held on to the houseplant like it was the only thing grounding her to the planet.

"I'm sorry, bonbon. It got out," Landon replied, tossing a glance over his shoulder at Madelyn.

She was about to drop the plant and hightail it out of there when Mitch cleared his throat.

"There it is," the former hothead chef said under his breath as her friends nodded along with him.

Screw the getaway. What did these people think they had on her?

"What are you talking about, Mitch?" she asked, going into super-bitch mode.

When in doubt, heap on the attitude.

"It's how you addressed Landon and how he answered you," the chef replied with the ghost of a grin.

What the hell did she say? She couldn't even remember how she addressed him.

"You called him heartthrob, and he called you bonbon. You've already got pet names for each other," Raz supplied.

Well, shit.

It meant nothing. They were under duress.

"It was a slip of the tongue," she announced, her pitch climbing.

"And she's doing the opera voice," Penny whispered to Charlotte.

"I don't do an opera voice," she shrieked—in maybe, possibly, the worst impression of an opera voice ever attempted.

Landon took a step toward her. "Before you got here, the group asked Madelyn about my nanny match situation."

Double shit.

"And?" she eked out.

"And," Madelyn interjected as she flipped her signature scarlet scarf over her shoulder like a Greek heiress, "the situation has changed," she purred in that rich Eastern European accent.

Here it comes.

"How so?" she asked, three octaves higher than normal speech. At this point, she was also communicating with dogs and possibly extra-terrestrial beings.

"I work exclusively with *single* male caregivers. It's my niche," the woman explained with a sly twist to her lips.

She looked from Madelyn to Landon.

Her pop star set the empty bottle of beer on the table. "I'm not single anymore."

No shit, Sherlock. She knew that much.

What she didn't know was if everyone knew she was the gal who'd taken him off the market.

A spell of silence swallowed the room.

Just wait it out.

Say nothing.

Do not give yourself away.

A knot formed in her belly, and she shifted her stance.

Did they know? Did they not know?

The jarring anticipation had her on the cusp of going mad. The pressure was too much.

She marched across the deck and set the half-dead housewarming gift on the patio table. "It's me," she announced. "I married Landon, and I hope you like the plant. Happy housewarming."

Dammit, so much for waiting it out and keeping her cool.

"Yes, of course, it's you, Harper," Madelyn answered smoothly. The matchmaker removed her cell phone from her bag and tapped the screen.

"What are you looking at, Madelyn? Are you checking the weather?" she asked, still channeling an opera singer.

Madelyn held out her phone. "Not the weather, dear, a wedding. Your wedding. I've got photos from the Presley-Paige wedding, to be exact."

There were photos?

She froze like a cornered rabbit as Penny, Charlotte, and Libby swooped in and crowded in front of the phone.

"You married Landon and didn't tell us, H?" Char trilled.

Could a person combust from mortification?

"It just happened."

She wracked her brain. She couldn't remember anyone recording or taking pictures.

But she had to see for herself.

Landon had the same idea.

The girls moved aside so she and her heartthrob husband could see the screen. Madelyn's browser was open to an online celebrity page on LookyLoo, no less. A smattering of photos and video clips of their wedding dotted a paparazzi site.

"When did this go live?" she asked, losing the opera voice.

"About an hour ago," Madelyn answered.

What would Babs think?

Wait, Babs wouldn't know.

She was en route to her retreat, far away from the internet.

"Despite your unique attire, you both look quite happy," Madelyn observed.

The matchmaker wasn't wrong.

She'd been happy—no, blissfully ecstatic.

She scanned the photos and zeroed in on a shot of Landon smiling. Shirtless and looking delectable, the pop god grinned at her as she slipped the ring onto his finger.

Audio started playing, and the attention shifted to Rowen.

"I now pronounce you husband and wife. You may kiss the bride."

"I found a video of the ceremony online," Rowen said, holding up his phone as cheering and whooping sounds came from his cell.

"We love you, Harper and Bara-lala-meow."

She inhaled a shaky breath, recalling the drunk ballerinas and tipsy gladiators clapping and whistling as Landon gazed at her like she was the girl he'd been waiting his whole life to kiss.

She touched her chest and felt the rings through the T-shirt.

"How does getting married just happen?" Penny asked with her hand on her hip.

How was she supposed to explain it?

"Um…well…it's complicated," she stammered.

"We were double-dog dared," Landon answered, standing his ground by her side.

Butterflies fluttered in her belly.

It was a repeat of the moment when Mr. Handsy wouldn't buzz off and Landon had appeared.

Get a grip, woman.

"That's right," she said like dare-matrimony was a commonplace occurrence. Still, it was odd how a double-dog dare seemed to hold more weight in Vegas than on Libby and Raz's patio.

"Let me get this right. You were double-dog dared to get married?" Penny repeated.

It was time to double down on this double-dog dare.

"Yes, like you double-dog dared me to enter the talent contest in second grade, Penn Fenn. So, this is kind of your fault."

"My fault?" Penny replied, wide-eyed.

She shrugged. "From that moment on, I couldn't back down from a double-dog dare."

"In their defense, a double-dog dare is the ultimate level of dare," Raz remarked.

"Unless you increase the stakes and drop a triple-dog dare," Rowen countered.

Mitch shook his head. "I have to disagree. Once the dare starts getting too large, it loses its emphasis. I'm no fan of the triple-dog dare. Double is the ceiling when it comes to dares," the man finished as Raz nodded.

"I see your point," Rowen conceded, then returned to his phone.

"Enough with the dare factor," Charlotte chided. "How did this happen? Did you plan to get married? I didn't think you two liked each other that much."

"We ran into each other at a dance club in Las Vegas last week," Landon answered. "And..."

And they screwed on a public balcony.

And he'd made her body sing with his massive cock and masterful mouth.

And thanks to a porn contest mix-up going awry, she was Mrs. Landon Paige.

"And one thing led to another," she supplied, choosing to keep it short, sweet, and vague.

Madelyn's phone pinged, and the woman turned to read a

text message. "You'll have to excuse me. An issue with a client has arisen, and I must be off."

"What happens with the nanny match?" Landon asked as Madelyn retrieved her purse. "I take full custody of Aria soon."

The breath caught in her throat.

Aria?

A little girl.

What a beautiful name.

Is that why he'd overreacted in the convenience store when she'd said that word? It had to be.

Was Aria his daughter?

She'd been so focused on marrying the man, she'd forgotten why he was in search of a nanny.

Madelyn slipped the straps of her purse over her shoulder. "You can discuss Aria with your wife."

Wife.

It was one thing for her to throw around the word. It was a completely different ballgame to hear the sage matchmaker drop the big *W*.

"Wife," Landon repeated.

"Yes, your wife is now Aria's aunt," Madelyn clarified.

Aunt.

She was some kid's aunt?

And then it clicked. Aria was Landon's sister and his bandmate's daughter. She had to be. They'd died suddenly, but she never knew they'd had a child. Heartthrob Warfare had fallen off the scene around the time she went to college. While Landon was still visible, his sister, Leighton, and the bass player, Trey Grant, had disappeared from the music world. She'd figured they were taking a break or pursuing individual projects, but their disappearance wasn't for work. They'd had a baby.

Was Landon the only family the little girl had left?

She had so many questions.

"I'm sure you have a lot to talk about," the matchmaker said with a cat-who-ate-the-canary expression. "I can see myself out. Congratulations on your new home, Libby and Erasmus. It's lovely."

"Thanks for dropping by," Libby called.

Madelyn left the patio, and silence swallowed the group.

No one said a word until the click of the front door closing added a layer of titillating drama to the air. The energy on the porch shifted, and she steadied herself for the onslaught.

Three, two, one.

Gird up thy loins.

Here it comes.

Chapter 10

HARPER

Her friends started talking at once, and a verbal explosion hit the covered patio like a sonic boom.

"What the hell, H?"

"Is this for real?"

"You guys are married, actually married!"

"When were you guys going to tell us?" Charlotte exclaimed. Usually, Char opted for pervasive gentleness over outright force. But the redhead could turn up the heat when she wanted to.

"Dude, you can't go and marry your nanny on the first night," Rowen exclaimed.

"Yeah, there's a process, mate," Raz added. "You've got to have your arse handed to you a few times before you get the girl."

"It wasn't like that," Landon replied, gaze darting all over the place like he'd woken up on an alien planet. "We weren't matched up officially."

Mitch took a sip of his beer. "You guys have to be the last match."

It was time to shut this down, Harper Presley style.

She took a slow breath. It was as if she were back in grade school, where every lesson felt like the information was coming at her through a fire hose.

"Time out," she cried over the flurry of conversation, and the buzz of rapid-fire questions stopped.

She took a second to order her thoughts. "This marriage was an impulsive, spur-of-the-moment decision. When we got double-dog dared, everyone around us was hammered and partying. The atmosphere was surreal, like nothing counted, like a crazy dream. And we got caught up in the fervor and excitement, right?" she finished and turned to Landon.

He met her gaze, but he didn't say a word.

What did his silence mean? Did he view it as a stupid mistake—a terrible error in judgment—or not?

"But you really got married, H. You said 'I do.' You spoke vows to each other," Libby remarked with a Zen master grin.

"Yeah, I legally wed L. Bartholomew Paige seven days ago."

"Bartholomew?" Raz repeated.

"Landon Bartholomew Paige is my full name," her heart-throb husband added.

"I wondered what those half-naked dudes on the video were trying to say," Rowen murmured.

"Why were you going by your middle name?" Penny asked.

"So they wouldn't suspect I was Landon Paige, the musician," he answered.

"And it worked?" Mitch asked, skepticism coating the question.

"Like we said," Landon continued, "the people we were with were smashed. The bride, Katrina, almost outed me, but Harper made up a story on the fly and started calling me Bartholomew," he finished, then gifted her with the sweetest grin.

And here come the butterflies.

Her emotions were all over the place.

She held her breath.

Do not go into swoon mode.

"Bartholomew is a bloody mouthful, mate," Raz commented.

"Yep, those poor drunk gladiators are making a mess of it," Rowen remarked with eyes glued to his phone as the raucous hum of Jude's gladiators slurring the hell out of the name hung in the air.

"I still have questions," Charlotte said, sizing them up. "How do you go from attending a piano teacher conference to marrying Landon?"

The lie.

Her stomach dropped. Bye-bye, butterflies.

"You might as well tell them," Landon said gently.

Dammit, he was right.

She twisted the hem of the T-shirt. "As you know, Landon and I ran into each other in Las Vegas, but I wasn't there for a piano teacher conference."

Libby raised her hands and closed her eyes like she was receiving an incoming message from the great beyond. "Were you on a balcony with flashing lights?" She opened her eyes. "I know that sounds silly, but that night after Penn, Char, and I called you, that's what I kept picturing."

"Wow," Landon breathed.

Yeah, wow.

"You must be getting a vibe from the Luxe Grandiose," she answered.

"I thought you said you weren't at that hotel?" Penny pressed.

"I...I lied to you," she confessed. "I didn't want you guys to worry. I was at the Luxe for a contest."

Penny frowned. "A piano contest?"

She would have been absolutely fine with a bolt of lightning striking her right about now.

"It was a contest to become the internet's next hot online performer."

"Are you singing again?" Char asked.

Only while screwing Landon.

She couldn't say that.

"It wasn't like that." She shifted nervously, feeling Landon's smoldering gaze. "It's because of this," she replied and pulled the feathered mask from her tote.

Penny frowned. "You're dressing up like a bird?"

"It's part of a costume." She stared at the feathery array of browns and black before returning the mask to her bag. "I quit teaching in-person piano lessons a while back and started doing lessons online to help neurodivergent people learn how to read music. I wear this mask to keep my identity hidden, and I call myself Bonbon Barbie."

"Bonbons for your grandad and Barbie after Babs?" Char asked gently.

Her friends knew her well.

"Yeah, I thought I could quickly make a boatload of cash to help Babs. She got duped into taking out a sketchy loan to pay for repairs to her house and owes quite a bit of money." She left out the part about it being nearly fifty thousand dollars, as well as the part about being on the brink of eviction. Her pride wouldn't allow her to divulge the info.

"H, if you need anything, we're here for you," Libby offered.

"Always," Char echoed. "If you need cash, you only have to ask."

No way.

Heat rose to her cheeks. "I love you guys. I do. But I won't accept a dime. That's not how I'm built. I'll work it out. I always do. That's why I was in Vegas. I figured, if I won the contest, it wouldn't be long before I started making real money, and then I could pay off the loan. But the competition was for a different kind of online performer."

"What kind of online performer were they looking for?" Raz asked.

Now her cheeks burned for an entirely different reason.

"The people who put on the contest meant to invite a performer who goes by Bang Bang Barbie. I shouldn't have even been there in the first place. They got Bang Bang and Bonbon confused and forgot to tell me about the mistake."

"Bang Bang Barbie?" Mitch repeated. "That's a weird name."

"What does Bang Bang Barbie do?" Char asked, when Rowen gasped, then dropped his phone.

"Holy smokes!" the man exclaimed as he retrieved his cell.

Penny stared at her fiancé. "Are you okay, babe?"

"I googled Bang Bang Barbie, and she's definitely not teaching children how to read music. That's for sure."

Mitch glanced over Rowen's shoulder. "And she certainly knows her way around a bottle of body glitter."

"Body glitter?" Libby repeated.

Hello, humiliation, my old friend.

"It was a contest to pick the next up-and-coming adult star."

"A porn star?" Char blurted as Mitch nodded wide-eyed, next to an equally wide-eyed Rowen and Raz, as the men stared at the screen.

"Yeah," she replied with a weary sigh, "it was a porno tryout."

"There's more, though, isn't there?" Libby pressed, going all mind-reader. "Something else got under your skin, H. Something else upset you."

It really sucked balls to have an intuitive bestie some days.

"You guys were right about Vance. I ran into him, and it wasn't pretty."

Libby gasped. "H, that had to have been awful."

"Vance Vibe?" Landon asked, practically spitting out the syllables. "He's the musician who hurt you?" He looked ready to track down Vance and tear the d-bag from limb to limb.

She parted her lips, unsure of what she was about to say, but Penny beat her to the punch.

"Vance Viberenski, aka Vance Vibe, is the jerk who stole Harper's music, skipped town, and broke her heart. He's an absolute creep."

Libby pressed her hand to her chest. "Accidental porn mix-up and an ex run-in? Harper, you poor thing."

"Then Carol got towed, and I thought I'd hit rock-bottom. So I lied my way into a gladiator-ballerina-themed wedding at the hotel's dance club, and that's when Landon helped me get away from a handsy guy on the dance floor."

Char shared a look with Libby and Penny. "Landon came to your rescue?"

"It was more like I came to the guy's rescue," her heart-throb husband corrected as a heaviness seemed to lift from his demeanor. "Harper was ready to punch his lights out on the dance floor."

Charlotte chuckled. "That does sound like you, H."

"And after that, one thing led to another, and…" she trailed off, chancing a look at Landon, only to find him gazing at her.

"And I'd bet an entire drawer full of Post-it notes I know what's hanging from the chains beneath your shirts," Penny remarked, looking from her to the heartthrob.

"Let's see them," Char nudged.

Landon removed the simple platinum band, and she followed suit. Just touching the rings brought back the beautifully outrageous memories.

"That's some rock," Penny remarked.

It was. At nearly four carats, she couldn't believe Landon had chosen the glittery ring.

The Luxe Grandiose wedding experience was like sprinting through the world's most expensive sparkling maze. It was a one-stop marriage shop. They'd started with rings and sealed the deal with a kiss.

All it had taken was a few signatures and the swipe of Landon's credit card, and ten minutes later, she was Mrs. Paige.

It was a microwave marriage with a hefty helping of bling.

But when Landon had proposed with the diamond, then slipped a smaller platinum band that matched his onto her finger two minutes later during the wedding ceremony surrounded by a circus of smashed strangers, she'd felt a serene sense of balance, like standing in the eye of a hurricane when the wind and the roar dissipate and all that's left is a captivating calm.

"It's Vegas. It's a go big or go home city," Landon replied as the girls admired her ring.

"Are you going to stay married?" Libby asked.

That was the million-dollar question.

Landon returned the ring to its hiding place, stuffed his hands into his pockets, pulled them out, then fidgeted with his cap. "Yeah, about that…"

They couldn't stay married.

She knew this.

He was a musician, and she wasn't about to allow another crooning Casanova to break her heart.

But that didn't stop an icy chill from prickling through her veins.

She steadied herself. "There's no way we——"

"Christ, that's a lot of glitter," Mitch remarked, cutting her off.

The hothead, the nerd, and the beefcake were still glued to Rowen's phone with their jaws on the floor.

"What is it?" Libby asked.

"What are you watching?" Penny pressed.

The men clamped their mouths shut as an airy woman's voice emanated from the phone, followed by a chorus of sensual moans.

"It's a Bang Bang Barbie glitter party."

Thanks to her, the guys were watching Bang Bang Barbie porn. Now there's something you don't see at a housewarming shindig.

"All that glitter must be a real bitch to clean up," Mitch said, when a stampede of footsteps muffled the sparkly porn star's sexy sighs.

"Rowen, turn it off. The kids are coming," Penny called.

The man fumbled with his phone as Phoebe, Sebastian, and Oscar charged through the kitchen, then skidded to a halt once they hit the patio.

"We want to play, too," Sebastian said, grinning from ear to ear.

"What are you talking about, mate? You didn't hear anything inappropriate. I can guarantee that," Raz said, turning the color of a ripe tomato.

"Aren't you playing cops and robbers?" Oscar asked, holding up his camera and scanning the mortified adults through the viewfinder.

"Yeah, what's the bang-banging?" Phoebe asked, making little guns with her hands and pretending to shoot into the air like a little Annie Oakley.

"There's no banging going on whatsoever," Rowen stammered, pocketing his phone.

Mitch shifted his stance. "Nothing bang-able here."

"And absolutely no glitter either," Raz added, then cringed.

Jesus, these men.

The trio of children shared a look, then turned their appraising gazes her way and frowned.

What had she done to deserve that reception?

At least she hadn't been binging on porn two seconds before they arrived like their male caregivers.

"Harper," Sebastian said with a stern bend to his crisp British accent.

She straightened her posture. "Yes?" she answered warily.

"We heard you talking to your plant when you got here," Phoebe said with a heavy dose of side-eye.

Oscar nodded. "You said a bunch of bad words."

"Yep, you said the *B*-word, H," Phoebe added, shaking her head. "That's a bad choice."

It was the least bad choice she'd made in the last week, but she'd keep that nugget to herself.

She cleared her throat. "I don't think I said it twice."

"You called yourself a badass bitch," Phoebe belted.

"We heard it twice when we were leaving the donkeys' barn," Sebastian added.

"And you could have tapped them out," Phoebe continued, followed by a disapproving huff.

These three were a force to be reckoned with.

"Shit," she uttered, then gasped and surveyed her friends, who looked ready to laugh their badass bitch asses off, but they held it together.

"There's another one you should have tapped out," Oscar chided, shaking his head.

"Well," she began, then remembered the erasers. She plastered a grin on her face. It was time to turn the tables on the pint-sized language police. "I have presents for you guys."

At the *P*-word, the curse word brigade halted their interrogation.

"What did you bring us?" Sebastian trilled.

She knelt but kept the erasers hidden in her hand. "Are you

sure you want your present now?" she asked and jiggled her fist to heighten the anticipation.

"Yes, now, please," the kids hooted.

She glanced up to find Landon watching her again. With a neutral expression, he was probably calculating the date when he could divorce her cursing badass ass.

She returned her attention to the vibrating seven-year-olds and slowly opened her hand.

"Erasers!" Phoebe hollered, shooting off another round of fake bullets.

Ah, the power of cool school supplies.

"Here's a hot dog eraser for you, Miss Phoebe, a camera eraser for Oscar, our photographer, and a little donkey for our burro racer, Sebastian."

Phoebe and Oscar investigated their tiny treasure, but Sebastian frowned at his.

"This is a horse, not a donkey, Harper."

She took a closer look.

Damn, it was a horse.

"Horses are donkey cousins," she replied, hoping she was right.

"Who gets the piano?" Oscar asked, studying the lone eraser.

She stared at the teeny-tiny black and white keys. "I'm not sure."

Phoebe looked past her and gawked at Landon. "What's that in your pocket, Landon? Did you bring presents, too?"

"What?" the man quipped, then gasped, and stuffed a scrap of black lace back into his pocket.

This roller coaster of a day wasn't done with her yet.

"Holy shit," she uttered.

She knew that scrap of lace.

"There's another bad word. You're worse than my dad,"

Oscar commented, then tapped his foot to demonstrate how to curse without saying the word.

But she couldn't worry about her child-unfriendly language.

"Are those fancy underpants in your pocket?" Phoebe asked, eyeing Landon and doling out one whopper of a question.

The man turned a shade reminiscent of dirty dishwater. "No, it's a…doily. A black doily."

A doily?

Oscar scrunched up his face. "What's a doily?"

"It's a little lacy placemat," Landon stammered.

He had her panties in his pocket.

Her panties!

"Can we see it?" Oscar asked.

Landon's eyes nearly popped out of his head. "No, it's a private doily."

Who carried around women's panties?

She should have been disgusted or freaked out, but she wasn't. It was oddly hot.

"Your private doily looks like the stuff in Penny's fancy underpants drawer," Phoebe replied.

Oscar perked up. "My Charlotte has one of those drawers."

"Mibby, too," Sebastian chimed.

"You know about that drawer?" Penny asked the little girl.

"I go through the drawers because I'm trying to find that book on a high shelf you keep talking about, but you never have a book. So, I figured it was lost."

"You should see all the hot dog torpedoes Mibby's got in her drawer," Sebastian added.

"Those fancy underpants don't look comfortable," Phoebe continued. "One pair even had a hole in it. I think you should return those broken underpants, Penny."

Now, every adult's complexion matched Landon's seasick hue.

Things had gone downhill fast.

From porn stars to crotchless panties, this housewarming party had taken quite a turn.

"Do doilies have crotches, Landon? Are they private underwear for placemats?" Oscar asked, then held up his camera and snapped a picture of the horrified pop star.

This had to stop.

But it would take a real humdinger to derail this bonkers convo.

She scanned the mortified adults, then waved her hands like she was marooned on a desert island and a plane had just passed by. "Guess what, kids," she sang like a disheveled, smelly Mary Poppins. "I married Landon, and now I'm his wife, which also makes me his niece's aunt."

What had she said?

She didn't dare look Landon's way.

A heavy silence took hold until Oscar lifted his camera and snapped a Polaroid of her. "Yeah, we know you married him," the kid answered, unimpressed with her slightly psychotic declaration. "That's what you said to your plant between calling yourself the bad words."

"You can be an aunt and a nanny," Phoebe gushed. "You're doing a backward nanny-match."

A backward nanny-match?

Anything was possible. Her whole world had gone backward, sideways, and upside down.

"Landon does look at you a lot, Harper," Sebastian commented.

"What do you mean?" she asked as Landon's complexion went from an uneasy gray-green to beet-red.

"Anytime we're together, somebody else might be talking, but Landon doesn't look at them. He looks at you. He looks at you the same way Phoebe looks at hot dogs," Sebastian explained.

"Sweet, sweet hot dogs," the girl cooed, then pinned Landon with her gaze. "So, do you like Harper more than hot dogs? Is that how you know if you should marry somebody?"

"Or do you like girls who smell like chocolate? Because Harper smells like a candy store next to a landfill," Oscar added.

"Do you like smelly chocolate?" Sebastian pressed.

"Um…" Landon stammered.

MIA musician husband or not, she had to help the guy.

She fake-coughed into her elbow. "Change the subject," she said through the fakest cough in the history of phony throat clearing.

Landon, looking like a gobsmacked fish out of water, nodded. "My niece, Aria, is registered to go to your school."

The pint-size bringers of mortification paused.

One second passed, then two.

"Do you know what class she's in?" Phoebe asked as the color returned to Landon's cheeks.

"We're gonna be in Miss Carrie Mackendorfer's second-grade class," Sebastian said.

Landon nodded. "Yeah, Aria's in that class. That's what it said on the school paperwork."

"Can we meet Aria before school starts?" Phoebe asked with a clap.

"Sure, I don't see why not."

"Let's do it now," Phoebe instructed.

"Now?" her heartthrob husband sputtered.

"Oscar, Sebastian, and I are very busy people. We've got park play dates, and we help Sebastian take care of his donkeys. Call her on your phone and put her on video," Phoebe instructed with her hand on her hip.

"About that, I—" Landon began, but Oscar cut him off.

"Or do you want to talk more about how you like to look at Harper even though she smells bad?"

"Let's make that call," Landon announced and slipped his phone from his pocket—the one that didn't contain lacy panties.

"Hey, Tomàs, can Aria come to the phone?" he said, glancing from the screen to the three children.

Who was Tomàs?

"Yes, hold on, Landon," came a man's voice with a gentle Spanish accent.

"What is it, Uncle Landy?" came a sassy chirp of a voice.

Uncle Landy? That was surprisingly adorable.

"Hand me the phone," Phoebe directed with practiced ease as she held out her palm.

"Aria, I'd like you to meet some friends," Landon continued, then passed the phone to Phoebe.

"Are you Aria?" the little girl asked.

"Who's asking?" Aria shot back with a decidedly less chirpy tone.

"Me. I'm asking. I'm Phoebe Gale. Tell her who I am, Sebastian."

There was enough sass between Phoebe and Aria to power the city for a week.

She chanced a look at Landon. A sad smile pulled at the corners of his lips as he watched Phoebe interact with his niece.

"I'm not saying your hot dog title, Phoebe," Sebastian lamented. "You made me do it three times yesterday and twice today before you'd help me brush the donkeys."

"Introductions are important," the little miss bossy pants huffed. "Fine, I'll do it myself. Aria, I'm Phoebe, Princess of the Hot Dog Fairies, Bearer of Cookies, and Eater of Pizza. These are my friends, Sebastian and Oscar," she continued, holding out the phone so the boys could enter the shot. "Your uncle said that you'll be in second grade with us at Whitmore. That's the name of our school. Are you excited? We've got great swings on the playground, and sometimes Oscar's dad comes by in a food truck and makes us grilled cheese sandwiches. That's my second favorite food after hot dogs."

And nothing—nothing. Not a peep came from Aria's side of the conversation, but that didn't deter Phoebe.

"And congratulations, Aria," Phoebe continued.

"On what?" the girl threw back.

"On getting a new aunt and a nanny. That's like eating a hot dog for lunch and then getting pizza for dinner. Her name is Harper. She plays the piano. She likes to say bad words, and she smells like a garbage can. This is Harper." Phoebe turned the phone.

And that's when she got her first glimpse of Landon's niece.

The child scowled with a smudge of dirt on her cheek, or maybe it was chocolate. She looked like she lived with a pack of mountain lions. Her thick brown hair made a bird's-nest-like halo around her face. The kid had the aura of a brawler— a beautiful, blue-eyed brawler who shared Landon's striking features.

She waved to the child. "Hi, Aria. Phoebe's right. I'm Harper. Harper Presley."

Crap! She'd overdone it.

She'd never been a kid person. That's what was so great about teaching online. But a strange connection formed between herself and this little girl, who exuded the force of a tiny mob boss.

The connection, however, was one-sided.

Aria's scowl deepened. "Put that hot dog girl back on."

Yikes.

"It's nice to meet you," she sang, switching back to opera mode as Phoebe turned the phone around.

"That's the aunt?" Aria asked—no, growled.

"Yeah," Phoebe answered. "That's what happens when your uncle marries your nanny. You're like me, Aria. My uncle hasn't married my nanny yet, but he's going to. I helped him propose. Honestly, if it wasn't for me, my uncle would be a mopey, nerdy, working machine."

Rowen shrugged. "She's not wrong."

"So, Aria," Phoebe continued. "Do you like fairies? Do you like cameras? Want to learn how to ride a donkey? How many cookies can you eat in sixty seconds without puking?"

A heavy silence descended.

Maybe Aria needed a little time to warm up to the changes in her life.

She shared a look with Landon. His skin tone had reverted to seasick green.

Did he know something she didn't?

She gave him a weak grin. There was no reason to expect the worst. This video call might have been a good thing. She remembered how hard it was to start at a new school after learning she'd never be going home and would live permanently in Denver with her grandparents.

"Hey, Phoebe?" Aria said, piercing the bubble of silence.

"Yeah?"

"Can you give my uncle Landy a message?" the child asked sweetly.

"Um…duh, he's right here, silly. Of course I can."

"Tell him he can…eat worms, sucker!" the child cried at the top of her lungs.

She had a decent vocal range.

"Okay," Phoebe replied with a shrug.

"And tell him I'm not going to school ever, ever, ever. And he can't make me. And I don't want a smelly nanny aunt either."

Hello, Miss Hot Temper USA.

The video call ended, and you could hear a pin drop.

"Wow," Phoebe whispered, wonder coating the word as she handed Landon his phone.

"Yeah, wow," Landon replied and scrubbed his hands down his face.

"You're supposed to eat worms," Oscar said, relaying the message everyone within a thirty-mile radius had heard, loud and clear.

"I got it," Landon replied with a weak grin.

"You know what, Landon?" Phoebe said, eyeing the man.

"What?"

A wide grin stretched across Phoebe's face. "I like Aria," the child gushed.

Landon cocked his head to the side. "You do?"

"She's got energy, right, Libby?" Phoebe continued.

Libby pasted a grin on her face. "She's definitely got a vibe. I'll give you that, honey," her friend answered, sharing a *holy shit* look with Raz.

"Her chi is top-notch," Sebastian chimed.

"I know we'll be best friends," Oscar continued. "I wonder if she'll let me take her picture."

"And we'll be in the same class," Phoebe remarked.

"My heart goes out to that teacher," Mitch said under his breath.

"What are you doing, Rowen?" Penny asked as her fiancé hammered away on his cell. "Please tell me you're not watching the Barbie videos."

"No, I'm on Whitmore's website making an extra donation to the school."

"Would you mind adding me?" Landon asked, but Rowen waved him off.

"I'm two steps ahead of you, man," the tech nerd answered, eyes glued to his phone. "I added Phoebe and Aria's name to the donation."

Good call. A Phoebe, Aria, Sebastian, Oscar combo would surely test the limits of the modern education system.

She turned to Landon, again wanting to reach out and touch the man.

But she didn't.

"Change can be hard on kids," she said, when his phone rang, and everyone went stock-still.

"Is it her? Is she calling back? Maybe she wasn't done yelling," Phoebe offered, tapping her chin.

He checked his phone, and she could see the screen as an image of an older woman with short spiky hair and a no-nonsense twist to her lips flashed on the screen.

"It's my manager. I need to take this. Excuse me," he said with a troubled expression. He headed inside the house. "Hey, Mitzi," he mumbled before his voice faded.

Harper exhaled an audible breath as she deflated from the high-stakes video call. But her relief was short-lived as the weight of, at least on paper, being Aria's aunt set in.

"Come on, mates," Sebastian said to Phoebe and Oscar, cutting through the quiet. "I'll show you my new room."

The children set off into the house. Once the kids were gone, Penny, Char, and Libby broke out into bubbly giggles.

She stared at the women. "Why are you laughing?"

"Aria is a little Harper," Penny said.

"She sounds like you," Charlotte replied.

"I was not that angry and growly," she shot back.

Libby crossed her arms. "H, you punched a boy on the first day of kindergarten."

"Yeah, he was teasing you about liking ladybugs and butterflies at recess. Why wouldn't I have punched him?" she answered, then shut her trap.

OMG, her friends were right.

Landon returned, caught her eye, then zeroed in on Libby

and Raz. "Thank you for inviting me over. Unfortunately, something's come up, and I have to leave."

"Is everything all right, mate?" Raz asked as the group gathered around the heartthrob, but she hung back.

What was her role? What was she supposed to do?

She zigzagged around the patio, gathering empty beer bottles, trying to work out her nervous energy.

"The call was about an impromptu meeting regarding a deal my manager was working on. She didn't mention specifics."

"It could be a good thing, right, H?" Libby chirped.

She froze. "Yeah, I'm sure it'll be terrific. I'll take these inside and see if the kids want to play hide and seek." The last thing she wanted was for Landon to take off and leave her to field the wedding questions. She picked up another bottle and headed for the kitchen.

"Harper, hold on a second," Landon called, and the sound of her name on his lips sent a shiver down her spine.

"Yeah?" she asked, keeping her back to the group.

"You don't have time to play hide and seek with the kids."

She pegged him with her gaze. "What do you mean?"

"You're coming with me."

She nearly dropped the bottles. "Why would I do that?"

His throat constricted as he swallowed hard. "My manager said she needs to meet with me and my new wife."

Chapter 11
LANDON

"Is this a damage control meeting? Do you think your manager wants to meet because the wedding pictures and videos came out? I honestly can't remember anyone recording us," Harper said, rattling off questions and musings as she clutched the Volvo's steering wheel.

He made sure his seat belt was buckled and held on for dear life as his lead-footed wife weaved through traffic like she was on the final lap of the Indy 500. The Volvo creaked and groaned, then ground to a halt at a stop sign.

He fought the urge to squeeze his eyes shut and pray. "I wish you'd let me drive," he said through gritted teeth as she hit the gas, which, thank Christ, didn't do that much. Blessedly, for his safety and that of everyone else on the road, this car's get-up-and-go seemed to have got up and left. The engine grumbled and hissed as the vehicle heaved forward, barely building speed.

"You've been drinking. I haven't. It only makes sense."

"I had one beer, Harper."

"Yeah, and I watched you drink it like you were trying out for America's Next Frat Bro."

This woman.

"And I'm concerned about your state of mind," she continued.

"My state of mind?"

"You've got my panties in your pocket—or should I say the private lacy placemat doily?"

Dammit.

How was he supposed to respond?

He couldn't tell her he'd been through hell this past week, and the only peace he'd experienced had come when he felt her panties in his pocket.

"You're wearing my shirt," he shot back.

She didn't reply. She pursed her lips and stewed as the Volvo barreled through the streets of Denver like a burnt potato on wheels.

He braced himself. "Why didn't you want to drive the Porsche?"

"Because I'm not insured on it." She threw a dose of stink eye his way. "I'm not always a tutu party girl out to break every rule, heartthrob."

Heartthrob.

Even when she yelled the moniker at him, his pulse kicked up.

"I'm actually quasi-responsible when I want to be," she continued. "Like, if I married someone on a dare, I wouldn't sneak out in the dead of night without saying goodbye or leaving a note."

Shit.

He deserved that.

His actions had solidified her grudge against musicians, and she'd pegged him as an inconsiderate jerk.

But she was wrong.

Dead wrong.

The last thing he'd wanted was to leave her.

His heart broke the minute the suite's landline rang. When he picked it up and heard Tomás's voice, the bubble popped and reality hit with a one-two punch.

He didn't want to leave, but he had to go.

The situation with Aria wasn't good. The little girl had become angrier and more defiant as the date to take full custody grew closer and closer. He understood the behavior. He got her pain. If he had a magic wand, the first spell he'd cast would be to bring back her smile and resurrect her laughter.

After a hushed conversation with his foster dad, he'd hung up the phone and drank in his sleeping double-dog dare of a wife. She was a vision with her wavy hair and kiss-swollen lips. But it wasn't just her beauty. She brought out a side of him that he hadn't seen in years. And in that slip of time, a melody came to him. He tightened his hold on Harper's warm body and hummed as she slept in his arms. Words weren't enough to describe what it was like to be with a woman who made him feel like nothing could hold him back. The sensation deserved a song, a ballad, a declaration of devotion, and if he were a different man, he'd proclaim his feelings to the mountain tops without reservation.

But he couldn't. He'd already gone too far.

Still, he couldn't deny that his time with Harper had been the best night of his life.

And that was saying something.

He was a pop star. He'd traveled the world. Throngs of people chanted his name. But none of it held a candle to slipping a ring onto her finger and hearing her say the words he'd never expected anyone to say to him.

I do.

When they'd left the club and entered the sparkling Luxe Grandiose lobby, her chameleon eyes had left him spellbound. It was as if the shades of brown, gray, and blue had silenced the nagging voice in his head and allowed his heart to lead. Once he'd snapped the bouquet of white roses out of the air, he was a goner. Even if Katrina and Jude hadn't dropped the double-dog dare, he would have wanted to marry his panty-less siren.

And that's why he hadn't woken her before he'd left.

Waking her would have meant it was over.

With Harper still asleep, the dream of their night lived on.

It was an irrational presumption.

But when he'd pressed one last kiss to her temple and listened as she hummed a sleepy, sated sigh, whispers of the freedom and elation he'd experienced with her by his side remained.

But that's all it could be.

A moment in time.

A little slice of what life might have looked like had he been different.

With Trey and Leighton gone, he was who he was.

A loner.

He and Harper had gotten one night to pretend the world wasn't waiting for them. One night, where he feasted between her thighs and pumped his cock inside her sweet center until they were delirious with lust and begging for carnal release. One night when she was his—all his.

Jesus, stop!

He had to start thinking with his head and not his cock—or was that his heart?

It didn't matter.

They had to figure out what came next.

And that meant untangling this marriage.

That's what he wanted, right?

Wasn't that what Harper wanted?

He removed his cap and ran a hand through his hair.

Here's what he knew.

News of their wedding had started hitting the celebrity sites earlier today.

Mitzi had flown in from LA, and whatever she had to say, she wanted to do it in person.

Christ, the label might have sent a team of lawyers, too.

He put his hat back on, then jumped in his seat as Harper switched lanes and cut off a minivan. The blare of a horn pierced the air, and he braced for the worst. Not two seconds later, Harper hit the brakes and a flurry of lollipops and crinkly candy wrappers slid out from beneath his seat and accumulated around his feet.

"What the hell?" he uttered.

How many lollipops did she consume in a day?

A muscle ticked in her jaw. "I haven't had a chance to tidy up my car."

He collected the wrappers and stuffed them into the glove box. "What do you eat besides lollipops and bonbons?"

"This week? That's all I've been eating. And I would warn you not to critique a woman's diet while she's driving."

That was sage advice. Although, her driving couldn't get much worse. He sighed, then studied the dash display and wasn't surprised to see the check engine light illuminated.

"When was the last time you had your car serviced?"

She shrugged. "I don't know?"

"You don't know when you last had the oil changed?"

"Carol isn't bothered by things like oil and routine maintenance."

The high-pitched whine of Carol's failing serpentine belt begged to differ.

Harper hit the brakes at a red light and pinned him with her hazel gaze. "What exactly did your manager say when she called?"

Here they go again.

"It's like I told you before. She didn't say much. She gave

me the address and said we needed to meet her there for a meeting. She said time was of the essence and it couldn't wait."

"Am I about to encounter a gaggle of lawyers? Because, FYI," she announced, hitting a few high notes with her flustered opera voice, "I didn't marry you to steal your money. You don't have to worry. I'm not some gold digger. You can let your management team know that they can call it off if this is some shakedown. I don't want anything from you."

Her words hit like bullets to his chest. "I know you're not a gold digger," he said. "Mitzi, my manager, also said things would make sense once we met. I don't know if this is about a legal issue."

A legal issue.

Was that what Harper was to him now?

"This is why I don't date musicians," she muttered.

"Well, you married one," he grumbled.

She glanced at him, then hit the gas. "On a dare."

"Did you date Vance Vibe on a dare?" he bit out, and instantly wished he could take it back.

Her shoulders angled forward as if she were fighting the urge to collapse in on herself. "No," she said without an ounce of fight. "There was no dare. He fooled me into thinking he loved me."

Damned Vance Vibe. He really should have hit the guy when he had a chance.

"I'm sorry, Harper, that's rough."

She kept her gaze on the road.

He had to get her talking. "Penny said he stole your music. What song?"

She huffed a humorless little laugh. "The one that made him famous."

"You wrote 'Every Time You Break My Heart?'"

It was a decent Vance Vibe song. No, it was more than decent. It was damned good. A crow could screech it, and it would still be a hit because the lyrics and melody were what made the tune pure magic.

"And there's nothing I can do about it," she added with a dismissive flick of her wrist.

This woman was a fighter—a force to be reckoned with. How could someone like her give up?

"If you have proof that it's your work, there's plenty you can do."

"He took my journals and the recordings."

"Recordings, like in a studio?" he pressed.

"No, nothing fancy like that. I've always filmed myself writing and composing. Sometimes I made videos. Sometimes I recorded audio. But he deleted everything."

He should have hit the guy and then kneed him in the balls. "That's next level malicious."

"Vance Vibe might be a no-talent jerk, but he isn't an idiot. It would be me against his label. And isn't his label your label?" she asked as the fire returned to her tone.

"It is, but that doesn't mean anything. He's no friend of mine. I thought the guy was a fraud even before I learned what he did to you."

Harper didn't reply.

He shifted in his seat. "Why didn't you tell me he was the musician who hurt you?"

"Would it have mattered?" she answered, her voice a shaky rasp as she slowed for another stop sign. "Enough about Vance. Are you sure this is the right way? We're headed toward my house...my grandmother's house," she corrected, "in the Baxter Park neighborhood."

Baxter Park.

He'd been so focused on not dying in a car crash, he'd neglected the scenery.

This was where he and Leighton had lived with their parents before they passed away. He took in the leafy oaks lining the street. They added a small-town feel to the quaint bungalows and two-story Denver square homes tucked side by side beneath a canopy of branches.

"Hey, heartthrob, you're the navigator. Navigate."

Snap out of it.

He checked the map on his cell—one of the few functions he liked about smartphones.

"We're nearly there."

"Your manager wants to meet with us at a Cupid Bakery?" she asked as a brick building with a brown and white awning and a cupcake painted on the side came into view.

He recognized it.

The breath caught in his throat.

He recognized it. He used to come here with his family.

This was where Leighton fell in love with butterscotch bonbons.

He studied the building. Something was different about the place. "Was this always a Cupid Bakery?"

She glanced at him. "You know this area?"

"I lived here with my family before they passed away. We used to come here."

"The bakery was called the Baxter Park Bakery for as long as I can remember," she explained, her tone softening. "Last year, I'm not sure exactly when, they changed the name to Cupid Bakery. I think the owner is getting ready to retire and sold the shop to the Cupid Bakery franchise. My grandparents used to be friendly with him and his wife. Even though the name of the place changed, they still make the same bonbons. I've been getting them here since I was a girl."

He could hear the smile in her voice. "Mitzi must have googled places to get bonbons. She knows I like them."

"I know you like them," Harper tossed back with a shot of her signature sass, and he was grateful for the shift in her mood.

Not to mention, the purr of her voice had him rocking a semi.

Was she messing with him?

"Or," she continued, "your manager wants to get me good and sugared up before she makes me sign a stack of divorce papers."

He studied her profile as the sun lit her in a golden glow. "Is that what you want?"

She pulled into a parking spot in front of the bakery, then cut the ignition. She pegged him with her chameleon gaze. Her eyes had darkened. The blue edged out the brown, and the flecks of green and gold looked ready to ignite. "Isn't that what you want, heartthrob?"

What did he want?

Unable to stop, he twisted one of her chocolate locks of hair around his finger. "There's what I want, and then there's what I can have."

He hadn't meant to say it, but Harper could strip his defenses with one look.

She edged forward, assessing him with those chameleon eyes. "They're not the same?"

Don't say another word. Stop talking.

But she tempted him.

What if he could pretend that nothing else mattered?

No fans, no shaky career, no responsibilities, no personal issues. Just the two of them, living from one dare to the next, pushing life's limits.

It could never happen.

He needed to get his head and his heart on the same page.

But that was easier said than done.

His gaze dropped to her lips—lips he'd kissed and licked. Lips that appeared in his dreams. Lips that had wrapped around his—

Thunk, thunk, thunk, thunk!

Who was knocking on the car's window?

He released her lock of hair, and in the space of a breath, they pulled apart like horny teens caught making out.

Is that what had been about to happen?

He'd be a liar if he said he didn't want to kiss her.

He regained his bearings, then peered out the window and saw—

"Who's that woman, and what's Madelyn doing here?" Harper whispered.

Good questions.

With her red scarf billowing in the breeze, the nanny matchmaker stood next to Mitzi. The women stared into the car for a second, then two, before his manager scowled.

"Are you getting out, LB? I've got a flight back to LA in an hour."

"That's my manager," he said, glancing at Harper.

Harper chewed her lip. "She seems…direct."

"That's probably the nicest way to describe her. But she's a straight shooter. She's always been good to me. We should see what they want."

"Okay," Harper answered, her voice doing that uneasy octave jump.

"Are you nervous, bonbon?" he asked. The color had drained from her face, and she looked half ready to throw Carol in reverse and Indy 500-it out of there.

"No," she sang out in that adorably ridiculous opera voice. "Let's get on with it."

That's all they could do.

He gestured for Mitzi to step back and opened the car door.

The twitch of a grin pulled at the corners of his manager's mouth, but before she could utter a single syllable, she flinched and touched her jaw.

"Are you okay, Mitz?"

She rubbed her jaw, then dropped her hand to her side and looked past him, presumably to get a glimpse of his wife. "It's nothing." Her smirk returned. "You've been busy."

He kept his features neutral. "You could say that."

"Exchanging vows in Vegas is an interesting way to blow off a little steam," she lobbed back.

"To each his own," he answered cautiously. He'd expected the woman to be angry. He'd known Mitzi for a long time, and this was not her pissed-off face. She still dished out barbs and pointed looks, but she wasn't anxious like she'd been last time they'd spoken after his concert.

What kind of meeting was this?

Mitzi shared a curious look with Madelyn, which wasn't that odd. The women knew each other. His manager had connected him with the matchmaker, so the two of them getting together didn't strike him as out of the ordinary.

What was odd was being summoned to meet the women at a Cupid Bakery in Baxter Park.

What could they want, and why this location? It had to be more than a bonbon meetup.

Madelyn had already told him his married status precluded her from working with him.

Was this the meeting for them to break ties officially?

But why would Harper need to come along for that?

And speaking of Harper, where was she?

He looked from side to side, then glanced over his shoulder. She was still in the car.

What the hell was she doing in there?

"I should check on my…"

"Your wife?" Mitzi supplied, keeping her tone even, but he could tell she enjoyed this. "And you seem to have something coming out of your pocket."

Damn panties.

"It's a…private doily," he muttered, stuffing it away. God

help him! He gathered his wits and nodded to Madelyn, who appeared quite amused. Well, at least their situation was good for something. He jogged over to the driver's side door and opened it, but Harper didn't move. "Do you need help with your seat belt?"

Had her diet of lollipops and bonbons sent her into a sugar coma?

"No, I'm familiar with how seat belts work," she answered, gripping the steering wheel for dear life.

He crouched down. "It's safe to get out now."

Harper's gaze ping-ponged between the women and the bakery.

"Is there a problem, bonbon?" he pressed and looked her over. She appeared to be breathing and cognizant, but something was off. Then again, thanks to her unique hobo attire, she seemed more than just off by any standard. Truth be told, she was a goddamned mess. But at least for the time being, she was a goddamned mess who also happened to be wearing his T-shirt. And from the aroma, it was safe to say she'd been wearing it nonstop—and had possibly completed a marathon in it or encountered a family of skunks. Still, none of that detracted from her beauty—that fierce, sassy stubbornness that had enchanted him from the first moment he'd seen her.

Dirty or freshly laundered, he'd take her however he could get her. But he couldn't deny he liked seeing her in his shirt.

A shirt that had served as her wedding dress.

Jesus, it seemed insane to imagine it now, but marrying a panty-less Harper Presley, swimming in nothing but his shirt and a pair of boots while a bunch of drunk gladiators and tipsy ballerinas cheered, might have looked like a giant shit show, but it wasn't. It was magical—like walking into a dream. Everything about the night he'd married her had clicked into place.

They'd clicked.

That wary, gnawing voice in his head had gotten drowned out by the voice of a sharp-tongued angel.

She might turn on the snarky persona ninety-nine percent of the time, but she'd kept his shirt.

It was a sentimental choice.

Was there a chance she didn't regret marrying a musician?

And what did that mean?

Dammit! What did he think he was doing? Penning a love song about their whirlwind night of throwing caution to the wind?

It was a shirt. It didn't mean anything.

That night had been extraordinary not because he'd opened himself up but because he'd still been able to hide the part of him he couldn't allow others to see.

"They know me at this bakery," Harper whispered, pulling him from his thoughts.

"It's close to your place, isn't it? It's your neighborhood bakery," he offered, then noticed something strange.

A pair of teenage boys sitting on a bench by the entrance spotted Harper through the windshield. The kids shrieked, then took off like the building was on fire.

"That was weird," he commented as the pair disappeared around the corner.

Harper was back to chewing her lip. "Not really."

"People look at you and run?" he teased, trying to lighten the mood.

It worked.

She loosened her death grip on the steering wheel and gave him the hint of a smile. That smile could put a dent in his armor if he wasn't careful. Still, it felt like he'd won the lottery.

Her hazel eyes glinted with mischief. "It's been known to happen."

He didn't doubt it.

"Come, come, you two. Let's go inside. Mitzi just went in. They're expecting us," Madelyn crooned like it was common-place for her to frequent bakery parking lots to lure people out of their vehicles.

He started to stand, when something warm touched his arm. He looked down to see Harper's hand.

Jesus, he'd missed her touch.

"Landon?" she said, hitting a high C.

He took her hand in his and twined his fingers with hers. "Yeah?"

"No matter what happens, I want you to know I've had a rough couple of days."

Something had gone down here.

What the hell could have happened in a bonbon shop?

"All right," he answered and ran his thumb across the back of her wrist. Her pulse hammered. He needed to help her relax. "Hey, bonbon?"

"Yeah?"

"Do you yell at people in bakeries like you do in convenience stores? Is that what's going on here? You're not wanted for disturbing the bakery peace, are you?" He was kidding, but her wide-eyed expression hinted that he might not be far off the mark.

She cringed, looking adorably guilty as hell. "I can explain."

Chapter 12
LANDON

He stared at his wife. At this rate, she was in the running to steal the title of hothead away from Mitch.

"You caused a scene in a bakery? Is there anywhere in this town where you haven't blown a gasket?"

"I didn't cause a scene," she whisper-shouted. "There was no yelling or threatening of old people. But there have been bonbons. Many, many boxes of bonbons, and I've had to go to great lengths to get them," she answered, looping her tote over her shoulder as he helped her out of the car.

She had to be overreacting.

"You've indulged in bonbons more than usual. That's not a crime," he replied, tightening his hold on her hand. He should have let go, but he didn't.

And she didn't pull away. She stayed close to him—like she had in Las Vegas.

Madelyn headed inside, and they followed a few steps behind. Harper hummed a little tune, then tightened her grip on his hand like she wanted to break it.

What went down in this place?

They entered the shop, and he inhaled the heavenly scent

of sugar and chocolate. From decadent cakes piled high with pastel-colored frosting to cookies and cupcakes to the row upon row of bonbons, the confections looked almost too good to eat.

He glanced at his wife.

She hadn't bolted or belted opera.

So far, so good…until a man at the cash register looked up and zeroed in on her. He waved to a woman carrying a tray of macarons. "It's her! It's the Singing Bonbon Bandit."

Singing Bonbon Bandit? This had to be a joke.

"Oh shit," Harper whispered.

His jaw dropped. "Did you rob this place—while singing?"

"Of course not," she exclaimed.

"Did you raid their take-a-penny, leave-a-penny tray?" He couldn't put it past her. He'd seen her in action at the convenience store.

"No," she whisper-shouted, her cheeks blooming scarlet.

The guy behind the counter pointed to the piece of paper taped to the side of the register that looked a hell of a lot like a grainy surveillance photo…of Harper. He studied the image of his wife in an oversized black T-shirt holding a box of baked goods to her face.

She was chowing down like there was no tomorrow.

"What is that? The bakery version of an FBI Most Wanted poster?" he pressed.

"We had to cut her off from the bonbons, sir," the woman behind the counter explained. "Schuman's orders."

"Who's Schuman?" he asked.

This was getting crazier by the second.

"Schuman Sweet owns the bakery," Harper murmured.

The man behind the counter crossed his arms and peered at the Singing Bonbon Bandit. "Mr. Sweet said if you came in again, you'd need a note with your grandmother's permission to buy more bonbons."

Holy shit! His wife had been put on bonbon probation.

"Is Mr. Sweet here?" Harper asked, nervously glancing from side to side.

"No, he had an emergency and had to leave early. But we're on strict orders not to sell you any bonbons," the woman replied.

He studied the photo. "You really went for it. Did you even use your hands, or did you knock those bonbons back like you were downing a Big Gulp?"

Harper tucked a lock of hair behind her ear and lifted her chin. "The bonbons here are delicious. And as I mentioned before, I've had a rough week."

He stared at the case. It was just like he remembered.

"The boss doesn't want you to OD on sugar. He said you've been coming here with your grandparents since you were a little girl. A couple of days ago, he became concerned when you started showing up a few times a day and would sing about sweet treats while stuffing your face with butterscotch bonbons. We nicknamed you the Singing Bonbon Bandit after..." The female clerk paused.

"After, what?" he asked.

The woman cleared her throat and glanced out the shop's windows. "The incident."

Jesus Christ, Harper wasn't kidding about having a hard week.

"What incident?" he pressed.

"After Mr. Sweet told her she needed to take a bonbon break, she paid a few kids to come in here and buy them for her," the woman answered, eyeing Harper warily.

He turned to the bonbon freak of the week, aka, his wife. "The kids on the bench?"

She ran her hands down her face and groaned. "Yes."

"I'm sure Harper will be able to keep her cravings in check," Madelyn offered, then waved for them to follow her through a door leading to the back of the shop.

Harper turned to the clerks. "You don't have to worry about me. I'll be on my best behavior."

The man tossed a nervous glance toward the case lined with bonbons.

"I promise, my husband will make sure I control myself, right, Landon?" she answered, her eyes pleading with him like a bonbon junkie.

"We're good," he said, really liking the sound of her calling him her husband—even if she was a bonbon bandit who'd corrupted youth.

But just when he thought they were in the clear, Harper gazed at the bonbon case.

"Don't even think about it," he whispered.

She bit back a grin. "Oh, I'm thinking about it. Feel like joining me on the dark side? We could grab a few and hide them inside the private doily?"

And God help him, this woman was a piece of work—a piece of work he'd gladly join in ransacking every bonbon shop in the Denver metro area.

Hand in hand, they left the retail part of the store and entered the back of the bakery. It was a larger space than he'd anticipated. With two long tables in the center of the room and a wall of ovens across from a wall of refrigerators, the production area looked as if it had recently been updated. A baker worked in the back corner on what smelled like brownies, while a couple of people stirred a giant vat of frosting. He scanned the rest of the area and found his manager speaking with a man and a woman he didn't recognize.

Mitzi must have sensed he'd zeroed in on her. She looked up and nodded to him before alerting the couple to their presence.

"Who's your manager talking to?" Harper asked, still holding his hand.

"I don't know."

"Wait," his wife said with a touch of excitement. "I recognize the woman. I've seen her on LookyLoo."

"Is she in the music industry?" he asked and observed the couple. The man was in a tailored suit, and the woman wore a pair of slacks and a chic button-down.

"No, she's a baker. She does tutorials for Cupid Bakery. I think she's the CEO or some bigwig there, too. She's popped up on my LookyLoo feed."

Why would Mitzi set up a meeting with a bakery CEO?

The trio headed toward them, with his manager leading the way.

"You must be Harper," Mitzi said, eyeing the T-shirt. "I'm Mitzi Jones, Landon's manager. Sorry I couldn't greet you back at the car."

"It's nice to meet you," Harper replied, releasing his hand, and instantly, he missed her touch.

"We're to blame," the young woman said, gifting them with a warm smile. "I'm Bridget Dasher."

The man with her cleared his throat, then the pair shared a spirited look.

"I'm Bridget Dasher Traeger Rudolph. It's a mouthful," she added, sharing another coy look with her companion.

"It's the baggage she inherited when she married me," the man said with the ghost of a grin as he shook their hands. "I'm Soren Traeger-Rudolph. We're here representing Cupid Bakery. My wife is the CEO. We flew in from Boston earlier today."

That didn't answer much.

"What brings you to Colorado?" he asked.

"You, Mr. Paige," the woman replied, dialing up her grin. "But before we go on, I must say that I'm thrilled to meet you. I had a Heartthrob Warfare poster in my room when I was a teenager." She gasped as a blush graced her cheeks. "I probably sound ridiculous."

Was this an A-list meet and greet?

He threw Mitzi a what-the-hell look. These two Cupid Bakery people seemed normal, but there was no telling if they were the type to bust out a cross-stitch pillow with his face on it.

"You don't sound ridiculous at all. I have one, too," Harper offered.

Stop the presses! Harper has a poster of him—like, present tense?

He caught her eye, and she froze.

"What I meant to say was that I *had* one...when I was younger, of course," she blathered.

He threw another glance her way. Her cheeks were back to blooming an irresistible shade of pink.

She was a full-on poster-owning Heartthrob Warfare fan.

"Sorry, I've forgotten my manners," Mitzi said. "Soren and Bridget, you know Landon Paige. This is his new wife, Harper Presley."

"We know," Soren replied.

"We've been glued to social media. Your wedding was..." Bridget began, then tapped her chin.

Oh shit.

Harper inhaled a sharp breath.

"So beautiful," the baker CEO finished.

"Beautiful?" Harper echoed, relief coating the word.

"The way you looked at each other and the excitement of the ballerinas and the gladiators. It was so unique and a pure joy to watch."

It had been pure joy to live through.

Jesus, get it together.

"And you're still wearing the shirt," the woman gushed, then turned to Mitzi. "Mr. and Mrs. Luxe were right. Your client and his wife are excellent candidates for this project. I can feel it."

Mr. and Mrs. Luxe.

"Are you talking about the owners of the Luxe Grandiose?" he asked. Maybe this wasn't an A-list fan meet and greet.

"Yes, and they're the major shareholders in Luxe Media and Entertainment. They own the LookyLoo platform and are expanding its content. That's what we wanted to discuss with you. Cupid Bakery is one of the sponsors for a reality TV contest," Soren explained.

"A reality TV contest?" Harper repeated.

"Yes, and we hope you and your husband will sign on," the man replied.

"It's called Celebrity Charity Bake or Bust," the baking CEO supplied. "As the name implies, it's a baking contest that donates money to charities."

Had Harper crashed into a tree and this was some delusion he was having while hospitalized in a coma?

He shared a look with his bonbon bandit wife. "You want us to participate in a baking contest? I hate to break it to you, but we're not bakers."

"You don't have to be bakers—just celebrities with a connection to the music industry. That's the focus of this competition," Bridget answered. "Cupid Bakery will connect you with a baker to guide you through the competition and give you tips. That's why we're here. We wanted to introduce you to your baking mentor, but he had an emergency and can't be here."

"But I'm not a celebrity," Harper added, her voice kicking into opera mode.

"The internet begs to differ," Soren offered. "In the last few hours, news of your marriage has been splashed over every major media outlet. You're the mystery woman who married a pop star. The buzz online is electric." His phone pinged. He pulled his cell from his pocket and stared at the screen. "Perfect timing! The Luxe attorney should be here any minute. He's got the contracts and can provide further details. Unfortunately, Bridget and I need to get going. We've got a flight to catch."

"This whole reality show contest must seem like the last thing you'd want to do," Bridget began, "but after watching your wedding videos, we agree with Mr. and Mrs. Luxe. You're a fit. Please tell us you'll consider the proposal."

The woman seemed genuine, and if Mitzi wanted to get him in front of a new audience, he couldn't deny this was one way to do it.

"It sounds fascinating," Harper answered, her voice jumping another octave.

He couldn't blame her. It was as if they'd entered the twilight zone. Had someone told him this morning that he'd be offered a spot on a celebrity reality baking show, he'd have laughed his ass off.

A few seconds passed before a short man in a crisp black suit carrying a briefcase entered the bakery through the back door and strode toward them. They said their goodbyes to Soren and Bridget as the attorney set his briefcase on the table and removed a file.

Contracts.

He hated contracts.

"Mr. and Mrs. Paige, if you wouldn't mind, and your advisors as well," the attorney said and waved them over.

Mr. and Mrs. Paige?

Neither he nor Harper moved.

"That's the two of you," Madelyn supplied.

Christ, that's right! They were Mr. and Mrs. Paige—or Mr. and Mrs. Presley-Paige, or maybe Harper would stick with using her last name?

It didn't matter because this union couldn't last.

He joined the women at the table with the attorney and willed himself to keep his cool.

"I'm Paxton Cleary, one of the Luxe attorneys. I'm here to

explain the proposal. Would you like me to begin with an overview and then explain the parameters of the contest?" the attorney asked, plowing ahead.

"Yes, we are sorely lacking in details," he answered, tossing a sharp look at Mitzi.

A heads up from the woman would have been nice.

But his manager looked as pleased as punch—and this woman rarely exuded pleased as...anything. Before he could ask more about what she'd gotten him into, the attorney removed two packets from the folder and slid them across the table, one for him and one for Harper.

"This is the formal offer from Luxe Media and Entertainment to participate in the *Celebrity Bake or Bust*, which will be filmed here, in Denver, Colorado," the man explained. "By signing, you agree to participate in three baking challenges. The challenges entail preparing baked goods and delivering said goods to a local community group. You'll compete against another Celebrity Denver-based team. The winner of the challenge will be decided by the recipients of the baked goods via a taste test. Luxe Media and Entertainment will stream the events on their LookyLoo platform. You'll be provided with the recipes ahead of time. Cupid Bakery will supply a mentor baker, which you may accept or decline, as well as deliver the ingredients. You, in turn, agree to film yourselves preparing the items in your kitchen. Luxe Media and Entertainment will provide a crew to livestream the community event."

"You want us to bake and record ourselves?" Harper asked.

"Yes," the suit answered.

She cocked her head to the side. "Like with our cell phones?"

The man nodded. "Mr. and Mrs. Luxe have chosen to employ an informal style for the contest. This gives you control over what the viewers see as you bake. You can share more of your personality and give the viewers an intimate experience.

Mr. and Mrs. Luxe are interested in an unscripted feel. The three community groups participating will be gifted an automatic donation, and the team that wins two or more of the three challenges will secure an additional donation to their charity of choice. Of course, there's a compensation package for the winning team as well."

Harper perked up. "What's the compensation package?"

"A lump sum."

"The winners get a cash prize?" Harper asked, wide-eyed.

"They do." Paxton removed another sheet from the folder. "Regarding the timeline, this project will start in two weeks and end after approximately six weeks or so. We're able to work within the parameters of your schedule, Mr. Paige. Your manager provided the dates you'll be out of town, and the contest will wrap before the Red Rocks Unplugged event."

"You're performing at Red Rocks Unplugged?" Harper asked softly, curiosity coating the question.

He shifted his stance. He knew what she was thinking. This gathering of artists was the opposite of a glittery pop production. No backup dancers and no modulated sounds, just musicians, raw and unplugged.

"I'm debuting a new acoustic rock sound—that's evolving—and currently, nothing has been finalized regarding Red Rocks." Aka, he hadn't been invited, nor had he written anything new. But he left that part out.

"Shall we continue?" the attorney interjected, blessedly shifting the attention away from his faltering career.

"Go on," he said, willing his tone to remain even.

"Your manager has reviewed the contract, Mr. Paige," the man continued. "Would you like to look it over yourselves before you sign?" he asked, then retrieved two pens from his case.

Mitzi knew what was going down and said nothing. Why would she do that?

189

He blew out a frustrated breath and studied the top sheet. His vision went blurry as he stared at the jumble of words. "I'd like a moment to speak with my manager."

The suit nodded. "Of course."

He glanced at the contract again and felt Harper watching him.

"I'll skim over the paperwork while you speak with your manager," she offered.

He nodded, then pegged Mitzi with his gaze. "A word, Mitz."

"Why don't you join us, Madelyn," his manager said, then gestured with her chin to the other side of the room.

The two of them were in on it.

Once they were far enough away from Harper and the attorney, he crossed his arms. "You knew about this baking contest? Why didn't you mention it when you called?" he pressed, lowering his voice.

"Because you wouldn't have come if I'd told you."

Damn right.

"You did sign off on allowing me to pursue this opportunity," she added.

"When?"

"After your last concert."

"I didn't know what I was signing. I trust you to do what you know I can't. And as kind as the CEO of the Cupid Bakery and her husband were, this reality show contest is bullshit."

"It's not bullshit. It's brilliant," Mitzi tossed back. "You need this opportunity, Landon. The public sees you as a waning pop star. This will get you in front of a different crowd and let people see another side of you."

That's what he expected and feared she'd say.

He pinched the bridge of his nose. "What about my music?"

"What about it? You've had months, years, honestly, and you haven't come up with anything." She softened her expression. "Shaking things up could help."

Or it could ruin everything.

"Baking means following a recipe, and..." He couldn't say it.

"You heard the lawyer. You'll get the recipe ahead of time, and you'll have Harper with you every step of the way."

"What do you mean?"

Mitzi bit back a grin. "She's your wife. You're married to her. You're in this together."

Would they live together? He hadn't even considered it.

He blew out a pained breath. "I married her on a dare."

"I don't care why you married her. The buzz is real. Don't throw this opportunity away, Landon."

Mitzi had to mean the reality show, but he couldn't help wondering if she also meant Harper.

He took off his hat and ran his hands through his hair. "What made you look into a reality show baking contest for me?"

"Madelyn."

There it was—the matchmaker connection.

He eyed the woman. "This is your doing?"

She smoothed her scarf, unfazed by his irritation. "I know people who know people. I understand that you're looking to alter the trajectory of your career. I simply suggested Mitzi reach out to Luxe Media and Entertainment. I didn't realize they were looking for celebrity couples for this project. Isn't it a fortunate twist of fate that you now find yourself a celebrity married to the internet's newest It girl?"

"It's not a real marriage," he said, the words tasting like ash.

"I disagree," Madelyn replied. "There's a marriage certificate and video proof the world is feasting on as we speak. You're as married as married gets."

He pulled his cap low. "Why are you still helping me? You said you couldn't keep me on as a client."

"That's a fair point," Madelyn purred. "I might not have matched you officially, but I'm not one for waste. I've had quite a while to work on your case, Landon. I see no harm in allowing what's been put into place to run its course. And I can always lend my professional opinion."

"And what's that?"

The matchmaker leaned against the table. "I find that you're in an interesting predicament. You're due to take full custody of Aria, and you also need to write new songs. When do you need to send your music to your record label and the Red Rocks Unplugged organizers? I presume they'll want to hear it before they offer you a spot."

Mitzi must have shared that nugget of info with Madelyn.

"I've got a little over a month."

A month to pull together a fresh sound and new tracks. Jesus, could it even be done?

"And if they like what you send them, when would you perform at this unplugged concert?" Madelyn asked and turned to Mitzi like they'd rehearsed this bit.

"The concert is sixty days from today," his manager answered.

"How curious," Madelyn quipped like it was the least curious tidbit she'd ever heard. "That just happens to be the time frame for the nanny match trial period. But of course, you're married, so it doesn't officially apply to you. Still, if you and your wife require the assistance of a live-in nanny, I can put you in contact with another agency."

No more nanny-match bullshit.

"I'll figure out the childcare situation on my own," he answered, irritation slicing through his words. "What I'm trying to tell you is that I don't know what's going to happen with Harper. I don't know if she wants to stay married to me."

His chest tightened. Why did it hurt so much to state the truth?

"Here's how I see it," Madelyn continued. "I've met your darling Aria. You'll need an extra pair of hands to help with your niece. She's a spirited child."

He sighed. "I can't disagree with you on that."

"And you require time to focus on your music. Lucky for you, Harper seems to be a godsend. You've married an accomplished pianist. She majored in music in college and overcame quite a bit to earn her degree. On the childcare front, Phoebe, Oscar, and Sebastian are fond of her. I'm sure Aria will warm up to her aunt."

He stared at the fluorescent lights. "Maybe on paper we're legit, but our marriage isn't real."

"Then we'll pretend it's real."

He startled and turned to find Harper. With determination flashing in her eyes, she stared him down.

When had she joined them? And how much had she heard?

She handed him the contract and a pen. "Sign it, heartthrob. You and your wife are about to become reality TV stars."

She was okay with this?

"You want to stay married to me to compete in a reality show baking contest?" he asked as his phone buzzed. He ignored it. It was probably the guys, and there was no way he was reaching for his cell with Harper standing before him like she was ready to take on the world. If he checked his phone now, he'd bet everything he had she'd snatch it from his grasp and toss it in a vat of cupcake icing.

He could tell from the set of her jaw that she meant business. He'd seen that look when he'd intervened with the handsy guy on the dance floor.

She'd gone into badass Harper mode, and shit was about to get real.

She flicked a lock of hair over her shoulder, and her hazel eyes flashed with dogged determination. "Well?" she bit out.

"Well, what?"

"Did I not make myself clear when I handed you the pen and the contract and said sign it?"

"You understand that means we'll have to live together and you'll essentially be Aria's nanny, right? That's the situation." He needed to be crystal clear that she understood what she'd agreed to do.

She barked a little laugh. "I'm not your nanny, but I can help you with Aria if it means you'll agree to do the contest."

His phone buzzed again. The guys would have to wait.

He studied his wife. He couldn't get a read on her. Something else was going on. "I figured you'd hate the idea."

"I did until I read the contract. But I do need a little more information." She snapped her fingers. "Hey, Mr. Suit, how quickly could the fifty K get deposited into my account after we win?"

"*If* you win?" the man parried.

"When we win," she lobbed back.

Fifty thousand dollars?

He looked between his wife and the lawyer. "What fifty thousand dollars are you talking about?"

Harper pointed to the lawyer. "Break it down, Mr. Suit."

The flummoxed lawyer shot a nervous glance Harper's way. He understood the man's apprehension. A bossy Harper could be damned intimidating. But truth be told, it was hot as hell to watch the woman bark orders.

"The cash payout is built into the contract for the winning team," the attorney explained. "Each of the winning participants gets fifty thousand dollars. Most celebrities quietly donate the funds to a cause."

"Here's the thing," Harper said, excitement building in her voice. "I'm not most celebrities. I'm not even a real celebrity, but I sure have a cause. Let's talk dates. I need to know the exact date the winning team will get their cash prize. I didn't see that info in the contract."

The attorney scratched his head. "I believe the payment will be made within hours of the final challenge."

"Within hours," Harper exclaimed. "Okay, final question, suit, and this one's important. Will the final challenge be on or before October fifteenth?"

What was so special about October fifteenth?

The attorney opened the folder and skimmed a page. "The final challenge is October twelfth."

"I would have the money by the twelfth?" she asked, lighting up.

"If you win," the man corrected.

"When we win," Harper countered again.

The attorney tugged at his collar. "Two teams are competing in the *Celebrity Bake or Bust*, and whoever wins will have the funds in their account by close of business on the twelfth."

"I don't usually do public math, but I can safely say that October twelfth is three days before the fifteenth."

"It is," the man answered, confusion marring his features.

And he wasn't the only one who was perplexed.

"Three days before the fifteenth," she hooted and laughed like she'd lost her mind. She sniffed the air, then did a little skip dance over to the other table where a baker placed a tray of bonbons. She picked up a treat and held it in front of her face. "Three days," she announced to the chocolate before popping it into her mouth. She closed her eyes and sighed. "Butterscotch."

What the hell had gotten into her?

"Miss, you can't eat those," a woman in an apron said, eyeing his bonbon bandit as one would watch a rabid animal, which wasn't that off the mark.

Harper gasped. "Sorry, I was having a moment."

"We know about your bonbon moments," the baker mumbled, sliding the tray away from the Singing Bonbon Bandit.

"Give me the pen, Paxton," she crooned, prancing to their table. The lawyer handed her the pen, and she signed the contract. "There, I'm in. It's your turn, heartthrob."

He looked from the pen to the papers as a jolt of anxiety tore through him. "I can't do it."

"What?" Harper uttered as the excitement drained from her face.

He shook his head. "It's not a fit for me. I have too much going on."

"I can help you with your niece. You don't need a nanny," she pressed.

"No, I can't," he bit out. He hated to be a prick, but she didn't understand.

"Landon, this could be very good for your image," Mitzi added, but he couldn't concentrate.

"I'll pretend to be your loving wife," Harper pleaded. "I'll be crazy low maintenance. You won't have to bring me breakfast in bed or do anything on the romance scale of devotion."

What the hell was she talking about.

"Romance scale of what?"

She chewed her lip. "It measures romantic stuff like general courtship activities, trips to romantic locales, kisses in the rain, fireworks displays…"

He narrowed his gaze, not buying the scale business. "Fireworks?"

"Okay, the romance scale of devotion isn't an actual thing," she confessed. "Not to pat myself on the back or anything, but it's a decent measure of devotion. Still, I made it up to make a point. I'll do whatever it takes to help your career or your image or whatever. I'll help care for Aria. I need to win this money. I need it for…"

And then he remembered. "Your grandmother's house."

She nodded. "This money would keep the bank from repossessing it."

What the hell?

"You didn't say anything about losing the house back at Libby and Raz's place."

"I know," she answered, not meeting his eye. "I didn't mention it to my friends because I didn't want them to worry. But I'm out of options. We're in a bad spot, and time is running out. She owes a little over forty-eight thousand, and it's due—"

"—on October fifteenth," he answered as it came together. This was some serious shit. "I could give you the money. Fifty thousand dollars is nothing to me," he replied and instantly regretted it.

A blush colored her cheeks. "I don't take charity from anyone. That's not the person my grandparents raised me to be." She blew out a sharp breath. "What's going on, Landon? Why won't you do it? Even your manager agrees this would be good for your career. You can't lose."

Oh, but he could. This seemingly harmless venture could expose him. Every humiliation could be revealed.

Mitzi should have known better than to throw his name into the hat for something like this.

His damn phone buzzed again, and now he was ready to toss it into the cupcake frosting.

"Landon," Harper rasped as her bottom lip trembled. "I need you to agree to this."

He met her hazel gaze. Warm cocoa brown and cornflower blue pleaded with him as his phone buzzed again.

Christ, give it a rest, guys.

Agitation tore through him. A game of tug-of-war played out in his mind. He wanted to help her, but every fiber of his being begged him to chuck the pen across the room and tear the contract into shreds.

But he didn't.

For the first time in a long time, he fought the urge to flee and pushed past the fear.

She had no idea she was asking him to risk everything.

Still, he couldn't say no to her.

A heady mix of elation and trepidation flowed through him. "Where do I sign?" He could barely believe he'd spoken the words.

"On the second page, sir. There's a red sticker," the lawyer replied, and that's when he realized the suit, Madelyn, and Mitzi had had a front-row seat to that charged exchange.

Madelyn threw Mitzi a curious look.

He'd deal with them later.

He flipped the page, zeroed in on the slash of red cutting through the monotony of black and white, and signed the contract.

Landon Bartholomew Paige.

He handed the document and the pen to the lawyer as the muscles at the base of his neck tightened.

"Thank you," Harper said on a relieved breath and rested her head against his chest. And just like in the club in Las Vegas, he wrapped his arms around her, and the strain and stress dissipated.

Touching her did that to him.

"This arrangement can end after Red Rocks Unplugged. I'll stay with you until then if that's what you want," she said softly, her words vibrating against his torso.

What did he want?

What did she want?

Cash.

She needed cash.

"Look at this—a nanny match by way of marriage," Madelyn announced.

Harper's body stiffened, and she pulled out of his embrace. "This isn't a nanny match, Madelyn."

"Jesus, here we go," he muttered.

"I'm not his nanny. This is an arrangement. I need the winnings to help my grandmother, and Landon needs help with his niece and time to work on his music."

"An arrangement," Madelyn repeated. "And one that includes childcare assistance."

"Yes, that's what I said," Harper answered.

"So, you have nothing against being a nanny. You just don't want to be Landon's nanny."

"That's right," his bullheaded wife answered with a triumphant air. "And I already have a job teaching music online. There's no room in my life to work as a nanny."

"Ah, then I'm correct," Madelyn replied with a sly grin. "This is simply a semantics issue. You're able to complete nannying tasks, but you don't want to be labeled as the nanny? It's the word, not the meaning."

Harper frowned. "Are you trying to use your nanny-match ninja mind-control on me?"

Madelyn chuckled. "I'm simply noticing the obvious. You'll conceal your nanny duties under the guise of being the child's aunt."

"But I am her aunt—on paper," Harper fired back.

"Indeed, you are," Madelyn answered as her grin widened. "For the next sixty days."

"But not as a nanny-match." Harper turned to him. "It's a *dare-match.* I'm your sixty-day dare-match wife." The chain slipped out from the neck of the T-shirt and dangled between her breasts. The diamond glinted in the light. She looked down and touched the rings. "We should probably wear these, you know, for appearance's sake." She unclasped the chain and slid the rings into her palm. She started to put the wedding ring on, but he stopped her.

"Let me."

She watched him closely, then handed him the rings. "Give me your ring."

He removed the chain and handed her the matching platinum band.

"Put out your hand," she said, and just like the last time, well, minus the hoard of drunk ballerinas and bellowing gladiators, she gazed up at him. "Will you be my dare-match husband for the next sixty days?"

"I will. I mean, I do."

She slid the ring on his finger. He wasn't one for jewelry, but this ring was different.

"Your turn," she said.

He gazed at the rings, then swallowed hard. "Will you be my wife?"

She stared up at him with a creased brow.

"I mean, will you be my sixty-day dare-match wife?"

"I will," she answered, and in the middle of a bakery, he slipped the wedding ring and then the diamond ring onto her finger.

Harper glanced around the room and grinned. "We seem to do this in the strangest of circumstances."

He leaned in, wanting to kiss her and seal the temporary vow again. He'd probably lost his mind somewhere between the insanity of marrying Harper in Vegas and agreeing to do this contest. But he didn't care—not one bit. He didn't give a damn that a trio of bakers, some random lawyer, his manager, and the nanny matchmaker were standing a few feet away from them. With the scent of chocolate in the air, one fact bubbled to the surface in his scrambled brain.

Harper would be his for the next sixty days.

He was ready to give in and start pretending to be husband and wife, when Mitzi's phone chimed.

"Sorry," the woman said, then pulled her cell from her bag. She glanced at the screen and frowned. "It's Bess."

"Who's Bess?" Harper asked.

And the spell was broken. Bess had to be the one calling him, and there was only one reason she'd called several times in a row.

He released a pained breath.

Not again.

"Landon, what's going on? Who's Bess?"

"Bess is my foster mom."

Mitzi answered the call. "Hello, Bess," she said, then gasped. "Oh, dear! I think he turned it off. Okay, I'll let him know."

"Is it what I think it is?" he asked.

Mitzi nodded as worry clouded her expression. "Bess said she's been trying to call you."

"What is it?" Harper asked.

"It's Aria," he answered.

"What about her?"

He glanced at his manager, and she nodded, confirming what he already knew.

"She's run away."

Chapter 13
HARPER

Harper surveyed the commotion as Landon paced across the back of the bakery with his cell pressed to his ear.

"Did you check the treehouse, Bess? What about the attic?" the man asked with worry ingrained in his expression.

She stared down at the rings on her hand, and the gravity of the situation sank in.

This marriage wasn't only about her and Landon. This marriage wasn't just a dare taken too far or the catalyst to—hopefully—make some fast cash. There was a little girl, a real flesh and blood child to consider, and from the sounds of it, she was hurting.

She pulled her gaze from Landon and scanned the bakery.

What she needed was some information. She couldn't go into this Aria emergency flying blind.

Luckily, there were two people who might be able to shed light on the situation. She smoothed her shirt, which didn't do much to enhance her hobo-fabulous appearance, and sauntered over to where Mitzi and Madelyn spoke in hushed tones.

"I'm sorry to interrupt, but does this happen often?" she

inquired, gesturing with her chin toward her pacing dare-match husband.

Mitzi rubbed the back of her neck and shared a look with the matchmaker.

"Mitzi," Madelyn said, eyeing the woman. "Harper is Landon's wife. It would help her to have some insight into the little girl."

Mitzi threw a worried look toward Landon, then released an audible breath. "Aria started running away a week ago."

A week ago?

"I see," she repeated as the pieces came together.

Landon had skipped out on her a week ago, and she'd given him hell for it.

"Aria isn't thrilled about moving in with her uncle Landon," Mitzi continued. "After she ran away, he decided to spend a good chunk of this week easing her into the idea of leaving Tomás and Bess's place and starting a life with him. He's had her over to the house and gave her free rein to decorate her bedroom and stock the fridge with her favorite foods, but she's not having any of it. She wouldn't even get out of the car and go inside his Crystal Hills place."

Harper nodded as memories of the day she learned she wouldn't be returning to her home flashed in her mind—not pictures, exactly, but sensations of red-hot anger and gnawing powerlessness. She pushed her feelings aside and ignored the twist in her belly. "Are Bess and Tomás her grandparents?"

"They're Landon's foster parents. Aria knows them as Lolo and Lala. A kid version of *abuelo* and *abuela*—grandpa and grandma in Spanish. They've been caring for Aria for the last two years."

Interesting.

"Why can't they continue to care for her?"

"They're sculptors, and they've been invited to teach abroad in Italy. It's something they've always dreamed of doing, but they can't bring Aria along. It's time for Landon to take full custody," Mitzi explained.

"We've known about this transition for a while. It's quite delicate," Madelyn supplied.

"This week has been hard on them, and Aria's no wilting flower," Mitzi added. "If she doesn't like something, she'll let you know. She's also as stubborn as a bull. She's a lot like her mother," the woman finished with a sad smile.

Harper shifted her tote on her shoulder and tossed another curious look at Landon as a different picture of the man emerged. He masked his pain like she did. But she still needed more information. Whatever she was walking into, there was a decent amount of baggage involved, and the more she knew, the better.

She steadied herself. "I'm going to come out and ask this."

Mitzi cocked her head to the side. "Okay."

"Are Leighton Paige and Trey Grant Aria's parents?" She'd had a hunch it might be a touchy subject to bring up with her pop star.

Mitzi looked her over as if she were weighing whether to answer the question.

"Harper will know everything soon enough," Madelyn offered. "And remember what you said to me after seeing the wedding video."

The wedding video?

"Let me guess," she said, shaking her head. "You thought I was some gold digger."

"Quite the opposite." Mitzi tossed a glance at Landon, then lowered her voice. "I told Madelyn I hadn't seen Landon smile like that in years."

Wow.

She twisted the corner of Landon's shirt. "I don't know what to say to that."

Mitzi narrowed her gaze. "Say you'll do what you can to help Landon and his niece find their footing."

It didn't take a genius to comprehend what Mitzi wanted her to do. It was a tall order, but one she might be up for.

No, not *might* be up for it.

A sense of purpose washed over her.

She was up for it.

"I understand the marriage situation is unconventional, but if Landon's niece needs help figuring out her new life, I'll do what I can," she answered, and she meant it.

She was no fan of pint-sized nose pickers, but Aria didn't seem like most kids. She knew this as well as she knew her own name. From the moment that little sass pot had told her uncle Landy to eat worms, the kid had simultaneously freaked her out and taken up residence in her heart.

And what did she have to lose?

She had no idea what her life would look like in six months or six years, but she'd just signed a contract that laid out exactly where she'd be and who she'd be with for the next sixty days.

For the next two months, she'd be part of a trio.

She might be a broke, chocolate-obsessed, tutu-wearing train wreck of a woman, but she could be there for the kid.

She held the manager's gaze. Mitzi Jones was tough, but her eyes gave her away. The genuine worry welling there spoke volumes.

One thing was clear: Mitzi cared deeply for Landon and Aria.

But that didn't mean the woman was about to spill the beans to some chick Landon married on a dare in Vegas—no matter how happy the man had appeared or how many offers came his way, thanks to the leaked wedding videos. Still, Mitzi was the key to figuring out what was going on between Landon and Aria.

"Mitzi, I don't mean to pry," she continued. "I knew Landon had a connection to a child, since he was part of the nanny match men's group. I figured it might be some groupie's baby. The guys are tight-lipped about each other's situations. I didn't know Landon had a niece until today. A little background info could help me help them. We're stuck together for sixty days. If I understood what was going on, I think it would help."

The manager raised an eyebrow.

That was something.

"Here's what I know," she continued. It was time to level with the woman. "The entire planet went crazy when Heartthrob Warfare announced they were taking a break. But Landon remained in the spotlight. I always wondered what happened to Trey and Leighton. They seemed to drop off the face of the Earth."

Mitzi threw another look Landon's way. "Aria is Leighton and Trey's daughter, and they vowed to keep that part of their life private. Trey and Leighton were very much in love. And while everyone was thrilled about them having a baby on the way, when they found out Leighton was pregnant, it threw a wrench into the direction of the band's music. It was at the height of Heartthrob Warfare's success. The label had agreed to let them write and record the music they wanted to do. But Trey and Leighton wanted their child to have a normal life, away from the paparazzi and the pop world. So they left it all to live in the foothills tucked away in Evergreen, not far from Tomás and Bess. There was talk that, after a couple of years when Aria was older, they'd start making music again, but it never happened."

"I'd had no idea they'd had a child," she replied, shaking her head. "They did an amazing job keeping it quiet."

"They wanted a stable, happy life for their daughter. Trey

and Leighton stopped craving the spotlight the minute they found out she was pregnant."

"And what did Landon think about it?" she prodded.

"That's complicated," the manager replied, then flicked her gaze to Landon, still on the phone and about to wear a hole in the floor from his pacing. "You haven't met Aria yet, have you?"

"Actually, I met her today."

"When?" Mitzi asked, shock coating the word.

"She and Landon had a video call a little bit ago at a housewarming party. One of the kids asked Landon to call her. That's when I got a glimpse of her."

"Let me guess. The little girl was Phoebe?" Mitzi tossed out.

"You know her?"

"Landon's told me a bit about the families in the nanny match group. The women are your friends, right?"

"Charlotte, Penny, and Libby have been my best friends since we were five years old."

"In Miss Miliken's kindergarten class," Madelyn supplied.

The girls must have mentioned it to Madelyn. "God bless that woman for putting up with us." She chuckled. "Well, putting up with me. Penny, Char, and Libby were model students."

"I can imagine," Madelyn answered with her trademark sly smile.

But there was something else—something Madelyn wasn't saying. But before she could ask, Landon charged toward them.

"I have to head up to Tomás and Bess's place," he announced, jamming his phone into his pocket. "Are we done with the lawyer and the contest business?"

The suit.

She'd forgotten about the Luxe attorney. She peered at the

table and found the man on his phone, scribbling on a piece of paper.

"I believe we're done," Mitzi answered. "But I'll touch base with the attorney before heading to the airport."

Landon nodded as anguish welled in his eyes.

"What's the situation with Aria?" Madelyn pressed.

"She might have headed into the woods. Bess and Tomás aren't sure." He checked his watch. "It'll be dark soon, and we can't have her out there alone at night. I have to get up to Evergreen."

She glanced at Mitzi, recalling the woman's request.

What would a wife and an aunt do at a time like this?

And then it hit her. If he was going, she was going with him.

She reached into her pocket and pulled out her keys. "Let's go. I can drive."

He stared at her like she'd rattled off her statement in an alien language.

Did he *not* want her to come with him?

It didn't matter. If Aria was missing, they could use all the help they could get.

"Your car won't make it where we're going. Bess and Tomás live in the foothills outside the city in Evergreen. It's not city terrain. It's gravel roads and steep inclines."

Did he disrespect her Volvo?

Oh, hell no.

The man was distraught, and she could grant him some grace, but that was no reason to dis Carol.

"Carol will make it just fine."

"Carol barely made it here, Harper," he huffed. "Have you checked your belts?"

She gestured to her hobo-chic—okay, just hobo—attire. "Hello? I'm wearing sweatpants. I don't know what my lack of a belt has to do with my car?"

Landon looked at her like she'd blathered gibberish. He checked his watch and shook his head. "I can't chance getting stuck on the side of the road. This is too important."

"You could have just said that," she mumbled when Madelyn pulled a key fob from her handbag.

"Take the Lamborghini Urus."

The nanny car.

And heaven help her. She couldn't stop her stupid pulse from kicking up. The Lamborghini Urus was a sweet nanny-gig perk—not that she was anyone's nanny. Still, one by one, she'd looked on as her friends inherited a nanny credit card with a hella crazy limit, along with a swank SUV. As much as she believed in blazing her own trail, she couldn't deny that doing it in a car with consistent air-conditioning and squeaky-clean cupholders beat roasting in a sticky, lollipop-encrusted heap of metal.

Landon turned his attention to Madelyn. "Isn't that the vehicle for the nanny?"

"It is," she offered with a nonchalant little shrug. "I drove it here. I'm parked out back. I planned on returning it to the dealership since your situation has changed. However, you require a reliable car, and you've already paid the lease." She waved the fob like a hypnotist.

Harper forced herself to pull her attention from the fancy Lambo key.

Stop drooling over a key! It opened a car, not a magic room with unlimited bonbons.

"I haven't seen the car yet," Landon stammered, staring at the shiny thing. The man looked almost as mesmerized by the bit of metal as she was.

Madelyn rested the fob on her palm like the snake offering up an apple in the Garden of Eden. "Now's your chance."

Damn, that fob could glimmer.

She stared at the miniature metallic mass—that elusive

nanny Lamborghini Urus key fob emblazoned with a golden Lamborghini bull. She'd be lying if she said she hadn't been green with envy when she watched her besties pull up in the ritzy SUV.

"I'll drive the Lamborghini," she said, trying to play it off like people offered her Italian luxury cars every day and twice on Sundays.

Madelyn flashed her smirk of a smile and handed over the key.

"It really fits nicely in the palm of your hand," Harper remarked as Landon looked at her like she'd lost her mind.

"You're not coming with me," he barked.

Who did he think he was dealing with?

She lifted her chin. "I am."

"This is serious."

Um…yes, she knew that. She wasn't a moron.

"I get it, Landon. I was a kid once—a kid who ran away a time or two. I can provide insight."

He stared at the ceiling. "Jesus, Harper, this is not the time to act like—"

"Like what?"

He removed his hat and raked his hand through that thick mass of perfect pop star hair. "Like you! Pushy, aggressive, and bullheaded."

She puffed up like a peacock. "FYI, heartthrob, those are my best qualities, and see this bull?" She held up the fob. "We're one and the same. These bulls are a pair. Wherever it goes, I go."

Boom.

He placed the cap back on his head, then pinned her with his gaze. "You won't let up until I agree to bring you along, will you?"

The corners of her lips curled into the hint of a self-satisfied grin. "You're just now figuring this out about me?"

He exhaled a sharp breath. "All right, you can come. But I'm driving,"

"Who's stopping you?" she shot back and tossed him the fob. She understood the magnitude of this moment. Of course, the man needed to find his niece. Still, an odd partners-in-crime quality rose to the surface like they were in this together.

"Where's the car?" Landon asked.

"You can't miss it. It's in the alleyway," Madelyn replied.

"Let's head out," he said and started for the door.

She scanned the bakery. "Wait," she called, then zipped toward the tray of bonbons. She ogled the beautiful chocolate decadence. Topped with a sprinkling of sea salt, these had to be the butterscotch bonbon delights.

She looked from side to side, grabbed the tray, and took off like a shot.

In for a penny, in for a pound.

"You can't take those," a baker exclaimed.

Yes, she could.

If anyone needed an obscene amount of chocolate, it was the Singing Bonbon Bandit.

"We're representing Cupid Bakery in a baking contest. This is research for our reality show."

"What about your grandma? We need a note. Mr. Sweet's orders," the baker exclaimed.

"Grandma's out of town. And when Grandma's away, Harper will play. You can put these beauties on my husband's tab," she reeled off, moving like a lynx past a pair of slack-jawed bakers before nearly taking out the poor lawyer.

"Sorry, suit!" she called, working her way to the back door.

Did Landon even have a tab here?

No, why would he?

She honestly couldn't name any bakery that employed a tab system, but desperate times called for desperate measures.

"What the hell are you doing?" Landon exclaimed.

"Get the door. My hands are full," she answered, glancing over her shoulder. The bakers huddled together and threw incensed glances her way.

"With stolen bonbons," he answered.

"They're not stolen. They're putting them on your tab," she announced, loud enough for the bakers on the other side of the room to hear.

"I don't have a tab here."

She held up the tray. "You do now."

The man gave her a serious dose of stink eye.

"Now that we're doing a reality baking show sponsored by Cupid Bakery, we're basically employees."

"I doubt that the owner allows his employees to steal bonbons," Landon fired back.

She had to make him understand.

"We need sustenance. And Aria might be hungry. I would have sworn she had chocolate on her face during the video call. I know a bonbon girl when I see one."

"You plan on luring my niece out of hiding with bonbons?"

Yes, it was ridiculous. But a gal had to use what was on hand.

"What's your plan?"

"Shit," he whispered, then headed toward the door alongside her. "Mitzi," he called over his shoulder.

"I'll take care of the bonbons. Don't worry. Just get up to Tomás and Bess's place in one piece," the manager replied.

Having a manager really came in handy.

She looked over her shoulder again and caught Mitzi's eye. The woman tossed her a furtive wink before heading toward the gawking bakers.

Landon whipped open the door. They charged into the alleyway, then came to a screeching halt.

She gasped and almost dropped the tray. "It's…"

"A brown Lamborghini Urus?" Landon supplied.

"Candy Pearl Brown Sugar, to be exact. The dealership said it was a custom job," Madelyn offered from the doorway. "And Landon?"

"Yeah?"

"While your wife was stealing chocolates, I made a call and had my people add her to your car insurance."

"Thanks, Madelyn," she called, then gestured with her chin toward the sexiest brown car she'd ever laid eyes on. "I can drive if you want to hold the bonbons, since it's all official."

"There's no way you're driving," Landon said under his breath, shaking his head. He pressed the fob and unlocked the doors.

"I didn't even think people had brown cars on purpose anymore," she remarked as Landon opened the passenger door. "It is the nicest brown I've ever seen. Shiny, like…" She looked down at the chocolate shells. "That's weird."

"Harper," he lamented as she slid onto the sumptuous leather seat.

"Okay, I get it. I'll cut the bonbon talk."

He shut her door, jogged around to the driver's side, and got in.

She maneuvered the giant tray and fastened her seat belt.

And they were off.

She glanced at Landon as they headed down the alley. With the bonbons balanced on her legs, she sat back and deflated into the seat.

What a day, and it wasn't even over.

The hum of the luxury tires meeting the road lulled them into a tense silence. Frustration and worry rolled off her dare-match husband in choppy waves. She stared out the window as they merged onto the highway and drove west out of the city toward the foothills. After at least twenty minutes of sitting in silence, she slid her gaze from the road and studied her husband's profile. A muscle ticked in his jaw as the setting sun had him looking more *heartthrobby* than ever. She couldn't fixate on his chiseled features. But she also couldn't help noticing the guy was crazy tense. He'd grind his molars to dust if he didn't relax. She was about to suggest he take a breath—Libby would be so proud of her—when a glint of light caught her eye.

His wedding ring.

She peered down at her rings, and a surge of anxiety hit her system.

What would she say to Landon's foster parents and Aria?

Had they seen the video?

Aria had been taken aback by the video call, that much she could deduce, and Phoebe had thrown the little girl for a loop when she dished out the whole nanny-aunt situation.

Landon must not have told his family about her. She couldn't blame him. She hadn't told a soul about them either. But everything was different now. They had to figure out how they would navigate the next sixty days.

And what happened after that?

No one had mentioned it, but divorce had to be on the table.

She couldn't stay married to Landon, could she?

She examined the bonbons, and for the second time that day, the chocolate didn't provide any insight. But they looked delectable.

She cleared her throat. "So, yeah, I know I said I'd cut the bonbon talk, but..."

"What?" he rasped, worry coating the word. The guy was a mess.

"I think you need one."

He relaxed a fraction. "Why do you say that?"

"You look ready to pull the steering wheel off whatever you call what the steering wheel is attached to."

He chuckled.

The sensual cadence of his voice—even his laugh—had her squeezing her thighs together.

Pull yourself together, woman.

She plucked a bonbon from the tray. "Open your mouth."

He glanced at her. "You're going to feed me?"

"I could throw it at you."

He chuckled again, and the sound flowed through her like melted chocolate.

Stop swooning.

Still, she couldn't be too hard on herself. Between her heartthrob and the glut of bonbons on her lap, her brain was on sensory overload.

He opened his mouth, and she slipped a bonbon past his lips. "Butterscotch sea salt," he said, then hummed the sexiest sound. A sound she'd heard on her wedding night not once but more than a few times while the man's head was between her thighs. "They're so good," he crooned.

Hello, Swoon City.

She closed her eyes, recalling his magical tongue.

What would it be like to kiss this man while eating bonbons?

"Harper, are you okay?"

She snapped out of it. "I know that they're yummy because…I've had them before…yes…of course, I've tasted these bonbons. And when I eat them, I don't experience sexual urges. I can assure you of that."

What the hell?

"You should have one," he said, and she could hear the smile in his voice.

Chocolate to the rescue.

"Absolutely, I'll indulge in a sex-free bonbon," she blathered.

Crap! She had better shut her bonbon hole ASAP!

She swiped two from the tray and jammed them in her mouth like a squirrel, deep-throating acorns.

"Wow," Landon remarked, "that surveillance photo really caught the essence of how you consume bonbons."

Look who thought he was a funny guy.

But she didn't have the bandwidth to reply with a barb. Instead, she leaned back as the choc-deliciousness hit her system and noticed Landon's demeanor had softened.

"Can I ask you a question?"

"Sure," she replied through a mouthful of chocolate butterscotch bliss.

"You said you ran away when you were a kid."

"I did."

"Why?"

She didn't want to regurgitate the sad orphan Harper story, but she could provide general insight. She wiped the corners of her mouth. "Power, I guess. I didn't have much of a say about things when I was a kid, and when you're powerless, you find something to control."

He nodded. "I can understand that."

Of course, he could. He had foster parents. That's when a strange realization hit. She'd followed Heartthrob Warfare religiously when she was a teen, but she knew very little about his background. Whoever had overseen his PR had kept any substantive information away from the media. That was likely Mitzi's doing. Their fairy tale story centered on being a trio of kids in Colorado who were pulled from obscurity thanks to LookyLoo.

There was so much more to this man than she'd expected.

He hit the blinker, and they exited the highway. After a few twists and turns, the asphalt road gave way to the crunch of gravel. They passed a line of mailboxes, and she spied one with Fletcher-Medina painted along the side.

"Tomás and Bess live up this way," he said softly.

"Trey Grant lived up here, too, right?"

That was the other nugget of info broadcast about Heartthrob Warfare. A musically gifted brother and sister who teamed up with their neighbor—a teen named Trey Grant.

He didn't reply.

She shouldn't have brought it up.

"Sorry," she murmured. "I remembered reading about Trey being your neighbor. I think it was an article called *Ten Facts About Heartthrob Warfare*. It was online or something…years ago."

He glanced at her, and curiosity flashed in his eyes.

Ugh! She did not want to sound like a fangirl.

"Trey was our neighbor," Landon answered. "He lived with his aunt, but she passed away a while back." His posture stiffened. "We're almost to the house."

Time was up.

She popped another bonbon into her mouth. "What should we say about us?" she asked through a glut of caramel. "About the…"

"They know about our marriage. When I was on the phone with Bess, she asked me about it."

She was meeting her in-laws.

Holy shit, she had in-laws!

"Did Aria tell them after the video call?" She should figure out how they'd learned about the unorthodox union.

"They heard the call, and then they got online."

They must have seen the video.

Again, she thanked the stars Babs was cut off from the world.

"Were they upset?"

"Tomás and Bess are open-minded and have a 'go with the flow' attitude. They don't get upset, but Aria—"

"—ran away because not only does she have to live with you, but she also has a new aunt to contend with," she supplied, putting two and two together.

"Something like that," he conceded as they continued down a narrow gravel path.

Barely a minute had passed before a large two-story house covered in cedar shingles emerged from a sea of green foliage. A detached garage sat dark and dormant about twenty feet away from the main structure, with a realtor's sign in the yard between the buildings.

"For sale?" she read.

"My foster parents are getting older. This place is a lot for them to maintain. They're hoping it sells while they're in Italy."

Mitzi had mentioned Landon's parents were traveling abroad to teach.

"They're sculptors. They're leaving tomorrow to lead a sculpture workshop."

"Tomorrow?" she repeated. Mitzi had neglected to provide that nugget.

"Yeah, tomorrow's the day Aria's supposed to start living with me permanently, but we're going to try to have her come back to my place tonight. Tomás thinks it might be easier."

"Aria's returning to Denver with us…tonight?"

Was there even an *us*?

Was she moving in with him?

He parted his lips, but nothing came out. He hadn't thought it through either.

And what did that mean?

But her concerns evaporated when she pictured the little girl with ice-blue eyes, a rat's nest for hair, and a smudge of chocolate on her cheek. With her grandparents leaving, her home for sale, and being forced to move in with another relative, this kid had a lot on her plate.

"I'm willing to bet these bonbons that Aria didn't run away. She's probably hiding."

"Is that what you would do?" Landon pressed.

She pictured herself climbing the rafters in her grandparents' attic as they called out to her.

Harper Barbara, are you in here? Harper, let us know you're okay.

"It's strange to want all the attention and none of it simultaneously," she mused.

Landon cut the engine, and she studied the man. Those eyes, those soulful deep brown eyes, shone with emotion. The intensity in his gaze could swallow her whole, and the vulnerability etched on his face touched something deep within.

"What is it?" she whispered.

The muscles in his throat constricted as he swallowed. "I'm glad you're here."

And this is why he was the world's heartthrob.

Rendered temporarily mute, she nodded, feeling the weight of the moment. But she wasn't about to pile on more sap. That's not what he needed. The man required a dose of Harper sass to lift his spirits. "I am your wife. Of course, I'd accompany you to pick up your niece…our niece…the niece." She had to get it together. She ran her hand across the fancy dashboard. "And I really want to drive this sweet turd-colored Lambo." She tapped her chin. "Yes, that's it. I'm here for the car, the candy, and the cash," she whispered, doling out one heck of a steaming dose of smart-ass. "And if I wasn't here, I'd be—"

"—corrupting youth outside of bakeries," he supplied as the hint of a grin touched the corners of his mouth.

She'd done it. She'd gotten him out of his head. "I think you've figured me out." She couldn't stop herself from mirroring the expression. This man and his perfect pop star half-smile and killer bone structure turned her brain to mush.

But it was more than that.

This flash of raw vulnerability left her breathless. "I'm sure Aria is—" she began, but stopped talking when two figures, a man and a woman, emerged from behind the mountain home. "Those must be your foster parents."

"Yeah, it's them," he said and shook his head as if he'd woken up from a trance. He exited the vehicle and met the pair in front of the car.

The tall, slim Bess embraced Landon. Her long, dark auburn braid swished to the side as she pulled back, and the two spoke. Tomás patted Landon on his shoulder, and to her surprise, headed her way.

OMG! She was still in the car.

She reached for the handle, but Tomás got there first and opened the door.

"You must be Harper, Landon's wife," he said in a gentle Spanish accent.

She pasted a smile to her lips that could put a beauty queen to shame. "And you must be Tomás," she replied—to her freaking father-in-law—just as she remembered she looked like the opposite of a beauty queen.

But Tomás didn't seem to notice. Not to mention, the man didn't look overly concerned for the welfare of his grandchild. The man's vibe was pretty chill for someone who'd misplaced a kid. He had to be in his late sixties or possibly his early seventies. With kind eyes, silver hair, and a bushy mustache, Tomás was as round as Bess was slender. "And I see you brought snacks," he added and patted his belly.

"I thought Aria might like a bonbon." She glanced at the tray teeming with chocolates. Holy cocoa party! She'd stolen a bejesus load of sweets. "Or twenty. We've got enough chocolate to feed an army."

Deep lines near Tomás's eyes crinkled as he gifted her with a warm grin. "You and our granddaughter will get along just fine."

Score one for the Singing Bonbon Bandit.

"Have you found Aria?" she asked and glanced at Landon and Bess.

"Not yet, but I have a feeling she's close by. Bess, on the other hand, is worried she's gotten lost in the woods."

"But you're not concerned?"

"Like I said, I have a hunch she hasn't strayed far." He leaned in. "Bess thinks I'm crazy, but between you and me…"

"Yes?" she whispered.

Curiosity glinted in the man's almond-shaped eyes. "I believe you're the reason she's gone missing."

Chapter 14

HARPER

"Me? You think I'm to blame for Aria going missing?" She could barely believe her ears.

It was a wholly inadequate response. She understood how the news of Landon marrying some random chick in Vegas could set the kid off. But she couldn't understand why Tomás seemed good with the situation. Before she could press the man, the crunch of feet hitting gravel caught her attention.

"I'm sorry we have to meet on such a chaotic day, Harper," Bess sputtered, coming toward her. "And aren't you sweet? Look, Tomás, our daughter-in-law brought treats."

Daughter-in-law?

Her brain came back online and re-sent the "yes, *you're their daughter-in-law because you married their foster son*" memo.

She studied her in-laws. Landon wasn't kidding about his foster parents being open-minded. They didn't seem upset about Landon's change in marital status. They were downright welcoming. She glanced at the stolen bonbons. "I grabbed what was available. What can I do to help? Tomás tells me Aria is still missing."

"Our sweet, spirited girl," Bess replied and pressed her

hand to her chest. "Change is hard, and she's endured more than her share. But it'll be dark soon, and we can't have her out alone."

"Let's spread out and recheck Aria's favorite spots," Landon offered, peering down a path that led into a swath of dense foliage.

"Harper, could you wait on the porch while we walk the property?" Tomás asked. "We'd be so grateful if you could keep an eye out for her. You can't miss her. She looks like she's been living in a foxhole, and she may growl at you."

Now that was a description.

After seeing the child on the video call, she couldn't disagree with the characterization.

Bess rested her hand on Landon's arm. "Honey, can you check the trail that runs along the stream?"

"I was planning on it," he answered, worry creasing his brow.

"Tomás, you and I…"

"Can walk the ridge," the man supplied, taking his wife's hand.

"Are you sure you don't mind waiting here on your own?" Landon asked. Pain welled in his eyes.

Her heart ached for him. "I don't mind at all. Go do what you need to do."

"Thank you," he said on a relieved exhale, then cupped her cheek in his hand and pressed a kiss to her lips as if that was how they said goodbye.

Like they had *a goodbye* routine—or any routine, for that matter. But even more surprising than the quick peck was how natural it felt. It wasn't forced or awkward. She relaxed into it, pushing up on her toes to meet him halfway. Still, she was lucky she didn't drop the tray. The instant their lips met, the breath caught in her throat as a breezy, buzzy warmth spread through her.

And then he was gone.

His form disappeared as he sprinted down the trail.

With her lips tingling, a question formed in her mind.

Why had he kissed her goodbye?

Was it for show—a gesture for his parents to make them think they were happily married?

The kiss didn't feel artificial. Quite the opposite. It felt like…like home.

She peered down the trail.

That kiss really happened, right? It wasn't in her head.

She released a slow breath when her brain engaged, and she remembered she wasn't alone. Bess and Tomás watched her as one might observe an abstract art installation.

They'd seen the kiss.

It had happened.

But this wasn't the time to dissolve into a pool of swoony goo or try to untangle the knot of competing emotions.

She resurrected her beauty queen grin. "The porch. Me. I go there. Bring bonbons."

That tiny peck had rendered her a brain-scrambled, babbling cavewoman.

"We'll be back as soon as we can," Tomás said over his shoulder as he and Bess set off.

She nodded because her ability to form words wasn't working so well.

Take a second and pull yourself together.

She stood there, holding the tray of bonbons while surrounded by pine trees and swaying aspens, like the wilderness welcome wagon lady—minus the wagon.

"Sit on the porch and watch for the kid," she murmured, grateful she'd regained the ability to vocalize a cohesive thought.

She hadn't even taken a step when a faint rustling at her feet caught her attention, and…

"Snake," she yelped. Her opera voice kicked in, and it wasn't only dogs that could hear her high-pitched cry. Gray with a white stripe down its back, the snake slithered toward her like she'd called the damn thing.

Oh, hell no. No stupid snake was taking her down.

She grabbed two bonbons. "Back off, you douche nozzle of a snake," she growled and pelted the reptile with chocolate. "Don't even think about making me drop these." She raised the tray over her head and tiptoe-ran—which was way more challenging than one would expect—toward the house, shrieking like a whistling tea kettle, when a bubbly sound floated over on the breeze.

What was that?

She checked the ground. It wasn't the snake. The creature ignored the bonbons—his loss—and wound his way into the tall grasses.

"You're passing up a tasty treat, Mr. Douche Nozzle Snake," she taunted, reasonably sure there weren't more snakes waiting to ambush her on the path. With the snake situation under control, she took one careful step, then another, before the tittering sound returned.

And now she could identify it.

Fizzy little girl giggles.

And they were coming from the darkened garage.

Playing it cool, she casually glanced in the direction of the noise as a form zipped past the window.

Hello, Miss Eat Worms.

She could call out for Landon and his parents. And perhaps she should.

But she didn't.

If Tomás was right, and she suspected he was, the little-girl giggles were Aria's way of dropping catch-me-if-you-can breadcrumbs.

Sticking with her calm and collected tactics, she cleared her throat. "Everyone went to check the woods. I'll check the garage. But I'm sure Aria's not there. She's probably holed up with a pack of mountain lions."

Another round of giggles emanated from the darkened structure.

Tomás was right.

Aria had set this trap.

The game was on.

She meandered up the trail leading toward the house, then stopped at where it split. If she went right, she'd end up on the porch, and if she veered to the left, she'd end up at the garage.

Left it was.

It took a few seconds to make it to the structure's side door. She tucked the tray under her arm and gripped the doorknob. Just as she'd suspected, the door was unlocked. The hinges creaked their displeasure as she edged inside the musty space. In the waning light, she spied a string attached to a naked lightbulb.

"Let there be light," she murmured, but she didn't pull the string immediately. Instead, she listened for a peep or a giggle but was met with a blanket of silence.

Her runaway niece must have retreated to her hiding place.

She pulled the cord, and a soft glow lit the interior. There weren't any vehicles in this garage. Weathered boxes lined a wall, and a couple board games in tattered boxes sat atop a tower of folding chairs. A trombone and a guitar were propped near the entrance, along with a cluster of rusty shovels and spindly brooms. She waved away the dust dancing in the stagnate air and drank in the rest of the space. The garage wasn't so different from her attic, save for one thing. She spotted an upright piano next to a stack of milk crates on the far wall.

And then it hit her.

This was the birthplace of Heartthrob Warfare.

This was the garage where Leighton, Landon, and Trey

Grant had made music. She hadn't been sure that part of the Heartthrob Warfare origin story was true. Music labels and slick PR firms could spin fiction to make their artists appealing. Hell, people thought Vance was a poetry-spouting, lyrical genius which was a crock of shit. But here she was, standing in the place where three Colorado kids started a garage band, then made it big.

She set the tray on the piano bench and sat next to it. It didn't matter if she was seated in front of a pricy Steinway or a child's keyboard. She couldn't help but love being near the instrument. Resting her fingertips on the keys, she noticed something curious about this piano. She reached up and slid her index finger across the top of a crate and traced a line in the dust. A gray sheen covered the forgotten items in the garage, save for one thing.

The piano.

There wasn't a speck of dust on it.

Someone kept this instrument clean.

Someone cared for this piano. And she had a feeling she knew the identity of this mystery musical aficionado.

Her first clue came when a light sprinkling of dust from above tickled her nose and revealed the runaway's secret spot.

The rafters.

Smart kid.

Hardly anyone looked up when they checked a room.

But it was time to shake the pint-sized heathen from her perch.

She played the middle C key, and the note floated in the air with the flecks of swirling dust. Feeling Aria's eyes on her, she picked up a bonbon and theatrically waved it like her grandfather used to wave his conductor's baton. With an air of pomp and circumstance, she popped the chocolate into her mouth, and the lyrics came to her like they always did.

Sweet, so sweet, hello, to my favorite treat.

Her fingers fluttered across the keys, making up a melody to her bonbon jingle, when a tingle worked its way down her spine. Usually, her mind would open and merge with the music, but not today. Sitting on the bench with Aria scrutinizing her every move from above, her thoughts went to Leighton Paige, the girl's mother. The woman had sat here, at this very piano. She'd watched Leighton play on stage in countless videos. She'd connected with the pop star in the one-sided way regular people bonded with celebrities. Still, the connection never sent a shiver through her. But the sensation wasn't foreboding. Quite the opposite, it welcomed her like a friend. She lifted her hands from the keys and sat there for a beat, then two, waiting as a plume of silence filled the room.

"You're the nanny-aunt lady. Your name is Harper."

Hello, sassy tough gal.

Aria had barked the terse greeting like she'd been anticipating this moment.

She could respect the kid going to great lengths to arrange this meeting.

Biting back a grin, she looked over her shoulder at a pair of dangling shoelaces, then shrugged. "Yep, I'm Harper."

Best to play the aloof card for now.

"Are you scared of snakes, Harper, the Nanny Aunt?" the kid grumped. This child could lay on the surliness.

"No."

"You ran away from that garter snake like you had ants in your pants," Aria barked.

"You saw that, huh? Were you watching me, or were you waiting for me?" she tossed back, then returned to the keys. She played a rolling arpeggio scale in the key of C to give the girl a second to craft a response.

C, E, G.

C, E, G.

C, E, A,

C, E, A.

She flowed through the rolling progression, playing the simple separated chords, allowing the notes to rise and fall in a rhythmic stream of sound. She didn't have to see Aria's face to know the wheels in the kid's head were turning.

When she was that age, she'd been constantly sizing up a situation, and she could use a second herself to figure out what to say next. She'd be a part of this kid's life—at least for the next sixty days. She had to come up with a game plan, and she had to do it quickly.

Landon, Tomás, and Bess would be back soon. This might be the only sliver of time for them to feel each other out without an audience.

She finished the piano progression, then rested her hands in her lap. Barely a second of silence had passed before Aria drummed her fingers on the beam.

Was she copying the arpeggio on the wood?

She didn't have a chance to ask. A series of cracks and clunks replaced the gentle finger taps as the little girl traversed the high beam, then dropped like Spider-Man and hit the ground with a thump. Swooping in like she'd dismounted from a flying trapeze, the child studied her, then twisted her mouth into a scowl. "You married Uncle Landy with no pants on."

Damn the internet.

"Pants can be overrated," she replied with a shrug, keeping it casual.

Aria's gaze dropped to the tray. "Did he marry you for your bonbons?"

This little hellion had no idea.

"Maybe, but there are worse reasons to get married. Do you want a bonbon?" she asked, studying the girl. Despite the raised by wolves look, the child had inherited Leighton and Landon's symmetrically perfect features, but unlike her uncle, she had cornflower blue eyes like a prairie sky.

Aria crossed her arms. "I've got my own stash."

"Oh yeah? Let's see the goods."

Aria lifted the lid to the Scrabble board game and huffed. "I'm down to six lime lollipops."

"Ew," Harper moaned, "those are the worst."

"I'd eat a yellow before I'd eat green," the kid lamented.

"And yellows suck, too," she agreed.

"They totally *suck*," Aria replied, testing some salty language. The girl was doing her best to maintain an air of toughness, but she seemed more intrigued than angry.

And that had to count for something.

When she taught in-person piano lessons, it was rarely just her and the kid. A nanny or parent often lingered, tossing a suggestion here and there or chiding the child to pay attention or play better. There was no space to connect and get to know the kid without other adults intervening.

She glanced out the door. Neither Landon nor his parents were back.

Here goes nothing—or everything.

She slid over and made room for Aria to sit on the piano bench opposite the tray of chocolates. "Let's see how many bonbons you can eat. I stole them, and I could use some help disposing of the evidence."

The kid plopped onto the end of the bench and stared at the tray. "You stole this chocolate?"

"I'm a badass like that." She paused. It was one thing to dish out naughty language. It was another ball game to encourage a life of crime. "But you should never steal, like ever. Stealing is bad and super wrong."

Woohoo! She was already aunt-ing like a pro.

Aria sized her up. "But you said you stole these."

"It was more like borrowing."

"You can't borrow food, Harper...the Nanny Aunt." The

kid balked like she would have preferred to call her Harper, the Interloper.

"Fine, I stole them, but they're billing your uncle for it. So, it's only kind of stolen chocolate. Try one," she nudged.

Aria picked up a bonbon. "Are Lolo, Uncle Landy, and Lala looking for me?"

"They are," she answered, returning to the keys to riff on her "*Sweet, So, Sweet*" melody.

Aria popped the chocolate into her mouth. "These are butterscotch."

"Butterscotch, milk chocolate, and a little sea salt. Pretty good, huh?" she answered as the child ate another.

"Mom and Dad's favorite bonbon flavor was butterscotch."

"They were my grandpa's favorite, too."

"Were?" Aria asked.

"Yeah, he died."

She picked up another bonbon, then returned it to the tray. "My mom and dad died."

She had her talking.

"My parents died when I was five," she answered, surprised at how easy it was to speak the words that usually made her spitting mad. "I live with my grandma," she added.

The child retrieved the chocolate and popped it into her mouth. "But you're old," she said through the bite.

Oh, hell no!

She stopped playing. "I'm not that old. I'm twenty-six."

Aria wiped the back of her hand across her mouth. "When I'm twenty-six, I'm going to live in a hot air balloon. I'll go wherever I want, whenever I want. And nobody will be able to stop me."

"That's a pretty kick-ass plan."

"It's better than living in your grandma's house," the child muttered.

"You live in your grandparents' house," she quipped, then stuffed a bonbon in her mouth.

"Not anymore. I have to live with Uncle Landy."

She returned to the keys. "He's not so bad." She changed the melody from a jaunty major key to a darker minor key.

It was time for a song.

"*Uncle Landy doesn't have candy, so he eats all the worms, eats all the worms,*" she sang, making up a little tune.

Aria pressed her lips together and suppressed a grin.

"Are you going to watch me, or are you going to try to keep up with me?" she challenged.

The child frowned. "You want me to play the piano?"

"No, I want you to play a water buffalo," she tossed back and caught the hint of a smile on the girl's chocolate-lined lips. "Yes, I want to see what you've got unless you're too scared to play."

"I'm not scared of anything," Aria shot back, placing her fingers on the keys.

"Do you need me to teach you the notes?"

The kid pursed her lips. "I don't need to know the notes. I can do whatever you do."

"All right, let's see if you can repeat this." She banged out a tune—something light and hopping off the top of her head.

"Easy peasy, apple squeezy." Aria cracked her knuckles, lifted her chin, and repeated the notes. And not only that. She'd caught the nuances of the tune.

The kid could play by ear.

"Not bad," she replied, playing it close to the vest. "Can you play and sing at the same time?"

Aria turned away. "I don't sing anymore."

"Because you sound like a frog?"

When in doubt, revert to snark.

The child whipped around and scrunched her face. "No, I don't sound like a frog."

"Then let's hear what you've got."

Aria joined in on the piano, then inhaled a slow breath. *"Uncle Landy doesn't have candy, so he eats all the worms, eats all the worms."*

This kid wasn't only a piano-playing savant. She was the whole musical package.

"You've got perfect pitch, girl," she remarked, unable to disguise the amazement in her reply.

Aria smiled up at her, but as the girl drew a breath, another sound wove its way through the garage.

"What's this I hear about eating all the worms, eating all the worms?" sang a sensual, soulful voice—accompanied by a guitar.

Landon.

Her jaw dropped as she peered over her shoulder at her insanely sexy pop star.

Her nipples tightened into pearls as she drank him in. Thank God she was swimming in his T-shirt. But it wasn't only her horny boobs jonesing for the man. Her entire body buzzed electric.

Do not fall for the musician.

It wasn't lost on her that the musician in question was her husband, but she couldn't fall for him, for real. What they'd had on their wedding night was for one night only. It wasn't who they were in the real world. She'd be wise to remember that. Yes, yes, she knew this. She'd been feeding herself this mantra. But who could remain reasonable with Landon Paige sauntering through the room, guitar in hand and bursting into song? It was a scene straight out of her teenage fantasies.

Somehow, she kept playing. It must have been the muscle memory in her fingers because her brain was about as useful as a bowl of oatmeal.

And then another teenage fantasy came true.

Like they'd been playing together for decades, he knitted in the guitar's brassy tones with her melody as he continued toward them.

He was just walking while playing the guitar.

He was putting one foot in front of the other and moving his hands.

He wasn't solving the climate crisis or even bringing her chocolate.

And it was hella *H* to the *O* to the *T*, hot, hot, hot.

Again, she thanked her stars she wasn't rocking a sheer tank top. Her nipples would have slashed through the fabric like diamonds splitting glass.

Forget the nips. Focus on the music. There was a child present.

She glanced at Aria, playing away like a mini-Mozart, then changed key and tweaked the melody, testing if uncle and niece could adapt.

The nimble musical ninjas didn't miss a beat.

But she still had a few tricks up her sleeve.

Strumming away, Landon joined them, standing a few feet from her. She glanced up at him and bit back a smirk, cooking up a tune that would surely throw him for a loop.

Her guitar-strapped dare-match husband wouldn't know what hit him.

Flexing her musical muscles, her fingers fluttered across the keys as she dialed up the tempo and increased the complexity.

To her delight, Aria hung in with her like a champ.

And what did Landon do?

He mirrored her smirk as if he thought her little *accelerando* was child's play. Like a mind reader, he followed her lead and even added his own side riff to the made-up song.

And then he parted his lips. "*Uncle Landy eats all the candy, and Harper and Aria have none. The girls have none.*"

She steadied herself.

He repeated the verse, then peered down at his niece. "Sing it with me, Aria," he crooned, and heaven help her. Thank God she was sitting. She might have passed out if she had to juggle the complexities of standing while listening to this man sing. His voice had her clenching her core, and her poor nips were done for.

Doubling her focus, she prepared to change up the melody again, ready to throw a few octave jumps into the mix, when her pint-sized partner in piano crime yanked her hands away and sucked in her cheeks like she'd been force-fed a bag of lime lollipops.

Before she could play another note, the mood shifted from light and jovial to dense and destructive.

And Aria wasn't the only sourpuss.

The brassy bray of the guitar disappeared.

Landon's expression darkened. He dropped his hands to his sides and stared at his niece.

What happened?

All he'd done was ask her to sing.

She stopped playing and looked between the suddenly sullen pair.

Say something.

"I found Aria in here," she said, stating the obvious. "We were messing around, making up songs until you and your parents returned."

He nodded as the joy glinting in his eyes petered out.

"You're not half bad on the guitar," she teased, trying to lighten the mood.

It didn't work.

She turned to Aria and gestured to the piano. "This is good stuff. We should write this song down. Do you have any blank pages of sheet music or a notebook handy?"

Aria huffed, then scrambled off the bench, scaled the boxes, and returned to her perch.

One hell of an angry cloud had settled over these two.

"I thought it would be fun to play this tune again," she offered. She didn't have the foggiest idea of what was going on.

Landon stared at the floor as a muscle ticked in his jaw.

"We don't like writing things down. That's for douche nozzles," Aria called from her spot on the beam.

That couldn't be the only thing that had set them off.

"Aria, you can't talk like that," Landon chided.

"Harper said it first. She called the snake Mr. Douche Nozzle."

Oh crap.

"The snake?" Landon repeated.

She waved him off. "It was nothing. There was one crossing the gravel drive. It caught me off guard, that's all. I threw a couple of bonbons at it and called it a douche nozzle, but I should have tapped out the naughty word." She glanced at Aria. "Tapping out bad words is a trick my friends and I started doing when we were around your age." She swiveled on the bench. "I'm going to say the word and tap the syllables. *Douche nozzle*," she announced, tapping her foot for each syllable, thinking she'd score points with the little girl.

She didn't.

"I don't like writing words, and I don't like tapping syllables. That's a stupid trick for stupid people," Aria snarled.

It was safe to say things had gone downhill fast.

Landon rested the guitar against the wall, then peered at his niece. "Aria, you need to climb down. It's time to go," he barked, exasperation coating the command.

"Nope," the kid countered and crossed her arms. "I'm staying here."

"You can't stay at the house. Lolo and Lala are leaving tomorrow for Italy."

"Then I'm going to Italy," the girl sassed back.

The man released a heavy sigh. "We've talked about this.

You're coming to live with me in the city. I know you'll miss Lolo and Lala. But we'll see them soon."

"Six weeks is not soon, Uncle Landy."

Six weeks?

"What happens in six weeks?" she asked, studying the man.

"We're headed to Italy to visit Bess and Tomás. They're renewing their vows while they're there at my vacation home in the northern part of the country, and Aria's staying another week with them."

Did the "we" include her? Did she want it to?

"Why can't we live here at Lolo and Lala's house?" Aria spouted.

Landon pinched the bridge of his nose. "We've gone over this. Your grandparents are selling the house. It's a lot for them to keep up with, and they won't allow me to pay for a house-keeper. They want to move to the city into a smaller place when they return from Italy. Then we'll all live in Denver. This is how it's going to be. My house is close to your new school. This is not a debate. I know you're unhappy, but this is what your mom and dad wanted. They wanted you to live with me if anything happened to them."

"Well, they're dead, and they're stupid to make me live with you, and I'm not leaving," Aria hollered and hugged the beam. "I won't live in your big stupid house in Denver, Uncle Landy. I won't do it."

Pain rolled off uncle and niece in heart-crushing waves as the two went back and forth, Landon telling Aria she had to live with him, followed by Aria shooting him down.

She had to do something. She had to say something to make it stop, to help them.

There had to be a middle ground.

And there was. She had the solution.

"Hey, I've got an idea," she said, but neither her heartthrob husband nor his hellion niece heard her over their arguing.

She plucked two bonbons from the tray and threw one at the red-faced pop star, then lobbed the other at his firecracker of a niece.

"What the hell?" Landon barked.

"Yeah, why are you being a bonbon-wasting douche nozzle?" Aria exclaimed.

"Because I have the answer," she tossed back, ignoring the kid's excellent use of the naughty words.

"And what's that?" Landon asked, skepticism coating his question.

She straightened her posture, feeling like a damned genius. "We'll live in my house."

For a good ten seconds, neither Landon nor Aria made a peep.

"You want us to move in with you?" Landon asked.

She shrugged. "Why not? There's plenty of room."

"You live with your grandma, Harper," Aria shot back, but she wasn't clinging to the beam for dear life anymore.

"My grandmother is out of town for the next several weeks playing her harp with her old lady music friends in New Mexico."

Aria's scowl smoothed into a smirk. "Your grandma plays the harp?"

"She does, and she's really, really good. She used to play with the Denver Symphony Orchestra."

"Did she really?" Landon replied, losing the grouch in his tone.

"Yes, really."

"Wait a second," Aria said, swinging her legs. "Your name is Harper, and your grandma plays the harp."

"Yeah, what about it?"

The little girl laughed, and the sparkling sound filled the room. "But you play the piano," she answered, barely able to contain her giggles.

What was so funny about that?

"I don't get it, kid. Why are you laughing?"

"You're named after your grandma's harp, and you play the piano," the girl crooned, holding her belly. "Your name should be *Piano-er*, not *Harp-er*."

That didn't make sense, but she'd rather see the child smile than scowl. The kid continued cracking up, and her laughter was contagious. The heaviness that had swallowed the garage lifted, and she met her dare-match husband's gaze.

"Piano-er?" she repeated, unable to hold back a chuckle.

Landon shook his head, laughing as he ran his hands down his face. "It is kind of hilarious."

"You're my Nanny-Aunt, and your name should be Piano-er," Aria trilled, rocking with laughter.

"I've been called a lot of things, Aria. But you are the first to throw that at me." She turned to the keys and made up a little melody for her new moniker. "*I'm Harper, the nanny-aunt piano-er, and I...*"

"*Have a big hole in my sock*," Aria finished, giggling as she added to the silly song.

She stopped playing and looked down at her big toe peeking out from beneath a sea of electric orange. "You noticed that?"

The girl flashed a hardcore *duh* expression. "It's hard not to see it."

"It is a pretty big hole," Landon added with a smirk.

"You can give Harper the sock in your pocket, Uncle Landy."

The lacy doily strikes again!

Her black underpants peeked out of the man's pocket.

"It's a sock, right?" the kid pressed.

The color drained from Landon's face. "Um...it's a..."

"It's a fancy doily. It's not a sock," she supplied.

"Yes, that's what it is," Landon agreed, stuffing it down into his pocket.

Those damned underpants seemed to have a mind of their own.

And just like that, the mood shifted. She caught Landon's eye, and there it was—the camaraderie, the crazy connection, the invisible thread that drew them together. The man gifted her with the kind of smile that could make a gal forget her marriage was on a sixty-day timetable.

"What do you say, Aria?" she asked, sliding her gaze from her pop star to the child. "Want to bunk at my place? There's a bakery close to my house. I'll let you walk in by yourself and buy bonbons," she added.

"Harper," Landon said with a thread of growly amusement.

"What?" she balked. "I'd be right outside."

"I'm not talking about your proclivity to corrupt youth. Are you serious about us moving in with you?"

"I think it's a pretty good temporary fix, and you both win. Aria doesn't have to move into your house yet, and you get to be in Denver. You guys can live with me until my grandma gets back." She tapped her chin. "You can stay until a day before my grandma returns. I'll need time to clean up."

"I don't know," Landon mumbled.

"I live in Baxter Park. It's as close to Whitmore as Crystal Hills is."

Why was she so keen to have them move in?

"Whitmore, that's the school with that hot dog girl, isn't it?" Aria asked from her perch.

"Yeah, that girl's name is Phoebe."

"Who's the boy with the camera?"

Well, well, well.

"Oscar Elliott," she supplied.

"Oscar Elliott," Aria whispered. "Will he be in my class?"

Look at that. Miss Aria might have a crush brewing.

"Yes, and Sebastian, too. All our friends' kids are in the same class," she said, looking at Landon and hating how much she liked the way *our friends* sounded.

Landon held her gaze. "Yes, Aria will be in the same second-grade class with our friends' kids."

Did he like the way it sounded, too?

The pitter-patter of Aria drumming her fingers on the beam pulled her attention from Landon.

The child chewed her lip and tapped out a melody. She was considering the offer.

This might work.

Perhaps her mind was clouded by the copious amounts of sugar and cocoa she'd ingested over the past week, but she wanted this. She wanted to take these two home like she'd rescued a pair of stray cats.

And then she remembered what every kid loved.

She had the power to seal the deal.

"And I almost forgot. I've got something for you, Aria."

"For me?" the girl said, shimmying down from her perch.

She reached into her pocket and removed the piano eraser.

Aria gasped. "It's a tiny piano."

"It's a tiny piano *eraser*."

"Whoa," the girl breathed.

What was it with cool school supplies?

A wide smile cracked the kid's stony expression, and she turned to Landon. "We should move in with Harper, Uncle Landy."

"I'm not sure about that," the man replied.

"Well, I'm moving in with her. She's my nanny-aunt, and I pick her." Aria met her gaze. "Got any more erasers, Harper?"

"No, but I know where to get them." She remembered the look on the clerk's face. "You'll probably have to go in on your own, though."

Landon paced across the garage. "It's not that simple, Aria. You can't make this decision on your own."

She observed her heartthrob's tense posture. The guy wasn't angry—he was afraid.

Why would he be afraid? Did he have something to hide?

Aria lifted her chin. "Then I double-dog dare you to move into Harper's grandma's house, too, Uncle Landy."

Landon stopped. "What did you say?"

"I said I double-dog dare you," the child repeated.

Whoa.

The universe had been throwing quite a few double-dog dares their way.

Landon flicked his gaze from his niece and caught her eye. "I can't turn down a double-dog dare."

"No, you can't," she answered, going back to the moment they were double-dog dared the first time.

"I'm gonna tell Lolo and Lala we're moving to Harper's house," the child said with a whoop.

"But remember, Aria, it's not for forever. It's temporary," Landon bit out like it hurt to say the words.

And it hurt to hear them, but she plastered on a grin.

"You understand that, don't you, Aria?" he pressed.

The hint of a grin pulled at the corners of the kid's mouth. "Okay, if you say so," she chimed, then reached up and removed the Scrabble box from its dusty resting place.

"What are you doing with that?" he rasped, wide-eyed like he'd seen a ghost.

"It's where I hide my treasures and my candy."

Landon stared at the box. "It is?"

"You'd know if you ever came in here," Aria replied. "Uncle Landy doesn't like the garage. He must have come in for you, Harper."

"Is that so?" she asked, sneaking a look at her husband.

Aria nodded and zeroed in on the bonbons. She opened

the Scrabble box and dumped the chocolates in with the tiles. "I'm gonna go see Lolo and Lala."

"I'm not sure if they're back yet," Landon answered, looking like he'd been through the wringer, and OMG, was this what it was like raising a kid? She felt like she'd lived a hundred lives over the last twenty minutes.

"They're back," Aria answered smoothly as she placed the piano eraser on the tip of her slim pinky finger. "They peeked in while we were playing the piano, and you were playing your old guitar," she added, grabbing the loot-filled Scrabble box.

Why hadn't they come into the garage?

"I'll get my bag and meet you at the poop-colored car," the child called as she skipped away.

And then it was the two of them.

She crossed, then uncrossed her arms, fidgeting like she'd just downed a triple espresso. "Aria's a hurricane packed into the body of a little girl, isn't she?" she offered, unsure of what to say.

Landon didn't answer. He stared at the crates where the Scrabble box had rested. "Why are you doing this, Harper? Why did you invite us to live at your place?"

Great question.

She formulated a few answers.

He was doing her a favor by agreeing to participate in the reality bake show. Or she could tell him she wanted to help Aria get used to her new life, but that wasn't the complete truth.

She pegged him with her gaze. "Do you want the long answer or the short answer?"

"Short."

She shrugged. "I'm not really sure."

"Then what's the long answer?"

She smiled up at him. "I don't have a long answer. Nobody ever asks for the long answer."

He chuckled and stared into her eyes as if he were searching for answers.

"But I do know one thing," she added, her voice a scrape of a sound.

"And what's that, bonbon?"

"We got double-dog dared again. And we don't back down from those."

He took a step toward her. The fear in his eyes disappeared, and he drank her in just as he had seconds after he'd caught the bouquet. "No, we don't."

She released a shaky breath.

Baxter Park better brace itself. The nanny-aunt, the heart-throb, and a whole lot of pint-sized trouble were headed its way.

Chapter 15

HARPER

"Harper Barbara Presley, what did you do?" she lamented and paced in front of her bedroom door.

Her locked bedroom door.

Except she wasn't the one inside her room.

Nope, she'd been relegated to the hallway.

She stopped pacing and perked up as a series of sounds came from the other side of the door.

Bump.

Thump.

Creak.

What was going on in there?

She knocked on the door. "Everything all right, Aria? Do you need help with your pajamas? Because that's what you're supposed to be doing in there. Putting on pajamas. It's pj time," she crooned, channeling a game show announcer.

"I don't need any help," the child replied, followed by a cascade of muffled scrapes.

"You can't miss your jammies," she continued. "I laid them on the bed—on my bed—well, your bed for now. They're right there, waiting for you to put them on."

"I put on different pajamas. I can do it by myself. I'm not a baby, Harper."

"Yep, you're a seven-year-old who can unlock the door, and now would be a great time to do just that. It's the only way out," she added, then gasped.

Unless…

She pressed her ear to the door. "You haven't opened the window, have you, Aria?"

"No," the child answered through a clunk.

Was the kid going through her closet?

"And remember," she said, her voice doing that crazy opera thing. "I'll move my stuff out tomorrow. You don't need to help me out with that. You don't need to bother yourself with any boxes or storage containers or notebooks or photographs. Nothing is exciting in my room. All boring stuff. Not to mention, it's your first night here. You should get a good night's sleep."

"Harper?" Aria called.

"Yeah?" she answered, heart racing as she listened at the door, trying to figure out what Aria was up to.

"Is Uncle Landy back yet?"

She glanced down the stairs. "No, I don't think so."

Another creak and a crash emanated from the room.

"What was that?"

A pause.

"Nothing," Aria answered like she was absolutely up to something.

There was no use in getting worked up. When she was that age, she'd spent hours in the attic, sifting through old letters, funny hats, photographs, and keepsakes from her grandparents' travels.

If the kid had a curious streak, she might as well let her get her fill.

Slumping against the wall, she checked her watch. It was

nearly ten o'clock on what had become the longest day of her life.

The kid would have to conk out sooner or later, right?

She rubbed her temples. She might as well take a second to catch her breath.

The past couple of hours had flown by in a blur.

Before she and Landon had left Tomás and Bess's garage, Aria had found her grandparents and spilled the beans regarding the temporary living arrangement in Baxter Park. Landon's parents were all for it, congratulating them on coming up with such a smart compromise, and between the four of them, they had Aria's things loaded in the bonbon-colored Lambo lickity-split.

And just like that, with Aria buckled into her booster seat in the back, they were a party of three.

When they pulled up to her house, the kid asked if she could pick her bedroom.

It seemed like a reasonable request, and she figured Aria would choose one of the two guest rooms.

She hadn't.

When she and Landon made it upstairs, only one bedroom door was open—and it was the one to her bedroom.

Aria had kicked off her shoes and flopped in the center of the bed—her childhood bed. The kid had made herself at home in ten seconds flat. And, as if she were a member of the royal family, the girl requested her Scrabble board game box be brought to *her* new room. Landon complied, and they looked on as the kid snacked on the stolen bonbons surrounded by pillows like a true lady of leisure.

That's when Landon excused himself to grab a few things from his place to get him through the night. The minute the door slammed, Aria asked if she could have a video call with Bess and Tomás to show them her new room. This turned out to be a godsend. She'd hit maximum hobo smell status and desperately needed a shower. She'd set the kid up with her phone, grabbed a pair of jean shorts and a tank top, then booked it to the bathroom to decontaminate under the hot spray. She'd barely zipped her fly when Her Majesty, Aria Queen of the Bonbons, knocked on the bathroom door and requested a bath.

Squeaky clean and wrapped in a fluffy white towel, the child had sprinted out of the bathroom, crossed the hallway, and was holed up behind a locked door in *her* new bedroom.

That kid could really move when she wanted to.

And now, she found herself locked out and listening to what sounded more like a family of raccoons ransacking the place rather than a little girl preparing for bed. She rolled her head from side to side to work out the kinks when Aria called to her.

"Are you still there, Harper?"

"I am. I'm waiting for you to open the door."

"Why do you have so many pictures of Uncle Landy?"

Oh shit!

The kid had found the box.

Her Landon Paige Heartthrob Warfare memorabilia box.

She peeled her body from the wall and bumped her head against the solid door, silently berating herself.

Move in with me until my grandma gets back.

It'll be great.

Let's cohabitate ASAP.

Here's the thing.

She didn't regret inviting Aria and Landon to move in with her, but what she hadn't considered was the state of the house. Not the cleanliness. The home itself was in great shape. Babs was a stickler for keeping the place spick-and-span. But she'd forgotten that her childhood bedroom contained some pretty embarrassing stuff, especially when it came to Landon.

"Are you dressed, Aria? Can I come in? I can help you

clean up. It sounds like you're really getting acquainted with your new room," she said, hoping if she ignored the question about the Landon pics, the kid wouldn't notice.

Her question was met with another crash.

Giving up, she resumed bumping her head against the door when a voice cut short her head banging session.

"Is there a problem?"

She shrieked and spun around to find Landon at the bottom of the steps peering up at her.

Had the man watched her knock her noggin against the door like she'd lost her marbles?

What did it matter at this point?

He'd already seen her lose her shit over eight cents and steal a tray of bonbons while dressed as a disheveled hobo. A little nightly headbanging had to be par for the course.

She rubbed her forehead. "I didn't hear you get back."

He started up the stairs with a duffel bag slung over his shoulder. "You changed?"

"Yeah, I thought I'd throw your shirt in the laundry—where clothes are washed."

OMG! Was she having a stroke, or had she totally lost her mind?

"Is Aria okay?" he asked.

"I think so. I gave her a bath, and now she's supposed to be putting on her pajamas."

"She locked herself in?" he asked as a sharp *thunk* came from her room.

They zipped to the door.

"Aria, what are you doing in there?" Landon called, trying the doorknob. "Are you hurt?"

The pitter-patter of feet rippled from the other side, followed by the click of the lock disengaging. The hinges whined as the door opened a few inches, and Aria peeked out.

"What happened in there?" Landon pressed.

"Uncle Landy, you've got to see this," the girl replied, awe coating her words as she opened the door.

But before they could set foot in the room, the child's attire rendered them slack-jawed.

"What are you wearing, Aria? Is that Harper's..." Landon stammered.

Oh dear!

"Yep," she answered, taking in the beaming child. "It's what you think it is."

The kid had not only raided her closet, the little snoop had rifled through her bottom dresser drawer reserved for Bonbon Barbie's attire.

But that wasn't the only eye-catching piece of her pj ensemble.

The top portion of her sleeping attire had come from the Landon Paige box. The child sported a T-shirt with Landon's face plastered across the front.

"I found a hair clip to make the tutu fit around my belly," Aria announced as she lifted the hem of the Landon Paige T-shirt to reveal the cinched waistline.

But the outfit was nothing compared to the foreboding pile in the center of the room. Empty boxes and plastic crates sat empty around the perimeter. Journals, pictures, and posters littered the center of the bedroom. Aria had dragged every box and storage container out of her closet, and as she'd suspected, the kid had gone to town, sifting through the items.

Remain calm. It can't be that bad.

It had been years since she'd looked inside those boxes. Sure, a few contained Heartthrob Warfare memorabilia, but perhaps there wasn't that much stuff. There was a good chance most of the keepsakes were school items like yearbooks and art projects.

She approached the pile like a soldier advancing on the enemy, and her worst nightmare became a reality.

There weren't any self-portraits or lopsided clay bowls. No glitter Valentines or hand-print Thanksgiving turkeys.

Nope, just a shit-ton of Heartthrob Warfare mementos piled in the center of her room like she was trying out for the Heartthrob Warfare edition of Hoarders.

This was not good.

"Wow, Aria, you've been busy," she said, doing the stupid octave thing. She was going for nonchalance but sounded more like a third grader playing the dreaded recorder.

"And your pajamas are…" Landon said, looking downright gobsmacked.

That made two of them.

"They're awesome," the child whooped, then spun like a deranged Landon-Paige-obsessed bonbon ballerina.

She stopped spinning in front of the pile. "There are like a million pictures of you, Uncle Landy. Look," the kid replied, then plucked a notebook from the floor. With *Harper Presley, age thirteen,* scribbled across the front, she knew exactly what the kid had found.

Her heart hammered away as hope of retaining a shred of dignity evaporated.

"That's junk. We should put it away. No, we should burn it. We could make a fire in the backyard," she blathered as Aria turned to the page with a photograph pasted onto the lined paper.

Landon leaned in to get a better look. "That's a picture of me and…" The man trailed off, and she could hear the amusement in his tone. He knew exactly what he was looking at.

This was worse than humiliating.

It was like having a dream where you're walking around naked and everyone is staring and laughing. She pinched herself. This was no dream. This epic humiliation was the real deal.

She had two choices.

The first was to grab the Scrabble box, steal what was left of the pilfered bonbons, run for the hills, and never stop.

Or she could own it and move on.

A badass bitch would choose number two.

She cleared her throat. "It's a picture of your uncle and some airhead model from a long time ago. I cut off her head and pasted mine in as an act of charity."

There, that wasn't so bad.

"An act of charity?" her pop star heartthrob echoed, enjoying this way too much.

This wasn't bad. It was awful—awful to the six thousandth power.

Heat rose to her cheeks as she scowled at her thirteen-year-old self, rocking a mouthful of metal and enough rouge and emerald-green eye shadow to put a circus clown to shame. But there was a perfectly good explanation. Well, perfectly good might be pushing it. There was an explanation.

"I borrowed my grandmother's makeup on picture day and put it on in the closet so she wouldn't see what I was doing. It was dark in there, and I might have overdone it."

Landon pegged her with his laughing brown eyes. "Might have?"

"You did that to your face on purpose?" Aria asked.

These two.

If they hadn't looked so adorable sporting the same what-the-hell expression, she might have pegged them with a few bonbons.

But she couldn't get too angry with them. They weren't wrong.

The picture was terrifying.

She glanced at the window. Stupid two-story home. If she jumped, she was sure to bust her ankle.

"I had no idea you were such a huge fan," Landon commented, biting back a grin.

"A fan of green eyeshadow and old lady rouge?" she tossed back.

"Of Heartthrob Warfare," he answered, his expression softening.

"She's a huge fan, Uncle Landy, like that lady who sewed your head onto a pillow," Aria blurted.

"She's seen the pillow?"

"I've got the pillow," Aria said and skipped to one of her suitcases.

"You gave her that thing?"

"She liked it," he answered with a shrug.

Aria yanked the pillow from her bag and held it up.

Landon reared back. "What did you do to it?"

The child admired her handiwork. "I gave you devil horns and cat whiskers with a marker. Sorry, Uncle Landy, I did it when I was mad about having to live in your house."

"I love it, Aria," she gushed, laying it on a bit thick before sealing her lips to stop from laughing her ass off.

But her respite from being called out as Landon's biggest fan ended when Aria tossed the pillow onto the bed and took her uncle's hand. She walked him around the pile of her childhood Landon Paige memorabilia collection that, from this day forward, would be known as the heap of complete and total mortification. "Forget the pillow. There are so many pictures of you in Harper's boxes," the child continued. "And the ones with girls in them either have their heads scratched out or have Harper's scary face taped on top."

Dear universe, a tsunami has never struck landlocked Colorado, but feel free to send one over right this very second to wash away the city of Denver.

She didn't dare look at Landon. Faced with the evidence strewn about the floor, there was no way to hide the truth.

"Look," Aria called. "Here's something that doesn't have Uncle Landy on it."

Thank God!

"It's a notebook with a picture of four girls on the front," the child added, then held it up. "Is that you, Harper?"

She grinned at the photo and accepted the notebook. Blessedly, she didn't look like the tween version of Tammy Faye Bakker in this one. "That's me and my friends, Charlotte, Penny, and Libby when we were in fourth or fifth grade," she answered, grateful the kid had found something without Landon's symmetrically perfect face plastered to it. She opened the notebook and cringed as the urge to throw herself out the window returned.

"Can you read what it says on the inside?" Aria asked, staring at the page.

"They're names of songs I wrote when I was a little girl."

"What are the titles?"

Her cheeks might as well have been on fire. "There are three songs," she began, tossing a glance at Landon. "The first is titled 'Charlotte's Dad Sucks.' The next is 'Penny's Sisters Can Suck a Dozen Eggs,' and the last song is called 'Libby Lamb, Stop Chasing Butterflies and Suck on a Lollipop.'"

Landon and Aria stared at her with their heads cocked to the side.

She flicked her gaze from the pair and studied a doodle she'd drawn of Penny's older twin sisters looking quite uncomfortable with eggs jammed into their mouths. "I dealt with a lot of negative emotions through song."

"And sucking," Landon muttered. The man's eyes watered as he pressed his lips into a tight line. Now her stupid heartthrob husband was the one who looked ready to explode with laughter.

But Aria wasn't laughing. She studied the page, then ran her fingertips across a line. "How did you make each line a different color? Did you use a highlighter?"

"That's exactly what I did. It helped my brain to do it that way," she answered, taking in the stripes of color. The neon highlighter had faded to a rainbow array of pastels.

"You highlighted the lines in a book, too," the little girl said, fishing a copy of one of the *Baby-Sitters' Club* books from the bottom of the pile.

"I forgot I still had these. My friends and I loved these books." She opened to a random page and took in another set of faded rainbow lines.

Aria came up next to her and scanned the page of text. "The color keeps the letters from jumping around all over the place."

She stared at the little girl. "What did you say?"

"The letters usually move when I look at them. But they're not so wiggly with the color. Can I see your notebook again?"

"Sure."

Aria opened to the first song and traced a line of text. "Penny's…sisters…are not…nice. They smell like…they live with a…family of…mice." She looked up. "Is that right?"

Aria had read them perfectly.

"It is."

The child beamed and set the notebook on the bed. "Sometimes, the letters flip around or parts of them break-away, but it's different with the color on top of the words."

Could Aria be a neurodivergent learner like her?

"The letters used to do that to me, too," she confessed.

"They did?" Aria exclaimed, wide-eyed.

"Yeah, words in books and musical notes. Musical notes used to be really tricky for me."

Aria nodded. "That's why I hate school and especially hate music class. I can play anything I hear on the piano. I used to play with Mommy before…" The child glanced at Landon, then trained her gaze on the notebook. "Anyway, at school, the teacher makes you practice writing the notes on paper and makes you look at them on the board. I can't do it. It's so easy for the other kids. That's why I had to punch Jason Huber when I was in first grade at my old school."

"Was he mean to you?" she asked, taking a knee to be at the girl's level.

Aria twisted the tutu's brown tulle. "He made me so, so mad. First, he laughed at me when I couldn't read the morning message on the board in the classroom, and then he called me stupid head when I couldn't name the notes my music teacher wrote on the staff where music goes. So I got up in the middle of class and punched him right in his belly. He fell on the floor and started crying like a big old baby," she finished, lifting her little chin.

The little brawler.

"And then you had to go to the principal's office, and the school called your grandparents and me," Landon added. His countenance had done a one-eighty. His laughing eyes darkened. And she had a feeling Aria's behavioral issues at school weren't the only thing weighing heavily on his heart.

"Yeah, I got in big trouble," Aria admitted, casting her eyes to the ground. "And they made me say sorry to stupid Jason Huber."

Poor thing.

She could sympathize. She'd pummeled her fair share of crummy kids who'd made fun of her or her friends. "You know what, Aria?"

"What?" the child asked, dragging her toes over the edge of the rug.

"Jason Huber sure sounds like a giant douche nozzle to me."

The girl stopped messing with the rug, and a mischievous twinkle glinted in her eyes.

Oh yeah, she'd dropped the douche nozzle, and Aria was there for it.

She feigned mock embarrassment. "I mean, I should say

that he sounds like a," she began, then tapped her foot three times and whispered, "douche nozzle."

It was seriously the best word for describing...well, douche nozzles.

"He's the king of the," Aria replied and knocked out three foot taps.

She smiled at the little scrapper, who also appeared to be a neurodivergent learner, just like the people she taught online.

Did Landon know? Did her old school know, or did they chalk up her troubles to a bad attitude?

The little girl retrieved the notebook and pored over the page. "Maybe I have rainbow reader eyes. Maybe the rainbows calm the letters down and keep them in their place."

"Rainbow reader eyes? I like that, but it might be something different called neuro—"

"It's getting late," Landon blurted, cutting her off. His muted expression had given way to a simmering fury. His eyes burned with it as he stared at the mess of empty boxes, papers, and notebooks. "Let's clean up and get you into bed. It's been a long day."

But she couldn't allow the man to cut short her conversation with Aria.

"Hold on. I want to show one last thing to Aria. It won't take long."

She took the girl's hand and brought her to the wall next to her desk. Her grandfather had installed a floor-to-ceiling magnetic whiteboard. This was where Babs had taught her to read music. Day after day, they'd practiced here, among her trinkets and treasures, using a set of multi-colored circular magnets. And now, this was where Bonbon Barbie taught when she wasn't stuck in her car in the Vegas heat waiting to be rejected from a porn contest.

She gathered a handful of magnets from her desk drawer,

then drew a makeshift musical staff with a curvy treble clef. "Do you know the names of the notes that go on each line?"

Aria's shoulders slumped. "My music teacher told us to say *every good boy does fine* to remember *E, G, B, D,* and *F.* But not every boy does fine. Jason Huber is super-duper terrible. He's the opposite of fine."

"I agree," Harper said, then pointed to the lines. "I use a different one. *Exceptional girls bake delicious fudge.* Who doesn't like fudge? It's the number two most delicious treat after bonbons." She thought the kid would get a kick out of her girl power acronym, but she didn't.

Aria shrugged. "I like that better because it's about girls, but the notes will still move around. And I don't like the notes, anyways. I can play anything I hear like my—"

"Aria," Landon cautioned.

What was up with him? She tried to read the guy. Was it anger? Was he tired?

"I need two more minutes," she said to her scowling husband, then turned to the child. "If the colored lines helped you read the song about Penny's stinky sisters, the colored magnets might help the notes stay in one spot."

Aria had to be a neurodivergent learner. Their similarities were too close to ignore.

She placed five magnets on different spots on the staff, then tapped the board. "Tell me the names of the notes," she prompted.

Aria concentrated. "Girl, delicious, fudge, exceptional, delicious. G, D, F, E, D?"

She got it.

"That is correct."

"Do I get fudge?" the kid asked, perking up.

"No," Landon answered, stepping in. "You get to clean up. And then you get to go to bed."

Why was he acting like a killjoy? Yes, it was late, but the kid just had a breakthrough.

"We can do more with your rainbow eyes tomorrow," she said, tossing another look at her sullen heartthrob. "Your uncle is right. It's getting late."

"Okay," the child murmured.

Despite Landon's cool reception, a spark had ignited within Aria.

And how did she know that?

When she was Aria's age, once her grandmother had shared these strategies, what Aria called using her rainbow eyes, making music and reading went from being a tedious chore to opening a world without limits.

The child skipped across the room and swiped the notebook off the bed. As she went to toss it into a box, the pages fluttered open, and a photo drifted to the floor. Aria picked it up and frowned. "Who's that guy with you?" she griped and held out the picture.

"It's Vance," she whispered. The image shattered the excitement welling within her. Just seeing her stupid smiling face next to his turned her stomach.

And what was it doing here?

She'd gone out of her way to feed every trace of the man to the paper shredder years ago.

"Was he your boyfriend, Harper?" the kid pressed.

Her boyfriend and her biggest mistake.

She swallowed past the lump in her throat. She could feel Landon's gaze.

Just play it cool.

"He was. But he wasn't a nice guy. He took something from me."

"Was he a…?" the child asked and tapped her foot three times.

"Yep," she replied, keeping her response short.

The last thing she wanted to do was discuss Vance.

Aria's gaze bounced between the photo and Landon. "Now you have Uncle Landy, and he's not a douche nozzle."

"Aria," Landon chided.

"I mean…" the kid said, then tapped her foot. "That's how it works, isn't it, Harper? I just have to tap it?"

She manufactured a grin. "Right, again."

Aria handed her the photo, then returned to the pile.

Her hand shook as she studied the image, hating how one photograph could usher in a flood of crushing emotions.

You're not that girl anymore. You're smarter. You keep your guard up. And you've sworn off musicians—except for the current marriage of convenience situation.

"I can take care of that for you," Landon said in a husky rasp.

Without thinking, she handed him the picture.

Why had she done that?

Did she want his help when it came to Vance?

Then again, there was no love lost between her pop star and the pop douche nozzle.

He'd probably just throw it out.

For the love of Christ! He simply offered to throw something away. Stop making a mountain out of a molehill.

She might be married to Landon, but she couldn't let the guy into her heart.

This was a business arrangement. She couldn't blur the lines with this man.

But she still had to be mindful of the promise she'd made to Mitzi.

And she would be.

She could help Landon and Aria transition into living together. Hell, she already had them under the same roof—her roof, well, Babs' roof, but it was a roof they were under and not yelling at each other.

But there was more, and it was the kind of more that made her want to look at that line and blur and blur and blur until she couldn't blur anymore.

She couldn't forget Mitzi's face when the woman said she hadn't seen Landon smile like he had in their wedding video.

As a Landon Paige fan on the down-low since she was a tween, she'd perused hundreds, possibly thousands of pictures of the man. She'd seen him smile in print and on TV. But she'd never seen the smile he flashed when he'd caught the bouquet and stared into her eyes. That dazzler of a grin was all for her.

At least, that's how it had felt.

"What are these for?" Aria asked, snapping her back from Lala Landon Land.

"What are you talking about?" she stammered.

Aria removed a hand-held video camera and a couple of old cell phones from the bottom of the heap.

She'd forgotten about those items.

She blinked, regaining her bearings. "I used to film myself when I was working on my music. Those probably have old recordings on them, but they're pretty much junk now."

"Can I play with them?" Aria asked, eyeing the old tech.

"Sure, if you can get them to work. The chargers should be—"

"I found them," the child answered, pulling a plastic bag teeming with white and black adapters and cords from the pile.

Aria retreated to the bed with the outdated electronics as she and Landon scooped up the remnants of her life and dumped the contents into the boxes and tubs. They worked in a strained silence. The guy had something on his mind. Sure, their day had been bonkers, but something gnawed at the man. She could feel it. But she couldn't allow the guy to brush off her breakthrough with his niece. Aria was a neurodivergent learner, and the sooner her primary caregiver understood that, the better.

And speaking of Aria. It had gotten awfully quiet. She glanced at the bed, and a warmth filled her chest.

She tapped Landon's shoulder. "Look at Aria," she whispered, gesturing with her chin toward the sleeping child sprawled across the comforter.

"She's always been a good sleeper. Leighton and Trey used to say…" he began, then stopped speaking and returned his attention to the boxes.

She felt for him. It couldn't be easy losing his sister and his best friend so suddenly. And she knew a thing or two about loss.

With the mess tidied up, they made their way to the bed. Aria's damp, dark hair spread across the pillow. The kid clutched the tiny piano eraser in one hand and an old adapter cord in the other.

Score another point for cute school supplies.

Landon removed the items from her grip and set them on the bedside table as she cleared away the camera and the dead cell phones.

"I'll pick her up if you could get the—"

"—blankets," she supplied, springing into action.

Gingerly, he lifted his niece in his arms. "Hey, little sack of potatoes, let's get you tucked in," he whispered as Aria rested her head in the crook of his neck.

Little sack of potatoes.

She couldn't stop herself from drinking in the scene.

He wasn't half-bad at this uncle business. He loved the kid. There was no denying it.

He caught her watching and smiled, but the grin didn't reach his eyes.

And again, she sensed fear. What was Landon afraid of? Was he worried about raising a child? No, it was more, and she had a feeling it had to do with how Aria's mind worked.

"Harper, the blankets."

"Yeah, right, sorry," she whispered. She pulled down the covers, and Landon slipped the sleeping child between them.

"Sing the Aria ABC song, Uncle Landy," the little girl murmured as she rubbed the back of her wrist across her forehead.

"It's late, little one."

"Just do *A*, *B*, and *C*," she mumbled, then rolled onto her side.

He sat on the edge of the bed. "A is for Aria," he sang softly.

OMG, the man was singing.

His smooth voice had her heart ready to burst.

"B is for butterscotch, C is for…" he trailed off, but she knew what should come next.

"Candy in a jar," she sang, joining him on the edge of the bed. She smoothed a few strands of the little girl's hair and tucked them behind her ear, then looked up and caught Landon watching her.

He devoured her with his gaze as if he were peering at forbidden fruit. Her breath caught in her throat, and she couldn't look away. Here, in her childhood bedroom where she'd pined over the pop star, it was surreal to think that he was her husband and they were in charge of not ruining a kid—at least for the next sixty days.

"Night, Uncle Landy. Night-night, Nanny Aunt Harper."

Nanny Aunt Harper?

That's who she was. Aria wasn't wrong.

She slid her gaze from Landon and concentrated on the little girl. "Sleep tight, little sack of potatoes."

A fierce need to protect the child flowed through her veins, and a realization hit.

She needed Landon to help her win the *Celebrity Bake or Bust* cash, but maybe he needed her, too.

No, he did need her.

She could help Aria like her grandmother had helped her. She'd use her Bonbon Barbie skills and help his niece.

Landon stood, picked up the Scrabble box, and headed for the door. "I need to work on my music."

Work on his music? Now?

Irritation prickled in her chest. She stroked Aria's cheek, then followed the man into the hallway. The guy had morphed from a pop star into a speed walker. Before she could say anything, he started down the stairs. The rattling Scrabble squares and loose bonbons punctuated the sound of his hasty departure.

"I'd like to speak with you, Landon," she said…to his back.

"I need to get my guitar. It's still in the car," he mumbled as he set the board game box on the kitchen table, then headed out the back door.

She wasn't about to put up with anyone, not even her pop star husband, acting like a haughty douche nozzle.

She stood at the door and watched as he removed the instrument case from the car.

He slammed the hatch, then grumbled back into the house, turning his hardened gaze toward anything but her.

One minute, he looked at her like she made up his world, and the next, he was as cold as ice.

He went into the living room, set his case on the couch, then removed his guitar.

"I need to talk to you about Aria. I can help her."

He looked up. "There's nothing wrong with her," he snarled.

This infuriating man.

"I agree," she shot back. "I'm not saying there is."

He strummed the guitar and frowned. "Then there's nothing to help her with."

Was he blind?

"You were right there, Landon. You heard Aria talk about

letters and musical notes wiggling and moving on the page. You saw her read the notes when I used colored magnets. She was able to read a line of text thanks to the highlighter."

"So?"

She pinned him with her gaze and turned up the Harper Presley sass. "So," she hissed, "your niece is a neurodivergent thinker. It's how her brain works and how she interacts with the world. There's no right or wrong. There's only finding what works and what brings her success. You want her to be successful, don't you?"

He fiddled with the guitar's tuning pegs. "The school says she has trouble with reading and behavioral issues because of the trauma of losing her parents. They didn't say anything about being a neuro-whatever."

She was ready to yank that guitar out of his hands and hit him upside the head with it.

She gathered herself. "The term is 'neurodivergent learner.' And if you love Aria, you'll let me help her, and let me show you how to help her, too. She doesn't have to be frustrated. She can thrive with the right tools."

"She'll be fine. She's a tough kid. If you haven't noticed, she can play anything she hears on the piano. She's also not half bad on the guitar either, and she's never taken a lesson."

He wasn't listening.

"I'm not denying or discounting that. I was with her in the garage. She's a musical prodigy, for sure, but she's also hurting. And she doesn't have to. She doesn't have to struggle or hide who she is."

"That's easy for you to say," he bit out, his words dripping with bitterness. "How many people scrutinize your every move?"

And then it came together.

Aria had mentioned she and Landon didn't like writing things down.

Landon hadn't put out any new tracks since Heartthrob Warfare took a break years ago.

And even with everything on the line, the man still hadn't written anything new for Red Rocks Unplugged.

"This isn't only about Aria, is it?" she pressed, studying her scowling husband.

The man didn't say a word. Not a single solitary sound passed his lips.

If he thought that playing the part of the aloof pop star would deter her, he was about to receive a rude awakening.

"Maybe you'll respond to this, *heartthrob*."

"And what's that, *bonbon*?" he snarled.

He wasn't softening her up with that smart-ass retort.

It was time to hit him with a zinger.

She looked him square in the eyes. "I know what you're hiding."

Chapter 16

LANDON

Was he breathing?

Where had the oxygen gone? And why was it so goddamned hot in this house?

His mind raced.

His throat grew dry.

It was as if the ground beneath his feet was about to give way.

He struggled to steady himself.

Calm the hell down.

She couldn't know what he was hiding. She was grasping at straws to get under his skin.

That was a lie.

Harper wasn't attacking him for the hell of it.

Sure, fury welled in her hazel eyes. He'd stormed off like a giant douche nozzle. That alone would have set off his firecracker of a wife.

But this was different.

She'd put it together. She'd figured out the truth. He'd feared this from the first time he'd laid eyes on her. If anyone could see into his soul, it would be her.

Behind the sass, the attitude, and the general air of complete Harper Presley insanity, empathy and a deep compassion lived in her heart.

And that emotion came to life through music.

After he'd searched the trail for his niece and doubled back, he'd heard the rise and fall of the notes dancing in the air as he approached the garage. There was no way to fight it. The melody had called to him.

And then two voices accompanied the tune.

Hearing Aria sing with Harper had eased the twisting anxiety that drained his creativity and left him a husk of a man. And just like on their wedding night, when they'd agreed to make every reckless choice and throw caution to the wind, a lightness had taken over. A euphoric bliss captured him and drove him to grab his old guitar and join them.

It was the first time he'd heard Aria sing since Trey and Leighton's passing. Despite clamming up the minute he coaxed her to continue, her spark had returned—even if it was only a brief flicker. The whole moment felt surreal like he straddled two worlds. One with Harper and Aria and the second with his sister and best friend. It was as if Trey and Leighton were with them in the garage. Their spirits were woven within the notes.

And that sense of belonging had lulled him into an unfamiliar contentment.

He'd never pictured himself living with anyone. Still, with Aria's spirits lifted and as Harper his wife, at least for the time being, he'd figured, what the hell. It was better than carrying a kicking and screaming Aria into his Crystal Hills mansion. Still, a more compliant and upbeat niece wasn't the only reason a sense of calm had washed over him when Harper had pointed to a welcoming two-story house with blond brick and a shady oak in the front yard and announced they were home.

Home.

He could try to deny it, but a part of him wanted to be

with her, wanted to play house, wanted to know she was close by. For the first time in a long time, he wouldn't be alone, and the part of him that craved connection couldn't help but see the Baxter Park living situation as a kind of respite.

But Harper was no fool.

That woman saw everything—or maybe he just couldn't hide from her.

Here's the thing. He understood Harper's impulse to help.

But that kind of shit would only draw more attention to Aria.

And to him.

A knot twisted in his belly as the shame that had been with him from the moment he realized he was different gathered around him like an invisible cloud, thick and weighty with fear and loathing. Like a boulder chained to his ankle, this emotion had the power to drag him into the depths of anguish and leave him gasping for air in a sea of self-loathing.

Do learning disabilities run in your family, Mr. Paige?

He could hear Aria's former principal asking the question.

And what had he done?

He'd lied.

He told himself he'd done it for Aria. But that wasn't the whole truth.

"You and Aria are similar, aren't you?" Harper pressed, yanking him from his spiraling thoughts. The venom in her tone had dissipated, and he wasn't sure what angered him more, her kindness or her boldness. When she was dishing out barbs, it was because she knew he could take it. This softening in her demeanor reeked of pity. And he sure as hell wasn't about to stand for that.

"Aria and I can play anything we hear by ear. If that's what you're asking about, then yeah, we're very much alike. My sister had the same gift."

His wife watched him like a hawk. "Did your sister have trouble reading, writing, or composing music?"

His pulse kicked up. "What does that matter?"

"My guess is that she didn't. I think she helped you get through school. And with Heartthrob Warfare, I have a feeling you brought the creativity, the lyrics, and the vision for the sound, but your sister, and probably Trey, too, pulled it together."

How the hell could she know that?

"I'm right, aren't I? You're a neurodivergent learner, and I'd bet my piano that you still struggle." She rested her hand on the shiny black Steinway in the corner of the living room like she was begging for him to try to deny it.

Struggle?

His life was the definition of struggle. Every damned day was a battle to conceal his shortcomings and fit in.

And it was exhausting.

This was why he didn't let anyone in.

This was why he had to keep his guard up.

He wanted to kick himself for thinking his time in her house would be a fairy-tale respite.

He schooled his features. With his defenses in place, he set down his guitar and crossed his arms. "What do you want me to say, Harper?"

"Try the truth?"

"The truth?" He huffed and shook his head.

"Yes, the truth. Do you have something against it?"

Hell yes, he did. But she had no right to lecture him on the truth.

"Let's talk about *you* living your truth," he remarked, walking past her as he sauntered into the kitchen. He shoved his hands in his pockets and felt Harper's panties in one and that damned picture he'd promised to dispose of in the other. A fresh jolt of snarling anger flooded his system.

"Go ahead. Let's hear what you think my truth is," she snapped, hot on his heels as she reverted to her feisty ways.

Good, this brush with vulnerability had him itching for a fight.

"Then you won't mind telling me what you've written since your split with Vance."

The thought of that prick being anywhere near her made him want to pound the guy into oblivion, but he kept his cool. This wasn't about the pop poser stealing her songs. It was about what she'd done after tragedy struck. And from the looks of it, she wasn't much different from him.

Anger burned in her eyes.

He'd hit a nerve.

Harper inhaled a fierce breath like she was gearing up to spew fire, but she didn't make a sound.

Was he playing dirty? You bet your ass he was.

He was in over his head, and if he was going under, so was she.

He paced the length of the kitchen and caught sight of a framed photo. A young girl, who couldn't have been much older than Aria, stood with two older adults. It had to be Harper and her grandparents. He concentrated on her grandmother—the woman on the brink of losing her home, the woman who'd left for a musicians' retreat.

A musicians' retreat?

It seemed like a strange choice to take off with her home on the line.

Unless the woman didn't know she was on the brink of losing it.

Christ, that was it.

That would explain why Harper had been so adamant about participating in the reality baking bullshit.

There was his ammunition.

If she could make assumptions about him, he could turn it around and question her motives.

"*I'm guessing*," he began, borrowing her words, "you haven't written anything. But let's put that aside for a sec and talk about the *Celebrity Bake or Bust.*"

She shrugged, trying to play it cool, but the unease in her chameleon eyes gave her away.

"You need cash, and you need it fast. You won't accept anything from your friends or me," he continued, circling her like a dogged detective interrogating a witness.

She tracked his movements. "Yeah, we've established that. So what?"

He leaned against the fridge and glanced at the photo. "What does your grandmother think?"

She went to the sink and picked up a dishcloth. She folded it once, then twice.

He had her on the defense.

"What do you mean?" she tossed back, taking another pass at folding the cloth.

"What happens if we don't win, *bonbon*?" he purred.

She abandoned the cloth and closed the distance between them. "We have to win."

"Does your grandmother know that her home is hanging in the balance?"

Harper's cheeks burned crimson.

"Look at that. I'm a mind reader, too," he barked.

She lifted her chin as defiance glinted in her eyes. "She knows there's an issue with the bank, but I told her I'd handle it. I don't want her to worry."

"So, you've hidden it from her and lied about the severity of the situation," he tossed back, raising an eyebrow.

"No, heartthrob, I'm *handling* it," she repeated, lowering her voice as she pressed onto her tiptoes and glared at him.

He leaned in. "It looks more like you're flailing." That was a shitty comment, but she had to see that he wasn't the only one who wanted to keep certain realities private.

He'd expected her to erupt into a verbal tirade, but that's not what he got. Instead, she smiled up at him like the cat who ate the canary.

What did she have up her sleeve?

"You'd know a thing or two about flailing, wouldn't you, Mr. Pop Star?" she crooned.

This woman was crafty as hell. He'd be wise to walk away and do whatever it took to end this conversation.

But he didn't. The buzz that took over when they were going at each other was too hard to resist.

He shifted his stance. "What is that supposed to mean?"

"You've been flailing for years," she tossed out, taking her turn to saunter around the room like a shark circling. "Your sister and Trey disappeared from the pop scene to raise Aria. She's seven. That means, for over seven years, you haven't made any new music."

It was actually longer, but he wasn't about to cop to that. "It's complicated."

"Oh yeah? Did they tell you that you couldn't write while they took a break to raise their little girl?"

Shit. "No."

"Would they have stopped you if you had?"

Double shit. "No."

"Then why didn't you? Why didn't you keep doing what you loved? You clearly had the vision and the time. You weren't raising a child. I remember seeing you splashed over the internet, dating a string of bubble-headed models. What's your truth, heartthrob? What kept you from making music?"

"Ladies first. What's your reason?" he shot back, deflecting her attack.

"You really want to know my truth?" she snapped.

"I wouldn't have asked if I didn't."

She nodded like she was harnessing her strength. "I haven't written anything since Vance broke my heart. You've got me there. And you're right about my grandma. I've kept her in the dark about the house because I love her. She's the only family I've got, and I'll do whatever it takes to save her home and give her peace of mind. I owe it to her."

Harper's eyes glittered with anguish, and his snarling energy shifted in the blink of an eye. The desire to go tit for tat with this woman disappeared.

He flicked his gaze to the framed photos. "I'm sorry. I shouldn't have come at you like that." He gestured to the pictures. "I get that you want to help your grandmother. Your grandparents took you in after your parents passed away, right?"

"What?" she breathed.

"I overheard you tell Aria that your parents had died. I figured that's why they raised you."

"Yes and no," she answered, her voice taking on a sharp edge. "When I was five, my mom and dad were very much alive when they handed me an envelope and a granola bar, then dumped me on my grandparents' porch."

"Where did they go?"

"They were musicians, and they took off with their band. I still remember when my grandparents got to the house and found me sitting on the porch steps. They were shocked to find me. It was a Saturday night, and they'd had a performance. I'd been there for hours. It had to be close to ten. They brought me inside and gave me a warm glass of milk. After that, a box of bonbons mysteriously appeared, and then they opened the envelope."

She'd lost the *I'm about to kick you in the balls* vibe.

"What was inside the envelope? Was it a note saying when they'd be back to get you?"

A muscle ticked in her jaw. "It was my birth certificate and my social security card."

He felt like an ass. "Harper, I'm sorry."

She returned to the dish towel. "A few days later, a police officer came to the house. He told us that the van my parents were traveling in had lost control and that they'd died when it jumped a guardrail." She stilled. "All I remember about that day is the officer at the door and then my grandparents taking me down to the bakery to get bonbons. It was a big deal to get treats again, since we'd also had bonbons the night I arrived."

"Is that when the bonbon infatuation started?" he asked, softening his tone. He hoped she'd see he was trying to make peace.

"It became our thing. It was a little escape. We'd walk to the shop and make up silly songs." She smiled like she'd slipped back in time. "My grandparents rearranged their lives to raise me. So you see, I owe it to my grandmother to save this house. They bought this place the day after they got married. My grandad wouldn't want her to lose it. And I'm here to make sure she doesn't."

She hid the pain so well.

She lifted her chin and captured him with her shining chameleon eyes. "Now you know my truth, heartthrob. What's yours? Why haven't you written anything? I've told you my secrets. I want to hear it from you. I dare you to tell me. No," she continued, narrowing her gaze, "I double-dog dare you."

Chapter 17
LANDON

Another double-dog dare.

His pulse hammered. His mouth grew dry.

Unable to stop himself, he cupped her face in his hands.

Was she trembling?

No, that was him.

Adrenaline pumped through his veins, and he concentrated on her chameleon eyes.

If she wanted the ugly truth, he'd serve it up on a platter.

"Everything you've said about me is true," he rasped, willing his voice not to shake. "I can't transfer my ideas to paper, and composing is out of the question. I have a hell of a time reading, and when I try to decipher sheet music, it might as well be a pinball machine with hundreds of black balls skittering on the page. I was never diagnosed with a learning disability or being a neuro…"

"Neurodivergent learner," she supplied.

He nodded and stroked her cheek with his thumb, then something surprising happened. While the rush of shame hadn't receded, it also hadn't pulled him under—not when Harper was a breath away.

He concentrated on her face and let the bullshit in his periphery go blurry. "My parents died of carbon monoxide poisoning when I was eleven and Leighton was ten. We lived not far from your place on the other side of the Baxter Park neighborhood. They'd left us with my grandmother to have an anniversary weekend away in the mountains." He swallowed past the lump in his throat. "The cabin they'd rented had just had a new roof installed. Something got sealed that shouldn't have. They went to bed and never woke up. It's strange to even think of what life was like with my parents. It feels almost like somebody else's life."

"I'm so sorry," she whispered and pressed her hands to his chest.

Her touch soothed his battered heart. "After that, we lived with my grandmother until she passed away, and then we got thrown into the foster care system. We had a rough couple of years. School was hell. We moved around quite a bit, and the teachers chalked up my poor test scores to bouncing around from placement to placement. I figured out ways to get by, and just like you guessed, Leighton helped me with my homework."

Harper held his gaze. There was no pity in her eyes, only concern. "How old were you when Bess and Tomás took you in?"

"Fourteen. I'd pretty much mastered the art of how to barely pass classes. But the misery of school wasn't so bad because I'd found something I loved."

"Music?" she offered.

"Yeah, Tomás and Bess had a ton of old instruments. They encouraged us to experiment and explore. That's when Leighton and I discovered we could play by ear. I gravitated to the guitar. She liked the piano. Trey lived on the next property over with his aunt. He played bass. We became fast friends, formed Heartthrob Warfare, and the rest is history."

"You didn't mind your best friend falling for your sister?"

"I couldn't have picked a better man for her than Trey. He adored her. She could have told him she wanted a rock off the moon, and he'd have gone searching for a spaceship. And he loved being a dad." Emotion cracked his voice. It had been ages since he'd allowed himself to remember the happy times.

"Can I ask you another question? It's kind of off-topic."

"Sure."

"Why did you call yourselves Heartthrob Warfare? I always wondered. It's such a unique name."

He smiled, remembering the day they'd adopted the name. "Scrabble," he replied and gestured with his chin toward the box on the kitchen table.

She raised a skeptical eyebrow. "Scrabble?"

"Leighton and Trey liked to play when we needed a break from the music. I hated Scrabble, for obvious reasons, but Leighton was a whiz. One day, *heartthrob* and *warfare* made it on the board, and Leighton decided that would be our name."

"She sounds bossy and domineering."

He chuckled. "You could say that."

"That's my kind of gal," Harper added with a pinch of snark.

He twisted a lock of her hair between his fingers. "I haven't been able to make music without Trey and Leighton. That's my truth. That's what keeps me up at night. It's what eats at my soul."

Those very words cycled through his mind like an album set on repeat. But he'd never said them aloud, never admitted the truth to anyone. A roaring torrent of angst tempered by an unusual sense of relief churned inside him.

Harper slid her hands down his abdomen, then wrapped her arms around his waist. He drew her into an embrace and held on to her like she was the only thing keeping him afloat.

Maybe she was.

But there was more, and he couldn't hold back now.

"I was a real ass to them," he confessed.

"To Leighton and Trey?"

"Yes, and I can never take back what I said."

He was venturing into uncharted territory, but in this cozy kitchen with Harper in his arms and Aria sleeping peacefully upstairs, the pain of his past didn't sting quite as much.

Harper traced lazy circles on his back. "Musicians have disagreements. Even my grandparents, who were crazy about each other, would get into it, especially when it came to music. When they were working on a piece, they'd go into the sound-proof practice room in the basement and be there for hours."

What he wouldn't give for it to have been a quibble over a refrain or a dispute about lyrics.

"This wasn't a disagreement. It cut deeper." He exhaled a heavy breath. "At first, I was fine with them taking time off to raise Aria. We went from being a garage band to playing sold-out shows across the globe within a matter of months. We needed a break. But one year became two, then three, then four. I was playing shows on my own, but it had lost the magic. When they told me they were leaving Aria with Tomás and Bess to take a trip, it sent me over the edge. Trey had gotten his pilot's license, and they'd bought a little Cessna. Looking back, I shouldn't have cared about them taking a few more days off. But it felt like another delay, another weight on my shoulders to continue to carry the band and keep promoting our music. I decided to confront them and made sure to be there when they dropped off Aria. I waited until she was inside with my foster parents, and then I went off on them."

Concern marred Harper's expression. "What did you say?"

He could still recall the chill in the mountain air and the fire burning through his veins as he raged at his sister and best friend.

"I told them I thought they were selfish. I said I was keeping the band alive and that they owed it to me to get back to work.

Leighton kept saying they'd start the next album after she and Trey returned from their trip. She begged me to believe her. Trey said they were ready to collaborate, but they wanted a little time to themselves. I should have been elated, but I wasn't. I don't even think I was mad at them. I was mad at myself for not being able to do it on my own. I hated that I needed them."

"What happened after they left? Were you able to work it out?"

He pulled her in closer. "I stayed up at my parents' place that night to help with Aria. I'd been a shit uncle and hadn't spent much time with her. I was still living in LA and commuting back and forth, but that's no excuse. That night, Aria and I made up the ABC song and played piano until way past her bedtime. And then I got it. I understood why they wanted uninterrupted time with her. She's amazing, Harper. That voice, that talent."

"Yeah, I noticed it, too. She's got perfect pitch. She's quite a kid."

He couldn't help but smile, thinking back on the joyful night and how he'd thought everything would be okay in the morning. "I tucked Aria into bed. She asked me to sing her a lullaby, then conked out halfway through our made-up ABC song. And then I watched her sleep and worked out what I needed to say to apologize to Trey and my sister. But I never got the chance. They were already gone."

"Landon, that was the plane crash?" Harper asked softly.

He could see the headline.

Pop Sensations Perish in Plane Crash Caused by Inclement Weather over the Rocky Mountains.

"I can't take back what I said to them, and I can't tell them how much they meant to me. I owe it to my sister and my best friend to give Aria a good life. I owe it to them to make the kind of music that honors their legacy and shows the world that Heartthrob Warfare is more than bubblegum pop. But I don't know how I'll do it. With Trey and Leighton, it clicked. And I'm running out of time."

He tensed. Had he said too much?

Nobody knew about the fight he'd had with Trey and Leighton. He hadn't even told Mitzi they'd quarreled, but Harper had cracked him open and peeled back the layers with nothing but a dare.

Maybe it was her chameleon eyes drawing him in or the genuine concern etched on her face, but he wanted, no, he needed to put the pain he'd carried into words.

"I made them a promise at their funeral. I told them I'd write the music we wanted to get back to. I'd figure out a way to do it for them and for Aria. But after their death, everything fell apart. As hard as I've tried, I can't even come up with a decent melody or a single refrain. And worse than that, Aria stopped singing and started hating me."

Harper continued tracing soothing circles on his back. "I don't think she hates you. Sometimes, it's easier to be mad than sad. I know that's true for me."

That made a hell of a lot of sense. He'd had the same reaction. But it had come at a price. Allowing anger and bitterness to touch every aspect of his life had changed his relationship with music. It had gone from being his greatest passion to an invisible prison.

"How do I change course? How do I fix it?"

What if there wasn't a solution? What if this was it?

"Can I tell you a story, heartthrob?" she asked with a mischievous lilt to her voice.

He rested his chin on the top of her head, welcoming the return of her sassy side. "Okay," he answered, grateful to focus on something besides his shitstorm of a life.

"It's about a bright-eyed hellion of a girl named Harper

Barbara Presley, and it'll come as no surprise to you that she got into loads of trouble in elementary school."

He hummed his amusement. "Go on."

"School didn't come easy for me either. I used to copy off Penny, Charlotte, and Libby as far back as kindergarten," she shared, her tone losing the snark and taking on a contemplative quality. "Back then, I didn't realize my brain worked differently. It wasn't until third grade or fourth grade when it really hit. My friends were into those Baby-Sitter Club books, and I didn't want to be left out. But I couldn't understand how they could read them so quickly. I didn't know what was wrong with me, and I didn't want them to see me as different. And this frustration didn't help me make good choices. It's safe to say I was a bit of a menace."

"A menace? You?" he teased.

"Okay, an epically gigantic menace," she conceded with a hum of a laugh. "My teachers equated my learning issues with my bad behavior. They would tell me I'd be fine if I paid attention and tried my hardest. But what they didn't realize was that it took an insane amount of energy and concentration for me to do any academic task. It was exhausting, and then I figured out that if I got in trouble, I'd get sent to the principal's office instead of having to complete the assignments. But then, everything changed."

"What happened?"

"One day, after my grandmother had to pick me up from the principal's office for the gazillionth time, she asked why I couldn't follow the rules. I told her it wasn't the rules. It was me. I couldn't do what my friends could do, and I needed a way to make the letters stop shifting. That's when she told me that letters and music notes used to do that to her. Back when she was a kid, nobody discussed neurodiversity. She happened upon underlining with colored pencils when she was in sixth grade, and that's how she coped. It gave her brain a structure.

She did the same thing with music and figured out a way to thrive. She's played all over the world. She's a success by any measure."

He weaved his hand into her hair and played with the silky tendrils. "I understand what you're trying to tell me. But you were a kid when you found a system that worked for you, and so was your grandmother. I'm thirty-three years old, Harper. I don't know how to move forward."

There it was.

His dark truth.

It was like being trapped between the voice in his head, telling him he couldn't do it, and the pull of his heartstrings, urging him to make good on the promise he'd made to Leighton and Trey.

He released his hold on her and scrubbed his hands down his jawline. "I've had years to write. If I couldn't do it then, what's different about now? And honestly, would anyone even care if I faded into obscurity?"

The compassion in her expression hardened into irritation. "You promised the people you loved the most that you'd try. Promises matter. Not to mention, your fans would care."

"My fans embroider my face onto cushions."

She poked him in the chest. "Don't do that. Don't be a giant prick and talk shit about the people who love your music."

"I'm not saving the world, Harper. I'm just singing songs."

She plucked a bonbon from the Scrabble box and jammed it in her mouth. "You can really be a first-class douche nozzle when you want to," she replied through her rage chewing.

"What are you talking about? I just spilled my guts to you."

"Yeah, I heard you, and my heart goes out to you. But you need to get one thing straight, mister."

"And what's that?" he fired back.

"Your music is important to millions of people. And if you

couldn't tell from the giant pile of Heartthrob Warfare memorabilia in my room, your music is important to me. My grandfather and I used to listen to your albums in the car."

Fat chance of that!

"Your grandfather, a symphony conductor, listened to a pop band?"

She had to be making it up.

"Yeah," she snapped, looking ready to snap his neck. "Every Tuesday and Thursday night when my grandfather schlepped me across town to my piano lessons."

"You got him to listen to Heartthrob Warfare in the car?"

"I did. And he loved every minute of it. We'd sing along, harmonizing with you, and then when he died..." She paused, then rested her palms on the counter and studied the row of photos on the windowsill.

"What happened after he passed away?" he asked gently, coming to her side.

"Your music got me through that time. It reminded me of how much I loved my grandfather. That's the power of your music. You can't give up, Landon. You can't throw it away."

He took off his cap, set it on the table, and ran his hands through his hair. "But I also can't let the world know I have a problem."

She retrieved another bonbon and chucked it at him. "What the hell?" he bit out, snapping the chocolate out of the air before it whacked him in the nose. "What is it with you and your friends throwing random objects at us?"

She huffed an incensed puff of sound. "It's because you and your nanny match-buddies are infuriating. You don't have a problem, Landon. Your mind works differently. That's all."

She didn't understand the level of scrutiny he lived with.

"Do you know how the press will spin it? They'll call me damaged. They'll speculate that I didn't write any of the old songs. People will never look at me the same."

"Do you believe you're damaged?" she pressed.

He flicked his gaze to the floor.

"Do you think Aria and I are damaged?" she continued.

He had to make her understand. "People will talk, Harper. I'm a celebrity. The press and the assholes online would love to get ahold of this and blast it on every celebrity site on the internet."

"Why do you care about those people? Forget them."

"I can't forget them," he hissed. "My label could drop me. My career could come crashing down. I need to save Heartthrob Warfare's legacy, not burn it to the ground."

"I can help you. We'll figure out a way. We'll make our own path. I can even show you strategies to get past what's blocking your ability to put what's in your head on paper."

He held up the chocolate. "I'm not one of your Bonbon Barbie students."

She reared back. "Maybe you should be. You might learn something. You can be a real spoiled celebrity when you want to."

"What does that mean?" he quipped, then jammed the chocolate into his mouth and scarfed it down like a rabid dog.

There really was something satisfying about rage eating decadent chocolate.

"First," Harper said, gearing up, "you say you'll do anything to start making music again, but when I offer possible solutions, you shoot them down."

He threw up his hands. "What do you want me to say? What do you want me to do?"

"Be honest with me. What's going on in your head? That night in Vegas, you said what you want and what you can have are two different things. What does that even mean?"

He paced like a caged animal. "You want to know what's going on inside my jacked-up mind? I'm terrified I'll screw up Aria. I'm heartsick because there's a chance I'll never make the kind of music Trey, Leighton, and I dreamed of writing. And then there's you."

Christ, he'd said it.

"Me?" she blasted.

He couldn't hold back, not with those hazel eyes challenging him. He caught the glint of her wedding ring, then held her fiery gaze. "Yeah, you, *bonbon.* From the moment I first saw you that night when Rowen decided to show up at that bar to freak the shit out of Penny, I couldn't get you out of my head. You sang that little song about Penny and the weirdos, and it was like time stopped."

"You heard that?"

"Yeah, you've got the voice of an angel. Packed stadiums teeming with fans would fall to their knees to hear you sing. And then there are your eyes."

"My eyes?"

"Damn right, your eyes," he rasped. "It's like you can see through me with those chameleon eyes."

"What the hell are chameleon eyes, heartthrob? Are you calling me a reptile?" she barked.

"No, are you crazy? I'm not calling you a reptile. What I mean is that they're mysterious. I don't know if they're gray, blue, or brown. Hell, there's green and gold in there, too. They change with your mood and the light. They're beguiling and haunting, and every time I look in your eyes, it's like discovering something new. You're like no one I've ever met, and the minute that drunk gladiator dared us to get married, it was the first thing I wanted, really wanted, in years."

There it was. The truth.

Breathless from his tirade, he observed her from across the kitchen, waiting for her to say something or throw something.

It could go either way with Harper.

She plucked another chocolate from the box.

Look out! Incoming bonbon.

But she didn't lob it at him. No, she gripped the treat in her left hand between her thumb and index finger, then held it in front of her chest as a sexy little smirk curled the corners of her mouth. "And I thought you only married me for my bonbons."

This damned woman would be the end of him.

With one sassy retort, she brought him back from the brink, back from an emotional overload threatening to tear him apart.

He concentrated on the diamond glinting on her hand. "What the hell happens next? Where do we go from here?"

She drummed her fingers on the counter, then glanced toward the staircase. "First, we make sure we do everything we can for Aria. I want her to be happy while she's here."

He hadn't expected that.

But he should have.

He'd sensed the girls' connection when he'd observed them playing piano in the garage.

He nodded, regaining his bearings. "She's what matters the most."

And if he meant that, really meant that, he had to do what was best for her. He swallowed past the lump in his throat, then peered across the kitchen and eyed the Steinway. "And maybe you could work with her on the neurodivergent learning stuff."

"I'd love to. And it's no trouble. It's what I do with my online students," she replied, then frowned.

What was that face for?

He took a step toward her. "Is something wrong?"

"I know what to do when it comes to music, but I'm not as well-versed in how to help her with reading and writing. I know what worked for me, but it may be different for her. With school starting soon, we should mention her learning style to her teacher."

Dammit.

She'd push him. That's what she did.

"Harper, I'm not sure—"

"Landon," she said, cutting him off. "If she had asthma and needed an inhaler to breathe, we'd tell the teacher, wouldn't we? We want her to have every opportunity to succeed, and if, in Aria's case, that meant highlighters, some learning interventions, and more time to complete assignments, we'd give her that."

How could he argue with her?

"We would," he conceded, and despite the unease roiling in his chest, he couldn't deny that he liked this *we* talk.

"And on the bright side," Harper continued, resurrecting her devilish smirk, "even if Aria does act up at school, we'll know that she won't be the only sassy kid in second grade."

"How would we know that?"

"She's assigned to the same class as Phoebe Gale, right?"

He laughed. "She is."

"That poor teacher. We'll have to make sure we shower that woman with kindness," she mused, then glanced at her left hand, and her expression grew pensive.

"What is it?" he asked.

"This next part is important. In fact, it's imperative."

"Okay," he breathed.

Jesus, what was she about to say?

She touched the platinum wedding band. "We have to commit to each other. And it can't be for show. It has to be for real."

Chapter 18
LANDON

Commit to each other—for real?

Was she saying what he thought she was saying?

Did Harper want more?

"I mean." She cleared her throat. "For the next sixty days, we commit to helping each other. We've got to be all in, no holds barred. I help you with Aria and your music. You can trust me not to say anything about your process. I understand that you've never worked with anyone besides your sister and Trey, but it's worth a shot, isn't it? Lucky for you, I'm your wife. I'm pretty sure a judge couldn't make me testify against you in a court of law, so you don't have to worry about your secret getting out. I'm legally bound to keep my big trap shut. But I need your commitment for..."

"For..." he stammered.

Forever?

Was that what he wanted to say?

What was going on with him?

"For the baking contest," she clarified.

He shifted his stance like a nervous teenager. "Absolutely,

the reality baking contest. That's what I was alluding to. But I have to warn you, I don't know shit about baking."

She studied the bonbon. "I don't either, but if we give it everything we've got and do whatever our baking mentor tells us to do, I'm sure we'll win. We're up against some other pop star team. I doubt they're master bakers."

"Master bakers?" he repeated and bit back a grin.

She threw him a dose of stink eye. "How old are you? Twelve? You know what I mean. And come to think of it, baking might be a good thing for your music."

He lost the master-baker smile. "How could baking help with making music?"

"My grandpa used to say that his best compositions came together when he least expected it, like when he was in the garden or driving or when he and my grandmother went on a walk. Creativity isn't a faucet you can turn on and off. You can't force a masterpiece. And if you're stuck and something's not working, try another melody, but never stop making music. You've got to open your mind to every possibility, and that can require a distraction," she finished, looking quite satisfied with that little speech as she hoisted herself onto the edge of the countertop.

"A distraction," he echoed, recalling how he'd pegged her as a beautiful distraction before his defenses broke down and he kissed her in the club.

"Yes, a distraction to usher in a release to get past whatever's blocking the flow of ideas," she replied, waving the bonbon to punctuate her declaration.

He prowled toward her as images of their first reckless kiss flashed through his mind. "Are you saying you'll be that distraction for me for the next sixty days?"

She flashed a sly smirk and crossed her legs. "It would be the wifely thing to do. Call me the nanny-aunt-wife sixty-day distraction."

He drank her in. She was the epitome of a distraction in those barely-there jean shorts and sheer tank top. "And how do you plan on distracting me, Mrs. Paige?"

Jesus, he liked the way that sounded.

She pressed the tip of the chocolate to her lips and hummed, cooking up a reply. "When was the last time you felt free, like you could do anything?"

That was easy to answer. "Our wedding night in Vegas."

"Me too, and I think I know why."

"Because I made you come until you were delirious."

A blush graced her cheeks. "Because we told the voices in our heads to shut up and we lived like tomorrow would never come. We didn't worry about the consequences. We took risks. We distracted each other from the bullshit. There was no fear, just…"

Love.

Why was that the first thing that popped into his mind?

Could this be love? No, this was lust. Pure, temporary lust.

And it was getting harder to fight.

He caged her in, pressing a palm on either side of her. "Just what?"

She brushed the bonbon across her lips. "Complete permission to do whatever we want. Total creative freedom."

Oh yeah, from the balcony sex to the way they'd defiled his suite at the Luxe, they'd gotten quite creative on their wedding night.

He stared at her mouth as she continued to slide the bonbon across her bottom lip. He'd never been more jealous of a piece of candy. "What are you proposing, bonbon? I want to be crystal clear on the parameters."

"Before we get into that, you know that I have a rule against dating musicians."

This again.

He released a weary breath. "I am aware."

"And while marriage isn't dating, I am breaking my rule by being with you. But you and I aren't a forever kind of thing, right?"

This was getting dicey.

What the hell did he want?

Not to look like a fool was a good start.

"Agreed. We're on the same page. I'm not a fan of marriage."

He wasn't. He'd decided long ago it wasn't for him. He'd be wise to remember that.

"We need our time as man and wife to end with cash in my pocket and new songs in your catalog," she mused, then frowned.

"What is it? That sounds like exactly what we need. Are we forgetting something?"

"Aria."

Aria.

What would their arrangement do to the kid? The child had no idea this was a temporary marriage. How the hell would he explain that to her?

But perhaps there was a workaround.

"My friends are your friends. You wouldn't be out of her life when this ends," he offered as a knot tightened in his belly.

"True," she conceded. "We'll still see each other, and I can help Aria with piano. When this is over, we could tell her we decided we were better as friends. And then nobody gets hurt," Harper added. She didn't sound one hundred percent sure of that, but she plastered on a smile.

He matched her plastic grin with one of his own.

This was how it had to be.

"Right, we can be friends," he repeated.

"But in the meantime," she continued, returning to torturing him by brushing the bonbon against her lips, "we should make a temporary exception to engage in a mutually beneficial arrangement that includes marital benefits."

Now she was talking.

He leaned in. "And what kind of marital benefits are you alluding to?"

"For the next sixty days, we allow ourselves to indulge the same way we did on our wedding night."

"Can you be more specific?"

"I'm proposing we take part in consensual stress-relieving activities to distract us from the pressure that may result from our situation and act as a diversion to usher in creativity and productivity," she prattled, then chewed her lip.

That was one hell of a word salad.

"So...sex?" He needed clarification.

She flashed a coy grin, held up her left hand, and wiggled her ring finger. "You buy the ticket. You take the ride. Or in our case," she purred. "You marry the bonbon. You enjoy every single morsel of its marital sweetness."

His cock came to attention, ready to indulge in every dirty desire their temporary matrimony afforded.

"That's a pretty sweet deal," he rasped.

"I'm a pretty amazing temporary wife," she tossed back.

He gripped her ass and slid her forward. "I agree."

Wide-eyed, Harper teetered on the edge of the counter, and before she could stop him, he plucked the chocolate from her grip.

"Hey, that's my bonbon," she quipped with an adorable pout that had him itching to kiss the expression clean off her face.

"You marry the bonbon. You enjoy every single morsel of its wifely sweetness, right?"

"Yes."

"That starts now," he growled. "I'm cashing in on those marital benefits."

"I didn't realize I had such a demanding husband."

She had no idea.

With nothing holding him back and permission to do whatever he wanted, an intoxicating boldness took hold. His mind emptied, and his worries drifted away as the lyrics to "No Fear" came to him. He'd sung them thousands of times to millions of cheering fans. But at this moment, a breath away from the woman he desired, they took on a new meaning.

"*Nothing to fear with you sitting here. Nothing to hide with you by my side*," he whispered, singing the first lines of the song against her lips.

"*We fly above the pain. Soaring like a bird. Open hearts. Open minds*," she continued as they swayed and set a sensual tempo.

"*Baby, baby, when it's all the line, no fear can keep me from claiming what's truly mine*," he finished, then held her gaze. "That's it."

She cocked her head to the side. "What are you talking about?"

"For the next sixty days, you're mine to do with as I please, Mrs. Paige."

"I disagree. For the next sixty days, you're *mine* to do with as I please, *Mr. Paige*," she countered.

She didn't give an inch, and it only made him want her more.

"Open your mouth, wife," he ordered.

She watched him for a beat, eyes glittering with desire, then slowly parted her lips.

And Jesus, that mouth.

He held up the bonbon. "Lick it."

Without hesitating, she leaned forward and ran her tongue across the tip.

God help him.

This woman was the definition of a temptress.

His cock wept to feel her wet heat. The anticipation was almost unbearable.

He slipped the bonbon past her lips and listened as she sighed her satisfaction. With the heat of her body and the scent of chocolate, he succumbed to a heady buzz. Palming her ass, he held her body flush with his. With their bodies pressed together, he rolled his hips, setting a sinfully slow pace as he rocked against her. She hummed a sexy melody as she feasted on the decadent treat and moved with him.

"Swallow it," he whispered.

Those chameleon eyes, full of dirty promises, glittered as she complied.

With nothing off-limits, he dialed up his pace. She closed her eyes and pressed against his hard length. He'd never been a fan of dry humping until today. Consumed with yearning, he leaned in, ready to capture her bonbon mouth in a kiss, when she hummed that catchy melody again.

"What tune is that?" he whispered.

She wrapped her arms around his neck as the friction built between them. "*Sweet, so sweet, hello to my favorite treat*," she sang against his lips.

He didn't know if she had a next line. But he did. It was the first burst of creativity he'd had in ages. "*What is this bliss? A dream girl with a bonbon kiss*," he finished, then gazed into her chameleon eyes. "Sing it back to me," he breathed, lust building as a sensual rhythm took over.

"*Sweet, so sweet, hello to my favorite treat. What is this bliss? A dream girl with a bonbon kiss*," she sang, changing up the melody to make the lyrics flow. "Should I write it down? It's not bad," she moaned, rocking her hips in time with his.

He brushed her hair to the side and kissed the smooth skin below her earlobe. "I won't forget it."

He wouldn't.

He wasn't replaying the lyrics in his head. They'd gone straight to his heart.

And like when he'd kissed her in the club, a rush of longing coupled with the spark of undeniable attraction left him with no choice. If he didn't kiss this woman, he'd combust right there in her kitchen. He dipped his head and ended his agony. Their lips met, and like the lyrics promised, her bonbon kiss was heavenly bliss. He devoured her mouth, tasting and exploring. Nothing existed but the two of them and the symphony of sensations they unleashed when they gave in to desire.

Deeper and deeper, he fell under her chocolate-laced spell. He gripped her hips, helped her off the counter, then dropped to his knees.

"What are you doing down there, Mr. Paige?"

"I want to taste every inch of you," he answered, unbuttoning her jean shorts, and he made a discovery that might keep him rock hard for the next decade. "You're not wearing underwear."

A sexy blush graced her cheeks. "I was in a hurry to shower and get dressed while Aria was on the phone with your foster parents. I forgot to put them on," she replied when her sly smirk returned. "But I know where I could find a pair."

"Oh yeah?" he replied and rubbed slow circles against her most sensitive place through the denim.

She moaned and clutched the edge of the counter. "My husband likes to carry them around in his pocket."

She had him there.

"I'd like to propose an addendum to our arrangement."

"I'm listening," she panted as he dialed up his pace.

"You won't have to worry about me pocketing your panties if you stop wearing them."

"What kind of wife would I be if I went commando all over town?" she purred.

"The best kind," he answered, lifting her tank top to press a kiss to her stomach.

She swayed her hips, bucking as her pleasure heightened. "If I give up panties, you have to do something for me."

He licked a line to her hip. "Name it."

"You'll let me work a little Bonbon Barbie magic on you and agree to try some of my strategies."

This woman had some restraint. She was on the cusp of flying over the edge, and she could still drive a hard bargain.

"I'd rather you work a little Bang-Bang Barbie magic on me."

"I bet you would," she moaned. "Do we have a deal?"

She was close, so close to sweet release.

"Landon?" she breathed.

"Deal," he growled.

He'd come out ahead in this bargain. Messing around with some highlighters and colored magnets seemed like a small price to pay to know he and his sixty-day bride could knock out a quickie lickety-split. He helped her lose the jean shorts, then slipped her leg over his shoulder, and feasted on his wife. "*Sweet, so sweet, Harper Paige is my favorite treat*," he sang against her as he licked, sucked, and worked the woman into a frenzy.

"I think," she said on a heated moan, "I want to be called Harper Presley-Paige."

He looked up at her. "I'm about to make you come, and you're talking about your name?"

"Then get up here and shut me up," she challenged.

She didn't have to ask twice.

He stripped off his T-shirt, lost his shoes, and shrugged his jeans to his ankles. His cock stood at attention as an electric current traveled down his spine. Want and insatiable need consumed his every thought.

"Take a breath, wife. I'm about to bang the words right out of you."

"We could call you Bang-Bang Bart," Harper teased as she flung her tank top onto the floor.

And hello, voluptuous breasts.

"If music is a bust, at least I have a killer porn name."

She stared at his cock. "You've certainly got the equipment."

The sexy banter with this woman sent a buzzy euphoria popping and whizzing through his body.

She flashed him a naughty smirk, then turned to grip the lip of the sink. He inhaled a tight breath as she presented him with an ass so goddamned gorgeous, it should be illegal. He gave his cock two rough pumps as he drank in his goddess of a wife.

He came up behind her and caught their reflection in the window.

She met his gaze. "I know you like to watch."

Hell yes, he did.

He positioned himself at her entrance, then slid his hands up her torso and cupped her breasts. "I could watch you come over and over and never get bored."

She arched her back. "I know. I'm amazing like that."

"Somebody needs to bang the sass right out of you, Mrs. Presley-Paige."

"Let's see what you've got," she replied, holding his gaze and challenging him like no one ever had.

He released her breasts, twisted her mass of chocolate locks in his fist, then gripped her ass. He thrust his hips and entered Nirvana. He tightened his hold on her hair, savoring the first seconds of sliding balls deep into his wife. He stilled and studied her reflection. Head back and lips parted, this stunning woman took his breath away.

He slid his hand between her thighs and massaged her sweet bud. She bit her lip and purred her pleasure. Ballads should be written about this woman. From the swell of her breasts to her soft curves, a man could easily lose himself to a woman with chameleon eyes.

She hummed the melody to the "*Sweet, So Sweet*" tune they'd crafted, and he rocked his hips in time with the beat.

Bodies swaying to the rhythm, he pumped his cock in smooth strokes as he worked her with his hand.

"Just like that. I'm so close," she said, arching her back and meeting him blow for blow.

And then a switch flipped, and he relinquished control to the slap of skin on skin. They were no longer two people craving carnal release. They'd become one, making music with their heated breaths and lusty gasps. Every muscle in his body stiffened as he hovered on the edge of release. Harper tightened around him, crashing into oblivion. He watched her lose control, bucking and writhing. She reached between her thighs and threaded her hand with his. Her fingertips brushed against his thrusting cock, and he couldn't hold back. His orgasm hit like a wildfire ravaging a hillside, consuming everything in its path. Pumping and grinding, he worked her body, lengthening her release and ensuring she experienced every lip-biting, toe-curling sensation.

He rested his head on her shoulder as they returned to their bodies, and their panting breaths slowed.

"I think you de-sassed me," she said on a sweet, sated breath.

He pulled out and then scooped her into his arms.

She gasped and giggled. "What are you doing?"

"I'm examining your chameleon eyes, and I've got bad news."

"What's that?"

He licked his lips. "I still see some sass in there."

She gifted him with that dirty smirk that got him hard and ready to bring this party upstairs. "Looks like you've got more work to do, pop star. Are you up for it?"

He held her securely with one arm and grabbed the bonbon-filled Scrabble box. "Mrs. Presley-Paige?" he said, ready to devour her and a box of chocolates.

"Yes, heartthrob husband?" she sassed, and Christ, he'd take her feisty any day of the week.

"You better fuel up with a bonbon or two. You'll need your strength."

"And why is that?" she purred.

He drank her in. "I'm not even close to being done with you yet."

Chapter 19
HARPER

Harper pressed her hand to her chest. Her heart pounded as the bubbly cries of boys and girls carried on the early September breeze. The crisp tap of a jump rope grazing the schoolyard blacktop mingled with the metallic creak of the swing set. The hinges whined as kids pumped their legs and soared through the air. Awash in shiny lunch boxes and snow-white sneakers, the atmosphere pulsed with excitement as adults congregated in groups and children burned off restless energy before the bell rang, signaling the start of the first day of the new term at Whitmore Country Day.

Aka, Aria goes to school.

"I feel like it's my first day," she said to Landon, then tossed a glance at Aria. With her lunch box in one hand and the other crammed into the pocket of her shorts, the kid schooled her features and lifted her chin. She was putting on her tough-girl front, but she'd rejected the idea of hitting the playground and hadn't budged from their side since they'd arrived.

New city. New school. New teachers. New caregivers.

Swap out an aunt and an uncle for a grandma and a grandpa, and Aria could be her.

But there were signs the girl was warming to the idea of her new life in Denver.

While she hadn't carried a tune since the day they met in Tomás and Bess's garage, the kid's icy demeanor had thawed. From the three of them munching on bowls of cereal at breakfast to hours spent riffing on the piano to Landon singing her to sleep—and thanks to a decent amount of chocolate consumption—Aria had rolled with the punches.

They all had.

She'd never expected she'd like having a pop star and nose picker living under her roof. Still, a strange harmony descended on the house.

And for the last fourteen days, it had been just the three of them.

From work to last-minute getaways, their friends had left the city the day after the infamous housewarming party. When she learned they were getting out of Dodge and wouldn't return until the day before classes started, she wasn't sure what she'd do with a temporary husband and a spirited niece. But it turned out to be a godsend. Without the distraction of the others, they'd found a rhythm. These past two weeks could only be described as a strange bliss.

Two weeks.

A period that felt like both an eternity and a split second.

She peered at the rings on her hand. It blew her mind that she could hardly remember what life was like before she gained a husband and a niece.

The unexpected thing about the situation was how normal it had become—how easily they fit together. How her heart expanded in her chest when she heard little feet padding down the steps.

That is, until today. Today, they'd woken up in an alternate universe.

This was when shit got real and their Baxter Park bubble popped.

Aria started school, and the next day, they embarked on their first celebrity baking challenge.

And from the curious glances being tossed at them from the other Whitmore parents, it was safe to assume everyone had learned of their Vegas nuptials, thanks to the internet.

They'd shunned the media and hadn't gone online once since becoming a trio. It wasn't a conscious choice—or maybe it was. Perhaps they understood that those two precious weeks were the calm before the storm.

Now that Aria's routine included school, they'd need to get serious about pulling together his new sound. They'd written snippets of lyrics and played with melodies, but they hadn't pulled an entire composition together to create a song. And she needed to record more Bonbon Barbie tutorials ASAP—and watch a baking tutorial or two. She could cram her face with delicious confections, but she was woefully at a loss when it came to making them.

First, they had to get through the Whitmore school drop-off.

Landon crossed and uncrossed his arms as a crease formed between his brows. "You're sure this is where everyone is supposed to meet?"

She nodded. "Penny texted early this morning and said this was the spot."

"What do you think, Aria?" Landon asked nervously and gave the girl's shoulder a gentle squeeze. "It seems like a good school."

"It's a dumb old school," she grumped, then lifted her foot and smashed a dandelion growing in the sidewalk crack.

"You won't be the only new kid. Sebastian Cress is starting here today, too. Do you remember him from the video call?" she asked, trying to put the kid at ease.

Aria shrugged and focused on the smashed dandelion. "I don't know why I have to go to school anyway. School is stupid. I like being at the house, I like playing the piano, and I like walking to the Cupid Bakery by myself and ordering butter-scotch bonbons."

Shit!

She could feel Landon's eyes on her.

"You sent Aria to the bakery to buy bonbons even after I picked up a couple of boxes?"

She waved him off. "Only once, maybe twice. And I was always right outside."

Right outside, hiding in the bushes.

Thanks to not having a note from Babs and stealing an entire tray of bonbons, she'd bet her weight in chocolate she was still persona non grata at Cupid Bakery.

"It was five times, Aunt Harper," Aria corrected. "I went by myself five times."

And yeah, the kid had started calling her Aunt Harper, which kind of felt amazing.

"Five times?" Landon repeated, blasting her auntie-fuzzy-feelings to bits.

"Yeah, we went really quick when you were out on your runs getting exercise," Aria answered with a devious smirk.

The adorable little snitch.

"We were bonding," she countered. "Yes, it was aunt and niece bonding time."

"Or you were using a child to further your bonbon addiction in my absence," he replied, but she could hear the delight in his voice.

At least he had a sense of humor about her borderline criminal behavior.

She raised an eyebrow. "You didn't seem to mind my bonbon addiction last night."

With that snarky comeback, what remained of Landon's initial irritation gave way to smoldering mischief. "Look who hasn't lost her sass."

And somebody hand Harper Presley a fan.

Her pop star could smolder.

Landon's soulful brown eyes darkened, and she did everything in her power to refrain from combusting into sexually satisfied dust or beautifully boinked cocoa powder. At this point, thanks to the numerous bonbon runs, her body was at least fifty percent chocolate, and the other fifty, good old sass. And if she'd learned one thing about Landon Paige these past two weeks, it was that he took banging the ever-lovin' panty-less sass out of her to a new level.

And she was there for it.

Sweet holy chocolate-flavored multiple orgasms, she was.

And last night had been no exception.

His chocolate kisses had led to her giving the man a cocoa-licious BJ, which then resulted in him climbing on top of her and rocking those pop star hips until she saw stars.

There was a good chance she'd never be able to eat chocolate again without flying over the edge into Ecstasy Junction. But there were worse burdens to bear.

"Forget school. We should get out of here and stuff our faces with lollipops. I've got better things to do," Aria griped.

And OMG, Aria.

And double OMG, she'd had a sexcapades space-out in front of an elementary school.

Blinking like she'd been returned to her body by aliens, she put the kibosh on her deliciously dirty thoughts and focused on the kid. "What was that, honey?"

"I have an idea for a song," Aria answered. "And I want to keep practicing with the magnets so I can copy it into my music notebook. I won't bother you, and I can get you bonbons whenever you want, Aunt Harper. All we have to do is get back into the poop-colored car and bust out of here."

It was a tempting proposition.

She studied the nanny Lamborghini parked in the school lot. "It's not poop-brown. It's candy pearl brown sugar. And I'm not going to lie, kid, we've had a great time together. I love that you're writing music and figuring out how to transfer your ideas to your notebook, but I have a feeling you'll like this school. The kids you met on that video call a few weeks ago will be here any minute. I'm sure they're excited to meet you in real life," she said, but Aria wasn't buying it.

The little girl smooshed another dandelion and fiddled with whatever was in her pocket.

"All right," she said, trying to engage the kid. "Let's do one last school supply check. Did you pack your pencils and crayons?"

Aria made a face like she'd been forced to eat stewed cabbage. "Yes, Aunt Harper."

"And your folders?" Landon added, joining in.

"Yes, Uncle Landy."

"What about your water bottle?" he pressed.

The child turned and flashed the shiny silver bottle secured inside a mesh pocket of her new backpack. Aria twisted to touch the cap. "And it's still cold."

The girl wasn't pleased, but at least they had the kid talking —and not murdering unsuspecting sidewalk vegetation.

She met Aria's cornflower blue gaze. "And the highlighters? Just in case you want to use them."

The Bonbon Barbie method of utilizing color to ground musical notes had clicked with the kid. But it was one thing for Aria to use highlighters when it was just the two of them at home. She wasn't sure if the child would feel comfortable trying them out at school.

Aria blew out an exasperated breath. "I've got them in

yellow, orange, blue, green, purple, and pink, Aunt Harper," she replied, then gave her guardians a suspicious once-over. "Why are you asking about what's in my backpack again? We checked it two times before we left for school and three times last night."

"I thought we only checked it twice last night," Landon replied.

Aria puffed up. "I checked it by myself. I came down to the kitchen, but you guys were busy in the music practice room in the basement."

This wasn't good.

She froze and plastered on a nervous grin.

"We thought you were asleep," Landon said and tossed a *holy shit* look her way.

And holy shit was right.

After rethinking getting freaky in the kitchen with a seven-year-old in the house, they'd spent the last two weeks taking advantage of the soundproof practice room in the basement, which clearly wasn't as noise-tight as she'd thought.

She widened her plastic expression. "You didn't hear anything, did you, Aria? You just checked your backpack, then skedaddled back to bed, right?"

Had she just used the word skedaddled?

Aria scratched her chin. "I heard a little bit of a song you were singing, Auntie Harper. It went like this: '*Yes, yes, yes…oh, yes,*'" the child crooned like she was narrating erotica.

And oh no.

A few parents glanced their way.

They could not be pegged as the porno people.

"You could call it the 'Oh Yes' song," Aria added, her voice echoing from sea to shining sea. At least, that's how it felt.

"Yes, oh yes," Landon blurted toward the group of judgy-eyed parents. He removed his cap, revealing his identity. "That's what we were doing, working on a song. I'm a musician. I'm pop star Landon Paige, and that's what I do. Yes, oh, yes."

What a time for the usually incognito celebrity to blow a gasket. But in for a penny, in for a pound.

"Yep, we were working on a song. A lively song with a vigorous beat and the repeated use of the word *yes*," she added like she was trying out for an infomercial.

Aria stared at them as if they required immediate psychiatric intervention—which was debatable. The child twisted her lips into a smirk. "I know what you were really doing down there."

No, no, no, this had gone from bad to worse.

The kid couldn't know, could she?

She glanced at her husband. The man stood stock-still with his mouth hanging open.

Point of clarification.

It cannot be overstated that they had really, really, really taken advantage of their marital benefits agreement. They'd been knocking boots so often she was lucky she wasn't walking around Denver bow-legged like she'd traversed the state bareback on a wild stallion.

"Aria, what do you think we were doing?" she asked, and hello, opera voice.

The girl narrowed her gaze. "You guys are staying up past your bedtime, and I bet you're eating bonbons down there."

And bonbon addiction for the save.

Crisis averted.

"That's exactly what we were doing," Landon gushed, finding his voice.

She shared a relieved look with the man. "Yep, you caught us."

"What did you catch, Harper? Was it a D?"

What the hell?

She gasped and peered down to find a bright-eyed Phoebe Gale.

Where did she come from? And the kid couldn't be referring to the cock kind of D.

"What do you mean, 'was it a *D*?'" she stammered.

Wide-eyed parents in the vicinity paused their conversations. If the Whitmore community didn't already think she and Landon were sexual deviants, they did now.

"A *dog*, like in *hot dog*. What did you think I meant?" the child quipped.

She wasn't about to go there.

"When did you get here, Phoebe?" she asked, changing tack.

"I've been here a while. You didn't notice me because I was behind that bush. I've been practicing spying."

Spying? Had she heard the kid correctly?

"Hey there, strangers," Penny called, then yawned as she and Rowen joined them on the sidewalk.

"Did Phoebe sneak up on you?" Rowen asked, looking exasperated for barely nine in the morning.

"She did. She said she's—"

"Spying?" Penny supplied.

"Yes."

"I've been spying for ten days straight," the girl announced. "I spied while we were on our big boat in Cabba Being."

"The Caribbean," Rowen corrected and rubbed his temples.

"That's what I said, Uncle Row," the child replied, not missing a beat. "The whole time we were floating around in the ocean, I practiced being a super spy. Super spies have to pay attention to details, and they have to be good at surprising people when it's time to catch the bad guys. And boy, oh boy, how I've gotten good at sneaking up on Uncle Row and Penny. That's how I woke them up this morning."

309

"At three thirty a.m.," Penny added through another yawn.

Rowen patted his beaming niece's head. "Which translates into constant bouts of Phoebe appearing out of nowhere and yelling—"

"Surprise!" the child bellowed. "It's Phoebe, the hot dog fairy princess secret agent."

"We've read Phoebe a few spy books for kids," Penny explained.

"And now I'm a secret spy agent on the lookout for—" Phoebe gasped when she noticed Aria. "Wait a second. It's you."

"Me?" Aria huffed, lifting her chin like she was preparing to throw down.

"It's the *eat worms* girl. You're here. Remember me from the video call? I'm Phoebe. You're going to be my new best friend."

"Says who?" Aria shot back with a smidge less beat-down to her tone.

"Me," the little girl replied, undeterred. "I told you. I'm Phoebe."

Aria looked Phoebe up and down. "You never said what you were on the lookout for."

Phoebe turned. "Hot dogs," she answered, showing off her bag covered in tiny dancing wieners. "I'm also on the lookout for cookies."

"What do you think of this?" Aria mimicked Phoebe's moves and showed off her backpack.

Phoebe's jaw nearly hit the ground. "It's covered in cookies and cupcakes."

"And bonbons. Those are the little chocolates." She waved Phoebe in and held up her lunch box. "When my uncle and aunt were in the basement last night, I dumped my carrot sticks into the garbage and filled the container with super chocolatey bonbons."

"We're gonna be the bestest of best friends," Phoebe exclaimed, then grew serious. "What's your name again?"

Aria flicked one of her pigtails over her shoulder. "Aria Paige-Grant."

Wide-eyed, Phoebe took a step back. "Wow, that's a super-star name."

The hint of a grin pulled on the corners of Aria's mouth. "Yeah, that's what I'm gonna be when I grow up."

"I'm gonna be the queen of the hot dog fairies. I'm just a princess super spy now," Phoebe replied, then gasped as she peered past her uncle. This kid clearly lived on a steady supply of adrenaline, sugar, and processed meats. "I see Oscar and Sebastian. They're playing hopscotch. Can me and Aria play, too?"

"Go ahead," Penny answered.

"Uncle Landy, Aunt Harper, can I go with this crazy weird hot dog girl?" Aria asked, but the grin on her face canceled out the snark in her request.

"Sure," Landon answered, "but stay where we can see you," he added, puffing up like Aria had, and for a good reason.

That was some solid parenting.

He glanced at her, and she nodded approvingly.

Look at them. Take away the porno innuendos, and they weren't half bad at not ruining a child.

Phoebe grabbed Aria's hand, and the girls headed off, pigtails swinging, as they sprinted toward the boys. The duo zoomed past Charlotte, Mitch, Libby, and Erasmus, who chuckled at the enthusiastic girls.

"The whole gang's here," Rowen said as the foursome joined them.

"How is newlywed life?" Mitch asked as everyone stared at her and Landon.

She glanced at her husband. "We're...great."

"Yes, great," Landon repeated.

And she knew he was thinking the same thing she was.

They hadn't discussed what they would say about their situation. They hadn't had much time to chat between all the sex and working their hardest to be decent parental figures.

Libby pegged Landon with her gaze. "We stopped by your place in Crystal Hills last night on our way back from Rickety Rock to say hello, but you guys must have been out."

If anybody could read the situation, it was their resident metaphysical yogi, Libby Lamb.

"You had a bunch of flyers and leaflets stuck to your door, and we tossed them in the bin for you," Raz added with a curious lilt to his voice.

She hadn't mentioned the living situation to her girls, and from the looks of it, Landon hadn't said anything either.

But in her defense, no one had asked—specifically.

"We're not living in Crystal Hills," Landon replied.

Raz shared a look with the others. "Where are you living?"

Here comes the onslaught of questions.

"We're staying at my place," she answered.

Charlotte cocked her head to the side. "At Babs' house?"

"Why not? She's out of town for the next several weeks, and Aria wasn't keen on moving into Landon's place, so I offered my home. A totally reasonable living accommodation because we are…"

"Taking complete advantage of marital benefits," Landon blurted.

Dammit.

She threw WTF eye daggers at the man.

"I mean, we're married," he corrected. "Yep, you know the story. I got double-dog dared, so I put a ring on it," he added and held up her left hand like she was a prize-fighter to show off the gargantuan diamond. "And now, like my wife said, we're living at her place. What's mine is hers, and what's hers is mine. Yeah, that's it."

Where was a roll of duct tape when a gal needed it?

"You guys are really doing the marriage thing?" Mitch asked. "Like for real?"

She shared another look with Landon and shrugged. After his word salad of a reply, there was no sense in lying about their situation.

"The day of the housewarming, we agreed to cohabitate for the next sixty days," she replied.

"Isn't that interesting? That's the same amount of time as the nanny match trial period." Charlotte shared a look with the girls.

Of course, her friends would make the connection. But she had to set the record straight.

"I'm not his nanny. We're helping each other with our personal and professional lives. It's a purely practical agreement."

"Are you guys working on music together?" Penny asked.

Landon tensed. She could feel the anxiety rolling off the guy.

"Not that Landon needs any help," she began, "but if he did require a pianist, I've offered to lend a hand, and of course, I'm helping care for Aria."

"Harper is quite a musician," her husband added. "I'm lucky she's agreed to work with me."

Did he mean it?

"You're writing songs again, H!" Libby exclaimed with a little clap. "That's wonderful!"

"More like dabbling. I wouldn't say that—"

Libby cut her off. "The whole time we were out of town, I could feel your energy, Harper. I could tell you were harnessing your inner musical goddess. It was the same vibe I used to get years ago when you were writing and composing."

"That's what she kept telling me," Raz confirmed. "All sorts of Harper vibes. And weren't you also seeing rocks and stones, plum?"

Libby's gaze widened. "Yes."

Charlotte perked up. "Libbs, you must have been remembering Harper's Red Rocks dream."

"Red Rocks like the amphitheater?" Landon asked.

"That's right," Penny answered, nodding. "Back in elementary school, Harper would ditch her schoolwork and draw pictures of red rocks. She'd take them home and tape them onto her wall to make it look like she was performing outdoors at the Red Rocks Amphitheater with those beautiful sandstone boulders framing the stage."

Landon turned to her. "I didn't know that was your dream."

"Oh yeah, since she was five," Charlotte answered. "It started after she wrote her first song in kindergarten for our teacher."

"No, it wasn't for our teacher," Penny corrected, twisting a lock of her blonde hair. "It was for somebody in Miss Miliken's family. Something like that."

"I remember," Charlotte trilled. "You sang it for the class. Miss Miliken recorded you. I'm so glad you're following your heart."

Feeling her cheeks heat, she waved off her friends. "It was a silly pipe dream."

"No way, H. You're incredibly talented," Char added, reaching out and squeezing her hand.

"It's great that you're working on music again," Libby offered.

Penny turned to Landon. "Have you heard her sing?"

"I have, and—"

"And the kids might be stuck in detention on the first day

of school," Rowen remarked, cutting off Landon and shifting the attention away from her.

But her relief was short-lived.

Rowen gestured toward where the kids should have been playing hopscotch.

Red-faced, the foursome appeared to be on the brink of a brawl.

Chapter 20
HARPER

Aria, Phoebe, Oscar, and Sebastian circled a boy almost twice their size. The quartet tapped their feet. And from the looks of it, they were tapping out a boatload of profanity.

"They're using the tap trick on Grover," Charlotte announced with a devious smirk, which was odd for the woman. Out of their foursome, Char was the sweet one.

"Who's Grover?" Landon asked.

"Grover Cleveland Schulte. He's a bit of a bully and not kind to mermaids," Charlotte answered.

Landon turned to her. "Mermaids?"

"Long story," Mitch replied with a wide grin, then wrapped his arm around Charlotte.

"The kids are holding their own," Raz said, crossing his arms. "Grover looks ready to crap his trousers. Nobody's throwing punches. As a former professional boxer, I say we let it play out."

"Give them back to us, you," Aria hollered, then tapped three times.

Rowen glanced at Landon. "What's Aria's word?"

"Douche nozzle."

"She's not far off the mark with that kid," Mitch murmured.

"She's using a strategy to control her anger," Libby remarked.

"And she's got more self-control than Harper did at that age," Penny teased.

But her friend had spoken too soon.

Aria lifted her tapping foot and reared back. Aiming at Grover's shin, the kid was seconds away from making contact when Oscar dove in front of her and absorbed the blow.

"That was unexpected," Mitch uttered as a young woman with a clipboard walked up to the group.

"I don't think he wanted Aria to get into trouble," Charlotte replied.

Penny sucked in a tight breath. "Oh, boy, here we go. That's Carrie Mackendorfer. She's the kids' second-grade teacher."

Rowen pulled his phone from his pocket. "I'll make another donation to the school."

What a way for Aria to make a first impression.

Still, the girl wasn't one to get angry for nothing. Grover must have been asking for it.

They watched as Miss Mackendorfer pointed to Grover's hand. The kid huffed, then handed something small to each child. The teacher spoke to the bully, then the boy bolted toward the playground.

"What did Grover take from the kids?" Charlotte asked.

"I don't know," Libby answered as the teacher escorted the badass tappers toward them.

"Hi there, I'm Carrie Mackendorfer. You must be the parents and guardians of Phoebe, Aria, Sebastian, and Oscar."

"We are. Is everything okay?" Libby asked. "We noticed there was a bit of a scuffle."

"We've got it sorted," the teacher answered warmly.

And thank goodness this educator seemed pretty chill.

"Are you all right, Oscar? I didn't mean to kick you," Aria said as she chewed on the end of her pigtail.

"I'm great. I'm super great," the kid gushed, smiling at Aria like she'd gifted him with a new camera and not a kick to the leg.

"That's good to hear," the teacher answered.

"And we weren't saying any bad words to Grover," Oscar added.

"I noticed the tapping. Mrs. Bergen told me about how you tap out syllables instead of using inappropriate language. It's a great way to stay out of trouble and communicate displeasure. But we can't kick people at Whitmore," the woman added and patted Aria on the shoulder.

"But Miss Mackendorfer," Phoebe lamented, "Grover took our super special erasers. We were showing each other that we had them when Grover grabbed them like a real..." Phoebe tapped twice.

"The kid sounds like a..." Rowen said under his breath, then tapped twice for Phoebe's naughty word of choice, *butthole*.

"She's right on the mark with that kid," Charlotte whispered.

"Aria's reverse nanny aunt gave them to us," Phoebe continued.

"And we decided that we'd be the eraser club kids," Oscar added.

Then as if on cue, the children opened their palms to reveal the tiny piano, camera, hot dog, and the little donkey that looked more like a horse, but it was the thought that counted. And OMG, not only did they love the little eraser gifts, they'd also brought their special treasures to school.

Score a point for Harper Presley-Paige, the thoughtful guardian.

"Well, eraser club kids," Miss Mackendorfer said, glancing

around the group, "I see we've got two new students joining our class."

"Yep, Aria and Sebastian," Oscar chimed. "Sebastian has donkeys, and Aria is...perfect," the boy mooned, staring at Aria like she was made of sugar and spice and everything nice.

"Welcome to Whitmore," the teacher said. "Phoebe, could you be Aria's Whitmore special helper?" she asked, then reached into her pocket and produced a star sticker with the words *special helper* printed in gold.

Phoebe gripped Oscar's arm and tittered like her body was on the verge of exploding. "Yes, I will wear the special helper sticker proudly. I will make sure Aria doesn't get lost on the way to the bathroom, and I will share the extra cookies I jammed into my lunch box with her."

"Extra cookies?" Rowen groaned.

"And Oscar, can you be Sebastian's Whitmore special helper?" the teacher continued and slipped a second sticker out of her pocket.

The boy accepted it. "You can count on me, Miss Mackendorfer." He turned to Charlotte. "Can you take our picture and use your camera and my camera?"

"Absolutely," Charlotte replied and removed her camera and Oscar's Polaroid from her large tote.

"You can stand by me, Aria," Oscar offered, still dreamy-eyed.

Mitch clapped Landon on the shoulder. "Not that she'll need it, man," he began, lowering his voice as the kids clustered together, "but it appears Aria's got a protector."

Landon nodded as a grin stretched across his lips.

They looked on as the fearsome foursome stood shoulder to shoulder.

"Say, 'eraser club kids,'" Char called, first snapping a shot with the Polaroid, then switching to her fancy DSLR camera.

Miss Mackendorfer checked her watch. "We've got a few

minutes until the bell rings. This is a good time to say your goodbyes."

The kids peeled away from their spots on the sidewalk and headed toward their people for last-minute hugs.

"You don't have to get mushy-gushy and huggy," Aria said, resurrecting the tough girl act.

"What if we want to get mushy-gushy and huggy?" Landon replied.

Aria sighed. "One hug. No kisses."

"One hug, no kisses, coming up," Landon replied, taking a knee to embrace his niece. He held her a second longer than usual. "I have a feeling your mom and dad are looking down at you right now and feeling so proud of you. You're one brave kid."

Aria stepped out of his embrace, unclenched her fist, and held up the little piano. "If I feel like I want to punch some kid in the belly or kick that Grover, before I do it, I'll look at this and think of you guys and mom and dad and Lolo and Lala, and I'll try not to get into trouble." The little girl looked up at her. "And Aunt Harper?"

"Yes?" she answered, willing herself not to turn into a blubbering mess.

Jesus, what was going on? She was not one to lose her shit.

"Is that why you gave me the little piano eraser? To help me do good at school and not punch the meanies?"

Cue the waterworks.

She blinked back tears and stared at the piano's teensy-tiny keys. She didn't know why she'd bought the little piano eraser —or maybe she did. Perhaps it was one of those cosmic signs Libby always talked about.

"Something like that," she answered and smoothed the wisps of hair that had come loose from Aria's pigtails.

"Come on, Aria," Phoebe called. "I'll show you where we line up."

The glimmer of a grin pulled at the corners of Aria's mouth, and she joined the kids as they set off for the blacktop.

And boom, their little spitfire was gone.

"I didn't think I'd feel like this," she uttered, more to herself than anyone else when a warmth engulfed her hand, and the familiar zing of her pop star's touch sent a tingle to her fingertips. She glanced at the man. Did he realize he'd clasped her hand in his, or was it his reaction to the moment?

She exhaled a slow breath, then caught the teacher's eye.

And she knew what she had to do.

"Could we speak with you for a second, Miss Mackendorfer, regarding Aria's learning style?"

Landon threw her a pointed look, but he didn't let go of her hand. "What are you doing?"

She gave his hand a gentle squeeze. "What we agreed to do."

"Sure, let's chat over here," the teacher answered and led them a few feet away to a spot with fewer people milling around. "What would you like to share?"

"Aria may be a neurodivergent learner. I wondered if you had experience with that?" she began as Landon's grip tightened.

"I'm glad you brought that up. When I looked through Aria's file from her old school, I noticed she might be a neurodivergent learner as well."

All right, she wasn't off the mark.

"The last school said Aria's learning issues were due to her parents' deaths," Landon offered, his voice barely a rasp.

The teacher nodded. "I noticed that. But after looking at her work samples, I agree with your wife, Mr. Paige. From the little I've seen, I suspect dyslexia. It's a type of neurodiversity."

Landon's posture stiffened. "Whatever you think she has, I don't want any attention drawn to her. I don't want her to feel different or stupid," he finished, his voice thick with emotion.

The teacher held Landon's gaze. "I agree completely."

The man's jaw dropped. "You do?"

"Absolutely. My job is to build up Aria. At Whitmore, we employ a multi-sensory approach to learning. We've got color-coded keyboards and line readers that set off text and use OpenDyslexic font on our computers and e-readers. We've found that these strategies help every child learn, but they're especially effective teaching tools for kids with different learning styles."

"What's OpenDyslexic font?" he asked, his tone softening.

The teacher slipped her cell phone from her pocket, then tapped the web browser and opened Whitmore's webpage. She held her phone out for them to see. "I've got it on my phone in case I need to reference something quickly with a student. It's a special font that's easier to read, and it's free to download onto any device. The OpenDyslexic font overrides the fonts on the page and switches it to this. The letters are formed with heavier bottoms. It helps keep the letters grounded and stops them from—"

"—moving around," Landon supplied, awe coating his words as he stared at the screen.

"Exactly," the teacher replied. "Aria is in good hands. We've got instructional specialists here who work with every child. We'll make sure she gets the support she needs to succeed."

Where were the Miss Mackendorfers of the world when she was in school?

It didn't get much better than that.

Hopefully, Landon agreed.

She chanced a look at the man, who no longer appeared ready to pounce.

"It might help you to know," she said, meeting the teacher's gaze, "that I've been working with Aria at home—with music lessons. I can relate to Aria because I was, well, I am a neurodivergent learner. Highlighting line by line seems to help Aria and me—at least with reading music."

"That's quite helpful. I'll let our teaching aides and classroom volunteers know so we can continue the practice at school. We can meet in a few weeks after I've had some time to work with Aria and touch base," the teacher replied as the bell rang. "We'll talk soon."

Anxiety rippled in her chest. She'd still be Aria's aunt in a few weeks, but there was no guarantee she'd hold the title for much longer.

She swallowed past the lump in her throat. "Thank you, Miss Mackendorfer."

"Yeah, we're grateful. You sound like you know what you're doing," Landon added.

The teacher nodded, then headed toward the mass of children congregating outside the entrance.

"She'll be okay," Landon whispered. He glanced up, then gazed at the lines of children snaking across the blacktop.

She squeezed his hand, not wanting to interrupt this moment when Raz's voice cut through the hum of children saying their goodbyes.

"Landon, mate!"

"Yeah?" he answered, snapping back.

"They're asking for parents and guardians to sign up for crossing guard duty, and Rowen's making us do it."

"Hey," the tech nerd chided, waving a finger at the men. "Had their teacher not intervened, our kids could have been seconds away from getting sent to the principal's office. We need to earn every brownie point we can."

Landon peered down at their joined hands. "I'm going to—"

"Of course, I'll wait with the girls."

He gave her hand a gentle squeeze, then hesitated before

he released it like he didn't want to let go. "Thanks for that, with the teacher."

"Go sign up for parent stuff," she replied, taking a page from Aria's playbook and doing all she could not to get mushy.

He nodded and joined the guys, and they set off toward a table near the edge of the parking lot as Penny, Libby, and Charlotte circled her like a trio of wild dogs.

She inhaled and counted down, waiting for her friends to explode with commentary.

Three.

Two.

One.

"Just look at our, Harper," Penny crooned.

"What about me?"

"She's got it," Charlotte chimed.

Libby nodded. "Yes, she does."

These women.

She groaned. "If I didn't love you guys so much, I'd pull an Aria and kick each of you in the shins. What are you talking about?"

Libby raised her hands like she was receiving a message from the great beyond. "Your banging nanny glow."

"I'm not officially the nanny," she countered.

"You're hanging out with Aria?" Penny offered.

"Yes."

Charlotte cocked her head to the side. "You care for her?"

"Obviously—she's the meanest seven-year-old this side of the Mississippi. I'm crazy about her."

Libby gestured with her chin toward the parking lot. "I've got a hunch that's your chocolate-colored Lamborghini Urus."

"The nanny SUV of choice for the nanny-match candidates," Penny quipped.

Her friends were enjoying this.

"Yes, I'm driving a Lamborghini."

Charlotte cleared her throat and glanced away. "And you're banging your boss?"

"Hell yes, I am," she fired back, then clapped her hand over her mouth. "Oh, crap."

Her friends shared a trio of knowing glances.

"Don't get any lofty ideas," she cautioned. "This isn't a perfect nanny match. It's not a nanny match at all. For the next six weeks, I'm Landon's temporary wife, his quasi-nanny, and his musical assistant."

Libby narrowed her gaze. "You and Landon agreed to get a divorce?"

She chewed her lip. She'd pushed that thought aside for the past fourteen days.

She waved them off, trying to play it cool. "We'll figure it out."

"And what about Aria?" Libby pressed.

"Whatever happens, I'll still see her. I'll just be her piano teacher. And there's something else. Landon's helping me by—"

"Providing you with multiple orgasms?" Charlotte interrupted.

She ignored the redhead.

"And what's with this six-week timeframe?" Penny asked.

"We're competing in a celebrity reality baking contest. If we win, there's prize money I can use to pay off Babs' debt. It starts tomorrow with the first of three challenges and concludes in about six weeks."

Crickets.

Her friends stood there, slack-jawed, until Penny turned to Libby and Charlotte. "We can never *not* talk to H for two weeks again."

"You're doing a reality show?" Charlotte pressed.

Penny tapped her chin. "Is that why you had to leave the

housewarming with Landon? Was that what his manager wanted to discuss?"

"Yes."

"But you don't bake, H," Charlotte added.

Like she didn't know that.

"I eat baked goods. How hard can it be to bake them?"

"You can pack away the bonbons—not that I'm blaming you. The bakery by your grandma's place makes delectable confections," Libby offered.

Penny crossed her arms. "Are you serious? This is for real?"

"Yes, it's real. A lawyer was there. It's legit. We just have to beat some other celebrity team."

"Are you sure you won't let us help you with the house? It's not a burden," Charlotte offered.

"Oh no," Libby breathed, taking a step back. "You've done it now, Char. H's aura shifted."

"Yeah, my aura shifted. Like I told you before, I'm handling the situation—on my own," she answered.

"Then we wish you luck. If anyone can kick ass in a reality show, it's you, H," Penny added.

Libby did that thing with her hands where she looked like she was communing with the universe. "I agree. I'm picking up a good vibe. You've got this."

"And we've got to get to the office," Rowen said to his fiancée. "Video games don't make themselves."

"And I've got an appointment with a gallery," Charlotte trilled. "And you've got food truck chefs-in-training to oversee," she finished, taking Mitch's hand.

"We beat you all," Raz announced with a shit-eating grin. "We're testing vibrator prototypes."

Libby shook her head. "You love announcing that, don't you, beefcake?"

"You bet your arse I do," he answered and wrapped his arm around his fiancée.

Their friends dispersed and left in their corresponding Lamborghinis.

Landon took her hand and brought it to his lips. The man kissed her knuckles.

"What was that for?" she asked as they headed toward the car.

He opened the passenger side door for her, beaming like a kid on Christmas. "I'm damned happy. We're not bad at this, are we?"

The warmth of his expression and the magnetism of his grin drew her in. It was easy to see why the man had legions of fans.

"Aria's off to a good start," she answered. She wanted to bask in this *we* moment, but a twinge of unease held her back.

Landon got in the car, and they headed to her place in Baxter Park.

She stared out the window at the familiar landmarks as a comfortable silence settled.

Landon's grin widened as he tapped his fingers on the steering wheel, keeping the beat to the song on the radio. She had a good idea of what was on her pop star's mind.

Leighton and Trey.

They pulled into the driveway, and Landon cut the ignition. But neither moved.

She sat back and drank in his profile. "What was it like when you, Leighton, and Trey were just starting out and entire stadiums would chant your name?"

He turned and pegged her with his gaze. The darkness that often preceded him talking about Heartthrob Warfare didn't appear. "It's like electricity taking over your body—a pulse that connects you to something greater than yourself. I didn't think there was anything like it until…"

She watched him closely. "Until what?"

"Until…you." He cupped her face in his hands, and his

dreamy brown eyes were damned near hypnotizing. "Thank you for today."

And she was speechless.

The girl who was always armed with a snarky comeback sat there, doe-eyed and ecstatic—really freaking ecstatic. There was no use fighting it. She blocked out the whispers in her head, reminding her that this guy was still a musician.

He pressed a kiss to the corner of her mouth. "I thought of something."

"Oh yeah? And what's that?"

"We're alone," he answered with a devilish twist to his lips. Before she could blink, he released his hold on her cheek. In one swift movement, he unbuckled her seat belt, lifted her across the console, and hoisted her onto his lap.

She gasped and steadied herself by gripping the side of the door. She hit the button that lowered the window a few inches, then feigned indignation as the breeze lifted the tendrils that framed her face. "What's going on here?" But she couldn't deny being manhandled by this big, strong, gorgeous celebrity was a crazy hot turn-on.

"It's about me wanting you right this very second," he said and slipped his hands beneath her skirt. He palmed her ass, and a primal yearning glimmered in his eyes. "You're not wearing underwear."

She tossed his ball cap onto the passenger seat and wrapped her arms around his neck. "I am not."

"You are a woman of her word."

"And speaking of keeping one's word," she said and plucked his phone from the center console.

"What are you doing?" he asked.

She rocked her hips, grinding into him as she did a quick internet search and found what she was looking for. "A deal is a deal. I'm putting the OpenDyslexic font on your phone. Remember, I go commando, and you—"

"—go crazy wanting to screw your brains out."

She hit install, then tossed his phone onto the seat next to his cap. "Got to give a little to get a little, Mr. Heartthrob." She swayed her hips. While he hadn't exactly sat down with her to talk strategies for reading and writing music, he was never far from her when she worked with Aria. And that had to count for something.

"I've got something to give you," he rasped, pressing his fingertips into her ass.

She rubbed against him as their bodies created delicious friction. "Do you like that?" she teased.

"It's sweet, so sweet. Hello to my favorite treat," he sang.

And hello, Swoon City.

The world melted away when this man sang to her.

"What is this bliss? It's Harper with a bonbon kiss."

With his cock stroking her sweet spot and his voice in her ear, he could order her to jump, and she'd ask how high.

"How do you do it?" she purred between kisses.

"It's a pop god perk," he answered, then kissed her with the intensity of a pop god with one thing on his mind.

And what was that one thing?

Total carnal release.

And she could say with one hundred percent certainty she was on the same page as this Paige.

Her body burned for the man.

She tangled her fingers in the hair at the nape of his neck and rattled off one glorious moan as they dry-humped away in the driveway.

"Look who's singing for me," he rasped.

There was a decent helping of maddening arrogance in his tone, but the guy wasn't wrong.

"Should we take this inside and get down and dirty on every flat surface?" she teased.

"Yeah…about that," came a voice that didn't belong to her or her heartthrob.

She and Landon froze, then slowly turned to look out the half-opened window.

A lanky guy wearing sunglasses and a beanie with a large box in his hands peered in at them.

"Sorry, dudes," he crooned like he'd been sent by central casting for the part of gnarly surfer. "I hate to crash your free-love vibe, but it's time to get baked."

Chapter 21
HARPER

Harper studied the dude.

It was time to turn on the charm.

She channeled Aria's *eat worms* expression. "Who the hell are you?"

"I'm Tanner, dude," the guy replied with a surfer-tastic bend to the words.

"That doesn't mean anything to me, *dude*," she fired back. She glanced at Landon. The man sat there slack-jawed like he wasn't sure this was really happening.

Neither was she.

"Are you lost?" Landon asked.

"Aren't we all a little lost, dude? Like, metaphorically?" the guy mused, stretching each syllable as his grin widened.

What was happening?

She met Landon's gaze. "Did we get into a car crash on the way home, and now we're experiencing head trauma? Or maybe some chemical got released into the air, and we're hallucinating?"

The surfer-voice dude shifted the box in his arms. "Those can be excellent for creativity."

"Car crashes?" she posited.

"Hallucinations," he countered.

Hello, Mr. Weirdo.

She looked him over. He had dark sunglasses, and tufts of brown hair peeked out of a green beanie. He didn't look dangerous, but she couldn't tell what was inside the decent-sized box in his hands.

He shifted his load to the crook of one arm and lowered his sunglasses. "Aren't you the eight cents lady, or am I hallucinating?"

What?

She leaned in toward her heartthrob and lowered her voice. "This guy is either totally out of his mind, or I'm right. We're dead and we've landed in some bizarro purgatory."

Landon peered at the guy. "Wait, you're high AF, right?"

Her gaze ping-ponged between the men.

Did everyone with a Y chromosome suddenly lose their mind?

"I mean, not yet, dude, but the day will proceed as the day proceeds. And what is meant to happen will likely happen," the guy replied.

She stared at her husband. "You know him?"

"I recognize him from the convenience store."

The convenience store?

She studied the dude, then gasped. It was the clerk who wouldn't let her take eight pennies from the take a penny, leave a penny dish.

Why would he come to her house?

She had a hunch, but it wasn't good.

"Did that old bag turn me in or file a report with the cops because of the plant scuffle?"

Dammit, this is what she gets for threatening senior citizens.

"What, dude?" the dude replied.

"The convenience store, where you work?" she clarified.

"I don't work there. I was filling in for a friend that day."

"Can you do that?"

He shrugged. "Why not? I did. I'm a jack of all trades, dabbling in many pursuits, including several agricultural endeavors."

What the actual F did that mean?

She cocked her head to the side. "If you're not here to serve me with a convenience store restraining order, what brings you to my house?"

"My nephew, Tanner Baker, is assisting me, so I can help you," came another man's voice. This voice didn't contain the same hang ten cadence as the dude staring into the Lambo, but she recognized it, nonetheless.

And if she'd thought she was busted before, she was really in trouble now.

Tanner stepped out of the way, revealing a slight, older gentleman with a bald head and a white handlebar mustache.

Schuman Sweet.

The same Mr. Schuman Sweet who owned the Baxter Park Bakery, which had recently become a Cupid Bakery.

The man who, alongside his wife, had sold her family bonbons for the better part of her life.

And the person who'd banned her from the shop, pending a note from her grandmother.

"Mr. Sweet?" she eked out, hitting a high C.

"You're the bakery owner, aren't you?" Landon asked, studying the man.

She returned her attention to her husband. "You know him?"

"I recognize him."

"As you should," Mr. Sweet said matter-of-factly in his gentle German accent. "Many years ago, you used to come into the bakery with your sister and your parents, Mr. Paige."

That's right! Landon had mentioned he'd lived in the area before his parents died.

"I think your wife used to slip an extra bonbon into our order. That was your wife, wasn't it, sir?" Landon asked, wonder coating his words like he'd opened a door in his mind that had been previously jammed shut.

The old man glanced away. "Yes, that was her. She liked to sweeten people's orders with an extra bonbon or two. She's...fine."

Yikes, had there been a falling out between the Sweets?

Come to think of it. She hadn't seen the woman in a while.

Still, Mr. Sweet's lovelife wasn't any of her business, and she'd had enough of the small talk.

She needed to know why Mr. Sweet had crashed her place with his surfer-dude nephew.

"It's lovely to see you, sir," she began. "What brings you to my house? I'm not in trouble, am I? Landon's agent said she'd pay for the bonbons I...borrowed."

"Stole," the man corrected, "along with one of my baking sheets."

How much did the man know about her shady bakery undertakings?

"Let's not get into specifics," she replied, going for nonchalance. "And just as a side note—I absolutely haven't had a child purchasing bonbons for me without my grandmother's permission."

Might as well cover her bases for the recent bonbon mischief.

"You mean Aria?" the man replied with a twitch of a grin.

"How do you know her name?" she shot back.

"I asked her. She's been in five times in two weeks to purchase bonbons while you hide in the bushes. She's a regular now."

She felt her cheeks heat. "I wasn't hiding in the bushes."

The man removed a folded sheet of paper from his pocket and handed it through the half-open window. She straightened and mustered as much dignity as one caught mid-bump-and-grind could and unfolded the sheet.

"We have cameras inside and outside the shop," Schuman said as she gazed at a lunatic, aka, herself, wedged between a pair of juniper hedges.

She had two choices: 'fess up to being the bonbon bandit and apologize for her chocolate indiscretions or add a layer of sass to her demeanor.

"Well, my grandma's not here, Mr. Sweet," she huffed like a cantankerous child, choosing the latter approach. "So you'll have to wait a few weeks to tattle on the singing bonbon bandit."

"I'm not here to tattle on you," the man answered.

"Then why are you here?" she asked, losing the sass.

"I told them we're getting baked today, Uncle Schuman," Tanner said, shifting the box and revealing a rather large bag of lollipops.

She could go for one of those.

"We're not getting baked, Tanner. We're baking," Schuman corrected. "I'm the baking coach for the *Celebrity Bake or Bust* contest," the man replied through a yawn.

What the hell?

"You are?" Landon asked.

"I am, Mr. Paige. I'm sorry I couldn't meet with you a few weeks ago. I was called away on an emergency."

This must be a meet and greet to prepare for tomorrow's challenge. Why hadn't she put it together?

It made sense that Mr. Sweet would be their coach now that the Baxter Park bakery had joined the Cupid Bakery family, and that's where they'd met with the Luxe lawyer. Then again, she'd seen Mr. Sweet less and less over the last few years. When she was a kid, he'd socialize with customers. Nowadays, not so much.

"Didn't you see the emails from Luxe Media and Entertainment and the LookyLoo peeps? They moved up the first challenge to today," Tanner explained.

"They did what?" she exclaimed.

Tanner shifted the box, and several lollipops trickled out of the bag. "They changed the date. That's why I'm wearing these," he added and tapped the glasses.

"You wear sunglasses when you bake?" she uttered.

"No, I wear them for audio-visual purposes."

Her jaw dropped. "You're recording us?"

"No," the dude answered, stretching the syllable.

"Thank goodness," she replied on a relieved breath.

"I'm livestreaming straight to LookyLoo."

Oh shit!

She blocked the sun and craned her neck to get a better look at the glasses.

There it was—a tiny camera lens built into the bridge above his nose.

Her heart hammered. "Did you film us…"

"Sucking face?" Tanner supplied.

"Yeah."

"Not on purpose. When most people pull into their driveway, they get out of the car. They don't get freaky and—"

"Okay, man, we get it," Landon said, cutting off Tanner's commentary.

Welp, the world had watched a shirtless Landon Paige wed her in nothing but his T-shirt and a pair of boots. As far as the media was concerned, getting caught making out in a Lambo wasn't that big a deal.

"If you wouldn't mind exiting the vehicle," Mr. Sweet said, checking his watch. "We don't have much time until you're due to present your baked goods at the first challenge."

Then it clicked.

This was it. This was part one of the opportunity to make fifty large for Babs, and she needed to bring her A game ASAP.

She grabbed Landon's hat, plopped it on his head, and shimmied off his lap. "Are you ready?"

"Do we have a choice?" he tossed back.

"Good point." She grabbed her tote, scrambled out of the car, and smoothed her skirt, which didn't release the mega-make-out wrinkles.

No bother. She might be commando, but at least she'd showered that morning. That had to be a good omen.

She brushed her hair over her shoulders.

It was go-time.

She had to play the part. She had to be the baker.

She needed to harness the energy of Katrina and the Waves' hit "Walking on Sunshine" but make it the baking version.

She replayed the song's peppy tempo and upbeat lyrics in her head.

Yes, this was the vibe.

She grinned like an idiot and directed her attention to the sunglasses' camera. "Right this way," she crooned and gestured toward the house. "We're walking on sunshine and ready to rock this baking challenge." She glanced at Landon. "Was that too much? Am I laying it on too thick?"

He chuckled. "I'm good with the 'Walking on Sunshine' shout-out, but it doesn't matter now, bonbon."

"Why not?"

He gestured toward Tanner. "This is a livestream event, emphasis on *live*."

She stared into the sunglasses' cam. "Shit," she hissed, then gasped. "I mean, whoops-a-daisy, not shit. Shit is a bad word."

Pull yourself together, woman.

Like a deranged realtor, she led everyone to the backdoor and welcomed Schuman and Tanner into the kitchen as Landon shut the door and mouthed, "*What are you doing?*"

She was going with the flow.

"Here we are," she announced, gesturing to the kitchen as she continued her deranged realtor shtick. "This is where the magic happens." She glanced at the sink, recalling the magical orgasmic explosion that had occurred there. And blast her crazy lady nerves. She couldn't have the livestream viewers think she was talking about sex. After catching them sucking face in the driveway, it was a logical conclusion and one she had to snuff out. "And when I say magic," she crooned, "I mean baking magic, not sex magic. Nope, no sex magic in this kitchen. We save that for the soundproof room in the basement or the bedroom."

Landon gawked at her—and rightly so.

She had to get control of her naughty-word spewing, sex-talking mouth.

She stared at her husband like a deer caught in the head-lights and made *help-me* eyes at him, praying he'd decipher her ocular cry for assistance.

He strode toward her and flashed his dreamy pop star half-grin at Tanner and his livestreaming glasses. "Why don't we turn this over to our baking coach, Mr. Schuman Sweet, from Cupid Bakery. We're so grateful to have him here, and he can fill everyone in on the first challenge," Landon said with prac-ticed ease. Then again, he was a pop star. He had experience speaking to the masses—and thank God for that.

"Thank you, Landon," the baking coach replied, watching her for a beat as one would regard a shrieking hyena. He slipped a card from his pocket, then focused on Tanner's camera glasses. "The first challenge is the sugar cookie chal-lenge," he read. "Today, our celebrity contestants are tasked with preparing this bakery staple to celebrate the one-year anniversary of..." The man cleared his throat. "Of Denver's Singing Grannies Choral Group."

Was this guy getting emotional about old ladies singing?

Stop and focus.

"Cookies for singing grannies, okay," she whispered as Landon took her hand and led her to the corner of the room.

"What's going on?" he whispered as Schuman addressed the camera.

"What do you mean?" She leaned against the counter, trying to play it cool, but she hadn't noticed Tanner's box perched on the edge. She startled when her elbow bumped the cardboard surface.

"You appear to be a little jumpy."

"I do?"

"You do."

She fiddled with the corner of the cardboard box. "Anytime I've been on camera, I've worn a mask. It must be nerves."

"Relax, take a breath. People are watching because they want to be entertained. They want to escape through you," Landon said calmly, as though when he wasn't living the life of a pop star, he enjoyed moonlighting as a hostage negotiator.

She nodded and exhaled a slow breath, then scanned the items in the box and noticed the lollipops.

Thank you, candy gods.

She plucked a red one from a plastic bag and jammed it into her mouth.

Landon watched her go to town on the sucker. "Do you think you should be eating those?"

"I'm sure one won't hurt, and I could use the hit of sugar." She stilled. "Hmm, it tastes...odd," she noted, then continued sucking away like she'd entered a lollipop eating contest.

Landon eyed her warily. "Is something wrong with it?"

"It's cherry, but it's got a peculiarly earthy flavor," she answered as Landon glanced at Mr. Sweet.

He pressed his hand to her back and leaned in. "Get your earthy lollipop fill, bonbon. It sounds like our baking coach is wrapping up his intro."

A strange calmness came over her as she chomped the sucker into tiny slivers, swallowed down the sugar-laden treat, then tossed the stick behind the toaster to dispose of the evidence.

Thank you, cherry-flavored sugar.

Libby would be impressed with her Zen master skills.

She focused on Mr. Sweet, and just like Landon had guessed, the man was wrapping up his commentary. He crossed the kitchen, entered the living room, and settled himself on the couch. The man expelled one hell of a yawn as he positioned a throw pillow behind his neck.

At least he was making himself at home. Surely he'd perk up when it was time to bake.

But there wasn't any time to worry about Schuman Sweet chill-laxing in her house. Tanner turned to them, and she turned up the wattage on her grin, but the guy removed the glasses and slipped them into his pocket.

"You're done livestreaming?" Landon asked.

"What happens next? Do we need to continue the livestream on our phones?" she asked, recalling the attorney's description of the challenge, when a rhythmic snuffling floated into the kitchen. She glanced into the living room and found the source of the sound. "Your uncle is asleep," she whispered, stating the obvious as Schuman's head drooped to the side.

The baker was out for the count.

Tanner nodded. "He's had a lot going on. That's why I'm here helping out."

Landon looked between the uncle and the nephew. "So, you know how to bake?"

"Totally," Tanner whispered. "Back in Kringle Mountain —that's where I'm from—I work at the Cupid Bakery in town, and I help in the kitchen at Kringle Mountain House. I also oversee other agricultural endeavors utilizing candy and baked goods."

There he was with that cryptic "agricultural endeavors" lingo again.

Whatever! She had to put that out of her head.

"I'm glad you know how to bake, because we don't know anything about making cookies from scratch." She pointed to the box. "Is that everything we'll need?"

"That's right, take-a-penny-leave-a-penny lady. Those are the ingredients."

Landon scanned the items. "Can you help us get started?"

Tanner's easygoing disposition darkened. "Ooh, dude, that's a no."

"No?" she and Landon chimed.

"I have to leave. I've got an MJ issue to address," the guy said, edging toward the door. "You know, a *Mary Jane* situation."

It wasn't a surprising issue for a guy with a beanie reading High AF.

Tanner reached into the box and removed the plastic bag filled with lollipops.

"What should we do?" she asked, eyeing the suckers.

She could really go for another.

Tanner removed a timer from the box and handed it to Landon. The device flashed one hour and twenty-four minutes.

No, one hour and twenty-three minutes.

"Is this how much time we have to bake?" Landon asked.

"This is how much time you have to bake and drive to the challenge," Tanner explained.

She shared a look with her heartthrob. "That doesn't seem like a lot of time."

"You'll be cutting it close, but it's doable. Follow the recipe. You're making Uncle Schuman's famous sugar cookies. The contest people should have emailed the deets."

She nodded. Oddly, she wasn't as freaked out as she thought she would be.

Maybe she was walking on baking sunshine.

And the thought of making cookies now sounded hella amazing.

She'd never been a fan of sugar cookies. She was a chocolate girl through and through, but she could sure chow down on a half dozen cookies or so.

Landon checked his phone. "I see the email," he said, staring at the screen like he'd opened the message that contained the answer to the meaning of life.

Another good sign.

"Good luck, dudes. Catch you later," Tanner called, tucking the plastic bag beneath his shirt.

"Wait, what about your uncle?" Landon called, tossing a glance at the snoring baker.

"I'd let him sleep. This isn't a tricky recipe. Make sure you follow every instruction to a T," the guy replied, then slipped out the door.

She scanned the kitchen and zeroed in on one appliance.

The oven.

It was as if the shiny metal box called to her.

Bake in me, Harper.

Fill me with sugary deliciousness.

"I hear you, oven," she whispered.

Landon watched her closely. "What did you say?"

"I'm connecting with the oven," she answered, then slid her gaze to Tanner's box of ingredients. She peered inside, suddenly fascinated with all things baking-related, and spied a rainbow of color scattered about the bottom. "A bunch of lollipops fell out of Tanner's plastic bag," she said, choosing a pink one. She sampled the sucker. "Watermelon. It's so watermelon-y but still a touch earthy," she gushed, then concentrated on the contents. "What do you think the number one cookie cutter is for?"

Landon cocked his head to the side. "To cut the cookies

into the shape of a number one. Are you sure you're okay? Schuman went over that in his intro."

"Oops, my mind's on candy and cookies. Mm-hmm," she hummed, sucking the daylights out of the watermelon lollipop. "Let's get this baking show on the road."

Landon scanned his phone. "Recap, Miss Lollipop Lover, we're baking sugar cookies for an organization that's turning one today. Hence, the number one cookie cutter."

"Hence," she giggled. "You sound like Shakespeare."

Was her husband always this funny?

"Harper, focus," the man chided.

That's precisely what she needed to do.

"Sugar helps my focus," she replied. She plucked a purple lollipop from the box and slipped it into her mouth. "What do we do first, heartthrob?"

"Get your phone and open it to the email with the livestream link. We can film using yours and follow the recipe on mine."

She retrieved her cell from her tote and opened her email. After scrolling through a digital mountain of junk, she spied a message from Luxe Media and Entertainment. "Are you sure you don't want me to do the reading?"

The man grinned, and she could feel the elation coming off him like rays of sunshine.

More sunshine.

"I'm good," he said, wonder coating his words. "This new font is—"

"—the cat's meow. *Meow, wow, wow, wow,*" she meowed, punctuating each *ow* by waving the lolly like she was conducting a feline quartet. She stuck the candy into her mouth. "I don't know why I'm talking like a cat."

"It's probably nerves," Landon replied, tucking a lock of her hair behind her ear. "You're a pianist. What do you usually do before you perform to work out the anxious energy?"

"It's been a while. I haven't performed since Vance left me," she admitted.

Had it been that long?

Landon's eyes glowed with a fiery intensity. "What did you do before that douche nozzle?"

She pushed aside the rush of angry Vance Vibe vibes and thought back to her childhood. "I'd sing. I'd make up songs just like I used to do with my grandparents on our walks to the bakery."

Landon held her gaze. "Then that's what we'll do," he directed, turning his attention to her cell phone. He gently removed it from her grasp. "We'll sing and bake."

"On the livestream?" she stammered.

"It's livestream or bust, bonbon. Think of your grandmother. You want to win, don't you?"

They had to win, and that meant doing whatever it took.

She finished her third lollipop and flicked the stick into the garbage. "*I,*" she sang with a shimmy shake, "*want to win,*" she continued adding a soft clap. "*I want to win. Win, win, win, win, win, win, win, win, win.*" She eyed her husband. "What do you think? It's like I can taste the notes."

Landon set the phones down on the counter and took her into his arms. "This is what I think whenever you sing," he answered and pressed his lips to hers.

And holy, pump up the volume! She dissolved into his embrace. His kiss penetrated her soul. Gentle and reverent, it buzzed through her like a swarm of music-loving, giant, fuzzy bumblebees.

"However," he crooned against her mouth as the vibration of his words mingled with her fuzzy bumblebee buzz.

"However?" she repeated.

"*Since this is supposed to be for charity,*" he sang.

His voice had her ready to remind the man she wasn't wearing panties.

"Yes?" she whispered, exercising considerable restraint.

"Try substituting *bake* for *win*."

She smiled against his mouth. "This is why you're the lyrical genius," she replied, feeling the baking rhythm in her bones.

Landon raised an eyebrow. "Lyrical genius? What's gotten into you?"

"Sugar," she answered, flashing a devilish grin.

He drank her in with those dreamy brown eyes. "Are you ready?"

"I am."

The kitchen pulsed around her, or it could have been Mr. Sweet snoring. Whatever it was, a lightness worked its way through her body.

Landon retrieved her phone. "I'll count you down, then set the phone on the window ledge to get a wide-angle view of the kitchen."

"Okay." If she didn't know better, she'd assume she'd left her body to float around the space like a baking spirit.

Harper, Patron Saint of Culinary Confections.

Landon held up the phone. "Three, two, one."

She stared into the camera. "*Hello, LookyLoo, I'm Harper Presley-Paige, and I'm here to bake. To bake. I want to bake, bake, bake, bake, bake,*" she chanted. "I'm with Landon Paige. And we're making music and sugar cookies."

Damn, girl, that was some smooth talking!

She'd need to thank her tongue, which was quite tingly.

It had to be the excitement.

Landon put his arm around her and held the phone in front of them as a bevy of heart emojis flooded the screen.

"They like us?" he asked as a flurry of thumbs-up and a continuous flow of hearts answered his question.

And her silly heart skipped a beat.

"Here we go," Landon said, setting her phone on the ledge and swiping his from the counter.

He looked at the camera. "First thing, preheat the oven to three seventy-five."

"On it," she sang, skipping across the kitchen to tap her favorite oven. "Next."

"Cream the sugar and the butter. But the butter needs to be soft," Landon read, grinning ear to ear. His joy rays positively lit up the space.

She retrieved the two sticks of butter, then banged them on the counter, doing a little drum solo. "They're pretty stiff."

He bit back a grin, and she struggled to keep a straight face.

She stared at the sticks. "How soft is soft when it comes to butter?"

The man cringed. "I don't know."

But the microwave knew. It whispered to her in a husky rasp.

I can soften your butter, Harper.

When did the appliances become so intuitive?

She dashed across the kitchen, grabbed a bowl, then unwrapped the sticks of butter and plopped them in. "I'll microwave them for a minute. No, I'll do two minutes to make sure they're super soft." She concentrated on the keypad. "You know what to do, don't you?"

"Who are you talking to, bonbon?" Landon asked.

"Myself," she answered, tossing the microwave a wink, then glided to the box. She eyed the lollipops scattered among the ingredients. She plucked another cherry one from the bottom and held it up. "Do you want one? There are a bunch in here."

He waved her off. "No, I'm good."

"And these are so good," she crowed, working on lollipop number four when the timer beeped. It was her buddy, the microwave. She twirled across the floor, retrieved the bowl, and stared at the butter. She frowned. The butter no longer looked like butter. "It's pretty liquidy."

"The recipe says to make sure it's softened. What could be softer than liquid?" Landon replied.

This would be a great time to get some input from their baking coach.

She peered past Landon into the living room. They weren't about to get any expert advice. With his hands folded on his belly, Schuman dozed peacefully.

Liquid butter it was, and the microwave wouldn't do her wrong.

In all the years she'd lived in this house, she'd never experienced the sheer power of the kitchen.

Following Landon's directions, she busted out Babs' mixer. Like two baking machines, they creamed the butter and sugar, added the vanilla extract and the eggs, then whipped it up. Incorporating the flour, baking soda, and salt, she had a good feeling—a really good feeling.

She hummed and twirled. The room swayed and breathed along with her.

"What next?" she asked, staring at the dough.

"We need to form it into a ball, wrap it in plastic, then pop it in the fridge for an hour." He frowned and checked the clock. "We've got less than an hour before the challenge ends."

And that's when the next appliance sent her a secret.

I'm here, and I'm so very cold.

"Freezer, fifteen minutes," she exclaimed.

Landon flashed her that pop star smile. "Works for me."

She grabbed the plastic wrap from the box and tossed it to him. The man scooped the dough from the mixing bowl, formed it into a ball, and wrapped the shit out of it.

Maybe they were better bakers than she'd realized.

She drummed a beat on the counter as the man worked.

"I didn't know you played drums," he said, glancing over his shoulder.

"I don't. I'm getting a vibe from the dough. I've never been more connected to a kitchen in my entire life," she replied, snagging a spatula and a whisk from the drawer to add texture to the sound.

Boom, boom, chick, boom, boom.

Landon placed the dough in the freezer, then grabbed his guitar from the corner of the room.

"Are you feeling this, heartthrob?" she asked, switching up the beat.

Boom, chick, boom, boom, chick, boom, boom.

He strummed the guitar and layered in a catchy melody. "*Come on, dough, get cold,*" he sang, serenading the freezer.

"*Come on, dough, get cold,*" she added, harmonizing with the man.

Not only could she feel the music, but she could also taste it and smell it. And their voices came together like two lyrical vines wrapping around each other. She closed her eyes, and a pair of images materialized.

Landon and Aria.

She fixated on the vision as a fluttering tingle took over.

Was she floating?

Was she flying?

Could she feel her tongue?

Those were weird questions.

She eased into the vision, walking on sunshine, twirling on cookies, and singing with bonbons. She'd fallen into a dreamy Candy Land with her pop star and her niece, skipping along a rainbow path, laughing and singing as their lyrics lingered in the rays of light.

"Harper, can you hear me?"

"Yeah?" she answered.

"Something is wrong with the cookies."

Landon sounded awful.

She blinked. "We haven't baked the cookies. We're waiting for the dough to cool."

"That was over thirty minutes ago."

"Over thirty minutes ago?" she exclaimed, welcoming her opera voice. "How could that much time have passed?"

"You spaced out when you started humming a slow and damned catchy melody. So I kept going. I followed the recipe, rolled out the dough, and made a bunch of number ones."

"No, that can't be. I closed my eyes for a few seconds to visit Candy Land. You were there, and so was Aria."

"Harper, what are you talking about? I made the cookies, but they don't look right."

"It's the butter," came Mr. Sweet's voice.

Look who woke up.

He stood at the counter, then turned to face them.

She crossed the kitchen, then touched the tip of his handlebar mustache.

The man reared back. "What are you doing?"

What the hell was she doing?

"Sorry, I've wanted to do that since I was five years old." She shook her head, still quite lightheaded. "What's wrong with the butter, and what happened to the cookies?"

"How soft was the butter when you combined it with the sugar?" Schuman pressed.

"It was completely melted," Landon answered.

"That explains it," the man huffed.

"I don't understand," she replied when Mr. Sweet stepped out of the way, revealing the baking pan filled with row upon row of...

She glanced at the phone on the ledge. There was no way it could see the cookies. She waved in her husband. "Holy baking fail, pop star! Why did you make penis cookies?"

"I didn't," the man whispered back, tossing a worried look

at the livestreaming cell phone. "You and Mr. Sweet zonked out, so I did it myself. They looked like number ones when I used the cookie-cutter, but they baked into—"

"—tiny penises," she whispered and giggled. "Tiny penises with balls attached." She studied the penises and frowned. "Why does that look so familiar?" she mused.

One after another, golden-brown penises with golden-brown ball sacs graced the baking tray.

"Why did this happen, Mr. Sweet?" Landon asked with sheer horror written on his face.

"The recipe called for the butter to be softened, not liquified," Mr. Sweet said, shaking his head.

"Why does that matter?"

"Because when the butter is liquid, the dough enlarges and expands while baking, causing the tip of the number one to mushroom and the base of the number to…"

"Look like a ball sac," she whispered.

"Yes," the gentleman agreed.

"Landon Paige," she giggle-whispered, "you created cookie erections."

What was up with the giggling? She wasn't a giggler.

Landon went to the ledge and peered into the camera. "We hope you enjoyed the livestream, and we'll see you at the challenge." He pocketed the phone, then came to her side. "Harper, what is going on with you? You're not acting like yourself."

"What do you mean?" she said, then caught sight of the oven. "You, oven, were very naughty to give us cookie erections."

Mr. Sweet walked up to her with the ingredients box in his hands. "There were lollipops in here. You didn't eat one, did you?"

"Oh, I ate more than one, and they were *dee-la-la-la-la-*

licious," she sang, and again, she wasn't sure what was going on with her tongue. It was Tingle City inside her mouth.

"How many have you had?" Schuman pressed.

"She's had four," Landon answered.

"Four?" Schuman bellowed.

"What's wrong with the lollipops?" her heartthrob pressed.

These men needed to chill. Those lollipops were out of this world.

"Are the lollipops making my tongue tingle?" she asked and pressed the tip of her tongue to the kitchen table, then to the chair, then to the toaster. "Weird, everything tastes like buzzy sunshine."

"Buzzy sunshine?" Landon exclaimed. "Harper, stop licking the table!"

"I'm not licking the table. I'm testing my tongue and sampling sunshine."

Yeah, she understood that tongue testing was a little strange, but so was communicating with ovens and microwaves, and that had been a lovely experience.

Schuman tossed a nervous glance her way, then eyed the timer. "Pack up the cookies, kids. We've got to go. I'll tell you everything in the car."

Chapter 22

LANDON

"I need answers, Mr. Sweet. Harper is not one to lick furniture and talk to appliances."

Well, there's a sentence he'd never expected to utter.

This day had taken a turn he sure as hell hadn't expected, and he had to know what he was dealing with.

There was too much at stake, and he doubted that the woman who'd kissed her toaster goodbye was in the appropriate state of mind to be in it to win it.

Schuman Sweet had some explaining to do.

He glanced at the man seated in the passenger seat as they traveled the city streets.

"This is not Harper. She doesn't commune with can openers. She's a get-in-your-face and tell-you-where-you-can-shove-it kind of woman."

Schuman Sweet chuckled. "She's been like that since she was a little girl."

He didn't doubt it, but this wasn't the time to trade Harper stories. "What's happened to her? Why is she acting like she's lost her mind? What is in those lollipops?" he pressed, lowering his voice. He checked the rearview mirror to confirm his wife was still breathing in the back seat. Harper sat stock-still and gazed at her left hand like it was made of bonbons—which she might believe it was.

Still, despite the bizarro behavior, she appeared rather content.

Schuman drummed his fingers on the plastic container that held the penis competition cookies.

Penis competition cookies.

And there was another string of words he'd never imagined putting together.

"Should we head to the hospital?"

"No, she doesn't need a hospital," Mr. Sweet answered. "For all intents and purposes, she's fine. She's simply in an altered state."

He checked the mirror again and found Harper trying to touch her tongue to the tip of her nose. "I need more information than that, sir."

Schuman nodded. The guy appeared pretty damned chill for dropping the *your wife is in an altered state* bomb. "Harper ingested an edible candy infused with fungi," the man continued.

"Fungi?"

"Fungi," Schuman repeated.

"Mushrooms?"

"Yes," the baker agreed.

And now, his wife's behavior made sense. "The lollipops contained mushrooms, and I'm guessing they're not the kind of fungi mushrooms you pick up at the grocery store and sauté with garlic as a side dish."

"Correct, Mr. Paige."

"Harper's on shrooms?"

The old man cringed. "That's such a derogatory term. But yes, those weren't Portobello mushrooms mixed into the lollipops. She's been exposed to a micro-dose of psilocybin—

possibly a bit more than a micro-dose, thanks to how many lollipops she consumed," he replied, then pointed to the traffic light. "It's green, Mr. Paige. You should go before people start honking."

"Call me Landon," he said, blowing out a tight breath. This was no time to adhere to niceties. His wife was macro-tripping on magic-mushroom lollipops, and they were about to be in front of cameras.

Drivers honking at him were the least of his problems.

He turned his attention to the road and hit the gas.

The emotional roller coaster of dropping Aria off for her first day of school and then getting ambushed in the driveway mid-make-out and now contending with a shroomed-up wife might drive him over the edge.

No…wait.

He couldn't lose his mind. Harper had gone full-on cuckoo, and one of them had to keep this crazy train on the tracks.

"Hey, heartthrob?" she sang from the back seat.

At least she was in good spirits.

"Yeah, how are you feeling?"

"Terrific," she cheered. "My left hand can talk to my right hand. Look, if I do this, it's like they are little mouths at the end of my wrists instead of fingers." She raised her hands and opened and closed them as her gaze bounced from hand to hand. "Hello, right hand. Hello, left hand," she greeted, then gasped and held her left hand to her ear. "Wait, what's that, lefty? You want to be called Joyce? That's a beautiful name, Joyce. And you have something to tell me, too?" she exclaimed, her expression awash with surprise as she directed her attention to her right hand. "You want to be called Bartholomew. That's my husband's middle name. Well, he's not my real husband. He's my double-dog dare sixty-day husband—with benefits, the naughty kind."

Sweet Christ!

Harper giggled. "Joyce and Bartholomew, you two know about the marital benefits because I use you when I run my hands down Landon's rock-hard abs and reach for his giant—"

"And…look at that lamppost, people," he blurted, pointing out the first thing he saw to cut off the X-rated commentary.

He could feel Schuman's eyes on him. But there was no way he was about to explain their marital situation. Hell, he wasn't even sure what was going on between them. But now wasn't the time to untangle his whirlwind of emotions.

"Tell me more about these shroom-pops," he said, steering the conversation away from his private parts. "Are there any other substances mixed in I should know about?"

"No, of course not. They're quite safe when used correctly. My nephew makes them for medicinal purposes," Schuman explained. "They're not meant to be scarfed down, though. Consuming one or even half of one is plenty to get a calming, mind-opening effect."

"What will four do?" he pressed, then glanced in the rearview mirror and caught his wife testing out her tongue again. "Harper, don't eat the seat belt."

"But it wants to be tasted, heartthrob. It wants to be tasted and valued and loved. And…heartthrob?"

"Yeah?"

"Could I have a penis cookie?"

How was this their life?

He glanced at Schuman, and the man shook his head. "The contest expressly states we need to submit two dozen. That's all we've got."

He caught her eye in the mirror. "Sorry, bonbon, the cookies are for the contest. Remember the contest—the baking contest?"

"Yes, I remember. The oven wouldn't stop talking about it before we left, right, Joyce?" Harper replied as she conversed with her hand. "One more thing, heartthrob?"

As long as it didn't have to do with a penis, she could ask any question she wanted. "What is it?"

She tapped her chin. "What about a ball sac?"

He swerved and nearly hit the curb. "Jesus, Harper!"

His wife cleared her throat. "Maybe," she began, employing a French accent while opening and closing her left hand like a delirious ventriloquist, "there's a broken penis cookie, and Harper can eat the ball sac part," the hand finished in a rather convincing Parisian cadence.

Come on, universe. If he could make it through this day without hearing his wife say *penis* or *ball sac* again, he'd donate a million bucks to some worthy penis and ball sac foundation.

"Sorry, Joyce, we don't have any extra *number one* cookies," he replied, addressing Harper's left hand.

Yep, things were getting nuttier by the minute.

No, not nuts. Nuts were another euphemism for ball sac.

Things were getting *crazier* by the minute.

Was he losing his mind?

He stopped at another light and regained his bearings.

This situation might be insane, but at least they didn't have to go live during the drive.

He turned to Schuman. "How long will this altered state last?"

"A couple of hours…possibly more."

"Hours?" he echoed.

"And we're almost to the community center where the Denver Singing Grannies Choral group practices," the man continued. "You'll want to take the next right."

They were minutes away. How would they pull this off?

They had to show up. They couldn't forfeit the first challenge.

He glanced in the rearview mirror. Harper had zoned out. And that might not be a bad thing. He'd take her Zen and contemplative over her noshing on the door handles or conversing with body parts.

"Are you familiar with this choral group, besides it being their first anniversary?" he asked. He might as well pick Schuman's brain.

"I was, but I'm not anymore," the man answered.

That was an odd response.

"Did you get to read the email that explained the contest's format?" Schuman asked.

"I read it while the cookies were baking."

While he and his double-dog dare wife might be minutes away from walking into a giant livestreamed clusterfuck, Mr. Sweet's question didn't freak him out. Usually, when someone had asked if he'd read something, his chest tightened and his pulse raced.

But not today.

And he had the tripping beauty in the back seat to thank for it.

When she'd asked the teacher to chat about Aria's learning style, every cell in his body was ready to explode. Heart pounding, it felt as if a spotlight had been directed toward his deficiencies. But when Aria's teacher held out her phone, he could barely believe his eyes.

Welcome to Whitmore's Website.

It wasn't the banal message that blew him away but the ease with which he'd read it.

The OpenDyslexic font unscrambled his brain.

When he'd opened his email to check the contest messages, he'd had the same reaction. He wasn't greeted with a spaghetti maze of lines, spaces, and curves. Thanks to Harper loading the font onto his phone, checking his email was no longer a nightmare. Akin to what it must be like for a person with blurred vision to slip on a pair of prescription glasses, everything came into focus. It wasn't perfect. There were a few flipped letters, but skimming the text no longer felt like gazing into a bowl of alphabet soup.

Still, he wasn't about to shout his excitement from the rooftops. No, he still needed to keep his neurodivergent learning status under wraps and far from the prying eyes of the inquisitive tabloids and internet trolls.

"There's the community center," Schuman said, cutting into his thoughts, as a sprawling one-story brick building shaded by towering oaks came into view.

He nodded. "The email said to park in the back, and a production assistant would meet us at the door. How are we on time?"

Schuman pulled the timer from the box placed next to his feet. "Four minutes. We made it."

That was a good sign.

They sailed through the packed lot and found the space behind the building buzzing with activity. Men and women crossed the pavement, removing lighting equipment from a trailer with *Celebrity Bake or Bust* emblazoned across the side.

A young man in a Bake or Bust T-shirt with an iPad waved for him to stop. "Landon Paige and Harper Presley, you made it with two minutes to go," the guy said as he tapped the screen. "Park here, and a PA will be out to get you when they're ready inside. It shouldn't be long."

He nodded to the guy, then pulled into the parking space and cut the engine. He swiveled in his seat to check on his strangely silent wife. "Harper, we're here."

As if she were channeling a Tibetan monk, his wife sat with her hands folded in her lap and her eyes closed.

"Are you awake?"

She opened her eyes. "I am, and I see everything." Flecks of gold glinted in her chameleon gaze. "Landon?" she continued, her voice quietly commanding.

"Yeah?"

"Don't be afraid to let people see the real you, the whole you, the complete Landon Bartholomew Paige."

Where the hell did that come from?

A scintillating tingle ran down his spine as if she were communicating with his soul.

He stared into her pools of hazel.

Was it even possible for him to comply with her altered-state declaration?

Could he let people see him, flaws and all?

Hell no.

She was high, and that was simply more crazy shroom talk.

He shook off the sensation. "We need to go inside that building. Can you walk?"

She fluttered her fingers. "I feel like I can fly."

He released a tight breath. "Let's focus on walking."

He exited the car and helped her out as Schuman joined them.

He waved the older man in. "Is this normal?" he asked and nodded toward his unusually meditative wife. She'd gone from licking seat belts, conversing with her hands, and requesting edible ball sacs to rocking a Jedi vibe.

"Some people become introspective after they ingest Tanner's lollipops," the man replied when his beanie-wearing nephew raced toward them.

What was this dude up to?

"What are you doing here, Tanner? You went to check on…" Mr. Sweet said, then tossed a pensive look his way.

"I did," Tanner answered. "It's all good on the Mary Jane front."

Mary Jane, like pot?

The dude did say he dabbled in agricultural endeavors, and it was legal in Colorado.

Tanner turned to him. "Dude, I caught part of the livestream. Did your wife sample the lollipops?"

Before he could answer, Harper reached up and patted Tanner's cheek. "In a world of take a penny, leave a penny, you're a silver dollar."

"That answers my question," Tanner replied as Harper traced his face with her fingertips.

If she kept talking like that, they were screwed.

He removed Harper's hands from the man's face.

"Your hands are warm," she said like she was imparting the information to defuse a ticking time bomb. "Mine are cold like lemons."

Shit! That didn't make any sense.

He looked between Schuman and Tanner. "Mr. Sweet, could you help Harper get her sweater out of the back? So she isn't…"

"Lemony," his wife supplied.

Double shit.

Maybe she'd go catatonic again. He could only hope.

"I'd be happy to help." Schuman handed him the container with the cookies, then guided Harper to the back of the Lamborghini.

He pegged Tanner with his gaze. "You should have mentioned the lollipops weren't regular candy."

Tanner removed his beanie and ran his hands through his hair. "Totally, dude. I'm crazy sorry, man. That's why I left my appointment with Mary Jane and rushed over. I wanted to make sure Harper was okay. I can't believe this happened again."

"Again?"

Tanner flinched. "Yeah, man, again. Back in Kringle Mountain, where I'm from, I left a bag of medicinal gummy bears out, and a lady hoovered the whole thing."

"Was she okay?"

"Yeah, but if you could *not* mention this little lollipop mix-up to Bridget and Soren, you know, the Cupid Bakery CEO and her husband, I'd be grateful."

There had to be a story behind that admission, but he didn't have time to ask as Schuman returned with Harper by his side.

He took in his wife.

"This is the quiet cardigan," she whispered.

If she could stay in this quiet cardigan zone, they might get through the competition.

Things were looking up.

But just as the thought crossed his mind, a grating voice sliced through the air and sent the hairs on the back of his neck on end.

"I'm so glad you love my hit song, 'Every Time You Break My Heart.' I'm stoked to join the lineup. Keep fighting the good fight and vibe on."

Chapter 23

LANDON

His heart nearly stopped.

Could that be pop's biggest douche nozzle, Vance Vibe?

He turned toward the syrupy slimeball of a sound blathering that ridiculous catchphrase.

At first, he didn't see anything. Two men carrying a large screen walked by, blocking his line of sight.

But as the pair moved out of the way, he realized his ears hadn't deceived him.

Like a curtain revealing the worst grand prize ever, the douche himself, Vance Vibe, strode toward them with a leggy blonde in a micro-mini skirt and a tube top by his side. And for the second time in a handful of seconds, his jaw hit the ground. He not only recognized Vance—thanks to Rowen's internet search the day of Raz and Libby's housewarming party, he identified the scantily clad woman carrying a Tupperware container while teetering on sky-high heels as she hurried to keep up with Vance.

"It's Bang Bang Barbie and Vance Viberenski," Harper supplied. Her voice was calmly eerie as the singer and the porn star headed their way.

He studied his wife, surprised at her low-key reaction, when a realization hit and his heart leaped into his throat.

There was only one reason Vance would be here.

"Vance and Bang Bang Barbie must be the other *Celebrity Bake or Bust* team," Harper remarked as if she'd read his mind.

It was a baking battle of the pop stars.

Jesus, what the hell kind of twist was this?

Had Mitzi known?

He didn't have time to consider how the teams had been chosen or who had masterminded this matchup. The shock that had hit his system at the sound of the pop poser's voice swiftly made way for a roiling burst of anger.

He'd disliked Vance Vibe before Harper had shared how he'd wronged her. Now, he absolutely despised the man. Straight-up fury pulsed through his veins. If they didn't need those penis cookies so badly, he'd hurl the container at the lyrical thief.

With his cell pressed to his ear, Vance slung his arm around Bang Bang Barbie. A grin slithered across his face as he blabbered into his phone while a young man in a Bake or Bust T-shirt trailed behind the couple.

"Mr. Vibe, I'm sorry to interrupt your call, but you're not supposed to interact with the other contestants until you're on stage. Sir, if you'd come with me, we could get you settled," the production assistant pleaded, but Vance didn't give the man a second look. And just as the Bake or Bust kid slinked away, the pop fraud set his gaze on Harper.

The nerve of this poser.

He saw red as the need to protect Harper from this jerk consumed him.

Forget fury. A homicidal rush threatened to take over.

He hadn't resorted to violence since his days in foster care placements. If faced with the choice of fight-or-flight, he was ready to throw down and send Vance Vibe packing with a pair of black eyes. He glanced at the tub of cookies in his hands. It took every ounce of self-control to refrain from cramming a dozen baked penises down this grinning d-bag's throat.

"What a douche nozzle," Harper remarked like she'd read his mind again, but her voice calmed him. It brought him back to himself. He wouldn't allow the man to get under his skin.

"That's right, bonbon. Here comes the King of the Douche Nozzles." In a possessive caveman move to protect what was his, he inched toward her. Shoulder to shoulder with her he schooled his features. Hopefully, the quiet cardigan would keep working, and Harper wouldn't say anything bonkers to give away her condition.

"Well, look at this. Landon Paige, we meet again," Vance cooed, lowering his phone while attempting to play it cool. But a thin line of perspiration glimmering on the man's top lip gave away his unease. He held up his cell phone. "I was on the phone with Red Rocks Unplugged management. They offered me a spot."

What the hell?

"It's not a pop concert," he replied, watching the man closely. "Why would they offer you a spot?"

Vance shrugged, an aloof twitch of his shoulder. "I'm switching things up and working on a few instrumental versions of my hits."

His hits?

"I heard through the grapevine you were gunning for a spot at Red Rocks Unplugged, too," Vance continued. "I'll put in a good word for you," he added with a smarmy wink.

Don't let the guy blow your cool.

"Big things are happening in the music world," Vance continued. "Luxe Media and Entertainment acquired Red Rocks Unplugged, and there's talk that they're in negotiations to buy our label. I'm sure you've heard about it."

He hadn't heard a peep.

Truth be told, he'd been living the last few weeks in complete radio silence. He'd disregarded the media, and it had been true bliss not fretting over his followers on social media or sulking about sinking record sales. He didn't know a damn thing about the changes, but he wasn't about to show it.

"The music world is a volatile place," he said, answering but saying nothing.

"For sure, one day you're at the top, and the next, you're not," Vance spat back.

Don't take the bait.

He stood his ground and didn't utter a word. Vance tugged at his collar, and again, like the guy couldn't stop himself, he stole a look at Harper. His gaze dropped to her left hand as the clouds parted and a ray of sunshine hit her ring. The giant rock glinted like it was taunting the jerk.

Yep, Harper's taken, you lyrical loser.

Vance cleared his throat. "Harper, I had no idea you knew Landon," the guy uttered, losing his cocksure air as he attempted to appear nonchalant.

But it didn't work.

He could see the wheels turning in Vance's head. The guy was trying to figure out if Harper had spilled the details regarding their breakup and the stolen music.

But this wasn't the time to accuse the man of theft—especially without proof.

Harper didn't make a sound. Instead, she crinkled her nose and observed Vance like she was deciding between a day-old egg salad sandwich or a soggy tuna melt.

Stick with the silent treatment, bonbon. Good call.

"Obviously, she knows me, Vance. I married her," he replied, then glanced at his wife. The woman's chameleon eyes sparkled with mischief, but she still didn't make a peep.

That cardigan was doing one hell of a job.

"We're both married men now," Vance said, plowing

ahead. "I'm sure you've heard the news of our recent wedding. This is my wife, Barbie."

"We hadn't heard the news. Congratulations," he replied, remaining calm and collected as he held the man's gaze.

"It's a beautiful story," Barbie trilled. "We met at the Luxe Grandiose after I came in second place in The Next Hot Online Performer contest. Double-Jointed Delilah took the first prize, but your costume was my favorite, Bonbon Barbie," the woman added, turning her attention to Harper. "I recognize you. Do you remember me? We met in the hallway."

Harper channeled a Zen-master vibe. "I remember, and my name isn't Bonbon Barbie. It's Harper Presley-Paige."

Damn right it was.

"Well, Harper Presley-Paige, my name is Barbie Viberenski," the woman continued, grinning like an overinflated sex doll as her tube top bounced as she spoke. "Our love story is so sweet. I'd lost a pasty in the lobby, and Vance found it for me."

Okay.

"How romantic," he deadpanned.

"It was. I really loved that glitter pastie," the woman answered with a dreamy sigh.

While Bang Bang Barbie didn't seem to be firing on all cylinders in the brain-brain department, he got the feeling she wasn't a conniving bottom-dweller like her new husband.

"Vance and I got married two weeks ago at the same chapel at the Luxe Grandiose as you guys did," Barbie gushed in a high girlish chirp. "Vance surprised me with a proposal. I wasn't expecting it at all. We were in his suite, and I was experimenting with a new edible body glitter when our phones started blowing up with news of your wedding. It was all over the internet. Vance must have watched the ceremony video at least fifty times, and then he was like, grab your pasties, Barbie, we're getting married."

That was an interesting little nugget of info.

"When it's true love, it's true love," Vance replied. His words carried an exaggerated saccharin sentiment, but his gaze hardened as he glanced at Harper.

If the dude didn't stop sneaking looks at his wife, he might have to glue his eyelids shut.

"And then," Bang Bang Barbie chattered, "Vance's manager called and told us about the celebrity baking contest. And here we are." She held out her container of cookies— cookies in the shape of actual number ones. And they had fancy shiny frosting.

"Is that glitter?" he asked.

Barbie lit up. "It's edible glitter. I'm really good with it."

He zeroed in on her tub of cookies. They looked more like art than baked goods. That woman didn't mess around when it came to the sparkly stuff.

Barbie studied the tub of misshapen cookies in his hands. "Trouble with the butter, or was it too much sugar?" she asked with a little pout.

He stared at the array of cookie cocks. "Butter."

Vance zeroed in on the penis cookies and resurrected his slippery grin. "Those are some interesting cookies. Barbie grew up working in her parents' bakery, isn't that right, baby?" the douche purred. "We don't need help in the kitchen," the man added, tossing a glance Schuman's way.

Schuman and Tanner had stepped aside, giving them privacy to converse with Vance and Barbie. But the old man looked none too pleased with Vance's boasting.

Good!

Perhaps Vance's arrogance would light a fire under their sleepy baker.

It also wouldn't hurt to make sure he had triple espressos on hand before the next challenge.

But he couldn't get ahead of himself. He had to focus on the challenge at hand.

"Hmm," Harper hummed, glancing between their penis cookies and Vance.

The pop douche shifted his weight from foot to foot. "What are you looking at, Harper? Is there something you want to say?"

Say nothing, say nothing. Come on, quiet cardigan.

Yes, this douche nozzle had broken her heart and stolen her music, but that didn't mean he wanted her to berate him using Joyce and Bartholomew or start licking random objects. It would only hurt her if anyone found out she was blitzed.

He braced himself, ready to throw her over his shoulder and head for the hills if he had to, but Harper remained Jedi-still and gave Vance the once-over. "Hey, heartthrob?" she purred.

God help him. Here it comes.

"Yeah?"

A devious grin pulled at the corners of her mouth. "I remember why our cookies looked so familiar."

Score one for his sassy wife. This woman could cut glass throwing out barbs like that.

Even stoned out of her mind, she could drop one doozy of a zinger.

And while the last thing he wanted was to picture Vance Vibe's junk, receiving confirmation that the d-nozzle wasn't packing much below the belt didn't surprise him.

Nor did Harper's comment seem to surprise the douche canoe in question.

The man's cheeks burned crimson.

It appeared as if his wife's assessment was spot-on.

Now he was the one sporting a cocksure grin.

"I'll take the baked goods," a woman wearing a headset and a Bake or Bust shirt called as she jogged toward them, shifting the attention from Vance's less than stellar equipment. "Mr. Vibe, the PA in the Bake or Bust shirt by the door will get you and your wife settled inside. And I'll be escorting Mr. Paige and his wife. Mr. Sweet, you and your guest can go in through the main doors. We've got saved seats in the front row of the auditorium for you," the woman finished. She collected the tubs, put a blue sticker on their container, then pressed a red tag on the other.

"Good luck," Schuman said as he and Tanner set off for the front of the building.

"They'll need it," Vance shot back, cheeks flushed ruby-red from getting called out for being a class A weenie with a tiny peenie.

"Bye-bye," Barbie called, blissfully clueless as she teetered on her heels a few steps behind her fuming husband.

He watched the pair disappear when Harper giggled.

"I know, I know," she uttered.

"Who are you talking to, bonbon?"

She grinned. "It's Joyce. She agreed with my comment about the size of Vance's—"

"Let's forget about that," he blurted, taking her hand.

She laced her fingers with his. And just like the first time he'd held her hand in Las Vegas, the urge to never let go tore through him. He stared into her chameleon eyes, enamored with her spirit, when another production assistant appeared and took the cookies from the headset lady.

"Follow me, please," the PA said as the other assistant hoofed it into the building with the tubs of baked goods.

He glanced at the PA striding a few feet ahead of them, then turned to his wife. "Are you all right?" he asked, lowering his voice. "You put up a killer front, but it couldn't have been easy to see Vance."

"Why would you say that?" she asked. "My eyes are working just fine. Better than fine. Things have never been so clear or so translucent. I can read people, Landon. I can see into them and hear their thoughts."

It was safe to say the hallucinogenic effects of the shroom-pops hadn't diminished.

"This way, Mr. and Mrs. Paige," the PA said, interrupting their brief interaction. She led them down a hall to a small exercise studio with mirrored walls. "Wait here. Another PA will return when it's time to go onstage."

She turned to leave, but he stopped her.

"Can you tell us the format of the contest? The emails didn't mention how it would go once we were at the venue."

"You read the emails in your new fancy font, and it wasn't scary, was it?" Harper remarked.

The breath caught in his throat. While the font had been a game changer, he couldn't have her telling the world about his…issues. He gave her hand a gentle squeeze. "Let's focus on the contest."

The PA's gaze danced between them. "Donna and Damien Diamond are hosting."

He frowned. "I've never heard of them."

"I believe they're friends of Mr. and Mrs. Luxe. They'll make sure everything runs smoothly. First, they'll introduce the choir, then the members will do a taste test and choose the winner."

He was pretty sure he knew who would win, but he had to stay positive.

"After the winner is chosen, the choir will perform a rendition of one of the winning team's songs—a Vance Vibe song or one of yours, Mr. Paige," the woman continued. "There's an issue with the choir's pianist, but that's not your concern. We're working on it. Any other questions?"

"I have a question about the ceiling," Harper replied.

Oh, no.

"The ceiling?" the woman repeated.

His wife nodded. "Is it made of cake?"

Damn those lollipops.

He parted his lips, unsure of how to respond, when the PA laughed.

"You're hilarious! And by the way, your wedding was so romantic. I must have watched the clip on LookyLoo a hundred times," she replied, then sailed out of the room.

He released a relieved breath.

That was close.

"Harper, you can't mention my..." He trailed off.

She watched him like a hawk. "Your what?"

It would be a fool's errand to go there while she was in this state.

"Listen, Harper, those lollipops have made you a little loopy," he explained, changing tack.

"I don't feel loopy, but I would like a piece of the ceiling cake unless you've got bonbons or a hidden penis cookie in your pocket."

He should be recording this to show her later.

He patted his empty pockets, then peered around the room. "No hidden cookies and no ladder to reach the ceiling cake."

She sighed. "We'll have to see if there are any penises or ball sacs left over after the contest. I'm famished."

"Speaking of after the contest," he began, "I'm not sure how our cookies will stack up against Vance and Barbie's batch. If they taste as good as they look, there's a good chance we'll lose."

She didn't reply.

A knot formed in his belly. "Harper, do you understand what I'm saying? We might not win this challenge."

She held his gaze as that sly twist of a grin graced her lips. "Kiss me."

What did she say?

"You want me to kiss you?" he repeated.

"Yes, kiss me. That's what you want to do. You've wanted to kiss me since we heard Vance's voice in the parking lot."

Was that true?

He couldn't deny that when Vance stared at her hand, he'd felt a dizzying rush of triumph.

And again, just like the first night he'd laid eyes on her months ago, he couldn't look away. He lost himself in her beguiling chameleon eyes. "How do you know I want to kiss you?"

She pressed her hand to his chest. "You know how I can talk to my hands?"

"Yeah," he answered, suppressing a grin.

"It turns out I can talk to parts of you, and your heart told me."

"You can hear my heart?" he asked, his voice a creaky rasp as he wrapped his arms around her.

"Yes, and I can hear your lips." She lowered her voice. "They really want to kiss me."

The woman might be talking to body parts and jonesing to chow down on a slice of the ceiling, but she wasn't wrong about what he wanted.

He kissed the corner of her mouth, and she hummed a deliciously sweet sigh.

"What are my lips saying now?" he whispered.

"They're saying, 'thank you for kissing your wife.'"

She'd nailed it.

"You taste like sugar and sunshine," he breathed, bringing her in another inch as his worries disintegrated.

She smiled against his mouth. "You taste like every dream I never thought could be a reality. Each note and every lyric I've written has landed me here, in your arms."

Even high as a kite, she could weave lyrics together like a musical maverick.

"Are you writing a song?" he asked and dropped a kiss beneath her earlobe.

"We're always writing a song with kisses and stolen glances and the way you tuck wayward locks of my hair behind my ear. Everything about us can be distilled into a melody."

"How do you do it?" he asked, returning to her lips. "Where do you get your magic?"

She gifted him with another smile. "Chocolate."

"Chocolate?"

"*The girl of your dreams comes with a bonbon kiss,*" she sang, and damn, that voice.

He couldn't hold back.

Hungrily, he kissed her and devoured her sweetness. It was as if he saw her anew and viewed their union with fresh eyes.

And that begged the question.

Could this union last?

Don't think...just kiss her. She's yours...for now.

He deepened the kiss, falling into the well that was everything Harper Presley.

No, Harper Presley-Paige.

"Harper Presley-Paige," he whispered as an invisible thread formed between them, lassoing his heart.

What was this? What was happening to him?

"Look at these newlyweds, Damien," a woman remarked with a near-comical buttery southern drawl.

"Bless their little hearts. Aren't they so sweet?"

Who the hell was that?

He broke their kiss, then stared at the shimmery senior citizens standing in the doorway.

He blinked. Could he have gotten secondhand shroom exposure from kissing Harper?

Was that a possibility?

It sure felt like it.

The people standing before them looked like they'd stepped out of a hallucination.

"Sorry, y'all, we didn't mean to interrupt," the striking woman donning a giant Dolly Parton-like wig crooned.

"Young love, there's nothing like it," the man next to her remarked in the same exaggerated accent, stretching out each syllable.

Dressed in matching jumpsuits that glittered like diamonds, the older couple looked poised to fall back in time and hit the disco circa 1972.

"We're Donna and Damien Diamond," the woman said with a little curtsey.

The name made sense.

"Mr. and Mrs. Luxe hired us to host the *Celebrity Bake or Bust*," the man explained.

Harper's gaze moved between the couple. "It's nice to see you both again."

Again?

Harper cocked her head to the side and stared at Damien. "This coat is very shiny. Shiny coats work for you."

Cue the hallucinations.

"What my wife means is that it's nice to meet you, for the first time," he said, swooping in as Donna and Damien exchanged a nervous glance.

What could they be nervous about?

If anyone should be nervous, it was the team with the penis-shaped cookies.

Damien cleared his throat. "We wanted to say hello," the man continued, "and let you know the singing granny choir is excited to meet y'all and sample the cookies."

"Yours are…unique," Donna added when a man in a Bake or Bust T-shirt entered the room.

"Mr. and Mrs. Diamond, the choir is in position. They're

ready for you on the stage. And Mr. and Mrs. Paige, we're ready for you as well."

A warmth engulfed his hand. He looked down to find Harper's delicate fingers laced with his.

The dreamy expression on her face put him at ease. Maybe getting your ass handed to you in a cookie baking competition was better done while experiencing the effects of copious amounts of shroom-spiked candies.

He tightened his grip, and hand in hand, they followed the PA as the low murmur of voices drifted toward them. They turned a corner, and a stage came into view. This wasn't a grand concert hall. The community center's setup resembled a high school's auditorium, but the place was packed. Cameras lined the periphery, and the lights brightened as Donna and Damien took the stage. The pair greeted the audience and introduced the choir.

He released a slow breath. They had some time to kill.

He scanned the seats and found Schuman in the front row.

The man blotted his cheek with a handkerchief, then stuffed it into his pocket as he gazed at the choir.

Had he shed a tear over their cookie catastrophe, or was something else making the man emotional?

The guy had a connection to this group. It didn't take a genius to figure that out. But he didn't have time to ponder the inner workings of their baking coach.

"Let's welcome Heartthrob Warfare's platinum bestselling artist, Landon Paige, and his wife, musician Harper Presley."

The PA pointed to them. "That's your cue. Go to the table with your nameplate."

"Harper, are you ready?" he asked as applause echoed through the space.

She looked up at him as fear welled in her gaze. "I'm scared."

Did she suffer from stage fright, or was her altered state throwing her off?

She had told him she hadn't performed since Vance broke her heart.

"You're not alone. I'm right here. We can do this together," he said and squeezed her hand.

She squeezed back with the strength of a gladiator as they walked onto the stage. But as quickly as she clutched his hand, her death grip loosened. "I remember this. I forgot how much I loved feeling the warmth on my face," she whispered, gazing up at the constellation of lighting fixtures as he led her to their table.

Panic rippled through his chest. He could not have her conversing with the spotlight.

"Focus on your quiet cardigan," he offered through a forced grin, waving to the audience and members of the choir.

There was no turning back now.

They arrived at their spot, and Harper leaned into him, staring at the crowd with awe written on her face. Okay, he could work with that. There was nothing weird about a woman smiling at the audience.

Donna and Damien announced Vance and Barbie, giving him a moment to take in the scene. The choir of about twenty or so women stood on a set of curved risers near the back of the stage. A shiny Steinway sat in the center of the space, with two trays of cookies on a table nearby. Their spot was on the far-left side of the stage. Vance and Barbie were situated across from them on the far right.

"We're here to celebrate the first anniversary of the Singing Grannies Choral group," Donna said, addressing the cameras. "It's a pleasure to shine a light on those bringing joy to their city. These senior songbirds regularly serenade the residents at local nursing homes and share their love of music with the community. And while I'm told their founding member can't be here. They wanted to dedicate this performance to her."

"Let's get this Bake or Bust started. The singing grannies will decide which celebrity team baked the tastiest confection," Damien added.

The sparkly couple stood at the cookie table and invited the choir members to leave their perch and sample the baked goods. The ladies peered from tray to tray, some chuckling as they sampled the plain cookie penises. Others held up the masterfully decorated number one treats, oohing and aahing after each bite.

"Ladies, you've had a chance to sample the goods," Donna drawled as the grannies returned to the risers.

The members nodded.

Donna tipped the red tray—Vance and Barbie's tray— toward the audience.

"Raise your hand if your top choice was from this tray," Damien called.

Landon braced himself. He knew what was coming.

A sea of hands went up.

"What about the blue tray?" Damien crooned.

One hand.

A little old lady in the front.

"I'm Granny B, and I like the shape of the cookies on the blue tray," she blurted as the grannies giggled.

Well, they got one vote. At least it wasn't a shutout.

Donna held up the red tray. "Vance and Barbie, you have won the first *Celebrity Bake or Bust* challenge. The singing grannies will now perform their rendition of Vance Vibe's 'Every Time You Break My Heart.'"

It was as if the walls were closing in on them.

No, not that song.

He turned to his wife and prepared for the worst.

Chapter 24
LANDON

He held his breath.

It was one thing to listen to "Every Time You Break My Heart" on the radio.

How would Harper react to hearing her song performed with Vance standing across from her?

He checked his wife.

Surprisingly, she'd barely batted an eyelash.

Maybe a super-dose of psychedelics was what she needed to get through this.

"Harper," he said softly, when Barbie squealed. The annoying trill echoed through the auditorium as she danced around, tube top jiggling like a plate of Jell-O.

"Woo-hoo for Vancey-Poo," the bouncy blonde gushed.

And what about Vance's response?

That smug prick donned an arrogant smirk.

He really was the King of the Douche Nozzles.

A pale woman with sheet music in her hands emerged from backstage and started toward the piano. She'd almost made it when she heaved and produced a guttural gag. In the blink of an eye, her dishwater-gray skin gave way to a pallid puce hue.

She heaved again, pressed her hand to her lips, and booked it off the stage.

"We need a bucket," called a PA somewhere behind the curtains.

Ew!

The audience expelled a collective gasp.

"My goodness, it appears the choir's pianist isn't feeling well," Donna drawled as the gasps coming from the audience morphed into a low murmur.

Maybe they'd have to cut the choir's rendition of Vance's—no—*Harper's* song.

He turned to his wife, hoping to get a read on her, when the warmth that had engulfed his hand gave way to a cool chill. Breezy, like blades of grass carried on calm winds, she let go. She pushed onto her tiptoes, kissed his cheek, then glided across the stage and headed for the Steinway.

"What are you doing?" he whispered as the cameras followed her.

"I can accompany you," she offered, addressing the choir. "I know 'Every Time You Break My Heart' like it was my own."

Damn!

"No, you don't have to do that," Vance blathered. His cocksure expression dissolved as he bolted toward the piano. "Harper, go back to your table. They can sing it without the accompaniment."

Oh, hell no!

He didn't know what in God's name Harper was up to, but he wasn't about to let Vance Vibe get in her way.

Striding like he owned the stage, he blocked the pop douche's path. "Don't move," he seethed and sized up the man. "I'm not kidding when I say that if you take one more step toward my wife, it will be your last."

Was this an over-the-top display of a pop star swinging around his dick?

You bet your ball sac, penis-shaped cookies it was.

But was it an exaggeration?

Nope.

He wasn't about to let Vance Vibe call the shots.

The pop tool glanced at the myriad of cameras livestreaming on LookyLoo. He mustered a weak grin and leaned in. "Whatever Harper told you, she lied."

What a moron! Did he want to leave this place with a limp? Didn't he realize his nervous blathering was an admission of his guilt?

It was a damned shame Harper didn't have proof.

"Are you calling my wife a liar?" he growled in a hushed rasp.

"What do we have here, fellas? A little pop star comradery?" Donna crooned. The woman grinned, but concern clouded her gaze.

"We're…" Vance stammered, but the guy had turned green. He looked almost as bad as the pianist who'd run offstage to puke her guts out.

Clearly, this guy could only perform with a fog machine cranked up to the max and Auto-Tune altering his voice.

It was time to show this poser how a real artist treated an audience and drop a little *Professional Entertainer 101* on the guy.

"I'm letting Vance know what I think of him."

Vance's eyes widened.

"On behalf of myself and my wife," he continued, "I want to congratulate Vance and Barbie on their cookie victory. I'd also like to thank the choir and their families and friends for coming out today to support the community." He leaned in toward Vance. "Listen and learn, dude. You can't steal songs and Auto-Tune your way through this industry. That shit will catch up to you."

Was he being a hypocrite?

Possibly.

Sure, he had secrets he didn't want the world to know about. But that was personal.

Vance's offenses and misdeeds were criminal.

The douche's gaze hardened, but he didn't reply. It was the first smart choice he'd made all day.

"And a special thanks to the competition's baking coach, Schuman Sweet, and to Cupid Bakery for sponsoring the contest along with Luxe Media and Entertainment," Damien added, piggybacking on his sentiments.

The host had barely finished speaking when the rich tones of the rolling arpeggio scale echoed through the space. Progressing from a low rumble to a high-pitched tinkling, the pleasing sound drew the crowd's attention. The cameras lost interest in him and Vance and zeroed in on the beguiling brunette working her way through a warm-up.

She was going for it.

"Harper..." Vance eked out.

Could this guy not take a hint?

He slung his arm around the pop poser like they were old chums. "Harper, we double-dog dare you to play your version of the song. Don't we, Mr. Keep Fighting the Good Fight and Vibe On?"

"Um..." Vance stuttered.

"Vibe on, vibe on," the audience chanted, and holy hell, it felt freaking amazing to hear Vance's stupid catchphrase used against him.

Harper nodded to the audience, and the chants died down. She removed her quiet cardigan, then tossed him a flirty wink. "We don't turn down double-dog dares, do we, heartthrob?"

"No, bonbon, we do not," he answered, bursting with pride.

Even flying high on God knows how many psilocybin

micro-dosed lollipops, the woman still kicked ass and took names.

She inhaled a slow breath as her fingertips hovered over the keys.

Anticipation crackled in the air, and the room stilled.

Vance opened his big mouth, but before he could protest, Harper's fingers danced across the keys as she played the first few bars of "Every Time You Break My Heart."

While similar to Vance's pop tune, Harper's instrumental version slowed the tempo and brought a raw delicacy to the song.

She caressed the keys, riffing the intro, and turned to the audience. "To me, 'Every Time You Break My Heart' is a ballad," she explained, then directed her attention toward the choir. "I'll sing the first verse. You can join in at the refrain. You'll hear the changes. You'll feel how the lyrics are meant to be sung."

He removed his arm from Vance's shoulders and left the man sucking his cheeks like a sulking toddler.

And then he forgot about Vance Vibe, and time stopped.

Harper parted her lips and turned a catchy pop song into a tapestry of lyrical bliss. Between her voice and the rich notes flowing from the piano, everyone, even the Bake or Bust PAs who'd been zipping around backstage, froze. Harper seduced the room with her voice. And just like she'd promised, the choir knew when to come in. Their combined sounds layered into a haunting ballad, complementing Harper's rich, melodious tone as she sang lead vocals.

It was like watching music turn into magic.

And that was the beauty of a well-crafted song.

It elevated one's mood.

It triggered inspiration.

It altered lives.

The masses didn't hear this transcendent song.

They felt it.

They breathed it.

They lived it along with the musician.

Note by note, word by word, the verses entwined with the soul. Harmony and melody united like perfect lyrical chaos. And the result was a spark that ignited pure, untainted awe.

If someone in the auditorium had screamed *fire*, nobody would have moved a muscle.

Every person within earshot of Harper was unequivocally and indisputably starstruck. As if he were observing the human embodiment of song, she swayed and surrendered herself to the beat.

And one overwhelming truth prevailed.

Harper Presley was a take-your-breath-away showstopper.

Just when he thought the muscles in his face might snap from smiling, the song ended as powerfully and delicately as it had begun.

The choir stood motionless, and Harper rested her hands in her lap as the final chord hung in the air, a ribbon of sound drifting higher and higher, until it was gone, like a dream.

The room was rendered speechless as every pair of eyes focused on the songbird perched on the piano bench and bathed in the golden spotlight.

"She's a star," Donna whispered to Damien.

Damn right.

The air crackled and was on the brink of detonating into a burst of applause when Vance turned on his heel and bumped the table with the trays. The scrape of the table legs skidding across the weathered hardwood screeched through the auditorium, but no one paid any attention. The audience was mesmerized by Harper's performance and didn't give a damn about the crabby Vance Vibe.

"Come on, Barbie, we're out of here," he barked, rubbing

the spot on his hip where he'd struck the table as he stormed off the stage.

Oblivious to her asshat husband's antics, Barbie blew a kiss to the audience. "Bye-bye," she chirped and teetered off.

As if the room had been waiting for Vance to leave, the crowd went wild the second the winning couple disappeared. People sprang to their feet, clapping, whistling, and hooting. The applause resonated like a living organism. He surveyed the sea of smiling faces and met Schuman's gaze. Eyes shining, the old man's grin lit up his face as Tanner flashed two thumbs-up.

They'd lost, but Christ, it felt like a win.

But they still had a chance.

They'd have to win the following two challenges. It wouldn't be easy. Especially going up against Vance and his bouncy baker wife. But from the look of teary joy on Schuman's face, it appeared as if the man might do more than sleep through the next baking task.

Harper stood and gestured to the choir, acknowledging their performance, then turned her attention to the ceiling.

Oh no, bonbon, please don't see cake in the rafters.

"This contest certainly brought out the drama and the fireworks. I'm sure Vance Vibe was so moved he required a moment to reflect in private," Damien announced with a hint of glee in his tone.

Interesting.

Donna tossed a curious glance at Harper, who kept her gaze trained on the ceiling. "Harper, darlin', your rendition of 'Every Time You Break My Heart' knocked it out of the park."

"Unlike our cookies," he interjected, joining his wife center-stage.

The choir and the crowd chuckled at his comment, but Harper remained fixated on the rafters.

"Is something up there? Maybe one of the high notes is still floating around," Damien ad-libbed.

Harper shook her head, then glanced from hand to hand. "No, it's cake. This building is made of cake. Joyce and Bartholomew were right."

Shit.

"That's quite an observation. You must have baking on your mind," Donna replied, sharing a perplexed look with Damien.

"Harper and I are raring to go for the next baking challenge, aren't we?" he offered, praying she'd nod.

But Harper didn't reply. She glanced over her shoulder at the table. He followed her gaze and spotted a piece of one of their cookies. No, not just a piece, a ball sac.

She smacked her lips. "I could sure go for a delicious ball s—"

No, no, no!

He could not allow the words *ball sac cookie* to pass her lips on a livestream.

He twirled her into his arms and cut off her confession with a kiss.

And the crowd was there for it. They broke out into another round of applause.

"And sealed with a cookie-loving kiss, we thank everyone for joining us here in Denver, Colorado, and on the LookyLoo livestream," Donna proclaimed.

"Let's get out of here, bonbon," he said, smiling against her lips.

She gazed at him with those chameleon eyes. "Want me to fly us home?"

He suppressed a grin. "Maybe next time. I'm sure Joyce and Bartholomew could use a break."

"And it might get drafty to fly without panties," she mused.

"Then allow me to provide the transport." He flung her cardigan over his shoulder, then scooped her into his arms

385

carefully, making damn sure he was the only one to know his crooner of a wife was going commando.

With a breathy yip, Harper waved to the adoring crowd while he moved like a man who desperately needed to extricate his shroomed-up wife from the spotlight.

But they'd done it.

They'd gotten through the challenge in one piece.

He zipped past a slew of Bake or Bust PAs, then bolted out the backdoor, hightailing it to the Lamborghini.

"This is the way to get around," Harper remarked as he helped her into the car and handed her the cardigan.

He jogged around to his side, fired up the engine, and hit the gas.

They might have lost, but they'd gone out in style.

Relief and a buzzy euphoria flooded his system as he navigated through the lot and maneuvered the car onto the street.

"The audience loved you," he raved. "Your rendition of the song took my breath away."

"It's not *my* rendition. It's the original version," she corrected.

How had he not put that together?

He reached over and held her hand. "That makes sense. When you sing it, it's got a heart and a soul. It was you, through and through. And Vance—"

"—looked ready to poop his pants," she answered with a rhyme and a giggle. But the bubbly reaction was short-lived. She stared at their joined hands. "We didn't win."

"We didn't. But we got one vote from a granny named Granny B."

She sighed. "And we forgot to take a piece of ceiling cake with us."

"We've got bonbons at home."

She lit up. "And lollipops."

"No," he replied, stretching the syllable. "We're laying off the lollipops for the rest of today and probably for the better part of the next decade."

The next decade?

They'd agreed to sixty days, not over three thousand.

Did he want three thousand more days with her? Was that possible?

She released his hand. "Where's my bag, heartthrob?"

He glanced at her and pushed aside the wistful thoughts of a decade by her side.

"It's in the back. But I don't think there's any cake in there unless you travel with a slice."

It was a possibility. The woman was a baked goods super freak.

"There's no cake in my bag. The cake was in the auditorium." She twisted in her seat, grabbed her tote, then proceeded to whip out her brown feathery mask and her laptop.

"What are you doing with those?"

"It's time for Bonbon Barbie to teach a lesson," she answered smoothly. "I'm going over exceptional girls bake delicious fudge. You know, *E*, *G*, *B*, *D*, and *F*, the notes on the lines of the treble clef."

"You plan on doing that in the car?" he exclaimed.

He'd hardly come down from the Bake or Bust adrenaline rush. He needed a second to catch his breath.

"Sure, I've done it before."

He'd bet his villa in Italy she'd never taught a class while under the influence of a hallucinogenic substance that made her think buildings were made of cake.

"Harper, hold on. We're almost home." He pulled into the driveway and cut the engine.

She yawned. "Maybe I shouldn't teach today."

"Good call," he replied on a relieved breath as he exited the vehicle.

"I'll let Joyce and Bartholomew do the lesson," she answered as he helped her out.

He couldn't let her do that either.

Think, think, think.

He unlocked the door and held it for her. "Let me teach the lesson. I can be..." He wracked his brain. "Landy Candy. What do you say? You rest, and I'll give teaching a whirl?"

He'd never taught a day in his life, but he couldn't do worse than someone who talked to their hands and, if given the opportunity, would take a bite out of the rafters.

She handed him her tote, plopped onto the couch, then studied her hand. "Joyce agrees with you. She thinks you'd be a terrific teacher."

"Really? Joyce said that?" He'd never been so happy to have an appendage in his corner.

"I'll rest my eyes for a minute, then we'll eat some ceiling cake and figure out where Babs has the unicorns hidden. I think Aria would like a unicorn."

"Who wouldn't?" he answered, gazing down at this amazing spitfire of a woman.

"Everything you need is on top of the piano. And you start by singing, 'do, re, mi, sing with me,'" she instructed, curling up like a cat.

He grabbed a quilt off a chair and covered her.

She hummed a contented little sound. "I can see why those fans have signs at your concerts that say *Marry Me, Landon Paige.* You're a pretty good husband...for a musician."

"Pretty good?" he teased, feeling a pang in his chest as he stroked her cheek.

The whisper of a sassy smirk pulled at the corners of her lips before her features relaxed and her breathing slowed.

Hopefully, she'd wake up and ask for bonbons instead of ceiling cake and ball sac cookies.

He blew out a slow breath, then took her laptop to the piano. Something odd happened as he settled himself on the bench. A lightness took over. Thanks to his learning issues, he'd never enjoyed school, but he genuinely wanted to teach this music lesson. He opened her laptop, downloaded the helpful font recommended by Aria's teacher, then went to Harper's LookyLoo page. The *live video* button flashed at the bottom as if it were challenging him.

His pulse kicked up. But it wasn't the usual anxiety he experienced when it came to learning.

No, this wasn't fear. It was excitement.

He hovered the cursor over the flashing live-video button, held his breath, and clicked it.

A recording icon flashed at the top of the screen as a gentle ping announced the arrival of viewers.

And there was no turning back now.

He dialed up his grin. "Do, re, mi, sing with me. Hey there, musicians, I'm Landy Candy."

Chapter 25

HARPER

Harper rubbed her eyes and rolled over, savoring the cozy warmth. She snuggled beneath the quilt and tucked the edge under her chin. Relaxed and at ease, she sighed. Boy, she'd had the loopiest dreams—dreams where she'd smelled colors, tasted sounds, and heard inanimate objects. She'd floated through the day, observing herself from above. There, but not there, engaged but delightfully aloof.

She yawned and burrowed into the softness when muffled voices followed by a bout of laughter drifted down from the second floor.

Was she still dreaming?

And then a song played. A song with a punk rock edge she recognized.

Penny's sisters can suck an egg, suck an egg, a dozen eggs.

Penny's sisters can suck those eggs. Suck them until chickens hatch in your mouth.

The lyrics were rough, childish, and ridiculous, but she'd been a rough, ridiculous child when she'd written them.

Wait, why was she hearing a song she'd written almost twenty years ago?

She shot up and tossed the quilt to the floor, bolting from her comfortable cocoon.

The snippet of the song played again. And again, it was met with rolling laughter.

Had she fallen through a rip in the universe, broken the laws of physics, and gone back in time?

She sure as hell better not be trapped in the kid version of herself.

No, that was crazy talk. But as her brain haze cleared, flashes of cookies and a choir carouseled through her mind.

She rubbed her temples, then spied two items in front of her on the coffee table.

A glass of water and a rectangular pastry box.

She focused on the glass of water. It had a note with *drink me* taped to the side.

Weird.

She slid her gaze to the box—a box from Cupid Bakery with a Post-it note printed with *eat me* taped to the top.

This was one hell of an Alice in Wonderland moment.

Her stomach growled in response.

There was the answer.

She opened the delicate box and feasted her eyes on half a dozen chocolates.

This was the way to wake up.

She helped herself to two butterscotch bonbons and washed them down with the water.

The sugar hit her system, and she reclined onto the sofa.

What time was it?

What day was it?

It was as if she'd lived a thousand lifetimes across the cosmos and had returned to her body here on earth.

A ping caught her attention, and she gazed toward where the sound had originated.

She rose from the sofa, shlepped into the kitchen, and

noticed her cell phone on the table. The device pinged again. She picked it up and cocked her head to the side.

Thirty-seven missed text messages from Penny, Charlotte, and Libby and eleven missed calls.

Her friends were in serious freak-out mode.

She scanned the messages, picking up bits and pieces.

Charlotte 11:06 a.m.: Harper, you were amazing. OMG, you killed it on LookyLoo!

Penny 11:08 a.m.: Vance's expression was price-less. Grr, I hate that guy.

Libby: 11:09 a.m.: Holy cosmic creativity. H, you are hella connected to your chi. Your energy is off the charts. Also, what are you on?

What was she on?

She gasped.

The lollipops.

Everything had gone sideways after she'd binged the sweet earthy treats.

Holy psychedelic head trip! Tanner's lollipops must have been laced with something. That was the only explanation.

And then, like one of those optical illusion pictures where you stare and stare until an image emerges, her brain fog burned off and the day's events rose to her consciousness.

She studied her hands—hands that had been rather chatty earlier. But they didn't make a sound, thank God. She exhaled a relieved breath when the muffled laughter caught her attention again.

She wasn't alone.

It was Landon and Aria.

Of course, it was Landon and Aria. They lived here.

"Come on, brain, you've got to kick it into high gear. And no more talking appendages," she whispered with a minute shake of her head, then checked the time.

8:45 p.m.

Where the hell had the day gone?

As if her brain had decided to comply with her request, a flood of images flashed through her mind like one of those olden days cameras that created an explosion of light.

Flash!

Aria, with her pigtails bouncing and backpack swaying, as she ran toward her new school with Phoebe, Oscar, and Sebastian.

Flash!

Schuman Sweet, sleeping in her living room as she and Landon baked penis cookies.

Flash!

Vance's face when she started singing "Every Time You Break My Heart."

Vance!

He and Bang Bang Barbie were their Bake or Bust competitors. That was even trippier than whatever was in those spiked lollipops.

The breath caught in her throat as the next rush of memories roared in like a tsunami.

She'd sung in front of an audience while being broadcast on the LookyLoo livestream.

That had really happened.

And the crowd had loved her.

She hadn't heard their applause exactly. She'd absorbed it, consumed it. She'd allowed the adulation to swirl around like a tangible tornado of sun-kissed honey.

Disbelief and amazement swelled in her chest when another jarring realization hit.

Either she couldn't remember doing it, which would be quite bad, or she'd slept through picking up Aria from her first day of school.

What kind of nanny-aunt did that?

In a state of panic, she dropped her cell on the counter.

Taking the stairs two at a time, she flew up the steps and plowed into Aria's room. "I'm here. I'm awake. Are you okay? Did you like your school?" She surveyed the room, expecting chaos, but found Aria sitting in bed with Landon perched on the edge with an e-reader in his hands. Her old camcorder, from years ago, rested on top of the covers next to Aria.

"We're okay, sleeping beauty. The million-dollar question is, are you okay?" Landon asked, looking her over as concern clouded his gaze.

She glanced at her crumpled outfit. "Yeah, I think so."

"Look up," he instructed.

What?

She cocked her head to the side. "At the ceiling?"

"Yes, and tell me what you see," he pressed, straight-faced.

She indulged the man. "I see a...wait for it...a ceiling."

"Does it appear appetizing?" He raised an eyebrow, studying her like a science project.

This would have been an insane line of questioning under normal circumstances. But today had been anything but ordinary.

And just like that, her brain cranked out another bonkers recollection.

And that loopy revelation had everything to do with cake.

She really needed to address her baked goods addiction.

Anyone who could believe—even under the influence— that the ceiling was made of cake really had it bad for confectionary treats. But it had seemed like a reasonable observation at the time.

She crossed the room and sat down on the edge of the bed near Landon. "No, the ceiling does not look appetizing."

"Thank God," he answered as relief softened his expression.

"What's on the ceiling?" Aria asked with a furrowed brow as she scanned the flat surface.

"Nothing is on the ceiling. Your uncle is being silly." She tapped the tip of Aria's nose, then honed in on the old camcorder. She picked up the old recording device. "This is what I heard, isn't it?"

"It's you, Aunt Harper, when you were a little girl singing that song about your friend's sisters sucking eggs. I'll show you," Aria said, taking the camcorder, and hitting play.

And hello, mortification.

She felt her cheeks heat as she watched the little girl version of herself rage-singing and dancing in the very room they were in right now.

She chuckled and shook her head. She could either laugh or cry at the embarrassing performance. "I can't even imagine what else is on those old tapes."

"It's you, singing all sorts of songs. I like your voice," the little girl replied.

"I like your voice. I liked singing with you at your grandparents' house. I wish you'd sing more," she added when Landon and Aria shared a curious look.

She observed the pair. "What?"

"Tell her, Aria," Landon nudged

"We had music class today, and now that I'm a big kid in second grade, I have to make a music goal."

"What did you pick?" she asked, catching Landon's wide grin out of the corner of her eye.

"I'm going to sing a song for Lolo and Lala when we go see them in Italy for their second wedding."

"It's called a vow renewal," Landon corrected.

"I like second wedding better," Aria tossed back, always the ball-buster, bless her heart.

Ball-busting aside, this was a big deal. These last few weeks, they'd played the piano together, and Aria had pretty much mastered the guitar, but she wouldn't sing.

"I can't wait to hear it. I'm sure your grandparents will be thrilled with that gift" she replied when Landon shifted his weight, and she got a look at the e-reader in his hand. "Hold on a hot second. Is that a Babysitters Club e-book?"

"Yeah, it is," Aria beamed. "We started reading it tonight."

Landon held it up. "Aria's school gave each student one to use at home."

"And I asked Uncle Landy to get the first book in the series on my fancy computer book because you didn't have that one in the pile of notebooks and Uncle Landy pictures."

Ah, the pile of mortification.

But she didn't have a second to be embarrassed about her childhood crush on her current husband. Not when something quite extraordinary had happened.

She peered at the tablet, noting the special font and high-lighted text. "You're reading to Aria?"

He gave her the heartthrob sexy little half smile. "I am."

Before today, that task had fallen to her each night. They'd tag team bedtime. After Aria was out of the tub and ready for bed, she would read the child a story, and Landon would sing a lullaby. But the brightness in his eyes would dim the moment she'd cuddle up with Aria and crack open a book.

Tonight, there was nothing subdued about the man. A boyish grin spread across his face, and God help her. The warmth in his expression had her feeling almost as unsteady as someone who'd ingested drug-laced lollipops.

Aria pointed to the e-reader. "It's got special letters that don't wiggle. My old school didn't have that. They had wiggle words, and it made me mad when the letters wouldn't keep still."

"I bet," she replied, squeezing the girl's hand.

"I asked Uncle Landy to wake you up to read to me like we always do, but he said to let you sleep and that he'd read to me."

"That was really sweet of your uncle," she answered and met her husband's gaze.

Was he starting to understand that he wasn't broken? Could he see there was nothing wrong with him? Did he realize there was nothing shameful about being a neurodivergent learner?

"Aunt Harper?" Aria said and scooted toward her. The kid narrowed her gaze and looked her over like Landon had a few minutes ago.

"What's with the full-body scan, kid?" she teased.

"Uncle Landy said you ate a bunch of lollipops that made you feel topsy-turvy."

Topsy-turvy was one way to put it.

She smoothed the upturned sleeve on Aria's pajama top. "I feel much better, but I'll be laying off the lollipops."

"We'll stick to bonbons," Aria replied. "You can never go wrong with those. They're our favorite, right, Uncle Landy?"

"They sure are," he answered as he slid his attention from Aria and set his sights on her. "They sure are."

Hello, belly butterflies.

Crank up the air-conditioning and give this gal something to hold on to. The heat in his soulful brown eyes made her head feel as if it were filled with helium and brought back the topsy-turvy tingles dancing through her limbs and settled between her thighs.

Pull it together and focus on the kid. Jesus, this is bedtime, not bang time.

"Speaking of school," she said, ignoring her libido, "how was your first day at Whitmore? I'm sorry I wasn't there to pick you up."

"That's okay. There are plenty more days of school. My teacher said that we'll have one hundred and ninety-two school days. Then she had us write that number, and I wrote the numbers the right way using colored pencils."

She high-fived the wiz. "That's amazing!"

"There was a slight hiccup," Landon added, sharing another look with his niece.

Oh no.

"What happened?" she pressed, working to keep her voice even and leaving out the wholly inappropriate *whose ass do I need to kick* question. The thought of some bully giving Aria trouble had her prepared to grab a pitchfork and hunt this nose picker down.

"A boy named Tucker made fun of me for making the *r* in *Aria* backward."

Tucker, you little douche nozzle, you're going down.

"What happened after he made fun of you?" she asked instead, exercising exceptional restraint.

"Tell her, Aria," Landon coaxed.

The child lifted her chin and sported a haughty smirk. "I didn't punch him."

Well, look at that.

She gifted the kid with a second high five. "I'm proud of you, Aria."

"Oscar did," she tossed back. The girl's eyes glittered with a mix of pride and mischief.

Oscar Elliott punched a kid? No way.

On second thought, Oscar's dad was a former hothead. Still, the boy was a sweetheart, through and through. The kid was an artist, passionate about his photography, and fiercely loyal to his friends.

Then again, he'd basically had hearts in his eyes when he looked at Aria.

She couldn't deny she loved the thought of the Tuckers of this world getting a taste of their own medicine. Oscar was the son of a famous chef. If any kid had the DNA to cook up a slice of comeuppance, it was him, and there was something heartwarming about the boy sticking up for Aria. She wanted to call Char, get Oscar on the line, and tell the kid he was a total badass, but advocating violence probably wasn't the best example. Instead, she employed a parental facade.

"Is Tucker all right?" she asked, feigning concern.

He still was a kid, albeit a real douche nozzle of a kid.

Aria waved her off. "Yeah, he's fine. It was a love tap."

"A love tap?"

"Uh-huh, it's a real soft tap right in your belly. Oscar said that Sebastian's dad, who's a big, tough boxer, taught Sebastian how to do it. And then Sebastian taught Oscar. But Sebastian and Oscar said that they're yoga boxers. So, after Oscar gave Tucker the love tap, he and Sebastian pressed their hands together like they were praying and said go eat hay."

Go eat hay?

"Namaste. The boys said namaste after Oscar punched Tucker," Landon countered, his cheeks growing rosy as he pressed his lips together, clearly working to suppress a bout of laughter.

"Oscar punched a kid, then bid him namaste?" she asked, picturing the scene and nearly losing it.

Landon nodded, his eyes watering.

"Yeah, Sebastian said Oscar had to balance his chi-chis, or something like that. And to balance his chis-chis he had to do a nice thing like telling Tucker to go eat hay. Then Sebastian started talking about the universe and bings and bangs."

"Yin and yang," Landon supplied, brushing a tear from his cheek as he harnessed Herculean strength not to laugh at Aria's earnest yet off-the-wall commentary. She had to hand it to him. He was doing a remarkable job. She, on the other hand, tittered on the edge of a complete giggle explosion. She pressed her hand to her mouth to hold back the tidal wave of laughter threatening to break through.

"That's what I said, Uncle Landy, bing and bang," Aria corrected—incorrectly—dishing out a dash of hilarious side-eye. "So I just nodded at Sebastian because if people want to eat hay, they should eat hay. Goats eat hay, and they like it. Anyway, Phoebe kept looking at Sebastian like he was a hot dog she wanted to eat, and then Tucker ran away, and we decided to hang upside-down from the monkey bars for the rest of recess."

This kid was something else.

And this Aria, Phoebe, Oscar, and Sebastian foursome were a force to be reckoned with.

The last thing she wanted to do was laugh at the kid. She met Landon's gaze as they worked to keep their expressions neutral. A cocoon of sweet cotton candy silliness engulfed the room, intoxicating in its beautiful absurdity.

She cleared her throat, intent on keeping a straight face. "I should probably call Charlotte and see if Oscar got in trouble."

"It's taken care of," Landon replied, his hold-back-the-giggles face smoothing into a relaxed, self-assured expression. "I saw Mitch and Charlotte at pickup. We talked with the teacher. After recess, the boys worked it out with her, and this Tucker kid apologized to Aria."

She sat back. "Look at you, navigating parenthood like a pro."

"It's unclehood, Aunt Harper," the pint-sized amateur linguist corrected. "He's my uncle Landon, and you're my aunt Harper. So, your thing is aunthood," she added with a resolute nod.

And despite aunthood not being a real word, she wasn't about to correct the kid.

"But then," Aria continued, her brow crinkling as she brought the drama, "it got serious."

"What happened?"

"We had a class meeting. That's just school words for having a big talk about being respectful and kind," Aria explained. "My teacher says we have things we're good at, and we have things we're working on. She says you have to be brave and work on the hard stuff even if it makes you grumpy or if it makes you want to give up. Then I raised my hand and said I bet we have brave muscles, and I bet they're in our heart because being brave must come from there. And then I thought some more and raised my hand again and said that everybody's brave muscles must be a little different. My teacher nodded her head a whole bunch and said she thought I was right, and then she said it would be a boring world if we were all the same and that working on the hard stuff gives us a chance to grow into who we're supposed to be. Then Phoebe tapped my arm and showed me the cookie she had hidden in her pocket, and I don't remember what anybody said after that."

"A bravery muscle in your heart, huh? I like that," she answered as Aria yawned.

The child rubbed her eyes. "Tucker can make his brave muscles strong to stop acting like a…" She kicked her foot three times, most likely kicking out the syllables in douche nozzle. "And I'm going to use my brave muscles when I sing a song for Lolo and Lala," she added and sank into her pillow. "I think I'm done talking now," she murmured as her head lolled to the side.

"Sweet dreams, Aria," she whispered and smoothed the girl's dark hair.

"Sing to me before you go," the child mumbled.

"What song would you like?" Landon asked, fixing her covers.

She yawned again. "I want you and Harper to sing the song about Penny's sisters sucking eggs."

Oh, sweet Jesus.

"You want us to sing a duet?" Landon asked as he turned off the little lamp on the bedside table.

"No, I want you and Harper to sing a song at the same time together."

Even half-conscious, she was a little spitfire.

But how were they supposed to sing a song that was meant to be…well, screeched?

She tapped the bed as an idea for a workaround popped into her head. "We could sing it to the tune of Row, Row, Row Your Boat to make it a little less…"

"Psychotic?" Landon supplied.

"Gentler," she countered. "I'll go high. You can go low."

"We know you can go high," he murmured, biting back what had to be grin number three thousand of the night.

She took a page out of Aria's playbook, followed Aria's lead, and shot the man a healthy dose of stink eye, then tapped her foot and set the tempo.

What happened next was nothing short of mind-blowing.

Chapter 26
HARPER

A shiver danced down her spine, and goose bumps peppered her skin.

Lit only by the nightlight and the moon's silvery glow, she and Landon sang the silly lyrics to the familiar children's nursery rhyme, but the sound was anything but immature.

Of course, they'd been working on music, but they hadn't sung a duet. She'd harmonized with Landon Paige on the radio, alone in her car, belting out Heartthrob Warfare hits for a decent chunk of her life, but singing with the man in real life was like something out of her teenage daydreams.

Still, it went beyond starstruck.

Their voices came together and created a rich, honest sound. Raw yet refined, their duet was the audible equivalent of a diamond in the rough. Its beauty came naturally. Neither competed to be heard. Nothing was forced with this collaboration. Just two people whose voices ebbed and flowed like the song of the ocean or the medley of the breeze passing through a cluster of aspen trees. Easy and natural, their voices didn't require booming bass or techno overtones to garner attention.

They sang the lines of the song once, twice, then a third

time before bringing it to a close. Shimmery anticipation hung in the air like the house needed a few seconds to absorb the sound and pay homage to the vibrations echoing within its walls. Never had such an ordinary girl's room held such melodic magic. Only Aria's even breathing could be heard as they lingered, gazes locked in a dreamlike haze. She wanted to remember every detail about this moment—the scent of Aria's shampoo in the air and the slight tap of the old elm needling at the bedroom window. She didn't look away, scared that the spell would be broken if she did. Warmth engulfed her hand as Landon tightened his grip. The heat of his touch added to the swell of energy pulsing between them. Somewhere between singing about chickens hatching in Penny's sisters' mouths, their fingers had twined together. Like the curved line of the musical slur symbol connecting notes beneath its arc to create one continuous trail of sound, her connection to Landon had never been stronger.

"Harper," he rasped, and his voice sent a delicious tingle through her body. It was as if her name held the key to his heart. He didn't speak the syllables. He breathed life into them.

She parted her lips, unsure what was about to come out, when Aria sighed deeply, and the puff of sound snapped them back.

"Looks like our girl is out for the count," Landon whispered.

Our girl?

Was that a slip of the tongue?

Lit only by the faint glow of the nightlight and the watery-blue haze of the full moon, she gazed at the little girl, and her heart ached. What would life be like when Aria didn't conk out in her bed? She'd grown to love watching the child's brow smooth and her expression soften as she drifted off each night.

And then an agonizing question echoed in her mind.

What would life be like when Landon and Aria moved on without her?

Was that what she wanted, or was that how it had to be?

Did she want to put her heart on the line and break her hard and fast rule to keep her from falling hard and fast for another musician?

Stop! He's your sixty-day husband. That was the deal.

She swallowed past the lump in her throat. "We should let her sleep."

"Yeah," Landon answered softly and released her hand.

It took everything she had not to reach out and lace her fingers with his again.

Just be the nanny-aunt.

After two weeks, they'd mastered the art of exiting the room without waking the unconscious seven-year-old. They followed the same steps. First, she rose to her feet, then he followed. But this wasn't like any night they'd shared. Something had changed. With her heart in her throat, she tiptoed out of the room a few steps ahead of Landon. He closed the bedroom door, then stood before her in the darkened hallway.

What if she was wrong?

What if nothing had changed?

Stop!

To maintain her sanity, she'd need to speak first and stick to business. "You should have gotten me up. I didn't mean to sleep all day."

"You needed to rest," he replied, his voice a sexy rumble.

She leaned against the door to the guest room that doubled as their bedroom. "It was the lollipops, right? They weren't regular lollipops, were they?"

He caged her in. "No, they most definitely were not normal lollipops. They had micro-doses of psilocybin—you know, the chemical in magic mushrooms that makes people hallucinate."

"Shrooms?"

"Uh-huh. Move over Lucy in the Sky with Diamonds and make way for Harper in the Kitchen Baking Penis Cookies," he teased, moving in closer.

This man.

She sighed, trying to hold it together as she savored the heat of his body. "I should have known better than to snack on anything left by a guy with High AF embroidered on his beanie. And that explains the taste, too, and why I thought my hands had names and why I wanted to eat buildings."

"Just ceilings," he corrected, then took her hand in his. "Did you see the bonbons on the coffee table?"

"I did."

"Are there any left?"

She scoffed. "You really think I'd eat a whole box?"

Damn, she would. There was surveillance video proof.

"Don't answer that," she added. "And yes, quite a few are left in the box."

"Aria had the idea to put the notes on them," he said, leading her downstairs.

"Did you stop by the bakery after school?"

"No, Schuman brought them over. He stayed with you while I went to pick up Aria from Whitmore."

"Schuman Sweet?" she repeated as they entered the kitchen.

"The one and only."

She retrieved the box of chocolates and returned to the kitchen. "I hope he doesn't tell my grandma I got high as a kite. Babs is nonjudgmental when it comes to an artist's process, but I think she'd draw the line at tripping while being broadcast across the globe."

Landon took a bonbon from the box. "I doubt he'll do that."

She joined him in indulging and popped one into her mouth. "True, the lollipops belonged to his nephew."

Landon drank her in. "I think it's more than that. You won him over."

She froze mid-chew. "How? By gorging on lollipops and baking cookies that resembled the male anatomy?"

"No, when you sang with the choir. The guy got emotional."

Her memories of the competition were more akin to spending a few hours in a funhouse rather than putting on a performance.

"He did?"

"Yeah, I think I saw him wipe a tear from his cheek."

She leaned against the counter. "Do you know why?"

"He didn't say anything, but your performance was breathtaking. Nobody in the entire auditorium could take their eyes off you. Not even Vance."

An odd sensation overtook her. Usually, any mention of Vance got her hot under the collar and ready to spit nails. But not anymore. It wasn't like she'd forgiven him. What he'd done was unforgivable. But under the influence of the psychedelic candy, she'd seen the small, jealous man within. He knew he was a fraud but didn't see any other way forward.

Still, something else softened the blow of competing against her ex.

She rubbed her temples. "Everything about the contest felt surreal."

"I was worried about you," he said, taking a step toward her. "I didn't know how you'd react to Vance being there. It blew me away to see him and Bang Bang Barbie, and I was stone-cold sober."

"When I ran into him in Vegas, he was a real douchebag. I alluded to him stealing my music, and he threatened me."

"What?" Landon bit out, his posture stiffening.

"Not with physical harm. Vance is too much of a pussy for that. I could kick his ass with my hands tied behind my back."

She blew out a heavy breath. "He said he'd sic his label's lawyers on me if I said anything."

Landon shook his head. "He's a slimeball. I knew from the second I met him that he was a poser. I hate that we're with the same label."

"But seeing him today was different," she said as a realization hit.

"Was it because you were on a crazy high dose of hallucinogenic mushrooms?"

"Maybe, that helped soften the blow, but I think I was okay because I was with you. Because you make me…"

He made her…what?

Believe in the strength of their hasty union?

That was only a temporary arrangement.

Still, having him by her side had sustained her. It had made her feel solid even when she thought the ceiling was made of sugar, flour, and eggs, and her hands insisted on being addressed as Joyce and Bartholomew. Landon's presence had kept her tethered to a base of inner strength she hadn't tapped in years.

"Come with me and bring the bonbons," he said, pulling her from her thoughts. She grabbed the box as he took her hand and led her toward the not-so soundproof room.

"Is this a bonbon booty call?" she asked, trying to change the subject and get out of her head.

What was she about to say?

Landon Paige, you complete me.

Landon Paige, you make me stronger.

Landon Paige, I'm not sure who I am without you.

"This isn't a booty call, Harper," he bit out, irritation laced into the reply.

What had gotten into him? He seemed as off-balance as she did.

"You don't want to…" she began.

"I always want to," he blurted. "Jesus, that came out wrong. I want to show you something—something I did today. Something you inspired me to do."

They entered the quasi-soundproof room, and she spied his guitar in the corner. Sheet music and a bevy of markers littered the small table. He gestured for her to sit on the bed as he retrieved her notebook where she'd jotted notes and lyrics from their sessions. It wasn't anything formal or official. They hadn't completed any songs. They were in the brainstorming phase, recording ideas and musings. He slipped a laptop from his satchel on the ground next to the keyboard.

She sat cross-legged on the bed and placed the box of chocolates in the center as Landon settled himself across from her. He set the laptop and the notebook next to the bonbons, wrung his hands, then took a bonbon and popped it into his mouth.

Was he nervous?

"I'm just going to say it," he announced.

What was going on with the man? Had he gotten into the lollipops?

"You're freaking me out, heartthrob."

"Sorry, sorry," he replied on a shaky exhale. "After I taught your LookyLoo class, I worked on our music."

"Rewind," she exclaimed. "You really taught on my channel?"

She had a vague recollection of the man suggesting she take a nap but parsing what wasn't a product of her psychedelic state still wasn't easy.

"I uploaded that special font, and it made it easier."

Wow.

"Who did you say you were?" she asked, and that question elicited a cocksure grin from her husband.

"I said I was Landy Candy, filling in for Bonbon Barbie."

This guy was full of surprises.

"Not bad, and you stuck with the sweets theme. Did anyone recognize you?"

The boyish half grin returned. "I started the lesson teaching the notes of the treble clef with a little more than a couple dozen viewers and ended it with a few thousand."

"A few thousand?" she shot back, wide-eyed. She'd never gotten close to that number.

He shrugged. "Give or take."

"Give me your laptop. I need to look at my page." She opened the internet browser and found her page—which had clearly gotten a bump from Landon Paige. Her likes and follows had exploded. She scanned the screen, found his lesson, and hit play.

A bubbly happiness took over as the lesson unfolded.

Landon was a natural.

That smile. The honesty in his eyes. The warmth in his tone. He beamed as he placed the magnets on the board and taught the *exceptional girls bake delicious fudge* acronym.

She couldn't have done a better job if she'd planned for a week.

"You're good at this."

"Yeah?"

"Have you ever thought about teaching?"

He looked at her as if she'd suggested he swim a few laps in piranha-infested waters. "Um…no. I hated school. You know that."

She looked up from the laptop. "What do you call what you did today?"

"Filling in for you." He shrugged, but the hint of a grin pulled at the corners of his lips. "I have to admit, it was kind of exhilarating. I was a little freaked out, but I've watched you tape a few lessons, and you're always working with Aria. I must have picked up a little Bonbon Barbie magic."

It blew her mind to think she'd pegged him as a self-absorbed musician once upon a time. But this double-dog dare of a marriage had given her another perspective on the man.

Could this be more than a marriage of convenience?

"And there's more," he said softly.

At the mention of *more*, she startled.

Was he reading her mind?

"What more is there?" she asked, pushing the more thoughts aside.

Honestly, what *more* did she want him to say?

She couldn't let her heart override her head. Even with the shroom-pops and Landon's presence lessening the impact, what she'd lived through with Vance was proof of what happened when she ignored her head and gave in to her heart. She couldn't put herself in the position to be used and abandoned again. Enough damage had been done by her parents and her ex.

Landon leaned forward and tapped the side of the laptop. "Open the file on the desktop labeled *New Tracks*."

She closed her LookyLoo page and clicked on the file.

"I finished three songs, and they're pretty damn good. I recorded a rough cut for Mitzi and sent it to her to take a listen. For one, I used the melody you hummed when I was baking the cookies."

That had to be the song in her head when she'd pictured Candy Land. Had she been humming it?

Forget the psychedelic Candy Land trip. Landon had pulled together three songs.

That was freaking huge.

Her jaw dropped. "You taught a music lesson and wrote three complete songs while I was asleep?"

Landon channeled his smirking niece, mirroring her haughty disposition. "And I picked up Aria from school, and I made dinner, and I did bath time, and—"

"*And*...I get it," she deadpanned. "You're a super uncle."

She couldn't let the man get too big for his britches. It wasn't like she'd spent the day intentionally slacking off, eating bonbons in bed, and watching trash TV. No, she'd spent it—accidentally—high as a kite.

"I took the lyrics and melodies we've worked on, played around with them on blank sheet music pages, then scanned in the sheets and added the lyrics using the OpenDyslexic font."

"That's amazing," she breathed, scrolling down the page. He'd color-coded each section. The intro was gray, and the verses were light blue. He'd made the chorus a light brown, the bridge was gold, and the outro was dark green.

"After watching you perform, it inspired me to give it a go. I figured out a system, thanks to that special font and messing with highlighters and different colored markers."

"Why did you choose those colors?" she asked, eyes glued to the screen as she read the lyrics—the damned good lyrics—and followed along, seeing the guitar and piano notes in her head.

"Isn't it obvious?" he asked.

She looked up, and the man nearly swallowed her with his gaze. He took the laptop and set it aside.

Her heartbeat quickened. "No, it's not obvious. Am I missing something?"

He slipped his cell from his pocket, then handed it to her. She stared down at his phone in selfie camera mode.

Why did he do that?

She cocked her head to the side. "You want me to take my picture?"

"I want you to look at yourself and tell me what you see."

She chewed her lip. What was he playing at? "Landon, I—"

"Just do it, bonbon," he coaxed in his velvet voice.

How could she say no with him calling her bonbon and

looking at her like he wanted to devour her like a box of Mr. Sweet's chocolates?

She held up the phone and was met with messy chocolate waves, smudged mascara, and cheeks dusted with freckles. She stared at herself, at this woman who'd become a nanny-aunt, a wife, and maybe, a singer and songwriter.

Could that dream become a reality?

Or was she still the girl people left behind?

She swallowed past the lump in her throat. "What am I supposed to see?"

"Blues, toffee browns, steel grays, and shimmering gold. The mix of hues that darken and lighten with your mood. Blues and grays so faint, they mirror the sky after a storm, seconds before the golden sun peeks through the clouds. Warm shades of cinnamon, cocoa, and maple so rich a man could drown in the depths. And a dash of green like spring flowers pushing through a blanket of snow. I want you to see your chameleon eyes—the eyes I haven't been able to get out of my head for months."

She stared, transfixed.

How could he see all that?

She was about to ask if he'd gotten into Tanner's lollipops when the rhythmic strum of a guitar resonated through the snug space. She lowered the phone. Awestruck, she observed as Landon sat on the edge of the bed and played a melody they'd been toying with for the Bonbon Kiss song.

But he wasn't messing around anymore.

He'd shifted the key and slowed the tempo, allowing the music to unfold like a story, note by note. He'd also borrowed an intro she'd come up with on the piano a few days ago. She hadn't thought it would work with "Bonbon Kiss," but it fit beautifully. Like a musical chemist, he'd taken snippets of sounds and portions of lyrics and entwined them to create something new. This heartfelt ballad stripped away the layers of the mega pop star and uncovered the artist—the rock star.

He played the intro, held her gaze, then parted his lips.

My bonbon baby, she makes me go crazy.

Taste your chocolate kisses, breathe your sweet promises.

Losing my mind, bonbon baby, say you'll be mine.

If she were a cartoon character, her eyes would have transformed into hearts.

This wasn't the first time she'd heard him sing. They'd been working on music, riffing, and experimenting with lyrics and melodies. But that wasn't what was happening now.

In this cozy room, tucked in the corner of the basement, he serenaded her.

Her first impulse was to say something snarky to get him to stop—not because she didn't like it, but because she wasn't sure if her heart could take it. The intensity of his gaze left her speechless.

His voice, that velvet voice that rasped in all the right places, sparked a deep, visceral longing. Elegant in its simplicity, anyone who heard this song would believe without a doubt that they were Landon Paige's bonbon baby. He'd connected with fans as the lead singer of Heartthrob Warfare. Now, he was about to bare his soul. Acoustic, raw, and unfiltered, the world was about to fall even harder for this heartthrob.

He played the final chord. It hung in the air like fireflies hovering in the summer sky. She closed her eyes, locking in the sound.

"What do you think?" he asked as he propped his guitar in the corner.

Her eyes fluttered open, but she didn't say a word.

Who could think after being the first person on the planet to hear Landon Paige's new sound? Not to mention, how could she string a cohesive thought together after this man had strapped on his guitar and sung his heart out for her.

"Say something," he pressed.

Now he wanted her to speak?

There was only one language appropriate to convey her feelings.

She stood and walked in front of him.

"What are you doing?" he asked, confusion marring his expression.

She couldn't explain it. She could only act on what he'd ignited inside her.

As if she were caught in a dream, she slipped off her top and removed her bra. The chilly basement air hit her skin, but it couldn't cool her desire. She skimmed her skirt down her thighs, allowing it to pool at her ankles, and stood before the man, naked and exposed.

"Harper," he breathed, but she pressed her fingertips to his lips.

"This is what the song did to me. It stripped me of all pretenses. I watched you take off your mask and lay your heart on the line. I saw every part of you. My heart beat with the strum of your guitar. Your voice swelled through my body, touching every part. It amplified my senses. It made me want to…"

"To what?" he pressed.

"To believe in you."

And there she was, taking off her mask and allowing her heart to override her head.

Yeah, her admission might sound cheesy as hell, but that's what a powerful song could do.

And Landon Paige had nailed it.

In the space of a breath, Landon's gaze darkened. He gripped the hem of his T-shirt, pulled it over his head, and dropped it to the ground. He stood before her, muscles rippling and abs flexed. Of course, she'd seen him like this. She'd spent every night in bed with the pop god since he and Aria had moved in. The sex had been mind-blowing. He made her purr, gasp, and cry out loud enough to permeate a soundproof box, but the yearning ablaze in his eyes had her wet and aching for him.

He drew her into his embrace, and she sighed, reveling in the contact. He lowered his head and tasted her mouth, licking a slow trail across the seam of her lips. A move that had her weak in the knees within seconds.

"That means everything to me," he said, his words bathing her in a shimmery cascade of sound. "You make me better. You made me believe I could do it. You're magic—crazy, beautiful, chameleon-eyed magic. It's always you. It'll always be you."

What does a girl say to something like that?

Nothing.

She wrapped her arms around his neck and kissed him like the world was about to end and she wasn't sure if the sun would rise again. Urgent and unyielding, she held on to him, pressing her body to his as if she feared he might disappear— as if she were afraid she'd wake up alone in her bed, rubbing her eyes in a silent house, and her time with Landon and Aria would have only been a dream.

In a desperate fury to absorb the full impact of this moment, she reached between them, palmed his cock, and found him rock-hard. His response to her touch ushered in a flood of heady excitement as she stroked his hard length. His kisses intensified, owning her with each brush of his lips. He tangled his hand in her hair, lifted her chin, and took control. A dizzying current thrummed from the top of her head to the tips of her toes. She wasn't one to submit, but a switch had flipped, and she took comfort in knowing he owned her pleasure and could have her gasping on the edge of ecstasy. She wanted him to take and take and take and kiss her until she couldn't see straight.

His heated breaths sent a shiver through her as he kissed a path to her earlobe. "Harper," he whispered, and again, the voice that had gotten her through some of the most challenging times of her life sent her reeling.

Landon Paige wanted her and only her.

The goddess Aphrodite could walk in, flaunting her otherworldly appeal and all-encompassing allure, and Landon wouldn't give the Greek beauty a second glance.

His gaze would remain focused on her and her chameleon eyes.

The truth of that revelation seemed almost too good to believe.

Believe.

There was that word again. Like the perfect lyric materializing, it had to be a sign.

Could her husband be the one for her even though he was everything she'd promised herself she'd shy away from?

She could do it. She could break her rule for him. She could take her battered heart, with its faults, cracks, and scars, and allow him to see every bruise and examine each blemish.

But the time for talking about what was to come had to wait.

The heat between her thighs and the drive to feel this man fill her to the hilt pushed aside the nagging questions and what ifs. He'd shattered her resolve with the song, and his kisses proved to be the final blow.

She couldn't wait for a second longer.

She required one thing and one thing only.

This man and his glorious cock.

"Make love to me," she pleaded, her words floating like flower petals dancing in the air. "Make love to me and show me what it means to be yours, all yours, with nothing holding us back."

It was terrifying to admit it. But the truth was inevitable. She'd never wanted anything more.

Forget about Landon professing how he never wanted to marry.

Forget about Babs' house on the brink of foreclosure.

Forget about Vance stealing her work.

Forget about being left on her grandparents' stoop and watching her parents' van disappear.

He pulled back, and she studied his face, concentrating on the storm brewing in his eyes.

He wanted to forget, too.

And isn't that how this started.

She'd begged him to make her forget.

He lifted her into his arms and gently set her on the bed. Without a word, he shrugged out of his jeans, then prowled the length of her body. Each brush of skin on skin heightened her arousal. They'd made love in the practice room plenty of times, but tonight, after a whirlwind day, their tempo as a couple had changed. He moved slowly, kissing her forehead, then her nose, then her neck, as he positioned himself at her entrance. This wasn't frantic, frenzied love-making that had him pumping his cock as he gripped her ponytail and took her hard and fast from behind.

Eye to eye, there was nowhere to hide.

"You feel it, don't you?" he asked.

His question sent a shiver down her spine.

Yes, she felt it.

The shift. The change in the air. The change in them.

She not only felt it, she craved it, needed it…*loved it.*

She rested her hands on the pillow, one on each side of her head, and allowed her knees to fall to the sides. Like a flower drawn to the sun's warmth, she opened to him. He lowered himself, and when his body covered hers in his masculine embrace, he laced their fingers as if he wanted to maintain as many points of contact as possible. He rocked his hips, sliding in slowly, gently, deliberately.

The man knew every inch of her body. Now, he possessed it.

She inhaled a sharp breath, savoring the connection as they moved in an unhurried, easy like Sunday morning cadence. They didn't need music to set a sensual pace. Their bodies found the perfect rhythm—their rhythm.

Still, it was hard to hold back. It took concentration not to dig her nails into his skin and beg him to make her come.

Methodical and measured, the intensity built slowly like the lines of a song.

The old bedsprings creaked beneath them as their bodies grew slick with sweat and their lusty breaths punctuated the air. She arched her back, trembling beneath him, and he dialed up his pace, giving her what she needed. She tightened around him, no longer in control, unable to hold back.

"Please," she moaned, not sure if she was on the edge of ecstasy or agony.

Every muscle in his body tightened as he made love to her like his life depended on it.

Thrust after powerful thrust, they accelerated toward the crescendo like a freight train thundering down the track.

She ran her hands down his back, delighting in the hard contours beneath his smooth skin.

But he didn't kiss her lips. He didn't nip at her neck. He didn't lick the lily-white skin beneath her earlobe.

He simply stared into her eyes, and the intensity of his focus set her on fire.

"I see you. I see all of you," he bit out, passion and fury swirling in his gaze as he surrendered to their demanding, delirious rhythm. The mechanics of their lovemaking came together like the elements in a song. A verse comprised of hip thrusts. The slick sweat between them made up the bridge. He hit the chorus and worked her in decisive, deliberate strokes, grinding against her most sensitive place, knowing how she liked it.

Her breasts heaved. Her nipples tightened into pearls, and her body quaked as they neared the crescendo.

More, harder, deeper.

The pure carnal gratification built between them as the friction of their bodies sizzled with unadulterated lust. The bedsprings noted the quickening tempo and teased the grand finale like a sexual metronome keeping time.

She was close—so close.

He pinned her hands above her head and altered the angle of penetration. "Believe in this. Believe in us. Let me see you. Let me hear you."

With those words, her last remaining defenses crumbled.

She cried out, swallowed by the crush of her orgasm. Wave after wave and thrust after thrust, their breaths mingled in the inches between them. Hot and demanding, he spilled inside her, pumping furiously as they hovered in that space between heaven and earth where time stood still, and pleasure rained down, hot, wet, and unrelenting.

She clung to him, riding out the surge of endorphins flooding her system until her muscles could no longer comply. Loose-limbed, she sighed as he shifted his body and gathered her into his arms. He stroked her cheek and gave her that boyish grin that had made her weak in the knees for over a decade, except it was just for her.

"What happens now?" she asked, panting to catch her breath.

"I think we know what happens."

She rested her head against his chest.

Was this the real thing?

Was she falling in love with her husband?

He hummed the melody—their melody.

The vibrations wrapped them in an invisible symphony of sound.

Stop asking questions, let go of the fear, and believe.

She inhaled his scent and concentrated on the rise and fall of his chest, then closed her eyes and drifted off to sleep, nestled in his strong embrace.

Chapter 27
HARPER

"Welcome to the second *Celebrity Bake or Bust* challenge, brought to you by Cupid Bakeries and LookyLoo," Donna Diamond announced in her buttery southern accent.

Harper caught her husband's eye as they waited backstage in the shadows alongside a set of pleated red velvet stage curtains, waiting for the hosts to invite them on stage.

"We've got this," he said under his breath, looking cocky as hell as he tossed her a wink.

She bit her lip. Be still her beating heart.

Cocky Landon in a button-up with the sleeves rolled just enough to incite drooling over his sexy as hell forearms was a sight to see.

And yeah, the man was right. They totally had this challenge.

She held a tray of skillfully prepared cocoa-licious macarons with chocolate ganache filling.

Fancy-pants baking, for sure!

Thanks to her ability to refrain from gorging on hallucinogenic lollipops and Schuman's capacity to remain conscious during their bake time, under the man's watchful eye, she and Landon had baked their asses off.

In her not-so-humble opinion, they'd knocked this macaron challenge out of the confectionary park.

And if she thought that she and Landon were on fire in the kitchen, to her delight, Mr. Sweet brought his own brand of heat.

The baker had guided her as she whipped up the macaron batter and baked up the delicate cookies while Landon filmed for the livestream. They'd changed places, and Landon had stepped in to rock the filling. With Schuman by his side, he prepared the ganache like a chocolate cream-making machine. And heaven help her, her husband was a phenom with the filling. Who would have thought Landon Paige could bang out a masterpiece with a few cups of cream and some chopped-up dark chocolate? Now, thanks to the LookyLoo livestream, the world would see Landon wasn't only a velvet-voiced crooner but a fancy cookie-making connoisseur.

When the cookies and filling were ready to be assembled into bite-sized masterpieces, Schuman had taken over filming as she and Landon sandwiched the dainty chocolate shells with the creamy filling, constructing French delicacy after French delicacy. They'd done a hell of a job preparing the best macarons ever made in the history of mankind—or baking-kind, if that was a thing, which it should be.

Okay, that might be a slight exaggeration.

But she'd had an inkling things were going well when Schuman's handlebar mustache seemed to smile along with the man. When she'd pulled the tray of sinfully scrumptious smelling cookie shells from the oven with no cracks, no bumps, or tiny air bubbles rippling on the surface, she could feel the pride coming off the old baker in cocoa-scented waves as he nodded approvingly at the cookies' toasty-brown coloring and smooth as silk finish. Mr. Sweet had been so impressed, he'd said he might consider hiring her to work for him if he wasn't so worried she'd bulldoze through the bonbons and eat herself into a sugar coma on her first day, which was a legitimate concern. She couldn't deny it. No bonbon was safe when she was nearby.

But it wasn't only her quasi-homicidal penchant for devouring chocolate delights that kept her from taking the man up on his comical offer.

Besides baking for the contest, she didn't have a moment to spare.

She and Landon had turned a corner in their double-dog dare of a marriage.

Had they talked specifics?

No.

But there had been a shift.

The night they'd made love after the first challenge had ushered in an age of bliss like she'd never known, which was scary but exhilarating. From an early age, she'd learned to keep her guard up and protect her heart. She'd made a mistake with Vance, but Landon wasn't the scheming, conniving thief Vance Viberenski was. Landon was...

Her silly heart skipped a beat.

Landon was someone she believed in.

And he believed in her.

Was it love?

Neither had mentioned the four-letter *L* word.

She shied away from it because she'd wasted it on Vance and she didn't want to jinx the magic she and Landon had created over the past three weeks by giving it a label.

But did she want a label? Did she yearn for a declaration?

Or were his actions speaking louder than words?

Whatever they'd become, it had worked its way into her heart.

She wasn't easily rendered starry-eyed. Snark, sass, and a

general attitude of badassery were her modus operandi.

Emphasis on the word *were*.

Now, she was the living embodiment of walking on sunshine.

Spending each night in Landon's arms and waking to him humming a melody against her neck as they greeted the day wrapped around each other, gasping, and drenched in moan-inducing ecstasy, felt as close to completely and insanely happy as one could get.

But it wasn't the core-clenchingly amazing feats between the sheets that had her floating through the days.

Making music with the man was as much of a turn-on as when he'd turned his soulful brown eyes on her, peeled off her clothing, then make her hit those opera high notes as she flew over the edge into Orgasm Country, USA.

They'd been working around the clock writing and composing additional songs over these last few weeks. They had twelve new tracks—a solid set by any standard.

The only time they took a break from eating, breathing, and sleeping music was when they were with Aria, which wasn't exactly a true break from music. It was more like a shift to Aria-centered music.

And how was the toe-tapping seven-year-old badass doing?

Pretty freaking great.

The kid thrived at her new school.

She had friends and was slaying the second-grade curriculum, thanks to the educational modifications at Whitmore. That, however, didn't mean she'd lost her surly edge. The girl was still a force to be reckoned with and could serve up a helping of side-eye like nobody's business, but the undercurrent of anger that had permeated every aspect of her life didn't bubble to the surface quite as much anymore. A contented rhythm had taken over. And while she wouldn't sing with them or at school in her music class, the kid had started to sing when she was alone. Landon had caught it first. After school about a week ago, Aria had bolted out of the car and hightailed it up to her room. Their first clue she was up to something was a keep-out sign the kid had hastily taped to the door. Risking life and limb, Landon had disregarded the warning. He peeked inside the room as Aria slipped into the closet and closed herself inside the snug space. Then, like the nosiest aunt and uncle on the planet, they stood in the hallway, straining to listen to the child hum and, finally, sing. In a rich, rolling tone, Aria started with the song about Penny's sisters, then veered off, toying with rhyming lyrics about Phoebe and Sebastian and Oscar.

Oscar Elliott is not so smelly-it. He gives me his dessert every day.

It had taken everything they had to hold back their giggles, but they were teary-eyed as they listened to the little girl pour her heart into her sweetly silly songs.

If it wasn't entirely obvious, an enthralling happiness had taken over the house. The rhythm they'd settled into was a balm to her heart. Granted, she had to come up with almost fifty thousand dollars to save it, and she remained bull-headed and wouldn't accept a penny from Landon or her friends. Still, their little trio possessed an unstoppable quality that made her believe it would be all right.

And there was that word again.

Believe.

She stole a glance at her husband as the glowing lights coming from the stage warmed his chiseled features.

With the scent of chocolate in the air, she sighed a dreamy rush of breath, knowing she'd fallen hard for the guy.

Just as the thought took hold, a reflex kicked in—a practiced reaction that triggered a faraway voice in the back of her mind to send out a series of alerts whenever anything seemed too good to be true.

Protect your heart.

Don't forget, you're the girl nobody wanted.

You'll never be good enough. Cut your losses before you lose everything.

"Earth to Harper, are you with me, Harper?" came a low, velvety voice.

She blinked. "Yeah, of course, I am. I was thinking about…"

"Yeah?" He sized her up.

She held his gaze, and the prickly whispers in her head quieted. "I was thinking about how we're going to kick some baking butt in this challenge."

"That's not all you were thinking about," he replied with a wicked grin that had her pulse hammering.

Now she was the one doing the sizing up. "How do you know that, heartthrob?"

He leaned in and twisted a lock of her hair around his finger. "You bit your lip. When you do that, I know you're thinking about the ways I can make you—"

"Scream!" came Damien's voice, twanging the word into two syllables, and the crowd went wild.

"That was frighteningly accurate," Landon murmured, rocking a shit-eating grin.

"You're terrible. And for your information," she said, turning on the sass, "I was thinking about Aria and how well she's doing."

It wasn't the whole truth, but it wasn't officially a lie.

The man raised an eyebrow. "That's it?"

"Yep," she replied, then bit her lip—because why not. If she was a little hot and bothered, it only made sense for the man to share in the agony, and it sure helped shut down the doomsday voices in her head.

A rapid peppering of footsteps pulled her attention from her pop star as a production assistant hurried toward them.

"I can take the macarons," the man said, eyeing the cookies. "Wow, these look amazing, unlike…"

Unlike?

He had to be talking about Barbie and Vance's entry.

That was a freaking great sign.

"I mean," the guy said and cleared his throat. "You've got about seven minutes till Donna and Damien invite you onto the stage. They're introducing a few volunteer instructors and talking about the music program," he explained, lowering his voice.

The second challenge had brought them to an abandoned tire factory that had been renovated, but there wasn't a tire in sight. With a banner attached to the front of the structure with the words *New Beats Music Center* printed in bold lettering, rows of instruments had replaced the assembly lines. The place wasn't far from the Helping Hands Shelter and Community Center in a rougher but rapidly evolving part of the city. A volunteer from the organization had greeted them when they'd arrived and explained that the sprawling brick building had recently been converted into a musical artists' enclave, serving teens and young adults who had found themselves on the wrong side of the law and needed a change in their life trajectory. And from what little she'd seen of it, she was already impressed with the assortment of practice rooms, casual seating areas perfect for collaborating, and where they were now—an intimate indoor concert hall.

She craned her neck to see what was happening on stage and caught a glimpse of several older adults fanned out around Donna and Damien. She narrowed her gaze. A few of the people looked familiar, but she couldn't quite place how she knew them.

"Several of the students wanted to know if you'd be able to stay for a Q and A session after the contest portion of the livestream. Would you be up for that?" the production assistant asked.

That was pretty awesome.

"Look at that," she teased, tapping Landon's arm. "The

youth of today want to pick your brain."

"And yours as well," the PA added, turning to her.

She wasn't expecting that.

"Could you spare a few minutes after the competition?" the guy pressed.

Landon checked his watch. "We need to leave no later than three o'clock to pick up our niece from school."

Our niece.

There it was again—two words that made her heart go all gushy and gooey like chocolate ganache filling.

"That should be plenty of time. Thanks, Mr. Paige. Thanks, Mrs. Presley-Paige."

Mrs. Presley-Paige.

And just as the warm fuzzies nearly had her melting into a pool of goo, that little gnawing voice inside her head returned, whispering the million-dollar question.

How much longer will you be Mrs. Presley-Paige?

She shooed the thought away.

And what about Italy?

Her absolute bitch of an inner voice wouldn't let up.

But it was a legitimate question.

Tomás and Bess's vow renewal celebration was days away.

Had she packed or prepared?

No.

She'd pushed the Italy trip out of her mind.

And why had she done that?

Neither Aria nor her husband had mentioned it.

When she'd pressed Landon about it last week, he'd blown off the question, then said he had to run to the bakery and grab a box of bonbons. Aria had agreed and joined the man on the outing, leaving her wondering what was going on.

Was she going with them or not?

She'd considered asking him point-blank when he returned with the chocolate treats.

But she hadn't followed through.

A memory had percolated to the surface of her consciousness—a recollection that had kept her lips sealed.

A cold stoop. A granola bar and a creased envelope. A van disappearing down the street.

The little girl who was left behind.

"Donna and Damien's outfits are a little over-the-top. Don't you think?" Landon offered with a chuckle.

His words were a lifeline, bringing her back to the here and now.

And currently, her here and now included a life with Landon and Aria.

Focus on the good stuff.

She mustered a grin and studied the hosts' theatrical ensemble. Sporting red shimmery berets and black and white striped shirts crafted with glittery sequins, the pair looked like the children's coloring book version of a mime-inspired French couple.

"Are you telling me you don't have a red bedazzled beret hidden in your dresser?" she joked, when a smattering of clickety clacking and high-pitched sniffling caught her attention. She glanced around the stage curtain and spied Bang Bang Barbie.

But there was nothing bang-bang about her. The blonde appeared distraught and deflated as she wobbled behind a scowling Vance.

Barbie wiped tears from her cheeks with the back of her wrist. "Vancey-Poo," she blubbered, "my grandparents didn't make macarons at their bakery. I never learned how to prepare them. I did my best."

"You said you could bake," Vance hissed.

And holy douche nozzle, she recognized the condescending tone of the pop poser.

Landon pressed his hand to her back. "They must think

they're alone," he whispered.

She nodded. "Vance's smiles are for show. He's a real jerk."

He was. Lazy, moody, and always looking for the easy out. How had she not seen it?

"I can bake," Barbie sobbed. "I won the first challenge for you."

"You sure as hell didn't deliver on the second. You saw the assistant go by with Harper and Landon's macarons. Ours look like a shit show compared to theirs. We should have done what I suggested we do."

Barbie's shoulders slumped forward. "But that would have been cheat—"

Vance pressed his hand to Barbie's mouth, cutting off the woman's words.

The absolute creep.

Anger tore through her like a tornado. Bang Bang Barbie didn't deserve to take Vance's shit.

Nobody did.

"Take your hands off of her, you giant phony prick," she growled as she emerged from behind the curtain to confront her bully of an ex.

"Mind your own business, Harper. Doesn't it get exhausting pretending to be such a badass when you're the girl nobody wants?" He took a menacing step toward her as he spat the harsh words, going for the jugular.

"If I were you, Vance, I'd think very carefully about your next move and even more carefully about what bullshit comes out of your mouth," Landon warned, emerging from behind the curtain.

His tone positively dripped with fuck around and find out energy, and holy hot hell-raising heartthrob. she was there for it.

And one thing was for sure.

They were about to put the bust in *Celebrity Bake or Bust.*

Chapter 28
HARPER

Harper scrutinized her asshat of an ex. "How do you like them apples, Vance?" she crowed because, one, she was a sassy bitch. Two, she'd always wanted to drop that line. And three, it was hella satisfying to watch Vance Vibe squirm under Landon's hardened gaze.

And speaking of Landon. Her husband stood by her side, a pillar of strength, as they knocked Vance down a few pegs and came to Barbie's defense.

Did she need a man by her side to dish out a healthy serving of sass and stand up for a fellow woman?

No.

She could fight her own battles. But Landon's steady presence didn't carry the air of a protector but rather that of a partner. Her little finger brushed his, and he laced his fingers with hers, strengthening their wall of solidarity.

"It's my fault," Barbie sobbed. "We saw the PA go by with your macarons. They look amazing, by the way. Ours look like—"

"—total shit," Vance seethed and tossed a sharp glance at his weeping wife.

With his jaw set, Landon glared at the douche nozzle. "The only thing that's total shit in this place is you, Vance."

She pasted a sugary sweet smile to her lips. "Agreed."

Vance took a step back and glanced around like a caged rat looking for the fastest way out. "This whole thing is bullshit," he muttered like a sullen teenager as Barbie wiped her wrist across her dripping nose.

Poor thing.

And Vance wasn't about to lift a finger to comfort her.

She scanned the backstage area, searching for some tissues, and noticed a slew of Bake or Bust production assistants filming the encounter on their cell phones.

Dammit!

"Put those away. Don't record her. Can't you see she's upset?" she chided, giving them her best Harper Presley stink-eye.

"Yeah, give the lady some privacy," Landon agreed, backing her up.

The PAs dispersed, and she spied a roll of paper towels on a nearby table.

It was better than nothing.

She released her husband's hand, grabbed a few sheets, and handed them to Vance's sniffling wife.

"Thanks," Barbie sobbed, dabbing at her cheeks with the wad.

Vance paced, widening the distance between them. But Landon hadn't let up—not yet. He peered at the man as one would regard a steaming pile of horseshit before he joined her at Barbie's side.

"Are you okay, Barbie? Did Vance hurt you?" Landon asked, softening his tone.

"I'm fine," Barbie blubbered and glanced Vance's way. Cast in the red glow of the exit sign, the man sulked next to the stage door as he stared at his phone. "Vance really wants to beat you guys. It's all he talks about," Barbie added as she wiped her nose.

The man had already stolen her music. Now he was hell-bent on beating her at a charity baking contest? What a tool!

"From one Barbie to another," she said, patting the woman's back, "take care of yourself. Vance isn't the kind of guy you can depend on."

"What's this?" Schuman asked, taking in the scene. The man had said he needed to make a quick stop before joining them at the challenge location, so they'd driven separately. He zeroed in on Barbie and pulled a handkerchief from his pocket. "Here, dear, this will work better than those. What are the tears for?"

"My macaron shells came out bumpy, and now my Vancey-Poo is upset," Barbie bawled, accepting the folded square. "I'm a baking failure."

In a fatherly gesture, Schuman wrapped his arm around her shoulders. "Your sugar cookies were topnotch. I couldn't have done better with the piping or the icing, and I've been a baker since I was eight years old."

"That's when I started helping in my family's bakery," Barbie replied through a weak grin.

"Those cookies alone would have persuaded me to offer you a job on the spot. You're a talented baker, miss. And I know Mrs. Sweet would agree. Beautifully decorated sugar cookies were always her favorite. She'd spend hours piping intricate designs onto the cookies."

That's right! Mrs. Sweet was a sugar cookie decorating maven.

When she was a girl, Schuman's bakery used to have tray after tray of ornately decorated cookies—cookies so gorgeous, it felt like a shame to eat them. And that was saying something, coming from someone like her, who'd happily tear into a box of baked goods like a raccoon hitting a fast-food restaurant dumpster.

Come to think of it, it had been a while since she'd seen the beautifully decorated cookies in the bakery.

Barbie's expression brightened at Mr. Sweet's kind words. Her lips tipped upward as she gifted the man with a grin, when Vance stormed over.

"We're leaving, Barbie. Screw this challenge. They can do it without us," he grumped, stuffing his phone into his pocket.

So much for his stupid catchphrase *keep fighting the good fight and vibe on*. The guy wouldn't know the first thing about fighting for anything that didn't benefit him. He was and would always be a petty prick.

Barbie returned the handkerchief to Schuman. "You're a sweet man, Mr. Sweet." She giggled. "And Landon and Harper?"

"Yeah, Barbie?" Landon replied, patting the woman's shoulder.

"You two make a great couple." She nodded, then teetered off, clickity-clacking behind Vance.

"She's a good kid. It's a shame she's with Vance. But you'd know what that's like," Mr. Sweet continued. "He was your beau for a while, if I remember correctly."

She wasn't expecting the baker to say that.

"I dated him when I was in college. How did you know that?"

"Your grandmother mentioned a Vance to me and Mrs. Sweet when she was in the shop years ago."

"Did she?"

"She wasn't fond of him."

"Babs is a good judge of character."

Mr. Sweet slid his gaze to Landon. "And what does Barbara Presley think of Landon?"

That was a great question, but she wasn't about to cop to Babs not knowing a damn thing.

"Well..." she began, but applause broke out in the concert hall and saved her from answering.

"That's your cue," a production assistant whisper-shouted and waved them toward the stage.

Saved by the baking challenge.

Her husband took her hand and leaned toward her as they made their way toward the bright lights. "Don't worry about your grandma. I slay with the grandmas. They're crazy about me. They embroider my face on pillows."

This man.

He was in rare form today.

A wide grin stretched across her face. Hand in hand, she and Landon emerged from the shadows and stepped into the spotlight.

"We heard there were some fireworks backstage," Donna drawled with a twitch of a grin.

"Never a dull moment with the *Celebrity Bake or Bust.* Nevertheless, we're excited to be here, right, Mrs. Presley-Paige?" Landon replied, the consummate performer. But he wasn't yucking it up for the cameras. He looked down and met her gaze.

All she saw was...

Her heart swelled in her chest.

It had to be the four-letter word she'd sworn she'd never utter to another musician.

Butterflies tickled her belly.

Pull it together.

She nodded. "Yes...we've heard great things about New Beats."

"And the show must go on," Damien remarked in a pleasing drawl. "A little dust-up won't stop us from sampling these chocolate macarons and choosing a winner."

"Michel Laurent," Donna continued, "since we're highlighting your remarkable music program and celebrating your French cuisine, why don't you lead your teachers in judging which team made the best macarons."

Michel Laurent. Why did that sound so familiar?

With their backs to her, the four volunteer instructors descended on the table sporting two trays of the tiny delicacies. She took a moment to survey her surroundings. A piano, a few acoustic guitars, several stools, and a drum kit sat silently in the shadows near the back of the stage. She squinted and studied the crowd, then almost fell over when she spied the nanny matchmaker, Madelyn Malone, among the young people packed into the hall.

What was she doing here?

Checking up on them?

She wasn't their nanny matchmaker.

She'd made it abundantly clear she couldn't work with Landon.

Perhaps she had an interest in music. She had visited with her grandmother, which was still quite odd and didn't make much sense.

"The choice is easy," Monsieur Laurent announced. At the sound of the man's voice, she forgot about Madelyn's surprise appearance and stared at the man. "We agree," the Frenchman continued. "While both trays of macarons are delicious, the macarons on the blue tray are *c'est magnifique*."

"That's us, Harper. We won!" Landon exclaimed, but she couldn't concentrate on his words or that they'd won. The crowd clapped as she took in the Frenchman's slender build and put together why this man seemed so familiar.

She knew him.

"Mishy?" she blurted as the crowd in the concert hall died down, and a slew of memories coupled with sensations flooded her mind.

An empty symphony hall cast in an ethereal blue hue.

Lemon-scented wood polish mingling with the papery comforting aroma of old sheet music.

The hollow, pleasing pop of a mallet striking the circle of timpani drums followed by a cascade of shimmery chimes.

Her foot, tapping out not a naughty word but a thumping, rollicking rhythm that worked its way through the floor from the soles of her feet to the tips of her little fingers.

"*Mishy*, how I loved that you used to call me that," Michel Laurent said in the same elegant French accent she remembered. "I wondered if you would recognize me, Harper Barbara."

"Us, actually," another instructor, a woman with her hair pulled into a tight silver bun, added in a smooth Italian accent —another accent she recognized.

She gazed down the line of adults. "Mishy, Maria Magdalena, Hans, and Yusuf?"

"You know the instructors?" Landon asked with a crease to his brow.

"We've known Harper Barbara since she hid in the symphony's percussion closet and knocked every chime off the wall," Mishy, no, Michel Laurent, the acclaimed percussionist, said with a wide grin.

"No, no," corrected the woman, Maria Magdalena Bianchi, a world-renowned violinist. "We've known Harper Barbara since she decided to take my violin strings and lace her tiny shoes with them. Remember what you told me after you did that?" the woman asked, raising a jet-black eyebrow.

Oh, she remembered.

It all came back to her. The instructors' faces had unlocked a door to her past.

A door that led to quite a few innocently menacing behaviors.

She felt her cheeks heat.

"Harper Barbara said, 'Señora Maria Magdalena, your strings look better on my shoes. You can use my laces to practice.'"

The audience gave a collective chuckle.

"I was a bit sassy back then," she conceded.

"Back then?" Landon uttered under his breath but loud enough for the audience and everyone on stage to hear.

She cocked her head to the side, eyeing her husband as amusement sparkled in his eyes.

"Look at this, LookyLoo! We've got a surprise reunion at our Bake or Bust," Donna crooned, but her southern accent wasn't quite as pronounced. Indeed, there was something about her voice she recognized.

"You must share how you know each other with the audience and our LookyLoo viewers," Damien insisted, pulling her attention from Donna as he gestured to the cameras and the packed house before peering into the audience. The man took a few steps forward and appeared to look directly at Madelyn. The nanny matchmaker smoothed her signature scarlet scarf as what looked like a ghost of a grin graced the woman's lips.

What the heck was this?

Madelyn did seem to know everyone. Maybe she knew Damien and Donna, or perhaps it was nothing. One never knew with the mysterious Ms. Malone.

"Many years ago," Michel explained, "we played with the Denver Symphony Orchestra."

"Under the direction of Harper's grandfather, Reeves Presley," supplied Yusuf Ali, a gifted cellist from Bahrain.

"And alongside the great harpist and Reeve's wife, Barbara Presley," Hans Pedersen, a gifted trombone player, added in a crisp Swedish tongue.

It had been nearly twenty years, but she recognized them

like she was still the little girl who used to run a zigzag pattern through the sprawling maze of red-cushioned seats that spread out from the stage like waves of crimson around a grand wooden platform.

"I can't believe that you're all in Denver. That's amazing," she exclaimed, crossing the stage to embrace them, one by one.

"They came at my request. The teachers at New Beats volunteer their time on a rotating schedule," Michel explained. "We could use a harpist on our faculty."

Babs would love that.

"My grandmother is kind of off the grid at a musicians' retreat in New Mexico and can't be reached easily, but I'm sure she'd love to catch up once she returns."

"It seems as if you've been busy as well," Michel Laurent said, taking her left hand into his to get a better look at the giant diamond twinkling under the stage lights.

"About that," she replied and glanced over her shoulder at Landon.

"No explanation is needed, *amore mio*," Maria Magdalena said warmly.

"Maria Magdalena is correct," Hans agreed. "We have grown grandchildren now. They showed us the footage of your...unique nuptials. We know about your wild Vegas wedding."

"Gladiators and ballerinas are an eclectic touch," Yosef remarked with the twitch of a grin.

"It was a spur-of-the-moment decision," she replied as the memories of Landon sliding the platinum band onto her finger made her lightheaded with buzzy happiness.

"I did not have to ask my grandchildren about Harper's wedding," Maria Magdalena chided, waving her finger. "I found out about it on my own. I received an email alert from the Landon Paige fan club. Our president, Norma, keeps us up to date on all pertinent Landon Paige news."

"You're a fan?" Landon blurted, awe coating the question.

She would never have pegged the haughty-in-the-best-way former first chair violinist as a pop aficionado.

"*Heartthrob warfare,*" the woman sang, her Italian accent growing thicker as she adopted an adorably comical cadence. "*I'm fighting for your love.*"

The audience erupted into applause as Maria Magdalena busted out the first line of the pop song.

"Your grandmother introduced me to his music, Harper Barbara. She said you'd played it nearly nonstop when you were a teenager," Maria Magdalena explained.

A wide, boyish grin spread across Landon's lips.

This man didn't need more proof she'd mooned over him for a decent portion of her life, but it was beautifully poetic.

"As you can tell," Michel cut in, "we're excited to have an artist from the world of contemporary pop and rock music grace our intimate concert hall. Our students are eager and excited to ask you questions. We're classically trained," the man continued, nodding to the instructors, "and while that is all well and good, many of our students are interested in music from—"

"—this century," a member of the audience called playfully and elicited another round of laughter.

"Exactly," Michel agreed.

"That's the perfect transition for the impromptu question and answer segment of this most unique baking challenge," Donna offered as another row of lights warmed the stage.

A trio of PAs scurried out. One grabbed a stool and an acoustic guitar, while the other two unlocked the wheels on the shiny black grand piano and pushed the musical beast toward center stage next to the stool. It happened to be the exact set-up they used when working on music in her living room.

"We figured you'd be most comfortable in your element,"

Damien said, escorting her to the piano as Donna walked Landon to his stool and handed the man the guitar and a pick.

She settled herself on the bench and listened as Landon plucked the low E string and moved his way up, tuning the guitar to his liking. The familiar sound of her husband strumming and tweaking the strings set her at ease as she ran her fingers along the keys to get a feel for the instrument. The last time she'd played for an audience, she'd thought the ceiling was made of cake. She said a prayer, looked up, and saw only...beams, lights, and a boring old ceiling.

Phew!

"Are you good, bonbon, or do you want me to ask Schuman if he's got any of Tanner's special lollipops," Landon teased, keeping his voice low.

"I'll try to get through this without talking to my hands or licking the building," she replied, then studied her hands. "Joyce, Bartholomew, does that sound good to you?"

"So damned sassy," he mouthed, pegging her with his darkened gaze. And hello, tightened nipples and below-the-belly tingles. His sexy as hell demeanor helped alleviate her nerves, but it also had her clenching the muscles between her thighs.

And look at that.

Turning into a raging hornball snuffed out stage fright.

With every pair of eyes in the concert hall trained on them, a buzzy euphoria washed over her, along with a feeling she hadn't known in ages.

Confidence.

She liked having the crowd in the palm of her hand.

The bubbly euphoria morphed into a slow, steady thrum of self-assurance that matched the beat of her heart.

Starting at one end of the piano and ending on the opposite side, she played a rich, flowing arpeggio scale, then caught her husband watching her. "Are you going to stare at me all day, heartthrob, or are you going to take some questions?" she goaded with a smirk.

Once you cashed in your ticket on the Harper Sass Express, you might as well sit back and enjoy the ride.

Landon tossed her a wink, eating up every morsel of her sass cake, and turned to the audience. "Why don't we keep this informal," he began, strumming as he spoke. "Feel free to call out questions, and Harper and I will do our best to answer them," he finished and met her gaze. "Does that work for you, bonbon?"

Thank God she was seated. Observing the man on stage in his element and taking control would have made her weak in the knees. She'd be puckering up to the parquet floor without that piano bench.

"I can live with that format," she answered softly, pressing the piano keys as she joined his guitar riff when a voice called out from the back of the hall.

"I've got a question. What's it like to get married half-naked in Vegas?"

A round of good-natured chuckling broke out, breaking the ice.

Their reputation had preceded them, and it offered her a chance to put her mouth to good use.

"It's cold," she answered and was met by rumbling laughter. "They really pump out the air-conditioning in those Vegas hotels, especially at the Luxe Grandiose." She glanced over at Donna and Damien. "You work for Mr. and Mrs. Luxe, right?"

"We do," Damien answered.

"Please, tell them that Harper says to turn up the thermostat a few notches. Oh, and ask them to say hello to a big burly bellman and one of the hostesses with long silver hair for me. I wished I had caught their names. They were truly kind on my last visit to the hotel."

"We'll pass along the temperature suggestion and the senti-ments," Donna replied with a coy grin.

What was up with the coy grins today?

First, Madelyn had busted out one, and now Donna. But before she could ponder the puzzling expressions, a young woman in the front row raised her hand.

"This question is for Harper," a young woman with pink braids trailing past her shoulders asked. "Are you the online music teacher Bonbon Barbie?"

Oh, boy.

"I only ask, well, we're asking," the girl continued and looked to her left toward a group of young women, "because we follow Bonbon Barbie on LookyLoo."

What a crazy coincidence!

"You're kidding."

"That's how we learned to read music before coming to New Beats. And when we saw Landy Candy fill in a few weeks ago, we figured you had to be Bonbon Barbie or else..." The gal trailed off.

"Or else Landon was messing around with another bonbon," she supplied.

The girls giggled.

"Something like that," the one with pink braids answered.

"You figured it out. I'm Bonbon Barbie."

"And the only bonbon I'm messing around with," Landon chimed with a twinkle in his eyes.

The audience was eating this up.

"Is there a lesson that stood out to you?" she asked the young woman.

The girls leaned in toward each other and conducted a brief tête-à tête.

"We like your videos," the pink-haired woman replied. "You've taught us so much, but Landy Candy is...wow."

Landy Candy.

Harper nodded, knowing that it wasn't Landon's killer good looks that impressed the young women. "He's an excellent teacher, isn't he?" she replied because he was. She'd watched his video at least a dozen times. He'd pulled off a phenomenal lesson with zero prep and no teaching experience.

Landon waved her off, but the grin stretched across his face couldn't hide his delight. "I don't know if I'd call it excellent, but I enjoyed filling in."

The woman seated next to the girl with pink braids raised her hand. "Are you two writing music together?"

"We are," she answered, unable to hold back a coquettish grin.

"More pop music tracks?" came a young man's voice from the other side of the hall.

Landon met her eye, and she nodded, letting him know she had no issue with him sharing about the new music—that is, if he didn't mind. It couldn't hurt to let the students know what was coming from Landon Paige. This event was being livestreamed. The publicity could be good for him.

And possibly for her.

Is that what she wanted—to be in the spotlight?

To be a star?

She knew the answer. It had lived in her heart for as long as she could remember.

"While pop music will always be near to my heart," Landon answered, his words snapping her back, "Harper and I have been working on some new tracks with an acoustic rock sound."

A low murmur simmered in the hall as the news of Landon's shift in musical genre had people raising their eyebrows.

A girl a few rows back waved. "Does that mean you'll have a new album coming out?"

At the young woman's question, titillating excitement

zinged through her body. The songs they'd written were good. No, they were works of lyrical and melodic mastery, and she couldn't wait for the world to embrace their new sound.

Their sound?

Or was it his sound?

Knock it off, girl.

"That's the plan," Landon answered, playing it a lot cooler than she was. Had she answered, there was a decent chance her shrill and insanely disconcerting opera voice would have burst the audience's eardrums.

"This question is for Harper," a woman toward the back called. "You're married to a famous singer, and we heard you sing during the first Bake or Bust Challenge."

"Okay," she replied, feeling her nerves kick in.

"Do you have plans to record and perform your own music?"

"Um…" She hesitated.

What the hell was wrong with her?

The answer was yes. Yes, she'd dreamed of being a star until…

Until a douche nozzle and the memory of a crumpled envelope made her doubt herself.

"We'll have to see what the future holds," she stammered and wanted to punch herself in the mouth. She could feel Landon's gaze, but she didn't meet his eye.

This isn't you, Harper Barbara.

She wasn't timid and soft-spoken, or maybe she was when it came to striving for her goals.

But before she could give her pathetic answer another thought, a woman with dark ringlets framing her face raised her hand.

"I have a question for Landon Paige," she chimed. "What's the most challenging part of being a famous musician?"

And for the second time in under ten seconds, anxiety rippled through her chest.

How would he handle this question?

Would he lay it all on the line and disclose his struggles?

Her stomach tightened into a twisted knot.

Was Landon about to come clean and let the world see the real person behind the pop star facade?

Chapter 29
HARPER

A palpable shift rippled through the concert hall.

With her heart in her throat, she observed Landon as the young woman's question lingered in the air, and a thread of silence wove its way through the space.

But she wasn't preoccupied with the student's question.

What she wanted to know was how her husband would answer it.

Landon nodded to the woman, politely acknowledging her, but he didn't speak. He strummed the guitar, toying with a melody. He picked at the strings and riffed an intricate, pebbly cascade of calming notes. She recognized his behavior. This was his reflective artist mode.

Anticipation built in her chest.

Would he share what it was like to be a neurodivergent artist?

Is that what he was considering?

She scanned the array of cameras and people holding up their smartphones.

He could do so much good by disclosing his struggles on a global livestream.

He plucked a few more notes, then pressed his hands to the strings, muting the sound.

He flashed the young woman his pop star grin. "How about I tell you how I discovered my passion for music instead. It's a better story," he answered, pivoting from the student's question.

Thanks to Landon's hypnotic persona and celebrity charm, the woman nodded as a dreamy expression took hold.

But he'd dodged the question.

And her heart sank.

A part of her wanted him to come clean. With his global popularity, he could inspire others. He could act as a role model to kids who struggled with the same issues. If she'd known that the singer she'd idolized had learning issues like she did, it would have comforted her and minimized the sting of the stigma.

"My foster parents had a garage filled with old instruments. My sister, Leighton, and I learned quickly that we could play just about any song on any instrument by ear," he explained.

"You play by ear?" the girl pressed as the ringlets brushed the apples of her cheeks.

"I'd never touched an instrument before we set foot in that garage. It only took a few hours before I was pretty decent on the guitar, and my sister could knock out just about any tune on the piano. Music and our foster parents became our refuge."

"You were in the foster care system?" a skinny guy with a punk rock vibe and spiky blond hair asked with a skeptical bend to his question.

She studied the audience and found several students slack-jawed.

And then it hit. He might not have disclosed his neurodiversity, but he had dropped the foster kid bombshell.

"I've never talked about it publicly, but yeah, my sister and I were placed in the system."

"Many of us here have been in and out of foster care placements," the girl with the ringlets commented as at least half the young adults in the audience nodded.

"And then in and out of juvie and jail," another voice supplied.

"Why is this the first time you've mentioned it publicly?" a kid with a mop of dark hair asked.

Landon strummed a gentle, delicate melody. "It wasn't a conscious choice. When Trey, Leighton, and I signed with our label, the PR people wanted to play up our youth and brand us as light and energetic."

"You were okay with that? Or were you embarrassed by who you were and where you came from?" the blond spikes kid replied with a distinct edge to his tone, but Landon didn't react.

He repeated the gentle, comforting melody. He played it a few more times, allowing the notes to hang in the air like a balm. It seemed to soothe the punk rocker. The young man's shoulders had almost touched his ears when he'd hurled the questions. Now, with every strum of the guitar and each soul-satisfying rise and fall of sound, the tightened coil within the kid loosened. He uncrossed his arms and relaxed into his chair, waiting for Landon's reply.

"That's a fair question," Landon replied.

She had to admit, even though he hadn't gone as far as sharing about his neurodiversity, he was good at connecting with these teens and young adults, who clearly came from challenging backgrounds. Then again, maybe it wasn't such a stretch. He'd done a hell of a job as the online music substitute teacher, Landy Candy.

"At the time," Landon continued, "we were just kids who were excited to have gotten picked up by a record company. We didn't dwell on what they wanted us to promote and what they wanted us to leave out. We were grateful to be making music and gaining fans. But we weren't completely naïve. We understood that they wanted to project an image. We knew our parts. Trey was the cool bass player. Leighton brought the edge, and I was the—"

"—heartthrob," Maria Magdalena supplied, lightening the mood.

Landon nodded. "Yes, the heartthrob. We took on these personas and went from zero to sixty in what felt like a matter of seconds. There are still days when I can hardly believe it happened the way it did."

"But it's just you now. You and your niece, right? I read something on the internet that said you'd taken custody of her," the spiky-haired guy posited.

The kid didn't appear to have an agenda. The stillness of the room and not one person's face illuminated by a cell phone spoke to the fact that these people were genuinely interested in how Landon was doing.

Her husband must have gotten the same vibe. He didn't tense, and the telltale muscle that ticked in his jaw when he was about to lose his cool hadn't twitched. "Losing my sister and Trey was hard. And yes, I'm raising my niece, but I'm not alone," he added and tossed her one heck of a panty-melting grin.

And hello, Swoon City.

Again, she gave thanks for the piano bench.

But was he telling the whole truth, or was he playing to the audience? It wasn't like he could tell them their marriage was one of convenience.

"Mr. Paige, what do you want this next chapter of your music career to look like?" called a person from the back of the hall.

Landon didn't turn toward the source of the question. Instead, he kept his attention fixed on her.

Despite promising herself she'd never fall for a musician again, she had.

"I want to make the kind of music that inspires people to believe in themselves and believe in the people they care about," he said, pegging her with his gaze, and cue the swoon. Her battered heart collected his words like audible treasures. He turned to the crowd, and the spotlight warmed his beautiful face. "I want to pen songs that don't just play on the radio or blast into your earphones to be forgotten seconds later when the next track plays. I want to make the kind of music that frames moments and captures memories."

Sweet lyrical gods, this man had a way with words.

"We've got time for one more question," Donna said, guiding the conversation.

"What do you do when you're blocked and the music won't come?" came a voice from somewhere in the middle of the hall.

"That's a good question," Landon answered. "Back when my sister, Trey, and I were starting out, sometimes the lyrics and melodies wouldn't flow. My sister and Trey liked to play Scrabble. And we'd do this thing where we'd pick a word from the board, then start riffing on it."

"Can you and Harper demonstrate?" came the rich, rolling Eastern European accent belonging to Madelyn Malone.

Landon raised his hand to shield his eyes and peered out into the audience. He turned to her. "Is that who I think it is?" he said under his breath.

"Uh-huh," she answered with a smile pasted to her face while her eyes said, that's crazy, right? What's the red-scarved wonder doing here?

He eye-replied back with, yeah, it's bonkers-ville, but we're being livestreamed worldwide, so keep grinning.

Just keep grinning.

"Do you want to give it a go to see if we're any good on the fly?" he asked her loud enough for the audience to hear.

"Right here? Right now?" she tossed back, giving the crowd a little banter to gobble up. She held his gaze and saw nothing but gratitude in his eyes—gratitude for her.

There was no going back.

"Throw out some suggestions," Landon said, speaking to the crowd.

"Romance," Michel Laurent suggested and got a few cat calls from the crowd.

"Devotion," came the rich rolling voice of the nanny matchmaker.

"My goodness, love appears to be in the air," Damien remarked as he draped his arm around Donna's shoulders.

Love.

The word sent her pulse racing.

"Those are perfect, and we can use both," Landon said, looking like the cat who ate the canary.

What prompted that response?

"I've got a *scale* that works with those words," he added, strumming a rollicking, buoyant melody.

And then it hit.

It had to be the romance scale of devotion—the bullshit concept she'd pulled out of her ass at the bakery to get Landon to go along with doing the reality show.

That day felt like it had happened eons ago.

But this was no time to take a walk down memory lane. They had an audience watching their every move.

"I see where you're going with this scale business," she said, joining in on the piano and marrying her harmony to his melody.

The audience clapped along as Landon parted his lips and broke out into song.

"She's a girl with chameleon eyes,

Her laughter's full of surprises.

Sign me up for the romance scale of devotion.

Tell me, baby, what you need.

I won't stop till I succeed, working my way through the scale of devotion.

Breakfast in bed, flowers in a vase, chocolate bonbons are no disgrace.

Baby's got a scale of devotion."

"Not bad," she said, playing it cool, but she was holding it together by a thread.

Landon Paige was singing about her.

Her.

Did she want to utilize her opera voice and shriek like she was a thirteen-year-old at a...Landon Paige Heartthrob Warfare concert?

You bet your ass she did.

Harper, aged thirteen, would have lost her ever-lovin' mind.

But she couldn't anymore—not in front of the students and everyone watching online.

Use the power of the sass.

She pegged the guy with her gaze. "That was cute and all, heartthrob, but you're missing a line."

"Am I?" he tossed back with a devilish grin.

Heaven help her. This was fun.

She nodded, then turned to the audience. "Should I finish the song for him?"

The students answered with a rousing eruption of applause.

Landon stopped playing and allowed the piano to carry the tune. She closed her eyes and concentrated on the chords and surrendered to the inflection and intonation of each note as the lyrics came to her.

"But it's not things that she really needs. It's the unspoken promise, the

tender deeds that show her what she really means, baby, on the romance scale of devotion," she belted, hitting each note like her sole purpose on this planet was to sing those precise lyrics in this exact concert hall with Landon Paige by her side.

She exhaled a slow breath as the students rose to their feet, clapping, hooting, and cheering as if they'd witnessed a miracle —and maybe they had because she could feel it, too. The magic, the energy, the instant where a song stopped being a collection of notes and words and became a vessel capturing a moment, just like Landon had talked about.

And if that wasn't momentous enough, another shift occurred. The roar of the crowd faded the second she met her husband's gaze. Owning her with his soulful brown eyes, he came to his feet, rested the guitar against the stool, then strode the few steps between them.

"You're spellbinding," he breathed as he took her hands and helped her to her feet.

Electricity sparked inside her like she was part human and part firework. She gave the man her best feisty smirk. "You're not so bad yourself, heart—"

Landon cupped her face in his hands before she could get out the last sass-infused syllable. "Always so damned sassy," he breathed, then shut her up with a kiss.

And like the first time their lips locked, time and space meant nothing when his lips met hers.

Here's the thing. They might have been standing in the spotlight, but this kiss wasn't for the crowd or those tuning in on LookyLoo.

This kiss was for them and for them alone. She felt the intensity and the intimacy with every fiber of her being.

She sighed as he slid his hands into her hair and the concert hall whirled around them, and a cacophony of sparkling exuberance took hold. The man had most certainly sampled the chocolate ganache filling, and his chocolatey-sweet kiss melded with the vibrations of their music lingering in the charged air. It was a palpable presence, unyielding and enduring like the ground beneath her. There was a permanence to it, a solidity, a strength.

Did he feel it, too?

Landon pulled back, and the warmth of his cocoa-licious breath tickled her lips. "You're vibrating."

She opened her eyes as a reverberation rippled through her. "That might be true, but you're vibrating, too."

Another low buzz zinged through her, and...shit!

Those vibrations weren't due to their musical magic.

"We're both vibrating," she exclaimed as the swirl of tasty kisses and rolling melodies vanished in a puff of chocolate-laced air. "It's our cell phones. It's our school pickup alarms for Aria."

He checked his watch, then cursed under his breath. "We need to hit the road. We can't be late—not today."

"We could text Char and Mitch or any of our friends and ask them to pick up Aria—or wait with her at school until we get there," she offered.

"No, it has to be us, and we have to be on time."

That was odd.

Picking up Aria right after the school bell rang was important, but it wasn't like the kid would be left out in the cold in a seedy part of town. It was early October in Denver. The temperature sat at a comfortable sixty-five degrees, and their friends would be there. They wouldn't allow Aria to wait by herself. Not to mention, Whitmore was surrounded by multi-million-dollar homes. Aria had a better chance of being cooked a gourmet meal and gifted a jeweled tiara than having any actual harm befalling her in that neck of the woods.

"I'm going to wrap up this livestream pop-star style, and then we're booking it out the back," Landon whispered against the shell of her ear.

"I still don't think we have to run," she replied and checked the time on her phone. Granted, they were on the other side of town and it would take longer to get to Whitmore, but not that much longer.

"Trust me, bonbon. We've got to go." He paused. "Are you wearing underwear?"

What?

He was all we-gotta-hurry five seconds ago, and now he was doing a panty check?

She cocked her head to the side. "I am panty-less per our agreement."

"Okay, I'll have to be careful," he mused, eyeing her dress that hit mid-calf.

Before she could ask if he'd snuck a psychedelic lollipop during their performance while she wasn't looking, he took a step toward the audience.

"We've got to bring this to a close. Thank you, New Beats students and faculty. You've been an amazing crowd. We want to give a heartfelt shoutout to our baking coach, Schuman Sweet, and Cupid Bakery and Luxe Media and Entertainment. We wouldn't be here without them and everyone working behind the scenes. See you for the next challenge on Looky-Loo," he added, looking into the camera, then turned on his heel and scooped her into his arms—just like he'd done after the last challenge.

"Landon," she yipped. "Why are you carrying me...again?"

"We're making a grand exit. It only makes sense. We left the first challenge this way. Think of it as me getting you out of here in style," he replied, hoofing it off the stage.

"You call this in style?" she shot back, holding on to the man for dear life as she bounced around like a sack of potatoes in his arms. It didn't feel quite as jarring as last time—though she had been high as a kite then. "And what's the hurry?" she pressed as some poor dude opened the door leading to the parking lot.

"Hold that for us," Landon ordered, bulldozing through.

In what could only be described as the craziest non-getaway getaway, her husband plopped her into the passenger seat of the Lamborghini SUV, then got in and took off like they'd robbed a bank.

"You're taking school pickup to the next level. And when I say 'the next level,' heartthrob. I mean 'completely psychotic,'" she shrieked, gripping the Lamborghini's oh-shit handle because, oh shit, her husband was a maniac behind the wheel.

They zoomed through the city, catching green light after green light. She needed to distract herself, or she'd pull a stunt-woman move and barrel out of the car like it was about to plunge off a cliff and she needed to make a hasty escape.

She had to distract herself from Landon's manic moves behind the wheel.

She closed her eyes and went over the rollercoaster of events.

Vance was a terrible husband—not a shocker—and douche. But that was nothing new.

Barbie was a sweet chick with more depth than she'd given the glitter-master baker.

Speaking of baking…they'd won the second challenge.

They'd freaking won.

Babs' house would be free and clear if they continued their streak and killed it in the final challenge.

That was terrific news.

And then, what?

Shit, she'd opened the doom and gloom floodgates.

Would their nanny-aunt arrangement come to an end?

And what about Italy?

If Landon and Aria wanted her to join them, they would have said something by now, right?

Her stomach twisted into an anxiety-ridden knot.

Her emotional pendulum was working overtime, swinging from one extreme to another.

"Why do you think Madelyn was at New Beats today?" Landon asked, cutting into her angst-ridden musings.

She opened her eyes. "I don't know. Maybe she donates to the organization. She does seem to know everyone," she answered when Landon's phone vibrated like it was going into convulsions.

"Don't worry about that," he said, eyes trained on the road as he hit the gas.

She scoffed.

Didn't this man know the first rule of phone etiquette?

If someone says to ignore a phone, the first thing the other person wants to do is ogle the screen.

Bzzz.

Bzzz.

Bzzz.

His phone never went off like that.

She disregarded her husband's suggestion and concentrated on the screen.

Text from Mitzi.

Text from Charlotte.

Text from Libby.

Text from Penny.

"There's a text from Mitzi and three more from my friends. Why are my friends texting you?"

He cleared his throat as they sailed through a yellow light. "Open Mitzi's message."

She tapped the icon. "She's at the oral surgeon's office and writes that she's having an emergency root canal. She says that everything is taken care of for Italy." She paused.

Italy.

"Is there more?" Landon pressed.

459

She stared at the message. "Contracts coming. She says you need to talk with her once she's recovered. What contracts?" she asked. But that wasn't what she wanted to ask.

"Probably routine stuff," he answered, then a text from Rowen rolled in.

She glanced at Landon. The man was fixated on the road as he sped down the street. She chewed her lip, then opened Rowen's text.

Rowen: We've got the snacks you and Aria requested for your trip.

Snacks for the trip...for Aria and Landon?

Not for her.

They were leaving.

Had she misjudged everything about the last few weeks?

"I asked your friends a few questions about clothing," Landon said.

She gasped and dropped his phone into her lap. "Clothing?"

"Women's clothing," he added, taking a corner like a speed racer as he turned onto the road that led to Whitmore.

He wasn't making any sense.

"What is happening here, Landon?"

"I promised I wouldn't say anything."

About Italy—about her not going?

"We're here. We made it," he said, breathless as they pulled into the school parking lot.

They exited the vehicle as the school bell rang and children poured out of the building.

It didn't take long before Aria tore out of the building with Phoebe, Sebastian, and Oscar.

She spied their friends on the far side of the building.

Why had they chosen to wait over there? Every other day of the school year, they'd waited for the kids in this spot.

Before she could whip out her phone and send a WTF text,

the kids stopped running at the halfway mark and clustered together. Phoebe unzipped Aria's backpack and handed the little girl something. Then the foursome huddled for a few seconds more.

This was not the usual routine by a long shot.

Her mouth grew dry. Her hands trembled. She stuffed them into the pockets of her dress.

The clawing voice in her head returned.

They're leaving you because you were never good enough—even the douche nozzle Vance knew that.

She focused on Aria, praying that would quiet her overactive brain. The little girl waved goodbye to her friends. Oscar, Phoebe, and Sebastian set off in the other direction toward their families, and Aria headed their way with a swishy swagger to her step.

"Did I miss something?" she asked, working to keep her voice even.

"Aria's probably just saying goodbye," Landon answered. His posture stiffened. He dug his hands into his pockets and glanced away. "She won't see her friends for a couple of weeks."

Great, he'd decided to pull the aloof pop star card.

Why was the man acting like he had something to hide?

It had to be Italy. They must be leaving today.

"It's Thursday," she said, her voice rising an octave. "There's school tomorrow. The fall break doesn't start until after school tomorrow."

"Not for Aria," he answered, staring at a point in the distance.

The little girl ran up to them and eyed Landon. "Did you tell her, Uncle Landy?" the child demanded.

Landon's features relaxed. "No, ma'am, I did not."

Aria tossed a furtive look toward Landon and waved him in. "She doesn't know what we're doing?"

"She does not," he confirmed.

"Because I saw you whisper stuff to her."

"I didn't whisper about this."

Whatever *this* was, it didn't sound good.

She glanced toward where her friends had gathered, but they were gone.

Aria turned her steely gaze her way. "Aunt Harper, you don't look so good. Did you eat too many lollipops again?"

"I'm fine. I'm terrific, fantastic," she blathered, taking a knee to be at the girl's level.

"If you're not about to puke like Phoebe does every time she eats too many hot dogs, close your eyes and put out your hand," Aria instructed.

She followed the kid's instructions, then felt paper touch her skin. She opened her eyes and stared at the wrinkled envelope.

The breath caught in her throat as memories of the last time someone had handed her a sealed envelope reared their ugly head.

"Should I open it?" she asked, working to keep her voice even.

"Not yet. First, I have to show you this." Aria held up a drawing of a half-circle divided into five different colored segments with a moveable needle in the center. It resembled a speedometer, but there were no numbers, only five blocks of color with faces drawn in, ranging from frowns to wide grins. "It's a Likert scale. I bet you don't know what that is," the child spouted like a pint-sized professor.

"I don't."

"My teacher said most people don't know about these scales. It's a special second-grade thing we make at my new school, and I wanted it to be a surprise for you."

"I'm surprised, for sure, but I'm not sure I understand what I'm looking at."

"These scales can help you understand when you're sad about something or when you're super happy. And that made me think about you, Aunt Harper."

"Me?"

"Yeah, so I asked Uncle Landy to help me make mine because I had to do it for homework on the first day of school, and you couldn't help because you were really sleepy because you ate too much candy. That's when I decided to make it a surprise."

Landon had mentioned he'd helped Aria with her homework, but she hadn't heard anything about this fancy scale.

"Uncle Landy was confused when I told him about my homework," Aria continued. "So, I did what my teacher did. I asked him if he'd ever used a scale to figure out information—like a scale to weigh yourself. And he said you'd mentioned a scale. Something mushy and gushy called the romance scale of…What was it again?" she asked Landon.

"Romance scale of devotion," she supplied before the man could answer.

"It must be an aunt and uncle thing," Aria shot back, unimpressed with the example—the exact example—they'd sung about at New Beats.

What were the chances?

"One, two, three, eyes on me. Are you listening, Aunt Harper?" Aria chided.

She must have picked that up at school, too.

"I am," she replied, snapping back from putting the pieces together.

"Anyway, I had to make a scale to help with feelings. Knowing how you're feeling is really important in second grade. It's called emotional intelligence."

Whitmore was one hell of a good school.

"I didn't learn anything like that in second grade."

"My teacher says we're a brilliant class, so she can teach us this higher-level stuff," Aria answered with a hefty slice of swagger. Still, she'd gladly take the kid's swagger. It was a godsend to see the girl so confident when it came to academics.

"This scale starts with green," Aria explained. "It's green because we think lime lollipops are the worst. Remember, you told me that you didn't like the green ones either the first time I met you, and we played on my mom's piano."

She'd never forget the tangled-haired mini heathen perched in the garage rafters.

"I remember."

"So green is grouchy because I was real grouchy that day." She tapped the next segment with a slightly less angry expression. "The next part is yellow because we don't like yellow lollipops that much either. That means sort of grouchy. I was a yellow last week when Oscar stood next to Cassie Klein in line to go to lunch."

"Okay," she answered, unsure if she was holding back laughter or tears.

"Red is for cherry," Aria continued. "We like cherry lollipops."

"We do," she answered, her throat thickening with emotion.

"Yeah, we really do. Especially when we're in dance clubs," Landon added, referencing the night in the club when he charged in to save her from Mr. Handsy Drunk. She'd been noshing on one of the bridal party's cherry treats.

That first cherry chocolate kiss had changed the trajectory of her life.

"What are the light and dark brown parts for?" she asked, touching the segments with smiley faces.

The girl grinned, and her whole face lit up. "Bonbons, of course. They're our favorites, right, Uncle Landy?"

"They are. I don't think we could live without them."

She looked up at him and found him glassy-eyed. "You don't?"

He shook his head. "You must know how crazy Aria and I are about bonbons."

"I think I do," she answered and blinked back tears.

She wasn't one for becoming a blubbering mess, but the sweetness factor of Aria's scale and Landon's display of devotion spoke to the kernel of hope in her chest that yearned to be loved and wanted.

"The dark section is for dark chocolate, which is okay chocolate, but not super-duper delicious chocolate. It gets a happy face. But I like the light brown ones better. The ones with caramel and a little bit of salt. That's why it's on the end with a super-duper happy face."

"Those are my favorite. I've loved them for as long as I can remember."

And there was something else she loved—two things, to be exact. She'd felt it with every breath she took.

"When I met you, Aunt Harper, I was here," Aria continued, touching the green frowny face section.

"Where are you now on your Likert scale?" she asked.

A sassy smirk bloomed on the child's lips. "To find out, you have to open the envelope."

The envelope.

Carefully, she untucked the flap and removed the rectangular contents. The first sheet had a picture of an airplane with *Passenger Aria Paige-Grant* written in blue crayon next to a green, white, and red flag. The child printed *from Denver to Italy* in pencil. She moved the top sheet to the back of the slim stack and read the information printed on the next sheet.

Passenger Uncle Landy.

There was one sheet left to view. She slid Landon's ticket to the back of the pile. With trembling hands, she peered at the last ticket.

Passenger Nanny-Aunt Harper. She doesn't play the harp. She plays the piano.

She chuckled at Aria's description, and her heart swelled.

They weren't leaving without her.

"Oops, I forgot to do something," the child said and reached into her pocket. Producing the tiny piano eraser, Aria erased the word *nanny*. "You can be just my aunt. I feel like this when I think about you being just my aunt," Aria said and tapped the light brown square.

"I like being just your aunt," she replied, her voice a hoarse whisper.

"I typed out what I wanted to say in my special reader font on my tablet, then copied it onto the tickets," Aria reported. "I had my friends double-check my writing at recess. Phoebe, Oscar, and Sebastian said I got every letter right."

"You did," she answered as a few droplets splashed on the child-made ticket. She checked the sky, but there wasn't a cloud to be found.

"Those are happy tears, H," a voice called—Penny's voice.

"My friends are over there with their dads and uncles and soon-to-be-moms and soon-to-be-aunts," Aria explained and waved toward their friends, standing near the parking lot. She tapped her chin. "We're kind of a cool bunch, aren't we? Like mishmash families."

"We sure are," she eked out, emotion clogging her throat as she glanced toward her girls.

Penny, Charlotte, and Libby held up three Cupid Bakery boxes.

Aria did a happy dance. "They remembered to bring the bonbon snacks."

"Just three boxes for a flight across the ocean?" Harper teased through tears.

"Rowen," Landon called. "Open her up."

Two car alarm chirps nipped the air, and the hatch on Penny's Lamborghini opened. A wall of cupid bakery boxes filled every nook and cranny of the space.

"Wow," she breathed.

"You know you can always trust me to do the right thing when it comes to bonbons."

She stared at her husband's beautiful face. "I *believe* I can."

There was that word again.

Believe.

"And Oscar's recording everything on the camcorder you let me play with. I asked him to do it," Aria added. The kid gestured toward a cluster of leafy dogwood bushes, and the little boy emerged. Camera in hand, he sprinted toward them and came in for a closeup.

"Want me to record your aunt crying some more?" Oscar asked.

Aria glanced at the screen. "No, that's enough crying. Now film me," the little girl directed.

Oscar pointed the camera at her.

"Harper likes her surprise so much she's crying like a baby. The end," Aria announced, then twirled.

Attitude for miles with this one.

Oscar closed the viewfinder and returned the camera to the girl. "That was an awesome ending," the boy cooed.

"I know," Aria replied, not lacking in confidence. "I'm gonna go say goodbye to Sebastian and Phoebe and sneak us some bonbons for the car ride to the airport," Aria announced. "Will you be okay, Aunt Harper? You're still kind of crying like Tucker in my class did when I told him he smelled like cafeteria tuna noodle casserole."

This sass-pot of a kid.

She gathered her wits. "It's like Penny said, honey. These are happy tears."

"And don't worry if you lose the tickets and the envelope," Aria added. "We don't really need them. Uncle Landy is rich and has his own plane."

She pressed the items to her heart. "This envelope and these tickets are the best surprises anyone has ever given me. There's no way I'd misplace them."

A feisty smirk returned to Aria's lips, and the child leaned in. "I knew you'd like my surprise. I love you, Aunt Harper," she whispered before taking Oscar's hand. The pair bolted before she could return the sentiment.

She loved that mouthy mini beast.

She rose to her feet and brushed the tears away.

"Did you think we'd leave without you?" Landon asked gently, touching her moist cheek.

She swallowed past the lump in her throat. "I wasn't sure."

"I'm not going anywhere without my double-dog dare wife. We make a good team."

They did.

"I believe we do," she answered.

He brushed his thumb across her lips and twisted his into a sexy smirk. "Maybe it's not so terrible being with a musician?"

"Maybe it's not," she breathed, pressing onto her toes, ready to kiss the cocky expression off the man's face when the pound of footsteps on the pavement popped their swoon bubble.

"Hey," Aria bellowed, skidding to a stop with three boxes of bonbons in her arms. "There's no time to get mushy-gushy. Save your romance scale of devotion kissy faces for later. We've got enough bonbons to give us tummy aches for days, and the plane's waiting to take us to see Lolo and Lala."

"Raincheck on the mushy-gushy stuff?" Landon asked.

Pure joy radiated from every cell in her body.

"You better believe it, heartthrob."

Aria handed her the boxes of bonbons and patted

Landon's arm. "Will you pick me up? I need to say something."

Landon raised an eyebrow. And rightly so. Pure mischief glimmered in the child's eyes.

"Who do you need to say something to?" he inquired.

"Everyone," the kid answered with a shrug.

Aria had something up her sleeve.

The man sighed, then lifted his niece into his arms. There was no use resisting.

The child beamed. "You can eat worms," she announced, laughing as she addressed the greater Denver metro area. "My family is going to Italy!"

Chapter 30

LANDON

"Look this way, per favore, Signore e Signora Paige."

He tightened his grip on Harper's waist. The cut of her dress revealed her back, and he held her close, feeling the heat of her body against his chest. A strand of her loose chocolate-brown locks caught the breeze and tickled his chin, and he reveled in the bliss of her nearness. He inhaled her delectable scent and kept her close as the pops of light ignited around them.

"Smile for the Italian press, bonbon."

"I'm trying to, heartthrob," his wife murmured. "But it's awfully hard to concentrate."

"Why is that?"

"Between dinner and dessert, you must have wandered into that giant Italian villa study of yours and slipped a pencil into your pocket." She shifted her hips enough to brush her supple ass against him. And his cock took notice. But how could she blame him? He did have the sexiest woman on the planet in his arms.

Still, he had to address her incorrect choice of descriptors.

"A pencil?" he purred as the paparazzi jockeyed around

them and snapped photo after photo. The rapid-fire clicks and flashes of the dozens of cameras peppered the crisp dusk air, but they couldn't blot out its serenity. Italian evenings could be categorized as the Eighth Wonder of the World. The scent of wisteria and the hint of Harper's chocolate breath teased his senses as the lake lapping against the shore provided a soothing, textured sound to the whirl of activity.

Harper swayed her hips, and the movement sent another jolt of lust through him. "How about a banana? Or would you prefer I compare you to a zucchini? On second thought, we are in Italy. How about a cannoli?"

This woman.

He peeled his gaze from her face and observed the frenzied press. While he was used to photographers hounding him, he didn't live for the exposure anymore. Sure, he'd worried about his dwindling record sales and his waning reputation in the music world. He'd spent years agonizing over the promise he'd made to make Heartthrob Warfare everything he, Leighton, and Trey had dreamed it could be. But since they'd arrived in Italy five days ago, the nagging voices in his head had quieted.

And it was thanks to Harper Presley.

No, Harper Presley-Paige.

His wife.

Emphasis on *his*.

He'd be making his intentions regarding their marital status perfectly clear tonight.

He slid his hands from her waist and allowed them to rest below her navel. All the press could see were two newlyweds embracing like a corny prom photo. There was nothing obscene about it, but the desire surging through him made him want to test the limits of modesty.

He pressed his hard length against her and moved his hands lower as he followed her curves, preparing to make her just as hot and bothered as he was.

And he knew precisely how to do it.

Harper had paired a shawl with her dress to stave off the night chill. The thin fabric draped past her shoulders and hit mid-thigh.

It provided the perfect cover.

He slipped his hands beneath it and skimmed farther down her torso.

"What are you and your cannoli up to, heartthrob?"

He answered by making barely perceptible circles with the pad of his middle finger above her tight bundle of nerves.

If she could provoke him with her gorgeous as hell ass, he could do a little taunting of his own.

Two could play at this game.

Harper inhaled a sharp breath, and that slight hitch signaled he'd gotten her attention. She rested her hands on top of his and swayed again. Her high heels scraped against the courtyard's stone patio as she arched her back.

"You're playing dirty, Mrs. Paige," he murmured.

"It's Mrs. Presley-Paige, and playing dirty is my middle name."

"Nope, it's Barbara," he countered.

She responded by swishing her sweet ass against his cock, and the press was none the wiser to their sexy challenge of who could drive the other crazy the fastest.

"Fine, it's *playing dirty*. I concede. Are you happy to be here, Mrs. Playing Dirty?" he pressed. He needed to hear her say it.

She relaxed against him. "You know I'm happy."

He did because he could relate. He felt the same way. "Forget the vegetables and the cannoli comparisons. Let's try sports. How about a bat?" he suggested.

"You're comparing your"—she rolled her hips and teased his cock—"to a baseball bat?" she whispered. "You're definitely not a challenge-number-one cookie. I'll give you that, heartthrob. But a baseball bat? What do you think you are? A wild stallion?"

Hell yes, he was. "It's not that far-fetched. A certain someone rode me all night long. A stallion isn't that much of a stretch."

She turned and wrapped her arms around his neck. The paparazzi frenzy intensified as the men and women calling out to them in a wash of English and Italian tussled to get a shot of them in a different pose.

"You've got me there." She ran her hand down the scruff on his cheek. "I might be a dirty cowgirl, but you're a very, very naughty rock star."

"Rock star?" he repeated.

"That's your sound now, isn't it?" she challenged. "Acoustic rock with an alternative edge."

Just hearing her say it gave him a boost. "It will be, thanks to you."

And if everything went as planned, he'd be showcasing his new sound at Red Rocks Unplugged.

The concert was drawing closer. He'd sent the rough tracks of his new music to his label. He hadn't heard back, but he had a feeling that would work out—a brighter outlook he hadn't harnessed in years.

Honestly, he should be a shoo-in if they'd offered Vance-freaking-Vibe a spot.

Still, it didn't help that a couple of days ago, Mitzi called to tell him she couldn't join them in Italy to celebrate Tomás and Bess's vow renewal. The slight pain in her jaw she'd written off as nothing had become a full-fledged dental emergency, and she'd required surgery. The woman was a force to be reckoned with, but even she was a mere mortal and couldn't go toe-to-toe with the powers that be when she was nursing a throbbing jaw.

He had to keep the faith and believe.

He gazed into his wife's eyes.

Believe.

That was their word.

The music they'd collaborated on was good—no, it was a game changer.

But he needed the street cred of the Red Rocks Unplugged platform to successfully make the switch from bubble gum pop to becoming a bona fide rock star.

Once he made the change, there was no going back—no Plan B, no second-guessing.

This was his shot to deliver on a promise that meant everything.

Don't screw it up.

"Where did you go?" Harper asked, tracing a line down his cheek as she pulled him back from the brink.

"I was thinking about tonight," he lied. He couldn't share his fears with her—not tonight.

Harper's face lit up. "More romance scale of devotion stuff?"

He stroked her cheek. "Something like that."

"You've spoiled me with picnics and breakfast in bed. Would tonight's installment have anything to do with the commotion I noticed at the boathouse?"

He mimicked zipping his lips, but his observant wife wasn't far off the mark.

When Aria had asked him to keep the Italy trip a surprise, he wasn't sure if it was a good idea. But watching tears stream down his wife's cheeks when his niece dropped the whole Likert scale business solidified what he already knew in his heart.

His niece was crazy about the woman, and he was, too.

No, he was more than crazy about her, and so was Aria. It was the real thing—and tonight, he'd let her know the extent of his devotion.

"*Ancora un minuto, gente.* One more minute, people," the head of his villa security, a stout meaty man, called to the press.

And yes, he had security.

A skeleton crew maintained his Italian residence while he was in the US. But when he was here, he needed help protecting his privacy.

The camera flashes intensified as the photographers got in their final shots.

Harper gazed at the wall of media and squinted. "We've done this a few times since we've arrived. You'd think I'd get used to it. But this is quite a circus. This is really your life?"

He couldn't tell if she was asking a question or making a statement.

He glanced at the wall of media. "It's our life—at least, while we're in Italy. Years ago, I tried ignoring the press here, but it was a disaster. Mitzi and I decided to schedule these pop-in photo ops to keep the paparazzi from scaling the walls and hiding behind deck chairs to get a shot of me."

"It blows my mind to think stuff like that really happens to celebrities," she mused and tossed another look at the media circus. "It's like we're fish in a bowl."

"It's part of the job," he answered and tried to get a read on her.

The celebrity existence wasn't for the faint of heart. The highs were high, but the lows were low.

"It's not usually this raucous. They're really champing at the bit over this visit," he remarked.

"Because of little old me?" she crooned with a sexy twist of a smirk.

"Because of little old you," he echoed, then tipped her chin and pressed a whisper-soft kiss to her lips, and the photographers went wild. Lit in bursts of white light, he hummed against her mouth, savoring her touch, so grateful to have her with him.

Tonight, Bess and Tomás had renewed their vows at his villa on the lake, with northern Italy's mountainous greenery as the backdrop. It had been a beautiful, intimate gathering of the five of them. He sure as hell didn't want to discover a wayward paparazzi hiding in the bushes during the ceremony. And with news of his marriage to Harper, the Italian press had clamored for pictures of his new wife from the moment they stepped off his private jet.

But he shouldn't have expected any less.

He'd been lifted to mega-star status in the country shortly after Heartthrob Warfare exploded onto the music scene. His sister used to give him grief about it, and Trey had jokingly dubbed him Mr. I-Pop, playing off K-Pop. But the people of Italy had rallied around him with a fervor akin to Norma Rae and her cross-stitch pillows. Not to mention, the amount of money he'd made from endorsements and commercials in the country had allowed him to purchase a private jet at the tender age of twenty-two. Italy loved him, and he loved Italy. From the food to the people to the open and welcoming culture, he felt a connection to this place. Once he had the cash, it made sense to buy a vacation home here.

But *vacation home* might not be the best way to describe the ten-bedroom mansion built into the hillside overlooking a lake.

When Tomás and Bess mentioned they wanted to renew their vows in Italy, he offered the villa. Truth be told, he'd offered to buy his foster parents a place of their own, but they'd declined like they always declined when he offered to shower them with his wealth.

The last five nights, they'd feasted as a family on dinners prepared by local chefs and indulged in the region's wines. Mother Nature had gifted them with mild weather for early October. While Bess and Tomás strolled through the village, he and Harper had spent their days with Aria, riding bikes, sailing on the lake, and playing tag on the pebbled beaches.

Life was good.

And if tonight went the way he hoped, it might end up being one of the best evenings of his life.

"Signore Paige, there was a call. I have a message for you," one of the villa butlers called from a side door.

Harper frowned. "What could that be about?"

He didn't have a clue.

He turned to the press. "That's all for tonight. Thank you for coming out." He nodded to his head of security. The man strode to the center of the courtyard as a trio of guards escorted the paparazzi off the property.

He took Harper's hand and led her into the main house.

"Who called the villa?" he asked the waiting butler.

"An attorney, sir," the slim man answered in a thick Italian accent. "The caller said he was with your record label. They're having trouble sending you documents. There have been issues with the internet in the region. A courier is supposed to drop off some papers, and you are to call this number when the documents arrive."

"Did the lawyer say anything else?" He studied the slip of paper. The scrawled digits looked more like chicken scratch than numbers. His chest tightened as he stuffed the note into his pocket.

"It's a little late for business, isn't it?" Harper remarked.

"Not in the States. California is seven hours behind Italy."

Still, what could be so important that they had to contact him while he was on vacation?

Was his label dropping him? Did they hate the new tracks?

Music was a dog-eat-dog industry.

If Mitzi wasn't recuperating from her surgery, she'd be all over this.

Whatever the label wanted, he was flying solo to figure it out.

"Uncle Landy, Aunt Harper, are the photographer people gone?" Aria called, sprinting toward them.

"We just wrapped up," he replied and whisked the child into his arms as the trio made their way to the patio.

"We're done with dessert, and Lolo and Lala were asking about you. They've got something they want to say," Aria reported.

His staff had set up a celebration dinner on the patio next to the pool overlooking the lake. They'd oohed and ahhed over a delectable five-course meal after the nuptials, but the media had arrived early for the photo op, and he and Harper were forced to excuse themselves from the festivities before dessert was served.

"How was dessert?" Harper asked.

Aria grinned from ear to ear. "They brought up a bunch of different kinds of bonbons and there was a cake."

"That sounds delicious."

"The bonbons were good. But I like Mr. Sweet's bonbons the best."

Harper chuckled. "What about the cake?"

"It was super yummy. There were layers of Cream of Wheat in it."

Cream of Wheat?

"Crème brûlée," he corrected, pretty damned sure the cake didn't include creamy breakfast porridge.

"Yeah, Cream of Wheat brûlée," the little girl quipped.

He shared a look with Harper, taking in her easy grin. Italy suited her. Being an aunt suited her. Being a wife—his wife —suited her.

"We saved some for you. It's in the kitchen."

"Did you eat all the bonbons, Miss Paige-Grant?" he teased.

"I wanted to," Aria confessed with an adorable shrug. "But then Lala got an idea and told the waiter guy to put some bonbons in a box for you to eat when you're at the secret location," the kid finished, whisper-shouting the *secret location* part.

"Secret location," Harper repeated. "Tell me more."

"It's for your kissy face romance scale stuff," Aria answered, then gasped. "I don't think I was supposed to say that."

Harper raised an eyebrow. "More romance scale of devotion?"

He winked at his niece. "You've said the right amount."

"She could say a little more," his wife prodded.

"Nope," he replied as they entered the sprawling living room overlooking the patio.

But something was off.

The grand piano in the corner of the room had been moved to the center of the space.

"The villa helper people put it here for me," Aria explained as he set her down.

The instrument sat adjacent to the French doors leading outside. With the starry sky reflecting off the piano's shiny black surface, the instrument took on an ethereal quality.

"I see you found your aunt and uncle," Tomás remarked, smiling through his bushy beard as he and Bess joined them next to the glimmering Steinway.

"She sure did," Harper answered. "Is this what I think it is? Are you ready?"

Aria exhaled a slow breath and nodded. "I'm ready to do my song." She tapped the piano. "I wanted to play the piano here because it looks like I'm playing a concert and I wanted to make this night super special since it's the last night before you and Uncle Landy go back to Colorado, and me, Lolo, and Lala go to their university, and I get to help them with their sculptures."

Bess smoothed a lock of the little girl's hair. "We can't wait to hear your song."

Aria chewed her lip.

"Are you nervous?" Harper asked, rubbing the girl's back.

The child reached into her pocket and removed the tiny piano eraser Harper had given her. "When I hold my eraser, it makes me feel better," Aria explained, touching the miniature item reverently before returning it to her pocket. "I'm a little scared, but that's what my song is about."

Aria hadn't shared much about the song. He and Harper had heard her singing in her closet, and he'd found her in her room scribbling in her music notebook, surrounded by a sea of highlighters. He figured the song might follow in Harper's silly-friends-songs footsteps, but it appeared the child had gone in another direction.

"We can't wait to hear it," Tomás chimed.

"I'm gonna play the piano and sing at the same time like Harper and my mom." Aria beamed, which was a departure from her usually sour demeanor when she mentioned her parents.

The hot-tempered, quick-to-anger kid had bloomed into a little girl exploring her love of music.

How he wished Trey and Leighton could be here.

He scanned the room, searching for ghosts. It seemed like only yesterday the trio sat in this very room, lounging on the couches, taking in the beauty of Italy, and riffing the hours away.

"Before you start, dear, Tomás and I would like to make a toast," Bess said warmly as a maid entered the room with a tray of champagne and a glass of apple juice. Once everyone had a drink in hand, Bess raised hers. "To family and to Landon. Thank you for graciously offering up your villa."

"You know it's yours anytime you want," he answered, embracing his foster mother.

"Returning to Italy to teach and sculpt has been a longtime dream of ours. And we're grateful to be with the people we hold in our hearts," she continued.

"We also wanted to take a moment to remember the two people who aren't with us tonight," Tomás added.

"My mom and dad?" Aria supplied.

Tomás nodded. "We miss them and think of them every day."

"To Leighton and Trey," Bess said, and they clinked glasses.

"We see so much of them inside you, Aria," Tomás remarked after taking a sip.

The kid gulped her juice. "You do?"

"Your spirit and fearlessness are so much like your mother," Bess answered. "And your thoughtful, passionate side is so much like your father."

Aria rested her hand on the pocket containing the piano eraser. "Sometimes, I forget what it was like to have a mom and a dad. But now I'm like my friend Phoebe. Phoebe and I are the only two kids in my class who don't have a mom or a dad. We have an uncle and an aunt. Well, she's got an uncle and an almost-aunt. Phoebe says her almost-aunt is real nice, but she can't reach stuff on shelves and clogs the sink in her bathroom a lot. I told her my aunt has lots and lots of recordings of herself singing and playing the piano, and she also keeps boxes and boxes of Uncle Landy's picture."

Harper blushed and shook her head.

"Aunts and almost-aunts are kind of weird but really awesome," the kid mused.

He chuckled, but a lump formed in his throat. He understood Aria's feelings. His life with his mother, father, and then his grandmother seemed like a distant memory after he and Leighton entered their first foster placement.

He needed to do more to keep his sister and Trey's memory alive for the girl.

His own grief had held him back.

It was time to do better.

He glanced at Harper—at the sassy, snark-wielding woman he'd married on a double-dog dare.

She brushed a tear from her cheek, and Aria took notice.

"Are you crying again, Aunt Harper?"

"No, I'm not crying. This isn't crying," the weepy woman replied through a sniffle.

"It looks like crying," Aria commented, scrunching up her face. "You've been crying a bunch lately. You cried at my school, and then cried during Lolo and Lala's second wedding, and then I think I heard you cry last night."

Harper cocked her head to the side. "Last night?"

"I went to get a glass of water real, real late, and you were making this noise." Aria threw her head back. "'Ooh, ahh, ohhh!' You were bawling up a storm."

Ooh, ahh, and holy bawling shit!

Harper's cheeks went from a dusty pink to deep scarlet.

How the hell were they supposed to respond to that?

"I think you were dreaming about horses and talking in your sleep, too," Aria mused. "You said I want to ride you all night long, and you sounded like you were running a race and couldn't catch your breath. Did you dream that you were running a race against a horse?"

Harper turned to him. Her mouth opened and closed like a befuddled flounder while her eyes screamed *help me.*

"That's exactly what she was dreaming about," he supplied, throwing his wife a lifeline. "You mentioned it to me this morning."

"Yep, I was dreaming about horses," Harper rattled off. "Aria Paige-Grant, you're one smart kid with impeccable hearing. You should play your song or I might start crying again. We can't wait for another second to hear her song, can we?"

She could have suggested they walk barefoot across hot coals, and he would have kicked off his shoes. He was up for anything that steered the conversation away from their sex life.

"Go for it, kid. Let's hear that song and never talk about your aunt Harper's dreams again," he added and walked his niece to the piano bench while Harper lifted the lid protecting the keys.

Aria shot him a perplexed look before eyeing her grandparents. "Lolo, Lala?"

"Yes, *amor*?" Tomás answered.

"Is something wrong with my aunt and uncle?"

"On the contrary, dear," Bess answered, gifting him and Harper with a knowing grin. "There appears to be something extraordinarily right with them."

"Adults are weird," Aria huffed, but her comical agitation dissolved when she scooted forward on the bench and concentrated on the keys.

It was as if time stopped, or maybe he'd gone back in time.

Aria's posture and focus matched Leighton's to a T. The child inhaled a slow breath, then appeared to morph into Harper as she warmed up with a rolling arpeggio scale. Hand over hand, the child worked her way up and down the keys in a graceful sway. Aria mesmerized everyone in the room as her brief warmup ended, and she played a delicate melody. Elegant in its simplicity, he listened as the child hummed the first few bars.

"This song is called 'Brave Heart Muscles,'" she revealed, repeating the intro as she spoke.

Déjà vu hit him like a punch to the gut.

Aria sounded so much like her mother when Leighton would introduce a song to the audience.

"*Sometimes life is scary. Sometimes you feel alone,*" she began, dropping the lyrics softly like a feather floating to the ground.

He wrapped his arm around Harper's shoulders. He needed to anchor himself to this moment. And he was glad he'd done it because he nearly fall on his ass as Aria sang on.

He knew the kid had perfect pitch, but her talent went

beyond mechanics. She melded with the melody, becoming one with the music like her mother and her aunt.

"But your brave heart muscles are stronger than your bones."

Brave heart muscles?

And then he remembered Aria telling them about how she'd come up with the term on the first day of school.

"They're there when you are worried or when you feel afraid. Your brave heart muscles help you out when you're scared you'll get a bad grade."

Harper leaned into him.

"But if you get stuck, and run out of luck, don't feel like a creep. You can ask your aunt or uncle for help unless it's just your uncle because your aunt ate too many lollipops and needs to sleep."

This kid.

"So, if you're frustrated or angry or if you're feeling blue. Find the people you love and trust and let your brave heart muscles work to help to get you through. I think that's what mom would say. And my daddy would agree, and that's all the words I have in this, my first whole song written by Aria Paige-Grant. That's me."

He closed his eyes as the endearing lyrics washed over him.

"Uncle Landy's doing it now," Aria remarked.

He opened his eyes and blinked away the bleariness.

Why were his eyes bleary?

"Doing what?" he asked and cleared his clogged throat.

Harper patted his cheek. "You're crying."

"Like a baby," Aria added, not holding back. "You're crying like Harper cried when I told her we were taking her to Italy."

"A beautiful song can do that, Aria," a misty-eyed Bess commented.

Tomás pressed his hand to his heart and knelt next to the child. "What a gift it is to hear you sing. Like sculpting, music is art. Art is connection, and it reveals the truth inside the artist's heart. An artist cannot hide behind a mask. An artist cannot pretend. Artists take risks and reveal their soul, and that kind of art is what turns a song into an experience."

An artist cannot hide behind a mask.

A grating uneasiness came over him, and a question formed in his mind.

Was he still hiding?

He knew the answer. He felt it scratch in the darkest parts of his heart but ignored the prickly sensation.

"I did that?" Aria asked, wide-eyed. "I revealed my soul?"

Tomás grinned through his bushy beard. "Indeed, you did."

"I felt every word. I lived for every note. Your song touched my heart," Harper gushed.

He patted his niece's shoulder and ignored the vexing agitation.

This was not the night to fall prey to those wretchedly familiar ruminations.

"Take a bow, Aria. You're a star," he said and instantly remembered when Donna had spoken the exact words about Harper after the first challenge.

Get out of your head, man.

Aria beamed as she stood next to the piano. She bowed and blew kisses, hamming it up, when the grandfather clock in the corner of the room chimed nine times.

The little girl stared out the French doors, observed the night sky, then bolted to his side. "Uncle Landy, it's about to start. You better get Aunt Harper to the mushy gushy spot."

The kid was right.

"What's about to start, and what kind of spot is mushy-gushy?" Harper asked.

"You'll see," Aria teased. "I helped set it up when you were in the bathtub. I acted super-secret like Phoebe does when she pretends to be a spy."

Harper raised an eyebrow. "This sounds pretty fancy."

"And fluffy," the kid remarked.

Tomás picked up a small pastry box and handed it to him. "Don't forget your bonbon dessert."

"And have fun, my dears," Bess added. "We'll help Aria get ready for bed after the—"

"Don't say it, Lala. It's the surprise," Aria chirped, then wrapped her little arms around his waist. "I love you, Uncle Landy. Love you, Aunt Harper," the kid continued, embracing her aunt.

Harper tapped Aria's nose. "We love you, too."

"Love is in the air," Tomás remarked.

Yes, it was.

He took Harper's hand and led her past the pool and down the stone steps. The moon slipped behind the clouds as they followed the winding path cloaked in a blanket of darkness. The lap of the lake kissing the shore set a peaceful soundscape, but his pulse had kicked up despite the calming surroundings.

He'd never done what he was about to do.

"Aria's song was amazing," Harper said, emotion coating her words. "She's a gifted artist."

"She's so much like Trey and Leighton."

"And you, Landon. Your niece is a lot like you."

The muscles in his chest tightened. "I don't know if that's such a good thing."

"Of course, it's a good thing," she countered.

He nodded. Better to agree with her. The last thing he wanted to do was bring up his learning issues.

A chilly breeze rolled in off the lake, and Harper pulled her shawl around her shoulders. "Are you sure a backless dress is appropriate for this mushy-gushy outing?" she pressed as they continued down the path.

He was grateful for the topic shift.

"A backless dress is exactly what this outing calls for, but this will help for now." He slipped off his sports coat and draped it over her shoulders.

"You know, heartthrob, I'm not wearing underwear either."

He was well aware of that.

"That was by design, bonbon. I told your friends not to pack any."

She nuzzled into him. "I'm surprised they didn't ask why."

"Oh, they asked."

"What did you say, Landon?"

He shrugged. "I said it was our thing."

He waited for her to lob some prime sass his way.

Three, two, one...

"You've got a point, heartthrob. You did have my panties in your pocket at the housewarming. Maybe they assumed you'd have a pair—or six—already stuffed into your bag."

"I think your memory is a little fuzzy," he snarked back, taking her hand as they continued toward the water's edge. "I told everyone I had a fancy doily in my pocket."

"Because you're a celebrity who carries a spare grandma doily—very believable," she dead-panned.

"Hey, I'm a hit with grandmas, and you never know when you'll walk into a doily emergency."

Harper giggled. "Look who's vying for the title of Mr. Sassy Pants. Luckily, my friends can't tease me too much about my commando status. Between Libby and Raz and their vibrator situation, Charlotte and Mitch doing God knows what with popsicles and grilled cheese sandwiches, and Penny and Rowen cosplaying their way through video games, forgoing panties is pretty tame."

They had a thing—a silly couple's thing.

"We do have one thing that they don't—at least at the moment," she offered, and he sensed a touch of hesitation in her tone.

"And what's that?"

The clouds parted, and moonlight bathed her in an ethereal glow. "We're married. I mean, we're married...for now."

He bit back a mischievous grin.

She couldn't have given him a more perfect segue.

"Speaking of marriage," he replied, keeping his tone neutral, "we should talk. There's something I need to make abundantly clear regarding our situation."

"All right, what is it?" she whispered.

He schooled his features. "We can't go on like this."

Chapter 31

LANDON

He'd dropped a doozy.

He'd wanted to get her attention.

He was walking a thin line. Pissing off Harper Presley was like kicking a hornet's nest, but he had a feeling this gamble would pay off.

The muscles in Harper's throat constricted as she swallowed. She dropped his hand and lifted her chin. He knew this posture. She was putting up her defenses—playing the part of the tough girl.

But he saw past her ruse.

What gave her away?

Her bottom lip had trembled.

It was a barely perceptible move, but he caught it.

She cocked her head to the side. "What does that mean?"

That fine line he was walking got a little—no, a lot thinner.

He slipped his phone from his pocket and checked the time.

"Do you have somewhere to go, heartthrob? Plans for later?" she snapped.

Hell, yes, he had plans—plans that should be going off any minute.

"I'm checking on a...bang." He cringed. Dammit, now he'd really be skating on thin ice.

His goose might be cooked.

His wife looked ready to knee him in the balls. "A bang?" she snarled. "Are you telling me you've got an Italian harem with legions of women waiting for a bang?"

"Not that kind of bang," he answered when—thank God —three jarring pops sliced through the night air.

Harper shrieked and clutched his arm, nearly knocking the pastry box out of his hand as white light illuminated her face and shimmering firecrackers pierced the sky.

"Is this the bang?" she whispered as four rapid cracks answered her question and, again, the sky glittered in a barrage of color.

He breathed a sigh of relief.

Her tone had lost the homicidal bend—his ball sac was safe, for now.

"What's this for?" she pressed.

"It's for you."

"For me?"

"I arranged it. Because you asked for it."

A trio of sharp pops sent a field of green glittering above them.

"Why?" she breathed.

"You mentioned that fireworks were a part of your romance scale of devotion."

"Let me get this straight. The fireworks are for me because of a fictional scale I made up on the fly?" she asked as pops of light rained into the lake.

He nodded.

Was he crazy to do this?

Maybe.

But he had to make her understand what she meant to him.

She peered into the sky. "They're beautiful. I've always had a thing for fireworks. I'm sorry I almost ripped your head off."

"I was more concerned for my balls."

"Those were next," she quipped, but there was no bite to her bark. "No one has ever…" She trailed off as a ribbon of shimmery purple faded into the night.

"No one has ever bribed the local authorities to send a man onto a boat loaded with explosives and shoot them off from mini cannons?"

She laughed and shook her head. "You bribed local officials?"

"I donated a substantial amount to a local arts program. After that, the city officials were happy to accommodate my request. They're kind of crazy about me around here. Anything else you want? A lifetime supply of cannolis? I can make it happen," he teased.

"This is plenty, and I love it." She glanced around. "Should we sit and watch the show? Is this the secret mushy-gushy location Aria mentioned?"

"Almost." He took her hand and led her to the end of the dock. With his niece's help, he'd covered the wood planks with blankets, pillows, and flower petals. Aria had the idea to grab a few candles from the villa to round out the romantic snuggle spot. He set the pastry box to the side and removed a packet of matches from his pocket as the sky shimmered above them.

Harper gazed at the sparkling scene, then picked up a throw pillow. "What's this for?"

He lit the candles as the fireworks showered the heavens with shimmering light. "Isn't it obvious?"

"No." She held the pillow to her chest as if she were guarding her heart.

He helped her to the ground, then wrapped his arm around her.

"I'm devoted to making you happy, Harper."

She stroked his cheek. "Is that so?"

He nodded. "And there's more."

"More?" she breathed.

He tensed as the familiar shameful fear he'd carried for as long as he could remember settled like a knot in his belly.

Ignore it.

Tell her what's in your heart.

"You make me better, Harper. There'd be no new music—no new sound without you. I'll keep my promise to Trey and Leighton because of you."

"Is that all?" she asked, injecting a dash of her trademark sass, but she couldn't fool him. Her eyes shined with tears every time the sky came alive with color.

"No, that's not all."

His heart pounded.

Say the words.

His lips parted just as a splash of hot pink points of fiery light formed a heart.

It had to be a sign.

Harper reclined onto her elbows. Silently, they observed as the pink pops of color faded into the inky canvas.

"You have it, Harper."

She turned toward him as another shower of sparks lit her in a rosy glow. "What do I have?"

"My heart," he rasped. "I love you, and I think you love me."

He'd done it. He'd never expected this day to come, never thought he'd let anyone in, never believed he could trust someone with his secret.

"That's a bold assertion, heartthrob. The deal was a sixty-day marriage." She was talking tough, but he could hear the vulnerability in her voice.

"Then I want to readdress the double-dog dare marriage terms."

She reclined onto the bed of pillows. "What are you proposing?"

He touched her knee and drew his fingertips along her inner thigh, lifting the fabric of her dress as he worked his way up. "I want more."

She closed her eyes and parted her legs as he continued his ascent. "Do you?"

He gazed at her. This was how she looked every morning. He'd crack open his eyes, and joy would overtake him at the sight of his wife. With her hair in a wavy halo of chocolate brown, he'd twist a lock between his fingers and watch her sleep.

He pressed a kiss to her left eye as his hand grew closer to her sweet center. "What if I told you I needed you?" He kissed her cheek. "What if I told you that you made me whole?" She smiled, and he kissed the corner of her mouth. "What if I told you that you're the song I can't get out of my head? I don't want to be without you, Harper. If that's not love, then I don't know what is."

The sky shimmered with bursts of light, and every star in the sky twinkled like a sea of diamonds bearing witness to his words.

She opened her eyes but remained silent, giving him space to speak.

He exhaled a slow breath. "What if I told you that you could trust me? What if I promised I'd never be reckless with your heart? What would you say to that? Could you let yourself love a musician?"

He drew tiny circles on her inner thigh.

Anticipation mingled in the air with the fireworks' sulfur scent.

"Is this real?" she whispered as the air cracked with color. "Or am I about to wake up in my car parked outside the Luxe Grandiose, and this will have been a wild dream?"

He slipped his hand between her thighs and rocked his palm against her. "Does this feel like you're dreaming?"

She bit her lip and expelled a breathy moan.

"It's not a dream, Harper. I love you. I love what we are together."

"You love me," she whispered on a sexy sigh.

He studied her face as a rush of pops and booms ushered in the fireworks finale. The sky sizzled with torrents of glittering light. But that wasn't the real show. The good stuff wasn't in the sky but here, writhing beneath his touch. He concentrated on his wife's face. The lights from the neighboring docks cast enough of a glow for him to drink in her apple cheeks, appreciate her stubborn slice of a nose, and lust over her lips that beckoned to be kissed.

He saw all of her—this woman who'd saved him from himself.

"I've loved you from the moment I heard your sweet, sassy voice," he confessed as he worked her in smooth, deliberate strokes.

"Landon," she breathed, rolling her hips as she rode his hand.

He dialed up the pressure, and she trembled beneath his touch. She was almost there—so close to falling to pieces. She arched her back as she inched closer and closer to the edge. Pleasure radiated from her body, and she grew hot and slick. She moaned a deliciously dirty sound, and her sultry voice fed his desire.

He increased the pressure, finding the perfect rhythm. Watching her writhe beneath his touch, gasping and moaning, had him rock-hard. He could do this all day. But as much as he loved making her body sing, he needed more. He fought every impulse to shrug down his pants and thrust his cock into her slick center. He needed to hear her say those three words. "Say it, Harper. Tell me you feel it, too."

"I love you." The words tumbled past her lips in a heated breath. "I love you, Landon Bartholomew Paige."

Her proclamation unleashed a surge of elation as a greedy yearning tore through him.

Harper gasped and surrendered to his touch. "Don't stop, please don't stop."

He wasn't about to, but he'd explode if he didn't have a taste. Without missing a beat, he worked her with his hand, then ran his tongue along her delicate folds.

"Yes, yes," she cried, tangling her fingers in his hair as he hummed his delight.

Going downtown like he was born to do nothing else, he set a titillating tempo. He feasted on his wife like a starving man ravaging a table teeming with decadent platters piled high with sweet ambrosia. Near delirious with desire, his senses heightened, and tunnel vision took over.

He had one goal, one purpose, one explicit objective.

Make his wife come...hard.

It was a challenge he was ready to meet.

Again, he hummed against her tight bundle of nerves, allowing the vibration to take her higher.

"That's...so...good," she whimpered.

He gripped her ass, relishing the feel of her supple skin. She cried out on the cusp of losing control.

He lived to please this woman.

"Heartthrob, you might just kill me," she cried.

Hell yes!

He had her right where he wanted her.

Through ragged, wanton breaths, every muscle in her body

clenched as a firestorm of moans and sensual cries mingled in the air. Harper tumbled into the hot wet depths of carnal bliss, and it had him raring to go. He squeezed her ass, holding on tighter and not letting up. He hummed against her again, prolonging her pleasure as he devoured her sweetness and savored the erotic victory of reducing his wife into a satisfaction-consuming seductress.

But their connection was more than physical.

From their first kiss, it had always been more.

Still, tonight was a momentous night.

He needed to sear these sensations into her soul.

Tonight was the night he claimed her—not as a sixty-day dare-match wife and not as a temporary nanny-aunt—but as his, and his alone.

Harper relaxed into the sea of pillows, gasping as she worked to catch her breath. "Are the fireworks over?"

He pressed a kiss to her inner thigh. "They're just beginning. You'll be seeing stars all night long."

She pushed onto her elbows. "Then get up here."

He wasn't about to make her ask twice.

Punch-drunk from listening to her lusty whimpers, his cock strained against his pants.

He wiped his wrist across his lips, savoring her taste, then undid his trousers and pumped his weeping cock.

"No boxer briefs, heartthrob? Riding the commando train, are we?" she teased with a dirty grin.

"I did it as a show of solidarity with my wife."

"And maybe because you also hoped you'd get lucky."

He loved that sharp-witted tongue. "So damned sassy." He gazed into her eyes. The clouds had rolled in, and it was too dark to admire the hazel ocean of browns, blues, grays, greens, and flecks of gold, but he didn't need light to know what was right in front of him.

Harper was the best thing that had ever happened to him.

She made him believe in love and led him back to music.

She was the catalyst.

He framed her face with his hands and pressed the tip of his cock against her entrance as he etched this moment in his mind. A tremor ran through his body, goading him to thrust his hips and fill her to the hilt. He couldn't deny that he craved the snug caress of her sweet center, but this wasn't the time for a hard and fast screw.

"Did you mean what you said?" she asked, running her hands down his back.

"Every word. I love you. I don't want to be without you."

He stroked her cheek, then captured her mouth, tasting her sunshine and reveling in her spice. His abdominal muscles tightened, working overtime to employ self-control, only to heighten his yearning. He inhaled a sharp breath and forced himself to move slowly, deliberately, and mindfully. Their bodies came together like an intricately crafted ballad. Every punctuated thrust led to the next, like the notes in a song. The rhythm of their lovemaking took over. They became one instrument, one creative force composing a sensual sound. Their heated breaths, ravenous kisses, and proclamations of love formed an invisible thread that bound them to this time, this place, and to each other.

"Believe in me," he whispered against her lips like a plea or a prayer—he wasn't sure which.

They moved like a rolling arpeggio scale, building up and coming down only to start again. With each wave of passion, the tempo dialed up. He could hear the music—the hypnotic song of their bodies. The rhythm flowed through him. Pumping his cock, he lost himself in the poetry of their gasps and cries. Measure by measure, they grew closer to the finale—to that final note capable of driving them into a sea of ecstasy. She tightened around him and gripped his shoulders, flying over the cliff. He wanted to hold back. He longed to gather these precious seconds. He yearned to collect them like treasured mementos. But he was powerless against her breathy cries and sensual moans. The symphony of sounds carried him over the edge. He disappeared into the throes of passion and crashed head-on into his release. As he pistoned his hips and pumped his cock, a lightness took over as the fears that plagued him disintegrated with each erotic slap of skin on skin.

Harper was his safe harbor, his glorious reprieve.

Nothing could touch him when she was by his side.

Nothing could hold him back.

The dizzying spiral of carnal release slowed, and he returned to his body. His arms trembled from the exertion, and he rested his forehead against hers. He cherished these precious seconds where they hovered in a sacred in-between space. He concentrated on the sound of her breathing as a cool pitter-patter peppered the air. He was ready to roll onto his side, sink into the pillows, and gather Harper into his arms when she tensed.

"What is it?" he asked through a kiss.

"Rain."

"Rain?" he repeated, confusion laced into the word. His foggy, sex-fueled mind still wasn't firing on all cylinders.

"It started raining." She giggled. "You didn't notice?"

And then his brain kicked in. "That's great!"

"It's wet, and it's chilly," she countered. "I don't know if that counts as great."

"Kisses in the rain," he exclaimed.

She held his face in her hands. "Are you okay, heartthrob?"

"This is on the scale. You said kisses in the rain were part of the romance scale of devotion."

It had to be another sign.

He leaned in, and adhering to the romance scale of devotion, he kissed her in the rain as the rhythmic smattering of droplets sprinkled to the ground.

"You've got some memory, heartthrob," she teased as the sky opened and the gentle tap amplified into a pounding wall of sound. "Oh no!" she cried through a bout of laughter.

He pulled out and maneuvered to his knees. Wobbling and damn near crashing on top of his wife, he fastened his pants as Harper's uncontrollable giggles became contagious.

"Gentle rain works great for romance," he laughed. "A torrential downpour—"

"Not so much," she finished.

He scrambled to his feet and helped Harper from the bed of pillows. He held his sports coat over their heads. She wrapped her arms around his waist, and they were off. But there was nothing romantic about their trek to the villa. They moved like the spastic contestants in a three-legged race, laughing and shrieking thanks to the slippery stone pavers.

"Tell me the truth, heartthrob. Did you plan the romantic rainstorm? Is Mother Nature another one of your superfans?" she teased as they clambered toward the villa.

"Mother Nature is about four billion years old. That's the median age of my fanbase. So, yeah, she was more than happy to accommodate," he sassed right back.

They were almost home.

He spied the staff entrance that led into the kitchen. He swung open the door. The chef and a few of the housekeepers gasped as they charged inside.

"We're so sorry to frighten you," Harper said, tucking a wet strand of hair behind her ear.

One of the housekeepers handed them each a dishtowel. "Here, here, dry off. And there is a call for you, Signore Paige. There have been many calls."

What could be so important?

He reached for his cell, but it was gone.

Shit.

"Your phone?" Harper lamented as thunder rumbled and the pound of rain intensified. "It's back at the dock, isn't it?"

"Or I dropped it on our way back. With this rain, it appears I'll be getting a new one. We're heading back to Colorado tomorrow. I can survive without a phone for a day," he said and patted dry her cheeks, when one of the butlers entered the kitchen.

"Ah, Signore Paige, a man on the line from your record label. He says it is important that he speak with you. He's called a few times. I'm so sorry to bother you."

Jesus, why was the label hounding him?

He glanced at Harper. He wasn't about to leave her side for a second. "Tell them I'll call them once I'm back in the States."

"No, take the call. I'll check on Aria," she said, soaking wet and looking even more beautiful.

"Aria fell asleep during the fireworks," the butler offered. "Ms. Fletcher and Mr. Medina put her to bed. They have also adjourned to their room for the evening."

"I'd like to check on Aria," Harper said, wiping the rain from her shoulders. "You should see what the lawyer wants. It could be good news."

Christ, how did he get so lucky?

Maybe it was a Vegas thing.

Sin City was where Lady Luck could change a person's life in the blink of an eye, a roll of the dice, or the twirl of a beautiful bonbon dancing in a brown tutu.

A crazy confluence of events had brought them together.

He lifted her left hand to his lips and kissed her knuckles.

Her diamond glittered like the fireworks, and the warmth in his chest penetrated his cold, wet clothing. That ring wasn't temporary. It wasn't for show. It wasn't the object of a double-dog dare. The bands on their fingers weren't about to expire after sixty days.

Harper was his wife to have and to hold.

Those were the vows.

"I'll have hot tea sent to your room," the butler added, then hesitated. "But the call, signore."

Dammit, the last thing he wanted to do was talk to some suit, but it was his job.

"I'm sorry if they've been badgering you. My manager usually takes care of these things. I'll take the call in my study."

"Very good. I'll let the caller know you'll be with them momentarily," the man replied.

He pressed another kiss to Harper's hand, then let go. Instantly, he missed her touch. "I'll meet you upstairs."

"FYI, heartthrob," she said and tossed him a flirty wink. "After I make sure our little music prodigy niece is fast asleep, there's a good chance I'll be in the bath. All alone in that big tub," she mused, the naughty vixen, then sailed through the room toward the staircase.

A hot bath with the woman of his dreams was precisely what the doctor ordered.

First, he had to take care of business.

He started for his study when the butler picked up a file from the counter. "A courier left this for you," he said, handing it over.

Panic rippled through his chest, edging out the warmth.

He set off for his study and cracked open the manilla folder, and his anxiety intensified. He peered at the mess of lines and curves. Damn, his damaged brain! He'd figured out a color-coding strategy for making music, but he'd relied on the OpenDyslexic font for reading.

How was he supposed to go over the contract?

He closed the file, entered the study, and sank into the chair at his desk. He pinched the bridge of his nose and stared at the blinking light on the phone.

Just get through the call.

He hit the button and engaged the speakerphone. "This is

Landon Paige."

"Mr. Paige, this is Paxton Cleary."

Paxton Cleary? Why did that name ring a bell?

"We met a little over a month ago when you and your wife signed the contracts to participate in the *Celebrity Bake or Bust Challenge.*"

There it was.

"Yes, I remember, but aren't you an attorney for Luxe Media and Entertainment?"

"I am."

"I was told this was a call from my record label."

"It is. Mr. and Mrs. Luxe have acquired your label. The details haven't been made public yet. But we notified your manager late last night. However, we haven't heard back."

"She's had some medical issues. She's indisposed at the moment."

"Ah, well, Mr. Paige, we'd like to act quickly."

He glared at the folder. "Regarding?"

"Two items, sir. But before we begin, I was told by your staff that there was an issue with your internet. We usually do these things electronically, but we've taken other steps due to the urgency of the situation. Did you receive the paper copy of the contract via courier?"

He opened the folder and stared at the sea of infuriating squiggles. "I'm looking at it now."

"Mr. and Mrs. Luxe are excited about the new direction you're taking with your music."

His anxiety dialed back a fraction. "That's good to hear."

"They'd like you to perform at Red Rocks Unplugged. Are you familiar with the event?"

Hell yes, he was familiar with it.

"I know all about it and accept their invitation." He couldn't wait to share the news with Harper. The trepidation welling in his chest receded.

What a night!

"Is the paperwork you sent over for Red Rocks?" he asked. If it was, he didn't have to worry about deciphering each line.

But the lawyer didn't answer immediately. "No, sir, it's not. You do have the contract in front of you, correct?"

Dammit! He couldn't let this guy know he wasn't able to read the lines and curves on the page.

"This legal jargon is Greek to me," he said, trying to cover. "Could you go over the main points of the contract?"

There, now, he didn't sound like a complete dumbass.

"Sure, the contract focuses on the new songs you've written. Mr. and Mrs. Luxe are offering the same terms as your last contract. You'll retain the rights to the composition and the sound recordings. If you're comfortable, you can skim over the first page, then initial at the bottom."

Shit!

He cleared his throat. "About that…"

"Is there an issue, Mr. Paige?"

There was a huge issue. It would take him hours if he tried to go line by line. He opened the drawer and eyed a neon yellow highlighter. He reached for it, then froze. A familiar shame left an acrid taste in his mouth. He couldn't highlight a contract. It wasn't a child's coloring book. It was a legal document.

"We've got a courier en route to retrieve the papers as soon as you sign. As I mentioned, time is of the essence. We've got a lot of moving parts, thanks to the merger," the lawyer clarified.

The muscles in his chest tightened. "I understand."

"Initial next to the red arrow, Mr. Paige."

He stared at the sheet covered in a blurry wash of black and white gobbledygook. Robotically, he flipped the pages and spied the red arrow. At least his messed-up mind could find that. He bypassed the highlighter and removed a pen from the drawer. Staring at the sticker, he held the pen's tip above the line. It hovered a millimeter from the page, poised to sign. All it would take were a few strokes, but he hesitated.

What the hell was happening?

He'd wanted this ever since he, Trey, and Leighton had formed Heartthrob Warfare. He'd promised them he'd do what it took to get to this point. But he couldn't sign the document.

"If you've initialed, sir, go ahead and turn to the last page," the attorney directed, when muffled voices on the other end of the line began speaking again.

Utterances that had an oddly familiar ring to them. Did he know the people in the room with the Luxe attorney?

He leaned in as a few words filtered through the speaker.

Harper.

Buzz.

Star potential.

Representation and promotion.

"Mr. Paige," the attorney continued as the side conversation stopped. "I apologize for the interruption. My colleagues reminded me of one last item to address. Has your wife expressed interest in becoming a recording artist? My colleagues cited significant buzz around her thanks to her performance at the first and the second *Celebrity Bake or Bust* challenges. We understand that you collaborate with her, but we're curious whether your wife has had thoughts regarding her own recording career. My colleagues are interested in your take on the situation."

How was he supposed to answer that?

It was Harper's dream, but was she ready?

His pulse kicked up as he looked from the phone to the contract he couldn't read, and another question lingered in his mind—a selfish question that triggered his deepest fears.

Harper had been the magic behind his success.

Could he transition to a new genre of music without her by his side?

Chapter 32

LANDON

Unable to speak, he peered at his wedding band. His throat tightened.

How was he supposed to answer the attorney's question?

"Mr. Paige, are you there? Did we lose the connection?"

He could hang up on the lawyer and blame it on a bad telephone line.

But he didn't.

"Yes, I'm here. Can you give me a second?"

"Take your time."

He had to think this through carefully.

Was Harper ready for the spotlight?

Perhaps, she wasn't.

She'd been skittish with the press. And while she'd overcome her bout of stage fright during the first challenge, due largely to a massive accidental psychedelic substance intake, he wasn't sure she was prepared for what would be required. It might appear glamorous, but life as a budding recording artist was a grind. Not only that—they'd gotten into a rhythm with their music. They'd become a family of three, and he wasn't sure if Aria could handle more changes in her life. Less than an hour ago, he'd professed his love. Less than an hour ago, he'd thought he had it worked out. They'd reside in Denver. They'd continue crafting his new sound. And if the crowd loved his new tracks at Red Rocks Unplugged, which he was sure they would, that would spark a tour and more recording sessions to capitalize on the momentum.

That was the reality of their situation, but it didn't stop a hollowness from settling in his chest.

This was what he wanted, right?

He craved the stage.

He wanted to shed the bubble gum pop star image and start anew.

Or did he?

He closed his eyes, and an image of a stage materialized. It wasn't a stage that faced a sprawling stadium packed with screaming fans. The stage that had come to mind was significantly smaller and packed with young adults.

He'd pictured the stage inside the intimate concert hall at New Beats.

The hollowness in his chest subsided as he pictured himself and Harper fielding questions from the audience. He recalled the relief and lightness he experienced when he'd spoken about his life in the foster care system. He'd relished the excitement of creating a dialogue with the young budding musicians. He'd sat in the spotlight not as the heartthrob but as an artist and a guest lecturer.

Did he want to play the part of a heartthrob rock star?

Was that still his dream?

He pictured Trey and Leighton. There was only one answer to that question.

He had to follow through for them.

He opened his eyes, returned his gaze to his wedding ring, then stuffed his left hand into his damp pocket.

Had guilt caused him to do it?

Maybe, but he had to stick with the plan of focusing on his new sound.

Life would get hectic once things took off.

They'd be wise to take it one step at a time.

Harper would understand, and perhaps watching him jump through the hoops of promoting a new album would give her more confidence in knowing what to expect.

It made perfect sense. He was being pragmatic, but it didn't loosen the knot in his belly.

"Let's put Harper's prospects on hold for the time being and focus on the new music—my new music. That would be the best choice for my family at this time." He sat stock-still, waiting for the attorney to speak. "Mr. Cleary?" he said, half praying the line had disconnected and his words had gone no farther than this room.

"I'm here, Mr. Paige. I was jotting down a note. I appreciate you taking my call and sharing your insight. The courier should arrive within the hour—possibly sooner—to pick up the paperwork. Please remember to initial at the first red arrow, then sign the last page if you haven't already, and we'll proceed accordingly. Mr. and Mrs. Luxe look forward to working with you and, perhaps someday, your wife. There's a business card in the folder. It's got Mr. and Mrs. Luxe's private cell number. They asked if you'd pass it along to your wife so she can contact them when she's ready."

He flipped a few pages, and a glossy black card slipped from between the sheets. "I see it," he answered, then flicked his gaze to the red arrow.

Everything he'd ever wanted hinged on signing on a dotted line.

"Thank you for your time, Mr. Paige, and I apologize for contacting you during your vacation. I'll be in contact with you and your manager soon."

The line went dead. He removed his hand from his pocket

and drummed his fingers on the desk. The glint from his wedding band caught his eye, and his gaze ping-ponged between the platinum ring and the red arrow.

Had he done the right thing?

He exhaled a pained breath, when the door to his study slammed, and an icy chill spider-crawled down his spine. He didn't have to look up to know that a pair of chameleon eyes were sizing him up.

His stomach dropped.

How much of the conversation had Harper heard?

And if he was asking himself that question, what did it say about him?

Roiling shame scorched his veins, and his skin prickled as if it were repulsed to be attached to him.

Dammit.

He'd professed his love. He'd pulled out all the stops to show her he was the man for her. He could only pray she'd hear him out. He studied her muted expression. She'd changed out of her dress and stood before him in gray yoga pants and a hoodie with his black T-shirt underneath. The sight of his wife wearing his shirt was nearly enough to ease his conflicted mind ,until he caught sight of a crumpled cardboard box and a cell phone in her hands—his phone.

"Where have you been?" He kept his tone neutral.

She sauntered into the room. "I checked on Aria. She's sleeping like an angel with her piano eraser clutched in her hand." She glanced away, and the ghost of a sad grin pulled at the corner of her mouth. But by the time she met his gaze, the warmth in her expression had faded. "Then I threw on dry clothes," she continued. "Do you recognize this shirt?"

"It's my shirt. The shirt you wore…"

"For our wedding," she supplied, but there was nothing coy or flirty in her tone. The stern set of her jaw made sure of that. "After I made sure Aria was okay, I decided to look for your phone—you know, to be considerate. And when I went to leave through the kitchen, one of the staff came in from the rain and handed these to me. It's awfully nice how people like to do things for you because you're a big, famous heartthrob."

He was screwed.

"As you can see, the nice man retrieved the bonbons as well," she added with a saccharine smile, holding up the darkened pastry box.

He nodded. Maybe she wasn't that upset.

"Would you like your phone? I'm not sure if it's salvageable. It's pretty water-logged."

Was that a trick question? "Sure," he answered carefully.

Her syrupy smile dissolved into a scowl as she reared back and chucked the device at him.

"Jesus Christ, Harper!" he cried and snapped his cell out of the air before it whacked him in the forehead.

It was safe to say his wife looked ready to tear him limb from limb.

She made a beeline for his desk, slammed the pastry box onto the surface, then popped the top and peered inside. The rain had soaked the cardboard, and the once sturdy container had caved in on itself.

"What luck! They're still dry." She plucked a bonbon from the box and slipped it into her mouth. She chewed slowly, watching him with her hazel eyes like she was deciding upon the best form of torture.

He'd seen her angry, and he'd seen her sassy, but he'd never seen her like this. Bottled fury stood before him, and like the fireworks, his wife was on the cusp of exploding.

She swallowed the chocolate, dabbed at the corners of her mouth, then crossed her arms. "You don't think I have what it takes to make it in the music industry. But I'm good enough to write songs with you. Is that where we stand?"

The ferocity and the snark factor were off the charts. But he hadn't said those things to hurt her.

He came around the desk, and she snagged another bonbon.

He raised his hands defensively. "Let's talk about this. I'm sorry you heard that."

She scoffed. "You're sorry I found out how you really feel? Maybe you didn't mean for me to hear it, but you think it, Landon. You *believe* it. You told a lawyer as much."

He took a hesitant step toward her. "Harper, you're misconstruing what I said."

"Am I?" she quipped before plucking another bonbon from the box and popping it into her mouth.

At least she didn't throw it at him.

"I have your best interests at heart," he reasoned. "I'm thinking about us—about the three of us."

She barked a mirthless laugh. "You're thinking about us by signing a contract you haven't even read. Wait—not haven't read, you can't read it because you won't take the time to give your brain what it needs to do it."

Jesus, they were back to this.

"I can't let anyone know about that. How do you still not understand?" He didn't mean to come off like an ass, but he'd been clear about his need to maintain his secret.

She shook her head. "How do you not understand that there's nothing wrong with you—well, apart from being a self-serving douche nozzle. You're a neurodivergent learner, Landon."

"Can you not say that word?"

"It's not a bad word," she shot back. "Your niece is a neurodivergent learner. I'm a neurodivergent learner. We don't have cooties. We process information differently." She swiped the contract from the table and studied the document. "You've got to be kidding me," she whispered. The anger in her eyes glittered with disbelief.

"What?" he asked, staring at the mess of text.

She flipped the pages, trailing her hand line by line. "My name isn't on here anywhere. It states that the new songs we wrote are solely yours. We never discussed attribution or copyrights, but I figured I could trust you."

Heat colored his cheeks. Shame held him in its relentless clutches. It made him damn near sick to his stomach.

"It's got to be a typo," he rasped as humiliation seeped into every cell in his body. "And I haven't signed it yet."

She tossed the papers onto the desk. "What would have happened if I hadn't come to your office?"

He didn't answer.

"I'll tell you. You would have signed the contract. You'd rather screw me over than reveal you need help."

He concentrated on a spot on the wall, unable to look her in the eye. "That's not true."

"It's one hundred percent true, and you know it. You're no different from Vance."

That accusation cut to the bone. "I'm not like Vance," he growled, taking her hands. "I'll make a call and ask them to amend the contract. This can be fixed."

"No, it can't be fixed," she whispered as her bottom lip trembled and she slipped her hands out of his grip.

"Why not?"

"Because you think you love me, but you only love what I can do for you and what you can take from me. I'm a crutch, a substitution for your sister and Trey."

"That's not true," he fired back.

Or was it?

He had to do something.

"You heard the conversation. You know I've been invited to perform at Red Rocks Unplugged. The Luxes have acquired my label and have given the green light for my new sound. This is everything I've been working for."

She crossed her arms and lifted her chin. "And thanks to me, you got it."

She wasn't wrong.

He paced like a boxed-in tiger. "We work as a team. It's you and me. I told you, I'll fix this. If you want to pursue your career, then we can figure that out, too."

She stared at him and said nothing.

"Isn't that what you want, Harper?" he snarled.

"You hide behind a facade. You only need me so you can keep up the charade."

He threw up his hands. "What the hell does that mean?"

"It means you're a coward. It means stadiums can chant your name, and fans can cross-stitch your face onto pillows, and that adoration won't change the fact that you're afraid to let people see the real you."

Her words hit like a punch to the gut.

The only choice he had was to give her a taste of what she was dishing out.

"What about the real you, Harper?"

She narrowed her chameleon gaze and took a step toward him. "What about me?"

"You let one setback keep you from following your dreams. The music industry is rife with obstacles. You have to believe that you're good enough to be on that stage. Trey, Leighton, and I knew we were supposed to be there."

Her jaw dropped. "Are you saying you don't think I'm good enough?"

"No, we both know how talented you are."

"But?" she shot back.

He might as well say it.

"Fear holds you back."

"Fear?" she balked. "Do you want to talk about fear, heartthrob?"

He kept his trap shut.

"You're the one nursing one hell of a monster fear," she scolded. "You see your neurodiversity as a weakness. That's your kryptonite. That's your Achilles heel. It's not the neurodiversity. It's how you see yourself. You could do real good, Landon. You're famous. You have a platform. You could help kids and young adults. Look what happened at New Beats when you shared about being raised in the foster care system. Those kids connected with you. I could see it on their faces. They were thinking if he could make it, coming from a tough background, then so could I. You could tear down the stigma of living with dyslexia or ADHD or being on the autism spectrum—just to name a few. You could show the world that thinking and learning differently isn't a deficiency but a strength. A strength that bolsters creativity and ingenuity. And the cherry on top is that you could be a role model for your niece." Her voice cracked. She blew out a tight breath. "Aria's doing well now, but there will be times when things are tough for her. Do you want her to feel ashamed when she needs more time to complete an assignment or requires an alternate way of finishing a project?"

He scrubbed his hands down the scruff on his cheeks.

She didn't get it. She didn't understand.

"I want to be respected as a legitimate artist, Harper. An artist who stands on his own two feet. This business is tough. The minute you show weakness—"

"—you prove you're a human being," she interrupted. "But here's the kicker. You'll never get the respect you want, because there's one person you need to win over to get it, and if you keep living the way you're living, you'll never do it."

"And who is this *one person*?" he snarled.

Her eyes glinted with emotion, and the saddest ghost of a grin bloomed on her lips. "It's you."

Speechless, all he could do was stand there.

"You'll never be enough, because you don't believe you're enough. Forget what the world would say about you. It doesn't matter if you're a pop star, a rock star, or just some guy walking down the street. You've already decided who you are and what you are." She touched the hem of the T-shirt. "I should have known better."

"Known better about what?"

But he knew what was coming.

"Trusting my heart with another musician."

He couldn't take any more. "It's not musicians, Harper. It's you. You think that if you cut something out of your life, it can't hurt you. If you take no risks, you'll never get burned, but you'll also never do anything more than teach kids online from behind a mask." He swiped the business card from the table and pressed it into her hand. "You heard the call. This is for you—for when you're ready to embark on your career." He pointed to the phone. "Make the damn call. I'm not stopping you."

He hadn't meant to be so cruel, but her accusations had hit too close to home. They echoed his worst fears about himself and triggered a jagged response.

It was as if they were standing in the eye of a hurricane. Chaos and destruction surrounded them as an eerie silence descended on the room. He held his wife's gaze, knowing he should say something, but he couldn't find the words.

Perhaps silence was better.

It kept them from pouring salt into their wounds.

"Landon," she breathed, and a kernel of hope formed in his chest. He took a step toward her, longing to hold her in his arms and promise they'd never talk of what had transpired in this room, when a sharp knock cut her off.

The door opened, and the housekeeper peered into the room. "A courier is here, sir. A taxi pulled up. He says you have papers for him."

He glanced at the damned contract. "Tell him to go."

"No," Harper countered and took a few steps toward the door. "Tell the taxi to wait."

He stared at his wife. "For what?"

"For me. Goodbye, Landon."

Goodbye?

His thoughts spiraled. His stomach dropped. His world descended into chaos.

"You're leaving now? What about your things? Where will you go?"

"To the airport, and then to my home—or at least my home for the next handful of days, depending on who wins the third challenge."

He raked his hands through his hair. "Harper, don't leave. We can work this out. I'm sorry. I shouldn't have…"

"Spoken what you believed about me?" she supplied, and his heart sank. She turned to the housekeeper. "Can you get my purse for me and meet me at the door?"

He stared out the window at the pouring rain. "What am I supposed to say to Aria?"

Christ, he'd ruined everything.

"We were leaving tomorrow, as it is. Tell her something came up and I had to return to Denver a little earlier."

"Just stay the night, and we'll leave together as planned."

"I can't stay. Tell Aria I left early to visit my grandmother, or tell her there was a tutu and lollipop convention I couldn't miss. Tell her whatever excuse you want, but let her know that I love her, and I'll see her soon."

"As her aunt?" He had to know the extent of separation she was talking about.

She stared at the business card. "I don't know."

Like the damned bonbon box, his world was collapsing in on him.

"I never used you, Harper. I'll fix the contract. Don't walk out that door. I love you," he pleaded.

"Maybe you think you do, but I've been burned by love like this."

"Harper…" he rasped. "I never meant to hurt you."

She resurrected that sad ghost of a grin. "How about this, heartthrob? I double-dog dare you to prove me wrong."

Chapter 33
HARPER

"Do, re, mi, sing with me. Hey, everyone, it's Bonbon Barbie."

She said her welcoming line, but it took a hell of a lot of effort to deliver it with a smile.

She balanced her laptop on her knees and allowed it to rest against the Volvo's steering wheel.

Yep, that's right. She and Carol, the brown Volvo, had reunited, but unlike the song, it didn't feel so good.

She shifted in her seat, and her leg brushed against something crusty.

Ew!

It could be anything from a dollop of ketchup from 2010 to a piece of a lollipop from ten minutes ago. She missed the Lamborghini's buttery-soft leather. But there was no way she was about to drive the luxury nanny mobile. She turned up the dial on her manufactured grin, straightened her feathery mask, and stared into her laptop's camera. "Today, we'll do a quick lesson on the difference between the major and minor keys."

She could do it. She could go back to her old life.

What choice did she have?

She glanced past the screen as a fluttery striped awning caught her eye and she glimpsed Mr. Sweet's Cupid Bakery.

Okay, maybe this wasn't the greatest place to park and teach a lesson.

Granted, she was able to piggyback off their bakery Wi-Fi. However, this was in Denver. A person could trip and fall into half a dozen hipster-owned coffee shops with perfectly adequate internet service.

Why was she here?

The easy answer was bonbons. But the real reason stung too much to dwell on.

She shifted again, trying to steady the laptop or, possibly, herself.

At this point, it was a toss-up.

She squirmed like the internet's version of the Princess and the Pea. It wasn't like she had a lot of room in there—especially with a stack of empty pastry boxes littered across the passenger seat.

She'd been wallowing in Pity Party Central while feasting on a hefty helping of rage-pie and had gone into serial bonbon consumption mode. If one of those Likert scales existed for a woman scorned and thoroughly pissed-off, she'd be off the charts.

She'd turned to the one thing that never let her down.

Chocolate.

Was it possible to eat away her sorrow?

She'd either find out or become the literal embodiment of death by chocolate.

Despite consuming close to the weight of an elephant in bonbons since she'd returned from Italy, she remained conscious, but the pain hadn't subsided.

Not even close.

She glanced at her phone, nestled among lollipop wrappers and sucker sticks dotted with candy remnants. There were about a bazillion missed calls and texts from her friends and a few messages from Schuman.

And what about Landon?

Had she heard from him?

Nope, not a text, call, or even an email.

Sure, his phone was out of commission. Still, one would assume a person with million-dollar homes spread across the globe could handle the cost of shelling out a little cash for a new device.

Emotionally, she was all over the place. Her emotions swung from being grateful he'd given her space to spitting mad that he hadn't even attempted to reach out.

And Aria?

The thought of the sweet sass-pot was enough to bring her to tears.

Luckily, Aria was spending this time with her grandparents, blissfully unaware of her aunt and uncle's impasse.

She should have said goodbye to the little girl before slipping out the door into the pouring rain. But as she collected her tote from the housekeeper and glanced up the staircase leading to Aria's bedroom, her wounded heart couldn't handle it. Just seeing the kid fast asleep with the piano eraser clutched in her hand would have been enough to keep her at the villa and agree to hear Landon out.

And she couldn't do that.

She couldn't allow another person to sell her out. Even if leaving her name off the contract was a typo, what wasn't a mistake was his feelings regarding her prospects as a recording artist.

While everything in her life seemed out of control, one thing remained constant: the ache in her chest.

But the pain was only part of her anguish.

She'd endured the blows dealt by her parents and Vance. She was no stranger to having her heart kicked around like a rusty can. She'd experienced emptiness. She'd been discarded and left behind like a half-eaten sandwich. But she'd never felt like a part of her was missing, like a thief had snuck in and stolen a piece of her soul.

She caught sight of a wrinkled envelope tucked beneath the empty pastry boxes, and another sliver of her soul slipped away.

Stop!

Teach the Bonbon Barbie lesson.

She sighed and gazed into the camera.

How was she back to square one?

She'd gone from being the definition of walking on sunshine to the poster child for eating your emotions. She'd become a bonbon fiend desperate for her next hit of cocoa, searching for anything that would distract her from the gaping hole in her heart.

And speaking of distractions, that was the reason she'd donned the feathery mask and hit the livestream button.

Was broadcasting to the world an insane thing to do under the circumstances?

Yes, absolutely.

In the high-tech world of instant messaging, everyone knew the rule about not texting while drunk.

There should probably be a second rule.

Never livestream after experiencing extreme heartbreak.

She'd be wise to take her own advice, but she wasn't operating on wisdom. There was too much sugar and disappointment in her bloodstream for that.

The anguish that had consumed her since she'd listened in on Landon's conversation with the Luxe lawyer was calling the shots.

She needed to do something that felt normal and reminded her of who she was before she became Landon Paige's double-dog dare nanny-aunt-wife.

And then, there was the Italian press—the reason she and Carol had been spending so much time together.

She hadn't thought about what would happen once she kicked the unsuspecting courier out of the taxi and demanded the driver take her to the nearest airport. The highly orchestrated villa photo ops had only given her a glimpse of Landon's celebrity status in the country. She learned the hard way that by being his wife, the frenzied excitement extended to her, and without a pack of security guards, she was left completely exposed.

Seconds after she stepped into the regional airport, a crowd of travelers recognized her. They'd swarmed around her like amped-up bees. All she could do was raise the hood on her sweatshirt and zigzag through the mass of people. They'd snapped pictures and filmed her on their smartphones while peppering her with a barrage of questions in broken English and Italian.

Her only saving grace was that she'd arrived in time to catch a direct flight to Denver and had the funds to purchase a first-class ticket. Landon's lesson on LookyLoo had garnered thousands of new followers and a few million video views, and the site had started paying her. She hated that the fresh infusion of cash came from riding Landon's coattails, and she hadn't made much. Still, relief washed over her when she checked her bank balance on her phone as the taxi pulled up to the airport.

Could she have called her friends and asked for help?

Yes.

But that wasn't how she operated. So, with a cluster of people filming her every move, she'd paid for the ticket, then barricaded herself in a bathroom stall until it was time to board.

A question had come to mind as she willed herself not to cry as she stood wedged between the toilet and the wall.

Was she cut out for fame?

Was Landon right about her not being ready?

Her laptop pinged, snapping her back. She startled, and her knee bumped the Volvo's console. A few wrappers fluttered onto the floorboards revealing a shiny black business card.

The Luxe's business card.

The card printed with the number she was supposed to call when she was ready to pursue a career as a recording artist.

She picked it up and brushed her thumb across the digits.

How could something so tiny feel as if it weighed a ton?

She exhaled a shaky sigh, then gasped when her laptop pinged again—and kept pinging.

Ping, ping, ping, ping.

The alerts piled up as people viewing her livestream posted comments.

She willed herself to pull it together, then mindlessly tucked the card into her shirt beneath her bra strap.

The pings kept coming, puncturing the air in a continuous thread of sound.

She skimmed the box teeming with messages.

Take off the mask, Harper. We know Bonbon Barbie is Harper Presley-Paige.

What happened in Italy?

Why were you crying at the airport?

Why were you at the airport alone?

You looked so happy in Italy.

I'll take Landon Paige if you're done with him.

Her stomach twisted into a knot, but she should have expected this.

When she'd stepped off the plane in Denver, she'd heard her name whispered and caught people filming her as she booked it out of the airport. And when the cab dropped her off at home, a handful of reporters had met her at the front door. The men and women had hurled questions like those popping up in the comments box. But she didn't have any answers on the day she'd gotten home, and she still didn't.

The incessant pinging continued as the comments box exploded with text. She caught one question before it got bounced up the ladder of messages.

Are you getting divorced?

Divorce.

Her traitorous mind conjured the image of Landon singing Aria to sleep as if it enjoyed torturing her by parsing through her memories and doling out doozies sure to ratchet up her anguish.

As much as she wanted to maintain that bubble of bliss the three of them had created, she couldn't stay with Landon.

When she'd written "Every Time You Break My Heart," little did she know she should have titled it "Every Time a *Musician* Breaks My Heart."

She'd broken her rule, and now everything was in jeopardy.

She'd put her worries of paying off Babs' loan on the back burner.

With the balance due in a week, and no guarantee that Landon would show up for the third challenge, she was well and truly screwed.

She'd lost focus.

She'd gotten sloppy.

She'd traded snark for sap and was paying the price.

And she had seven days to figure something out.

She scanned the comments, hoping there were one or two questions that didn't pertain to Landon Paige.

But nobody was there to take in a music class.

Sounding off at a rapid-fire pace, question after question hit like bullets to her heart.

But there was no way she could teach a lesson.

"On second thought, let's call it a day. See you next time. I'm Bonbon Barbie, making music sweeter and easier to understand. Remember, no matter your learning style, you can read and play music," she finished, sputtering her closing spiel, but the scripted ending rang hollow. She peeled off the mask and tossed it on the empty boxes. "Who am I kidding?" she said as the comments section registered a frenzy of activity. "I'm Harper Presley-Paige. At least, that's who I am for the time being, and I'm about to murder another box of bonbons."

She closed her laptop and slipped it inside her tote, along with her phone. She exhaled a weary breath, grateful for the break from the onslaught of pings and gnawing questions.

Get your chocolate fix, girl.

She looped the tote's strap over her shoulder and set her sights on the bakery.

Hello, sweet chocolatey relief.

She got out of the car, said goodbye to Carol, and smoothed her shirt.

But it wasn't *her* shirt.

The oversized black T-shirt that had doubled as her wedding attire belonged to Landon. But just like the week after her wedding, she hadn't taken it off.

After three days of eating, sleeping, and trying to get through the day in it, the smell was beginning to rival the week she'd lived in the shirt after returning from Las Vegas. Her head was all in on throwing the damn thing into the trash bin, but her heart couldn't bear to part with it—or even take it off.

And then there was the tutu.

She glanced at the brown ballet staple.

She'd put it on early this morning before sneaking out of the house to evade the reporters.

Blame the fashion-choice faux pas on her stupid heart.

Of course, the brown boots and the tutu were a combo, so she was also rocking the café-colored footwear.

Go big or go home—and she couldn't go home.

Lifting her chin, she strutted her stuff dressed as a cocoa-licious hooker ballerina and charged into the bakery. "This is a bonbon emergency. I'll take two dozen butterscotch STAT," she announced. She wasn't sure why she'd added the STAT part, but it appeared to fall on deaf ears.

The tall man and the petite woman working the counter ignored her.

Ugh!

These two again.

She was pretty sure these were the clerks who'd labeled her the Singing Bonbon Bandit.

She surveyed the shop. There wasn't a customer in sight.

"Hello, I'm the only person here, and I could use those bonbons ASAP."

Now she was talking like some jackass middle manager.

Get. It. Together.

The man shared a look with the woman. "We can't help you."

"Mr. Sweet's orders," the lady chimed.

"Then let me talk to him."

The male clerk fiddled with a stack of pastry boxes. "He's not here."

"Where is he? You know who I am, right?" Now she sounded like a mob boss.

The woman held up a grainy surveillance photo. "We know who you are. You're Harper Presley-Paige, the Singing Bonbon Bandit."

They were doing this song and dance again.

"That picture is from like a month and a half ago," she barked and waved a dismissive hand at the image.

The man reached beneath the counter and held up another photo. "This is the one from a month and a half ago."

"This one is from yesterday," the woman supplied. "It's a shot from when you dropped the pastry box and got down on your hands and knees to eat the bonbons off the ground."

Dammit! She couldn't dispute the proof.

But she wasn't defeated yet.

It was time to harness the full power of her snark and sass.

"I was playing a game," she sang like a deranged opera singer. "It's bobbing for bonbons. It's like bobbing for apples, but there's no barrel of water, and there aren't any apples."

Crickets.

Maybe she did need to be cut off.

Just when she thought she'd struck out, the door that led to the back of the bakery opened, and Tanner sauntered into the retail area.

Hallelujah!

She'd never been so happy to see the man or his High AF beanie.

"Take a penny, leave a penny lady. How are you doing, Harper? You sound like you might need one of my lollipops."

It wasn't a terrible idea.

What was wrong with her?

Actually, there was plenty wrong with her.

"No, I don't need any lollipops." She eyed the bonbon case. "What I need is two dozen butterscotch bonbons *S-T-A-T*, *A,- S-A-P*. Give. Them. To. Me."

Holy crazy talk! She'd gone from anxious opera voice to barking a disturbed cheerleader chant.

"I was kidding about the lollipops," Tanner replied, looking her over. "I saw the pictures online. You're on the celebrity gossip sites. There's speculation about you and Landon. Are you guys okay?" He glanced at the bobbing for bonbons surveillance picture. "Kinda looks like you're not so good."

Harper Barbara, act like a normal non-chocolate-obsessed person.

"Everything is fine. I'm fine. Totally and completely fine, fine, fine, fine."

Tanner scratched his chin. "People who are fine usually don't tell you they're fine six times in three seconds."

She grinned, praying there wasn't any chocolate wedged between her teeth from her last bonbon binge. "I'm peachy keen. Does that one work for you?"

"It's okay not to be okay," Tanner answered.

Why was it so hard to get some bonbons in this place?

"You can drop the fortune cookie advice, Tanner. What I really need is for you to tell these nice people to sell me some bonbons," she pressed, plowing ahead.

Tanner grimaced. "About that…" It appeared as if he was about to side with the clerks when the bakery telephone rang. He gestured for her to wait a minute and picked up the receiver. "Cupid Bakery, Baxter Park, it's your dude, Tanner."

She toyed with the tulle edge of her tutu and observed as his easy-going demeanor morphed into a befuddled expression. "Yeah, dude, she's right here," he answered, staring at her.

Who would call Cupid Bakery looking for her?

"Uh-huh," the man uttered, then glanced around the shop. "It's empty." A pause. "Okay, gotcha."

He hung up the phone.

And stood there.

And said nothing.

"Who was that? Was it the press?" she questioned.

She'd done a damned good job sneaking out the back this morning.

Had they tracked her down?

Tanner zoned out and stared out the shop's front window.

She snapped her fingers. "Tanner, who was on the phone? Were they asking about me?"

Before the man could answer, the door to the bakery swung open, and a whoosh of air sent a chill through her body. She'd barely had a second to react before a stampede of footsteps echoed through the snug space.

"There she is. Get her!"

Chapter 34
HARPER

Harper shrieked and nearly dropped her bag. She took an unsteady step backward as Penny, Charlotte, and Libby busted into the bakery. Dressed in head to toe black and laser-focused, they looked like the Charlie's Angels' version of a SWAT team.

But they weren't alone.

Libby's fiancé, Erasmus Cress, was a step behind, and while he wasn't dressed like a high-end cat burglar, he didn't look well. The man held his stomach and hobbled through the doorway.

"Get her, beefcake," Libby called as the women circled her.

When had her friends started acting like a chicly-dressed pack of wild dogs?

"What the hell is going on?" she cried. "And why does Raz look like he's about to puke?"

"I'm here as the muscle," the British boxer eked out. "But you scare the hell out of me, Harper."

"Raz, you used to fight people for a living," Libby chided.

"Yeah, I've gone up against some rough blokes, but Harper is—"

"I'm the scary bitch in this friendship foursome. And if

you're about to come between me and a bonbon, you should be scared, beefcake," she exclaimed as her friends closed in, tightening the circle. She scanned the femme fatales. "Have you guys lost your minds?"

"One might ask the same of a woman running around town in a brown tutu," Penny shot back.

"You guys," Charlotte crooned, "H is wearing Landon's shirt."

"Wouldn't you classify it as her wedding dress?" Libby mused. "Or would it be a wedding shirt or nuptial tunic because it's pretty big on her? Whatever it is," Libbs continued, "I can feel the vibes."

"No, plum," Raz whispered to his fiancée, then grimaced. "I don't think you're getting a vibe. It's the shirt's ripe scent."

"For real, Harper," Tanner agreed. "The stench is almost as bad as the day you came into the convenience store and almost attacked that old lady over a plant. Wait, that's the same shirt, isn't it? You must really have a thing for that shirt."

Enough of this.

"Rule number one: no more talk about the shirt. Rule number two: anyone with a ball sac needs to shut the hell up." She eyed her friends. "Why are you three bursting into bakeries dressed like hot Prada ninjas?"

Penny's pounce-demeanor diminished, and she lovingly touched a black fanny pack at her waist. "Do you like this belt bag, H? You're right. It's Prada." The blonde swished her hips to show off the accessory. "This personal shopper Rowen set me up with found it."

Harper narrowed her gaze and couldn't help but admire the compact design and the shimmery shine of the clasp. "It's hella cute, Penn Fenn. But again," she said, cranking up her bitch-factor, "what on God's green earth are you people doing here?"

"Um...Harper?" Tanner interrupted, raising his hand like

a schoolboy. "I know I have a ball sac, but I have an emergency."

"What is it, Tanner?" she barked.

He held up his phone. "I've gotta go. I've got a Mary Jane situation to address."

That wasn't too surprising for a guy with a High AF beanie.

She gestured to the door. "Do what you've got to do, Tanner."

"I hope you get this figured out," he replied and dashed out the entrance like the place was on fire.

She exhaled a weary breath and eyed her besties. "I am in no mood for shenanigans."

"Ignore the bonbon addict," Charlotte announced. "Ladies, maintain focus. We stick to the plan."

More of this nanny ninja nonsense?

"Why are you doing this?" she cried.

"This is what happens when you're splashed over the internet because the world is speculating on the status of your relationship and you don't text your friends back when they're trying to make sure you're okay," Penny replied.

These nutjob women.

She set her tote on the floor and scrubbed her hands down her face. "I'm okay. You guys don't have to worry about me. I can take care of myself. You know that."

"We know, H," Libby answered.

"We also know when you need us," Charlotte added.

She hated to admit it, but Char was right. The girls always knew.

As much as she wanted to throttle her friends, it was good to see them.

Raz raised his hand. "Is the ball sac rule still in place?"

"No, Raz, I rescind the ball sac rule. Do you have something to say?"

"I'm not trying to piss you off, Harper, but I can see why

your friends are worried," the man remarked. "You look like a right old state."

She reared back. "A right old what?"

"What he means is you appear slightly disheveled," Libby translated.

She stared down the boxer. "You think I'm disheveled, Raz?"

"Something like that…but worse." He sniffed the air. "And you smell like the donkeys."

Screw this!

Yes, it was good to see her friends, but she had a hell of a lot of wallowing and bonbon binging to get to.

"I don't know what this is," she began, gesturing to the petite ninja trio, "but it's not necessary. What is necessary is that I walk out of here with three dozen bonbons."

"You said two dozen when you came in," the man behind the counter called.

Men! She should have left the ball sac rule in place.

She threw the guy a slice of top-notch side-eye. "Well, now I'm a little pissed off and require more."

"H, close your eyes and press your hands into a prayer position," Libby coaxed.

It was like living in the twilight zone.

"Libby, I'm not meditating."

"I wasn't suggesting you meditate. With your hands in the prayer position, it would lessen the smell coming from your armpits."

"Libbs," she groaned.

"H, we're worried about you," Charlotte said, taking a step toward her as one would approach a wounded wild boar. "We saw the pictures of you from the Italian airport."

The last thing she wanted to talk about was Italy.

She waved off her friend. "That was nothing," she lied.

"It can't be nothing, Harper," Raz replied. "Landon won't

answer our calls or texts either. Rowen worked his computer nerd magic and tracked him to his house in Crystal Hills, but he won't answer the bloody door."

"Something happened, and we want to help," Libby added.

Her heart jumped into her throat.

Landon was in Denver.

Was he hurting, too?

Then it hit.

He was back in the city, and he hadn't dropped by—hadn't done anything to make sure she was okay. She allowed anger to edge out sympathy and doubled her resolve. She wasn't about to break down in the middle of a bakery.

"Is that how you found me?" she asked through pursed lips. "Did you have Rowen hack my cell phone?"

"No, we saw your livestream on LookyLoo and recognized the street in the background," Charlotte explained. "We grew up in Baxter Park, H. It's not like you're hiding out in the middle of nowhere. The shop is only five minutes from our places."

"Who said I was hiding out?" she fired back like a sullen toddler who'd been hiding out.

"All the gossip sites," Penny answered, then slipped her phone from the Prada fanny-pack-belt thingamajig and held it for her to see.

She peered at a picture of herself creeping out of the house, crawling on all fours toward the Volvo. "Dammit, I thought I was evading the press."

"You aren't, and you're coming with us," Penny replied, pocketing her cell.

She didn't have time for this. "What is this—an intervention?"

No one answered.

Jesus, it was an intervention!

"Listen, ladies, I want to get my chocolate and go home

and hide in the soundproof room. I appreciate you guys coming to check on me, but—"

"Now, Raz, grab her!" Libby exclaimed.

The lion of a man pitched forward, grabbed her around her waist, and hoisted her over his shoulder.

"Wait, I'm not wearing—" she cried, but it was too late.

"I forgot about the no underwear thing," Charlotte exclaimed.

Even though her relationship status with Landon wasn't clear, and she didn't have to abide by their panty agreement, the whole commando business was quite freeing and comfortable. That is, unless a giant heavyweight champion decided to throw you over his shoulder like a sack of potatoes. Thankfully, she felt something soft cover her ass a few seconds later.

"I took care of the bare ass situation," Charlotte chimed. "I'm so glad I decided to wear that wrap."

"It is adorable," Libby replied. "I'll have to borrow it sometime. I am always up for a cute wrap."

What was this—an abduction or a fashion discussion?

"Um…hello," she called from her potato-sack position.

Libby patted her back. "Sorry, H, desperate times and all. Lucky for you, inversion is the queen of all yoga poses. Allow the oxygenated blood to feed your mind and usher in a welcoming sense of calm."

"I'll show you a welcoming sense of calm," she growled and pounded her fists on Raz's muscled back.

"Let's get her into the Jeep before she totally loses it," Penny murmured.

"I'll get the bonbons and Harper's tote," Charlotte called as Raz hauled her commando ass out of the shop.

She stopped assaulting the man with her tiny fists. "Wait…I still get bonbons?"

"Only if you're good," Penny answered with a slap to her wrap-covered ass.

It was no use resisting.

She went limp and hung like a wet noodle, swaying from side to side as Raz left the bakery.

"Sorry about this, Harper," he said under his breath.

"Oh, you'll be sorry, Erasmus," she whispered-shouted, but it wasn't his fault. This cockamamie idea could have only been cooked up by her three insane besties.

It didn't take long before Raz stilled, and she stared at an upside-down turquoise Jeep.

"Penn, is that your old car?"

"It sure is. We had her repaired and tuned up. She runs like a dream."

Raz maneuvered her off his shoulder and placed her in the back seat.

She was about to hurl a few zingers his way when she ran her hands across the upholstered seat and settled into the spot that had been hers since she was sixteen. Her frustration gave way to a sentimental rush of emotions. How she loved Penny's Jeep. They must have racked up hundreds, maybe thousands of hours cruising through Denver. Laughing and chatting, Penn and Char sat upfront while she and Libbs reclined in the back and allowed the wind to blow through their ponytails. She was starting to feel that welcoming sense of calm Libby mentioned. There might just be something to being hauled around upside down while forgoing undergarments. She inhaled a steady breath, then coughed and gagged when she spied the items on Libby's spot.

"Zip ties?" she exclaimed. "You guys brought zip ties?"

"Bonbon her," Penny commanded from the front as Libby hopped into the back and shoved a chocolate into her mouth.

"Wha—tha—foo," she blurted through the hunk of deliciousness.

Libby dropped the zip ties onto the floorboards. "We only had them in case you tried to run."

She swallowed the bonbon. "What if I screamed?"

Charlotte held up a roll of duct tape.

She shouldn't have expected anything less from her girl gang. "You guys really thought through this whole abduction thing."

"I have some experience in the kidnapping department. I was abducted by Mitch," Char replied as Libby handed the redhead a bonbon.

Penny shook her head as they sailed out of the parking lot. "No, Char, you thought you were abducted."

"In those brief moments when I *thought* I'd been abducted," Charlotte clarified, "I thought a lot about abduction."

"No, sweetie, you were just a hungover ex-mermaid traveling in a luxury RV suffering from a mind-body disconnect," Libby corrected.

"How many people can say they've done that?" Penny mused, reaching back for Libby to bonbon her. "I should write that on a sticky note. If you ever want to write a memoir, Char, you should totally put that in a book."

God help her! These crazy girls!

For a beat, nobody spoke, and it was as if they'd been transported back in time. The muscles in her neck and shoulders relaxed, and she laughed for the first time in days. She laughed, and the warm vibration soothed her heart and her weary soul. Libby was next to join the giggle party, followed by Penny.

"What is so funny?" Char demanded. "I was terrified, you guys. I thought I'd been taken by a serial killer," she wailed, but the woman couldn't stay mad. It wasn't her nature.

It didn't take long before the redhead joined their giggle-fest, and for a few blissful seconds, she forgot about the hole in her heart.

They cruised through the Baxter Park neighborhood, and she glanced at the passing street signs.

She slipped on the ass-covering wrap and pegged Libby with her gaze. "What's the plan, Libbs? Where are you taking me?"

A coy smile bloomed on her friend's lips. "What makes you think we have a plan?"

"The outfits, the zip ties, the duct tape. The fact that you brought your beefcake of a fiancé along to throw me into the Jeep—oh, and Charlotte yelling for you to stick to the plan," she sassed back.

"We're going to where it started," Libby answered.

That could be anywhere. Every first she'd had happened in this town and most of them with these women.

Before she could protest, the Jeep slowed. They'd only been driving for a few minutes when Penny pulled onto the side of the road.

"We're here," the bubbly blonde called and engaged the brake.

That didn't take long.

She looked between the front seats and stared at a familiar rectangular one-story building.

A simple structure comprised of brick and cement. It wasn't flashy or any wonder of architectural design.

It was better than that.

It was the place that changed her life.

Baxter Park Elementary School.

The elementary school where Libby Lamb, Penelope Fennimore, Charlotte Ames, and Harper Presley had been seated at the same table in Miss Miliken's kindergarten class. It had been years since she'd driven by the building, tucked in the heart of the Baxter Park neighborhood. She rarely had a reason to head down this street. She stared across the baseball field at another building she hadn't seen in ages—the Baxter Park Assisted Living Center.

She surveyed the landscape. It was as if time had stood still.

She recognized every inch of the place. She drank in the metal monkey bars, the twisty slide, and her favorite—the swings. Metal chains and black, bendy rubber seats. So simple, yet it was where she'd formed a bond with her best friends.

"Whitmore and most Denver private schools had Fall Break last week. Public school is off this week. The playground is ours, ladies," Penny explained.

"I'll bring the bonbons," Libby chimed.

"I call my swing," Charlotte trilled as they hopped out of the Jeep and set off for the metal structure with four swings hanging there like they'd been waiting for them.

"And we don't need to scare off any kids to get our usual spots. Bonus," Libby called.

"That was H's job. You were so good at scaring the hell out of the bigger kids," Penny remarked as they trotted up to the playground equipment they'd visited every school day from kindergarten through fifth grade.

"Somebody had to be the tough girl," she replied, setting her tote on the ground, then gingerly touching the metal chain as each woman took their designated spot. Just like old times, Penny and Libby snagged an end swing while she and Charlotte snapped up the two in the center.

She settled herself, then pumped her legs and built a little momentum. Swinging in an adult-sized tutu—commando, no less—was surprisingly easier than she'd expected. For the first few minutes, the only sound came from the creak and whine of the old structure as the women glided through the air.

Libby slowed to a sway, then broke the silence once her feet were planted on the packed dirt. "You don't always have to be the tough girl, H. It's all right to let your guard down every now and then."

"I know," she answered, twisting from side to side like she used to do back when her legs dangled. "I appreciate this walk down memory lane, but why did you guys bring me here?"

"We're pretty sure you need a reminder," Penny answered.

"A reminder?"

Charlotte pointed to the end of the building. "Do you remember what's in that part of the school?"

Of course, she did.

"The auditorium? What's so special about it?"

"You," Penny answered.

"Me?"

"I double-dog dared you to do the talent show, right here in this very spot, when we were in second grade," Penny continued. "After recess was over, you marched up to the auditorium and wrote your name on the sign-up sheet posted on the door."

She stared at the building, recalling how she'd had to push onto her tiptoes to reach the sheet. She'd been practicing writing her letters correctly, and she'd made sure that her name was printed perfectly.

"And you won it," Charlotte added. "You won it by singing a song you wrote."

"Penny's sisters weren't happy with me about that," she replied, remembering how she'd turned the punk tune into a ballad for the talent show, which had sounded amazing and had the excellent effect of annoying Penny's always-perfect older twin sisters.

"The twins survived, and you were right. They totally sucked back then," Penny teased, but her expression grew pensive. "When you stepped onto the stage, H, the air shifted. I could feel the importance of the moment." She glanced at Charlotte and Libby, who nodded. "I think everyone in the auditorium could. You had this presence. You sat down on the piano bench, and from the second you played the first note and sang the first line, the entire place was captivated."

That was the moment she realized she wanted to be a professional musician and set her sights on the dream of becoming a star.

But it was a silly child's dream.

"I was a little kid," she replied but didn't pull her gaze from the building.

"That's what makes it even more special, H," Penny continued. "You only got better. You're a performer. You're an entertainer. You're a rare talent."

"I'm not sure what I am anymore."

It was the truth.

"We know what you are," Charlotte replied. "You're a star. We know this because we've been with you every step of the way."

Libby handed her a bonbon. "And we always will be, H."

They would.

She pictured the day of the talent contest. After she'd finished the song, she'd spied Penny, Libby, and Charlotte in the audience. The girls had sprung to their feet, clapping and cheering. The teacher tried to quiet them, but she couldn't get them to sit down as they gifted her with a standing ovation.

She brushed a tear from her cheek. "I almost forgive you guys for kidnapping me."

"Do you want to talk about what happened with Landon?" Libby asked gently. "We figured it was something related to the music."

"Do I have a choice?"

Charlotte brushed a lock of auburn hair from her cheek. "The guy cares about you, Harper. He and Aria were so excited to surprise you with the Italy trip."

"And you two looked so happy during the livestream of the second Bake or Bust Challenge and in the pictures from Italy. What made you leave? We know how much you care for Aria and Landon. Whatever happened, it rocked you to the core," Penny said, laying it out.

Her friend wasn't wrong.

But she didn't just care for Aria and Landon. She loved them. She loved them with a ferocity she'd never known.

Just tell them what happened.

"Landon pulled a Vance on me," she said. She wanted to inject fury or even indignation into her response. Instead, it came out cracked and broken.

Libby scrunched her nose. "Stupid Mr. Keep Fighting the Good Fight and Vibe On. His vibe is vile, by the way. But Landon's aura is nothing like Vance's energy."

Charlotte's jaw dropped. "Did Landon steal your music?"

How was she supposed to answer?

"Yes. No. Not really, but sort of." She gazed at the black T-shirt peeking through the chic wrap and sighed. "I need a bonbon."

Libby tossed her a treat, and she popped it into her mouth, but it didn't lessen the pain needling at her heart.

How could she explain what had happened without revealing Landon's neurodivergent learning style?

Give them the basics.

"The trouble started with Luxe Media and Entertainment acquiring Landon's music label."

Penny swiveled on her swing. "The same Luxe people who own LookyLoo and the Luxe Grandiose in Vegas?"

"Yeah, and whoever Mr. and Mrs. Luxe are, they stay off the radar, but at the same time, they appeared to have their fingers in quite a few pies. They also own the Red Rocks Unplugged concert event. I overheard Landon on the phone with a Luxe lawyer. He had the call on speakerphone, so I heard everything. They invited him to showcase his new sound at Red Rocks Unplugged in a few weeks."

Libby rocked back and forth, making circles with her heel in the packed dirt. "That's what you guys wanted, right?"

"Yeah," she answered, "but there's more. There was an issue with his contract regarding the new songs he and I wrote together. The contract listed Landon as the sole owner of the copyright and didn't mention me at all."

"It had to be a mistake," Libby offered, abandoning her circles.

"Maybe, probably. Landon said it was," she conceded.

"Then what happened that made you leave?" Char pressed.

This was a slippery slope. She trusted her friends. They knew about her neurodivergent learner status, but sharing Landon's wasn't her information to spread.

She focused on a few pebbles mixed into the dirt and nudged them with the toe of her boot. "The internet wasn't working at the villa. Landon's place is in a secluded location in northern Italy. I'm sure stuff like that happens all the time. The record label was having trouble sending the contract electronically. The lawyer seemed to be in a big hurry to tie up loose ends, and he sent a paper copy of the contract via courier to the house. Landon's manager was recovering from surgery and wasn't available. It fell on him to figure out what to do."

"A paper copy of the contract?" Charlotte repeated.

"Yes."

Char's brows knit together. "And let me guess. Landon had trouble reading it."

What. The. Hell.

She froze. "How would you know that, Char?"

Her friend rocked on the swings a few times. "Oscar mentioned something."

"Oscar?" she echoed.

"It was the day you left for Italy," her friend explained. "Aria and Oscar were buddy reading in class that day before school got out. Oscar shared that Aria uses her e-reader with the special font because it makes it easier to read. She told Oscar that she and her uncle liked this special font. She also told Oscar that Landon didn't like reading paper books to her because he had trouble making the letters stop wiggling. She said the e-reader made it easier for them. Oscar also said Aria was proud of being like her uncle with reading and proud of being like you when it came to writing music."

She blinked back tears. "Aria said that?"

Charlotte nodded.

The cat was out of the bag.

"Did you guys know about Landon's learning issues?" she asked, looking from Penny to Libby.

Penny nodded. "Aria said something similar to Phoebe."

"And she mentioned it to Sebastian, too," Libby volunteered.

"And it makes sense," Penny continued. "The guy only voice texts. He plays the vain celebrity role, like checking on his social media followers and thinking people are spotting him in a crowd. But the more we get to know him, the more we can tell he's not a shallow guy. He plays that part to distract others from seeing who he really is."

Penny had hit the mark.

She twisted the hem of his shirt. "Landon could do so much good for kids like Aria if he was open and honest about his struggles," she answered as a fresh wave of anger tinged with disappointment washed over her.

"Sometimes, it's not that easy," Libby supplied with a knowing grin. "Like Penn said, sometimes, people take on a persona to hide what's going on inside when they don't feel safe to reveal themselves—like, for example, playing the tough, snarky girl when you've got a heart of gold and a gentle spirit capable of writing beautiful music."

"Heart of gold?" she challenged.

"H, you've been in our corner for everything from kids trying to steal our swings in grade school to making sure Rowen, Raz, and Mitch were the right men for us," Penny answered.

"You terrify our fiancés. These guys are mavericks in their fields, and you don't back down because you love us and want the best for us. And that's what we want for you," Charlotte added and reached out to touch her knee.

Cue the waterworks.

Her gaze grew blurry. "Landon is a neurodiverse learner like Aria and me. But he thinks he has to hide it to save face in the music world. Here's the thing I can't get past: he would have signed that contract and sold me out instead of asking for help."

Charlotte leaned toward her. "Did he sign it? Does the record label have it?"

That was the million-dollar question.

She rocked back and forth. "I don't know. He hadn't when I was still there, but I left for the airport minutes after the call with the lawyer ended. And before you say I should give him another chance, there's more. There's something else."

Her friends sat silently, giving her space to gather her resolve.

"The record label attorney asked Landon if he thought I wanted to pursue my own music."

"Like as a solo recording artist?" Penny pressed.

"Yeah."

Libby leaned in. "What did he say?"

It was like her heart was breaking all over again.

"He said he didn't think it was the right time for me. With him making such a big change in his sound, he said that he thought we should wait on my prospects. After the call ended and I confronted him, he said he got the feeling that deep down, I didn't think I was ready, like something was holding me back." Her bottom lip trembled. "He doesn't believe in me —in my talent."

Believe.

That word had fed her soul. Now it tore it to shreds.

She'd been such a fool to fall for another musician.

"Harper, your talent is undeniable," Charlotte said, conviction brimming in her eyes. "When you sang 'Every Time You Break My Heart' the way you wrote it, it was a showstopper."

"That video has millions of views on LookyLoo. You know that, right?" Penny pressed.

Millions of views?

"No," she rattled, "we were so focused on Aria and the new music, we've completely ignored social media."

"I think you're wrong about Landon. He sure looks like a man who believes in you," Libby said and twisted her cascade of jet-black hair into a bun. "When you sang together at the last challenge, he gobbled you up with his eyes like you were the best thing since..." She held up a bonbon. "Since one of these."

That's how she'd felt in that dreamy, lyrical, cotton-candy encrusted moment.

Unstoppable.

Unbreakable.

But was it because she believed in herself or because Landon was by her side?

She'd spent the last few days furious with the man and hadn't allowed her mind to go there.

"What was the last thing you said to him?" Charlotte asked.

She closed her eyes and exhaled a shaky breath, recalling the pain etched in Landon's expression. "I told him that I believed he used me like Vance used me. I told him he was a coward for hiding his neurodiversity, and I told him that he doesn't really love me."

"Oh, H," Charlotte lamented.

"Then," she whispered, "I double-dog dared him to prove me wrong."

There it was. Another Harper and Landon double-dog dare. Would the man rise to it, or was this the end?

"Are you ready, H? If you got an offer from a music label today, what would you say?" Libby asked, watching her closely.

But she didn't have to wait for them to call. She leaned forward, and one of the corners of the business card poked her chest. She pulled it from its hiding spot. "This was in with the contract. The attorney told Landon to give it to me so I could contact the Luxes when I was ready. It's their direct number."

"Have you called them?" Penny asked.

How was she supposed to answer?

She had to go with the truth.

She turned the card over in her hands. "No."

"You haven't?" Charlotte exclaimed, wide-eyed.

She shook her head.

What was she waiting for?

This question had to be percolating in her friends' minds.

It had been rattling around hers from the moment she'd left the villa.

Why hadn't she gotten into that cab and called the second they'd pulled away?

Why hadn't she called when she returned to Denver?

Was Landon right?

Was she scared to take a risk?

Or was it worse?

The image of the city swallowing her parents' van as they drove away from her grandparents' house looped in her head.

If she were good enough, her mom and dad wouldn't have driven off, Vance wouldn't have left her behind, and Landon would have encouraged her to follow her dreams, right?

Was she destined to remain the girl who was left behind?

Or...had she cast herself in this role?

She'd accused Landon of being at war with himself. Was she any different?

Stop driving yourself crazy.

For a beat, her mind quieted as her thoughts shifted to Aria. She pictured the sweet heathen with her intelligent blue eyes, chestnut-colored hair that matched her uncle's dreamy heartthrob locks, and all that sass packed into one terrific kid.

Her stomach dropped as another question broke through.

Would Aria think she'd abandoned her?

She might.

The ache in her chest intensified.

How was she supposed to be there for the little girl and protect her heart from breaking into a thousand pieces?

Despite attempting to ward off the clawing queries, the questions piled up and weighed down her battered heart. She was on the cusp of cramming every bonbon in her mouth and praying for a sugar coma to hit when a series of honks snapped her back to reality. "What the hell is that?" she demanded. She craned her neck toward the sound when another round of *honk, honk, honk* rang out. "Is this part two of your abduction plan?" she pressed, but her friends looked as surprised as she was.

"I don't know why that car is honking at us," Charlotte answered.

Penny pointed to the vehicle. "Baxter Park Assisted Living Center Transport is written on the side. It must be somebody from that care facility on the other side of the field."

The tinted driver's side window lowered, and a man leaned out. "Have you seen an older woman in a pink shirt and khaki pants? She might be carrying one of those piping bags for frosting cakes and cookies."

There's a question you don't hear every day.

"One of our residents is missing. I'm a nurse from the assisted living community across the way," the man added.

They abandoned the swing and walked toward the SUV.

"No, we haven't seen anyone," Penny answered. "But we'll look around the school for you."

"Thank you. Mary doesn't usually wander too far, but she's one of our dementia residents. She can easily become confused and disoriented."

The SUV disappeared down the next block, and she turned to her friends. "Why don't we split up. I'll check the wooded area that runs along the creek, and you guys can take the school and check the block ahead."

"Sounds good. We'll meet back at the swings," Charlotte replied as they fanned out.

She tucked the business card into the waistband of her tutu and started walking. She looked down at her boots. There was a reason people didn't rock stilettos in the wilderness—or even in the woodsy patches dotting Metro Denver. It was hard as hell to move, but it was too late to assign this stretch of the school property to one of her ninja-clad friends. Continuing her trek, she listened for the creek. It was early October, and while the water wouldn't be raging like it did in the summer months, the unusually warm fall wouldn't have dried things up quite yet. A slight burble and splash caught her attention, but the faint sound of a woman singing stopped her in her tracks and had her jaw hitting the ground.

"Sweet, so sweet, hello to my favorite treat."

Chapter 35
HARPER

She froze. She had to be hearing things. But there it was again.

"Sweet, so sweet, hello to my favorite treat."

Who the heck would be singing her childhood bonbon jingle?

A flash of pink caught her eye through a sea of brown branches and willowy green aspens fluttering in the breeze. A woman in a pink blouse sat on a downed tree trunk. She had four flat rocks on her lap, and like the nurse in the SUV had mentioned, the woman had a piping bag in her hand.

What was she doing? Decorating rocks to look like sugar cookies?

"Sweet, so sweet, hello to my favorite treat," the woman sang again, then hummed the tune as she attended to her stones.

Harper narrowed her gaze. She recognized the woman.

"Mrs. Sweet?" she said, hardly able to believe her eyes. But it had to be her. She couldn't even count the number of times she'd been in the shop with her grandparents and seen the lady carrying out trays of meticulously decorated cookies.

The woman looked up. "Hello, Harper Barbara. I was just

singing. I do love to sing when I bake. Did you know I was a soloist in my high school's choir?"

That might be the oddest hello ever, but she decided to go with it.

"I…I didn't," she replied.

Mrs. Sweet brushed a lock of silver hair behind her ear. "Mr. Sweet just put out a tray of your grandpa's favorite bonbons." She surveyed her surroundings. "Where are your grandparents, dear? You're an independent little thing, but they usually accompany you."

What year did Mrs. Sweet think it was?

She didn't know much about dementia, but she figured it best to keep playing along.

"My grandparents are inside. It looks like you're doing your decorating outdoors today," she answered, unsure if that was the right thing to say, but she didn't want to upset the woman.

Mrs. Sweet glanced around, then chuckled. "Look at that! Mary Jane Sweet, how did you end up here?"

Mary Jane.

MJ.

It made sense now.

She'd totally forgotten the woman's first name. To her, she'd always been Mrs. Sweet.

Tanner's MJ emergencies had to be Mary Jane Sweet emergencies, and she'd bet that this was why Mr. Sweet was often called away from the bakery.

Mrs. Sweet returned to humming and attending to the objects on her lap.

Her heart broke for Mr. Sweet. When she was younger, she'd thought that the Sweets were attached at the hip inside the bakery. They'd seemed as much in love with each other as Babs and her grandpa Reeves.

But now wasn't the time to take a walk down memory lane.

While the woman appeared content and unharmed, she had to get her back to the assisted living facility.

"How about we head inside, Mrs. Sweet? I'll walk with you."

The baker surveyed her stone cookies. "I know sugar cookies aren't your favorite, dear, but would you help me carry them? I'll tell Mr. Sweet to add a few extra bonbons to your box for being such a good helper."

"I'm happy to help," she answered as Mary Jane handed her two rock cookies with the woman's trademark intricate piping designs.

They walked through the foliage and reached the clearing not far from the playground just as Penny, Libby, and Charlotte appeared.

"Your friends are here," Mrs. Sweet exclaimed. "Penny, your mother was in earlier picking up a cake for your sisters."

"What's going on, H?" Penny asked, confusion marring her features.

She had to get her friends on the same page without upsetting Mary Jane.

"It's Mrs. Sweet, Mrs. *Mary* Jane Sweet, from the Baxter Park Bakery. I'm sure you recognize her. She's wearing pink, and she needs to get these cookies back to the shop," she explained, hoping her friends would figure it out.

"Girls, this is your lucky day. You can each have a cookie," the baker said, handing Libby and Charlotte the decorated rocks. "Harper, you can give one of your cookies to Penny."

"Thank you, Mrs. Sweet," the girls replied, accepting the items and, blessedly, playing along.

"Are you taking ballet lessons, Harper Barbara?" Mary Jane Sweet asked, looking her over as they headed toward the care facility.

She'd almost forgotten she was dressed like a hooker ballerina.

"No, ma'am, but I'm still playing the piano."

Mrs. Sweet perked up. "And writing songs, I hope. I do love your *sweet-so-sweet* bakery tune. Mr. Sweet and I can always tell when you and your grandparents are nearby when that little song floats through the air."

Harper swallowed past the lump in her throat.

"I love walking with them to your shop and singing as we go," she answered as they approached the building.

Her gaze grew blurry. The Sweets had always been kind, but she'd had no idea they'd taken such an interest in her. She was just a kid—oblivious to the inner workings of the adult world—but it touched her deeply.

"Your grandparents are so proud of you, Harper," Mrs. Sweet continued. "Your grandmother was telling me you won your school's talent competition last week. What an accomplishment! You truly are the apple of their eye—or should I say the butterscotch bonbon of their eye?"

She was. Her eyes pricked with tears, and she took a second to bask in the nostalgia with the baker. "Yes, they were quite pleased. It was probably the first week my teacher didn't have to tell them I'd done something naughty," she said as a joyful sensation fluttered through her body.

"You're not naughty, dear. You're spirited. I told Mr. Sweet that if I had been able to have children, I would have loved to have had a daughter like you."

She swallowed past the lump in her throat. "That's very kind of you."

"It's terrible what happened to your parents," Mrs. Sweet continued. "I will always remember when your grandmother called down to the shop. It was late. We hardly ever answer the phone after closing, but Mr. Sweet and I were still in the back icing cupcakes, and something made my husband answer. I'm glad he did. Your grandmother said it was a bonbon emergency. They needed something sweet for their granddaughter who'd just come to live with them and needed to be cheered up. We set them on your doorstep on our way home from the bakery."

"I remember that night, but I didn't know you'd made a special trip to drop off the bonbons" she replied, recalling how that little bit of sweetness had lifted her spirits.

They started up the path to the care center's main entrance when the facility's sliding doors opened. A pale Mr. Sweet and two men in scrubs hurried toward them.

"Mary Jane, are you all right?" Schuman asked, taking the piping bag and handing it off to one of the nurses as they entered the building.

"Yes, of course, Schuman, I was decorating sugar cookies, and I must have wandered outside." Mary Jane looked around, and her smile dissolved. "Where are we? This isn't the bakery. What am I doing here?"

A nurse moved toward the woman. "Mrs. Sweet, let's get you back to your room."

She scowled at the man. "Who are you?"

"That's one of the nurses, Mary Jane," Mr. Sweet answered with a weary bend to the words as if he'd had this conversation more than once.

"I don't need a nurse, and these cookies won't decorate themselves. We have work to do and orders to fill."

Schuman shook his head. "No, not anymore, Mary Jane."

Mrs. Sweet's gaze darted around the room. "I want to go home. Why am I here? Why aren't we at the shop?"

Harper shared a heartbroken look with her friends.

"Did you know she was here?" Charlotte asked, lowering her voice as Mrs. Sweet grew angrier and more animated.

"No, I didn't work it out until I saw her by the creek."

Two more nurses joined the melee.

It was dreadful to see Mrs. Sweet so confused and distraught.

"I will not go to my room. I'm not a child. I don't live here," the woman argued, raising her voice.

"Poor thing," Libby lamented.

Harper looked on as Mr. Sweet tried to reason with his wife, but his words were getting lost between the nurses attempting to assist the woman.

"I wish we could do something," Penny said.

Do something.

She studied the space. The main entryway served as a gathering place. Clusters of intimate seating dotted the area, and a piano sat in the corner of the room.

A piano.

"I can help," she said, eyeing the instrument. She handed Penny her stone cookie and tote, then skirted by the group attempting to calm the woman.

She lowered herself onto the bench and rested her fingers on the keys. "Here we go," she whispered. She played a rolling arpeggio scale. Climbing then descending, the reverberation of the crisp notes ringing in a cascade of sound quieted the frenzied conversations.

She looked over her shoulder. "Mrs. Sweet, would you like to hear a new song I've been working on?"

The baker's pinched expression smoothed into a serene smile.

It was as if a switch had flipped.

"I'd be delighted, Harper Barbara," she replied and settled herself in a rocking chair next to the piano. "I'm ready, dear."

What song should she play?

Oddly, the decision wasn't hers.

As if Joyce and Bartholomew had reclaimed control of her hands, she played the intro to a tune that didn't even have a title—or a full set of lyrics. But the notes didn't come from her hands. They came from her heart.

"She's a girl with chameleon eyes,

Her laughter's full of surprises.
Sign me up for the romance scale of devotion."
The lyrics from the second challenge flowed past her lips.
She waited for heartbreak to set in.
But it didn't.
A steadiness took over.
"Tell me, baby, what you need.
I won't stop till I succeed, working my way through the scale of
devotion.
Breakfast in bed, flowers in a vase, chocolate bonbons are no disgrace.
Baby's got a scale of devotion."

She glanced up and caught Mrs. Sweet tapping her foot to
the beat. Mr. Sweet stood next to her, and Tanner was there,
too. The High AF dude nodded as he held up his cell phone.
The guy must be recording her. Why would he do that? Then
she noticed a few of the nurses doing the same thing.

Weird.

She returned her attention to the song and played the
melody again, humming along until the final lines.

The lines she'd added.

"But it's not things that she really needs. It's the unspoken promise, the
tender deeds that show her what she really means, baby, on the romance
scale of devotion."

She rested her hands in her lap. Applause broke out, along
with a few whispers.

That's her, right? It's Harper Presley-Paige?
Yeah, she was livestreaming on LookyLoo.

She'd almost forgotten. She was famous—well, infamous.

"Harper, I recognize that song. Schuman, Tanner, and I
watched you perform it on TV. You were playing the piano,
and your husband was strumming a guitar." Mrs. Sweet's face
lit up. She'd jumped in time to the present. "Congratulations
on your new marriage," she continued. "I can tell your
husband adores you by how he looked at you while you were

singing. Schuman tells me they call him the heartthrob. He's quite dreamy, like my Shooey was back when we were young."

Mr. Sweet blushed. "We showed Mary Jane the video on LookyLoo."

"I had one of Tanner's special lollipops that day. They open the mind," the woman added.

Hell yes, they did.

"I feel you on that one, Mrs. Sweet," she answered, then glanced at the small crowd in the lobby, continuing to film the moment.

Oddly, it didn't bother her.

She wanted as many people as possible to experience the power of music.

What was music for if not to calm the soul, reset the mind, and help others exist beyond themselves and live, thrive, and reminisce in the measures of a song.

She'd done that for Mrs. Sweet. Her music had done that.

Mrs. Sweet sighed, then closed her eyes and yawned.

It was time to allow the woman to rest.

She slid off the bench and knelt next to Mrs. Sweet's rocking chair. "We better be going, Mrs. Sweet. And you should put your feet up and relax after decorating those sugar cookies."

The woman yawned again. "I am rather tired. But I need to tell you something, dear," she said, clear-eyed and alert.

"You can tell me anything."

"Your music touches people, Harper. Don't let anyone dim your light. Your grandfather would want you to be true to yourself and your music."

She stared at the woman, and her breath caught in her throat. "You're right. He would."

Mrs. Sweet gifted her with a weary grin. "I have done quite a bit of work today. I do believe a nap is in order." She looked at her husband. "Shooey, you look like you could use some rest, too."

Schuman nodded. "I'd like that, but first, I'd like to see Harper and her friends out. Tanner, would you walk your aunt to her room?"

Tanner helped Mrs. Sweet to her feet. They took a few steps, but Mrs. Sweet stopped and looked over her shoulder. "Harper Barbara?" the woman called.

"Yes?" she breathed.

Mrs. Sweet gestured to the floor by the rocker. "You dropped something, dear."

It was the business card.

"You should call that number. It might change your life," Mary Jane Sweet added with an aura of calmness before hooking her arm with Tanner's and continuing down the hallway.

How would Mrs. Sweet know the importance of that card?

It was most likely the ramblings of a woman shifting between the past and present, but the baker wasn't wrong. The card had the potential to change everything for her.

"Ladies," Schuman said and gestured to the sliding doors.

Once they were outside, he turned to Penny, Charlotte, and Libby. "Thank you again for helping us find Mary Jane. Would you mind if I had a moment with Harper?"

"Not at all," Charlotte answered.

"We're glad your wife's safe," Libby added as the trio walked toward a cluster of benches down the path.

Schuman smoothed his handlebar mustache. "Thank you for what you did in there and for finding MJ. They let her help in the kitchen. It calms her. But she slipped out when nobody was looking."

She waved him off. "It was nothing."

The man's gaze sharpened. "No, it meant everything. It hasn't been easy for Mary Jane. It's not safe for her to live in our home. She can't sing with her friends anymore, and she can't work in the bakery. We've had many changes over the last several months. I needed help caring for her, and I couldn't run the business without her. That's why I joined the Cupid Bakery franchise. Tanner comes to town to help, but his life is in the mountains. We have no children of our own and wanted to make sure the bakery was able to thrive in Baxter Park."

The guy had it rough.

"I'm so sorry, Mr. Sweet."

"Don't be sorry. I'm not. This is where we are. And while some days are difficult, I treasure them. And I still get to hear her sing your little songs."

Her songs.

And then Mr. Sweet's strong reaction to the first challenge made sense.

"Mr. Sweet, did your wife start the Singing Grannies Choral group?"

He nodded.

Now the man's teary response made sense.

"If you don't mind me asking, why did she call it the singing grannies?"

Mr. Sweet's handlebar mustache twitched as the ghost of a grin graced his lips. "MJ thought the singing grannies sounded better than a bunch of old broads shrieking in an auditorium."

She chuckled, but the man's expression grew serious.

"The real reason is that, while we don't have any children or grandchildren, Mary Jane always thought of herself as a grandmother to the children who came into the shop." Mr. Sweet glanced away and cleared his throat. "She was particularly fond of you. She said you were a real scrapper. She didn't think there was much life could throw at you that you couldn't conquer."

Wow.

"I had no idea she believed in me like that."

Believed.

There was that word, but it didn't hurt to hear it.

Schuman looked toward her friends. "I think there are many people who believe in you."

She took in her bestie ninja brigade, and the whole world brightened.

The man was right.

"Thank you for what you did for my wife."

"I was happy to help. I'm glad she's okay."

The man shifted his stance. "And what about you? Are you okay?"

She'd almost forgotten that he'd left a few messages for her.

"Tanner tells me there's gossip about you and Landon online, and my staff tells me your bonbon consumption has increased exponentially."

She exhaled an audible breath like her body desperately needed to release a boatload of pent-up energy. "My life is a dumpster fire, Mr. Sweet." She couldn't lie, and she didn't want to sugar-coat the truth—not after witnessing such vulnerability from Schuman and his wife.

"Will I see you and Landon for the third challenge?" he asked. "Will you and Landon be competing together?"

The contest.

With all the craziness, she'd nearly forgotten they had one challenge left—and it was only a few days away. Not to mention, she needed to win the prize money to pay off Babs' place.

"I don't know what's in store for Landon and me."

Again, she couldn't lie.

It was more than hope, but she couldn't let her emotions get the best of her.

"Love has its ups and downs," Schuman said gently. "It reveals your greatest strengths and your most glaring faults. The trick to making it is simple yet complex."

"I'd love to know the trick," she replied through a teary chuckle.

"Vulnerability," he said gently. "You must be willing to risk it all while knowing there will be wins, and there will be losses, but you choose to walk that road together. You choose honesty and optimism over fear and regret." Schuman patted her shoulder. "And Mary Jane was right, by the way."

She cocked her head to the side. "What was she right about?"

"Your grandfather. He'd want you to be true to yourself."

If something isn't working, change the melody but keep making music.

The man's words extended far beyond crafting a song.

"He would," she agreed and glanced at the business card cradled in her hand.

"Mr. Sweet?" a nurse called from the entrance, puncturing their moment. "Do you have a second to chat?"

She shared one last look with the man. He nodded once, bidding her a silent goodbye, before heading inside.

She waved to her girls.

"Swings?" Charlotte asked.

"That's where I left the bonbons," Libby replied.

Too bad they didn't have anything stronger. Mr. Sweet had dropped quite the life lesson in her lap. She could sure go for a pitcher of margaritas.

"Swings it is," she replied, and the foursome returned to the playground.

She stared at the business card.

"What's kept you from calling, H?" Penny asked as their footsteps cut a path through the field that separated the assisted living center from the elementary school's property.

Mr. Sweet had mentioned it.

Fear.

She stared at the digits on the glossy rectangle. "The fear that I'm not good enough, but I'm tired of thinking of myself as the girl nobody wanted. That's not who I am," she said, believing it with every fiber of her being.

"Who are you, H?" Charlotte asked with a coy grin as they took their spots on the swings.

Who did she want to be?

The answer came easily and effortlessly.

She'd be a performer. A singer and a songwriter. A musician.

A star.

A star who wanted it all, and that included love.

"In a perfect world, I'd have a career in music, and I'd be Landon's wife and Aria's forever aunt. But I don't know if that's possible." She brushed a tear from her cheek, and Libby passed her a bonbon.

"Forget about Landon for a second," Libby began, "and think about what kind of qualities Aria's mom would want in a person who'd influence their daughter's life."

"We've asked ourselves this question, H. And the answer is as reassuring as it is distressing," Charlotte added.

"We had to become the person we're supposed to be," Penny answered.

Harper chuckled. "That's all?" she teased, but she shouldn't have been surprised by this. She'd been at her friends' sides when they'd stood at the crossroads.

"I know this sounds super Libby-ish—no offense, Libbs," she said, tossing her Zen bestie a wink.

"None taken," the raven-haired woman replied.

"But I felt Leighton's presence the first time I saw Aria in person," she continued. "Aria and I were singing and playing piano in Landon's foster parents' detached garage, and this weird sensation came over me like we weren't alone."

"It's not weird, and we've all experienced something similar," Penny replied, looking to the other women.

But what now? How did she move forward when her life was in limbo?

She concentrated on her wedding band—a ring placed on her finger thanks to an agreement to throw caution to the wind and a double-dog dare. "You guys took the risk, and it paid off. What if that doesn't happen for me? What if I don't get the nanny-match happily ever after? I'm not the Cinderella type. I'm more evil stepsister with a side of baked goods."

"Sorry to wreck your badass baked goods vibe, H, but you've got some Cinderella in there," Penny countered. "And by the way, Cinderella was no damsel in distress. She was a girl who took the risk. She broke the rules. She had a great group of friends—animal friends, but friends, no less, who were behind her every step of the way. She found true love. But she had to fight for it and push her limits. She didn't let fear win, and she never stopped believing in love. She believed."

Believe.

"You've got to believe in yourself before you can believe in anything or anyone else. It's the yin and yang of nanny matching, or nanny-aunt matching, in your case," Libby added, throwing a dash of Zen into the mix.

Penny tucked a lock of blonde hair behind her ear. "No happily ever after worth ever-aftering was ever easy."

Jesus, that was a mouthful.

"Ever-aftering?" she said, eyeing the woman.

Penny bit back a grin. "Yes, it's a word. I'm a writer. I know about these things."

Bullshit.

But she loved that she had friends who would give it to her straight.

It was time to act.

She had to take Schuman's advice and shed the snark and allow herself to be vulnerable to face her fears.

She had to look the little girl version of herself square in the eyes and make something perfectly clear. She might have been rejected, but she was surrounded by love. From her grandparents to her friends, to the kindness of people like the Sweets and the gifted musicians she'd met through her grandparents, there was good and happiness in this world, and she owed it to herself to go after a slice of that happy pie.

That was the kind of woman worthy of being Aria's aunt.

And what about Landon?

She loved the man but couldn't drag him kicking and screaming to accept what and who he was. That was his responsibility. His journey.

But he wasn't the only one at fault. He wasn't off the mark when he'd sensed she wasn't ready to pull the trigger on a career as a recording artist.

She had hesitated. She had been reluctant. She'd allowed rejection to send her to the sidelines.

Only one person could get her back in the game, and that was the woman she saw in the mirror.

She didn't know if she'd be happily ever-aftering it with Landon and Aria. All she knew was what she had to do to be the best version of herself.

One challenge remained. The final challenge was days away.

She'd show up.

She'd double-dog dared him to prove her wrong.

The question was, would he?

"Bonbon," she demanded like a surgeon requesting a scalpel.

Libby fulfilled the request.

She slipped the chocolate into her mouth. "*Cell-own*," she mumbled.

"You're lucky we speak bonbon," Charlotte teased before reaching into the tote. She plucked her cell from the bottom of the bag and handed it over.

She tapped the home button, and the screen came to life, but she took a second to drink in the moment.

The afternoon sun bathed the playground in golden light. The familiarity of their spot soothed her as she peered at the school's auditorium.

If something's not working, change the melody.

She pictured Landon and Aria, exhaled a steady breath, then pressed the telephone icon.

Her melody was about to get one heck of a transformation.

It was time to face her fears and believe in Harper Barbara Presley-Paige.

Chapter 36
LANDON

Sunlight streamed through the windows, and specks of dust swirled in the air. Whispers of laughter, rollicking melodies, and the click of tiny letter tiles carried on the breeze, or perhaps they were echoes of the past. Landon sat on a stack of milk crates and picked at his guitar. He riffed a scratchy, tumultuous tune. He couldn't get into the groove—couldn't find the balance his mind craved. Set in a foreboding minor key, the jagged, melancholy notes pricked the air judging him, and rightly so.

He was a damned fool.

He'd screwed up, and he couldn't see a path forward.

No wonder he couldn't conjure a tune to save his life. He'd lost the ability to tap into the joy of making music he'd rediscovered the night he'd laid eyes on a brunette beauty rocking a cocoa-brown tutu.

Caught between the desire to fulfill a promise and the need to hide his faults, he'd been living in hell for the past few days since he'd returned from Italy.

That's why he was sitting on a stack of milk crates.

He'd come to a place he'd hoped could offer a measure of peace.

The place where he and his sister had found music, friendship, fame, and love.

The detached garage on Tomás and Bess's foothills property.

The property was still on the market. No buyers had put in an offer. The realtor could turn up for a showing, but he'd decided he'd take his chances.

He stopped playing and stared at the piano against the wall, recalling when he'd walked in on Harper and Aria. The weight he'd carried for years had lifted when he'd heard them singing. He blinked, and in an instant, Harper and his niece disappeared. He pictured Trey tuning his bass and Leighton glancing over her shoulder and gifting him with a grin. A sinking feeling took over as the familiar heaviness set in under the strain of figuring out his next move.

If only he could turn back time.

He scrubbed his hands down the unruly scruff on his cheeks.

If only he could ask Trey and Leighton to help him solve the nagging problem that had kept him pacing the nights away since his separation from Harper.

How do I make it right and still protect my secret?

After a couple of sleepless nights in his Crystal Hills estate, he'd gotten in his car and started driving.

He hadn't planned on coming to Tomás and Bess's place.

His heart longed to return to a two-story, Denver-square house in Baxter Park. A structure with a quasi-soundproof room in the basement, a kitchen with a box of bonbons and lollipop wrappers on the table, and a piano in the living room with loose sheet music, highlighters, and colored magnets scattered about the space. A place resonating with Aria's laughter and Harper's sweet sighs as she drifted to sleep in his arms.

He'd driven by Harper's place, hoping it would lessen his anguish.

It hadn't.

He'd spied his wife's form in Aria's window. The curtains were closed, but he could see she was standing in a spot that allowed her to gaze at the bed. Was she missing Aria? Was she picturing the three of them snuggled up as they read bedtime stories and sang a goodnight song? Every cell in his body had urged him to get out of the damned car, sprint into the house, and take her into his arms.

But he hadn't given in to the gnawing compulsion.

And he knew better.

It wouldn't have been a warm welcome after what had happened in Italy.

Fighting the impulse to watch her like a Peeping Tom, he'd driven down the darkened road and almost turned onto the street that led to the house he'd lived in with his parents and Leighton.

But he didn't do that either.

Desperate to escape his demons, he'd hit the gas and headed for the highway. Near midnight, he'd arrived at Tomás and Bess's darkened home. He could have gone inside and slept in his old room. That's what a rational person would have done.

But he wasn't firing on all cylinders.

He decided to cloister himself away in the garage. He'd unfolded an old camping cot and retrieved a sleeping bag from one of the large cardboard boxes stacked in the corner. In the musty, darkened space, he'd fallen into a fitful sleep.

Plagued by dreams about a girl with chameleon eyes, he'd woken up a damned mess.

He was a pitiful squatter running on empty.

He needed a plan. He required direction. There was so

much on the line. But he couldn't see past the misery of his current situation.

He strummed the guitar and glanced at the papers next to the cot.

The contract.

The damned contract.

His ticket to everything he wanted.

It never made it to the courier.

The Luxe lawyer was probably going out of his mind. Mitzi probably knew by now.

There would surely be a shit-ton of messages on his phone. But the joke would be on the lawyers and his manager. His phone was blessedly out of commission, thanks to an Italian thunderstorm.

The only way someone could get him a message was via pigeon. And that's if they could figure out where he was.

For all intents and purposes, he'd been off the grid since returning to Denver.

He plucked the strings mindlessly, trying to piece together a melody that could save him from this agony, when his wedding band glinted in the hazy light.

The vice around his heart tightened.

He wasn't supposed to be living in this hellscape.

He was supposed to be living the good life as a loving husband.

He'd been so sure his romance scale of devotion gesture would have washed away the timestamp on their marriage and ushered in the beginning of their forever as a family of three.

Christ, he was wrong.

He'd lost a piece of his heart when she'd gotten into that cab.

Another slice had whittled away when he saw Aria the following day.

The kid had woken up bright-eyed and raring to take a morning walk along the water's edge with her aunt and her uncle and found only her gloomy uncle at the breakfast table. He'd manufactured a grin and told the kid her aunt had to go back to Denver early to take care of something for their new music.

It was a bullshit excuse.

But bullshit appeared to be his only currency.

Tomás and Bess had been there when he'd mumbled the words. He'd observed the concern etched on his foster parents' faces, but he didn't have the mental strength to make up anything better. Luckily, neither pressed for details.

And surprisingly, Aria hadn't either.

His niece had eyed him as one would assess a science project. He didn't have to be a genius to see the wheels turning in her head. Perhaps she'd picked up on his cardboard smile. He'd figured she would have called him out on it. Aria Paige-Grant wasn't one to hold back. He'd braced for her interrogation, but the child had said nothing. Instead, she'd slipped her hand into her pocket, fidgeted with something, then asked Bess if she could have leftover cake for breakfast.

His pint-sized ball-buster of a niece had let him off the hook. He didn't have the foggiest notion of why she'd given him a pass, but he was grateful, nevertheless.

He'd left a few hours later on a flight that was supposed to be the precursor to his next surprise.

With Aria missing school to spend more time in Italy with her grandparents, he'd planned a kid-free staycation at his Crystal Hills estate.

He'd assumed the sprawling mansion would become their home in the next few weeks. While in Italy, he'd arranged to have the place cleaned, the pool treated and ready for skinny-dipping. He'd stocked the pantry with their favorite bonbons. He'd pictured the moment he opened the front door, and Harper—being Harper—would give him shit for living in such a hoity-toity house with every fancy-pants convenience before wrapping her arms around his neck, twisting her lips into a sexy smirk, then demanding he screw her brains out on every flat surface.

If that wasn't one hell of a dream scenario, then he didn't know what was.

But none of that had transpired, and here he sat, alone in a dusty garage.

He cringed as he plucked at the strings like his fingers were covered in peanut butter.

"That sounds like absolute shit."

He startled, then peered at the doorway and nearly fell off the stack of crates. "Mitzi?"

"You're lucky it's me and not the crap music police," the woman fired back, but her sarcastic tone couldn't hide the concern in her gaze.

"How's the tooth? Shouldn't you be in bed?" he said, coming to his feet.

She waved him off. "I've got enough ibuprofen in me to lose a toe and not know it. I've rested long enough. We need to talk, LB. I've been looking for your ass for the last seventy-two hours. I was just at your house. Why haven't you responded to my emails, texts, and calls? I came up here as a last resort."

He looked away. "Me too."

She leaned against the door frame. "You're ignoring the world, is that it?"

He toyed with the guitar's C string, then fiddled with the tuning pegs. "I left my phone in the rain, and the water damaged it."

"You didn't think to get another one?"

He stopped tormenting the guitar. "I've been trying to limit my thinking."

"I figured as much," she murmured.

"What does that mean, Mitz?"

She cocked her head to the side. "You don't know, do you?"

Ice crackled down his spine.

Had something happened?

In his wallowing and self-loathing, his judgment had blurred, and he'd neglected his responsibilities. Aria was with Tomás and Bess, but he'd taken custody of the kid. He couldn't disappear like an indulgent pop prick anymore. Not to mention, he was still married. What kind of douche nozzle put his needs above his wife's happiness?

Oh, that's right, he was that type of douche nozzle.

"What's going on, Mitzi? Is it Aria?"

"Aria's fine. I spoke with Tomás yesterday." His manager pursed her lips. "It's Harper."

A knot formed in his belly. "Is she okay?" he rasped, his voice a scrape of a sound.

Mitzi dusted off a folding chair and took a seat. "That depends on how you define *okay*. She's all over the internet. The day before the two of you were set to head back to Denver, she showed up at an airport in northern Italy. From the looks of the pictures and videos splashed online, she was identified the minute she walked in. Word is, the Italian press and paparazzi were already camped out waiting to get shots of the two of you leaving the next day." Mitzi pulled her cell from her tote and handed it to him. "The press loves a lovers' quarrel. When Harper showed up by herself, looking distraught, they pounced on her. She put up a strong front. That gal has one hell of an iron resolve, but you know how the press can be. They hounded her. She ended up locking herself in a bathroom stall until her flight to Denver boarded. But they followed her into the ladies' room. There are pictures of her feet from where the photographers got down on the floor to get a shot."

He'd known that kind of hysteria, but he hadn't experienced it alone. He'd been with Trey and Leighton.

"Dammit," he whispered. He scrolled through the pictures,

and the screws on the vice clamped around his heart tightened. It killed him to see her like this. He handed Mitzi her phone. "Italy was supposed to be a game-changing trip for us."

His manager's expression softened. "The game changed, kid, but it doesn't look like it changed in your favor. What happened?"

"This happened," he answered and picked up the contract. "It's the contract for—"

"—the new music under Luxe Media and Entertainment. I know," she said, interrupting him. "I'm sorry I couldn't handle that for you."

"I get it. You were recovering. But I don't understand why it didn't mention Harper anywhere."

Mitzi reclined in the chair. "I'm not sure either. But it's an easy fix. I've already spoken to their legal team. You could have told Harper that."

Sure, if he'd been able to read it.

"I almost signed, Mitz. The lawyer said the legal team was in a hurry. He glossed over the terms. He said they were the same as what you'd negotiated for Heartthrob Warfare. They sent this paper copy to the house, and I..."

He couldn't go on, but Mitzi knew his secret.

"You couldn't read it," she supplied and narrowed her gaze. "You're not telling me everything."

He removed his cap and ran his hands through his hair. "I took the attorney's call on speakerphone. The guy mentioned that the Luxes were interested in Harper and wanted to know if she wanted to pursue her own music."

Mitzi crossed her arms. "Let me guess. You said it wasn't a good time."

She knew him—faults and all.

He returned his ball cap to his head and nodded.

"Is it that you don't think she has what it takes, or is it

something else?" his manager asked like she already knew what the *something else* was.

But it wasn't that goddamned easy to answer.

"It's a lot with the press and crowds and the fans."

"It was a lot for you, Trey, and Leighton in the beginning," Mitzi countered. "What's the real reason?"

"Do you want me to say it?"

"I'd like you to be honest with yourself," she fired back.

"If Harper started making her own music, she wouldn't be able to…" He trailed off as the acrid taste of shame flooded his mouth.

"To help you with yours and ensure your transition from pop to rock went smoothly because you can't ask anyone else for help," Mitzi supplied.

Those words had rattled around in his head since Harper had hurled them at him.

To hear Mitzi repeat it added salt to the wound, but the fear of his neurodiversity getting out still ran the show. He had to keep it hidden, but he needed Harper to do it. And she sure as hell wasn't about to help his self-serving ass. And yes, he was doing this for himself. But he was also doing this for Leighton, Trey—and even Aria.

It was a goddamned paradox.

"She also wants me to be more candid about my learning issues. I can't do it, Mitzi. I won't do it."

"It amazes me that you've always seen it as a problem," Mitzi mused.

He picked up the contract and held it in front of his face. "What the hell else would you call a grown man who would take hours to read this?" he hissed, then folded the damn thing and stuffed it into his pocket. He paced in front of the piano. "Could you leave me in peace, Mitz? I messed up. I can't be the man Harper wants me to be. I don't know how I'll keep the promise I made to Trey and Leighton. There's a great chance

I'm about to cost Aria the aunt she loves and adores. I can't deal with reality quite yet, and I—"

Mitzi's phone chimed like a buzzer cutting off his tirade. The woman scanned the screen. "No, I can't leave you in peace. You've got an event."

It was as if someone had doused him with a bucket of ice-cold water.

"Today?" he shot back, shock coating the word.

"At four o'clock."

"What time is it?"

"Almost four o'clock," she barked, going into no-nonsense manager mode. "Do you have a change of clothes?"

He pinched the bridge of his nose. "No."

She took a step back and looked him over. "You're lucky you're so good-looking. Get your guitar."

"Where are we going?"

"Denver."

"For what?" he pressed like a petulant child.

"A press engagement at a nonprofit."

"A meet and greet?"

"Something like that," she said, coming to her feet. "Luxe is announcing a partnership with a Denver organization and asked if you'd do a site visit and record a few promos."

"Is this really something I need to do?" He caught his reflection in the window. "I'm a walking disaster, Mitz."

"Yes, it is. You're on thin ice. Mr. and Mrs. Luxe are a little bent out of shape since you haven't gotten back to them regarding the contract—especially after they offered you a spot at Red Rocks Unplugged. It would be a good-faith gesture to do this for them."

She was right. This was a business, and music was his job. He couldn't afford to play the aloof celebrity.

She headed out the door. "I'll be in the car. There's something we need to talk about on the drive down."

He secured the guitar in its case and followed a few steps behind. "I can't talk about Harper. I don't know how to fix what I've done. I don't even know if she'd take me back. I don't deserve her."

He pictured the signs at his concerts.

Marry Me, Landon Paige.

And his canned, corny response:

I wouldn't dare. You're too good for me.

Little did he know how true those words would turn out to be.

"I don't need to speak with you about Harper," she replied and pressed a key fob to a beefy black SUV with tinted windows.

"Then what is it?" he asked as he set his guitar on the back seat.

Mitzi climbed into the driver's seat but didn't reply right away. She exhaled an audible breath and stared at the detached garage.

He joined her up front. "What, Mitzi?"

The woman was wrestling with something.

She pegged him with her steely gaze. "We need to talk about Trey and your sister."

Jesus, Christ!

"Mitz, not now! I can't stir up the past. Let me get my head in the game. Everything I'm doing is for them."

"That's why it has to be now," she replied, starting the vehicle, and shifting into drive.

What the hell did that mean?

Trey and Leighton had been dead and buried for over two years. What more was there to say?

The gravel and dirt crunched under the weight of the wheels as they drove in silence.

Perhaps she'd decided to grant him a reprieve.

"There's something you need to know about Leighton and

Trey's wishes," she said. Her voice cracked. That wasn't the Mitzi he knew. It sounded as if she were speaking under duress.

"I know their wishes," he said, his voice taking on an agitated edge. "Why the hell do you think I've been tying myself up in knots to make our dream of going back to our original sound a reality? They'd agreed to work on the new music. I was the last person to talk to them."

"No, you weren't. I was. They called me in the car on the way to the airport."

"You?" he fired back. "Why did they call you?"

Did Mitzi know about the fight?

She kept her gaze trained on the road as they merged onto the highway. "There's no easy way to say this."

He took off his cap and ran his hands through his dark mess of hair. "Just say it. Give it to me straight."

"Trey and your sister wanted out."

"Out of what?" he rasped.

"Out of the band. Out of Heartthrob Warfare."

Chapter 37

LANDON

What the hell was Mitzi talking about?

There was no way Leighton and Trey wanted out of Heartthrob Warfare.

Mitzi wasn't making any sense. She must be mistaken.

He'd parted with Trey and Leighton on good terms.

It was supposed to be the beginning of a new era for the band.

He shook his head. "That's not true, Mitzi. They couldn't want out."

"Honey, that's what they wanted."

Anger roiled in his chest. "The last time I spoke with Leighton and Trey, we'd argued."

"I know," she said gently.

"I was angry and unloaded on them, but we worked it out."

"I know that, too."

It was as if they were talking in circles.

He scrubbed his hands down his face, then returned his cap to his head. "Then why are you saying they wanted out?"

"Leighton and Trey were going to make the new album with you, and then they wanted out."

Her words hit like a punch to the gut.

Still, she had to be wrong.

"Mitz, it was our dream to go back to our old sound. It's all we talked about until..."

He clamped his mouth shut.

Until Leighton found out she was pregnant.

His manager glanced at him. "Trey and Leighton's dreams changed."

He was figuring that out. "What was their new dream?" he asked and deflated into the seat.

"They wanted to open a music school and teach."

"A school?" he fired back as his posture went rigid.

"More like a music center for children and teens who learn like Aria." Mitzi paused. "For people like you."

He swallowed hard. "I don't believe you."

"It's the truth. They hadn't purchased a building, but they'd scouted locations in the city."

He shook his head. "No."

"Trey and Leighton asked me to have the paperwork ready to dissolve the partnership and remove them from Heartthrob Warfare once you'd completed the new album. Like I said, they were doing it for you."

It was too much.

"Everything I've done since Leighton told me she was pregnant was for them. I carried the load. I kept us in the spotlight," he bit out, trembling with emotion. "Why didn't you tell me they didn't want to keep making music?"

"Your sister made me swear I wouldn't say anything until after the three of you made the rock album. By then, she would have had everything for the school in place."

"They wanted to trick me? To make a fool of me?" he rattled off.

"No, they loved you. They wanted to show you what was possible beyond singing in stadiums. They wanted this center for Aria. They didn't want their daughter to struggle the way you struggled. And they wanted you to help them run it."

They wanted him?

That was insane.

They knew about his learning problems. For Christ's sake, they'd helped him hide his shortcomings.

But just as the damning thought crossed his mind, he recalled filling in for Bonbon Barbie as Landy Candy. That joyful recollection almost cleared the haze of anger and betrayal. But that was a single lesson—a lesson where he'd regurgitated one of Harper's sessions that he'd overheard her do with Aria.

He couldn't teach on a regular basis. What if a kid wrote him a note? What if a student cracked open a music book and pointed to something? What if he had to write on a blackboard?

"What did they think I could do in a music school?" he mumbled. "Take out the trash? Clean the windows?"

"They wanted you to be an equal partner. They believed in you," Mitzi answered.

A muscle ticked in his jaw at the mention of that word.

Believe.

"There's a folder in the glove box," Mitzi said and pointed to the compartment in front of him. "Leighton emailed their business plan to me on the way to the airport. She wanted me to work on the legalities of opening a center."

He removed the folder and glared at it. "It'll take me hours to go through it."

"No, it won't," she countered. "It's printed in Open-Dyslexic font."

And the bombs kept dropping.

"How do you know about that?" he demanded.

"My friend volunteers at a school that uses it and told me about it."

He wasn't even about to open that can of worms. Instead, he opened the folder, and Mitzi was right. He could read it. He skimmed the first line as the SUV came to a stop.

Aria's Song Music Center

He traced his fingertips across the page. Leighton and Trey had outlined an entire program working with children from grade school to high school. From recruiting teachers to referencing articles on teaching music to neurodivergent learners, his sister and Trey had thought out the entire process. There was no doubting this was important to them.

He closed the folder. "Why tell me now, Mitzi?"

She cut the ignition and held his gaze. "Because you're at a crossroads. Because you need to think about what you really want in this life. People come and go, Landon. Some breeze in and out unnoticed. Others make an impact and change everything. Trey and Leighton came to that crossroads when Aria entered their lives. They knew what they wanted. But their dreams were cut short."

He closed his eyes. "What do you want me to do now?"

Bam, bam, bam, bam!

"Sign my shirt!" came a screeching voice, followed by another set of pounding *thunks*.

He startled and stared out the passenger window at a woman with her nose pressed to the glass.

"Landon Paige, sign my shirt," she shrieked and banged a marker against the glass.

"Where are we?" he asked, gazing at throngs of people and signs with his name printed in bold lettering.

"This is the place for the PR event," Mitzi explained as a few police officers surrounded the car and got control of the crowd. "Someone in the media must have let the cat out of the bag that you'd be here."

"We're not done talking about this," he said and passed her the folder. "You should have told me sooner." He glanced at the fans, then got a look at the building, and another surprise had his jaw in his lap. "We're at New Beats. This is where Harper and I had the second Bake or Bust competition."

"Yes, of course. Did I not mention that?" Mitzi answered with a sly twist to her lips.

"Mitz," he growled. What was she up to?

"Don't forget to take your guitar."

Before he could give her hell for the omission, she opened her car door and got out.

Dammit!

He hopped out, and the crowd roared as he retrieved his guitar case from the back.

Here we go.

The press hurled questions the second he closed the back door.

"Is it over between you and Harper Presley?"

"Are you getting divorced?"

"What did you fight about in Italy?"

"Did you break her heart?"

He froze and stared at the churning mass of bodies bobbing and weaving with cameras and cell phones pointed at him like a firing squad.

"Here, Landon!" a woman with a large tote cried, bolting past the police. She wore a T-shirt with his face on it.

Wait a damn second.

He'd seen her before. But where?

Grinning from ear to ear, she reached into her bag and pressed a small cushion to his chest. "I made one for Harper. Don't let her get away," the woman said before a police officer escorted her back to the area taped off for fans.

He peered at the item in his hands. It wasn't a cushion. It

was a pillow—a pillow with Harper's face cross-stitched into the fabric.

The gift-giver was Norma Rae from Vegas. He searched the crowd to thank the woman when an airy voice called out to him.

"Landon, Landon Paige, I need to talk to you!"

He couldn't find Norma Rae, but he spied a blonde woman glistening—no, glittering—in the afternoon light.

Bang Bang Barbie?

Was that douche nozzle Vance Vibe here, too?

Mitzi came to his side.

"That's Vance's wife," he said and gestured with his chin.

"I know who she is. She's emailed me a few times."

"About what?"

"Hell if I know," Mitzi said, shaking her head. "The subject line said Naughty, Naughty Husband. God only knows what kind of virus I'd get from opening an email like that."

"Vance has no shame. Is he here?"

"No, the Luxes were very clear. They only wanted you."

Not Harper?

He stared at the cross-stitch rendering of his wife's face, and the vice gripping his heart clenched tighter.

They should be together. They were better together.

"There'll be a crew from LookyLoo inside," Mitzi said, hooking her arm with his as she gave him the rundown, and they headed toward the back entrance. "No other outside press was invited."

He nodded, then glanced over his shoulder at the sea of fans and felt...empty.

He'd loved the applause and attention when he'd shared the stage with his sister and Trey.

The same thing had happened with Harper by his side.

Why was that?

Stop!

Get out of your head and do your job. Be the heartthrob.

"Look who's here. How are you doing, honey?" Donna asked in a soothing drawl. The woman was decked out in a café-colored jumpsuit shimmering with gold and brown sequins. She looked like Bonbon Barbie's glitzy Vegas grandma.

"I've been better."

That was an understatement.

Damien joined them, sporting the matching men's version of the café-colored glitter costume. "We've seen the pictures of Harper," he said, his green eyes awash with concern.

"It's…complicated," he replied, unsure what to say about their situation.

"You look like you've lost your best friend, honey. But I believe in fate," Donna answered with a wink.

Damien nodded. "Sometimes, it requires a little facilitating."

Fate? Facilitating?

He pegged the sparkly pair with his gaze. "What did you say?"

"You look like you need something to go your way," Donna answered.

But that wasn't what they'd just said.

"You said facilitator of fate. I know someone who also uses that term," he answered and caught a glimpse of a flowing red scarf. He turned toward the flash of color, but all he saw was a group of cameramen and a woman carrying a large circular light reflector.

His gaze ping-ponged between the glittery hosts when a faint drumbeat peppered the air, followed by the strum of a guitar and then the lustrous vibration of a violin. He strained to listen as the trio played. The melody was almost there, but the instruments were competing, and the tempo was off. He glanced around. They were in the part of the building that housed the practice rooms. He and Harper had only glimpsed this area of the New Beats facility last time they were here, but he didn't see any musicians using the rooms.

A woman with a clipboard walked up to them. "Good, everyone's here. Today we'll be filming spots about LookyLoo and Luxe Media and Entertainment supporting this local music program. With Luxe's recent record label acquisition, Mr. and Mrs. Luxe tell us they'd like to highlight—"

"I'm sorry," he said, unable to focus on anything but the whispering melody, "you'll have to excuse me." He didn't want to be rude, but he knew exactly what tweaks the song needed.

"Landon?" Mitzi said with a crease on her brow.

"Give me a second." He tucked the pillow under his arm and followed the sound. Heading down a hallway, he snaked around the building until a pair of doors appeared and the sound intensified. He opened the door and slipped into the room.

He'd been here.

It was the intimate concert hall where the second challenge had taken place. He spied the musicians on stage, lit by the spotlight. It was odd to see it from this vantage point. He was always the one lit in a flurry of spotlights. He walked down the aisle toward the stage.

"Maybe we should try it in a different key?" a guy suggested from the second row.

It wasn't that.

"You're in the right key, and you've got a great post-grunge sound," he said, jogging down the aisle, then taking the steps to the stage. He set the pillow on a stool. "I'd suggest changing the tempo and fine-tuning the resonance. You're looking for harmony and balance, but I hear three distinct instruments, not one cohesive sound."

A young woman with pink braids holding a violin, a guy with spiky blond hair on the drums, and a woman with dark ringlets framing her face holding a guitar stared at him wide-eyed.

Holy shit! He recognized them. They'd asked questions during the Q and A.

"Do you remember me?" he asked.

"Everyone remembers you. You're Landon Paige. You're crazy famous," the girl with pink braids answered.

He could help them. But he had to put them at ease.

"Just think of me as another musician. What are your names?"

"I'm Kai," the guy said, looking shell-shocked. "DeeDee is on the violin, and May is on guitar."

"All right, Kai, DeeDee, and May, listen to this." He opened his guitar case and removed his instrument. "I'll play your original melody, but I'll slow it down. Kai, I want you to come in first. But you don't need to beat the hell out of the drum kit."

The kid chuckled.

"But don't be afraid to let me know you're there," he continued. "Imagine walking into a room and feeling out the vibe. That's the energy you want to put into it." He played the melody on his guitar, then nodded to Kai. The guy came in sharper and provided the perfect base layer. "That's it," he said, nodding to the drummer. "May, you're next. You're going to come in smooth. Picture gentle waters. There's nothing choppy. Only the ebb and flow."

"Got it," she said, joining in.

And there it was.

That tingle. That synergy of sound. The connectedness he'd felt with his sister, Trey, and Harper.

He swallowed past the emotion in his throat. "DeeDee, you're up. Start a measure behind. The contrast in the notes will add the right nuance."

The woman positioned the violin at her chin, raised the bow, and followed his instructions.

The air shimmered as ripples of sound pulsed through the space. The notes ceased being notes and became storytellers. They carried a narrative. They delivered an emotional message. The instruments melded together, and the melody expanded and contracted like a living organism.

He took a step back and stopped playing. "This is all you. Keep going," he said, tapping his foot and keeping the beat. "You found it. This is the sweet spot."

The musicians beamed and surrendered to the tweaked melody. They played it through once, twice, and a third time before he signaled for them to wrap it up.

Kai pressed his drumsticks to his chest. "That was incredible."

"How did we do that?" DeeDee asked, staring at her violin as if she were seeing it for the first time.

"That was taking a risk, facing what scared you, and following your gut. That was living your truth through music," he answered. He hadn't formulated the response. It hadn't come from his head—that's for damn sure. The words had come from his heart.

He pictured Harper's face.

When she visited him in his dreams, he could only see the anguish in her eyes. But the image that came to him now carried no pain or disappointment. He imagined watching her sleep during those few seconds before she would awaken each morning. He'd roll onto his side, gaze down at her, and twist a lock of her hair around his finger. She'd smile a sweet ghost of a grin as she open her eyes, and he'd see his forever in her pools of hazel.

"Mr. Paige, could you write that out for us?" Kai asked.

"What?" he stammered.

"We have a tough time doing that," May added and reached for a notebook.

He snapped back to reality, and the warmth of Harper's memory evaporated.

What was he supposed to do?

"You want me to write the notes because it's hard for you?" he asked, working to keep his voice even.

The teens stared at the floor. The crackle of excitement seeped out of the room as an emotion took hold—an emotion he knew well.

Shame.

May tugged at one of her ringlets. "We're kind of crap when it comes to getting out our ideas."

"What May means is that we're a bunch of dumbasses," DeeDee explained.

He could not allow them to see themselves this way. But he needed more information.

"Have you always had trouble getting your ideas out?" he asked gently.

The teens nodded.

"We met in remedial English Lit class last year when we were seniors in high school," Kai explained. "We bonded over being in the foster care system and pretty much sucking at school."

"School was never our thing," May continued. "We graduated by the skin of our teeth, got in a little trouble with the law, and ended up getting referred to New Beats."

Jesus, had he not had his sister to help him get through school, he could have had the same outcome.

DeeDee brushed her pink braids behind her shoulders. "We're trying to make it as a band, but it's hard when the notes in our heads don't translate to the page. It's even trickier to go back and remember a melody after we've changed it a bunch. That's why we like your wife's Bonbon Barbie channel on

LookyLoo. She breaks down reading music into manageable pieces."

"Our dream is to be a trio like Heartthrob Warfare," Kai added.

May twisted one of her ringlets. "But we might not make it."

He was so much like these kids.

He held the girl's gaze. "Why do you say that?"

"Everyone at New Beats is great, and we've learned a ton since we started coming here. But how can we say we're professional musicians if we can barely read music?"

The kids looked at him like he had all the answers.

They wanted his guidance.

He couldn't lie to them, and more than that, he understood the shame and fear.

One by one, he made eye contact with each teen. "Would you call me a professional musician?"

The kids laughed.

"Of course, you're Landon Paige," DeeDee answered. "You write lyrics and melodies people have loved for years and years. Your concerts sell out. You're known across the globe."

He stared at the young musicians, and he stood at a crossroads.

He remembered Mitzi's words.

A calmness washed over him.

He had two choices.

He could nod and allow the kids to believe he'd written the songs without help, or he could do something he'd never done. Something worthy of a double-dog dare. He could cast his fears aside and allow these teens to see the real Landon Paige.

He was a gifted musician.

And he was a neurodivergent learner.

For the first time, he understood that these truths could exist in tandem.

It didn't have to be one or the other.

What would the music world say?

He didn't care.

As long as he had the love and support of two feisty, spirited gals, he could claim musical victory.

This was the way to honor Trey and Leighton.

He glanced at the piano and pictured Harper.

If he wanted her to believe in him, he had to embrace the truth about who he was at his core and accept—no, embrace—how his mind worked.

He thought of Aria. The child was gifted beyond measure.

And she was like him.

If he wanted the kid to believe in herself, he had to lead by example.

And that started here with these teens.

"I didn't write the lyrics and music for Heartthrob Warfare on my own. My sister and my best friend were a huge part of the process. Like you, it's a struggle for me to read and write. That extends to penning musical notation."

"No way," Kai breathed, sharing a shocked look with the girls.

"You have a learning disability?" DeeDee asked.

"Someone much smarter than me doesn't call it a learning disability. She calls it neurodiversity. Our brains work a little differently than most people's minds," he answered.

"Are you talking about your wife?" May asked.

"I am."

DeeDee twisted the end of her braid. "Bonbon Barbie—well, Harper—never said you were like her."

Here it was. The moment of truth.

"I've never spoken about it because—up until about ten minutes ago—I thought it made me look weak. But being here with you, with other neurodiverse musicians, I see that neurodiversity isn't a weakness. It's a strength. Look at the music you made. That's a gift. What we have is a gift. And we have to see the value in ourselves. Otherwise, we're stuck. Creativity can't flow when we're worried about what others will think of us. We don't have to go it alone. We don't have to hide, and there's no shame in asking for help."

Faint applause echoed in the concert hall.

Who was here?

Besides the kids on the stage, the place had been empty when he'd entered.

Clearly, that had changed.

He shielded his eyes and watched Mitzi, Donna, and Damien clap as they made their way to the stage.

"That was quite a performance," Mitzi said and gifted him with a wide grin.

"These musicians are talented," he said, nodding to the teens.

Donna and Damien chatted with DeeDee, May, and Kai, while Mitzi made a beeline his way.

"That was some pep talk." She waved him down and lowered her voice. "Those kids could share what you've divulged with the press."

"They could."

"You're okay with that?"

"Yeah, I'm more than okay," he answered.

Donna yipped an excited yeehaw. "My, oh, my! Giddy up and go!" the glittery woman crooned, patting the teens on their cheeks. "I see rock stars in this room, Damien."

"As do I," her sparkly companion replied. "Do you kids have a LookyLoo page? You should share your music with the world."

The teens' wide grins disappeared.

"We shut ours down after Vance Vibe stole one of our songs," May said as the kids bristled.

Stop the goddamned presses.

"Vance stole your music?" he asked as a door somewhere behind the stage slammed shut.

"He's done it to lots of smaller artists," Kai explained. "People are too scared to go after the guy. Lawyers cost money, and we can barely scrape enough cash together to get bus fare to come here."

"Do you have proof? Video, audio, anything with time-stamps?" Mitzi asked.

"Yeah, we're nineteen. Our whole lives are on our phones," DeeDee answered as a familiar clickity-click echoed from backstage.

The velvet curtain behind the drum kit parted, and freaking Bang Bang Barbie appeared.

"It's true! What they're telling you is true," she exclaimed. "Sorry to break in like this. I snuck in through the stage door. But you need to know that Vance is a bad, bad man. He wanted to cheat and buy macarons from another bakery when my macarons didn't come out for the second challenge, and he spends hours online watching smaller, obscure bands. He takes their music and records it as his own. He's got it on his laptop."

He knew it! The guy was a fraud. And now, if Barbie was right, there was proof.

"Vance Vibe is a—" he began, but before he could say *douche nozzle*, the curtain parted again, and his jaw dropped.

"Vance Vibe is a cheater, cheater, pumpkin eater. He stole my aunt Harper's music, too, and I can prove it."

Chapter 38

LANDON

"Aria?" he exclaimed.

He didn't know how she'd gotten here from Italy, but his niece was a sight for sore eyes.

The kid ran toward him. Her backpack swayed from side to side. She moved like an Olympic sprinter, then threw herself into the air like she was going for a long jump record.

He scrambled to flip his guitar to his back and caught her as Bess and Tomás emerged from behind the curtain.

He embraced the little girl and pressed a kiss to the top of her head. "What are you doing here? You should be in Italy."

"We had to come back, Uncle Landy."

"Why?" he asked, turning to his foster parents.

"Because you need us, honey," Bess answered.

Tomás wrapped his arm around Bess. "We care about you and Harper, and we uncovered something that might help her."

What could they have uncovered?

Before he could ask, Aria peered into the audience and shielded her eyes. "Hey, Ms. Malone, special helper lady, are you coming?"

Special helper lady?

And just like that, Madelyn walked down the aisle. "Hello, Aria, dear. Nice to see you, Bess and Tomás. I hope you had a pleasant flight to Denver."

Madelyn was here. He wasn't crazy.

He turned to his niece. "Why did you call her special helper lady?"

"She comes into my class sometimes. Usually, this nice old lady called Mrs. Bergen helps my teacher. But a few times, Ms. Malone has come in."

"It's a community outreach partnership with Whitmore and Denver businesses. I've filled in a few times for my friend Harriett."

He didn't care if she was filling in for the Queen of England. He had no idea she'd been doing that. "You never mentioned any special helpers, Aria."

She gave him an Aria-special shoulder shrug. "I'm busy, Uncle Landy. I'm in second grade."

"Okay." He pegged Madelyn with his gaze. "You could have said something."

"I'm busy, Uncle Landy. I'm a nanny matchmaker," the smirking woman tossed back, channeling the Aria shrug.

God help him!

"Little lady, if you've got proof that Vance Vibe is stealing other artists' music, we need to see it," Damien said. Except, he'd lost the southern drawl. He tugged at his nose, and...holy hell...he popped the sucker clean off.

"What is that?" Aria exclaimed. "You've got two noses, mister!"

"It's a state-of-the-art prosthetic," the man replied. "I use them when I go undercover."

Undercover?

"Who are you, and what can you do about Vance Vibe?" he asked.

Before he could utter another word, Donna whipped the giant Dolly Parton wig clean off her head and revealed silver hair twisted into a low bun. "We can do quite a bit," she answered without a trace of her buttery southern accent.

Had he accidentally ingested thirty of Tanner's lollipops?

"Who are you people?"

Madelyn sauntered across the stage and stood between Donna and Damien. "Landon Paige, may I introduce Warren and Lizzy Luxe."

No way!

"You're Mr. and Mrs. Luxe? The owners of the Luxe Grandiose and LookyLoo?"

"We are," Donna—no, Lizzy—answered.

He still couldn't understand what they were doing, moonlighting as sparkly southern internet personalities.

"Why are you dressed like that?"

"Lizzy and I got our start in show business on the Strip in Vegas," Damien—no, freaking Warren Luxe—explained.

Lizzy Luxe nodded. "And we use our skills to covertly assess our investment endeavors."

"We don't get the full picture as Mr. and Mrs. Luxe," Warren continued. "But as reality show co-hosts or even working in our hotel as a bellhop or a hostess, we get an untainted view of our businesses."

Landon eyed the matchmaker. "And you knew about this?"

The woman offered another nonchalant shrug, then adjusted that damned red scarf. "I know many people. The Luxes have been friends of mine for years, and our *endeavors* aligned."

He could use thirty of Tanner's lollipops right about now. He was all for requesting a slice of ceiling cake and then being put to bed.

"We're also the new owners of the record label that represents you and Vance Vibe," Lizzy Luxe purred as she removed a prosthetic chin.

Her chin!

These people took hiding their identity to another level.

"Sparkly nose guy and chin lady," Aria called and wiggled out of his arms. "Check out my proof."

His niece unzipped her backpack and removed Harper's old video recorder and a photograph. He stared at the creased picture. It was the photo of Harper and Vance he'd seen the first night they'd spent in Baxter Park. He'd thrust the damn thing into his pocket. He was supposed to dispose of it, but he'd forgotten about it.

"Where did you get that, Aria?"

"Your pants. I also found some of Aunt Harper's underwear. I thought you said it was a doily."

Busted.

"What's so special about the picture, Aria?" Mrs. Luxe asked, pulling the attention from his panty problem.

"The date on the back of the picture. My friend Phoebe is practicing to be a secret spy, and she told me details matter."

Mr. Luxe nodded. "They most certainly do."

"The date on this picture matches the date that flashes on the video, and the people are wearing the same clothes. My Lolo and Lala helped me with the math. It's from six years and four days ago. Here, Uncle Landy."

Aria handed him the picture, opened the camcorder's viewfinder, and hit play.

A scowling Harper stared into the camera. "Vance, stop messing around with that old thing. I doubt it even works."

"Why? I'm bored," Vance whined.

"Well, I'm trying to work."

"I'm hungry. I'm getting a pizza."

"You don't want to help me write this song?"

"Nah, letting you do the work is more fun. Keep fighting the good fight, Harper."

Off-camera, a door opened and closed.

Harper shook her head and turned to her keyboard. Unaware that the device was still recording, she pulled out a highlighter, ran it across a page of sheet music, then proceeded to sing "Every Time You Break My Heart" just as she'd sung it during the first challenge.

"Look at the picture, Uncle Landy. The sheet music in the video has the same highlighter marks on it," Aria, the super-sleuth, explained. "Then me, Lolo, and Lala checked the internet. That mean old Vance Vibe came out with the song five years ago. He didn't write it. He took it and pretended it was his."

There was no disputing it. Aria had cracked the case.

"You're one smart cookie, Aria Paige-Grant," he said, smiling at this powerhouse of a kid.

She tapped her forehead. "It's my neurodivergent brain. It's like a secret weapon. Sometimes, it makes letters and numbers wiggle around, but it also helps me play music, write songs, and connect pieces of information."

Her secret weapon. He liked that.

Mrs. Luxe crossed her arms. "I had a bad feeling about that Vance Vibe."

"Can we borrow the video recorder and the photograph, young lady?" Mr. Luxe asked.

Aria eyed the glittery pair. "This stuff belongs to my Aunt Harper. She trusted me with it. Do you promise to give it back, sparkle people?" She pressed, giving them a slice of side-eye.

Mr. Luxe suppressed a grin and shared a look with his wife. "You have our word, Aria."

"Here," Barbie said, pulling a zip drive from her cleavage. "I almost forgot. There's more proof on this."

The Luxes thanked Barbie, then waved DeeDee, May, and

Kai over. "Could we talk privately? We'd like to hear more about Vance Vibe."

The group migrated to the side of the stage and spoke in hushed tones.

It gave him a second to catch his breath and take in his incredible niece. "You did something really kind for Harper."

A coy grin stretched across her lips. "You mean *Aunt* Harper."

He looked into her blue eyes, and his stomach dropped. "About that—"

"Oh, I know, Uncle Landy," she said, waving him off.

He frowned. "What do you think you know?"

"My friends told me to watch out because you were gonna mess up real bad with Aunt Harper."

"What?" he eked out.

"Yep, I was waiting for it. And then, in Italy, on the day you said Aunt Harper had to go back to Denver early, Phoebe emailed me a bunch of pictures of Harper hiding in the bathroom looking like she'd been crying a bunch—and not the happy kind of crying. I figured it was your fault," she finished rather brightly.

"Um…"

She narrowed her gaze. "Was it your fault, Uncle Landy?"

He couldn't lie to the kid. "Yes."

"Were you a…?" Aria asked and tapped three times for douche nozzle.

"Yeah."

The little girl nodded solemnly, then glanced at Madelyn. "Are they here?" Aria asked.

Madelyn slipped her cell from her purse. "They're arriving now."

Aria raised her hands and cupped them around her mouth. "Eraser club kids, it's time for operation Win Back the Aunt."

He was startled when the curtain flew open and Phoebe, Oscar, and Sebastian charged onto the stage.

That curtain was like one of those clown cars.

"Who else is back there?" he asked. "Santa Claus? The Tooth Fairy? The Easter Bunny?"

"No, mate," Raz said, pocketing his cell phone as he crossed the stage. "It's the nerd, the hothead, and the beefcake."

"Why are you guys here?" he asked, looking from Erasmus to Rowen and then to Mitch.

"Your niece," Mitch replied and shared a fist bump with Aria.

"She's quite a kid," Rowen added.

"Aria, what's going on?"

"We stopped at Whitmore after our plane got here. School was getting out, and I told them I needed reinforcements."

"Were you right, Aria? Was your uncle a?" Phoebe asked and tapped her little foot twice.

He looked to Rowen. "What's her word?"

"Butthole," the nerd whispered back.

"It's worse than that. I think my uncle was a..." Aria said to the kids and tapped five times.

They gasped.

What was five syllables that had these kids looking like he'd kicked a puppy?

"What did she tap?"

"A douche nozzle butthole," Phoebe translated, wide-eyed.

"That's super-duper bad," Oscar chimed and snapped a photo of him with his Polaroid camera.

Jesus, that thing was bright.

He blinked away the black spots from the powerful flash.

"But don't worry," Sebastian remarked, then pressed his hands into a prayer position. "The donkeys know."

Donkeys?

He stared·at the curtain. "Are your donkeys about to come out on stage?"

"No, I'm talking about your journey, boyo," Sebastian corrected, losing his prim British accent and speaking in his father's gruffer cadence. "You've got to harness your chi and change the trajectory of your energy. And if that doesn't work, do a handstand until you figure out what to do."

"Sebastian," Phoebe huffed, "donkey yoga stuff won't work for Aria's uncle. It worked for your dad. Aria's uncle's fix-it has to be special and just for him."

This was going off the rails fast.

"I'm confused," he said, looking from kid to kid when Phoebe released an exasperated groan.

The child checked her fingernails like she was bored to tears. "Our dads and uncles aren't super quick when it comes to this kind of stuff, are they, Ms. Classroom Helper Lady?" Phoebe finished, sharing a look with Madelyn Malone.

The nanny matchmaker replied with a little wink.

Who didn't have a secret side plan for his love life?

Aria took his hand and squeezed it. "You've got to do something big for Aunt Harper to prove you're not a douche nozzle butthole."

"And you've got a lot to prove, mate. I saw Harper a few hours ago," Raz added.

"You saw her?" he rasped, and his heart jumped into his throat.

The beefcake shifted his stance. "Don't get mad, but I helped kidnap her."

"What?"

He raised his hands defensively. "She's fine. She's not tied up in some basement. Libby, Penny, and Charlotte asked me to do it. They needed to talk to her, and she wasn't calling them back."

"Is she okay? How'd she look?"

Raz cringed. "Like a ballerina crossed with a chocolate-obsessed feral cat, but she was wearing your black shirt, mate. The one she married you in. That must count for something. And she smelled god-awful. So I assume she'd been wearing it for a while."

"That's good, Uncle Landy. That means she misses you."

"I miss her," he confessed.

"Let's get her back," Aria announced. "What do we need to do?" the kid asked her friends.

"What does she care about?" Oscar pressed and snapped another picture.

"What balances her chi?" Sebastian continued.

Aria tapped her chin. "She loves chocolate, but it has to be more than unlimited bonbons for the rest of her life. But... Uncle Landy?"

"Yeah?"

"I would like unlimited bonbons for the rest of my life for my birthday," the kid quipped.

"Noted," he answered.

This entire scene was bonkers, but the kids were right. Whatever he did, it had to be big.

"Maybe this will help," Rowen said, adjusting his glasses. "Penny's a writer, so Phoebe and I wrote a story about her and read it at the writing competition."

"Dude," he said, shaking his head. "I was there."

"And I started a whole charity and culinary education program because of Charlotte," Mitch added.

Did these guys have amnesia?

"Again, Mitch, I know. I was there. I set up the music for your big food truck reveal."

"And I'm a great big slice of beefcake. What woman wouldn't like that?" Raz snarked.

Everyone eyed the boxer.

"Fine, you blokes know what I did for Libby. I won the

bloody heavyweight championship and figured out a way to honor Meredith and be a better dad. Honestly, mates, we'd be lost without these women. They make us better men."

"Are they just figuring this out?" Phoebe asked the kids.

"Raz," he said, exasperation coating the word. "I was there. I've been there for all of you."

For a beat, no one spoke.

"And that's why we're here," Mitch said and clapped him on the shoulder. "We owe you, and we can't imagine having to hang out with your wife without you being around to run defense."

"She's terrifying, mate. I know she's a musician, but she'd kill it in the ring," Raz teased, but his expression grew earnest. "All kidding aside. We know one thing for sure. You and Harper are meant to be together, and we're here to help."

Who would have thought that the nerd, the hothead, the beefcake, and the heartthrob would go from being not-friends friends to the men who had each other's backs?

He nodded to the guys. "Thank you."

"All right, Uncle Landy, you love Aunt Harper," Aria mused as she paced across the stage. "What could you do that would make her cry happy tears like when I gave her the tickets to Italy? What's something she really wants with all her heart? Here," she said, removing the piano eraser from her pocket and handing it to him. "This will help you use your brave heart muscles."

He stared at the tiny thing.

"We should start thinking of ideas," Phoebe announced.

The space exploded with overlapping voices.

Everyone here was ready to help him.

A deep sense of gratitude washed over him as an idea sparked.

He scanned the space.

Mr. Luxe chatted with the New Beats students and Barbie, but Mrs. Luxe had stepped away to take a call.

He took a step back and concentrated on the piano—the same piano Harper had played during the second challenge when they'd come up with the romance scale of devotion tune. He could hear her voice.

"But it's not things that she really needs. It's the unspoken promise, the tender deeds that show her what she really means, baby, on the romance scale of devotion."

He knew how to show her what she meant to him.

She'd double-dog dared him to prove he was the man for her.

And that's what he was going to do.

Years ago, when his sister had looked at the Scrabble board and called out the words *heartthrob* and *warfare*, she'd said heartthrob warfare meant going to war to fight for what made your heart sing.

He was ready to fight for love.

He was prepared to face his fears and embrace his truth. And if that also allowed him to get revenge on the man who'd stolen his beloved wife's music—that was the icing on the ceiling cake.

"I've got it," he whispered as the plan came together, but the others didn't hear him. "It's not a thing. It's a double-dog dare," he cried at the top of his lungs.

The conversations stopped as all eyes fell on him.

"Do you have an idea, Uncle Landy? Can we go see Aunt Harper now?" Aria asked.

He shook his head. "Not quite yet." He crossed the stage. "Mr. Luxe, the third challenge is still on, right?"

"Yes, but we'll have to deal with the accusations regarding Vance right after."

"What if I had a plan to expose Vance, grab blockbuster

ratings for LookyLoo, and help me win my wife back?" he offered.

"This plan sounds awfully theatrical," Warren Luxe answered with a curious twist to his lips.

Good! The guy was intrigued.

"It's over-the-top. But I'd need to have input on the third Bake or Bust Challenge. I don't know what's happening with Vance and Barbie, but Harper needs the prize money to pay off a loan to keep her grandmother's house. We have to be able to compete."

Lizzie Luxe joined them. "Harper's financial situation has changed dramatically."

"How would you know that?"

"I just got off the phone with her."

"She called you."

A smile spread across the woman's face. "She did. She's a showstopper, the real deal. She's going to be a star."

A star.

Harper had done it. She'd faced her fears and taken the leap. His heart swelled. But he couldn't get too caught up in the moment. He needed to set the stage and turn up the dial on the romance scale of devotion.

"Mr. and Mrs. Luxe, my niece was right. I screwed up with Harper, and I have to prove what she means to me. But I'll need your help. We're four days away from the final challenge."

"We are," Lizzie Luxe replied.

"I've got an idea, but it hinges on the challenge. Can you share anything about it with me without breaking the rules?"

"The third challenge is the bonbon challenge," Warren Luxe replied.

"That's why we're wearing these fantastic sparkly, chocolate-inspired costumes. Donna and Damien were going to announce it today," Lizzie supplied.

"The bonbon challenge," he repeated.

It had to be a sign.

"Everyone, I'm going to need your help."

"Even us?" Kai asked.

"Absolutely."

Barbie cocked her head to the side. "And me, too?"

"You've really come through for us, Barbie. Thank you," he said, then scanned the group. Something felt off, and he knew why.

There was one other person he needed to pull this off.

He patted his pocket, feeling for his phone, and found the botched contract. He could deal with that as well. "Aria, I need you to hold onto this. We're going to fix it on the plane."

"The plane?" Aria echoed. "Are we going on a trip?"

"We sure are. I need to talk to somebody who loves your Aunt Harper. And I need a cell—"

He hadn't even gotten the word out when Rowen slipped a phone from his pocket. "You better answer this one."

"I will. Thank you." He turned to Mitzi. "Could you call the pilot and have my jet ready?"

"No need," Madelyn said smoothly as she adjusted her scarf. "My plane is fueled and on standby. All the pilot requires is a destination. I assume you're headed to New Mexico."

This woman was good.

"We are. Would I be correct in assuming that you have the address for where we need to go once we land?"

A sly grin spread across the woman's lips. "You would be correct."

He stared at the nanny matchmaker. "How did you orchestrate this? Does that scarf have magical powers?"

She chuckled. "I'm not a fairy godmother or a magician, and this scarf is just a scarf. I'm simply a facilitator of—"

"—fate," the guys answered.

She waved him in. "Sometimes, nanny matchmaking

requires the nuclear approach. I must say, your case offered more than a few obstacles."

"But you said you couldn't work with me because I wasn't a single male caregiver."

She shrugged. "You'd already paid, and my fee is nonrefundable. And I do love a good challenge. Go on. You and Aria have a date with destiny." She patted his cheek. "My work is done. Everything that happens from this point on depends solely upon you."

Chapter 39
HARPER

"Sweet, so sweet, hello, to my favorite treat."

With a box of bonbons, her cell phone, and an envelope tucked under her arm, Harper sang her bakery bonbon tune softly and stepped onto her front porch. She inhaled a breath of cool air.

Fall had arrived in the Mile-High City, and October in Denver might as well be called *Leaf-tober*. She peered down the tree-lined street, taking in the canopy of brilliant fiery reds, golden yellows, and burnt oranges. She'd rarely appreciated the view from this spot, which was a shame. From this west-facing vantage point, one could see the outline of the down-town skyscrapers with the white-tipped peaks of the Rocky Mountains framing the view. She turned her attention to the front steps—steps that used to be the reminder of the little girl nobody wanted.

Now, they were part of her story—a string of lyrics in her song.

A song that didn't have an ending...yet.

She sat on the middle step, set the bakery box and the envelope next to her, then tapped the email icon on her phone

KRISTA SANDOR

and scrolled to the message from Richard P. Snodgrass, previously known to her as the annoying jerk from the bank. His calls and emails used to trigger sheer panic, but not anymore. She opened an email from the day before and peered at the attached image of a loan statement.

Balance Due: $0.00

She reached into the pastry box, popped a sweet treat into her mouth, and let relief sink in.

Nobody, especially not some guy named Richard P. Snodgrass, had any claim to the house her grandparents had purchased years ago.

She'd done it. She'd saved the day.

Four days ago, sitting on a swing with the support of her friends, she'd called the number on the shiny black business card and told Mrs. Luxe she was ready to reach for the stars.

Hours later, she'd opened an email with the subject line: Luxe Media and Entertainment Contract. They'd offered the same terms as Landon's contract—full control of the rights to her songs and to the sound recordings. An artist couldn't ask for anything more.

But there was more.

A bonus.

A one hundred thousand dollar signing bonus.

That gave her plenty of cash to pay off Babs' loan and put a little money aside.

Was she relieved?

Of course.

Was she also shaking in her brown Bonbon Barbie boots over taking the leap to pursue her dreams of becoming a singer and songwriter?

Absolutely.

But her friends were right. It was up to her to decide who she was, and fear of rejection wouldn't hold her back.

She had to become the person she was supposed to be.

She had to believe in herself.

She closed the email and scrolled through her inbox. Today was supposed to be the day of the *Celebrity Bake or Bust's* third and final challenge, but she hadn't received any information, nor had she heard from Landon.

She set her phone on the step and gazed at the diamond on her left hand. Her heart ached for Landon and Aria. She'd spent the last four days holed up in the living room. She'd slept on the couch, not because she couldn't bear to go upstairs but because she'd channeled her emotions into music. Composing from early in the morning until late at night, she'd sit on the piano bench, where her legs once dangled, and allow her fingers to dance across the keys. Lyrics and melodies came to her faster than she could get them down.

But a girl had to eat...eventually.

Armed with bonbons, she'd wander upstairs, stand in her bedroom, and close her eyes. She could smell the scent of Aria's shampoo in the air and hear the whispers of Landon singing the girl to sleep. She'd give herself that moment to imagine their presence, and then she'd get back to her piano.

She'd been furious with Landon, but that anger had cooled into a guarded sense of hope—hope that the man, her husband, would see his value and embrace it.

She closed her eyes, inhaled the crisp fall air, then nearly jumped out of her skin when a voice called out, "Do you ever take off that shirt?"

She blinked and spied Schuman Sweet walking up the path toward the porch.

Relieved to see a friendly face, she smiled at the man and touched the hem of Landon's black shirt.

Yeah, she was still wearing it, but she'd tossed it in the washing machine last night.

She gathered her things and came to her feet. "Don't

worry, Mr. Sweet. It's clean. You won't drop dead from the smell."

"I see you got the delivery," he said and tapped the box. "Mary Jane insisted I send over some bonbons and a few extra for being a good helper."

"How's she doing?"

"She's been fairly lucid these past couple of days since your impromptu concert."

"I'm glad to hear it." She glanced down the road. She didn't see a car. Schuman must have walked here from the bakery. "Are you here for the third challenge? It's supposed to be today, but you don't have any ingredients. Is Tanner coming with them?"

He held her gaze, then turned his attention to the envelope. "What's that?" he asked, ignoring her questions.

She stared at Aria's handwriting. "Aria made it."

"May I take a look?"

She handed it over. Gently, Schuman removed the contents and studied the tickets.

"Your niece is a special little girl."

Your niece.

She wasn't sure how much longer she'd hold that title but steadied herself and mustered a grin. "She's a terrific kid."

Schuman glanced down the street, checked his watch, then shifted his stance. He handed back the tickets and gestured toward the front door. "I might have left something in your house when I was here for the last challenge."

It had been nearly two weeks since they'd made macarons in her kitchen.

She studied the man. "Okay."

"Do you mind if I take a look inside?"

The man was acting awfully strange.

"No, not at all. Where are my manners? Would you like a drink?" she asked and started toward the porch.

"I'd take a glass of water."

She juggled the items in her hands, nudged open the door, then gestured for him to enter.

"I'll peek around," he said as she headed to the kitchen, and he peeled off toward the staircase.

She set her things on the table, grabbed a glass, and went to the faucet. As she turned on the tap, she heard footsteps above on the second floor.

She was pretty sure the man hadn't ventured upstairs the last time he was in the house.

"What do you think you left here, Mr. Sweet?" she called and filled the glass.

"I found what I needed and I do have information regarding the final challenge," he called from the hallway. "I'll meet you outside."

Outside?

"What about your drink?" she asked as the front door slammed.

Had this man gotten into Tanner's special lollipops?

She followed him onto the porch and nearly dropped the glass. Schuman Sweet stood in the middle of her front yard with a ladies' shoebox in his hands. And it didn't belong to him. She recognized the box. It held the black high-heeled shoes her grandmother used to wear when she was playing with the symphony.

What the hell did Mr. Sweet want with her grandmother's shoes?

"Listen, Mr. Sweet, if wearing ladies' heels is your thing, I'm totally good with that, but you don't have to steal my grandma's shoes."

There's a sentence she'd never expected to say.

The man's handlebar mustache twitched, and he broke out into laughter.

"You're kind of freaking me out. Did you get into your nephew's candy stash?"

"No, a friend asked for this. It'll help with the challenge."

Yep, this guy wasn't firing on all cylinders.

"Don't we need to start baking for the challenge?" She glanced at the house. "I'm not sure if Landon will show up, but I'm here, and you're here. We can do this together."

"Landon's taken care of everything. He's already prepared for the third challenge."

She took a step back. "What?"

"It's all in hand, Harper."

"Have you seen him?" she asked as the kernel of hope in her heart warmed.

"I have."

"And is he…? How does he…?" she blathered.

"Why don't you drink that glass of water," the man offered.

"Good idea," she said and downed the liquid.

"Landon's doing well. He's been busy."

"Will he be at the challenge?"

Schuman nodded.

"What's the challenge?"

A grin spread across the baker's face. "It's the bonbon challenge."

"Bonbons," she whispered as a black SUV barreled down the street, then came to a screeching halt in front of the house.

Mr. Sweet took the glass from her hand and set it on the porch. "By the way, that's our ride."

She eyed the beast of a vehicle. "Are you sure? Babs drilled into my head the lesson of not getting into a stranger's car."

As if on a creepy car cue, the back passenger side window lowered.

Now she understood how Charlotte thought she'd been kidnapped, because this whole scenario felt hella kidnapp-y.

She peered into the car but couldn't see the occupants.

"Hey, whoever you are, my grandmother taught me not to talk to strangers, so piss off."

"Watch your language, little miss."

Only one person on the planet called her little miss, and that person wasn't supposed to return from New Mexico for a week.

She jammed her left hand into the pocket of her jean shorts and glared at Mr. Sweet. "Did you tell on me about the bonbons?"

Babs leaned forward and looked out the window. "The bonbons are the least of your problems, missy. Get in."

Schuman opened the door for her, and she climbed into the SUV next to her grandmother as Schuman got into the front seat.

The window closed, and the car continued down the street.

What was she supposed to say?

What did Babs know?

And why had she rolled up in a beefy black SUV with tinted windows like a mafia boss?

"Harper Barbara," the woman said in her *you've got some explaining to do, young lady* voice.

She plastered a grin on her lips. "Hey, Babs! You're back a little early. How was New Mexico?"

"Enlightening, thanks to a visit I received a few days ago."

"Enlightening, how?" she pressed, going for nonchalance, but her octave-jumping opera voice killed the easy-going vibe.

Her grandmother crossed her arms. "Why did you tell me you had the loan situation under control? I assumed you were negotiating a payment plan. You should have told me how serious it was."

She gazed into her grandmother's hazel eyes. There wasn't much use in lying.

She leaned back into the plush leather seat. "I didn't want

you to worry. I wanted to take care of you like grandad would have."

"Your grandfather might have been better with numbers, but he would have told me. We were a team."

"I know. I'm sorry. But I was able to pay off the loan. I signed a contract with a record label, and they gave me a signing bonus."

Babs nodded. "We'll get to that, missy."

"You know about the contract?"

"I do, and there's another legal document I've recently learned about."

"Another legal document?"

Babs narrowed her gaze. "A marriage license."

Oh boy.

"Take your hand out of your pocket, Harper Barbara."

She complied and allowed her grandmother to inspect the rings.

"I don't even know where to start, Babs."

"Let me help you, dear. You married your teenage pop crush, Landon Bartholomew Paige, in Las Vegas, Nevada, after being rejected by an internet pornography performer competition."

Her jaw dropped. "Um...yeah, that's technically correct, but I'm going to have to ask that you never utter the words *internet pornography performer competition* ever again. And who have you been talking to?" She wracked her brain. She hadn't connected with her friends since they'd kidnapped her. She'd been so wrapped up in her music that she'd shut out the world. Could Penny, Charlotte, and Libby have gone to see Babs? If anyone could track a person down, it was Penny's tech nerd fiancé. But she had a feeling it wasn't them.

"You've been busy, little miss. Not only did you become Landon's wife, but you also became an aunt."

"I did," she answered, and her gaze grew glassy. "I became

Aria's aunt. She's a spitfire of a little thing. She's got attitude for miles. She loves bonbons as much as I do, and she's—"

"—a gifted musician," Babs supplied.

Did her grandmother suddenly become a mind reader?

"How would you know that, Babs?"

"I met her."

"When?"

"Three days ago. Aria finds it quite amusing that I play the harp, and your name is Harper, but you play the piano."

That kid.

"Yeah, she's funny like that." She brushed a tear from her cheek. "I'm guessing Aria didn't take a plane to New Mexico and track you down on her own."

"No, she came with her uncle."

"What did he say?"

"He apologized for marrying you without asking for my blessing."

"To be fair, it happened quickly. We got double-dog—"

"—dared," Babs said. "Yes, he showed me your wedding video and pictures from the event."

"It was a unique ceremony."

"That's one way to put it," Babs replied with a touch of amusement in her tone. "And I see you're wearing your wedding shirt. If I'm not mistaken, it's the same shirt you wore the week after you returned from Las Vegas."

She looked down at the black T-shirt. "How many women can get this much wear out of their wedding dress?" she teased, but her grandmother saw through her attempt to make a joke out of the situation.

"Landon also said he'd upset you and let you down."

Here it comes.

She folded her hands in her lap. "That's one way to put it. I love him, Babs. I thought he believed in me—in my talent. But he just needs me to help him hide…"

"Behind a mask, like Bonbon Barbie?" the woman answered.

"Why would you say that?"

"That feathery thing you said you wanted to show Libby wasn't just some random child's costume item you found in the attic. You wore it to teach people how to read and write music."

"But I wasn't hiding, Babs," she shot back. "Yes, I wore a mask, but I was open about being a neurodiverse learner. I didn't want you or my friends to find out what I was doing because I knew—"

"You knew we wouldn't let you carry the burden of the loan payment by yourself," Babs finished.

"I wanted to take care of it on my own," she answered as a tightness in her body took hold.

Her grandmother watched her closely. "You can stop trying to prove your worth to them, little miss."

She stared at the woman. "Who are you talking about?"

Babs' expression softened. "Your parents."

Her parents?

She swallowed past the lump in her throat. "I'm not trying to prove anything to them," she fired back, but her words didn't carry conviction. She glanced out the window. "The facts are the facts, Babs. They left me on your doorstep. And you and Grandad got stuck raising me."

"We didn't get stuck," she replied, then leaned forward. "Schuman, would you hand me the shoe box."

She'd forgotten the guy had it.

Schuman passed it back, and Babs removed the lid. The box was chock-full of papers, photographs, old birthday cards, and letters with postmarks dating back decades ago. "I need to show you something," she said and removed a slim ivory envelope.

Another damned envelope.

"What's that?"

"It's a letter from our attorney," her grandmother answered, then handed it over.

She checked the postmark. "It's from over twenty years ago."

"Open it, little miss."

She removed the folded page and skimmed the letter.

Reeves and Barbara Presley of Denver, Colorado, request physical custody of the minor, Harper Barbara Presley.

"Your grandfather and I petitioned the court and asked them to give us full custody."

"What? I thought my parents just left me on your porch."

"It's more complicated than that," the woman replied.

"Babs, I need more information than that."

Her grandmother released a pained breath. "Your father fell in with a rough crowd at a young age. He'd joined a band when he was sixteen and started binge-drinking and getting into all sorts of trouble. We tried getting him treatment, but he moved out when he turned eighteen and disappeared. We hadn't heard from him in many years until he called out of the blue. We were more than surprised when he told us that he was with a woman, and they had a daughter. Then he shared that he had no money to buy groceries or pay rent. We wired money to his bank account immediately, and he started bringing you by. You were almost four years old when we met you for the first time. We hoped that your parents were making better choices. But between their band and their drug and alcohol abuse, we feared for your safety."

She'd had no idea.

"I don't remember much from when I was little besides loud music and falling asleep on random couches. The clearest memory I have of my parents is when they told me to sit on the porch, eat my granola bar, and wait for you and Grandad."

Babs nodded. "Your parents received a copy of that letter

the day they left you on our porch. Your grandfather and I hadn't expected things to move so quickly. Our attorney said it could take months, but I will always be grateful to your mother and father. I know they loved you because they made the hard choice to give you a stable life. They may have made questionable decisions, but they knew you'd be safe with your grandfather and me. And had they not made that choice, there is a very good chance you would have been in that van with them when it went over the guardrails."

"Why are you telling me this now?"

"Because you should know that your parents tried to do right by you, Harper. They loved you, but they weren't in a place in their lives to care for you. They gave us a gift when they left you on the porch. We became a family. You were one heck of a piece of sassy work. My goodness, you had a mouth on you even then. But I wouldn't trade the life I shared with you and your grandfather for all the riches in the world. You have a chance at a life like that. You have nothing to prove when it comes to being worthy of love and happiness. Your parents would have wanted that for you."

Of course, she understood what the woman was saying, but it wasn't that easy.

"I want that too, Babs, and I want that with Aria and Landon. But I can't be with Landon if he won't accept who he is. He's a neurodivergent learner like his niece and me. I won't be the means that allows him to hide who he is. If he can't accept himself, then he can't believe in himself, and he can't believe in me—not the way Grandad would have wanted. I won't allow myself to be used or diminished. And I owe it to Aria to stand my ground on this. Grandad said if something isn't working, then change the melody, but keep making music. This is me, making a change, standing my ground, and making my music. I don't need to prove myself to anyone."

She held her grandmother's gaze as a weight she hadn't realized she'd been carrying lifted.

"That's my girl," Babs said, emotion coating the words.

That's my girl? What was this—some kind of test?

Babs slipped another envelope from the box and held it up.

And holy shit. She knew exactly what it was.

"You still have the letter I wrote to—"

"To your pop star heartthrob, Landon Paige?" Babs answered with a glimmer in her eyes. "Yes, I do. I want you to listen to what you wrote." Babs removed the page from the envelope. "You wrote, 'Dear Landon, My grandfather and I loved listening to your music. My grandpa believed in me. Your music reminds me of that. P.S. I'll be eighteen in a few years and then we can get married.'"

"I can't believe I wrote that."

"Landon told me you double-dog dared him to prove he could be the man you deserve," Babs said and returned the letter to the box.

"I did, but I'm not sure simply making a trip to meet you accomplishes that."

"What about something like this?" her grandmother said with a coy twist to her lips as she pointed out the window toward a large sign that read *Double-Dog Dare Music Festival.*

"What is that?" she asked as the SUV passed the sign and the sun illuminated slices of red boulders jutting out majestically from the earth into the sky.

She knew the location.

She'd drawn and colored red boulders and taped them to her wall.

They sat silently and stared out the window as the SUV headed toward Red Rocks Amphitheatre.

"What's going on here, Babs?"

"A music festival."

"I know of every music festival in Colorado. There's no Double-Dog Dare music festival," she fired back.

"There is now," Babs answered as the glimmer in her hazel eyes intensified.

The SUV sailed past packed parking lots surrounding the concert venue, and news vans lined the edges of the lots.

Whatever this Double-Dog Dare event was, it had garnered plenty of attention.

The SUV pulled up behind the stage. She'd never been to this part of the outdoor amphitheater.

It was reserved for performers.

"Here we are," the driver announced in a thick New York accent.

She stared at the back of the man's head. Why was his voice familiar?

Before she could get a word out, Babs opened the door. A catchy acoustic tune hung in the air as her grandmother, Schuman, and the driver exited the vehicle. She scrambled out behind them, when Bang Bang Barbie hurried toward them with a tray of bonbons in her hands. The woman had traded her tube top and heels for sneakers and a Cupid Bakery T-shirt.

"Mr. Sweet, we're running low on sugar cookies, and the glitter bonbons are a huge hit," the bubbly blonde gushed, then looked her way. "Hi, Harper, try one of my glitter treats."

"What are you doing here, Barbie?"

"I traded the bang-bang for bake-bake."

What?

"I hired Barbie," Schuman explained. "She's the new head baker at Cupid Bakery's Baxter Park location."

Had she fallen through a rip in the time-space continuum and landed in an alternate universe?

Schuman pointed to a white van. "Tanner's back with more cookies."

Mr. High AF jumped out of the vehicle. "Hey, Harper, have you tried one of Barbie's glitter bonbons? They're the bomb-bomb!"

"Tanner," Barbie cooed. "Aren't you the sweetest?"

Were the bonbons Mrs. Sweet had sent over laced with a psychedelic substance?

"I'm not one to turn down a bonbon, but isn't this the third challenge? Shouldn't you be with Vance?"

Barbie made a pouty face. "Vance is here, but I'm not with him."

"You're not?"

"No, and you were right about him," Barbie replied. "He's not someone I can count on. But he'll be getting a taste of his own medicine soon enough," the woman said with a devious grin.

"Come on, kids," Schuman said to Tanner and Barbie. "Let's unload the cookies and get them to the bakery booth. We've got hungry musicians to feed."

"Bakery booth? Hungry musicians? I'm at a loss," she said to her grandmother.

"Why are you at a loss, music teacher?" came the thick New York accent. "The first time we met, you told me you were a singer and a songwriter. Shouldn't a music festival be right up your alley?"

The bellhop.

She stared at the driver—the driver who also appeared to be the glittery hotel employee from the Luxe Grandiose.

"What are you doing here?"

"I'm doing a favor for a friend," he answered in a thick, syrupy southern accent.

"Damien?" she exclaimed, wide-eyed. She was ninety-nine percent sure she'd either experienced a psychotic break or was feeling the effects of finally consuming her body weight in chocolate. The sugar psychosis had to kick in at some point.

"Warren, give the poor girl a break. Can't you see she's overwhelmed?" said a woman with long silver hair, coming to the man's side.

Except, she recognized the woman. "You're from the Luxe, too. You're the hostess."

"And also own the place with my husband. I'm also Lizzie Luxe."

How many times was she going to have her mind blown today?

"We spoke on the phone a few days ago," she blurted.

"Yes, I know."

"I signed with your label."

"Again, dear," Mrs. Luxe replied and shared a look with her husband, "we know who you are."

"You're really Mr. and Mrs. Luxe? Why did you pretend to be other people?"

"Your husband can fill you in," Mr. Luxe answered with a coy grin.

"Landon's here?"

"Of course, he is, music teacher." The bellhop—no, Warren Luxe—answered. "This is his music festival."

"Landon has a music festival?" she repeated.

Lizzie Luxe nodded. "He's partnered with us at Luxe Media and Entertainment and with New Beats to create a music event highlighting up-and-coming bands and connecting them with mentors in the music industry."

"There's also an educational component," Warren Luxe added.

"And what's that?"

"Aria's Song," Lizzie replied.

"I don't know what that is?" she answered as the band stopped playing.

"I can help with that," Mitzi called, coming out of a door that led into the amphitheater complex, with Michel Laurent by her side.

Who wasn't here?

"Before their untimely death," Mitzi explained, "Leighton and Trey wanted to start a musical program teaching neurodivergent children how to read, write, and play music. We've worked out a deal for it to be housed in the New Beats building. We'll also have an outreach program to teach local music instructors how to work with neurodivergent learners, using many techniques and strategies you taught on your Bonbon Barbie channel."

"Oh," she answered, dumbstruck—no, freaking gobsmacked.

"*C'est magnifique, no?*" Michel sang. "You have a talented husband, Harper Barbara. We can't wait to welcome him as a new member of the New Beats staff. And Barbara, it's been so nice having you stay with me. We've been having such fun with our orchestra friends."

She stared at her grandmother. "You've been staying at Mishy's house?"

Babs shrugged. "Yes, I returned three days ago with Landon and Aria."

"And you didn't think to tell me you were in town," she fired back.

"We've been busy," Mishy answered. "Your husband is quite a driven man and very passionate about making music accessible to everyone. His personal story is quite inspiring."

His personal story?

She walked toward the back entrance and took in the enormous boulders framing the packed outdoor seating area. "How did Landon do this in a matter of days?"

"With a lot of help," her grandmother answered.

The announcer's voice rang out. "*Let's welcome Vance Vibe to the stage.*"

"That's our cue," Lizzie Luxe said to her husband and Mitzi.

Warren Luxe grinned. "Come on, music teacher, you don't want to miss this."

She and her grandmother walked behind the trio as they headed toward the backstage area.

"Babs," she said, lowering her voice, "why is Vance here? Landon despises the guy."

"I believe it's part of your husband's response to the double-dog dare."

That didn't make any sense.

She and Babs stood off to the side as Vance took to the stage with a guitar in his hand. "I'd like to start with a fan favorite. This is the acoustic version of 'Every Time You Break My Heart,'" he crowed into the microphone, but no one in the crowd seemed to be looking at him. A rumble of murmuring broke out as everyone stared at the jumbo screen situated off to the side on the stage.

She couldn't see what it was, but it had to be something worth gawking at. People pointed and gasped. She hurried toward the seating area and looked up to find a picture of her and Vance plastered across the jumbo screen. Her stomach dropped. She recognized the image. It was the photo Aria had plucked from the pile of mortification.

Vance craned his neck to see what everyone was looking at and inadvertently caught her eye. He frowned, then glanced at the screen and turned a ghostly shade of white.

"That's nothing. It's just an old picture. I used to know Harper Presley years ago—a lifetime ago," he stammered into the microphone, when the photo disappeared from the screen, and a video took its place.

A video she didn't recognize.

She watched herself on the screen as she composed "Every Time You Break My Heart."

"There's proof," she whispered.

And it had come from the old camcorder.

There was only one person who could have found it—one person who'd been playing her old videos and listening to her sing about stuff sucking.

And that person was her niece.

Her heart jumped into her throat as Mr. Luxe and his wife stepped onto the stage. "I'm Warren Luxe. My wife and I are the owners of Luxe Media and Entertainment. Vance Vibe, we must stop you from performing that song."

"It appears you stole it from another artist we represent," Mrs. Luxe added.

Vance's gaze whipped from the Luxes and he zeroed in on her. "You signed Harper?"

Before the Luxes could reply, voices called out from the audience.

"Vance Vibe copied my music!"

"He stole our stuff, too!" came another voice.

Vance peered into the crowd. "This is a misunderstanding. I've never stolen anybody's work."

As soon as the words fell from Vance's lips, a video with LookyLoo clips from other bands playing so-called Vance Vibe songs graced the screen with the video upload date printed at the bottom. Then a clip of Vance performing the song with the release date printed in red letters. Clip after clip proved that Vance had copied and stolen from dozens of artists.

The crowd booed every time Vance appeared, and rightly so.

The guy hadn't written anything original.

Nothing.

He'd stolen everything in his music catalog.

"You're a thief and a fraud, Vance Viberenski," Mrs. Luxe called in her buttery Donna voice.

"Your goose is cooked, son," Mr. Luxe exclaimed, following his wife's lead and reverting to Damien's drawl. "Vance the Cheat is no longer welcome at Luxe Media and Entertainment. Effective right this very second, he is banned from every Luxe hotel and media platform."

The fraud's jaw dropped as he connected Donna and Damien to the powerful Luxes.

"And he's not welcome at the Double-Dog Dare music festival either."

Landon.

She gasped as her husband walked onto the stage, owning the spotlight, and the crowd went wild. He scanned the area near the base of the jumbo screen and stilled when he met her gaze. Her pulse hammered, and her mouth went dry as Landon looked at her like nothing else existed. Holy hot rock star, she'd missed him. He smiled, and damn the man for tossing her that sexy as hell boyish half-grin.

Landon raised his hand, signaling for the crowd to quiet, and the amphitheater went from roaring cheers to hear-a-pin-drop silence.

"Hey, bonbon."

She swallowed past the lump in her throat. "Hey, heartthrob."

He looked her over. "I like your shirt."

She shrugged, playing it off. "I can't seem to get rid of it."

That boyish half-grin stretched to a wide, grateful smile.

"Hold up a second, Vance," Aria called, coming out of nowhere and skipping across the stage.

She'd nearly forgotten about the pop poser.

Vance looked ready to lose his lunch. "Yeah, kid?"

The child peered into the audience and waved. "Aunt Harper?"

"Yes?"

"This is for you," the girl said, then marched up to Vance and took the mic out of his hand. "Vance Vibe, keep fighting the good fight and vibe on, you butthole douche nozzle."

The kid had unleashed a firestorm of bad words, and she'd never been prouder of the girl.

Vance stared at the kid, wide-eyed, looking ready to crap his pants.

"And I almost forgot. Eat worms, sucker," Aria bellowed with her arm raised and pumped her fist like one of Jude's gladiators.

The amphitheater exploded with laughter and applause as the audience ate up the child's performance.

Vance, on the other hand, made like a cockroach seeing the light of day and bolted off the stage.

Aria dusted off her hands, hamming it up like a consummate performer, then turned to her. "Aunt Harper, Uncle Landy and I want you to join us on stage." She turned to the crowd. "Everybody, clap for my Aunt Harper."

"We love you, H!"

She turned and saw her friends, their fiancés, and her favorite little nose pickers in the crowd.

Libby pressed her hands into a prayer position.

Charlotte held up her camera and started snapping shots.

Penny smirked a devilish smile and mouthed, "How long have you been wearing that shirt?"

Heaven help her. She loved those women.

A flash of red caught her eye, and she spotted Madelyn. The woman smoothed her scarf, flashed that coy nanny matchmaker smirk, then tossed her a wink.

Had this been the woman's plan all along?

"Go on, little miss," her grandmother said. "I have a feeling your melody is about to change."

At the mention of her grandfather's words, a wave of emotion washed over her. Overwhelmed by the romance scale of devotion of Landon's response to her double-dog dare, she couldn't speak. She nodded to Babs and made her way to the steps leading to the stage. The crowd cheered as Aria took her hand and led her to the center of the space to stand next to Landon.

Staring into a sea of people was like something out of a dream.

No, this was her exact dream.

She took in the periphery of the seating area. Tents and vendors had been set up in the space. Tanner, Barbie, and Schuman waved from a Cupid Bakery stand. A mini Mr. Cheesy Forever food cart sat next to it.

And there was more.

She spied a tent with Pun-chi Yoga printed in swirly letters and several tables next to a sign reading Register for New Beats Music Programs Here.

"What do you think, bonbon?" Landon asked.

She parted her lips, unsure of what was about to come out, when a man's deep voice cut through the air.

"We love you, Harper and Bartho-lala-mama!"

Jude?

She studied the crowd and noticed a mass of gladiators and tutu-clad women waving and cheering. "Is that Katrina and Jude and the wedding party?"

"Yeah, the Luxes contacted them for me. I'm not sure why they showed up hammered and wearing their costumes. I guess that's how they roll. And you need to say hello to Grandma Bootsy."

Her jaw dropped. "Grandma Bootsy's alive?"

A tiny older woman wedged between Katrina and Jude and wearing a tutu and a tiara waved to them.

"She wasn't at the wedding because she was practicing with her choir," Landon explained.

For what had to be the millionth time that day, she gasped. "I recognize her, Landon. That's Granny B from the first challenge. She was the only one who voted for our penis and ball sac cookies. She's a singing granny who just happens to be

Jude's granny." She shook her head and laughed. "Hi, Granny Bootsy!"

The lady blew her a kiss as the ballerinas and gladiators hooted and hollered.

"This is kind of insane, heartthrob."

"Just wait," he said as Aria came to his side with an envelope in her hands.

"Here, Aunt Harper, I fixed Uncle Landy's contract."

"You fixed it?"

Aria beamed. "Open it."

She removed a wrinkled set of pages. It was the contract Landon almost signed in Italy.

"I crossed out Uncle Landy's name and wrote your name over it with my colored markers. I made every letter the right way."

"What does this mean?"

"The music belongs to you."

"No, we collaborated. It's your new sound. It's your dream. It's how you'll fulfill your promise to your sister and Trey."

"Dreams change. Leighton and Trey's dream was to start a music school for neurodivergent children. Making that happen is how I honor them. Plus, I'll be busy mentoring musicians at New Beats."

"This is what you want?"

The man's half-smile took on a cocky twist. "I've been told I'm quite the teacher. Just look how many views my Landy Candy lesson has gotten. Plus, you'll need the new songs for today and for Red Rocks Unplugged next week."

"What are you talking about, heartthrob?"

"Uncle Landy, it's time," Aria said and handed him the microphone as a few stagehands rolled a grand piano onto center stage. "Hold this," the little girl said and gave Landon the piano eraser. "And use your brave heart muscles."

Landon nodded to his niece, and the child skipped off the stage and took a seat in the front row with Bess and Tomás.

He took her hand, then turned to the audience. "Hello, Denver!" he called, and the crowd responded with a wave of applause. "It gives me great pleasure to be here among musicians, artists, educators, and volunteers. But I wouldn't be standing here if it wasn't for my wife."

"And a double-dog dare," Jude cried, then beat his chest.

"And a double-dog dare," Landon repeated and gazed into her eyes.

"Reading and writing have never come easily to me. I struggled through school and relied on my sister's help to get by. I didn't know it at the time, but I was…I am…a divergent learner. My brain works a little differently. It does amazing things like allowing me to write songs like 'Heartthrob Warfare' and 'No Fear,' but I still struggle with reading and writing music. I've lived in fear that my secret would get out. I felt shame about who I was. I believed I had a problem. I thought asking for help made me weak. My friends, there is no greater strength than embracing who you are, and there is no shame in asking for help. Look around. We're here today celebrating music and neurodiversity because people came together to help me prove to my wife that, despite being a musician, I believe in her. I believe in myself. I believe in all of you," he said, and the amphitheater shook with the crowd's boisterous response.

"You don't mess around when it comes to a double-dog dare, do you, heartthrob?" she sassed as tears rolled down her cheeks.

"I owe everything I am to you. You and Aria are my future and my forever. You are the lyrics whispering in the back of my mind. You're the melody I can't stop humming. You are the song in my heart. You are the crazy person wearing my shirts and yelling at old ladies in line at convenience stores."

She wiped her cheeks and chuckled as Aria ran back onto the stage.

The little girl waved her down. "Let me see, Aunt Harper."

"What are you looking for, honey?"

Aria grinned. "You did it, Uncle Landy. Those are Aunt Harper's happy tears."

Landon took her hands into his. "Music has been a part of my life since I was fourteen years old. But it became a part of my soul the minute I heard you sing."

This heartthrob.

"I love you," she whispered.

A sneaky smirk curled his lips, and he leaned in. "You might want to throttle me in a second, but just go with it. You have all the songs we wrote memorized, right?"

"I do," she answered.

"Ladies and gentlemen, in her debut performance, I give you the woman who is the love of my life, Harper Presley." He lowered the mic. "Break a leg, rock star."

She studied the grand piano, then gazed at the audience. "That was some fancy talking, heartthrob, but there's one little change I need to make."

"And what's that?"

"My name. It's Harper Presley-Paige."

Chapter 40
LANDON: THREE WEEKS LATER

Landon Paige licked his lips. "You taste better than bonbons, wife."

Harper propped herself up on her elbows. "Is that so?"

Yes, it was.

Situated between her thighs, he hummed against her most sensitive place. She sighed a sexy little sound, and he met his bonbon beauty's gaze. Those chameleon eyes got him every time. This woman had unlocked the music in his heart. She'd become a part of his soul. She'd freed him to be the man he was meant to be. And she believed in him and their love.

She also drove him insane with lust.

Harper Presley-Paige, with sex-mussed hair and a devious look in those hazel eyes, was the best thing a man could wake up to each day.

She tangled her fingers in his hair. "You did say you were in the mood for the romance scale of devotion staple, breakfast in bed. And as you know, my sole purpose on this planet is to make you happy, heartthrob. *Bon appétit.*"

He didn't believe he could get any more turned on.

He was wrong.

"So damned sassy," he growled. He kissed her hip, then continued the trail, licking and tasting until he reached the curve of her neck. His hard length pressed against her, and she rolled her hips.

"You know you like me sassy."

He drank in her kiss-swollen lips. "I wouldn't want you any other way."

A dirty smirk bloomed across her face, and his cock twitched.

"I can think of another way you'd want me," she teased.

She pressed her hands to his chest, and his cock twitched again, knowing exactly what was coming. He rolled onto his back and watched as his bossy, take-charge wife straddled him.

This morning was getting better by the second.

He ran his hands along her torso and drank in his sexy spouse.

Sweet Christ, he'd take this view any day.

"Going for a ride, rock star?" he asked, cupping her breasts in his hands.

"Rock star?" she purred.

"You better get used to the title."

"Rock star," she repeated, massaging the words with her erotic morning voice.

She positioned his cock at her entrance, then lowered herself. Humming her delight, she welcomed him into the sanctuary of her sweet, wet center. She tightened around him, and he inhaled a sharp breath. The intensity of becoming one with her never let up. He rocked his hips, barely able to hold back from thrusting like a carnal beast, but he gathered the strength to keep himself under control. This might be morning sex round two, but he wasn't about to cut the session short. Harper moaned, and the deliciously dirty sound was music to his ears. He palmed her ass and guided her body up and down in a slow, sensual motion.

"Just like that," she whispered, raising her arms and giving him the hottest view possible.

She bit her lip and moaned again before leaning forward to grab the headboard.

This bout of morning sex was about to get wild.

He devoured her body with his gaze. Her breasts bounced with each thrust of his cock. As if Mother Nature had turned on a spotlight, the rays of sunshine peeking through the curtains warmed the honey highlights in his wife's hair. Her diamond caught the light, and red-hot lust surged through him as a primal, caveman reaction took hold.

This glorious goddess of a songbird was his and his alone.

She arched her back, riding his cock like the naughtiest cowgirl on the ranch. "You better hold on tight, music teacher."

Music teacher.

He loved it when she called him that.

Still, it was a title he'd never dreamed he'd hold. But thanks to his wife challenging him to become the man she deserved, and the uncle Aria needed, he'd taken on the roles of running Aria's Song and working as a volunteer teacher and mentor at New Beats.

Three weeks had passed since the Double-Dog Dare Music Festival, and their lives had been a beautiful whirlwind of activity. Harper had blown away the crowd with her talent, not once, but again a week later at Red Rocks Unplugged. He'd insisted she take his spot, and Mr. and Mrs. Luxe had agreed. And it was the right call. Watching his wife fulfill her childhood dream of performing at the iconic outdoor amphitheater filled him with love, gratitude, and a steady sense of knowing who he was.

For the first time in a long time, he knew his purpose in this world.

He understood where he fit.

He didn't measure his worth by his number of fans or followers on social media. His value didn't hinge on whether he could transition from pop to rock. He'd spent so many years toiling, trying to honor Trey and Leighton's memory, but he'd allowed fear and shame to control his every move.

Not anymore.

There was nothing to hide.

He was a neurodivergent learner who embraced his individuality, treasured his uniqueness, and welcomed the creativity it afforded him. It was easier to close himself off and hide, but love and happiness didn't live in those dark corners. Strength of character was being terrified to take the leap and doing it anyway. After sharing his truth at the Double-Dog Dare Music festival, which had been livestreamed across the globe on LookyLoo, he'd been flooded with fan mail. Neurodivergent learners, parents of children who learned differently, and educators had reached out to thank him and share their stories. Harper was right. His celebrity status had afforded him wealth, security, and a platform to do some real good in this world. It was time to use that status to help others.

And to his surprise, being vulnerable sparked a joyfulness inside him that he could barely contain.

Just like the song playing in the convenience store the day he'd walked in to find Harper wearing his shirt, yelling at an old lady, and squabbling over eight cents, he was walking on sunshine.

However, not everyone was living the dream.

Vance Vibe's fall from grace had been deliciously swift and brutal. Not only had the man lost credibility in the music world, but he'd also been slapped with a bevy of lawsuits. Turns out, the hard drive Barbie had copied showed that the guy had also been evading his taxes.

Vance's days of vibing-on and stealing other artists' work were over.

Eat worms, sucker!

He wasn't a vindictive guy, but holy shit, he'd enjoyed playing the white knight and orchestrating the douche nozzle's fall. Now he was done worrying about the pop fraud—especially when he had rock's new It Girl rocking his world.

Thump, thump, thump, thump.

The headboard bumped against the wall as Harper's lips parted. "I could ride your cock all day long, music teacher."

He liked the sound of that.

He tightened his hold on her hips. It was time to take control. "Class is in session, bonbon, and you're about to get a lesson in Tempo 101." He shifted to a seated position and pulled her in close. Her breasts pressed against his chest, and he reveled in every point of contact. Thrusting his hips, he worked her in maddeningly measured strokes. "*Largo*," he whispered against her lips, busting out the Italian word for a slow, savory tempo.

And he sure as hell was savoring every damned second.

Harper purred her satisfaction.

But he had more for his wife.

"*Andantino*," he rasped, dialing up the pace. "But I have the feeling you want more."

"I double-dog dare you," she challenged.

And you bet your ass he was up for the job.

"Harper Presley-Paige, meet *allegro*," he bit out. He flipped his wife onto her back, pinned her hands above her head, and pistoned his hips, working her hard and fast like there was no tomorrow. Banging each other's brains out, they disintegrated into the flow and grind. The sensual soundscape of the sweat-slick slide of their bodies wove its way around the titillating slap of skin meeting skin.

Harper gasped and writhed beneath him. "I'm there. I'm there. Yes, yes, yes, yes!"

And he was right there with her.

Like the fireworks that had lit up the Italian sky, he exploded, coming hard with his wife. Their mouths came together in a heated clash of lips, teeth, and tongues as they met their release. The vibrations of their lovemaking echoed through the room, ricocheting like a ball of orgasmic energy—humming, throbbing, and pulsing with the intensity of their desire.

He released her wrists, and she wrapped her arms around him. He kissed the corner of her mouth, and she sighed.

She was his everything—his happiness, his home.

He stared into her pools of blue, grey, and brown and tried to count the flecks of green and gold.

"You're doing it again," she said with a sweet, sated smile.

"And what's that?"

"Mooning over me like a superfan," she teased.

"Damn right. I'm your number one fan," he replied, then glanced at the pillows scattered on the bed and bit back a devious grin. He snagged his favorite and held it up for Harper to admire. "I take back my superfan status. Anyone who takes the time to cross-stitch your face on a pillow deserves the title. Norma Rae is your number one."

Harper giggled. "I can't believe you like having that on our bed."

He admired the handiwork. "I like to think it helps muffle the sound. You're noisy in the sack, rock star," he teased. "It's a good thing we moved into my Crystal Hills place. If we were back at your grandmother's house, all of Baxter Park would have heard you moaning those sexy high notes."

"You like my sexy high notes," she said, and traced her finger down his jawline. "But you have a point. It might make family brunch a little awkward now that Bess and Tomás live down the block from Babs."

Yep, Tomás and Bess had moved into a snug bungalow. Their place in the foothills hadn't sold, but he'd come up with a creative compromise. He'd floated the idea of purchasing the home and donating it to New Beats to use as an artists' retreat.

He twisted a lock of Harper's hair. "I could listen to you purr all day." He shifted his hips. He hadn't pulled out yet, and it appeared he wouldn't need to. "Ready for round three, bonbon?"

"Round three?" came a little boy's voice with a crisp British accent from the other side of the door. "That must mean your aunt and uncle are boxing. That's a boxing word."

"But Aunt Harper was also singing her 'Yes, Yes, Yes' song," Aria fired back.

What the hell?

Harper's naughty-girl demeanor changed to wide-eyed, freaked-out-aunt mode.

"It's Aria," she whispered. "How long has she been out there?"

"I don't know."

"Did you lock the door?"

Oh shit!

"Uncle Landy?" the little girl called. "Are you and Aunt Harper boxing in there?"

Before he could figure out what to say, the doorknob turned.

"Landon, do something!" Harper whisper-shouted in the very same tone she'd used when she'd spoken similar words in the Vegas club when Katrina and Jude were on the cusp of figuring out that she'd crashed their wedding.

But this time, he couldn't get away with kissing her into oblivion—especially since he was naked as the day he was born.

He sprang off the bed and grabbed the closest item he could find. Harper, on the other hand, chose to stay put. In a movement that was comical and efficient, she rolled across the bed and turned herself into a mummified-looking sheet burrito.

His wife was damned inventive. But he couldn't dwell on the awesomeness of her quick thinking.

He set his sights on the door. It swung open with a whoosh of air just as he covered himself with…

He looked down.

He was hiding his junk with the Harper Presley-Paige cross-stitched pillow.

It was better than nothing.

He grinned like an idiot as Aria sauntered into the room with her iPad.

He held the pillow with one hand and propped his fist on his hip—going for creepy casual. "Hey, Aria!"

The little girl stared at Harper, then flicked her gaze to him and frowned.

He glanced at his wife and flashed her *what should we do* eyes.

She replied with *play it cool and act like this is normal.*

"Are your friends here? We heard voices," he asked, pretty damned proud of himself for keeping a straight face.

Aria's gaze ping-ponged between her burrito-mummy aunt and her pillow-junk-covering uncle. "No, they're on my iPad. We're having a video call because we all woke up and heard weird sounds in our houses," she answered, then turned so he could see the other kids, which meant they could see him.

Stay calm.

"At my house," Sebastian explained, "it was so noisy in my dad and Mibby's room that I thought the donkeys had gotten inside."

"And at my house, there were popsicle sticks everywhere in the kitchen, and fruit from the fruit bowl was all over the floor," Oscar added. "I took a bunch of pictures to show my dad and my Charlotte because I think raccoons or badgers got into the house."

"My uncle Row and Penny have been trying to get a book off a high shelf for the last twenty minutes." Phoebe cocked her head to the side. "Nice pillow. Is that a cross-stitch of Harper?"

He glanced down. "It is. The lady who makes them is pretty talented. The attention to detail is——"

"Heartthrob, zip it," Harper called from the edge of the bed.

"Hey, Aria?" Oscar said.

"Yeah?"

"Why is your uncle holding a pillow like that?"

Aria looked him over. "Probably because he's naked."

"No, your aunt and I were having a pillow fight."

The kid raised an eyebrow. "With no clothes on?"

"It's called a naked pillow fight."

"Landon," Harper shrieked.

Dammit! He sounded insane.

"I was about to get dressed for…"

"The playdate at the playground at the school Aunt Harper went to when she was my age," Aria supplied as the three children on the screen nodded.

"Yes," he exclaimed, nearly dropping the pillow. "The play-date at the playground—where people wear clothes."

Aria looked at him like he had shit for brains, which, at the moment, wasn't that off the mark.

"All right, guys," Aria said to her friends, "I need to get my aunt and uncle ready. Don't worry. We'll get to the park super-quick. My aunt Harper doesn't wear underpants, so she's super-fast at getting dressed."

He glanced at his wife, who'd turned beet-red.

"What if she wants her underpants, like if she wants to go upside-down on the monkey bars?" Phoebe asked.

"It's no big deal," Aria replied. "My uncle Landy has some for her. He carries them in his pocket. He calls them special private doilies, but they're just ladies' underpants."

Now it was his turn to blush like a ripe tomato.

"The word doily must be your uncle's codeword," Phoebe shot back. "It's like my codeword for when I want a hot dog. I say gimme a D. Boy, oh boy, do I need some D."

If he wasn't scared of dropping the pillow, he'd have beeen belly laughing his ass off.

"Go get your adults ready," Aria said, channeling an exhausted parent. "I'll see you guys in a little bit." The little girl ended the call, then pegged him with her gaze. "You and Aunt Harper have one minute to get yourselves ready," she chided, as her iPad pinged. Aria stared at the screen.

"What is it?" he asked.

"Phoebe just sent a message. She says that our sometimes-class-helper-lady, Ms. Malone, just told her uncle Rowen that she's going to meet us at the park, too."

Aria held up the iPad for him to see.

He skimmed the message, then met his wife's gaze. "Madelyn's joining us at the park, and she says she's got something to tell us, and she's bringing somebody special."

Chapter 41
HARPER: AN HOUR LATER

The car came to a stop, and Aria pressed her nose to the window. "Is that your old school, Aunt Harper?"

"It is. It's good ole Baxter Park Elementary. It's where I met Penny, Libby, and Charlotte."

"I see my friends. Oscar, Phoebe, and Sebastian are on the swings," the girl exclaimed. "Aunt Harper, will you hold my piano eraser and be super-duper extra careful with it?"

"Hand it over. You know it's safe with me," she replied and presented her palm.

Aria placed the tiny piano in the center and gave the little rubber item one last look. "Can I go play?"

"Go for it," Landon answered.

The kid whipped off her seat belt, bolted from the vehicle, and booked it toward the swing set.

The swing set.

Who would have thought creaky metal, rusty chains, and a few strips of rubber could hold such meaning?

She looked on as Aria ran past a cluster of benches and waved to their friends, who'd settled themselves under the shade of a towering oak. A reddish-brown leaf fluttered to the ground. She watched it dance in the air until it landed on the empty bench next to Penny and Rowen.

"Pretty soon, the trees will be bare," she said, and felt Landon's hand on her knee.

"Fall has always been my favorite season, especially in Colorado," he replied with a sweet, wistful quality to his voice. "If the seasons were a song, fall would make the perfect ending."

"What would spring be?" she asked as another leaf drifted to the ground.

"Spring would be the intro, alive with possibilities. Summer would be jam-packed with the verses, chorus, and the bridge, and then comes fall. When the leaves turn from green to an array of reds, browns, yellows, and burnt orange, fall reminds you of how far you've come."

She studied her friends.

They'd come so far since Madelyn Malone entered their lives.

"You forgot one. What about winter?"

"It's when life slows down and gives you time to dream of new melodies," her husband answered.

She rested her hand on top of his. "I like that, and it fits the eight of us. Penny was nanny-matched with Rowen in the spring. Then came Charlotte and Mitch in the late spring and early summer. Libby and Raz's match took up the rest of the summer."

"And we came along in the fall and threw one hell of a wrench into the nanny matchmaking process," Landon finished.

"Madelyn saved the best for last," she answered with a little smirk.

Landon squeezed her knee. "Speaking of last, we're the last to arrive."

She sighed. "After our video call disaster this morning, be

prepared for the firing squad, heartthrob. My friends can be relentless." She couldn't help smiling as she spoke the words.

"Oh, I know. I was with their fiancé's as they were being put through the wringer. You ladies are a force to be reckoned with."

She gazed into his soulful brown eyes. "It's been a wild ride for all of us, huh?"

He lifted her left hand to his lips and kissed her knuckles. "I'm just relieved we didn't get stuck with the donkey match."

"No kidding," she answered with a chuckle, but her throat had grown thick with emotion.

Perhaps the excitement of the last several weeks was catching up with her.

Most people don't go from being the infamous wife of a pop star to breaking out as a newly minted rock diva in a matter of days, but she was taking it in stride.

Luckily, she had a strong foundation to keep her grounded.

Of course, she had Landon, Aria, and Babs, but her family had expanded beyond blood and vows. Mitzi, the Luxes, Bess, Tomás, Schuman, Tanner, Mary Jane, and even Bang Bang Barbie had become treasured friends. Reconnecting with Babs' old symphony colleagues, who'd also become Landon's teaching colleagues, had also been a true gift.

And she'd always have her girls.

She blinked back tears.

What was going on with her?

She knew the answer to that question.

She was the person version of a bonbon. Hard on the outside and ooey-gooey on the inside.

But there was something about today that had her feeling more ooey-gooey than usual.

Landon hopped out of the car, opened her door, and offered his hand. "Are you ready, rock star?"

"Yeah, I am."

Hand in hand, they walked toward the cluster of five benches situated in the shape of a pentagon. It was set up to foster conversation, but she feared it might become the perfect location to get blasted by a verbal firing squad.

"Look who finally made it," Charlotte teased as they took a seat on the bench opposite Rowen and Penny.

"We figured you'd be the first family here since you forgo the lengthy step of putting on underwear," Penny added, piling on some sass.

"Is that a couple's thing? Is Landon commando as well?" Raz asked with a cocky bend to the question.

"Raz," she chided. "Do I need to enact the ball sac rule again?"

"The what?" Mitch blurted.

"No, ma'am, you do not," Raz answered, and it was funny as hell to see the beefcake of a boxer shaking in his boots.

She'd figured their friends would give them a hard time. Luckily, if anyone in this group of eight could dish out a serving of sassy pie, it was her.

"Hey," she said, eyeing the couples like a Victorian headmistress. "None of you have room to talk." She set her sights on Penny. "I don't know who you and Rowen think you're fooling with the book on a high shelf excuse, but Phoebe's got your number. That kid knows you're up to something."

Penny shared a look with her fiancé and shrugged. "You've got us there, H."

"And Char," she said, moving to the next bench.

"Here we go," Mitch muttered.

"One of these days, Oscar is going to walk in on your cherry popsicle, knocking fruit off the kitchen counter sexytimes sessions."

Charlotte twisted a lock of auburn hair and chewed her lip. "You're probably right. We leave that place looking like it's been hit by a—"

"—food truck," Mitch supplied.

"I was going to say tornado, hothead, but food truck is more our style," Charlotte answered, then pressed a kiss to Mitch's cheek.

"And Libbs and Erasmus," she continued.

"Bloody hell, she's scary," Raz said under his breath.

"What do you have for us?" Libby pressed. "I can feel your dragon rock star energy gearing up to toss out a doozy."

She winked at her yoga-fabulous friend. "One day, Sebastian will find out that the hot dog torpedoes he and the kids think are toys are actually giant vibrators created by his beloved Mibby, who just happens to sit atop a spiritual, sexual pleasure empire."

"Spiritual, sexual pleasure empire?" Libbs repeated.

"Fine," she quipped. "Call it a dildo factory."

"My vote is for spiritual, sexual pleasure empire," Raz said and wrapped his arm around his raven-haired fiancée.

"We get it, H," Penny remarked. "We all have our quirks."

"Indeed, you do," came a woman's voice with a rich Eastern European accent.

"Madelyn, it's so good to see you," Charlotte said, embracing the woman as the others welcomed the nanny-match maven.

"Your message said that you needed to speak with us," Rowen remarked as the matchmaker smoothed her trademark red scarf, and took a seat on the empty bench.

"And that you were bringing someone along," Penny added.

Madelyn gestured to a gray SUV parked behind Charlotte and Mitch's candy apple red Lamborghini Urus. "Yes, she's in the car finishing a call with one of her daughters. She'll be with us shortly." The woman took in each couple, then glanced at the children on the playground. "I must say, I do excellent work. It will be hard saying goodbye to Denver."

"You're leaving?" Landon asked.

"My work here is done, and my services are required elsewhere. It's part of the matchmaker's life." Madelyn turned her attention to the kids gliding through the air as they whooped and laughed on the swings. "I wanted to see you before I left. I wondered if you had any questions for me."

That would be a yes!

She shared a glance with Landon, then looked at each of her girls. She could tell they were thinking the same thing.

"The scarf," the four couples blurted in unison.

"Ah, the scarf. This piece of my nanny matchmaker attire has garnered interest."

"When you lent it to me a few months ago, I definitely picked up a powerful energy coming from it," Libby offered.

"It's magical, right? You found it in some temple on a mountain tucked away in the Himalayas?" Rowen posited.

"Babe, that's a great idea for a video game," Penny chimed as Madelyn laughed.

"It's an Hermès scarf. I believe it was purchased in Crystal Hills a little more than twenty years ago." She touched the silky material reverently. "What makes it uniquely enchanting is that it connects the four of you young women to me," Madelyn continued.

"Us?" Charlotte questioned.

"Yes," the matchmaker answered, then turned to Libby. "I'm sure you can enlighten everyone about the color red."

Libby leaned forward. "Red holds powerful energy. It demands action. It's the color of passion, strength, and courage."

"Correct," the matchmaker agreed. "This scarf was a gift —and gifts carry their own magic. It arrived with a letter and a photograph during a difficult time in my life two decades ago."

"What happened?" Landon asked.

"I was living on the East Coast and was in a terrible car

crash. My injuries were quite serious. There was damage to my spine, and I suffered a broken collarbone." Madelyn removed the red scarf. She gently pulled at the collar of her blouse, revealing a jagged silvery-white line. She turned her head and showed them a scar on the back of her neck. It started just below her hairline and continued down. "The doctors weren't sure if I'd be able to walk again. Every time I looked in the mirror, I grew angry and impatient. One day, a package arrived from my niece in Denver. It contained this scarf, a letter, and a photograph."

"I still don't understand how Harper, Libby, Charlotte, and I could be connected to a red scarf you received twenty years ago from your niece. We were young girls back then—only five or six years old at the time," Penny remarked.

"The letter contained a story about a young girl who wrote a song to cheer me up and her three friends. It seems this foursome was quite precocious and endlessly entertaining. Their teacher was quite fond of them."

It all made sense now.

"You're Miss Miliken's aunt? Is she still in Colorado?"

Madelyn's coy grin bloomed.

"Hello, girls, it's so very nice to see you again."

Holy kindergarten flashback!

She studied the newcomer. With her golden hair in a low bun and kind blue eyes, there was no doubt that this was their beloved teacher.

"Miss Miliken?"

"I wondered if you'd recognize me," the woman said as she embraced them one by one before settling next to Madelyn. "I go by Mrs. James, but please, call me Pamela."

"And you're really Madelyn's niece?" Charlotte asked.

"I am," their former teacher answered. "But I wasn't supposed to be."

"I'm not sure I'm following," Rowen said.

Pamela shared a knowing look with the matchmaker. "When I was six, my parents passed away in a boating accident, and I was sent to live with my only living relative—my mother's brother. My uncle Charles."

"Charles was my first client in the United States," Madelyn continued. "You see, I come from a long line of matchmakers. My grandmother was known throughout Europe. She'd made many influential matches and saw the gift in me. When I was a young woman, she sent me on my first matchmaking assignment. But it wasn't to make a love match. She'd asked me to match a wealthy single male caregiver with a nanny for his niece, but I failed."

"I don't know if I'd call it a failure, auntie," Pamela said, then squeezed Madelyn's hand.

"The man owned real estate across New England. When I met him, he was rigid, far too arrogant for my liking, and to my great irritation, devastatingly handsome. His name was Charles Malone."

"Malone?" Raz repeated.

"My uncle thought he needed a nanny, but what he required—what we both required—was love," Pamela finished.

"I broke the rules," Madelyn said with a coy grin. "I married my boss and became an aunt. I thought my grandmother would be livid. But she wasn't. She told me that I'd found my matchmaker's calling. You see, I don't believe in coincidences. A matchmaker is blessed with a sixth sense. We get a feeling when we meet people or even hear about them."

"And you got a feeling about us, didn't you?" Libby asked.

"I did. I learned about you through Pamela's letters. One day, she sent me a beautiful scarf along with a photo of her kindergarten class and a letter. Her words distracted me from the pain and made me laugh with tales from her first year of teaching kindergarten. A letter would arrive every week, and four little girls used to dominate the page. Penny Fennimore,

Charlotte Ames, Libby Lamb, and the often mischievous and always spirited Harper Presley."

Oh boy!

"Sassy since day one," Landon remarked, then kissed her temple.

"While I was undergoing physical therapy and learning to walk again," Madelyn continued, "I'd wear the red scarf and think of my dear Pamela and those four girls. You were never far from my thoughts. Every time I put on this scarf, I thought of you and wondered where you were in your lives. When my work brought me to Denver to match four single male care-givers, I knew it was fate."

"You knew from the start that our nanny matches would turn into love matches?" Charlotte asked.

Madelyn folded her hands in her lap. "Not necessarily. Finding love isn't about matching two people who automatically fit together. There's no person out there who can fill the hole in your heart. That work must be done by the individual. Sometimes, the work requires a spark—something earth-shattering and mind-blowing that makes you question everything you thought you knew about yourself, and that's precisely what these four men required. There's also a delicate balance when making a nanny love match because, of course, the child's needs supersede that of the adults. It takes a special person to love another woman's child like her own. There's always a risk, and true transformation isn't easy. It requires a challenge. Luckily, my grandmother seems to have been correct. I've got a knack for choosing which individuals will perfectly challenge each other."

"So there is some magic to it?" Penny pressed.

"Why, of course, there is. Look around. Look at your friends. Look at the children. Feel the bond you've created. Magic surrounds us. The trick is allowing yourself to see it and then giving yourself permission to believe in it."

"Wow," Libby whispered.

Raz sniffled. "That was bloody touching."

"Seriously, how do you do it, lady?" Mitch blubbered, crying like he'd been peeling onions.

Penny handed Rowen a tissue from her bag.

"How are you doing, heartthrob?" she asked, checking on her husband.

"You should write songs, Madelyn," he said and blinked back tears just as the children came running.

The kids stopped and scanned the group.

Aria propped her hand on her hip. "Aunt Harper, did you make the guys cry?"

"No, it wasn't me," she answered and bit back a grin.

"Madelyn," Phoebe said, wide-eyed, "did you use your nanny matchmaker powers to make the dads and uncles cry?"

"Something like that, Phoebe."

Phoebe eyed Pamela. "Who are you?"

"I'm Pamela, Madelyn's niece."

"Nice to meet you, Pamela, Madelyn's niece. I'm Phoebe Gale. Tell her my title, Sebastian," the child said, then nudged the boy.

"Do I have to?" Sebastian huffed.

Phoebe tossed a pigtail over her shoulder. "Yep, you do."

The boy sighed. "This is Phoebe, Princess of the Hot Dog Fairies, Bearer of Cookies, and Eater of Pizza."

"These are my friends. That's Aria. That's Oscar, and that's Sebastian," Phoebe said, introducing the brood to the kindergarten teacher.

"It's nice to meet you," Pamela said, gifting them the sweet kindergarten teacher smile.

"Ms. Malone, do you want to swing with us like you did at our school playground?" Oscar asked.

Madelyn slipped her scarf around her shoulders. "My dears, I must be going. Before I catch my plane leaving for the

Krista Sandor

coast, my niece and I are meeting Charlotte, Penny, Libby, and Harper for brunch."

Aria cocked her head to the side. "But Charlotte, Penny, Libby, and Harper are here."

"You are correct, but there are four girls with those names who also happen to be my great-nieces."

"You named your daughters after us?" Charlotte asked with a crack in her voice.

"Oh my gosh," Penny gushed and grabbed a tissue for herself and then handed one to Libby.

"As you can see, you four made quite an impression on me," Pamela answered.

And cue the waterworks.

"Are you crying, too, Aunt Harper?" Aria asked.

"Yeah, I am. Magical moments can do that."

"While everybody is crying," Phoebe said, "can I ask you a question, Madelyn?"

"Absolutely, dear."

"What will you do on the coast?"

Madelyn adjusted her scarf. "More matchmaking."

The little girl studied her friends. "What about for us? Do you know who our matches will be?" Phoebe pressed.

Madelyn leaned forward and waved in the children. "I do."

"You do?" the kids answered, wide-eyed.

"And I can tell you one thing about your matches. Are you ready?" she asked, surveying the adults before returning her attention to the children.

"We're ready" Aria answered and lifted her chin, always playing the tough girl.

Madelyn nodded. "Matches are a matter of the heart and don't always reveal themselves, but I believe I can make a prediction."

"What is it?" Oscar whispered and glanced at Aria.

650

"Yes, tell us, Madelyn," Phoebe pleaded and leaned into Sebastian.

The matchmaker smoothed her scarf. "Fate has much in store for you, and true love may be closer than you think."

"Why is that?" Phoebe asked.

"Because, my dears," Madelyn said as her lips twisted into a coy, knowing grin, "your matches have already been made."

THIS MIGHT BE the last book in The Nanny Love Match Series, but the love match legacy continues in The Sebastian Guarantee. Fast-forward sixteen years and the love match adventure continues with two of your favorites, Sebastian and Phoebe.

CROSSOVER ALERT: The Nanny Love Match Series features characters from the Bergen Brothers Series. If you enjoyed the Nanny Love Match books, you'll adore the Bergen Brothers. They're three billionaire brothers who are about to get schooled in the game of love. I double-dog dare you to check them out!

Also by Krista Sandor

The Nanny Love Match Series

A nanny/boss romantic comedy series

Book One: The Nanny and the Nerd

Book Two: The Nanny and the Hothead

Book Three: The Nanny and the Beefcake

Book Four: The Nanny and the Heartthrob

Love Match Legacy Books

The Nanny Love Match kids find their perfect match

The Sebastian Guarantee

The Bergen Brothers Series

A steamy billionaire brothers romantic comedy series

Book One: Man Fast

Book Two: Man Feast

Book Three: Man Find

Bergen Brothers: The Complete Series+Bonus Short Story

The Farm to Mabel Duet

A brother's best friend romance set in a small-town

Book One: Farm to Mabel

Book Two: Horn of Plenty

The Langley Park Series

A suspenseful, sexy second-chance at love series

Book One: The Road Home

Book Two: The Sound of Home

Book Three: The Beginning of Home

Book Four: The Measure of Home

Book Five: The Story of Home

Box Set (Books 1-5 + Bonus Scene)

Own the Eights Series

A delightfully sexy enemies-to-lovers series

Book One: Own the Eights

Book Two: Own the Eights Gets Married

Book Three: Own the Eights Maybe Baby

Box Set (Books 1-3)

STANDALONES

The Kiss Keeper

A toe-curlingly hot opposites attract romance

Not Your Average Vixen

An enemies-to-lovers super-steamy holiday romance

Sign up for Krista's newsletter to get all the up-to-date Krista Sandor Romance news!

Learn more at

www.KristaSandor.com

Acknowledgments

When I was in grad school earning a master's degree in early childhood special education, I had a professor I will never forget. Dr. Moore was fair, and he was also tough—so tough. I busted my butt in his class. One of the lessons that has stuck with me through the years is something he said during a conversation.

I was asking him about strategies to use when working with neurodivergent learners, then paused mid-question. I read the list of classroom modifications, and it hit me that these strategies could be applied to all kids. When I mentioned this to him, he smiled and said, "Now you get it."

I did.

Children are children. With or without a diagnosis, every child is unique and deserves classroom instruction that allows them to bloom into learners and thinkers and doers.

Now that I'm a mom raising a neurodivergent learner, I think about Dr. Moore quite often. I recall his compassion and how he encouraged me to do everything I could for those in my care. I draw on that in my life as a parent and my profession as a writer. Neurodiversity is a subject that is close to my heart. I understand the struggles and the victories.

And that brings us to The Nanny and the Heartthrob.

Back in December of 2020, I knew from the moment I was on the phone with my friend and author SE Rose, sharing my idea for a nanny romance series, that I would make one of the couples and their kiddo neurodivergent learners.

Along with the romance and the humor, I hope you

learned something. I hope this book gave you insight into minds that process the world a little differently. If you're a neurodivergent learner, I hope this book helped you see how extraordinary you are. We need your ideas and creativity.

Now, I'd like to thank a heck of a lot of people who assisted me in harnessing my ideas and creativity to write this book.

How about that for a transition? :)

I don't know where I'd be without my dear friend, author SE Rose. This woman is my romance rock. Thank you for putting up with me, my friend. Thank you for helping me be the best writer I can be.

Another amazing woman who puts up with my craziness is my sounding board and friend, Carrie. If my books make sense, it's because Carrie makes sure they do. Her suggestions and edits are spot-on. I treasure our book discussions. I value your input. I am so grateful to you.

And that brings us to Marla, Tera, and Erin. These are my trusted proofreaders. Thank you for combing through 175,000 words and finding those pesky edits.

I could not live without photographer Eric McKinney and designer Najla Qamber. Eric (6:12 Photography) captured the perfect heartthrob, and Najla crafted the exquisite cover.

These acknowledgments wouldn't be complete without thanking my husband and my boys. I have the best family a girl could ask for. I love you all so much.

And a special thank you to our newest family member—our rescue dog Huckleberry. Sweet Huck, thank you for reminding me to be patient, nap, and find joy in every moment. Here's our boy. I had to share his picture with you.

About the Author

If there's one thing Krista Sandor knows for sure, it's that romance saved her sanity. After she was diagnosed with Multiple Sclerosis in 2015, her world turned upside down. During those difficult first days, her dear friend sent her a romance novel. That kind gesture provided the escape she needed and ignited her love of the genre. Inspired by strong heroines and happily ever afters, Krista decided to write her own romance series. Today, she is an MS warrior, living life to the fullest. When she's not writing, you can find her running 5Ks with her husband and chasing after their growing boys in Denver, Colorado.

Never miss a release, contest, or author event! Visit Krista's website and sign up to receive her monthly update.

Made in the USA
Monee, IL
08 July 2022

99251645R00385